Lies & Liberation:
The Rape of Europa

a novel by
Barbara Bérot

This book is a work of fiction. Names, characters, businesses, organizations, places, events, and incidents are either the product of the author's imagination or are used fictitiously. Any similarity to living persons or actual events is coincidental and not intended by the author.

cover design by Ryan Feasel
photo of Ms. Bérot by Patricia Gershanick, C.P.P.

Published by Streetcar Books
Mechanicsville, Pennsylvania 18934

www.BarbaraBerot.com

ISBN 978-0-9748899-1-7

LCCN 2006908915

First Edition

Printed by BookMasters, Inc.,
in the United States of America

For Cynthia Bérot Miller,
my resilient sister,
whose courage and fortitude inspire me.

And for the patient and supportive fans of
When Europa Rode the Bull: I am deeply
grateful for your praise and encouragement.

Lies & Liberation:
The Rape of Europa

Of mortal creatures, all that breathe and move,
earth bears none frailer than mankind. What man
believes in woe to come, so long as valor
and tough knees are supplied him by the gods?
But when the gods in bliss bring miseries on,
then willy-nilly, blindly, he endures.
Our minds are as the days are, dark or bright,
blown over by the father of gods and men.

Homer, from The Odyssey

One

A nnie d'Inard stood alone on the West Sands of St. Andrews, with one hand raised and clawing at the sky. The helicopter, which was fast disappearing from view, was tugging at her insides, even as it seemed to be taking her very essence with it. When she could no longer see it, she leaned her back against the Aston Martin he had left her, then folded in on herself until she met the ground in a heap. How she would climb into the driver's seat and find her way back to Kingsbarns would remain to be seen.

As the helicopter sliced through the sea mist and lifted away from her, the passenger inside underwent a transformation. The place he was speeding off to, the wife and children he would be reunited with shortly, the very life he had so painstakingly constructed over twenty years — all flashed before him in images, some of them painful, some of them sweet — as though this life were coming to an end. But as the woman he was leaving faded into the misty backdrop, another image captured him: a most critical memory, one that he had managed to bury beneath the safety and predictability of the last twenty years. It was the picture of her, bare chested and dreamy, lying with him in a spring meadow. A stark reminder of what he had lost, the potent emotions that image generated all but expunged the others, which now seemed to huddle defensively, to coalesce into something alien and hostile, as though that part of his past — his life with Janet and the children — was mounting an attack against him.

When the aircraft finally maneuvered for landing, he sighed with resignation. Instead of the relief and warmth he would normally feel upon returning to his home, today Andrew Stuart-Gordon felt thwarted and defeated, like an escapee who had eluded capture for a few wondrous days of freedom, but was now being returned to the castle in shackles.

Although still a week away, preparations for the upcoming event at Crinan Castle were in full swing, and there was yet much to do. There were thirty-six guest bedrooms to be prepared, countless supplies to be laid in, and untold pieces of silver to be polished. Gardeners and groundskeepers pulled every stray blade of grass and plucked every spent blossom, giving meticulous attention to the more than twenty acres of formal gardens. Cook and her staff were having regular meetings with the catering firm from Glasgow that was to arrive next Friday, replete with refrigerated lorries filled to the brim, and the enclosed, heated tents that would be set up on the grounds. It was a massive undertaking that required constant supervision and attention to detail, and although Janet had only been in charge of it for the past four years, she managed it all with apparent ease.

But this year's celebration of Laird's Day would be unlike any other, and although her deportment bespoke confidence and control, inside she felt as jittery and uncertain as she had the day she married Andrew. And why she was so anxious on that day, only her late father-in-law knew. *Ne obliviscaris,* he had said to her, her Campbell clan's motto, which translated: Do not forget. He had a very particular reason for using that phrase, because he wanted her to remember the choice she had made and would have to live with the rest of her life. But she did not want to think of that, on this of all days, and chose to view it differently—with regard to her birthright—to remind herself that although she was not Andrew's choice in love, she was the one with the right to it, and anything she needed do to claim that right was justified. She had only to remember that she was the granddaughter of the Duke of Argyll, born to Inveraray Castle and educated at the finest schools. She had been groomed all her life for this role and one even greater; when her parents failed to produce a male heir, she, as the eldest daughter of the only heir, was in line to inherit her father's title. And her marriage to Andrew had been her right as well, something long hoped for, planned for, by both their families. So why she went about her tasks this day feeling somewhat off balance and with an anxious fluttering in her stomach was something she kept to herself, and was steadfastly determined to overcome.

A business crisis kept Andrew in Glasgow all day Friday and his return late that night went unnoticed. He slept in on Saturday morning, then joined his family for midday dinner. It was an enormous meal set out in the larger of the two family dining rooms and attended by all the important members of the household, including the estate manager and his wife; the head butler and housekeeper; Mrs. Ferguson, the cook; Nanny Whitburn, and the earl's personal secretary, Nigel Bain. This coming together was important to Andrew, and he usually made every effort to be in attendance.

The same meal was always set out in the servants' hall, after which all but a handful of staff were officially off until Monday morning. This weekend's respite was particularly looked forward to by the weary staff, for next weekend there would be no such luxury.

When the meal concluded, Andrew helped his mother with her chair and she excused herself, as was her custom, to retire to her separate abode for a nap. When Andrew's father died some five years earlier, Mary had been mistress of this enormous pile, but custom and respect for the sovereignty of her daughter-in-law had relegated her to a less significant albeit substantial dwelling, the comfortable Nethergate Lodge. Although still on the estate, having her own place afforded Mary the opportunity to run her household as she liked, while keeping close to her beloved grandchildren. And as large as it was by ordinary standards, its twenty rooms were quite manageable and easily maneuvered by Mary and her aging staff.

Andrew walked his mother to the west entrance, where her car and driver awaited her. Standing in the warming sunshine to watch her departure, Andrew and Janet decided not to take their after-dinner coffee in the drawing room, but to gather the family on the south terrace. As they enjoyed coffee and an assortment of delicate sweets, husband and wife glanced at each other frequently, smiling and talking casually in front of their five children, so that none of them had the slightest idea of where their father had been during the past week, or of how deeply his absence had affected their mother.

Cathy, the younger of the two girls, asked him, "Are you staying home tonight, Daddy?"

He beckoned her to sit beside him, as he answered, "Yes, I am, Cat darling."

"That's good, because I miss you when you're not around, you know."

"We've all missed you, Andrew," Janet added, with carefully disclosed disapproval. "We had hoped to have you home with us this week."

"I know and I apologize for that, but I intend on making it up," he told her. Then he asked the children, "What would you like to do today?"

"Sorry, Father," Donald, the oldest boy, answered quickly, "but I've plans for the rest of the day. As a matter of fact, I'd better be off."

"Where are you off to?" Andrew questioned. Both boys were returning to Eton tomorrow, and he had hoped to have time with them.

Donald avoided his father's eyes as he answered, "Ardfern."

Now Andrew understood. "To see that pretty brunette?"

Donald blushed and stood abruptly, while his brother Duncan suppressed a laugh. Donald shot his brother a disapproving glance and gestured nervously toward his mother, saying, "I don't see much of her anymore." That wasn't an outright lie, he consoled himself, just a misrepresentation of the truth. He was, after all, not home often enough to see her frequently.

"Oh? Sorry to hear that," his father offered. "She seemed quite charming. Well then, have a nice evening anyway, and don't be too late. We worry, you know."

"It won't be early," he warned. "Robin Malcolm's just had his yawl refitted at Ardfern, and he wants to take her out for a short run, then back to Crinan harbor."

Andrew lifted his eyes toward the sky before observing, "Should be a nice evening for sailing."

"Yes," Donald answered, with some awkwardness, "should be." He didn't like keeping things from his father, but with the way his mother felt about the girl, he wasn't about to announce that she would be sailing with them. Hesitantly, he moved toward his mother and kissed her cheek. When he approached his father, Andrew stood and wrapped his arms around him.

As they watched him traverse the lawn headed for the carriage house, Janet commented under her breath, "He's not fooling me for a minute."

"Let him make his own choices," Andrew told her, in that quietly commanding and terribly effective voice he had.

The cup and saucer she held in her hands began to rattle, as she mumbled to herself, "Yes, of course, there's no sense in trying to keep a Kilmartin heir from doing something that might ruin him, is there?"

Andrew clearly understood her meaning, and he responded with equal clarity. "Our interference is counterproductive. He needs to make his own decisions, and his own mistakes—that's how he'll become a man."

She knew she wasn't going to win this one, so Janet stood abruptly, asking, "Shall we go for a ride?"

"That sounds the thing," Andrew answered gratefully. "What do the rest of you say?"

Maggie suggested, "Let's take out the four-in-hand, Daddy. We've not done that in ages."

"That's a splendid idea," her father agreed. Andrew swept Malcolm up in his arms and took Cathy's hand as they headed for the stables.

Duncan took the reins of the marvelous old barouche, which was more than 150 years old and in perfect condition. It had belonged originally to the twentieth earl and had been used by him to visit the various tenants and different corners of the estate; it was drawn now by four perfectly matched horses, who carried themselves as regally as their occupants. Andrew sat up front with Duncan, Malcolm between them, while the ladies occupied the interior.

"It's not fair to let him drive," Maggie complained. "I can handle them as well, if not better."

Andrew already had a plan. "The gentlemen will take us out and the ladies will bring us in, all right?"

"All right, that's fair," Maggie conceded.

The afternoon was sunny and warm, and the breeze that blew in from the loch liberated the scent of wild myrtle. They took a leisurely two and a half hours for their excursion, following the well-worn lanes that crisscrossed the estate, through forest groves where deer and pheasant ruled and pastures speckled with grazing sheep.

When they returned to the stables, Andrew traversed the length of it to visit his favorite horse, noticing as he did that the stallion nicknamed "Rage" was bucking and kicking at his stall. He took long, angry strides back toward his wife who was now alone in the tack room, the children having already gone up to the house.

The tack room was arguably Janet's most favorite place on the estate. It was large and comfortably furnished, with a small, pullman-type kitchen that was always stocked with fruit and cheese and biscuits. After a long day riding, she liked to relax here in her dirty breeches, stretched out on one of the worn couches, near enough her beloved beasts to hear and smell them. And, too, it provided her shelter from the busy household, for unless it was an emergency, this was one place where she would not be disturbed, called upon by the housekeeper or estate manager to make some decision or other, or Nanny Whitburn to settle something about the children.

So when Andrew violated her sanctuary with, "I see that Satan is still with us," it set her off. But she was happy for the change in tone, for she'd grown weary of the pretense of calm and normalcy they'd carried on for the children's sake.

"And what would you have had me do," she asked him, "run out here the other night with a pistol?"

"Goddammit, Janet, you know that I despise that animal."

"There are a lot of things I despise," she retorted, "but I don't go around killing them." Pleased with her response, she turned her back on him to return a rope lead to its hook.

"That devil poses a danger to everyone," he insisted, "and most of all to you."

"He's not a devil, he's a stallion," she corrected. "Stallions can't help the way they behave. I should think you, of all people, would understand that." She was even more proud of herself for that one.

Her remarks were not lost on him, but for the moment he was more concerned about the danger in keeping the horse around. "We've no such problems with the other stallions, have we?"

She frowned her impatience. "He's high strung because he misses the chase. He lives to run and jump and he never gets enough of it. And he hasn't been put to stud enough, either."

"Then for Christ's sake, get him a mare he can have a go at!"

"I'm working on that very thing," she informed him. "I'm trying to locate one with the proper disposition, to temper his in the offspring. When it comes to breeding," she added, with a bitter grin, "one can't be too careful in choosing, you know."

Undeterred by her sarcasm, he continued, "Regardless of that, he's not a suitable mount for you. I can see something dreadful happening with him and I don't want to let it get that far."

She inquired flippantly, "Don't you?" then walked behind him and closed the door he'd come through. "Shall we have our talk now, since we're speaking of studs and dreadful things that could happen?"

He felt a sudden fatigue and sank into one of the leather club chairs. "There's no one about. Now's as good a time as any."

She strode casually toward the little kitchen area, asking, "Can I get you something?" as she opened the refrigerator.

"No, thank you," he answered, watching as she poured a glass of cranberry juice.

Janet didn't speak again until she had settled on the couch and propped herself with several pillows. The digs she'd already gotten in had emboldened her. "Tell me, Andrew, what's it like seeing her again, after all these years?"

Something about the manner in which she'd posed that question irritated him, but nevertheless, he answered grimly, "It was like exhuming something that had been buried alive."

Janet grimaced, then gulped some juice. "What a ghastly analogy; it sounds positively dreadful."

He kept his impatience with her in check. "I mean that it was painful to bury it to begin with, and it's just as painful to bring it out into the light again."

The sarcasm returned with her next question. "And what does it look like now that it's out?" Laughing slightly, she added, "I hope not like something from your grisly metaphor."

Before he answered he fortified himself with a deep breath. "At times it seems brand new, at others it looks hopeless."

"Sounds like quite the predicament," she quipped.

He was reaching the limits of his patience, and scoldingly informed her, "There are questions about her health, Janet."

She dropped her smug expression for the first time since the conversation had begun. "What questions?"

"I tell you this in the strictest confidence—"

"Now really," she bristled. "With whom would I speak about your mistress?"

There were certain things he was unwilling to tolerate, and this was one of them. "Her name is Annie," he said. "Calling her my mistress only demeans you."

Sipping nonchalantly at her juice, she responded with a barely discernible lift of her brow.

His voice deepened with sadness, for saying it aloud made it more real. "Annie may be infected with HIV."

As the words reached her ears, she gave herself a moment to repeat them in her head; they were that unexpected and incredible. "Good lord—good lord!!" she exclaimed, slamming her glass to the table in front of her. "You've not slept with her—please tell me you've not had sex with her!"

"She wouldn't allow it," he answered immediately. "I told you that. We've been together, though, we've been intimate, but safely intimate."

Was there such a thing? "Are you certain? Are you certain you were safe?"

"Yes."

"My God, Andrew!" The more it sank in, the more absurdly dangerous it seemed. "Do you think it wise to be with her in any way at all, considering?"

"There's nothing to worry about," he insisted. "I know enough about the disease to understand the way it's transmitted."

How could he not see it? "Nothing to worry about?" she shrieked. "My husband goes off and spends three days with a woman who could be infected with a disease—a contagious, fatal disease, mind you—how could I not worry? I'd have to be a bloody idiot to not worry!"

"Please keep your voice down," he asked gently. "The children might come looking for us."

"Keep my voice down?" As her anxiety grew, her eyes reflected it, lighting with the wildness of a madwoman. "Why don't I just shut the bloody hell up altogether? Yes, why don't I do that? Just sit quietly by while you destroy our marriage, our family, maybe even your own bloody life, all for the momentary satisfaction of sticking yourself in some diseased bit of ass. Yes, why don't I do that? That sounds the thing to do!"

Andrew rose from his chair and walked toward his wife. She braced herself when she saw him make a move for her—not that he'd ever laid a hand to her. She braced herself because of the raw emotion she'd discerned in his face; it was menacing and colored with fury as he stood over her, glaring down upon her as though he might lash out.

"Well? What are you going to do?" she screeched. "Tell me to take back what I said? Give me a good smack across the face? Tell me to mind my own damned business? What?"

In the last few minutes he'd been in the presence of the Janet he'd never liked: the one he always avoided, the woman whose bitter, sarcastic tongue had sent him out of his marriage in search of other, softer women. And it wasn't just the situation with Annie that had brought her out. That Janet was always there, lurking, simmering under the genteel facade.

When he didn't respond, she demanded again, "Well? What are you going to do?"

The tension between them was so tangible as to be inhaled; it was as thick as the scent of hay coming from the stalls.

"Nothing," he finally answered. "I'm not going to do anything. It was perfectly foolish of me to even think we could talk about this." The anger and revulsion that welled up within him made him turn on his heels and leave his wife.

With the sound of the slamming door, Janet felt her heart drop. *Stupid woman, stupid, bloody woman*—she cursed herself. *He wanted to talk with you, he was ready and willing to discuss this with you, but you wouldn't let him. You stupid, shortsighted woman. You wouldn't listen, and now you've sent him running back to her.*

After a light supper, the family gathered in an upstairs drawing room. Donald was still out and Andrew occupied the middle of the sofa, surrounded by the other four children: Malcolm asleep with his head in his father's lap, Duncan sprawled on the floor near his legs, and the girls flanking him. They watched a video and Janet joined them only briefly, sitting alone in a chair, staring at the five of them huddled together, and, strangely, feeling like an outsider.

When he retired to his room, Andrew picked up the telephone and dialed the number that he now knew by heart. He knew that her son Marc had arrived and he was hoping to catch her alone, after the boy had gone to bed. When she answered, he asked tenderly, "Did I wake you?"

"Oh no," she answered, sighing with gratitude at the sound of his voice. "Marc and I just got in from a late dinner. We drove to see Glamis Castle today. How are you?"

"Fine, just fine, darling," he answered, then questioned, "Why didn't you tell me you wanted to go there? I'd have arranged a private tour for you. They're my cousins, you know. My grandmother was a Bowes-Lyon."

Hearing that, she shook her head and smiled. "No, I didn't know," she responded. Throughout the tour, she had wondered if Crinan Castle was anything like Glamis, and upon hearing about the family, she'd also wondered if they were related.

"Is all well?" he asked her now.

She hesitated before answering, looking to see if her son was nearby. "Yes—but I miss you terribly," she whispered.

He sighed before admitting, "That was the second hardest parting of my life, Annie."

The line went intimately silent. After a time, Annie asked him, "How are your children?"

"Getting on. Donald's off sailing this evening and I spent most of the day with the others, who all seem to grow inches each time I'm away. How's Marc liking it so far?"

"He's having a great time, but I think he's most impressed with James Bond's car," she chuckled. "He said to thank you for that."

"I wish you would have let me do more," he told her.

Marc had been in his bedroom searching out something in his suitcases, but he came into the little parlor now.

"You'll call me in the morning?" she asked Andrew. It was little more than forty-eight hours since they'd parted, but he'd already called her five times.

"First thing," he answered. He knew that it was time to end the conversation, but before he could hang up, he had to say it again, "I love you, Annie."

"I know," she responded, "and I thank you for that."

"Marc's listening," he understood.

"That's right."

"Good night, my darling. I'll ring tomorrow."

When he turned off the bedside lamp and closed his eyes, Andrew traveled back in time, back to when he was a student and living at the Whaum. He saw with perfect clarity the details of the room where he had slept. He heard the creaking sound the rafters would make with the wind, envisioned the faded colors of the quilt, the chair near the wardrobe that was always piled high with his clothing. He could even conjure up the musty smell of the old cottage. But of all the memories that visited him on this spring evening, he recalled one more keenly than the others: He felt the emptiness, the unassuageable longing that he suffered at night, lying alone in his bed, separated from her. It was a pain that could only be endured by focusing on the next day, on the exact time in the afternoon when he would return from his lectures and find her waiting in the garden, her eyes as green and alive as the rose leaves: when they would come together and he would marvelously, miraculously, feel full and whole again.

As she readied herself for bed, Janet dressed in a negligee that Andrew had given her in better times, in times when he slept in her room, not in his. She sat at her dressing table and brushed her closely cropped red hair, hoping against hope that he might come to her tonight, that he might knock on her door and ask if they could try again. When she'd brushed her hair so much her arm ached, she settled into a chair and stared at the door that connected their rooms for what seemed an eternity. She finally turned off the lights after taking a sleeping pill, after listening at the door and hearing nothing, when being awake and alone was no longer to be borne.

Two

On Monday morning Andrew was up and dressed very early, and Janet caught him just as he was about to leave for Glasgow.

A little timidly, she questioned, "Will you be home tonight?"

His secretary Nigel had already gotten into the Range Rover and her husband was standing alone in the entrance hall, closing his attaché. He betrayed no emotion as he answered, "Yes, but late."

"Shall I hold supper?"

He responded casually, "If you like. I'll have Nigel ring and let you know when you can expect me." He offered her a small, tentative smile.

She lowered her eyes and then looked into his. "Do you think we might try to talk again tonight?"

Her request surprised him. "Do you want to?"

Nodding slightly, she said, "I do. It's just that what you told me about her health—it frightened me so. It's difficult to be rational when one is so frightened."

"I know," he answered, with a heaviness of heart.

Her arms were folded tightly around her middle, and she grasped the sides of her cashmere sweater. "I feel like I'm losing control sometimes. I feel like this whole thing is spinning out of control."

Moved by her frankness, Andrew left his case on the table and approached her. "You've an absolute right to be angry and it's perfectly reasonable for you to be afraid," he quietly acknowledged. "And I fully realize that talking about what's going on is difficult and hurtful, but it's important to include you, exactly so you *won't* feel it's out of your control. I want you to have a say, Janet; whatever happens, your voice should be heard as loudly and clearly as anyone's." As he finished saying this, he reached out and touched one of her hands.

His touch brought a rush of warmth to her frigid, numbed skin, and her voice relaxed as she responded, "I'll hold supper for you; no matter how late, I'll wait for you."

Smiling softly now, he answered, "Thank you, I'll look forward to it."

A silver tea service had been set in front of him, as was the morning custom, and the chairman and CEO of Nether Largie Incorporated asked his personal secretary to hold off the morning meeting while he made a phone call.

"Good morning, darling, how'd you sleep?"

"Good morning! I slept all right, and you?" Her son was having a bath, so she was free to talk.

"Reasonably," he answered. "How's the weather there? Will it be nice for your touring with Marc, do you think?"

"I haven't been out yet, but it looks like a fine day."

"Listen, darling," he told her. "I'm up against it just now, so I need to make this brief. I want to ask you a question, ask your permission about something."

"Yes?"

"You know I'm to be in New York on Wednesday. I've been thinking that I'd like to try and get together with your husband while I'm there."

She was caught completely off guard. "Why on earth do you want to do that?"

"I've a pressing need to understand what's going on with him," he explained, "why he kept the news about Glenn to himself. I'm very troubled by that, but if you think I'm interfering, I'll let it go."

Annie had been standing but she found herself needing to sit down. "No, I don't think that — I'd like to know the answer to that myself."

"So you don't mind if I contact him?"

"I'd just ask one thing of you," she decided. "Don't tell him about us, if it doesn't come up, that is. I don't want you to lie, I'd never ask you to lie, but if it doesn't come up then please don't offer it. I'm asking because I think it'd be better if I told him."

"I agree," he said. "And I'll be very careful about how I tackle the subject. He'll understand that I'm asking because I'm your friend, who wants to help bring some clarity to this situation."

Annie laughed nervously, before saying, "You're so consistent!"

"How do you mean?"

"I remember you trying to help patch things up with my friend Adam Wilson, all those years ago."

The memory made him smile. "I owed Adam. If it hadn't been for him inviting you to St. Andrews, you and I would never have met."

"No, we never would have," she realized, "because we lived in completely different worlds."

The idea of that gave him a cold shiver, but he comforted himself with this thought: "I might have met you now, though. You might have come to do the very thing you're doing for me in advertising. I wonder, would we have felt the same attraction we felt all those years ago, if we met today as perfect strangers?"

Smiling to herself, she answered, "Absolutely; it's something in our cells, I think, our chemistry. What do you think?"

"You'll get no argument from me on that."

They laughed together before she thought to advise him, "Better call Mike today, if you've any hope of getting squeezed into his schedule."

"I'll do that."

She was picturing the two of them meeting for the first time, when she added, "I think you'll like him. He's a very impressive, stand-up kind of guy."

"So I've heard." Nigel knocked gently at the office door, a signal that everyone was there and ready. "Look, darling, sorry, but I've got to ring off now."

"Have a wonderful day, Andrew."

"You, too, my love. Give my best to Marc."

Later that afternoon, Nigel Bain placed the call for him.

"Westfield, Brown, Fleming, and Rutledge. How may I direct your call?"

"Michael Rutledge please. The Earl of Kilmartin ringing, from Glasgow."

"One moment please."

"Good morning—Mr. Rutledge's office—"

"Good morning. Lord Kilmartin ringing for Mr. Rutledge."

"Mr. Rutledge is with a client. May I take a message?"

"This is his lordship's personal secretary, Mr. Bain. The earl would like to speak with Mr. Rutledge today."

"Yes, Mr. Bain. May I tell him what it's in reference to?"

"Yes, Ms. Annie d'Inard."

Vicky stepped out of character a moment. "Annie—is she all right?"

"Yes, I believe so," he answered flatly, then added what he'd been directed to say: "The earl is a personal friend of Ms. d'Inard's and he'd like to speak with Mr. Rutledge."

Her professional tone returned as she responded, "I'll see that he gets the message as soon as he's out of his meeting, Mr. Bain. May I have the number?"

After she'd hung up, Vicky was so worried by the call that she decided to interrupt her boss in his meeting.

He listened intently. "Did it sound urgent?"

"No, not really, but you know how laid-back those Brits are; it was hard to tell."

"Where do I know that name, that title, I mean, where do I know that from?" he asked her.

"I don't know" she answered. "I ran through your client file and it's not in there."

"I'm finishing up here," he told her now. "Don't get me involved in anything else until I've gotten back to him, all right?"

"Right," Vicky said.

As he waited for her to place the call, Mike felt his own anxiety mount. Just before they were put through, Mike finally connected on who the earl was, and he knew he'd never met him.

Andrew's voice was friendly and somewhat familiar when he greeted him. "Hello, Mike. Thanks for getting back so quickly."

"Of course," he responded, thinking how odd it was that he'd called him by his first name. "Forgive me," he said now, "but you seem to have the advantage. Have we met?"

"On the phone the other day," he told him. "I picked up when you rang Annie at her cottage."

It took a second to click. "Andrew? My secretary said you were the Earl of Kilmartin!"

With the ring of humor, he responded, "I'm that, too."

"Not the same one who runs Nether Largie?"

"The same."

Mike was overcome with a smile. "Well, I'll be damned. You didn't say that the other day."

"We spoke but briefly."

"I bought quite a few shares of your company," he told him now, "when you went public a few years back. I remember reading about you and thinking that you were going to take that business through the roof, and you've not disappointed me." He suddenly remembered that there might be a problem with Annie. "Is Annie all right?"

"Yes, fine, I spoke with her this morning."

Perhaps it was his stepson. "Is Marc all right?"

"Annie says he's having a marvelous time."

"Well, that's good, that's a relief."

Andrew cleared his throat. "I know you're busy and I don't want to keep you, but I'll be in New York on Wednesday and I was hoping I might persuade you to dine with me that evening."

"Wednesday, Wednesday dinner," he thought out loud. "I can't think of anything—can you hold while I check my schedule?" He was back very quickly. "Wednesday's good; when and where?"

"I don't suppose you could come to New York?"

"That would be difficult, I'm afraid."

"Never mind then, I'll come to you. Pencil me in for eight if that's all right, and I'll have my secretary get back to yours with the details."

"You're on. I'm looking forward to meeting you." Mike found himself having to suppress a chuckle. "I'm having trouble connecting the Andrew of the St. Andrews stories with the CEO of Nether Largie."

"The St. Andrews stories?"

"When Marc was little, Annie used to tell him bedtime stories about when she was in St. Andrews. You were the main character, the knight in shining armor. She never said that you were an earl, though."

It made him smile to know that; then he had to ask himself: How could he have believed that she'd forgotten him? "She didn't know," he explained. "I kept it a secret when I was at university."

"Really? That sounds like a story in itself. How'd you two get together again?"

"I'm the client she's consulting for."

"Well, I'll be damned." That bothered him a little, and he wanted to know more, but unfortunately he was pressed for time. "I'll look forward to hearing all about it when we meet," he told him.

"And I look forward to meeting you. Cheers, Mike."

"Cheers, Andrew. See you Wednesday."

It was just past nine when the helicopter set down on the south lawn of Crinan Castle. Janet had taken the Range Rover to meet her husband and was standing alongside it, smiling warmly as he made his way toward her. When he was near enough to hear, she greeted him with a very deliberate: "Welcome home."

They dined alone in the small dining room, formally known as the breakfast room, beside a fire and under candlelight. While the footmen were in the room with them, they made polite conversation.

"How are things going with the businesses?" she asked.

"Well enough," he answered. "We've a few problems just now but nothing that can't be handled."

"Surely a problem here and there is meaningless," she observed, "in the overall scheme of things."

"Yes and no," he answered thoughtfully. "Since I've changed the way the business is run, my attitude has changed, too. I'm of the mind now that every penny counts, and every decline in profits is money out of my employees' pockets, or money lost that might have gone to some needy person."

"I can see how you'd feel that way," she observed, "with so many charities depending on Nether Largie's largesse. Do you regret having done it," she wondered, "having gone public? I know your father would never have allowed it."

"My father's attitude toward the business was positively feudal," he said, then signaled to the footman that he was finished with his plate. "And no—I don't regret it. It's made for a better company, having everyone who works for Nether Largie own a bit of it. And the charity connection has given me the purpose I needed. Making money for money's sake never quite did it for me."

After they'd been served their cheese course, Janet dismissed the young men. She cast her eyes downward and spoke tenderly to her husband. "That part of you, that giving, generous aspect of you, it's something I've always admired."

He smiled warmly as he told her, "Thank you, Janet. That's nice to hear you say, because lately I've not felt as though there was much about me to be admired, not in your eyes at least."

Now that they were alone, she wanted to tell him, "Since I've had time to mull it over, I understand why you've needed to be with her, in light of her illness and all. It would be totally out of character for you to ignore her at a time like this." She nibbled at her crowdie and oatcake, but kept her eyes on her husband.

When he realized what she was saying to him, he dropped his smile. "I don't want to give you the wrong impression. Annie doesn't know if she is ill; in fact, there's rather a good chance she isn't."

Her brow knitted. "I don't understand. I thought you said—"

"The two men she's been with," he explained, "her husband and her lover, neither of those men appear to have the virus."

Janet was having trouble swallowing the dry oatcake, and she chased it with a large gulp of wine. "I take it she says there's been no one else."

"Yes."

Her softened demeanor was overcome by her skepticism. "And you believe her?"

"I do."

She shook her head and closed her eyes, muttering, "Yes, of course you would."

"She's no reason to lie about that," he protested. "She's nothing to gain from a lie. And if you're thinking that I'm with her now out of pity," he decided to add, "that's not the case. I'd be with her regardless."

Janet had spent the day convincing herself that it was her husband's compassion that compelled him to be with this woman. Now he sat in front of her saying this was not so, and her mind, which had been calmed by that idea, once again plunged into outrage.

The two footmen had noiselessly reentered the room. One removed their cheese plates while the other served their pudding. Janet and Andrew didn't speak while they were there, except to say thank you.

When they were gone again, she drank more wine and tried to keep from clenching her jaw as she informed her husband, "I've freed up two more bedrooms for this weekend."

He was happy for the change in subject. "Thank you, I appreciate your effort. How'd you manage?"

"I'm organizing dormitories for the children: girls in the nursery and boys in a third-floor drawing room. How old is her son?"

"Fourteen."

"That's what I thought. He'll be in the boy's dormitory."

"I really appreciate all of this, you know. I'm well aware of how difficult this is for you."

Janet set her glass on the table heavily, angrily, spilling some of its contents onto the damask cloth. "Are you? Well then, that makes it all better, doesn't it?"

Her reaction made him realize how foolish he'd been to think they'd moved on. He laid aside his utensils and settled deeper into his chair, saying to his wife, "That was a stupid statement and I apologize for it. I've no idea of how this is affecting you. Why don't you tell me so I'll understand?"

With a grim smile, she said, "I don't think you can. I think I could sit here all night, explaining it to you, and you still wouldn't understand."

He couldn't think how to respond, except to say, "I know how it feels to be terribly hurt by someone."

She almost laughed. "You do, don't you? And isn't it funny, that she's the very one who acquainted you with that feeling. Bloody ironic, isn't it?"

Calmly, he defended, "I was hurt because I had no access to the truth."

Her face flushed with angry disbelief as she questioned, "So that's why you feel so free to deliver your truth to me? You believe you're doing me a service, do you, protecting me in some odd way?"

With a slightly bowed head, he answered quietly, "Yes."

"Well," she fumed, barely able to restrain herself, "let me tell you something about your truth, Andrew. You run me through the gut with it!"

The air that escaped from his lungs was pure angst, and the words that followed were born of unfettered emotion. "What do you want me to do then, lie to you? Will that make it better? Tell me what it is you want," he insisted. "Do you want a divorce? If that's what you want, then do it! You can rake me over the coals, I'll take all the blame, I'll give you everything you ask for and not even make a sound in my own defense—but for Christ's sake, please don't keep punishing me for something I can no more help or change than these scars on my face!"

With the sting in her eyes and swelling in her throat, it was difficult to answer. "No, I don't want a divorce."

"What then?" he demanded. "Tell me what it is I can do!"

I will not cry, she told herself, *I will not let the threat of this woman reduce me to tears.* She lifted her chin in an effort to bolster her courage. "You can look at me," she said. "Look at me and see who I am and what we've meant to each other. Look long and hard at that before you go ahead with anything."

Meeting her eyes now, he spoke with more composure. "I am looking at you. I see you more and more clearly every day. I realize how important you are to me, I recognize the sacrifices you've made for me, and I ache for the pain I've caused you. But I won't turn away from her, Janet, I can't. I can't because I love her," he had to say. "I've never stopped loving her."

Once again, his frankness pierced her. "Then promise me something, Andrew," she pleaded. "Promise me you won't let that love blind you to all the other love in your life. Promise me that you'll do everything in your power to keep your eyes and mind open, to keep your heart open, even if it hurts, even if feels like it's killing you."

She was very right about that; it did feel at times as though these emotions might kill him. But if there was anything he understood about himself it was this: "I can't be open to anything if I can't be honest. You've got to give me that if you want the other."

"Then I do!" she nearly screamed. "Keep on with your infernal honesty, then!"

His expression softened and as he spoke, the flickering candlelight cast living shadows across his face: softly dancing, dark images that seemed to reflect what was going on inside of him. "I never wanted it to come to this," he told her. "But I accept and understand something about it that you don't. It's been looming out there all along, waiting for me, waiting to come back, like a storm that blew off the coast that I thought was gone, but it wasn't. It was still out there, churning itself over the water, and then one day it just blew back in, big as life, and there was nothing I could do to get out of its way." He continued to look deep into his wife, but he could find no more words to put to his feelings.

The room became quiet, save the occasional crack of the fire, as husband and wife looked into the other, hoping for understanding and drained from their efforts.

A comforting thought came to Janet in this moment, as she began to see the threat of Annie in the way her husband had just described: like a storm that was bearing down on them. She latched onto that idea, determining that she could survive it if she treated it as such, as something that would blow itself out eventually, something she could weather if she had the fortitude, if she had the tenacity, and if she battened down the hatches, secured the lines, and lashed herself to the main.

Three

It was just a small piece, barely two paragraphs, wedged between a Sussex woman's account of abduction and rape by aliens, and a slightly more plausible article about a male prostitution ring operated out of the House of Lords. But the title of it, "Earl on the Loose?" caught the eye of the young kitchen maid and she showed it to Mrs. Ferguson, the cook.

"Why do you waste your hard earned money on that rubbish?" she asked the girl.

"I only buy one now and again, Mrs. Ferguson," she blushed. "Really, only now and again."

"Just look at the rest of this rot! Do you think you can believe anything you see printed here?"

The girl wrinkled her nose as though she'd had a whiff of something foul. "No, guess not," she admitted.

"Give it to me," the older woman told her, "and don't say a word about it to anyone. It's going right into the rubbish heap with the rest of the trash."

Mrs. Ferguson sent the girl to fetch something from one of the pantries and while she was gone, the shrewd woman carefully folded the paper, tucked it into her desk drawer, and made a mental note to show it to Nigel Bain.

Nigel downplayed the significance of the article as he thanked Mrs. Ferguson, adding that he knew he could rely on her continued discretion. He then tucked the tabloid under an arm and went straight to the earl with it.

It was very late but Andrew was still in his study. Nigel stood across the desk from him, waiting while he read it. When he looked up, Nigel questioned, "How would you like me to handle this?"

Andrew's eyes returned to the paper in front of him, as he responded, "Handle it by ignoring it." He folded the tabloid and tossed it in his rubbish bin.

Nigel was obviously distressed. "But your lordship," he argued, "this kind of thing can be very damaging if it gets out of hand."

"It won't get out of hand," Andrew insisted. "I was a bit careless this past week but that won't happen again." Then, rather impatiently, he asked the younger man, "Is there anything else?"

Nigel didn't answer, and although he knew he was dismissed, he didn't leave.

Andrew looked up now, repeating, "Is there something else?"

"If you don't mind my speaking out on this —"

His secretary's persistence was grating on his nerves, but he fought the impulse to tell him that he did mind, and very much. "Go ahead," he said.

"I was afraid this sort of thing would happen," Nigel audaciously began. "And I must add, I'm quite disappointed that you didn't allow me to assist you in your arrangements. This might have been avoided if you had."

Andrew bristled. "This was personal, not at all the sort of thing that I cared to involve you or anyone else in. And while we're at it, let's get that clear for the future, shall we?"

Nigel's posture stiffened as he questioned, "The future?"

"Yes, the future," he flatly stated. "I plan to spend a great deal more time with Ms. d'Inard. As a matter of fact, she's to be a guest here this weekend with her son."

Nigel was stunned. "At Crinan Castle? In the presence of Lady Kilmartin, your lordship?"

With rare insolence, Andrew answered, "Yes, in everyone's presence."

"Excuse me, sir, but do you think that's wise?"

Andrew's conversation with Janet had left him exhausted and raw, and this intrusion into his private life was just too much. "Wise? Since when do you question my judgment? And why is it you insist upon involving yourself in this matter, when I've made it more than clear that this is my personal business?"

Nigel had been feeling a bit raw lately himself, and the contentious nature of their conversation was wounding him in ways he'd never dreamed possible. He should have ended it, he knew that, and later on, in the quiet of his rooms, he would wish with all his heart that he had. But still, he argued back, "I beg to differ, sir. It was you who involved me. You had me contact the lady's husband."

Andrew's response was swift and indignant. "If placing a phone call for me compromises you, then perhaps I should be looking for a new secretary."

Nigel was grievously injured by that statement, and it was in a less challenging manner that he continued to pursue the subject. "You've always relied on me in the past, your lordship. Have I done something that's led you to believe me incapable of handling these matters?"

Andrew chided, "Don't do that. Don't make this about you. And while we're at it—too often lately you're stepping out of your role to fuss over me like a bloody nanny. You and I need to stick to business, Nigel, it works much better that way." He had wanted to say that for some time, and having done it now gave him some measure of satisfaction.

His voice slightly tremulous, Nigel responded, "I apologize, sir; I don't mean to overstep my bounds. It's just my fondness for you—I care about you. I don't want to see you hurt."

Suddenly aware of how upset Nigel was, Andrew decided that he'd been unfairly harsh. He also recognized that it was his confrontation with Janet that had put him in this rancorous state. "Look, Nigel, I apologize for my mood," he told him. "I want you to know that I appreciate all your hard work; I don't know what I'd do without you. I'm sorry if my words hurt you. Forgive me."

The almost tender manner in which Andrew apologized opened the floodgate on Nigel's emotions, and with the rush of that tide, his better judgment was swept away. "I've never said that to you before," he uttered softly.

"That you're fond of me? You needn't, I know that you are."

"Do you sir? Do you really?"

Andrew's smile was conciliatory when he responded, "Yes, of course."

As the warmth of Andrew's smile reached him, a few tears chased down Nigel's cheeks. "I don't want anything to come between us," he told Andrew. "I'd never do anything to jeopardize what we have. Never, ever would I knowingly hurt you."

This sentimental display baffled Andrew. "What is it, what's bothering you?" he questioned. "You've not been yourself lately — do you need a rest? Am I pushing you too hard? Perhaps some extended time off would be the thing."

He lifted his shoulders and tried to sound brave, but the effort resulted in something other than what he'd intended; he stepped closer to Andrew with a twist of his upper body and a sensuous follow-up of his hips. "No, sir, being away from you is the last thing I need."

Andrew still wasn't getting it. "I think you're spending too much time here," he decided. "You need to be out and with your friends more. Perhaps you should spend more time in London, socializing with people your age."

Nigel had fought it for so many years now, telling himself how wrong it was. He'd had that first relationship at school, then another at university. And when he came to work for the earl, he told himself that it had to stop. But he'd allowed himself his feelings for Andrew, because they were different: unlike the others, it hadn't begun as a physical thing. It had been his intelligence and warmth, his kindness and generosity that had made him so irresistible. Sitting next to him at meetings, traveling with him, staying in hotels together, their rooms often adjoining — how could he not grow to love him? And he wasn't blind, anyone with eyes could tell that he was dissatisfied in his marriage. Why else would he take up with an American woman he'd only just met? Bolstering himself with these thoughts, Nigel's voice lowered into seduction when he said, "My time with you is all I need; I don't need anything else in my life." His tone was fluid and feminine.

That feminine tone sounded an alarm in Andrew and his eyes widened as the message finally came through. "No — stop!" he said, his body tensing into a rigid, defensive posture.

The idea that they might become lovers had taken such a hold upon Nigel's consciousness that it no longer seemed a fantasy, and that was why his heart fluttered uncontrollably when he next uttered the words he had so longed to say. "Don't turn me away, Andrew, you don't know how much I have to offer. I could make you happy in ways you never dreamed possible."

For a few seconds, the shock that overtook Andrew left him with but a single thought: that this was the first time Nigel had ever addressed him by his given name. But as the initial shock abated, another, more profound one settled in. For in the last few minutes, the young man with whom he'd worked so closely for more than four years had undergone a transformation, revealing a side of himself that Andrew had been foolishly unaware of. It was not unlike what had happened at Eton, with Philip, and it evoked wretchedly painful memories.

As his stomach turned queasy, Andrew raised his hands in front of him, his palms toward Nigel as though to halt his approach, telling him, "I want you to stop right there — don't say another word!"

This reaction was not what he had hoped for, and with the creeping awareness that he was being rejected, Nigel's pain and embarrassment welled up, exposing itself in a generalized flush.

The nausea was overcoming Andrew. He swallowed hard to keep it from moving up his throat, while his thoughts raced toward a crucial decision. Sternly, he told the young man, "Listen to me. I don't want to cause either of us any further embarrassment, so let's handle this matter carefully. On Monday next I want you to go on holiday, two weeks, three, whatever you need. I don't want you to worry over the expense, I'll make it a gift to you, a reward for all your hard work. Go someplace warm and sunny, make some new friends, then come back here and we'll talk. Hopefully we can forget this ever happened. If we can't — well — I'll give you references the prince would envy. Am I making myself clear?"

Nigel's shoulders drooped as his eyes filled and overflowed. "Perfectly, sir. I'm so dreadfully sorry for this."

Andrew spoke haltingly to add, "If I've led you — to believe. . . . I do apologize —"

"You haven't, sir, you haven't!" he protested. "It's all my doing."

"I feel the perfect fool," Andrew mumbled.

Nigel attempted a smile. "Please don't!"

"I'm afraid I never realized," Andrew continued. "I suppose I never really thought about it — about you. But now that I do, I don't believe I've ever seen you with a woman."

"I've tried being with women, your lordship, it's just never seemed to suit me."

His response struck a sympathetic cord in Andrew, for it was spoken in a forlorn, regretful manner. "Well then, I expect the thing to do is to simply be what you are, who you are," he offered. "Leave off trying to be something you're not." Thankfully, the queasiness was passing, but he was more anxious than ever to have this over. "Why don't you go on then," he told him. "It's very late and we could both use some rest. We've a full day tomorrow."

Nigel was immensely grateful for the dismissal, for he had a desperate need to be alone just now. "Yes, good night then, your lordship. I am so dreadfully sorry." He sucked in his chest and left the library, closing the door quietly.

When Andrew could no longer hear his footfalls, he exhaled, "Jesus!" As he sank into his chair, he said more fervently, "Jesus, bloody Christ!"

Andrew rang Annie early the next morning, saying only, "Oh, Annie," in answer to her hello.

She immediately discerned something in his voice and questioned, "What's wrong?"

He wanted to tell her, but not over the phone. "Nothing, really," he decided to say. "It's just been an exceptionally trying couple of days."

"Something is wrong," she persisted.

"We'll talk about it when I see you on Friday, all right?"

She guessed at the problem. "Don't let me make you miserable."

"How are you doing that?"

"By being in your life, that's how. Look, I don't need to come to Kilmartin; let's rethink this."

He was leaning over his desk and had both elbows on it, supporting his head with his free hand. He sat upright now to respond emphatically, "It's not you who's distressing me and I don't need to rethink anything. Knowing that I'll see you on Friday is what's keeping me together at this point."

She huddled against the wall and whispered into the receiver. "I know I'm screwing up your life. It makes me crazy, thinking what I'm doing to you."

His tender response gave her some reassurance. "What makes me crazy is being away from you."

Marc came into the room then, and Annie acknowledged him.

Realizing that he had to change the subject, Andrew asked her, "How was your day yesterday?"

"Wonderful. We went to Falkland Palace and stopped at the Angus Folk Museum, among other things."

"Marc still enjoying it?"

"Absolutely, but your car continues to be the big attraction. I went into a pub yesterday to ask directions, and when I came out he was behind the wheel, searching out the buttons for the ejector seat and bullet shield."

Upon hearing that, Marc frowned at his mother, asking, "Why'd you tell him that? It makes me sound like a little kid."

Andrew could hear his comment and he laughed before saying, "Tell him that when I first got the car, I looked for them, too." For one fleeting moment he wanted to drop everything and join them in their touring. And that image—of them together, like loving parents taking their child on holiday—brought on stabbing pains of regret. "I'm flying to London this morning," he continued. "I'll be staying at my Mayfair house tonight; the number is in that list I gave you. Then I'm off to New York."

"Are you still planning to see Mike?" she wondered.

"For dinner tomorrow," he answered her.

Annie remained silent as she watched her son go into the kitchen.

"You all right, darling?" he asked.

"Yeah, fine. I just miss you."

"And I you, more than you could possibly know," he sighed. "I'll ring tonight, after ten." He hesitated a moment before adding, "I do so love you."

Marc had returned to the parlor, so she cautiously answered, "Me, too."

Nigel carried on with a stiff upper lip and although he'd originally intended to accompany the earl to New York, he remained in London and distracted himself by poring over travel brochures.

Andrew caught a short nap on the Concorde going over, then went directly from the airport to meetings with the corporate lawyers at Nether Largie's North American headquarters in Manhattan. The remainder of the day he met with his executive staff. Just before seven a limousine whisked him to the downtown heliport, and an hour later he was in another limo headed for the Four Seasons Hotel in Philadelphia. He barely had time to shave and change his shirt before meeting Michael Rutledge.

He informed the concierge, who happened to be an English expatriate, that Michael Rutledge would be joining him for dinner.

The gentleman smiled. "Mr. Rutledge dines here frequently, your lordship. I'll direct him to you in the lounge."

He'd read his bio, even seen a photo of the man, so he knew what to expect. But when Andrew watched Mike traverse the lobby with the concierge, he was struck by his presence. A man slightly older than himself, he possessed a youthful air that blended the athleticism of a former football quarterback with the poise and intelligence that got him elected class president at Princeton. As he followed Mike's confident stride toward him, Andrew observed how casually he wore his professional success — how comfortable he seemed in his own skin — carrying off his custom-tailored pinstripe and crisp, white shirt with the same unstudied ease. And he pondered for a moment the contradiction in someone who obviously knew how to play the game, who clearly understood the benefits of conformity, yet chose Annie for a wife: Annie, whose individuality and rebelliousness always carried her outside the mainstream.

As the time for their meeting drew nearer, Mike grew less and less comfortable with the idea. Something in what was not said on the telephone nagged him, worried him, made him start to feel a little like he did when he agreed to meet Glenn. Coming over in the taxi, he had to remind himself that Andrew was an old love, not a current one, and tell himself how ridiculous it was to feel ill at ease. And yet he remained apprehensive, until the moment he spotted him.

Having looked at his photo in Nether Largie's annual report only this afternoon, Mike easily recognized Andrew. But there was more to the recognition than simply his physical features. Andrew was just as Mike imagined someone of his centuries-old pedigree would be, for there was a distinctive aura about him that set him apart from everyone else: an air of equanimity—the aplomb that comes from having no need to impress anyone, from knowing his place in the world and accepting it humbly, gracefully.

His apprehension dissolved, Mike held out his hand and greeted Andrew warmly. "It's truly a pleasure," he told him. "I'm sorry I wasn't able to come to New York, but I can't make it too late of a night. We're in the middle of something critical, and that means I meet with my team at six-thirty."

"That's perfectly all right," Andrew responded. "I've decided to stay here tonight, so it's worked out. Do you have far to go this evening?"

"No," he answered. "I'm staying in town, at the Bellevue. Our firm has an arrangement with them. We pay them an exorbitant corporate fee for the use of their athletic club, and they provide us with rooms when we need them." He chuckled slightly.

Andrew smiled as he said, "I suppose if you use them often enough, it works out. What are you having?"

Mike grinned as he questioned, "That wouldn't be Glen Cairn single malt you're drinking?"

Andrew's smile widened. "What else?"

"I'll have the same," he told the young man who'd been awaiting his order. "So at long last, I meet the famous Andrew. Tell me, you said on the phone that Annie didn't know who you were before, how was that?"

"It's rather a story," he began, "but the short of it is, I kept my identity hidden when I was at university. I didn't want the attention and as it was probably the last opportunity I'd ever have to just blend in, I decided to take full advantage."

"No one knew?"

"The university knew, of course, and they were under strict orders from my grandfather to keep it under wraps. My best friend also knew, he was my flat mate at the Whaum, and one or two others."

Mike repeated, "The Whaum," as though the place were dear to him, too. "How many times I've heard about the Whaum. Annie tells me it's still there and that she's been in it."

"Yes, it's still very much there," he answered, allowing his thoughts to drift a moment.

"And have you met Marc yet?" he wondered.

"No, not yet," he answered. "But he's enjoying himself immensely, I'm told."

"I'm happy to hear that. He was anxious to see his mother; he's really missed her."

Mike's drink arrived, and Andrew lifted his glass to say, "Good health!" His drink back on the table, he turned the glass several times, wondering if that were true: Was Mike in good health?

Mike had kept his glass in hand, and now, with downcast eyes, he said, "And to Annie, to her good health."

After drinking to her, Andrew offered softly, "It's been an awful time for her. Being away from her son was not what she wanted, but neither did she want him to see what she was going through."

It seemed a rather presumptive statement, and Mike was instantly irritated. He responded curtly, "I think I've understood that—better than anyone."

Recognizing that he had overstepped his bounds, Andrew stammered in embarrassment. "Of course, do forgive me."

His obvious sincerity allowed Mike to back off. "It's all right. I'm just touchy about this whole thing."

Andrew sought to explain. "Annie's honored me by sharing her confidence, but we needn't discuss any of this if it makes you uncomfortable."

Just then, an attractive young blonde, fashionably dressed and displaying abundant cleavage, entered the Swann Lounge with two male companions. As she passed their table she uttered a breathy, "Hi, Mike." He acknowledged her with a dismissive smile

and nod. The threesome occupied a nearby table, the woman placing herself so that she faced them, and Mike abruptly turned his
back on her. The way in which she sought Mike's attention and his
apparent determination to not give it to her, left Andrew wondering if she was the woman he'd slept with.

"One of the newer members of our firm," Mike muttered in
explanation, before taking to his whisky. Afraid of being overheard,
he softened his voice to continue. "I haven't really spoken to anyone about this, about our separation, I mean, and it's awkward." He
lowered his drink to the table then lifted a corner of the cocktail
napkin to flip it back and forth between his fingers.

Andrew studied Mike's face as he said those words and saw
how difficult they had been to say. "Annie has placed her trust in
me and I would never betray that trust," he told him. "I want you
to know that that extends to you as well."

Realizing how earnestly Andrew meant that, Mike responded,
"Thank you. I appreciate that."

The maitre d' came to inform them that their table was ready,
and as they left the lounge area, the young woman craned her neck
to follow them. Inside the Fountain Restaurant, two gentlemen at
a table they passed greeted Mike, and four others at another table
smiled and waved to him.

Andrew, who usually garnered all the attention, was amused
by this display. "You appear to know a few people, Mr. Rutledge."

"I grew up here, on the Main Line," he explained, "and I've
spent my entire legal career in this town. I've made my share of
friends, not to mention enemies."

As they took their seats at a window overlooking Logan Circle, Andrew observed, "That's the nature of the business you're in,
I imagine."

Unfolding his napkin and spreading it across his legs before
the waiter could, Mike grinned slightly. "One of the retired partners always says that if you don't make enemies along the way,
you're doing something wrong."

They chatted about business while they were being fussed
over, avoiding the true purpose of their meeting until they could be
assured of some privacy. Mike had many questions about Nether

Largie, Inc., and the direction it was taking. Andrew asked Mike if he foresaw the alcohol industry being drawn into the kind of litigation that the tobacco industry had. They went on this way for a good half hour or more, not mentioning Annie, until Mike brought her up again.

It was the nagging question that had arisen at the end of their telephone conversation. "How'd you come to hire my wife as a consultant?"

Andrew had relaxed during the last half hour, but that reference to Annie as Mike's wife gave rise to some discomfort. With uncharacteristic awkwardness, he answered, "Lynch and Collings has done the ad work for the company for many years. The present director is this chap, John Millar-Graham. We were talking one day and he mentioned that his best friend had attended St. Andrews, one thing led to another and we realized that we'd actually met once, and that we both knew Annie. Sometime after that he showed me the *Ad Week* article on her, and that was how I discovered that she was in the business." He deliberately left out the part about recognizing her on the plane, because it might take the conversation where Annie didn't want it to go.

Mike appeared disturbed by this information. "I knew all about the consulting, of course, but she never said a word about the two of you. And you being *the* Andrew, it doesn't make sense that she wouldn't," he realized.

"She told me that she's tried repeatedly to talk with you in recent weeks," Andrew said. "It seems you were mostly unavailable and seldom returned her calls."

Mike let his gaze fall to the table. "I can't deny that."

Andrew daringly continued, "And then, if you don't mind my speaking frankly, when she did finally reach you, you were with another woman."

Mike turned his head to the window view, though his mind's eye flashed on the naked image of the woman in the nearby lounge.

"Forgive my intrusiveness," Andrew apologized. "It's not my intention to place blame. I only mean to point out that it's been rather difficult for the two of you to discuss anything lately."

"Nothing to forgive," he said. If there was anything Mike admired in a person, it was honesty and candor. Lord knew he saw little enough of it in his professional dealings. "Even though she lost contact with you, Annie retained a fondness for you, the memories of you at least. Meeting you now, I can see why."

Andrew looked away from Mike as he carefully considered his words. "I never forgot Annie," he decided to tell him. "She's held a special place in my heart, too."

Coming from anyone else, that revelation might have disturbed Mike Rutledge. But it was strangely comforting and led him to muse, "She gets under your skin, doesn't she?"

Andrew smiled and looked away from Mike to observe a herd of taxis race through the yellow light.

The sommelier stopped at their table to discuss the wine, an excellent Petrus Andrew had chosen, while the wait staff cleared away the plates from their second course.

When they were alone again, Andrew said, "Mike, the reason I wanted to meet with you—it distresses me to see what's become of her. When I met Annie all those years ago, she was so very unique, so wonderfully open and full of life. She'd already been through some rough times, you know, but she'd remained strong and determined. She was courageous, and quite unlike any woman I'd ever met before, or since, for that matter. But the woman I see today is nothing at all like that. The Annie I see now . . ." he shook his head slightly, "she puts me in mind of a cowering, cornered animal, waiting for the final assault."

A waiter had returned and the men sat in silence while he delivered a second bottle of mineral water.

When he was gone, Mike said, "I never knew that young Annie. I wish I had. I only caught glimpses of her now and again, and it always made me happy to see that part of her."

Andrew wondered aloud, "Why was it, do you think, that she was never able to free herself of the terrible weight of losing her brother?"

Mike sighed before responding. "To begin with, I don't think she was on the most stable ground when it happened. She still suffered some unrecognized posttraumatic stress from the incident." He hesitated, then wondered, "Did she ever tell you what happened to her in her freshman year at college?"

Andrew's face turned grim as he responded, "The bad trip—the rape. That's what I was referring to when I said she'd already been through some rough times."

Mike's tone conveyed his respect for her when he next said, "It's amazing really, how well she did, considering she never got any professional treatment, any real help. And Timmy had been so important to her recovery, her stability. He wasn't just her brother, they were kindred spirits. You don't ever quite recover from a loss like that." He paused briefly, thinking of the loss of his own kindred spirit, his beloved Michele. "It wasn't long after that her grandfather died, and he was the only other person in the world with whom she felt a strong connection. Then her parents pulled up stakes and returned to New Orleans. She stayed on because she was in graduate school by then, and that's when she met Carlos. I think that's why she took up with him, because she felt abandoned, and his attention lessened that. But that was a complete disaster; did she tell you about it?"

Andrew shook his head.

That heartened Mike for some reason, perhaps because it meant they hadn't gotten as close as it seemed. "When I met Annie she was recently divorced and struggling to get by," he told Andrew, "while Carlos was living the good life married to a member of San Francisco society. I used to see her in this little park near my townhouse. She'd bring Marc and push him on the swing, or sit on a bench while he played in the sandbox. I'd watch them from the window; I was drawn to them for some reason. I realized afterward that it was because I could feel her anguish. From across the street, through the walls of my house, I could feel it." He sighed again. "And just before we actually met, Carlos had taken their son for a visit in San Francisco, then refused to return him to Annie."

Mike's gaze fell to the floor beside his chair as the memories carried him off, carried him back in time. He was at the window of his study watching them in the park, and he didn't just see it in his mind, he felt it in his heart: the quiet emptiness of the house, Michele's clothing still hanging in her closet, her perfume barely noticeable upon them, the scent fading with each passing hour. And with that brief but powerful recollection, he realized what he'd done — what his psychiatrist had been diligently trying to get him to see these many weeks — he understood that he'd taken up Annie's pain, in an effort to cast off his own.

Andrew could see that he was sorting through something in his mind, so he waited unobtrusively.

When Mike returned to the moment, he told Andrew, "I got Marc back for her, you know." He smiled slightly, thinking of it. "Carlos was threatening her, so I had our investigative firm do some digging on him. He's an investment banker who moved up the ladder rather quickly because of his heiress wife, and it took the investigators no time at all to find that he was already screwing around on her. So I took it upon myself to fly out there and have a little chat with him, and two days later he was winging it back to Philly with Marc."

Recognizing how significant Mike had been in Annie and Marc's lives made Andrew a little envious, but at the same time he was grateful that Mike had been there for them. "When you met her, that was after you'd lost your wife, wasn't it?" he asked now.

Mike averted his eyes, saying only, "That's right." It was clearly something he didn't want to discuss, and he lifted his glass to finish off the wine.

The bottle was empty and Andrew ordered another, with the excuse, "We're neither of us driving."

Their glasses filled again, Mike told him, "Damn good wine, this. As a rule I don't drink much, but this is so delicious."

Andrew had gathered that, for Mike seemed a little tipsy. "I'm glad you approve," he said, "but do go on with what you were saying." It was prying, he knew, but he needed to understand. "You came together during agonizing times, for both of you."

As he thought of Michele, Mike's necktie seemed suddenly tight. His hand went to the knot to loosen it, but then he seemed to change his mind. Still grasping the knot, he told Andrew, "I found a lot of satisfaction in taking care of Annie, in giving her and Marc a secure home. I loved seeing them happy." He let his words settle out of the air.

Andrew quietly observed, "But something went wrong."

The wine was going down easily and Mike was relaxing into it, emotions and all. "What has she told you about us?" he wondered, slurring slightly.

Andrew, too, was feeling the wine's effects, and his eyes now evidenced some fatigue. "She's said what a wonderful man you are, how much you've done for her and her son, how much she's loved you. But over the years—" He was suddenly too uncomfortable to continue, and asked himself: *What am I doing? How would I feel about a virtual stranger prying into my personal life, asking questions about my marriage?*

Mike wondered, "Why do you stop?"

His countenance struck Andrew; for all his composure and restraint, Mike Rutledge seemed terribly vulnerable at that moment. "I feel as though I'm intruding someplace I have no business," he explained. In truth, he felt as though he'd been peering into their bedroom: a voyeur to their marital struggles.

With someone else Mike would never have discussed these things; hell, he even had trouble talking to his psychiatrist about it. But for some inexplicable reason, this was different. Perhaps it was because Andrew had known her so long ago, had known the young Annie he'd always wanted to. "I'd like to know what she's told you," he encouraged Andrew. "I'd very much like to know how she sees all this."

"I don't want to say anything that may hurt you," Andrew responded, acknowledging, "you've had enough of that already."

They paused while their dinner plates were removed, and Mike reflected on how intimate their conversation had become: two complete strangers who had nothing in common but Annie d'Inard. But he'd allowed it to go that way, he knew, because his instincts told him that Andrew was someone he could trust, and that his purpose in being here tonight was to see if there were some way he might help Annie.

Alone again, Mike met Andrew's eyes to question, "You know how my first wife died?"

"Yes, and I'm awfully, terribly sorry for that," he rushed to say. "I can't imagine."

For weeks now, he had wanted to tell Annie this, but it was too damned awkward a thing to bring up. As he made the decision to confide in Andrew, he did so in the hope that he would pass it along to Annie. "I said I've not been able to talk to anyone about this, but that's not entirely true. I've been in therapy since Annie left." It was the first time he had told anyone. "Psychiatry wasn't anything I ever found much use for, even after I lost my first wife. But after Annie and I separated, well, I ah . . . I guess I needed something."

His revelation surprised Andrew, and he softly questioned, "Has it helped?"

He tried to smile. "It's made it a little easier for me to talk about my feelings, and probably more importantly, to recognize them in the first place." He had to get back to it now, because he had to know. "What did she tell you about us?"

It was clear that Mike would not let this go, so once again, he considered his response carefully. "She said although she loved you deeply, she never felt the kind of love from you that she needed. I'm oversimplifying it, of course."

That stung Mike, but still, he encouraged Andrew. "Go on."

He sighed now. "The affair was a way of taking care of her need. Foolishly perhaps, she'd hoped to keep on with you by going outside your marriage for what you couldn't give her." As misguided as it was, Andrew had no trouble understanding Annie's motivation, because it was what he had done with Janet.

Mike shifted uncomfortably in his chair. "There were signs, you know. I look back now and I see them. When it first started up with him, she would break into tears, every time we made love. When I asked what was wrong, she'd just tell me to hold her. She had wanted another baby and I told myself that was it, that's what was bothering her."

Andrew had asked her why they never had children together, and Annie's response had simply been: "Mike couldn't handle it." But he could tell from the heaviness in her voice that it had been deeply disappointing, even heartbreaking for her.

"From what she's told me, I think that was part of it," Andrew responded. "But there was also the fact that you wouldn't share things with her. She said you locked yourself away from her."

Mike sat very still now. "She did her best to get me to open up, to tell her what was going on inside. It was never something I could do, and her asking always seemed to have the opposite effect of what she wanted. I'm afraid it made me close up even more."

"I believe Annie understands why that was," he offered.

"Michele." As he said her name, his gaze dropped again to the table, and his voice fell into melancholy. "I worked too hard, I still do. I used my work as an excuse to be away from her." He took hold of his wine glass.

"She knows that, too."

"I've told myself it was for them, to provide for them."

Their waiter was at the table now, asking if they wanted dessert, and Andrew found the interruption irksome. "We could have coffee in my suite, if you'd like," he suggested.

The wine was Mike's excuse and he didn't want to leave it behind. "The place is emptying out now, we're fine." He buoyed himself with a few more sips, then nearly whispered, "She's always needed so much, I never trusted that I had enough to give her. I'd look inside of myself and I'd think, you can never be enough for her." After saying that, Mike couldn't believe he had, thinking: *If only that damned psychiatrist could hear me; maybe what I need is to get loaded for my next session.*

His brow raised slightly as Andrew marveled at the courage it had taken Mike to admit that. "So you worked harder and harder," he understood, "and went further and further away from her."

Mike smiled at him. "You sound as though you have personal experience with that."

He respected Mike's candor and although it was decidedly not in the nature of Brits to speak of such things, he wanted to reciprocate. "When my wife and I married, we weren't in love," he freely admitted, astounded by how easy that had been to say. "It was an arranged thing, something our families wanted. When she started to love me it frightened me, and I went running from it into my work. I continue to take refuge there, to keep from facing the facts about it." As a thought came to him, he found himself needing to suppress a chuckle.

"What's funny?" Mike questioned.

"Annie said something to me the other day; she said that the habit of hiding in work is a testosterone thing."

Mike smiled. "That sounds just like her." He realized then how much he missed her quirky perspective on things, remembering how she had always tried to make him laugh. He made his voice soft again to ask, "How is she, Andrew? How's she doing, really?"

Andrew swirled the wine in his glass, contemplating what he would say. "She's managing, but frankly, I'd say that's mostly because I've been with her recently. When I arrived last week she was in a very dangerous place," he wanted Mike to know. "Her friend, this chap Tom Keegan, he'd just died and she'd spent his last hours with him. To say that she was overwrought would be a grievous understatement. She had two episodes—terrifying episodes—where she couldn't get her breath."

Mike was instantly and genuinely concerned. "She's doing that again? God, I should have known. Did she bring the tranquilizers with her?"

Nodding, Andrew answered, "Yes, and she took them the first time it happened. She should have the second time, but I was unable to leave her to get them, the situation was that precarious."

Mike leaned an elbow on the table and propped his head with one hand. He was feeling slightly dizzy from the wine, and the next thing he said tumbled out of him without restraint. "When I think of her, I want to go to her, I want to help her. But my pride, my stupid pride forbids it, so I end up throwing myself into work to keep from even thinking about it."

The connection that had been established between them encouraged Andrew to take more of a risk now, and he led Mike with the statement; "And what she did—her betrayal—it must have cut you to the quick."

Abruptly, Mike straightened in his seat. As he had a few moments earlier, he sensed that Andrew spoke from experience. "Has your wife ever betrayed you?" he wondered.

"No," Andrew answered, feeling compelled to add, "but someone I loved very much did. And I believe I know how you feel, because a part of me understood why she did it, but my pride wouldn't let me forgive her. For many, many years I harbored tremendous animosity toward her." Andrew had to look away from Mike to keep from revealing himself.

But that evasive move alerted Mike's intuition. "Someone you loved very much, many years ago—" he echoed. "That wouldn't be Annie?"

Andrew remembered his promise to Annie, but he also recalled that she'd qualified the request, knowing that she would not want him to lie. "Yes, it was," he answered, and offered nothing more.

It was as though Andrew had opened a window on himself, and Mike began to see the silhouettes of things inside. "I've been talking to you like an old friend, and now I know why. We've quite a lot in common, don't we?"

"We have," he answered solemnly, and to himself he added: *More than you know.*

The tone of their conversation changed dramatically now, as Mike shifted from introspection to interrogation. "What happened with you two? She never really said much about how it ended, only that she left on the motorcycle and you were to meet her in France, I think, but never did."

Andrew felt the mounting tension, but he didn't look away. "I loved Annie but never told her. She loved me and let me know it— but I never said how I felt. On her last day in St. Andrews I was distant and cold and downright mean to her, because it was so bloody awful to have to say good-bye. I handled things very badly, I admit that, and she left feeling confused and hurt."

Mike was most curious to know, "How was it she betrayed you?"

Andrew exhaled as he answered, "John Millar-Graham."

Mike's jaw dropped. "The fellow from the ad agency?"

He nodded.

As that sank in, Mike looked away, shook his head slightly, then loosened his perfect Windsor knot. He leaned back in his chair and slipped his hands into his pockets, something he tended to do when he was deep in thought, realizing: *That's why she didn't bring this up with me, the fact that she knew John and Andrew from before—she would have had to tell me the whole, sordid story.*

He met Andrew's eyes to say, "You'd have to believe that this is more than coincidence, the three of you coming together, after all this time."

Andrew answered, "Annie thinks that it was meant to be, that it was fate."

"Maybe it was," Mike mused. As he pondered the irony, he released the top button of his shirt. "So how did John enter into things?"

"He was visiting from Oxford," he explained, "and he asked Annie if she'd give him a lift back. She stayed with him in Oxford for a few days before she left for France."

"And slept with him," he scoffed, shaking his head again. "She loved you but she slept with him. That has a familiar ring, doesn't it?"

"It was one of her desperate moves," Andrew defended, "when she throws herself into something to keep from feeling the pain of something else."

Mike blinked slowly and muttered under his breath, "I'm well acquainted with that pattern of behavior."

They sat in silence for a few moments, each seemingly focused on the table.

"And have you forgiven her?" Mike wanted to know now. "It sounds as though you have."

"I have," he answered, "but only because I recognized my part in things. I let her go—no, more than that—I pushed her away. I have to take responsibility for that." He spoke of himself, but he also wanted to convey that message to Mike. "It may not be my place to say this, but after talking with you tonight, I sincerely believe that if you could find a way to do that—to forgive her—you'd feel worlds better, as I do now. That acrimony, that resentment, it does no one any good."

Mike motioned for the waiter. "I could use some coffee," he said. "How about you?"

"No, thanks, it'll keep me up."

Mike ran his hand through his hair, hair that had become more gray since Annie's departure. His eyes were now slightly bloodshot, and the circles that were forming there were like dark clouds, gathering beneath them. "It's not as though I haven't realized that," he told Andrew. "On some level I do understand that. There's just this roadblock of pride or whatever it is; every time I try to get around it I find it's right in front of me again, dead ahead."

Recognizing how fatigued he was and that he'd had too much to drink, Andrew hesitated before saying this. But it was, after all, the reason he'd come, so he went ahead anyway. "It's late, and I don't want to keep you any longer, but if you'll allow me one more liberty, there's something I need to ask before we call it a night."

Mike sipped at his steaming coffee. He was ready to go, to end this emotionally draining conversation, but out of respect for his host, he stayed put. Cradling the cup between his hands he took another sip, then told him, "Ask away."

It had grown quite late and they were now virtually alone in the dining room, but Andrew leaned closer to Mike. In a voice that was nearly a whisper, he said, "At my insistence Annie finally called Glenn, and she discovered that you've known, for some time now, that he isn't ill. Why haven't you told her?"

Upon hearing the question, Mike's first instinct was to tell him that it was none of his business, and who was he to put him on the spot like that? He set his coffee cup down, looked away briefly, but then went back to meet Andrew's scrutinizing gaze. Decidedly miffed, he answered, "I wanted to, I should have. But there was something about him. I took an immediate dislike to him and it wasn't because of the situation. He reminded me of the slippery characters I'm forced to deal with in my profession, the kind who refuse to accept an ounce of responsibility. I couldn't trust him. He questioned me, he even tried to cast suspicion on her. He insinuated that there'd been others she hadn't told me about."

"That must have pissed you off," Andrew realized, "it would have done me."

"He pissed me off, all right. It was all I could do to keep from decking him. It disgusted me to think of her wasting herself on a man like that." He spat the words. "He'd been her friend and she'd put her trust in him, then he screwed some total stranger without protection. Some might say Annie got what she deserved, but I don't see it that way." He thought about it a second, then added, "I may be looking at this in a totally bizarre way, but I do believe that even in a duplicitous situation like that there's room for honor. At the very least, there should be trust."

Andrew nodded. "I agree with you, but if he were telling the truth . . ."

Still upset, though decidedly less angry, Mike admitted, "I know it doesn't make sense. I should have reported back to her, told her what he'd said, regardless of what I thought about him, but it was just too damned hard. And what if he were lying? What would that do to her? I didn't want to hold out false hope only to have the rug ripped from under her again."

"I understand that, I really do," Andrew assured him. "But Mike—the stakes! You don't know what might have happened in the meantime. She's been so alone and desperate, anything might have happened."

"I didn't allow myself to think in those terms," he said flatly, giving up on the coffee and going back to his wine. "But I did consider the stakes—my stakes." He looked into Andrew's eyes again. "If he were telling the truth it would have set her free, wouldn't it? It would have cut the rope and set her free."

"Yes," he answered, although he didn't understand.

The response came directly from Mike's heart, and it surprised the man who said it, as well as the one who heard it. "I guess I didn't want that." The darkness under his eyes seemed to intensify, and he looked away again, toward the now deserted street.

With that admission, the scattered doubts and detached facts that had been whirling around Andrew's head melded into sharp, clear focus. "I see," he said, solemnly.

Mike looked off into the distance and failed to say anything more. Andrew could see him closing down and locking things up, right there in front of him, worrying that he'd revealed too much.

Andrew signed the check and after walking into the lobby and going through the usual social platitudes, the two men bid each other good night. Mike intended on walking back to his hotel, but Andrew was concerned about him and wouldn't hear of it. He asked the doorman to bring a car around for him, then accompanied Mike to it, watching until the driver made the turn onto Market Street and the car disappeared from view.

As he lay in his bed, Andrew mulled over their meeting. Mike's desire to know how Annie was and what she had said about him, as well as the deep-rooted grief he still carried over the loss of his first wife, evoked his sympathy, and he was impressed by the courage it had taken to share those things with him. He regretted not having been as forthcoming, chastising himself for not telling Mike straight off that he loved Annie, that his need to be with her was the strongest thing he'd ever felt, that they had already been together as lovers. He recalled Mike's words: *Even in a situation like that there's room for honor, at the very least there should be trust.* Shame crept over his heart and wrapped itself around it, like a wildly growing vine.

There were three messages for Mike at the lobby desk, two having to do with tomorrow's case and one that had been dropped off by the sexy young lawyer he'd seen in the bar, asking him to call when he got in, no matter how late. It had annoyed him that she'd followed him to the Four Seasons, but the fact that she had had the gall to come by the Bellevue looking for him really ticked him off. He'd explained that something important had come up as he bowed out of dinner plans with her, but that explanation apparently hadn't been good enough — she had to see for herself. *Annie would never have done that,* he reminded himself, *she would have trusted me. When did I stop trusting her?*

He crumpled up the note as he walked toward the elevator, then hurled it in the trash.

Before he left Philadelphia, Andrew placed a call to Mike's law offices. He was put through immediately.

He began with, "I won't keep you, I know you're preparing for court."

Mike responded politely. "I've got a minute. I enjoyed our dinner last night, I'm glad we got together. I've a slight headache this morning, though."

Andrew's tone lightened when he admitted, "Me, too, I'm afraid. Listen, Mike, I just want to say one more thing. I strongly urge you to make every effort to see Annie, and soon. There's so much you two need to talk about—and I don't believe either of you are going to be all right until you do. I'm taking her to see that doctor in France on Tuesday. I don't know what he'll find, of course, though I do believe it'll be good news. After that I'm going to invite her stay at a place I have in France, for as long as she likes, because whatever the verdict, I think she'll need the rest. It's very near where her cousins live and not that far from Barcelona," he explained. "Maybe you could make plans to visit her there, spend a few days. Perhaps even make a holiday of it with Marc, if you like."

Mike sighed, thinking that that would be a nice thing to do, but knowing it would be difficult to fit into his schedule. "Thanks, Andrew. That's a nice offer. I'll give it some thought. Will you have her call me, let me know what happens with the doctor?"

"I will," he answered, "or I'll ring you myself."

It wasn't the easiest thing for Mike to say, but nevertheless, he wanted him to know this. "I'm grateful to you for being there for Annie, for being with her now. I'm glad she has a friend."

"I owe her, Mike," he responded, and stopped himself from saying more. "Think about my offer, will you? Think about what I said."

"I'll do that." He considered it a moment, then decided to tell him, "Last night did me some good, I think. It helped me get some things off my chest."

"I'm glad of that, I truly am." Andrew's own need to unburden himself made him add one more thing. "And Mike, after you've spoken with Annie, we'll talk again, too. There's more that needs saying between us."

Mike experienced some discomfort with that last remark, but in the interest of time he had to let it go.

The valet had come for his bags, and he couldn't help but notice how distressed Andrew seemed as he replaced the receiver.

"Everything all right, sir?" the young man asked.

Andrew could barely nod, his mind was that full, that troubled.

Four

The driver who'd been sent for them was a sweet, older Scots-man, who treated Annie and Marc like royalty and entertained them with the stories of his life. At Edinburgh airport he drove them directly onto the tarmac and into the area designated for private jets. The Earl of Kilmartin's had already arrived, and a uniformed crewman stood watch at the foot of the descended gangway. As the car drew to a stop, he greeted them with, "Afternoon, madam, sir. May I escort you on board?"

At first sight of the sleek Nether Largie jet, emblazoned with its tasteful company logo and three flags—the Union Jack, the Rampant Lion, and the blue and white cross of St. Andrew—Annie was dumbstruck. She pondered the absurdity of this situation: of being reunited with someone she had always loved and longed for but had never really known, who had turned out to be one of the most wealthy and influential men in Britain.

When they had mounted the steps, the cabin steward smiled pleasantly as he led them to the elegantly equipped seating area, which was more like a posh office and boardroom than an airplane.

Andrew quickly ended his phone call and stood to greet them. "Welcome aboard," he told them. "Well, Marc, what a pleasure it is to meet you at last." They joined in a firm handshake.

"Thanks, your, ah, your lordship," Marc responded awkwardly. "I'm not sure what to call you." His cheeks flushed pink.

"How about Andrew? That's what your mother's always called me."

"OK, Andrew. You sure that's all right?"

"Positive. Now, mind if I give your mum a hug?"

"Nah, go ahead," he grinned.

He reached his arms around Annie and rubbed her back. "And how are you, my friend? All's well with you?"

With his touch, her discomfort dissolved, and she breathed into his ear, "Yes." Their embrace was compelling and difficult to break off.

When he released her, Andrew turned again to Marc. "And you, young man, you resemble your mother quite strongly."

He blushed again. "Mom tells me I look just like my uncle Timmy."

That seemed terribly poignant, and Andrew wondered how difficult it had been for her to be so consistently reminded of her brother.

Marc told him, "It's pretty cool that you came for us on your jet. Mom says we're going to Barcelona on it, too."

"That's right—hope you don't mind." He smiled and turned toward the first officer, asking, "Are their bags stowed?"

"Yes, your lordship."

"Then tell the captain we're ready for takeoff."

"Very good, your lordship."

As Andrew beckoned them to their seats, Annie noticed his impressive desk, which was a three-sided piece, built into the bulkhead. It was fashioned of burled walnut, and there were two prominent features attached to it, one the Stuart-Gordon coat of arms and crest with its earl's coronet, and the other a posed, portraitlike photograph of his five children.

She suppressed her desire to take a closer look. "I was surprised when you called and said you'd be on the flight with us," she told him. "I didn't think you'd have the time."

"I made the time, because I want to be with you when you first see Crinan Castle."

They both glanced at Marc, who was looking out the window.

Andrew turned his attention to him. "Once we're underway, how would you like to sit in the cockpit?"

"That'd be awesome!"

"Consider it done, then."

Since it was such a short flight, the first officer came for Marc within minutes. Once the cockpit door closed, the steward made himself scarce, so that they were able to speak in private.

They moved to a small couch and Andrew wrapped an arm around her, drawing her close.

"Did you see Mike?" she asked, then watched him nod pensively. "How was it?"

He grasped one of her hands and answered, "Disturbing."

"Why?"

"He's struggling." He could think of no better way to put it.

Unease made her shift her position on the seat, and she began to twist the rings she still wore, the ones Mike had given her. "With what?"

"His feelings for you."

She thought she understood. "He must still be so angry."

"I think the anger's abated for the most part," he ventured. "I think it's something other than that now."

"I'm afraid to ask."

He released her hand and turned to face her more directly. "I satisfied myself that he wasn't keeping something from you. I was concerned about that, you know."

"I have to admit, the thought had crossed my mind, too."

"I'm reasonably confident that that's not the case," he continued. "But I came away with a very strong opinion on something else." He hesitated briefly. "I think what kept him from telling you about his meeting with Glenn was his fear of losing you."

She frowned slightly, because it didn't make sense. "How's that?"

Increasingly thoughtful, he explained, "I understand the twisted logic of it, and I think he does, too, at least he does now. He may not have understood at the time, though."

Still twirling and pulling at her rings, she said, "I'm not following you."

He laid a hand upon hers, to calm her nervous movements. "He believed that telling you was going to be the send-off, that when you learned you were all right you'd be on your way, and that would be the end of your marriage."

That made even less sense. "Why would he think that? It would have been the opposite. Knowing I wasn't sick would have given me the courage to ask if we could try again. Thinking that I was kept me from doing that."

"But that's not all there is to it," he said more solemnly. "There's another reason, Annie. He doesn't trust Glenn, he's not convinced that he's telling the truth."

The muscles in her neck and shoulders tensed, so she reached to rub them. "Why?"

"Instincts, mostly."

"Oh." She frowned and looked away. "That's worrisome; Mike's instincts are very good."

It had troubled him as well, but he was not going to let her know that. "We mustn't become discouraged. We'll stay positive because we've no reason not to be, but we won't get too excited just yet. We'll keep our focus on your visit to that doctor, and wait for his pronouncement."

A knot twisted up her neck and sent shooting pain into the back of Annie's head. She moaned slightly as she rubbed at the spot.

"Please try to relax, my love. We're going to get through this." He nudged her into turning her back to him and began massaging her shoulders. "Are you anxious about meeting Janet?"

"Oh no, not at all," she scoffed. "Why would I be nervous about that?"

"Janet will behave decently," he assured her. "She'll be cordial and won't make a scene."

She didn't want to discuss Andrew's wife just now, because she was consumed with thoughts of her husband. "Can we get back to Mike? It's not like him to be so open. The things he told you . . ."

"I gathered that," he said. "But we put away nearly two bottles of Petrus—that helped, I'm sure. And did you know he's been in therapy since you left?"

"Therapy? Mike?"

"That's what I meant when I said he's struggling. He's struggling to make some difficult changes."

She whirled around to face him again. "What kind of changes?"

"He didn't spell them out," he explained. "But he understands that the distance he kept from you set things up to fail."

"He does?"

"I think he's very aware of that."

She frowned again. "He's no reason to feel guilty. What happened — it's my responsibility — I made the choice to be with Glenn. Just like before, just like with you."

"The guilt is not yours alone to bear," he responded sternly. "Mike acted, you acted, you both reacted. It was the sum of those actions that led you both to where you are now, not a single act or choice made by either of you. And the same holds true for us, for what happened between us all those years ago."

"Guilt is an awfully hard thing to let go of, Andrew."

"I know. I have my own problems with that." They sat in silence for a time before he added, "There's one more thing about our meeting you should know. I urged him to come over and spend some time with you, so you can talk. I urged that very strongly."

"Why?"

It was bad enough that he'd had to think it, but saying it out loud was surprisingly difficult. "Because you both still love each other, and leaving things as they are is not right for either of you."

Shaking her head, she responded, "We can never go back — too much has happened."

"Should going back be what you want?" he wondered. "I should think if there's any hope, it's in finding a new way to move ahead."

Completely befuddled by that comment, she questioned, "Finding a new way? Move ahead?"

Admittedly, he was no less confused than she. "I know it sounds hypocritical, but I liked your husband very much: I felt an affinity for him. I'd like to see things work out more happily for him, for both of you."

"Really? At what price? At the price of our relationship?"

The response came swiftly and easily. "No, not at that price. I'm not prepared to pay that."

"Then what? You've lost me, Andrew."

"I don't know," he answered, his sense of frustration growing. "It's something I feel but don't understand, like my relationship with Janet. I want somehow to keep that, but at the same time I need to be with you, I need to love you."

"And how are we going to do that?" she questioned.

He reached and pulled her to his chest. "Is it selfishness that drives me?" he wondered. "I worry about that, I worry that I'm being selfish. More than anything I've ever wanted in my life I want to be with you, but at the same time I want to protect Janet. And now that I've met your husband, I'm worried about him as well, because I don't want to hurt him. Instead of thinking about how we can be together, maybe what I should be doing is everything in my power to get you back to him, and everything in my power to stay with my wife."

As she lay pressed against his heart, his arms clutching her, Annie could suddenly see what had been eluding him. For she, too, had been plagued with the same disquietude, the unsettling knowledge that in seeking their happiness, they would likely bring misery to others. But on this day, after being apart for only a week and missing him as though it had been years, she came to understand a simple truth: Time was running out for them and they could not — should not — sacrifice their happiness again, even if it hurt the people they wanted most to protect, even if it turned their worlds on end — they could not say good-bye again, not now. They had gone too far, drunk too deeply of the sweetness of being together.

She pushed herself off his chest to search the endless blue of his eyes. "But we've already tried that, haven't we? All those years ago we tried to do the right thing — you, with your sense of duty and responsibility, me, not wanting to take you away from that. And where did it get us?" Shaking her head, she said adamantly, "Nowhere, it got us nowhere. Remember how it was, saying good-bye? And how miserable would we be this time? I can't imagine surviving it." She closed her eyes as she conjured up the wretchedly painful scene. "No. Whatever we have to do, whatever we have to go through, we can't let that happen to us again."

His heart knew that she was right, but even as he accepted that it must be that way, he felt a sudden, urgent need to protect her, for in this moment he experienced pangs of despair over their future. He pulled her close to him again and offered up a silent prayer, thanking the powers-that-be for bringing her to him, hoping that his gratitude might somehow placate them, but knowing full well that when they were ready, they would exact their price.

The steward interrupted them with a discreet cough. "Excuse me your lordship, the young man is returning, we're about to land."

They brought their lips together briefly, and he whispered to her, "Never leave me."

"I won't," she sighed, and with that simple promise, she sealed their fate.

When Annie realized that they would be completing their journey in a helicopter, she grew uneasy.

Marc laughed at her. "My mom's afraid of everything. She won't even put her face under the water."

"I remember a time when your mother wasn't afraid of anything," Andrew told him. "She had more guts than most of the men I knew, myself included."

Andrew held her hand tightly throughout the flight, and tried to distract her by pointing out the various landmarks they overflew. After a while she actually seemed to enjoy the experience.

They wore headphones and used a microphone to communicate, which meant that everyone else in the helicopter was privy to their exchange. "This isn't where you grew up, is it?"

"I was born here," he responded. "We remained at Crinan Castle until I was about eight. Look," he said, pointing toward the north, "you can just see the turrets now."

"Wow!" Marc exclaimed. "Awesome castle; is that your house?"

They had overflown Crinan canal and Crinan harbor, filled with anchored sailing yachts, and when she looked north from the harbor, Annie saw it for the first time.

With auspicious presence Crinan Castle commanded a seaside promontory, overlooking the loch to the south and west, and rolling green pastures to the east. A dark and dense woods sheltered it from the north winds, but a series of terraces and walls on the west opened it to the sea, with a pair of matching curved stairs that led down to the formal gardens. To the east, a straight and wide gravel drive was lined with graceful beech trees that guided visitors toward the courtyard entrance, strikingly designated by a clock tower that rose higher than the turrets. There was an ample lodge standing guard over the main entrance at the narrow country road, and to the southeast, an enormous barn was flanked on either side by matching three-story houses, living quarters for the help, that were fashioned of the same ivory and gray stones as the castle. A Palladian conservatory attached to the south facade of the castle by means of a breezeway glimmered in the afternoon light, like a diamond pendant, dangling on a beautiful bosom.

As they drew nearer, they could see that the doors of the conservatory were opened upon a terrace that overlooked the formal gardens, all bursting with the colors of the West Highland spring. The white gravel car park near the barns was filled with the lorries of caterers and grocers today; from the air people could be seen hustling in and out of the tradesmen's entrance, like two-legged worker ants carrying food to their queen.

Annie was at a loss for words. Andrew instructed the pilot to fly over once and then to circle back, to give them a good, encompassing view of the estate, especially the castle, which rose five stories and closed around itself with flanking wings.

Andrew removed his headphones and then hers, so he could ask into her ear, "What do you think?"

"I'm awestruck," she answered him. "It's a fairy tale—a dream!"

As they settled in for their landing, he was reminded of his own dream, the one he'd had repeatedly at Crofthill while he was recovering from his injuries: the one that had sustained him through that awful time. Annie came with him to Crinan Castle in that dream, when he took his place as the twenty-fourth earl. She stood beside him, her dark hair tumbling over bare shoulders, her eyes reflecting the green of the lawns, and as she took hold of his hand, he felt empowered by her touch. Watching her face as she saw the castle for the first time, he wanted to tell her this, but he couldn't, not here, not with the incessant noise, and not in front of the crew and her son. Instead, he grasped her hand the way she'd always done his—in the dream—and swallowed back the emotions.

The helicopter eased itself onto its landing pad, bowing the heads of the thousands of tulips that bore witness to their arrival.

The Countess of Kilmartin had them lined up and ready: the children beneath the coat of arms that decorated the entrance hall fireplace, with the eldest, Viscount Donald, on Janet's right, and her mother-in-law, the dowager countess, on her left. Nigel was also called into duty, for this was a diplomatic mission, intended to leave an impression of power; he stood at attention near the base of the marble staircase, as though guarding to see that no one uninvited mounted it. Even the family pets were on hand, two placid old Scottish Deerhounds that had been the favored companions of Andrew's father, and an excessively friendly Gordon Setter named Dumfrie. There was also a contingent of household staff opposite the family, including the housekeeper and head butler.

"My!" Andrew exclaimed, as they entered the hall.

The younger children wanted to break ranks and run to their father, but one look from their mother warned them against it. The Gordon Setter, however, who adored his master, could not be restrained.

Janet's tactics were not lost on Andrew and he laughed in embarrassment. "What a reception!" he exclaimed, as he vigorously rubbed Dumfrie. "Is this for us, or is the Princess of Wales arriving early?"

"Darling," Janet responded, as she stepped away from the troops and kissed her husband's cheeks, "don't they deserve a proper welcome?" She offered a limp, cold hand to Annie. "How do you do?"

"Well, thank you," she answered. "And you?" She gripped the flaccid hand firmly as she waited for a response—none came. *Oh God*, Annie bemoaned, *this is going to be excruciating. Why ever in God's name did I let him talk me into it?* "I thank you for your gracious invitation, Lady Kilmartin," she managed to say. "I'm honored to be invited into your home." She thought it wise to acknowledge that right up front, and wondered if she'd emphasized *your home* adequately.

Janet stared at her as though she were speaking an unfamiliar language, then recovered her hand and moved toward Marc. "And you must be Marc. Welcome to Crinan Castle." With all deliberateness she had extended the welcome to him, not his mother.

Quietly, Andrew fumed over his wife's flagrantly discourteous behavior, and Annie could see it happening.

"Thank you, Countess," Marc responded. "I'm very happy to be here, thanks for inviting us." He smiled a devilish, little boy grin, which charmed Janet in spite of herself.

Her frown barely disguised, Janet examined Annie while her husband continued the introductions, scrutinizing her clothing, her figure, even her makeup and jewelry. *Well, at last,* she told herself, *at last the woman in the flesh. She's not so very much to get excited about,* she decided quickly, *altogether too American and casual for my taste: Whatever does he see in her?*

"This is my mother, Lady Mary, Dowager Countess of Kilmartin. Mother, this is Annie d'Inard."

With a calculated adjustment to her half-glasses, she responded, "Annie d'Inard—have we met before? Your name is familiar."

"No, your ladyship, we haven't."

Janet saw her opportunity and seized it. "You'll be remembering the name from years ago, Lady Mary, while Andrew was at university."

"Oh? You're American, aren't you? Were you an exchange student, my dear?"

"No, your ladyship. But I had a friend who was, and I was in St. Andrews to visit him. I met Andrew then."

"Annie d'Inard," she repeated. "I do believe I've heard the name."

Andrew touched her forearm. "Later, Mother, we'll go into this later."

"Now I remember," she said, with some enthusiasm. "You took her to a ball. I sent my car for you to take her to a ball."

"Yes, Mother, that's right." Andrew moved away and guided Annie toward his oldest son.

Lady Mary's eyes squeezed into tight slits as she recalled more about this woman, and Janet grinned to see it happen.

"This is the Viscount Donald."

"Welcome to Crinan Castle, Ms. d'Inard." His greeting was not unfriendly, but typically expressionless in the way of British upper class.

Annie smiled at him. "Seeing you is like seeing your father as a student again." She watched him blush in response.

"And Lord Duncan."

"Welcome, Miss." He had a nicely firm handshake and was more animated than his brother.

"The Ladies Margaret and Catherine." They curtsied and smiled politely at Annie, but rather coquettishly at Marc.

"And Lord Malcolm."

The little man held one arm behind his back and the other across his abdomen as he bowed toward Annie, saying, "How do you do?"

She broke into an enormous smile. "Very well indeed, thank you."

Nigel had been patiently waiting his turn. "And this is Nigel Bain, my personal secretary."

She extended her hand, saying, "It's nice to meet you." His handshake was more limp than Janet's.

Nigel grinned briefly and rather oddly. "Very pleased to meet you, Ms. d'Inard."

With the introductions complete and the staff dismissed, Marc was whisked off by Donald and Duncan. The girls followed, intrigued as they were by the cute American boy. Nigel accompanied Lady Mary to one of the drawing rooms, where tea would be served. Annie was left standing in front of little Malcolm, whose large, sapphire eyes she could not get away from. She crouched down to speak with him, while Andrew took Janet aside.

The sight of him filled her heart, and Annie smiled tenderly as she asked, "Do you have any idea how much you look like your daddy?"

His voice sweetly melodic, he answered, "Yes, everyone tells me that."

"Everyone is right. I can't get over it, Malcolm." While all the children resembled Andrew in one way or another, Malcolm was his clone.

"Do you know my daddy?" he wondered.

"Yes, very well. I'm his old friend."

"You don't look old," he wisely observed.

Her smile broadened. "Thank you, Malcolm. Neither do you." She noticed the reddened area near his hairline, and asked, "How's your head? Does it hurt much?"

"Only a little. Want to see?" He pushed back his curly, blonde locks and held them there. "They took the stucking out."

"The stucking," she chuckled. "I see that! It looks as though it'll heal very nicely. Your daddy says you were incredibly brave through all of this."

"I only cried once."

She smiled again. "Well, even if you cried ten times, that'd be all right, too."

He returned her smile as though they shared a secret. "Would you like to see the nursery? Mummy's put lots of beds in it because I'm going to have company this weekend."

"I'd love to see your room, but can we wait and go there with your daddy?"

"All right."

His dear, accented voice played like music to Annie's ears.

Andrew had taken Janet into an antechamber just off the entrance hall, the luggage room that led to a service stairs for the upper floors. As soon as they were out of earshot, he scolded, "That was disgraceful. I've never known you to treat a guest that way."

"I've never known you to bring your mistress home before," she retorted.

"She's not my mistress," he reminded her, "and she's a guest in this house."

"She's not *my* guest."

"No, you're right, she's *our* guest, and Stuart-Gordon tradition demands that you be gracious."

With a grim smile, she responded, "I did the best I could. Sorry if it didn't cut the mustard."

"She was anxious about this," he wanted her to know. "She didn't want to come. I assured her that you'd be cordial, but you weren't even civil!"

"What the bloody hell do you want from me?" she screeched. "Shall I embrace her and kiss her cheeks?"

They stared at one another as they both struggled to bring themselves under control.

"Where have you put them?" he demanded to know.

She took a deep breath, then answered through clenched teeth. "Marc is in a third-floor sitting room with two other boys his age, and I've put her in Donald's room."

"Where have you moved Donald?"

"To your room."

"And where am I to sleep?"

"With your wife, of course." A self-satisfied grin punctuated her reply.

Andrew gave her a hard look. After her clever maneuverings he knew she wasn't going to like this, but that didn't stop him. "Leave Donald in his own room, put Annie in mine," he ordered.

"Not on your life!" she blurted.

"I'm not asking, Janet."

"You're not going to do that here!"

"Do what?"

"Sleep with her!"

He was only slightly more conciliatory as he told her, "You're right, I'm not. I'm going to sleep with you, as you wish, but I want her in my room, all right?"

She glared at him to say, "Fine, so long as we understand each other."

"We do."

"Don't push me, Andrew," she scowled.

"Don't make me have to," he rejoined, as he walked away.

He found Annie still crouched in front of Malcolm.

The child exclaimed when he saw him, "She's your old friend!"

"Yes, she is," he answered, bending to embrace his son.

Annie grinned from ear to ear to see the two faces next to one another.

"And do you like my old friend, Malcolm?" he asked.

"She's very pretty, Daddy, and she's going to come see the nursery."

Andrew smiled at her, then asked his son, "Shall we give her some tea and cakes first?"

"Yes, Daddy."

Malcolm placed one small hand in his father's then held his other out for Annie; together the three mounted the marble staircase, with the dogs happily following.

Having given herself some moments to cool down, Janet emerged from the luggage room in time to observe this scene. She saw her baby take to Annie in a way he seldom did with strangers. She recognized how naturally and easily this woman related to her husband, how his smile seemed different with her, how there seemed to pass between them some mysterious, unspoken communication. As she watched them reach the first floor with a chuckling burst of laughter over Dumfrie's antics, a chill originated in Janet's spine that shot through to her extremities, firing little electric shocks in her nerve endings that were like the triggering of an alarm.

Five

Lady Mary was seated at an exquisite antique table, her arms draped over a tapestried chair, looking the perfect matriarch. Her carefully maintained blonde hair was pulled away from her face to a tight bun at the back of her head, but her appearance was softened by a pretty scarf that overflowed the top of her buttoned-up Chanel jacket. Baroque pearl earrings complemented her creamy complexion and her skirt was carefully fanned out around her legs, which were crossed only at the ankles, as though to display her expensive Italian shoes to best advantage.

Nigel stood next to her, and when Annie entered with Andrew and Malcolm, he straightened from the slightly bent position he'd been in as he whispered to Lady Mary. His dark hair and eyes stood him apart in this household of blondes and redheads, but he was like the family in manner, in the self-possessed, dignified way that he carried himself. He was nearly as tall as Andrew and dressed in the same stylish though understated fashion, and Annie might have found him attractive had he not regarded her so severely. And too, there was something amiss in the way that he and Andrew avoided looking at one another, as though they'd had a recent tiff. Andrew, she was certain, would not be angry with him without good reason.

Lady Mary greeted her with less warmth than she had earlier. "Come in my dear," she told her. "Have a seat. You may bring the tea now, William."

The butler bowed his head to acknowledge the request, and left the room.

As he had been directed to, Nigel helped Annie into a chair immediately across from Lady Mary, a location that made her feel as though she was in the woman's line of fire.

"I remember more about you now," she informed Annie. "It took me a few moments, but I remember now." She turned to Andrew to add, "I thought you'd lost contact with her."

Noticeably perturbed, he responded tersely, "We haven't seen each other for twenty-two years, Mother."

"I see." She looked again at Annie. "And how did you come to meet again?"

"I hired her as an advertising consultant."

"Can't she speak for herself, Andrew?"

Quietly, Annie answered, "I can, Lady Mary," then bemoaned — *Oh God*. She had picked up on the tension between mother and son and assumed correctly that she was the cause of it.

Glaring over the rim of her half-glasses, Mary told her, "I'm happy to know that, Ms. d'Inard," with a tone meant to convey anything but happiness.

The woman's haughty, baronial manner was decidedly off-putting, but she reminded herself to be nice, for this was Andrew's mother. "Please call me Annie," she asked her.

Three servants brought the elaborate tea service into the room and organized the sandwiches and cakes for the dowager countess to serve. Light filtered in through a long window and shone directly on the silver, setting it to sparkle with almost blinding brilliance.

"How do you take your tea, Annie?" Mary asked, then motioned to the underbutler to draw the drapes.

"Milk and one sugar, please," she answered, grateful that the intense reflection had been eliminated.

"I thought Americans preferred lemon," Lady Mary observed, barely moving her mouth when she spoke. Looking to Annie's left hand, she scrutinized her rings before asking, "Will your husband be joining us for the weekend?"

Meekly, she responded, "I'm separated from my husband, your ladyship."

She lifted a single brow, stared at Annie a moment, then handed over the tea she had prepared for her. "Oh dear, that's dreadful business," she said. "That must be very hard on your son, I imagine."

"I'm separated from my second husband and Marc is his stepson. But, yes, it is hard, on all of us."

Lady Mary glared her disapproval, thinking: *So young and al-ready through two husbands — I do hope she's not here in search of a third.*

Andrew used his commanding, no-nonsense voice to say, "Your questions are overly personal, Mother. Let's discuss something else, shall we?"

With a wicked grin she responded, "Whatever you say, Andrew."

Janet entered the room then, clutching notepads and an organizer. Her face was flushed and when she spoke it was with an abruptness that was born of her discomfort. "Do forgive me all, there are just so many last-minute details to attend to. I'm afraid I won't be able to give you much of my attention this afternoon, Ms. d'Inard."

Janet's unease was not lost on Annie, and had she had her druthers, she would have liked to gather up Marc just now, and leave. But politeness compelled her to stay put and to say as graciously as she could, "Lady Mary has been kind enough to call me by my first name, I hope you will, too."

Janet preferred to decline the offer, but one look from her husband made her answer, "Very well — Annie."

"And you needn't worry about entertaining me."

Andrew interjected, "No, you needn't, because I'm going to give her the grand tour before dinner."

"Oh, thank you, Andrew, that's good of you," Janet answered, with a saccharine smile. "That makes everything fine, then."

The other children returned with Marc, generating a happy noise as they bounded down the gallery and into the drawing room. Their demeanor changed abruptly, however, and they quieted and stiffened once they were in the presence of their grandmother.

Marc reported to his mother. "What an awesome place! There's this really neat room they call the armory, and it's got swords and muskets and all kinds of old weapons on the walls. And there's a gym and an indoor pool, and even a dungeon!"

Looking to Andrew, Annie teased, "A dungeon? Is it still put to use?"

"Not lately," he smiled. "When was the last time anyone was held there, Mother?"

Mary observed the playful, familiar manner in which the two interacted and was vexed by it. Her response was in dead earnest: "It's probably been four hundred years, I would imagine. But one of your ancestors was very fond of sending those who displeased him there, for a bit of a holiday." That last remark appeared directed toward Annie.

"Now there's a novel idea for a holiday," Annie jokingly responded. "For those who are tired of the same old spa scene: spend it in a medieval dungeon, on bread and water, chained to a wall. A fantastic way to slim down and cleanse the mind."

Andrew laughed and Janet suppressed a laugh, but Nigel scowled and Lady Mary was not amused.

When tea was over Lady Mary excused herself, but not before asking Andrew to visit her at Nethergate Lodge.

"After I get Annie settled," he told her.

"Are you ready to see your rooms, Annie?" Janet asked, once her mother-in-law had departed.

"Yes, if it's convenient."

"I'll attend to her," Andrew said. "I know you're quite busy."

Frowning slightly, Janet told him, "Allow me at least one act as her hostess, Andrew."

"It's no trouble for me—"

"I insist," she said. "You go along and have your chat with your mother. I'll take care of Annie." She knew that Mary was set to ream him out and she didn't want to delay that.

Janet began as though she was leading a public tour, and Annie was put in mind of the BBC documentary that Lena had told her about.

"The family has lived on this land longer than recorded history, and one of the oldest remaining structures is the twelfth-century castle keep, around which the eighteenth-century castle was built. Robert Adam was the architect of most of what you see. He designed the castle and park lands around the old keep."

"I was going to ask if it were Adam—the oval staircase seems trademark Adam."

"Are you familiar with him?"

"Of course. He had to have done this before Culzean," she realized, "because didn't he die right after Culzean was completed?"

Astounded that she knew this, Janet answered, "The work on the two coincided, actually, though Crinan Castle was begun years earlier. Adam would get something underway at Culzean, then dash up here to check on things, then back to London. He died from a bleeding ulcer, just after he completed Culzean. It was likely brought on by the stress of working on so many projects simultaneously." She was more comfortable now, feeling more in control. "There were additions and renovations afterward, of course. Sir Charles Barry more than doubled the size of the castle in the mid-nineteenth century, and Sir Robert Lorimer did the most recent work, after a fire in 1913. The clock tower, most noticeably, was designed by him."

As they traversed the long gallery, Janet identified the portraits of Andrew's ancestors that lined the walls. "These two are particularly fine, as they were done by Allan Ramsay." Stopping in front of another, she said, "But this one I'm especially fond of. He was the tenth Earl and the first Andrew. Wasn't he handsome?"

Annie smiled at the resemblance to Andrew, commenting, "Yes, very." Although his hair was dark, he had the same penetrating blue eyes.

"The fourteenth earl was also Andrew. He was reputed to be a great lady's man. The family doesn't like to say, but the countryside was apparently dotted with his illegitimate offspring."

Annie wondered: "Did he die young?"

Amazed by the question, she answered, "Why, yes, he did. Why do you ask?"

"That much activity usually does a man in," she responded. "It either takes its toll on his health or he meets the sword of a jealous husband."

With her first genuine smile since they'd met, Janet informed her, "They say he died from wounds sustained in a duel."

"There you go," Annie grinned.

They had reached the entrance to the south wing, referred to by the staff as the master's wing. "My husband's asked that you stay in his rooms this weekend. He'll be with me, of course," she thought it wise to add. "We've a bit of a crunch on for space. Being as isolated as we are, we offer rooms to as many of our guests as possible."

"Marc and I can share a room, if that would help."

Janet was relieved to know this, for it suggested that Annie had no intention of sneaking around with Andrew. "That won't be necessary. He'll be in a room with other boys his age, if that's all right with you."

"I'm sure he'll love it," she said.

Janet felt considerably more at ease with Annie now, which allowed her to offer a compliment. "He seems very nice, your son. My children have certainly taken to him."

They were now standing inside the master's wing. It consisted of their two, enormous bedrooms, an adjoining sitting room, his and hers dressing and bath areas that were nearly as large as the bedrooms, and a private study, which Janet used exclusively. The gilded ceilings were nearly two stories high, with many of the walls covered in either silk damask or tapestries, and the furnishings were impeccably maintained antique treasures. Janet gave Annie a complete tour and she was suitably impressed, though she had to wonder how Andrew could feel at home in such a museumlike environment.

"I have only one word," Annie said as they finished. "Wow!"

Janet smiled again. "I redid the suites just after Andrew became earl. The bedrooms are essentially unchanged but the baths were from the early 1900s and far too old and drafty. And there was a dreadful plumbing leak," she added, pulling a face. "We desperately needed to do something about that, as well as the dressing areas, which were altogether too cramped, so we annexed two adjacent servants' rooms to get the space we needed. Gone are the days when a gentleman's butler and a lady's maid sleep near them."

"You did a magnificent job," Annie told her, "because it looks as though it's always been this way."

"That was the challenge, of course, modernizing the facilities without compromising the historical integrity. You'll notice that despite changing the use of these spaces, we did very little to the supporting structures, in case our descendants ever want to restore them."

Annie wondered, "Did you take before photos?"

"Why, yes, I did."

"I'd like to see them if it's not too much trouble. My husband and I redid our old farmhouse, and I like to show people what we started with. You can't really appreciate what's been done until you see how it was at the beginning."

"They're in my study."

Her study was a tastefully decorated though unfeminine sort of space that reflected Janet's preference for all things equestrian.

"Have a seat," she told Annie, as she rifled a desk drawer.

As she watched her, Annie paid the most careful attention she had yet to Andrew's wife. Janet's pretty face was delicately featured, but because of the way she arranged herself, she gave the overall impression of being rather plain. Her red hair was cut in a short, practical style, she wore very little makeup, and despite having given birth to five children, she had a slim, boyish figure, with a small bosom and straight hips. She was clothed in pleated, masculine trousers and a buttoned-up blouse, with no jewelry save her rings, and Annie guessed correctly that this type of outfit was what she most frequently wore, what she was most at ease in. She was beginning to equate her to those Main Line Philadelphia types, the horsy set that she and Mike sometimes socialized with: restive women, who balked at their femininity.

Janet located the photos and brought them to Annie, who waited on a couch near the fireplace. Much to Annie's surprise, she sat next to her. The table in front of them held an enormous floral arrangement, predominately lilacs, and the heavy sweetness of them engulfed the women.

"Very, very nice," Annie commented, as she surveyed the photos. "Who was your architect?"

"Trevie MacLean. He's an Adam devotee and historical preservationist, but I did the original drawings and he followed them."

That impressed her. "I really like what you did."

"Thank you; that's kind of you to say. I'm not much of an artist, you understand, but the study of it was one of those college requisites." Out of politeness, she inquired, "What did you do at your house?" though she knew it could in no way compare.

"Everything," she answered. "First we ripped out the plumbing and wiring, then we took the plaster off some of the stone walls and ceilings, and then we got started," she laughed. "And, two years later, when we were finished inside, we got to work on the outside."

"Gracious. Sounds like quite the undertaking."

Annie's expression grew suddenly wistful. "It was, but it was a labor of love. I always wanted to live in a place like that and Mike bought it for me as a wedding present. We fixed it up together. We made all the decisions together, we even did some of the work together, especially in the gardens, and the decorating, of course."

Janet observed the change in her demeanor and offered, "It must have been difficult for you to leave."

She nodded, saying, "I dream about it now and again. Sometimes when I wake up, I think I'm still there."

She had been avoiding it, but Janet turned on the couch and looked directly at Annie, focusing on her almond-shaped eyes, their green and amber rimmed by thick, dark lashes. She understood why her husband would be captivated by them, and imagined a moment when they were young and in St. Andrews, hearing Andrew's voice as he told Annie how much he loved her eyes. She inhaled as though she were about to say something, but then she stopped herself.

Aware of her reticence, Annie urged her on. "Go ahead, say what's on your mind. I'm ready for it."

Janet had thought, at first, of playing this offhandedly, of affecting disinterest, as though Annie were a meaningless distraction. That worked with many of the wives she knew, the ones whose husbands played at sexual conquest as sport. But that would not work with her husband, nor with anyone who knew him, for Andrew was not given to shallowness, nor would he involve himself with anyone who was.

Janet took an abrupt breath before volunteering, "You're not what I expected."

"Is that good or bad?" Annie questioned.

She responded honestly, "I don't know."

Seizing this moment of relative openness, Annie determined to make the most of an opportunity that might not come again. "I tried not to have any preformed opinions about you," she told her, "but I have to be honest and say that I had them anyway. Andrew told me what a wonderful woman you are, what an excellent partner and mother you've been, and I can see that's true—not that I doubted him."

Janet pursed her lips and said nothing as she quietly fumed over hearing that description of herself coming from this woman, knowing all too well that they were her husband's words: that they were the same, passionless phrases he always applied to her.

"I want you to speak your mind, Janet, I really do," Annie encouraged. "It'll make this weekend easier, if we both feel we can do that, if we don't have to tiptoe around each other and pretend."

It ignited her suppressed anger that Annie had the effrontery to call her by her given name, without being invited to do so. "All right then, I will. Do you love my husband?"

Well, here you are—she told herself—*you asked for it, didn't you?* There was a simple answer to her question, and Annie voiced it willingly: "I do."

It wasn't as though Janet had anticipated another response, but it was still agonizingly difficult to hear. She demanded to know, "And what is it you want from him? What do you expect to get out of him?"

Naturally, she'd ask it that way—Annie realized—*of course she'd want to think of me in that grasping way.* "Beyond just spending some time with him, I'm not really certain," she told her. "But rest assured, it's not his money."

Janet's throat tightened in spasm and she blurted out, "Are you hoping to marry him?"

Jesus, Annie marveled, *when you ask for straight talk from this woman, you really get it.* Fortunately, she had no answer other than: "I've no hope of that."

Janet swallowed at her tension and moved away from Annie, more toward the end of the couch. Folding her arms defensively, she leaned into the pillows. "Why?"

It saddened Annie to think of this, and that heaviness of heart was evident in her voice. "Because any chance we ever had of that, we lost that summer."

Her response bolstered Janet, but she needed more. "Does Andrew feel that way, too?"

Since they hadn't discussed it, she could only respond, "He doesn't want to lose you."

A revealing sigh escaped Lady Kilmartin's lips, as she reached to reposition the pillow at her back. With artificial nonchalance, she now informed Annie, "He's said he's no intention of divorcing me, but that's been difficult for me to believe, seeing how much he cares for you." Those were her thoughts, though she hadn't intended to say them aloud. When she realized what she had done, she felt first ashamed, then angry, then, curiously, relieved.

"Well, you should believe it," Annie assured her. "He hasn't wavered on that." She looked into Janet's eyes for the first time and found them unsettling, for although their icy hue was the palest of blue, there seemed to be something white hot sparking within them.

The countess was feeling considerably more grounded now. "I know about the situation with your health and I must say it has me terribly concerned. Are you protecting him—are you keeping him safe?"

Annie dropped her gaze to answer, "I am." Unable to meet his wife's eyes again, she added for the record, "We've been intimate, but only in ways that won't allow for transmission of the virus—if I do have it."

Janet didn't want to appear heartless, so she offered, "I hope you don't."

Annie wasn't sure if that was for her sake or Andrew's, nevertheless she uttered in response, "Thank you," adding, "I would never endanger him, Janet. I hurt him so much in the past, the last thing I'd ever want is to hurt him again."

That reference was a spark, a flame put to the brittle, tinder dry memories of years gone by. Janet was now very glad they were speaking so openly, because it gave her leave to level a charge against this woman, one she never dreamed she'd have opportunity to voice. "You did hurt him—terribly, cruelly—and it didn't end there. Everyone who loved him got a piece of it. Completely innocent people, people who'd never even heard your name suffered because of what you did to him." As she recovered herself with deep breaths, the aroma of the lilacs filled her nostrils.

Annie looked away, quietly acknowledging, "You're referring to the accident."

"That had far-reaching consequences that you know nothing of," Janet said, her voice heavy and scornful. "And I've been the one who has had to live with the aftermath."

Annie wasn't certain it was wise, nonetheless, she said: "He's told me that he wasn't a very good husband to you."

"Not very good? He was dreadful! He was brimming over with anger and self-pity, and he lashed out at everyone who loved him. And if I'm to keep speaking my mind—"

Annie dreaded what was coming, but said, "Please do," anyway.

"Then I need to say that I despised you for what you did to him. I hated and despised you." Janet had to stop to catch her breath. "I knew him long before you did, since we were children. He was kind and gentle and loving then, and I felt very fortunate in those days to be the one who would marry him. But after you left him, he changed, he became unrecognizable." She seethed with the recollection.

Annie's immediate reaction was to apologize, but then something in her rebelled, reminding her: *I wasn't the one who kept him from pursuing his happiness. Yes, I hurt him, but it was his father who lied to him and kept us apart, it was his interference that set all of those horrible events in motion. So why should I take this from her? She's not the loser here—I am. She got him, his children, everything that should have been mine.*

She might have lashed out with exactly those words, but in the interest of peace—well, diplomacy anyway—Annie said instead, "We both did things we regret, but that's between us; that's for the two of us to work out."

Freshly infuriated by Annie's response, which seemed deliberately to exclude her, Janet insisted upon knowing, "Why have you come back? What is it you want from him now?" Her genteel veneer had been completely peeled away, and she was unashamedly displaying her belligerent, quarrelsome nature.

Reminding herself that she'd started this, Annie understood that Janet deserved an honest, straightforward answer. "I want time with him," she said stoically. "We had so little before, that's why everything got so confused and hurtful and completely screwed up. We never had the time we needed to go through things, to let things run their course."

Janet responded sneeringly, "That's vague and evasive, hardly an answer to my question."

Fueled by a growing sense of defiance, remembering what he had only recently told her, that all those years ago he had loved her, wanted to marry her, not Janet, she decided: *All right, to hell with diplomacy.* "I want what's mine," she said. "I want the part of him that's always belonged to me."

Janet marveled at the audacity of this woman. *Well, at least I know what it is I'm up against,* she consoled herself. *So she thinks she can turn back the clock, does she, pick up where they left off? We'll just see about that,* she scoffed, *we'll just bloody see.*

Worried now, about the repercussions of what she'd just said, Annie backed off slightly. "What I mean to say—I can't help but wonder, if we'd had that summer—had the chance to be together and finish things, to say good-bye at the end of it—if we might have been able to avoid all this hurt." Recalling a decision she'd made after she learned of Andrew's engagement, she added, "For what it's worth, that's what I'd intended. When it was over, I meant to send him back to you."

Grimacing in disbelief, Janet responded with biting sarcasm. "How very generous of you!"

They were both still seated on the couch, but Annie suddenly rose to her feet. "I didn't mean it that way," she insisted. "I only meant that even then I knew I couldn't have him. I understood that."

She would not have Annie looking down upon her, so Janet also stood, saying with bitterness, "If only it had worked that way, how different things would have been—for all of us."

They were face to face now, and when she became aware of the weakness in her knees, Annie regretted having gotten up. "And I have to wonder," she forged ahead, "if maybe what we need now is to do just that, to let it run its course, to let happen what was prevented from happening before."

Janet was doubtful but intrigued. "What are you suggesting?"

"I'm not sure," she answered, because she wasn't. "I only know that I need to be with him, and I believe he shares that need."

Janet sighed loudly. "That need is what terrifies me the most," she admitted. "It could wreak bloody havoc on all of us, including the five innocent children who are now part of this equation."

That struck a blow, and Annie responded defensively. "He's had other relationships during your marriage, and you seem to have managed in spite of those."

Janet folded her arms again. "They were none of them threatening. I knew what he was after with them—and so did he."

"I'm not a threat to you," Annie told her. "I don't want to be, anyway." The heady aroma of lilacs was thickening the air and laboring her breaths.

"Oh?" Once again, Janet saw her opportunity and seized it. "Tell me then, just how much do you love him? Do you love him enough to walk away before it's too late, to save him from being damaged all over again by you?"

Annie had been keeping it together thus far, but the very mention of giving Andrew up made her airway tight. She wrapped her arms around her middle and concentrated on keeping her breathing in check, imagining him breathing with her.

"I don't want to hurt your family," she said, in a timid, apologetic tone. "I look into your little Malcolm's face and I know I would never want to do anything that might cause him to suffer. But I wonder, Janet, I really wonder: Is denying it really the ultimate expression of love?"

Janet raised a single brow, saying, "Perhaps, but I'm no expert on the subject." That was one of the most honest, revealing statements she'd made.

The lilac air she was taking in seemed to be growing more dense, and Annie wished she could open a window. But she kept it together—barely—and managed to respond, "Then I guess the answer to your question is no, I don't—not that much."

Janet scowled, shook her head, then walked to her desk. Positioning herself at the window behind it, she turned her back to Annie, so that she might survey her domain. This particular window was a canted bay, offering an expansive view of the estate, all the

way to the village of Kilmartin and beyond, as far as the acres of tim-
ber they owned on the rugged slopes to the east. When she needed
to reflect on something she often did it here, because this view reinforced her sense of authority and command, her feeling of control.

Annie remained where she was, breathing deeply, anxiously
awaiting her reply. After a time the two women were looking at one
another again.

Aware now that Annie's breaths were labored, Janet asked,
"What's wrong with you?"

"Nothing," Annie answered. "I have a touch of asthma, that's
all. It's probably the flowers."

"Do you need to take something?"

"No, I'm OK," she said, plopping herself onto the couch again.

Janet's mood had changed dramatically, and she appeared
sanguine when she next said, "Well then, at least we know where it
is we stand." She moved to take the flowers away, and carried them
to a table in the far corner.

With puzzlement, Annie questioned, "Where's that?"

Turning back to her, Janet answered placidly, "On common
ground, because I don't love him enough to give him up to you."

The flood of despair that Annie had experienced over the idea
of losing Andrew increased tenfold, and she knew she must do
whatever she could to prevent that from happening. But having
seen for herself what a formidable opponent Janet would be, she
made a rapid and fateful decision. For in their half hour together,
she had come to recognize that with her marriage and social status
at stake—not to mention the well-being of her children—Lady Kilmartin would likely fight to the death. The fallout from that would
cause Andrew such misery, she knew, it would destroy their happiness and, very possibly, ruin him.

Through utter determination and nothing more, Annie regained control of her breathing. Making certain she caught Janet's
eyes, she said now, "An impasse isn't going to get either of us anywhere. You and I need to strike a deal."

That statement tantalized her. "What sort of deal?"

"If you back off for now and let us be together, I'll make you a
promise," Annie proposed. "Should it prove to be too much, if things

begin to fall apart — for you, the children, for him, whomever — I'll give you my word that I'll go quietly."

"How do you mean, quietly?"

It nearly killed Annie to say this, but she knew she had to make concessions or risk losing everything. "I'll break it off and send him back to you. I'll let him go without a fight and make it as easy for him as I possibly can."

"And why would you do that?" Janet questioned.

"I'd do it in exchange for time."

Annie was being vague again and that wouldn't do. "How much time?" Janet asked.

What Annie felt for Andrew, what she needed from him — it was impossible to quantify. "Whatever I can get," she reluctantly conceded.

They focused intently on one another in what amounted to a stare down.

The simplicity of that request left Janet amazed, and unable to believe her good fortune. She already knew there was nothing she could do to stop her husband from being with Annie, and anyway, she had acquiesced to pretty much the same arrangement with Andrew. *The woman doesn't know this,* she gloated, *but I forfeit nothing by agreeing to her terms.*

As for Annie, all she could think in this wrenching moment was that she would do whatever she must to be with Andrew, for however long they could manage, because she would collapse and die if she had to say good-bye to him now. But the way it felt, having agreed to put a limit on the time they would have together, Janet might just as well have taken her to their dungeon and cut out her heart.

There was a knock on the door that opened into the hallway; it was Andrew, asking if he might come in.

"Just a moment, darling," Janet called to him, then lowered her voice to say, "All right, you have your deal. And don't think for one bloody minute I won't hold you to it." She was a Campbell, after all, who lived by her family motto: Do not forget.

Annie muttered, "I expect you to."

There was another slogan frequently associated with Janet's family: Stroke not the cat against the grain. It was in this light that she warned Annie, "Mind you: Don't make the mistake of messing about with me. I can be quite vicious if I'm crossed."

Annie had already surmised that. "It won't come to that," she told her.

"He's sleeping with me while you're here."

She readily agreed. "That's where he should be."

"You're not to carry on under my roof and in the presence of my children," Janet said. "Because he wants it, you'll be in his bed, but you'll sleep alone, understand?"

"That's close enough for me. I never dreamed to get this far."

The countess affected an oddly serious smile, saying, "Neither did I." She moved to open the door but turned back before she reached it. There was one fly in the ointment, she realized suddenly: What if Annie told Andrew of their arrangement? "He can't know of this," she insisted now.

Annie protested. "But I can't keep anything from him."

"You'll have to," she said. "If he knows, he'll view this in the same way he saw his father's interference, and we'll end with the same disastrous results." What she knew was that it would turn her husband against her, not Annie.

Annie's eyes fell to the floor when she realized that Janet was probably right. The last thing he needed or wanted was for anyone else to make decisions for him. "OK," came out of her, against her will. The sound of her complicity resonated in her, making it feel as though she was nothing but hollow inside.

The white heat in Janet's eyes made them sparkle in triumph, for she knew she had negotiated a bargain that was all to her advantage. Her enjoyment of the moment was spoiled, however, by a nagging bit of conscience, a twinge of compassion for a woman who had everything to lose; it drove her to make one last comment—an acknowledgment, actually—before letting her husband into the room.

Janet mumbled dispassionately, "I suppose you do after all."

Annie would not respond, but in her heart she cried: *Yes, oh yes—I love him so much, so very much—enough to give him up if I have to, enough to die from heartache if I lose him.*

Her face went pale and her heart almost still when she looked up and saw Andrew then, standing in the doorway.

Six

Before finding his wife and Annie in Janet's study, Andrew had gone to see his mother at Nethergate Lodge.

Lady Mary paced in her sitting room while she awaited her son. When he finally arrived, it was with such casual ease that it turned her simmering resentment into vexation.

"And just what do you think you're doing?" she demanded of him.

He took a seat and smiled up at her. "I don't know what you mean, Mother."

She snorted exasperation. "You know damned well what I mean! What the bloody hell do you mean bringing that woman here?"

"Now, Mother, mind yourself," he chided. "Such unladylike language is most unbecoming."

"My language can't begin to express how I feel about her being here!"

He remained stolidly impertinent. "And why is that, Mother? Why would you have such strong feelings about someone you don't even know?"

"I don't need to know her; I know what she did."

"Ah, I see. And just what was that?" he inquired.

"There are times, Andrew," she fumed, "when you far exceed your father's capacity for obstinacy."

"I'm simply trying to understand what it is you think you know about her; is that being obstinate?" He grinned condescendingly, and that expression, so like his father's, roiled her all the more.

"We both know the situation well, there's no need to dredge it all up again."

"But that's where you're wrong," he countered. "I've only just recently learned the truth about the so-called situation, and what I learned made me realize that what I thought was truth was actually nothing but cruel deception."

"Don't be evasive."

"Evasive is hardly what I'm being."

"Then what are you?"

"What am I?" In a slow, exaggerated gesture, he brought a hand to his chin and lifted his eyes toward the ceiling. "Well now, let me think; does honest ring a bell?"

Confusion was now conquering her wrath, and she regarded him with a confounded look.

"Come, now," he told her. "You're not going to tell me that you had no idea what Father did with the letters."

"What letters?"

He grimaced in disbelief, but when he began to speak of it, his composure slipped. "My letters, letters that belonged to me, that no other person on the face of this earth save Annie had any right to. Is any of this jogging the old memory, Mum?"

As she realized what he was referring to, Lady Mary averted her eyes and arched her brow.

"Still too foggy?" he wondered, though he could tell by the change in her mood that it was coming back. "Let me see if I can clear it up for you: the letters I wrote to Annie and the ones she wrote to me, that were intercepted and never reached their destinations. You wouldn't know how that came to be, would you?"

Lady Mary had been standing throughout this exchange, but now she lowered herself into her favorite chair. *How in God's name did he find out?* she wondered. *It must have been that woman, that damned woman—but how did she know?*

"Donald thought it best," she murmured in response.

His face flushed with stinging heat. "That's right; good old Donald thought it best. My father, my loving father—at the lowest point of my life, mind you—decided to keep me from the woman I loved, the woman I needed more than anything—more than air to breathe, more than water to drink. Remember that now, do you?"

Mary would not give in to his bullying, and said resentfully, "She told you."

He voiced his contempt with an abrupt scoff. "No, she did not. She was as much in the dark as I."

"Then how did you find out?" she demanded to know, but the astonishing answer came to her even as she formed the words. "That's why you went to see Ambrose."

He nodded first, then he glared at his mother. "He didn't burn the letters," he informed her, "he saved them, and he gave them to me."

In spite of herself, Mary gasped. "I don't believe it," she insisted. "Ambrose would never have disobeyed your father."

His acrid response left no room for doubt. "His conscience prohibited him from complying with Father's wishes on this one, Mother dear. You see, there are some things that are just so wrong, so insidiously evil, no person of conscience could follow orders and do."

She responded with the tried and true. "Your father was acting in what he knew to be your best interest."

He forced an awkward laugh, but wasn't at all amused. "My best interest—that's a good one! You can try, but you can't attach noble motive to an act that was nothing but cruel and calculating. My best interest was the furthest thing from Donald's mind: The family interest, his legacy, his precious estate, that's all he cared about."

"You were too young and naive to make those decisions for yourself," she defended.

That was so ludicrous it made him wince. "To decide whom to give my love to?"

"You were ready to break off your engagement," she reminded him.

"As though that would have been the end of life as we knew it! You know, I couldn't understand it then, but now that I'm a parent, I understand it even less; under no circumstances could I ever do to my children what was done to me."

"She wasn't suitable," she persisted.

Disbelief colored his cheeks. "And how would you know that? Neither you nor Father had ever even met her!"

Mary stood her ground. "We didn't need to meet her to know she wasn't an appropriate match. But now that I have, I can see with my own eyes that we were correct in our assumptions."

It was incredible. "Because she doesn't walk around with her nose in the air, looking as though she's had a whiff of something foul?"

"She's no background, no breeding—that's plain to see."

He mocked her haughtiness as he responded, "Well do pardon me for saying so, but some of the most obnoxious, wicked, arrogant people I know are the result of that ill-advised breeding. Take Father's crony, Alfred Cowan, for example."

She retorted, "You're a product of that breeding, Andrew, and don't ever forget it!"

"Christ—how could I?"

With renewed ire, she proclaimed, "You should never have brought her here. It's an insult to your wife and children, and it's a hateful defamation of your father's memory. He must be turning over in his grave."

"I hope he is; in fact, I hope he climbs right out of it. I'd love the chance to have this out with him!"

She was appalled. "Andrew! How dare you speak so!"

"I make no apology for my feelings."

"And I make none for myself—or for your father, for that matter. Look at you, look at your life, at what you've become. Why, in the five years that you've been earl you've far surpassed anything your father or grandfather ever accomplished. The businesses have never been healthier, your generosity has kept numerous charities afloat, your presence in the House of Lords has been enlightening and important, and not the least of it, you're raising a magnificent family!"

He sneered at her remarks.

Her eyes widened in shock. "How dare you denigrate those achievements! How dare you!"

"I don't belittle them," he wanted her to know, "but I resent your citing them to excuse what you and Father did to me."

"I do nothing of the kind," she argued. "I bow down to you in acknowledging what you've made of yourself. I must be the proudest mother in all of Britain, Andrew."

Recognizing her sincerity, he softened somewhat. "There's no telling how much more I might have been able to accomplish, had I been allowed to be with the woman I loved."

It was her turn to scoff. "The woman you loved! She was just a girl, a mere girl, and you, barely a man."

"She was young, Mother, and so was I, but in age only. We'd both already been through hell by then."

She knitted her brow. "How had you been through hell? You knew nothing of life then."

"Were you so oblivious to what was happening?"

"Lord, but you're making me angry! What on earth are you talking about now?"

Bristling impatience, he told her, "About school, Mother, about Eton."

"I do wish you'd stop making these nebulous statements; it's so damned maddening."

He studied her face a moment, looking for signs of recognition, but Mary remained befuddled.

"Well, are you going to explain?" she demanded.

"You really don't know?"

"I don't know how your life was hell before you met her, but I know it was afterward!"

He closed his eyes and shook his head, saying, "Never mind, then."

"Never mind what? Tell me!"

"Let's drop it."

This was the first thing he said that she was actually happy to hear. "Fine, but I'll say one more thing to you." She paused for emphasis, then said with dramatic gravity, "Remember who you are and what you are. Look well to your family, your public life, your responsibilities—they're the substantive parts of life, the things that nourish and comfort us in the end. Passionate love is mercurial, Andrew, and it can be terribly dangerous. That's what your father knew; he understood that, you didn't. That's why he acted to protect you."

"He knew those things, did he? Why then, did he philander his way through your marriage, then meet his end on a hilltop in Rannoch Moor, sneaking off with another woman?"

Mary's lower jaw dropped. "That's not a proper thing to discuss. Let your father rest in peace, Andrew."

Andrew's caustic laugh had an unsettling effect on his mother.

"Very well," she conceded. "If we must discuss it let me say that Donald didn't want his son to follow his example, he wanted to spare you that kind of life."

Soberly now, he asked his mother, "Shall I tell you what else Ambrose revealed? He told me that dear old Donald regretted what he'd done. Not long before the crash he made a statement regarding that very thing to Ambrose. He said he regretted having taken Annie from me."

Mary frowned. "I don't believe it!"

"Do you think Ambrose lied?"

"He's old, his memory is likely defective."

Andrew frowned back at her, saying, "Sorry, Mother, it's not. His recollections are quite clear."

"Why would your father say such a thing? That flies in the face of everything he wanted for you."

Andrew took two deep breaths to quell his irritation. "Because he finally realized what it had done to me," he answered. "He was watching me with Janet and the children one day and it came to him that he had taken something very precious from me, something I could never get back." His voice deepened with the grief that overcame him now, as he added, "He experienced a moment's remorse, and he confided it to Ambrose."

She shook her head in denial. "That just doesn't make any sense, not any sense at all for him to say such a thing."

"Well he did, Mother, and knowing that now is the only thing keeping me from despising him; at least he recognized it, even if it was too late. But I tell you, I hope he felt bloody awful about it, I hope it haunted him to his grave."

Mary didn't know how to answer, or even if she should, as she grappled with her conscience, vividly recalling the day twenty-two years earlier when Donald made the fateful decision to lock his son's passport away. She remembered her deep sense of foreboding when he told her what he'd done, and she'd had to live every day since regretting that she hadn't tried harder to dissuade him. But she also recalled her fury, her outburst of rage and despair when Donald told her of the accident, those first brutal moments that found her screaming and pounding his chest with her fists, crying: "What have you done, what have you done?" She'd sat in stunned silence afterward, on the long journey from Mull, dreading the discovery they would make when they reached the hospital in Glasgow: the absolute terror she could not shake, that her husband's impetuous actions had caused the death of their only son.

Andrew stood staring at his mother, watching her eyes dart back and forth with her thoughts. There was more he might have said but there was nothing to be gained from it, so he waited for her to speak. When he realized she would not, he turned away and left without another word, feeling strangely energized by the encounter, as though he'd been relieved of a cumbersome burden.

The Dowager Countess of Kilmartin remained in her favorite chair for quite some time afterward, staring at a photograph of her husband taken just three short weeks before he passed away: before he burned to death in that horrible plane crash, when, without regard for himself, he went back into the wreckage, in an attempt to save the life of the woman he loved.

The sight of his wife and Annie together was unsettling, to say the least.

"Everything all right?" Andrew had to ask, although he could see that it wasn't.

"Fine, dear, we were just having a sit down," Janet answered.

Annie stood again but her knees were still wobbly, and she grasped the sofa arm to steady herself.

Andrew witnessed her awkward movements and understood them well enough to know that she'd been having trouble breathing. He closed the door and made his way to her, then protectively took hold of her hand. Janet's face went beet red when he did this, and her body stiffened with indignation.

"What happened?" he asked Annie.

Janet answered before she could. "I told you, we had a chat."

He looked at Annie as she confirmed, "That's right, we talked."

"About what?" he wanted to know.

Annie answered now, "About Janet's letting you and me spend time together."

He had trouble believing his ears. "What?"

"And she's agreed to it," she said, then lowered her gaze.

He was astonished, and demanded to know, "Why, Janet?" because there had to be a catch.

Thinking on her feet, she told him, "Because I believe you'll tire of it all and come to your senses — if you want the truth — as you have before. And more importantly, I trust you to do the right thing by your family." She was pleased with herself for having put it that way; reminding him of his responsibilities was always a good way to keep him in line.

Andrew continued to hold Annie's hand, and this tender display hammered at Janet's very foundation.

But in spite of that, she rallied herself to add, "And I think Annie's a sensible woman who won't let it get out of hand. Isn't that right, Annie?" Her eyes settled on their clamped hands.

Annie understood what she wanted, and removed her hand from Andrew's. "Yes, that's right. I've promised Janet that we'll be very discreet."

Andrew moved closer to his wife now. He knew her well enough to realize that she had more up her sleeve, but still, he wanted to believe, so he told her, "Thank you, Janet. You're being very generous, and I appreciate it more than I can say." He grasped her upper arms gently, then bent to kiss her forehead.

A dismissive kiss to the forehead was not what she wanted, and Janet lifted her face and put her lips to his, briefly letting them linger before saying, "I still want you in my bed this weekend, Andrew," and it was mostly for Annie's benefit.

Her kiss was stinging and cold, and he backed away from it. "I told you that I'd sleep with you, and I will," he said, without emotion.

"Fine," Janet responded, then touched his cheek for effect. She next inquired of Annie, "Do you require anything, is there something you may have forgotten to bring with you, perhaps?"

"No, thank you," she answered, her voice barely audible. "I think I've everything I need."

"Then if you'll excuse me, I need to see Cook about this evening's dinner. We'll dine early, Andrew, before our guests arrive."

Flatly, he responded, "I assumed."

Seeking to exert her control again, she asked the ludicrous question, "Can I count on you to entertain Annie until then?"

Because her question didn't deserve a response, Andrew merely closed his eyes in a sustained blink. Janet smiled at them both, but neither one could return it.

When Janet was gone Andrew took Annie in an embrace; she felt limp and defeated, her rag-doll posture supported completely by his arms.

He whispered to her as he kissed her neck. "I'm so very sorry. I know this is impossibly difficult for you."

"Maybe it's better if Marc and I leave now."

He held her at arm's length so that he might see her face, and pleaded, "Please don't—please stay—there's so much I want to show you, to share with you."

The strain made her sound slightly hoarse. "All right, I won't go," she answered, mostly because she didn't have the strength to do otherwise.

He suddenly remembered that they were standing in the middle of his wife's study and it prompted him to say, "Come on—let's get out of here and go someplace where we can breathe." He grasped her hand again and pulled her toward the door.

Seven

They left the castle through the open conservatory doors and descended the terrace steps, but not before pausing to take in the view. The gardens below were arranged in the Italianate style, reminiscent of Versailles, with three box-edged parterres and center fountains, planted now with masses of tulips and iris. As they reached the castle bank, the divine euphony of fountains and delicate scents drifting on the salt air transported Annie, and she was instantly cleansed of her distress. For in the presence of such serene beauty, it was difficult, if not impossible, to harbor any worries or unhappy thoughts.

Rose beds cut into diamond shapes by gravel paths and artistically sculpted evergreens created a sense of order, along with the twenty large wooden pyramid plant supports that cascaded with clematis blossoms of all varieties. Lavender borders, not yet in bloom, promised the hum of bees on a warm afternoon. Squares of emerald grass with carefully placed benches invited daydreaming and frolicking children, while a croquet lawn evoked images of white-clad players, passing through time. Annie was especially enchanted by a sweet summer house, tucked into the natural wood that defined the garden's southern border, that whispered of cream teas under the wisteria and moonlit trysts enticed by the scent of honeysuckle. The entire space was sheltered by high, handcrafted walls on three sides, and to complete the enclosure, a massive undertaking of terracing and stone steps that supported the castle, on a high pedestal it seemed, against a background of sky.

Duncan had brought Marc to show him around the garden as well, and when they met up with Annie and Andrew, the boys were invited to come along for the rest of the tour. So that they would not have to mount the hundreds of steps they had descended, Andrew had a car waiting on a service road that ran from the loch to the greenhouses; as they headed away from the castle and down the long drive, Andrew spotted Dumfrie in the rearview mirror, running and barking after the Range Rover. He halted the car to let him in and when he opened the tailgate, the Gordon Setter licked his face with such ebullient gratitude, it made Annie and the boys break into laughter.

But as spectacular as the manicured lawns and gardens had been, what Annie saw of the estate grounds nearly took her breath away. Softly glowing yellow gorse lined paths and wagon roads, and wood anemones in all the colors of the rainbow, peeked out from behind the trunks of ancient oaks. There was an abundance of primrose and wild hyacinth adorning sun-speckled woods of hazel and ash, pastures of bluebells that coddled white, fluffy sheep, and carpets of baby fern unfurling amid stands of silvery birch. Choruses of birdsong erupted wherever they lingered, and throughout the drive they were treated to the scents of wild thyme and myrtle. But most noticeably of all there was green — green in every shade imaginable, in textures and transparencies, accented with the warm hues of earth and stone, all of it set against the breathtaking blue of loch and sky.

After a time, Andrew asked her, "Do you like it?"

"I'm absolutely in love with it," she sighed.

They went next to Duntrune, with its generous view of Loch Crinan, and Andrew handed her a pair of binoculars he kept in the glove box. There were at least thirty yachts anchored in the center of the harbor, away from the shallows of the shoreline, and pointing toward the largest one near them, he asked her, "Can you read the name on that one?"

"Lady of Mull," she answered.

"That's the family yacht," he informed her. "It's a hundred-year-old, mahogany schooner that had originally belonged to my great-grandfather. And do you see the smaller one near it?"

"Yes," she responded.

"That's mine," he explained, looking at the sailboat to avoid her eyes. "It was given to me by my grandfather, after my engagement to Janet was formally announced. It's one I can manage on my own, without a crew, and my favorite place to be, when life becomes too much."

In a quiet voice, she said to him, "I didn't know you were a sailor."

"We're all of us sailors, and always have been," he responded. "You need only look around to see why. And many of the Kilmartin earls have had commissions in the Royal Navy, you know. I'm one of the few who hasn't."

"Why's that?" she wondered.

With discernible regret, he answered simply, "The injuries I sustained in the accident." He lifted his gaze toward his yacht again. "I'll never forget what my grandfather told me, the day he gave her to me. He said, 'Andrew, there will be days when the responsibilities will overwhelm you and you'll want to chuck it all and walk away. On those days,' he said, 'put on your sailing clothes and take her out, sail her 'round the islands—feel the wind in your face and tackle the sea one on one. Out there you'll realize that all the things you were fretting over aren't that significant, and you'll come to understand what is.'" He looked to Annie now to say, "I didn't give her a name until I'd taken her out the first time. Can you make it out?"

She put the binoculars to her eyes again. After swallowing hard, she didn't read the name aloud, but said instead, "I am the daughter, of earth and water, and the nursling of the sky." It was her favorite Shelley poem, the one that had brought them together in the garden at the Whaum.

"I named her *The Cloud* because of the freedom she affords me," he explained.

But it was more than that and she knew it: It was a name that would always remind him of Annie, of those precious weeks of freedom he'd shared with her.

The boys were standing near them so they were unable to say anything else. With the boys chatting away, they all returned to the vehicle, but Andrew and Annie walked slowly, and remained gripped by pregnant silence.

They drove through the Moine Mhor, or Crinan Moss as it was mostly called by the locals, which Andrew explained was one of the last remaining raised bogs in Scotland. Ahead of them now was a rocky crag that lay upon the flat, verdant fields like a giant lion, napping in the sunshine.

"What's that?" Annie asked.

Andrew grinned as he turned to her, saying, "I'll tell you when we get up there."

She saw the Historic Scotland signs regarding Dunadd but refrained from reading them, knowing that he had a special reason for waiting to tell her about the place. After a short hike to the top, they arrived at a rocky plateau that afforded them a spectacular view of the moss and loch, and also Crinan Castle with its park lands. Duncan had taken Marc ahead and was already explaining to him what Annie could not hear.

They were alone there, the four of them and Dumfrie, and Andrew was happy for that, for this was a day he had long wished for; he was glad he didn't have to share it with strangers. In a quietly proud voice, he told her, "We're standing where many of the early Scottish kings were crowned, we're standing atop Dunadd Fort, the very heart of Dalriada, the earliest kingdom of the Scots, which dates back to the fifth century A.D. It was here that my family had its beginnings."

Something she saw in his face and heard in his voice made her heart beat faster, and she listened intently.

His smile deepened when he asked her, "Have you ever heard of the Stone of Scone?"

She nodded, "I've heard the name, but I'm not sure what it is."

"It sits under the coronation chair," he explained, "the one that's been used to crown British kings and queens since 1308. It was stolen from the Scots in 1296 but its history in Scotland emanates from the Celtic tribes of Dalriada, who came here from Ireland."

"What is it?" she questioned.

"A sacred rock," he answered, "that is purported to have been brought here by the founders of Dalriada; the earliest Scottish kings were crowned with their feet on it. There are many stories about it, including one incident in 1950, when some students from Glasgow broke into Westminster Abbey and stole it. But most of its known history begins with King Kenneth MacAlpin when he moved it and his capital to Scone in 843—that's how it came by its present name. It was used for coronations hundreds of years before that time and had been called the Fatal Stone or the Stone of Destiny." He looked to the ancient coronation site with its carved basin and cup and ring markings.

She wondered, "Was your present queen crowned over it?"

He tried to hide his smile by bending to give Dumfrie a good rubbing under his chin. "She was."

Annie could see that he was enjoying a private joke, so she asked, "What's funny?"

His face seemed full of mischief when he straightened again. "There are some who say that the Stone of Scone is not the true Destiny Stone at all. Many Scots adhere to the belief that in 1296, some loyalists—who learned that the English meant to steal it—replaced it with a worthless lump of rock, then hid the true Stone away. The one under the British throne is rather plain, you see, and the Destiny Stone was purported to have been inscribed with ogham—inscriptions from ancient Celtic times."

She liked that story. "Really? Is that true, do you think?"

He shrugged but continued to smile, saying, "Who knows?" although he gave the impression that he did.

Aware of the contradictory messages he was sending, she asked, "Are you one of those who believe that?"

He couldn't meet her eyes as he answered, "If indeed it was secreted away, it's been well hidden for a very long time."

"Well, I for one hope the English don't have it," she declared emphatically, "because they've no right to it. They stole your country and oppressed your people—why'd they have to take that, too?"

More soberly now, he told her, "It's not enough for conquerors to take the land from the people, they need to break the people's spirit so there will be no uprisings. The Stone was an important symbol that Scots would rally around and the English understood that."

She grinned wickedly. "Then it's a great joke on them, isn't it, if what they've been crowning their monarchs with since 1308 is merely an ordinary piece of rock?"

He smiled again. "Many Scots like to think of it in that way."

"I like the original names better," she said. "Well, not Fatal Stone so much. But the Stone of Destiny, I like that one. It sounds so heavy and important."

Andrew laughed at her.

"I've never heard of King Kenneth MacAlpin," she said now. "Was he significant?"

He led her to the site of the coronations where the intended king would place his foot into a space carved out for it, to symbolize both his dominion over the land and his union with it. "MacAlpin united the Scotti and the Picts to create what was called Alba and is now most of Highland Scotland," he informed her. "His descendent, Malcolm the Second, brought Lothian under his control and his grandson Duncan brought the rest of what is now this country into the fold. More than any others, these Celtic kings created this country, not single-handedly of course, but through their leadership and valor. They fought the Vikings, the Angles and the Britons, and their own warring factions to do it, but what they accomplished so long ago still stands as their monument."

As he was explaining this to Annie, Duncan and Marc joined them.

"The remains of some of the more important Celtic kings lie in sacred burial ground on Iona," he continued, "but their predecessors and descendants lived and reigned here, in Kilmartin Glen. The earliest kings were buried on the grounds of our ancestral home and the Stuart-Gordons have guarded their resting place for more than a millennium, sometimes at the cost of our lives." He pointed now to the carving of a wild boar etched into the stone, asking her, "Does this look familiar?"

It took a few seconds, but then it registered. "It's like the boar in your family coat of arms."

"That's right," he smiled. "We bear that coat of arms because we are their descendants, our bloodline springs from Scotland's first kings."

Annie was astounded. "Jesus, Andrew—that is so cool!"

Marc, who'd been listening intently, had to add, "Man, that's totally awesome!"

Duncan smiled proudly but held back some laughter, entertained as he was by their reactions.

"And it's not as dilute as you might expect," Andrew added. "Careful, strategic blood-alliances have been made throughout the centuries. My mother was a distant cousin to my father, as Janet is to me, as my grandparents were to each other, and so on."

Annie raised a single brow and nodded twice, commenting, "That certainly puts things into perspective."

Quietly, he said to her, "I thought it might."

Still grinning, Duncan asked his father, "Are we going to take them to see the Temple Wood and Nether Largie?"

"Let's do that," he answered him.

As they returned to the car Annie was visited with a clear recollection, which prompted her to ask Andrew, "Do you remember when you took me to the Kate Kennedy Ball?"

Sighing slightly, he responded, "I've never forgotten it."

"I remember how striking you were in your kilt," she told him. "I said you looked like a Highland prince and you reacted in an odd way—you asked me why I would say something like that. Now I know why it threw you. You're exactly that, aren't you? If history had taken a different turn, I'd be speaking to the King of Scotland now, instead of the Earl of Kilmartin."

Andrew didn't answer, but he smiled genially and helped her into the car.

They went first into the wee village of Kilmartin, where everyone who saw them greeted Andrew with genuine smiles and "Afternoon, your lordship." He showed Annie and her son Kilmartin House, which was the just-completed center for tourism that he'd been instrumental in creating. They next saw Kilmartin Church with its extensive collection of medieval grave slabs, then they traveled up the road to see the ruins of Carnassarie Castle, which Duncan told her had been built by his mother's ancestors. It was not without envy that Annie heard this, recognizing how connected Janet and Andrew were, not only through the here and now, but through their common heritage as well.

On the way back, Andrew took them into the Kilmartin Hotel for a quick pint and soft drinks for the boys. When they entered the pub, she was surprised to see the clientele stand in respectful greeting, and she absolutely loved that he seemed to know them all by name. He even asked about their families, remembering that this daughter had gone to university in England or that son had taken a new position in Glasgow.

They next drove past the Nether Largie Cairns for which Andrew had named his company, but there wasn't time to explore them. Their last stop before returning to the castle was the Temple Wood, a mysterious place for which Andrew had a particular fondness, having loved to play there as a child.

"This ritual site was used for more than two thousand years," he told her, "beginning in about 3500 B.C."

She walked to the center of the pebbled circle, which was surrounded by standing stones. Lemon-colored gillyflowers, redolent in the afternoon sun, seemed to sprout from the very rocks. "What did they do here," she wondered, "make offerings to the gods?"

"Most likely," he answered, smiling. "They did find human bones when they excavated, those of an adult female and those of a tiny child."

Just then, a cuckoo called from the wood beyond the circle and Annie was overcome by a strong feeling of déjà vu. Still standing in the center of the site, she wrapped her arms around herself to suppress a shiver. "Were they sacrificed?" she asked him.

"Probably. But there's also the chance that this was an elaborate memorial. They may have been the wife and child of an important chief." Because Duncan and Marc had wandered off with Dumfrie, he was free to come behind her and enclose her in his arms. "Does this place frighten you?"

"No," she answered, "not like our Celtic place near St. Andrews; that place reeks of death. And I guess I'm more comfortable here because of you, because this place is such a part of you. But I had the strangest sensation just now, like I knew the woman and child whose bones they found, like I had some connection with them. How weird is that?"

He released her now, for he heard Dumfrie's bark coming toward them. They walked away from the circle and into the grove, which was carpeted with the indigo of wild iris. "I wish there was more time," he told her, "because there's still so much to see. And God, but I'd love to take you sailing 'round the Hebrides."

Thinking of that made her sigh, for nothing would give her more pleasure than to be alone with him just now, letting the wind take them where it would. But she needed to get that idea out of her mind, because it make her heart ache with longing.

"Tell me something," she said to change the subject. "Your last names: I take it it's not just the Celtic kings that you come from."

"We're Stuarts as well, of course," he told her. "Mary, Queen of Scots, Bonnie Prince Charlie and company, who were also descendants of Duncan the first, as is the present queen."

"Wasn't that spelled differently?"

"Initially it was spelled S-T-E-W-A-R-T, but it was changed quite a long while ago to distinguish our family from all the other Stewarts in Scotland."

"And the Gordons? Who were they?"

"Another noble family who brought us into the whisky business and were related, actually, to George Gordon. Do you remember who he was?"

"George Gordon? Not Percy's good friend and fellow poet . . ."

Andrew was delighted that she knew this. "Yes! George Gordon was Lord Byron. I so wanted to tell you that back in St. Andrews all those years ago, when you told me how much you loved Percy Shelley."

"I've always sensed the poet in you, Andrew," she smiled.

"You've no idea how wonderful it is for me, having you here at long last."

"It's more wonderful for me—it brings me that much closer to you." All this talk of ancestors made her think of something she wanted to share with him. "You know, the d'Inards have some history, too. Nothing like yours, of course, but we're from what used to be the tiny, independent country of Béarn in southwest France. My great-grandparents were the first in the family to leave the region and that's saying something, because my cousin Jean-Marc has traced the family back to 1253."

Smiling broadly now, he exclaimed, "How wonderful!"

"And in doing that," she continued, "he discovered how we came to bear our name."

"How was that?"

"It was actually the name of a baron," she informed him. "An ancestress of mine was the passionate love interest of this man, Baron d'Inard. She bore his son and he in return made a gift to her of a small château and many hectares of good farmland. My cousins still live on some of that land. He also gave his name to her son, hence, our ascendancy."

"Is that documented?"

She nodded. "Jean-Marc has a copy of the deed that details that. Unlike a lot of places where the town halls were burned to the ground during the revolution, that part of France was virtually untouched by the violence, so many of the official records remain intact. Jean-Marc spent several years sorting through it all and compiling the information—which wasn't easy. It was written in Béarnais and they seldom spelled a word the same way twice."

"When did this occur, with the baron?" he wanted to know.

"In 1583."

"The Scots and the French were great allies then—I wonder if any of my forbearers knew him." His expression grew wistful. "What was her name, your ancestress?"

"Audine Laborde-Hourcade."

"What a beautiful name!" he exclaimed. "So the Baron d'Inard loved Audine. He must have loved her very much, to have done all that."

Searching his eyes, she told him, "It's my fantasy that theirs was a great love, that the baron loved her deeply."

With quiet certainty, he responded, "If she was anything at all like her descendent, I understand him perfectly."

"I love you so much," she whispered to him.

Andrew couldn't answer her, for he'd heard the dog's bark again and noticed the boys almost upon them. But he captured her eyes with his and tenderly whispered, "Audine," as though he were her lover.

Eight

To receive their guests this evening, the earl and countess had opened the doors between two grand drawing rooms. In one of the two rooms, a late supper buffet had been laid out, along with a dessert table and coffee. Liveried servants waltzed amid the clusters of important people and celebrities, serving them drinks and whatever their hearts desired. Robin Keay and his wife Loreena were among the early arrivals and Andrew brought Robin immediately over to Annie, who had been sitting by herself, nursing a glass of single malt.

Trying hard to contain his smile, Andrew asked, "Robin, do you remember this lady?"

He smiled politely, saying, "I'm afraid you have the advantage."

"I did some gardening for you once," she said, as she rose to her feet, "at the Whaum."

"Oh my!" he gasped. "My word—it isn't! Is it? Is it you, Annie?"

"In the flesh," she responded.

He embraced her warmly, before asking Andrew, "How on earth?"

"I've engaged her to do some consulting for me," he explained, "on the advertising end of things."

"Oh, that's marvelous!" he exclaimed. "I can't get over it—I just can't get over it." He lifted his hands to Annie's and Andrew's shoulders and gave them each a squeeze. "It feels as though I've taken a tumble back in time—the three of us, standing here like this. We should be heading out to The Russell for a pint or to a ceilidh at the town hall."

They shared the laugh, before Andrew reluctantly left them to greet other guests.

"You look remarkably well," Robin told her, "remarkably."

"Thank you," she answered, "and so do you." But in truth she was astounded by how much he'd changed, going from the thin, retiring young man he was to this pot-bellied, balding businessman, who was showing the tell-tale signs of enjoying his drink too much.

"Let me introduce you to my wife. Loreena, dear—"

The dour-looking woman turned away from the couple she was conversing with to half-smile, half-frown at Annie.

"Annie was an astounding American," he informed her, "who came to visit St. Andrews and purchased an old motorbike, then took off for parts unknown."

"Really? How interesting." It was obvious that Loreena didn't find it interesting at all.

Seemingly oblivious to his wife's sullen mood, Robin eagerly questioned, "Where'd you go after you left? How'd you get on?"

In an effort to include Loreena, Annie offered her a warm smile. "From St. Andrews I went to Oxford, you may recall, and then to France. I spent the entire summer tooling around, up to the Netherlands, then Germany and Switzerland, then all around southern France. After Bastille Day I went to Italy and spent the remainder of the summer there."

"Lord, that sounds like a brilliant holiday. When did you go home and what did you do with your motorbike—what did you call it?"

"Percy B."

"That's right, old Percy!"

"Old Percy died on me in the Pyrénées," she informed him. "I was on my way to Andorra on some treacherous mountain roads when the throttle stuck. I almost went hurtling over the side of a mountain."

"No! How'd you manage?"

"When I realized what was happening, I pulled off the road into a steep incline," she recalled. "That slowed me down and I had the presence of mind to turn off the switch. I was traveling with some American boys I'd met who were all on fancy new motorcycles, and they helped me fix him enough to drive back to the nearest mechanic. I never made it to Andorra, though. I limped into Montpelier and left Percy at a shop, and I never rode him again."

"What a story—but I imagine you had quite a few adventures that summer."

"I did, Robin, more than I'd bargained for."

Loreena seemed painfully bored and she interrupted them now. "Do forgive me, but some people have arrived who we need to greet, Robin."

"Let's have a drink together later, shall we?" he proposed to Annie.

Despite the disapproving glare from his wife, she leaned and kissed his cheek, telling him, "I'll look forward to it."

Andrew put considerable effort into introducing Annie to his friends, especially to the less stuffy ones whom he felt would be more accepting of her; she chatted congenially with most of them, remembering names and faces with ease. Her son was kept busy by Andrew's children and once the guests began arriving, she only caught glimpses of him now and again; he'd give her a wink or a smile to let her know that he was OK.

Having driven up from Oxford, John and Lena were among the last to arrive that evening, and Annie was especially delighted to see Lena again.

Lena embraced her and kissed her cheeks, exclaiming, "I see you've worked things out with Andrew!"

Annie returned her kisses. "It's so good to see you—I've missed you."

"And we've missed you," John answered. "It was altogether too quiet after you left."

"I imagine so," she realized. "Sorry about all the ruckus."

"Don't be." Lena took Annie's hand in hers and patted it. "It gave us something to talk about and anyway, I couldn't be more thrilled to have been invited here. Isn't this place magnificent? I can't wait to see the grounds."

"The gardens are perfection," she told them, "and the estate grounds are glorious."

"Where are you sleeping? Where've they put you?" Lena wanted to know.

"In Andrew's room."

"Oh my! Really?" That seemed odd to Lena, and she displayed puzzlement. "It must be very grand."

"It is that." Annie understood her confusion, but would explain later. "And you? Where are you?"

"The third floor—we haven't been up yet, but we were told. How many guests are they expecting?"

"I think there are more than sixty who will be staying over. As for the events themselves, several hundred I think."

"Is the Princess of Wales really coming?"

"Tomorrow afternoon," Annie told her, "and she's staying through Sunday evening, according to Andrew."

"I never dreamed to be included in a weekend house party that included Diana," Lena gushed. "And—oh my lord—is that Sting and Trudie?"

Annie laughed at her. "Steady on, old girl."

As they chatted, Janet came upon them to introduce her parents, the Marquess and Marchioness of Ardgour; they had surely been briefed on who Annie was, because the very air about them caused her to shiver. They stayed but a moment and were distinctly more cordial to John and Lena, but when they walked away Lena expressed her disapproval, saying to Annie, "What is it you do to people to make them react so? For the life of me, I can't see it."

John was sipping at a whisky, when he wisely observed from the rim of the glass, "It's not that difficult to guess. It's what she meant to Andrew at one time."

"But that's in the past," Lena protested.

Annie looked away from them to hide her face, but they both witnessed her cheeks going pink.

John and Lena retired soon after, for it had been a grueling drive up. As midnight drew near, the crowd thinned considerably and Robin's wife excused herself, claiming a need for beauty rest. Robin and Annie were left on their own and moved to the music room, where they settled into a cushioned window seat flanked by an eighteenth-century French harpsichord and baroque-style grand piano. A talented young pianist had been playing there these last three hours, but she packed up her sheet music now and bid everyone good night.

While Robin had always shown some reticence in their interactions of the past, that seemed to have been forgotten, and tonight he treated Annie in the warm and comfortable manner of an old friend. It wasn't long before Andrew joined them, looking rather spent. He seated himself at the grand piano and brushed his fingertips over the keys, then played the beginnings of a Debussy piece with amazing skill.

Annie was astonished. "I had no idea you played!"

"Play at it, is all I do," he said. "It was a monumental waste of time, forcing me to sit here on a beautiful day when I would have much preferred to be climbing trees."

Robin grinned and scoffed. "Never mind that, I've heard you play and I'd beg to differ. Will you have a drink with us now, old man?"

"I'm afraid I'll have to pass," he told him. "It's been a long week and Janet's insisting we go up so I won't run out of steam tomorrow."

Robin's drink-flushed face beamed excitement. "It's brilliant, isn't it, seeing Annie again? Too many years have passed."

"Yes, far too many," Andrew answered, hinting at melancholy.

"I cherished those times in St. Andrews," Annie said, briefly catching Andrew's eyes. "And I did so love the Whaum." Then to Robin, she added, "I've been in it, you know."

"You haven't! What's it like now? Who owns it?"

"A lovely English couple, the Hamptons," she answered. "I stopped by there one day when Mrs. Hampton was working in the front garden. I told her my connection to the place, and she was gracious enough to invite me in. They've changed it quite a bit, but mostly for the better, I think."

"I do hope they've installed some modern plumbing," he chuckled.

"I think they must have," she smiled. "They remodeled the kitchen and added a sunroom just off it—where the mudroom used to be. They have their meals there, because they use the dining room as a study."

He lifted his eyes to the ceiling as he imagined it. "That should be nice, because of the garden views. Is that as it was?"

"It's been entirely revamped," she said. "They had professional landscapers in and terraced it, with a lovely slate patio for a table and chairs; there's also a smallish lawn and new flower beds along the walls. It's very nice what they did, very practical for the space, but—"

"But what?"

"But there are no more roses."

Robin looked distressed. "Oh dear, my aunt's roses gone. That's rather sad, isn't it?"

She nodded pensively.

Andrew's fatigue kept him from participating in the conversation and that was for the best, he knew, because he hadn't the strength to keep his emotions disguised. He and Annie made eye contact again, and she suggested, "Why don't you go on up? You needn't keep us entertained."

He was clearly struggling with something he wanted to say, and managed only, "It's so long since the three of us were together. It's quite extraordinary, being like this again."

"We'll have other opportunities this weekend, old chap," Robin offered. "Go on, now, the lovely countess calls." He gestured his chin in the direction of Janet, who was conversing with someone in the corridor, just outside the open music room doors.

When Andrew left with his wife, Annie was struck by the way he carried himself, which put her in mind of a prisoner being returned to his cell, after an all-too-brief visit with loved ones.

"Lovely woman, that," Robin said of Janet. "She's made quite a job of it, too, what with the five children and all. She holds up her end astoundingly well, seeing to the charities and all the social obligations, and it's no small task, let me tell you. Andrew made quite a good match for himself."

"Made quite a good match for himself?" she mocked. "Come on, Robin, it's me you're talking to."

He was momentarily flabbergasted, for he'd forgotten just how bluntly honest she could be. "It's just a manner of speaking—

making a match for oneself—it's merely an expression. No, he didn't make that choice for himself, did he?"

She kept what would have been a scathing comment to herself.

"Actually," he said, then looked around to make certain no one else heard, "you and I know that he went kicking and screaming." It gave him something of a thrill to be able to say this aloud, for it was a secret he'd carried around for years. "But I'm sure he sees now, as we all do, that it was for the best."

She closed her eyes and sighed.

"It must have been that odd for you," he ventured, "when you saw him again, when you found out who he was, after all this time. You hadn't known, had you?"

Her response betrayed her bitterness. "I was completely in the dark."

"It wasn't easy for him, you know, keeping it from you."

With a measure of sarcasm, she questioned, "You helped him with that, did you?"

"I tried to keep him focused."

She found that response irksome, but let it slide.

A footman had crept up on them, to ask if they needed anything; Robin relinquished his empty snifter, and the young man left to refill it.

When he was gone, Annie asked, "And my friend Susannah Barclay, she helped, too, didn't she?"

His brow knitted. "If I remember correctly, she learned of it quite by accident. But she wanted to tell you, she thought you should know. I think it was Andrew who persuaded her not to."

She frowned at him. "It was quite a little conspiracy, wasn't it?"

"But totally without malicious intent. We were, after all, friends, were we not?"

She seized on that remark. "Then tell me something, old friend. Didn't Susannah know what had happened to him; didn't she know about his accident? I distinctly remember asking her in my letters if she'd seen him and she wrote back that he hadn't returned to university. It was as though he'd dropped off the face of the earth."

He answered carefully. "She must have known, everyone in St. Andrews did. His picture had been in all the papers when it happened and everyone realized who he was. For a time, it was all anyone talked about."

She shook her head despairingly. "I just can't understand why she didn't tell me; she knew how much I loved him. I met her and Mel in London, you know, just before I flew home. If she'd told me then as she should have, I would have gone to him."

Robin's drink arrived and he set it on the table next to He crossed his legs, then grasped hold of one knee with both h in what seemed a thoughtful moment. "I can't speak for h course, but maybe that was just it," he speculated. "Maybe knew you'd try to go to him, and that his father would have you barred at the gate."

"God!" she exclaimed, feeling as though she wanted to punch something. "The whole thing's so damned maddening!"

"I can understand your bitterness, Annie," he told her. "He carries some, too, you know. It comes out now and again." As he sipped at his brandy, his eyelids began to droop. "Every so often, over the years, we've had occasion to discuss it, when we're alone and we've had a wee dram too many."

Recovering herself, she asked, "What was it like for him afterward? How long did his recuperation take?"

His expression saddened with the recollection, and he answered somberly, "I read about it in the papers; I read that he was near death in hospital at Glasgow, and that the family were keeping vigil. I went as soon as I could, and when they finally let me in I sobbed to see what had happened to him: his face gashed and swollen, his leg so horribly broken, his whole body bruised and battered and punctured. It was nothing short of a miracle that he survived." He had to pause and shake the image from his head.

Annie's pulse began to throb in her ears and she grasped the pillowed cushion beneath her, until her knuckles blanched and smarted. The pulsing throbbed out what she couldn't say to Robin: that the picture of Andrew so wounded, so damaged and full of pain made her want to scream, made her want to claw at the walls of time and tear them down, as though she might somehow get back to him.

"When he was back at Crofthill," he continued, "I visited almost every Sunday that summer. His father would send a car for me and I'd bring him books and records and sit with him for the afternoon. I'd play the records for him, because he was so long getting to do things like that for himself." He allowed himself a moment's silent contemplation, and it was then that a particular memory surfaced. "There was one song he'd have me play over and over. He'd go far away in his mind while he listened, you could tell that, and then he'd come back at the end and tell me to play it again."

In her gut, she knew the answer to this question, but she asked anyway, "Which song was that, Robin?"

"A Van Morrison song, 'Into the Mystic.' Do you remember it?"

She nodded and as she did, her heart filled with the memory of that long-ago afternoon in the meadow, when they almost made love. Since that day, every time she'd heard that song she had remembered him, longed for him, lamented the loss of him. It heartened her to know that the song had also affected him, even as the pain of knowing that now tore through her insides.

"He never said, but I thought it had something to do with you," Robin informed her. "Anyway, time went on, he got better and stronger, and I had to go back to St. Andrews. We wrote, we never lost touch. Eventually his father brought in tutors and arranged for him to finish his studies at home. He only went back to St. Andrews to sit for his final examinations, you know."

"No, I didn't know," she sighed.

"Going back there was just too difficult for him to even consider," he explained. "He was getting better, but he was still limping badly and needed physical therapy every day, you see. The next time I saw him was at Hogmanay at Crofthill," he recalled now. "He was with Janet and they were doing all right."

"Hogmanay?"

"It's a Scottish New Year tradition. It's basically an excuse for a party, but it's also a symbolic occasion, a time for putting the past behind you and getting on with things. People even throw things out that have to do with the old year, as a gesture."

Annie murmured, "Oh."

"He wasn't the same old Andrew," he told her, shaking his head slightly, "not at all, but he was much improved from the last time I'd seen him. And then the next time, he was even better. By the following summer it was clear that he meant to put everything behind him and get on with the business of things." He considered the wisdom of saying this, knowing that she might not like hearing it, but something told him to go ahead. "I tell you this, because I think you should know that his present state was terribly hard in the gaining, Annie, that he paid a great price for it. But that's the way life is, isn't it? I mean, none of us realized it at the time, we were that young, but that's the way of things. Most of what we value in life we've had to pay dearly for, one way or another."

In her exhaustion and despair, her restraint had been wiped out, and she responded to him with undisguised emotion. "There are some things," she said quietly, "that come to us as gifts, as pure, heavenly gifts, that we've neither paid for nor deserve. Those gifts, Robin, matter the most."

He sighed before responding. "I'm no theologian, so I don't know about that. Perhaps I'm just too much of a Calvinist to see things in that way." He ended with a small, nervous laugh.

And because her restraint was gone, she could not help asking this, although she knew it would likely distress her all the more. "Were you at their wedding?"

With a less than genuine smile, he answered, "Of course. I wouldn't have missed it for the world."

"What was it like, I mean, what was he like?"

He furrowed his brow. "Well, let's see, it was in August, two years after the car crash. The ceremony was in Glasgow at the cathedral, there were five or six hundred guests, to be sure. You can imagine who was there, what with his family and Janet being the granddaughter of the Duke of Argyll: everyone from the Prince of Wales to the Prime Minister. The queen was there as well," he informed her, with curious pride. "After the initial reception in Glasgow, the family and closest friends came up here, to Crinan Castle, where the celebration continued through the weekend. I was hungover for fully a week."

She asked impatiently, "What about Andrew? How was he?"

Still holding his crossed leg, he tossed his head backward and looked toward the ceiling, as though he needed to jog his memory. "Solemn, comes to mind, solemn and resigned. At least until it was over, then he tied one on with the rest of us."

Disappointment creeping into her tone, she questioned, "Is that all you can remember?"

He inhaled as one does before speaking, but then he released his breath suddenly and without a word.

"What is it?" she demanded. "Is there something else?"

"Just a passing thought."

"Tell me, Robin," she insisted.

"I haven't thought about it in years, I suppose I deliberately put it from my mind." He released his captive knee and rubbed at his chin, looking suddenly anxious. "Sorry, Annie, but I really shouldn't say."

"No, not to just anyone you shouldn't, but you can tell me," she said, then reminded him, "because I'm not just anyone." She was prying, she knew, but she had to learn everything she could about that time, because it was a deep, painful void in her that needed filling.

He attempted to diminish the importance of it by saying, "It's nothing I know for certain, it was just an impression that I had," while avoiding her eyes.

She could tell by the change in his behavior that whatever it was was significant. And she could also see that he had decided against telling her, so she tried another approach. "After what went on before, don't you think I'm owed some honesty now? Don't you think I deserve to hear the truth? That's why Andrew's invited me here, you know, to tell me the truth about himself, finally."

"Really?" he questioned. Then as he considered it, he said, "I can see that—I can see him wanting to set the record straight. That's the kind of person he is."

"Then why don't you do that, too?" she encouraged. "Why don't you tell me what it is you know?"

He knew he shouldn't, he knew this was something better kept to himself, but there was a part of him that itched to tell her. He scanned the area around them, making certain no one was near, then in a low, conspiratorial tone, he said, "It was getting to the wee hours and all the ladies had retired, so there was a lot of randy behavior among the remaining lads. There was a lass, a very pretty lass, with the catering firm; she had long dark hair and green eyes and all the men were on about her."

Her heart pounding again, she questioned, "What about this girl?"

"Andrew was the most taken with her," he whispered, "and the more he drank, the more he went after her. Everyone saw it as a great joke and prodded him, teasing him about being a married man and all that."

"And?"

He had meant to stop there, to say only that, but the next thing just sort of popped out: "Come to think of it, she looked quite like you, Annie."

She had already gathered that from his description. "And?"

"I really shouldn't say more," he realized, looking around again and seeming increasingly jittery.

She would not let up, and pressed him. "Did he make a pass at her, fondle her? What'd he do, Robin?"

He reached for his brandy again, and gulped the remainder of it. "I can't be certain, I was bloody well pissed by then, myself."

"Can't be certain of what?"

He shifted his position, crossing and uncrossing his legs. "I don't know this for certain," he offered as preface. "But it was his wedding night and it struck me that he was paying more attention to that young lass than to his new wife. And then he disappeared, he just up and disappeared about the time the caterer was leaving. I had the distinct impression—no," he halted, then said, "let me re-phrase that. It occurred to me that he might have gone off with her. Of course he never said and I never asked; it wasn't the sort of thing we'd discuss, you see."

It had been deliciously terrifying, saying that aloud, tantaliz-ingly dangerous. But the rush of excitement it gave him faded quickly, when he was overcome with worry that she might convey this to Andrew. "I really shouldn't have said this to you; I don't know why I did. Please don't tell him that I have."

Annie closed her eyes.

Robin continued his wary scan of their vicinity, asking her, "You won't say, will you?"

Her hand brushed at her cheeks and caught two large droplets. "No, I won't say," she assured him.

He was so concerned about being overheard that he hadn't noticed she was crying. "I don't know why I've told you. I suppose it's because I recalled thinking at the time that he was after her because she resembled you. I remembered feeling very sorry for him at that moment, very sorry indeed. Here he was, the envy of most of the men in Scotland—in Britain for that matter—and I was probably the only person there who knew what he was really about, who understood that he had not married the girl he loved."

With that acknowledgment, Annie had reached her breaking point. "I'd better get to bed, I'm very tired," she fumbled out, then tried to stand, but the welling pain and nausea caused her to sink back into the window seat.

"What is it, are you faint?" he asked her.

She would have liked to say what it was she really felt: that the agonizing pain of learning these things so many years later—so far past the point where anything could be done about them—was some of the worst she had ever experienced. It was right up there with losing Andrew to begin with. "It must be the Scotch," she lied, "I've no stomach for it."

"Better not let Andrew hear you say that," he said, trying to laugh but not quite managing. "Shall I ask them to bring you something, an Alka-Seltzer perhaps?"

"No, thanks, I'll be all right once I get to bed."

"I'll head up with you," he responded, and sprang to his feet.

She wished she could put her head in her lap and sob until all her breath was gone, but she stood, too, praying that the wrenching ache in her chest would ease up enough for her to make it to Andrew's room.

Her mind was so full, her heart so burdened, she didn't remember getting there, nor did she recall saying good night to Robin. It was decidedly too much, this day, what with her encounter with Janet and everything she had learned about the Andrew she never knew. And not the least of it, there was the sailboat he had named in memory of her. And as though those things weren't enough, there were Robin's revelations.

And here she was now, finding her way to his bedroom, in this incredible castle that had belonged to his family for centuries, that—had fate taken a different turn—might have been her home. But it wasn't, she reminded herself, he had a wife and five children who lived here, who belonged here, and she questioned her motives, wondering what on earth had possessed her to take up with him again, when it was clearly such a risk.

The fire was ablaze and its flames lit the room; the bed had been turned back and a tray with hot milk and delicate biscuits left near the hearth. A card embossed with the family crest was left on her pillow, and although unsigned, it was most certainly written by Andrew: Sweet dreams—was what he wished her. She was touched by his thoughtfulness, though still deeply distressed, and stared into the flames as she changed into her nightgown. But as she pulled the folds of soft flannel over her head, something mystical happened that drew her to a window.

The piper stood alone on white marble terracing that glowed as brightly as the moon, paying tribute to the falling of the Argyll night. It was part of the old tradition, to be piped asleep and then piped awake, and it was one that Andrew particularly loved. The lullaby he played tonight was especially sweet and Annie listened, not just with her ears, but with all her sense and emotion to the traditional "Sleep Dearie, Sleep." She was all goose pimples and memory as she recalled the lone piper on the battlement of St. Andrews Castle, that May morning so very long ago, as she stood between Andrew and Susannah, holding their hands.

They had passed the night together, snuggled into one another on the beach, sharing their thoughts without speaking. Andrew had been kissing her, gently caressing her body. Susannah had come for warmth and melted right into them, putting her own lips to Annie's. Andrew had reached his arms around both of them and gone on with his kissing, each touch of his lips more tender than the last, each connection more powerful than the one before. There had been no shame, no embarrassment, no denial of emotion: only hearts laid open and vulnerable, safe in one another's company.

She easily recalled how that night had felt, how everything took on the rare and blissful aura of perfection, and how she had pleaded with the gods to slow it down, to make it last. And in remembering those feelings, she understood why it was worth the risk to be with him again.

For it was in their love for one another that the young Annie and Andrew had found meaning in their otherwise bereft lives; it was that brief, rhapsodic moment in their youth that gave point to what had happened to them before, and made bearable everything that followed. And it was in coming together again, she realized, in knowing once again the peace that their love bestowed, that they would find the healing they both sorely needed, and the courage to face whatever lay ahead for them.

But as the piper finished his tribute, the mournful, concluding wail of his pipe reminded her of what she first came begrudgingly to acknowledge then, on that very morning in May, when she became sadly, sweetly aware of how fleeting joy is: when she first came to understand that happiness belongs to Time, and that Time always takes it with him.

Nine

Crinan Castle awoke to a lively reel, played by a quartet of pipers from the gardens outside the orangery. Inside the conservatory, gigantic flowering clivia, espaliered fruit trees, and fragrant azalea bloomed, where many of the early risen guests now strolled with their coffee. Nearby, in the larger of the two dining rooms, a breakfast was being set out that was reminiscent of the elaborate hunt breakfasts of the past.

The guests filtered down the Adam staircase to be greeted by serene servants and the hunger inducing scents of breakfast. Dressed in the causal garb of country gentry—estate tweeds and kilts on many of the gentlemen, the ladies mostly in skirts and sweaters—the invitees greeted one another with refined familiarity, an occasional peck on the cheek, a gentle slap on the back. Andrew came late to the room, wearing the family tartan, with apologies to his guests for having to take an important call.

Before Andrew made his entrance, Annie had wandered away from the crowd to stand near a window, her eyes captured by the crystalline morning light on the gardens. She hadn't wanted to fuss with her hair this morning, so she had twisted it up and secured it with a barrette, the way she used to as a young woman. She was reaching to the back of her neck to replace a fallen wisp, when Andrew came upon her.

He approached her unseen and spoke to the nape of her neck, saying, "Good morning, I hope you slept well," and wanting very badly to kiss the tiny mole he saw there.

When she turned around to greet him, the sight of him in his kilt made her flush with warmth. "I did, thank you—and you?"

"Tolerably," he told her. In truth, it had been an uncomfortable night, sleeping next to Janet, knowing that Annie lay alone in his bed. "Darling," he whispered, "before we're interrupted—I've just spoken to Dr. Coupau. You're to go to Versailles instead of Lyons—there's a clinic there that'll afford you more privacy. I've already spoken with the pilot and Nigel's seeing to your accommodation."

Anxiety caused her heart to pound. "Won't you be coming?"

"I'll meet you there in the evening," he told her. "Late probably, but I'll be there."

"Late Monday, or Tuesday?"

"Monday, my love, I won't let you go it alone." It was all he could do to keep from reaching his arms around her.

The lump in her throat was hard to speak over. "I'm so afraid, Andrew."

His voice was the softest whisper, as he acknowledged, "I know." Then he had a thought, and told her, "After breakfast, head up to my room and wait for me. I'll come to you."

John and Lena walked over to greet them, John calling out, "Good morning! Marvelous gathering, this, simply marvelous, your lordship."

"Good morning, Lena, John," he smiled. "I'm so happy it pleases you. And I do recall asking you to call me Andrew," he reminded them.

"Thank you ever so much for inviting us," Lena told him. "We're having a splendid time, everything is absolutely brilliant. This is such a beautiful place—and how I love the bagpipes. I was positively chilled last night, hearing that as we went to sleep."

"I'm glad you like them," he told her, "because you'll hear more than a bit of them this weekend. Aren't we fortunate with the weather? Last year it rained the entire time."

Someone else came over to them, a Lord Begley, asking if he might have a moment of Andrew's time.

When he left them, John asked Annie, "Peckish?"

"Yes, very. It smells awfully good."

Lena linked her arm in Annie's, saying, "Let's go see what lovely things they're offering us," as the three made their way to the dining room.

As they ate, Andrew watched Annie out of the corner of his eye, and Janet watched him. It did not escape her notice when Annie left and Andrew followed some ten minutes later. But, being the consummate hostess she was, she valiantly saw to her guests and did her best not to think about it.

His gentle knock on the connecting door made Annie's insides flutter with anticipation, and they embraced as though they'd not seen each other for weeks.

"It was so difficult last night, knowing that you were here, in my bed," he told her.

"How were things with Janet?" she wanted to know.

"Not easy, but then it wasn't as awful as it might have been." He pulled her over to the bed and together they sat on it.

"I can't imagine what it must be like for her," she said, "having me here, knowing how you feel about me. I can't imagine how painful it must be."

"It's painful for all of us," he knew.

"But we have each other for comfort—who comforts her?" she worried.

"I try to, I attempt it, anyway," he admitted, "though I know I'm not very successful." He took her hands in his. "Listen darling, I can't stay very long—talk to me about what you were feeling downstairs, when you said how frightened you were."

"It's nothing," she said, "it's just that when I think of seeing that doctor, I get panicky."

He reached his arms around her and rubbed her back. "It's going to be fine, you're going to be fine. And I'm going to be there for you, no matter what."

Annie rested her head against his chest. All she wanted just now, was to forget about Tuesday, and being this close to him was doing that for her. She ran her hand along one bare thigh, up under his kilt, stopping when she felt the edge of his boxer shorts. She tugged on them and teased, "Is this what Scotsmen wear under kilts?"

With deadpan delivery, he responded, "I don't know what others wear—I never ask and I never look." His answer made her laugh out loud, and as she did Andrew took her hand and brought it to the erection she had given him, saying, "What I wouldn't give, to lie you down on this bed and make love to you."

She kissed him, then spoke with her lips touching his. "We've promised Janet."

He merely sighed.

She sighed, too, and kissed him again, saying, "You should get back to your guests—you'll be missed."

They embraced in silence for a few more stolen minutes.

The guests were invited to explore the gardens and park lands after breakfast. Mounts were made available to those who wished to ride; some worked out in the gym while others played tennis or croquet, or swam laps in the pool. Duncan and Marc were among those in the pool, and Marc, who was a strong swimmer, made quite an impression. There was even the option of an organized tour of the historic sites in the area, for those who had not been there before. The vast majority of guests, however, seemed to find pleasure in simply sitting out the morning in pillowed chaises, watching as a small chamber orchestra set up for a concert on the upper south terrace. The musicians struck their first chords at precisely half past noon, just as waiters began to leave the castle in tag teams, carrying the drinks and hors d'oeuvres that were the prelude to luncheon.

Janet and Andrew hardly had chance to eat, making certain to spend time with each of their guests, asking all the polite questions about family and business and where they planned to holiday this year.

Just after three o'clock, as overfed guests strolled through the gardens, a Rolls made its way up the long drive. It was led and followed by two black cars filled with security officers, a hairdresser, a personal maid, and private secretary. The earl and countess had been notified that the Princess of Wales was near and were ready to greet her. When she stepped from the car, all eyes were upon her and she put her head down as she always seemed to do, in some embarrassment. Andrew greeted her with enviable familiarity, and kisses to both cheeks.

"Welcome, Diana. How was your journey?"

"Lovely, it's always a pleasure to come up here. And how are you, Janet? Everything looks splendid — the gardens are especially lovely this year."

"Thank you, Diana, I'm very well," Janet answered. "We've been most fortunate this spring with the weather, the gardeners have had an easy go of it."

Her eyes darting toward the guests who were gawking at her, she said, "I think we must have got your rain this year. It's been horribly gloomy in London."

Knowing that she wasn't that keen on socializing these days, Andrew suggested, "You must be tired after your journey — would you like to go to your rooms first?"

With noticeable relief, she answered, "Yes, I thought I would, and then come down later, if that wouldn't be too much trouble."

Andrew offered his arm, and responded jovially, "Your wish is my command — may I escort you up?"

The state bedroom at Crinan Castle was traditionally reserved for royalty but since Andrew had become earl, it had been used for anyone he considered a special friend. As the Princess of Wales was both, he was especially happy to have her staying there. When they arrived at the suite, Andrew was prepared to leave her and return to his other guests, when Diana dismissed her entourage so that she might speak to him in private.

"You're looking particularly well," he told her, remembering that the last time he saw her she had looked haggard. "Have you done something different with your hair?" he politely inquired.

"Why, yes, I have," she blushed, her hand rising to primp it. "Do you like it?"

"Very much," he said. "It's most becoming."

She lowered her head again. "I wonder, Andrew, do you have time to sit with me?"

"I'll make the time. Shall I ring for some refreshment?"

"No, thank you," she responded, then walked to a window to gaze upon the gardens.

Concerned by her somber mood, he asked her, "Are their royal highnesses well?"

Her back to him, she answered unconvincingly, "Yes, everyone's well."

"I meant your sons, particularly."

She turned to face him again, saying, "They're splendid, thank you, and growing in leaps and bounds."

"They tend to do that," he chuckled, "boys, especially."

Awkwardly, she moved to take a seat, then beckoned him to do the same.

Although she kept averting her eyes, he was watching Diana's troubled face, and it prompted him to say, "If there's anything I can do, you need only ask."

She sighed heavily. "Some days are just so horribly difficult."

"Is today one?" he wondered.

"No, not at all," she assured him. "In fact, it's something of a relief, being here. This is such a tranquil and special place."

"If you'd like to stay on after everyone's left," he thought to offer, "I'd see to it that no one bothers you. And I'd arrange for you to go sailing, if you'd like, or you could go to Mull, there's abundant privacy there."

She smiled at him, and it was the first genuine one he'd seen since she arrived. "That's very kind of you, but some other time, perhaps. I've obligations enough to keep me busy for weeks."

"But if you need a rest—"

"I think it's better that I keep busy." Her hands were in her lap, clasped together, and she began to twist and wring them. When she realized what she was doing, she put them instead to straightening the creases in her trousers. "Things just get worse and worse for me, you know, with each day that passes. The press is merciless, Charles is impossible, and *they*, well, need I say what they are?"

He smiled slightly, as he answered, "No." Although outwardly loyal to his sovereign, he was not her biggest fan.

"And that insufferable woman," she fumed, shoving her sweater sleeves to her elbows. "Everywhere I go I see a photo of her on some scandal sheet somewhere, rubbing my face in it. What am I to do? How am I to manage this awful mess? I see you and your lovely wife and children and how happy you all are, how right everything is with you, and I envy you so. What I wouldn't give for a relationship like yours—for a peaceful, normal life as a wife and a mother—for a husband who loved me the way you love Janet."

"Diana," he said quietly, "don't make us out to be some ideal couple; we're not that at all." It was now his turn to avert his eyes.

"Well, perhaps not ideal," she conceded, "no one is that, of course. But certainly stable and loving, certainly miles ahead of most of us."

"I'd never make that claim," he admitted, blushing slightly.

Smiling sweetly, she told him, "You're so modest, Andrew, perhaps that's your secret."

"I'm not being modest," he insisted, unable to return her smile. "You shouldn't envy us—we've problems of our own."

"But all marriages do, don't they? It's a matter of how you handle those problems," she understood, "of whether or not you decide to tough it out or turn to someone else. You've always seemed to me to be the sort who stands by his commitments, who doesn't throw in the towel." She suddenly remembered his compliment regarding her hair, and it prompted her to touch it again, lifting and smoothing it with her fingers.

"I've tried to honor my commitments, but I've been no saint," he responded, a hint of shame creeping into his tone. "I've been far from the ideal husband. My indiscretions haven't been made public, that's all."

She was blindsided by that, and questioned, "Your indiscretions?" even as she smiled to convey her disbelief.

"I've not been faithful to Janet," he admitted, "but I've been careful to not be found out. I haven't wanted her or the children to suffer because of me."

Diana had trouble believing her ears, and her smile now transformed to an incredulous, disappointed frown, one that said: *Dear God, not you, too?*

"I'm sorry to tell you this," he forged ahead, "I'm sorry to disillusion you, but it's not right for me to accept your praise when my behavior hasn't been worthy of it."

They were sitting across from one another and while they spoke, Diana had unconsciously leaned forward. But now, clearly stunned by what he'd just revealed, she braced herself against the back of the settee. "But why, Andrew? Why would you do such a thing? I mean, if you care so much about Janet's feelings, why would you act so? For the life of me, I don't understand."

He sighed before answering. "It's so damned complicated. It wasn't a matter of boredom or going through a bad patch, the roots of it go back a long way, since before our marriage." He was going to end it there and offer nothing further, but when he began to think of her painful predicament with her own husband, it dawned on him that knowing these things about someone else—someone other than Charles—might prove helpful. So he decided to try to explain it a little better. "I experienced something once," he quietly told her, "that was so compelling and powerful, it's difficult to know whether to call it blessing or curse. I could never forget it, nor could I stop wanting to have it again. It made me restless and dissatisfied, it sent me out of my marriage to see if I might find it again."

She questioned, "Are you talking about love or sex?"

He looked her directly in the eyes as he answered, "It was love, Diana."

"And, of course," she scoffed, "it couldn't have been your wife who made you feel that way."

His only defense was, "We don't plan these things."

"Good lord, Andrew—do you know whom you sound like?"

"Like Charles," he realized.

With considerable rancor, she exclaimed, "Exactly like Charles talking about that awful Camilla!" Then she demanded of him, "So why do you stay married?"

"For much the same reasons you do."

Seemingly more disturbed by this admission than the others, she stood abruptly and returned to the window. In a heavy, less angry voice, she stated emphatically, "Duty and responsibility offer cold comfort."

He had followed her movements with his eyes, but he dropped his gaze to the floor to respond, "I know." Then he added, "I can understand your being discouraged by what I've told you."

"It's very disheartening . . ." The tiny lump in her throat stopped her midsentence.

He considered the wisdom of what he was about to say, know-ing that it might antagonize her. But out of respect for their friend-ship, he determined to continue speaking frankly. "If what you wanted was someone perfect to hold yourself up to, to make your-self feel depressed over what he had that you didn't—then I've let you down terribly, and I offer my sincerest apology."

She spun around and flashed irritation at him.

He knew where he was going with this, so he continued un-daunted. "But if what you wanted was to share some of your anguish with a friend, a friend who really cares about you and can empathize with you, then I make no apology, for I believe I've been that."

She scowled at him. "How does knowing about your bad be-havior help me?"

"Because I'm real, my life is real, my struggles are real," he calmly explained, "and it's in reality that solutions to our problems lie, not in fantasy or idealism."

"What makes you think there are any solutions?" she coun-tered. "How do you know that life isn't just one struggle after an-other, piled on top of each other, so that in the final tally all one ends with is just some meaningless heap of rubbish?"

Amazed by the cynicism in her remarks, he asked her, "How can you, of all people, say that? When you've affected the lives of untold thousands for the better—how can you speak of a life with-out meaning?"

"Because I'm personally without it," she declared, folding her arms for emphasis.

"Because Charles loves someone else?" he questioned. "That leaves you purposeless?"

"That's the way it makes me feel," she pouted.

He couldn't help himself. "That's absurd!"

"I thought you understood—"

"But I do," he answered confidently. "I understand that self-worth is not something that should be gauged by the success or fail-ure of a relationship."

"Then how else to value oneself?" she asked, and it was evi-dent that her desire for an answer was sincere.

He could see how earnestly she wanted—needed—an answer. So he did his best to give her one. "I believe a person's worth is measured by the manner in which he lives his life," he told her. "The people I respect and admire aren't perfect specimens—they're often flawed and needy—but they rise above their own difficulties to do good for others. It's compassionate, conscience-directed individuals whose lives are about more than just themselves—people like you, Diana—whom I admire most."

With the great compliment he had just paid her, her tension began to ease, though she remained deeply troubled by his revelations of infidelity. She'd grown up with it of course, with that disturbingly common practice of the aristocracy—almost every couple she knew had been tainted by it—but she'd always refused to accept it as a fact of life. "And what about *your* conscience," she questioned, "how do you justify *your* actions?"

"I can't justify them," he admitted, frowning, "and in truth this conversation has made me feel a damned hypocrite. But I learned at a very tender age that I wouldn't always make the right choices and that life isn't the tidy affair we're brought up to expect, so I've stopped castigating myself for my human failings. And as I've matured, I've actually come to embrace life's mutability and reject the fanciful notion of control. Instead, I liken it to a garden, that's continually assailed by weeds and pests, or undone by droughts or deluge. You go on each day with the business of tending to it, some days more focused than others, other days with less care. There are times when the elements come together so perfectly that it seems you're in control, but there are also times when the forces of nature are so powerful, you have to just stand back and let happen what will."

"Let it all go to bloody hell? Is that what you're saying?"

"Sometimes, yes," he responded, "and you deal with the consequences later, you pick up the pieces later."

Hearing him speak this way made her heartsick for Janet. For while he may be prepared to "let things happen," she knew how important order and control were to his wife.

"I know how horrible it's been for you," he continued. "Every day you're publicly reminded of the mistakes you've made, something on the television or in the press, or some hurtful gossip on the lips of a not-so-well-meaning friend. But I've watched you stand up to them and persevere; I've seen you time and again suck it up and get on with the business of things. You've followed the edicts of your conscience and given of yourself 'til it hurts, and that's been no minor feat, what with all the obstacles that have been put in your way." He shook his head slightly.

Although still grappling with what he'd told her, she wondered now, "Do you really see me that way?" Her face softened to that sweet, childlike expression, full of innocence and charm, the one that always endeared her to people.

He frowned to show his disappointment. "You should know me well enough to realize that I wouldn't have said so if I didn't."

Wistfully, she responded, "I wish I could see myself like that—I've such an awful time liking myself."

"You're still so young," he understood. "Self-acceptance doesn't come that easily or that early on. In time you'll come to see things that you can't possibly see now, and that will make all the difference."

"And you're so terribly old!" she teased, laughing slightly. "What are you, a whole ten years older?"

"I've learned rather a lot in those ten years," he recognized. "In fact, I've learned considerably more in these last few weeks than I knew for many, many years. Life has that way of placating us sometimes, by bringing a little knowledge and wisdom in exchange for what time takes away."

Her curiosity was sparked. "What's happened in the past few weeks?"

He looked away from Diana for a moment, then back to her perceptive eyes, saying only, "I've been refocused."

"How?"

He hesitated, then admitted, "I've seen her again."

"Who—your Camilla?" she questioned, grimacing as she said her name.

He nodded.

"I see." She stared at him a moment, then she asked, "And what do you intend to do now that you have—or is that too personal a question?"

He prefaced his response with, "Forgive the cliché—but I don't know how else to say it. I intend to follow my heart and conscience, and pray that they don't lead me in opposite directions."

"And if they do?" she wondered.

"I'm counting on my conscience to keep me from disaster."

"Well, let's hope it does," she told him, exhaling. "I've been through the muck of a bad marriage on both ends, as a child and now as a woman, and let me tell you—I wouldn't wish it on my worst enemy."

With her admonition, Andrew's thoughts went running, contemplating how devastating a divorce would be to his children, how their loyalties would be torn, their stability shattered.

Diana's thoughts had gone elsewhere, too. "I suppose I ought to have a few minutes to get myself together before I come down to your guests."

"Take all the time you need," he told her, then added, "but if you'd rather have tea here on your own—"

"I hadn't wanted to ask," she answered nervously. "I know people are expecting me."

He stood now, and told her in no uncertain terms, "You're a guest in my home, Diana, and as such you may do as you please. You're not here to entertain the others."

She bit her lower lip, then blurted out, "I've done things I'm not entirely proud of, you know, things I wish I could undo—"

"You're human," he consoled, "and you've followed your heart—right or wrong. The heart doesn't always lead us where we'd like it to."

She seemed suddenly stronger and more sure of herself. "Women have needs, too, you know. Men aren't the only ones with needs. I don't think Charles understands that."

He smiled again, as he responded, "I believe that women are far better at knowing themselves and recognizing those needs than we are." That said, he moved toward the door, but just before he reached it, her timid voice called to him again.

"Thank you for talking with me like this," she said. "It's very rare for people to be so open with me; I want you to know that I treasure that, I treasure our friendship, Andrew."

"Thank you, Diana," he told her, "and I share your feelings. I'm so very sorry for all you're going through — I wish there was something I could do to help."

"You have helped," she realized. "You've caused me to see Charles in a more sympathetic light today, though I can't say how long that will last." The furrow in her brow added irony to her grin.

Andrew continued to smile warmly as he said, "I know you to be a beautiful and extraordinary woman, capable of great things, and I won't be the least bit surprised if Charles comes 'round one day to recognize that, too." He left before seeing the enormous smile his comment brought to her face.

Ten

Just after tea most of the female guests disappeared, and the wells that fed water to Crinan Castle were put to the test, as each of the twenty-five bathrooms became occupied, every tub filled with hot water, every basin tap opened. An orderly procession of chambermaids moved among the guest rooms, laying out evening clothes and steaming or pressing them when needed, running to fetch bath salts or hair dryers for those who'd forgotten to pack them. There were three hours before dinner but every minute of preparation was precious to ladies who wanted to look their very best.

Two touring-type buses drove onto the estate at that time, carrying the members of Her Majesty's Black Watch. They were escorted into the servants' hall and sat down to high tea for their supper, as they would be busy later when dinner was served. When they had dined sufficiently, they walked out among the now deserted gardens. Like guardians of former times, regally attired in their tartans and military embellishments, they were an imposing sight. Annie watched them from a window in Andrew's room, imagining what it must have been like at Crinan Castle when his ancestors wielded swords and fought on horseback, when they believed so strongly in their cause that they were willing to lay down their lives for it. She readily pictured Andrew among his ghostly forbearers, his eyes darkened by passion, his face set and determined, leading the charge.

The doors to the grand ballroom had been kept closed to allow the caterers adequate preparation time, and they remained closed as the house guests filtered down the Adam staircase in their expensive ball gowns and dress kilts. As they reached the first floor they were directed toward the long gallery, where the earl and his family formally received those newly arrived, as well as those who were staying at the castle.

Annie had been distracted in her preparation — Marc had come to her room to catch her up on all he'd been doing — so she didn't make the receiving line. By the time she came downstairs with her son, the ballroom was already filled and Andrew and Janet were nowhere to be seen. A livery-clad footman showed Marc to his table and another escorted Annie to hers. She was seated, not surprisingly, with John, Lena, Robin, and Loreena, and two other couples she'd met last evening.

She was dressed in a simple black gown, that clung to her form, scooped over her bosom and down to the small of her back, then trailed out a few inches behind her. For adornment, she wore only her rings and a matching set of diamond earrings and bracelet, and her hair was done in an ordinary French twist. Heads had turned when she entered the ballroom, broaching the sea of gilt and glittering colors like a sleek and dark apparition.

"Aren't you fabulous!" Lena exclaimed when she saw her.

John embraced her and kissed her cheeks. "Splendid gown," he commented, as he helped her with her chair.

"Thank you, it was a gift from my husband."

"Really? Had you seen it and told him you liked it?" Lena wondered.

"Thank you," she said first, to the waiter offering her a glass of champagne. Then to Lena, she explained, "No, actually he saw it in New York and brought it home as a surprise. He does that now and again."

"I'm impressed," Lena told her, adding with a sideways glance at her husband, "John's never bought anything like that for me."

John responded defensively. "Lena, dearest, in all fairness, everything I've bought you in the past you've seen fit to return."

"But you have such atrocious taste," she teased. "Perhaps you should spend some time with Annie's husband — you might learn something."

Seemingly irritated by the nature of this conversation, Loreena stated unequivocally, "I prefer to choose my own things."

Lena smiled politely as she questioned, "But isn't it fun to be surprised with a fabulous gift?"

"I don't need surprises," she said, mostly to her husband.

Lena turned away from her and rolled her eyes.

Annie told her, "Your gown is very lovely, Loreena."

She was wearing a full, silk, tartan skirt, with a sash draped across a white, taffeta blouse. "It's not from New York," she said defiantly. "It's from Glasgow and it's traditional."

Loreena seemed more cross than she had last evening, and Annie wondered if she was always this way. *Poor Robin*, she bemoaned. But in truth, Robin's wife might have been attractive, were it not for her scowl, her hopelessly dated hairstyle — probably the same one she had sported in secondary school — and her prematurely etched face, surely a result of her chronically disdainful condition.

"I do so love that tradition," Annie said sincerely. "I'll never forget the Kate Kennedy Ball and how wonderful everyone looked that night. Remember, Robin?"

He'd remained warily silent while his wife spoke, but now he readily responded, "Indeed I do!"

Loreena snapped her head around so quickly she might have injured her neck, demanding to know, "You took her to a ball?"

Robin tried to laugh off the severity of her reaction. "Oh no, dear, I wasn't her escort — Andrew was."

Her eyes wide with shock and disbelief, she questioned, "Lord Kilmartin took her to a ball?"

"Yes, Loreena — I told you they were close."

Lena covered her amusement with a cough and John reached under the table to squeeze her thigh. Loreena was speechless now, her eyes trained on Annie as she casually sipped her champagne.

John thought it wise to change the subject. "I wonder what marvelous things they're going to serve us."

Lena grinned, "I'm awfully peckish, but there's nothing unusual about that. I wonder where the princess is?"

"I believe she'll enter with the family," Robin answered her, "and from the looks of it, it should be any minute."

The long banquet table at the head of the dance floor had remained empty and now, as they spoke, there was a rustling of activity near the entry doors.

"Is there to be a grand entrance, Robin?" Lena wondered.

Robin hadn't time to answer. The captain of the Watch stood in the doorway and pounded the floor with a heavy staff, bringing the room to a hush.

"My lords, ladies, and gentlemen, honored guests of the House of Stuart-Gordon—Her Royal Highness, the Princess of Wales, escorted by his honour, Alfred, Lord Cowan!"

Everyone stood as Diana entered, attired in a vibrant blue that seemed reflected in her eyes, and the dapper Lord Cowan beamed with pride at having been chosen as her escort. The pair strode self-consciously across the floor to the banquet table and remained standing when they reached their seats, as all eyes turned toward the entrance once again.

"Is that the same Lord Cowan I met in St. Andrews?" Annie whispered to Robin, who nodded in response.

Then, each in their turn, Andrew's mother and sisters were announced, along with their husbands, before being escorted to their seats. Behind them the Black Watch gathered, four across, ready to march into the room. The Pipe Major held the Pipes and Drums at attention while the captain announced them.

"Your Royal Highness, my lords, ladies, and gentlemen, by special permission of Her Royal Highness, the Queen Mother, in honor of the twenty-fourth Earl and Countess of Kilmartin—may we present to you, the Black Watch—the Royal Highland Regiment!"

The drums rolled, the skirl from the pipes transfixed the room, and after the first few bars of music, the exquisitely uniformed soldiers marched onto the dance floor. They stepped four abreast and broke ranks in the middle to provide an escort for the countess, who was flanked by her daughters. They were all prettily dressed in traditional evening skirts of the family tartan, with plaids draped across their blouses. They smiled and moved gracefully amid the kilt-clad regiment, and didn't attempt to keep in step. Janet nodded occasionally to a particular guest and when they reached the table the Regiment broke away and turned back to the doorway, continuing to pipe their cheerful tune.

At its conclusion another more somber one was struck up, and a few bars into it young Malcolm came forward, in full dress kilt. His face beamed and he appeared delighted to be parading in front of the three hundred or so people who watched him. He was followed by his brother Duncan and then by the Viscount Donald, and all three marched across the floor, escorted by the Watch, the older two strikingly noble in their posture. Annie was a mass of gooseflesh as she watched Andrew's wife and children carry out this centuries-old tradition.

Having now delivered most of the family, the Pipes and Drums returned to the entrance once again. The Pipe Major turned toward the audience and pounded his staff before calling out, "Your Royal Highness, my lords, ladies, and gentlemen—Andrew, twenty-fourth Earl of Kilmartin, Viscount Rannoch, Baron Kilmartin of Mull, and Lord High Constable of Scotland!"

Lena leaned in and spoke to Annie's ear. "My God! So many titles!"

The drums rolled again and the pipes followed, with a chilling, long skirl, as Andrew stepped into the ranks of the Regiment. Annie was awestruck by the sight of him, so tall and proud and majestic, yet still so very kind and approachable, as only he could be. He wore a velvet doublet with his kilt, adorned with silver buttons and facings, and an elaborate sporran, which was fashioned of animal hair and appeared quite old. A sash was draped over one shoulder, that was virtually filled with gold and silver insignia of varying shapes and sizes, and the large, floppy hat on his head was trimmed in gold and adorned with an eagle's feather. He carried a wooden staff, the head of which was an intricately carved, silver thistle. He stood with patient regality, waiting for the first few bars of the song, his face wonderfully serene, and in the candlelit room it was impossible to make out the scars. To Annie's eyes he appeared as he had so many years ago, when he had come to take her to the Kate Kennedy Ball—so splendidly noble—like the Highland prince she now knew him to be.

The tune the Black Watch honored him with was called "The Skye Boat Song," which told of Bonnie Prince Charlie's exile to the Isle of Skye, and as they played he looked ahead with his right hand grasping the staff, the other behind his back. But just before they began to march him to his table, he turned his head to where he knew Annie to be seated. His eyes caught hers for an instant and when they met, hers filled with tears.

When he was at his seat, he removed his hat and handed it and the staff to an attendant. Someone shouted: "To the Prince over the sea!" and everyone raised their glasses and drank. Andrew made the next toast, which was to the princess, who sat next to him and whose hand he kissed. She then stood and offered her glass to him.

"I shall probably cause him great embarrassment," she began, and the guests laughed. "Those who know him know that he doesn't care at all for effusive praise. But I'd simply like to say that in all of Britain, I do not believe there to be a more generous or socially responsible individual, nor one who has carried out his noblesse oblige with more grace and humility, and I am terribly proud to be able to call him my friend. To the earl!" She would ordinarily have added what a wonderful husband and father he was, but tonight it didn't seem appropriate.

"The earl!" echoed throughout the room.

Andrew raised his glass again. "And in that it is all important to acknowledge the contributions of the Countess of Kilmartin, whose tireless devotion has allowed for the fulfillment of the many projects undertaken by the Kilmartin Trust. To the countess!"

Janet beamed and in an uncharacteristic display of emotion, she kissed her husband's cheek.

The Pipes and Drums had remained at attention during the toasts but struck up again when they were complete, continuing to play throughout the first course, before retiring to thunderous applause. The chamber orchestra who had entertained during luncheon then took their turn, and their soft accompaniment allowed more readily for dinner conversation.

"Wasn't that just splendid!" Lena exclaimed. "I do so love the pipes! My God, but wasn't that a thrilling thing to see, his lordship entering with his family like that? I felt as though we'd all slipped out of the twentieth century."

"Marvelous tradition," John agreed.

Annie merely nodded, being somewhat overwhelmed by the spectacle she had witnessed. And throughout the dinner, although she faced the table where they sat, she avoided looking at Andrew and Janet because every time she did, she felt anxious and uncomfortable.

After a time, she asked Robin, "What can we expect tomorrow?"

"After breakfast," he answered, "the estate will fill with neighbors—everyone from within a hundred miles will come—and there'll be food and drink and dancing 'til nightfall."

As the main course was being cleared up, Lord Cowan approached Janet. After a few minutes of quiet conversation, the two made their way to Annie's table.

Everyone stood to greet the countess, and John offered first, "Fabulous evening, Lady Kilmartin, thank you so much for your invitation."

With her thin smile, she responded, "I'm so happy to know that you're enjoying yourselves."

Lena's eyes widened as they fixed upon Janet's jewels, and she just had to say, "Your necklace is exquisite, Lady Kilmartin."

One hand went to her chest to touch the magnificent emeralds, as she responded blithely, "They've been a tradition of the earldom—they were originally a gift from the sixteenth earl to his lady, when she gave birth to their first son. Andrew presented them to me after our Donald was born." She glanced at Annie now, and allowed herself a momentary gloat, before saying, "May I introduce Lord Alfred Cowan to everyone—" saving Annie for last, "and this is Ms. d'Inard."

He took Annie's hand and kissed it, as he asked, "How do you do?"

"I'm well, thank you," she responded, "and you?"

"Lord Alfred," Robin grinned, "the two of you have met before."

Feigning surprise, he questioned, "We have?" still holding to her hand.

"Years ago, in St. Andrews," Robin reminded him. "She was Andrew's friend and you invited us to tea at The Rusacks when we'd finished our round on the Jubilee Course."

Cowan turned to Janet to see how she would handle this.

"Yes, Lord Alfred, that's right," she deemed it appropriate to say. "She was an acquaintance of my husband's when he was at university.

They've only just seen each other again after many years—he's employed her in some fashion or another." A slight degree of discomposure was evident in her voice.

"Really? How interesting," he said. "I do vaguely remember someone—but you mustn't be offended, Ms. d'Inard, if my memory is not what it used to be." His laugh sounded artificial.

Annie smiled. "I'm not at all offended, your lordship."

"Well then," he responded, "perhaps you'll allow me the honor of the first dance, which I believe will be any minute now, will it not?"

"Quite so," Janet told him, "and I should be returning to my husband for it."

The orchestra had vacated the bandstand and been replaced by a popular dance band from Glasgow, about whom the crowd seemed excited.

"This should be enjoyable," Cowan told her, "though I do hope they'll play something an older man can move to."

"You look to be in better shape than most of the young men," Annie observed. Cowan did seem extraordinarily fit for a man of his sixty-odd years; sporting his dress kilt with a rakish flair, he impressed her as the kind of man who employed a masseuse and frequently pampered himself at expensive spas. And when she glanced at his manicured hands, she knew that she was correct in that assumption.

The group's first number was an old standby of Scottish dances, a waltz that brought almost everyone to the floor. They moved into the thick of the crowd and as he took her into his arms, he grasped her tightly. After a few moments he spoke into her ear, saying, "Let's be honest, shall we?"

Nonplused, she responded, "I wasn't aware we weren't." Then, like a bolt of lightning striking in her memory, she vividly recalled the discomfort of their original meeting in St. Andrews, and how she'd been visited with a disturbing sense of déjà vu. She also remembered how very much Andrew had disliked him.

With peculiar rancor, he said now, "I remember you quite well, Annie, and if the twenty-third earl were alive, you would never have set foot in this place, lovely though you are." He squeezed her waist and pinched at her hip.

She pushed him away and stopped dancing, demanding of him, "What do you think you're doing?"

He urged her into dancing again, saying, "Let's not make a scene, shall we?" Showering her with breath that reeked of Scotch and garlic, he continued, "I was amusing myself with a bit of tabloid trash the other day, and lo and behold, what juicy little morsel do you think I happened across?"

She pressed her hands against his upper arms and shoved him away. "I haven't the slightest idea."

His tone saccharine and sexual, he questioned, "Haven't you? Perhaps you haven't. I imagine you've been rather busy these past weeks, and haven't had time to spend on such things, have you?" His salacious grin complimented his malodorous breath.

At that moment Annie saw Andrew and Janet, dancing closer to them. He had spotted her, too, and was trying not to focus on her, though he frequently cast his eyes in her direction. She wasn't certain, but he appeared to be deliberately coming nearer, and his facial expression indicated some concern.

She scowled at Cowan now, saying, "Whatever game you're playing, I'm not interested. Why don't you just say whatever it is you mean to, and get it over with?"

"Not here," he said, grasping her hand and leading her to the open terrace doors. Once outside and positioned out of earshot of the nearest people, he folded his arms and stared at her, and the sensuousness of her body, silhouetted against the moonlight, momentarily distracted from his purpose. When he spoke again, it was with more civility. "Our Andrew's a free man now, isn't he?"

She folded her own arms and frowned. "He's hardly free."

"I mean that he's free of his father," he calmly elucidated, "free to make his own mistakes—and it seems he's determined to do just that."

She understood his intention now, and it was starting to make her nervous. Still, she responded with bravado: "I fail to see how anything Andrew does or doesn't do is any of your concern, and I know for certain that any relationship I have with him is absolutely none of your business."

He chuckled, feeling slightly giddy from the pleasure of watching her squirm. "Isn't it, now? I'd beg to differ and say that I'm intimately involved in the matter, since it was I who alerted his father to the dangerous situation that was developing all those years ago."

He was too close to her, very much in her space, so she stepped back and glared at him, asking, "So we have you to thank, do we?"

He moved in again, knowing full well that his nearness was intimidating her, and enjoying every moment of it. "Perhaps you've no gratitude, but seeing Andrew today, I can't help but feel that he appreciates my efforts."

They had suddenly become engaged in a sort of psychological tango, as she once again stepped back. "You know," she told him, trying her best to cover her anxiety, "I find it very odd that a twenty-year-old American girl should have been considered important enough for all those machinations."

He now had her against the edge of the terrace, where the steps began. "Don't flatter yourself, my dear; the value lay in Andrew, not you. Your role might have been played by any pretty girl."

She marveled at the man's natural, effortless cruelty. Seeing that her only escape was to turn her back on him and descend the steps, she moved to do just that, but he grabbed her arm to halt her. With his touch, she hissed, "Get your hand off me —"

He kept hold of her, and far from being put off by her reaction, he seemed excited by it. "My, my — such passion! You know, I do believe you're even more beautiful when you're angry." He chuckled again. "There's no need for all this acrimony, you know — I'd like to be your friend, or more, if you'd allow me."

Her instincts would have had her deliver a powerful slap to his face, but she suppressed that desire and merely snarled at him.

He softened his tone, and the sleazy way in which he said this made her nauseous: "I must say, I find you even more delicious than I did when you were a young woman. I do so prefer women of passion and experience, they tend to be much more satisfying. Don't you find the same true of men?"

Although his remarks and behavior outraged her, something in his manner was also frightening her. "Experience can only improve what was good to begin with," she said, as she once again broke free of his grasp. "In some it makes for sour wine."

"And you're clever, too," he added sarcastically.

"Apparently not clever enough to have avoided you," she quipped.

He passed his eyes over her body, then settled them on her bosom, saying, "You shouldn't be so quick to judge me. I'm a single fellow, you know, and a wealthy, powerful man, with no reputation to lose and no pretenses to uphold. Isn't that more appealing to a woman like you than that overly obligated husband and father, whose every minute of time is accounted for over the next ten years?"

She suddenly felt as though he could see through her dress, and it made her shudder and feel sick inside. "The only thing about you that could possibly appeal to me is seeing the last of you," she managed to say. "I find you distasteful and officious, to say the very least, and the next time you touch me," she decided to add, "I'm going to scream bloody murder."

He tossed his head back and laughed, then caught her square in the eyes, like a viper ready to strike. "Careful, my girl, careful. My power and influence extend far and wide, and as pretty as you are, I'd not be averse to wielding it on you—should you provoke me."

The sincerity with which he'd delivered that warning played to her growing fear, and she deemed it safer to not respond.

His manner slightly less offensive, he now informed her, "The truth of the matter is that I had a discussion with Andrew's mother earlier, and she asked if I might reason with you, persuade you to leave Crinan Castle and her son's life. I didn't want to involve poor Janet, so I pretended to be taken with you and simply asked her for an introduction—although I must admit, it wasn't much of a pretense."

Christ, she thought, *Andrew's mother unleashed this odious man on me?* She realized she needed to consider her responses carefully, for they would certainly be reported back to Lady Mary. "What you don't seem to know is that Janet and I have had a very frank discussion, and she's all right with my being here. I wouldn't have come here but for her invitation." She folded her arms and bravely met his unsettling leer.

He grinned and eyed her breasts again, salivating over them as though they were edible. "Janet is a woman of grace and breeding, I'd expect nothing less from her," he was certain, "but I know for a fact that her largesse does not extend to her husband."

His persistence was exasperating. "Really, I do think you're butting into something that's none of your business."

Increasingly smug, he said to her, "This family is much more my business than it is yours, my dear. Donald and I were the closest of friends, you know." His eyes briefly lost their focus, as he mused, "We did have some fine old times together; we did enjoy life in those days."

Ugly images were conjured up in her mind, but she managed to laugh at him in spite of them. "Men like you are such hypocrites. You recognize the need for personal freedom, yet you derogate the women with whom you enjoy it."

"Is our Andrew enjoying the freedom of you?" he wanted to know.

She had led him to that question, and she cursed herself for it. "I won't dignify that with an answer."

His focus fully restored, he told her now, "The article I referred to questioned his indecorous behavior with you around the old gray town. And as you can plainly see, I wasn't born yesterday—I can fill in the blanks."

Defiantly, she admitted, "Andrew and I did spend time together in St. Andrews, and Janet's fully aware of that, too."

His left eyebrow lifted and arched as he said, "Well then, I'll advise you to be more careful in the future. Now that the hunters have had a whiff of indiscretion, they'll have sent in the bloodhounds. I'd not be surprised if there were one or two sniffing about tonight. He's a man of such reputation and importance, you see— the tabloids would dearly love to bring someone like him down, it's what they exist for, after all. And considering how protective of him you appear to be, I should think that you wouldn't want to assist them in that, would you?"

Annie glared at him but didn't respond, although what he'd said distressed and troubled her. She began to feel less put-upon and more guilty now, realizing that this possibility was probably what Andrew's mother was worried about.

He may have been overdoing it, he knew, and he might have left it at that. But intimidating women was, after all, one of his favorite pastimes, and he was so enjoying himself. "I've given you a lot to think about," he concluded, as a slow, malicious grin took shape. "But while you're mulling matters over, I'll advise you to reconsider your opinion of me, my dear, for there may well come a time when you need my help in this delicate matter, and I'm a better friend to have than enemy." He watched her pull in her lower lip and bite it nervously, and it sent a rush of sexual excitement surging through him. "Shall we go back in?" he offered. "You look as though you could use a drink."

When she was at her table again, Annie abruptly told John, "Dance with me."

"Of course!" As they moved onto the dance floor, he asked, "Is something bothering you? You seem perturbed."

"Do you think you might pull Andrew aside for a private word?" she wondered.

He brought his mouth very close to her ear, to question, "Is something going on between you two?"

"Please don't put me on the spot like that," she implored. "Just see if you can get him alone and tell him I need to speak with him, OK? I'd appreciate it."

The night wore on and although John tried, he was unable to speak to Andrew alone. At about two in the morning, the band from Glasgow closed their set with "Auld Lang Syne," and everyone joined in the singing. There wasn't a dry eye in the place, with the possible exception of the young people, who were either too embarrassed to cry or who had yet to understand the poignancy of the lyrics. As the band packed up, a disc jockey took over the entertainment. Many of the older guests retired then, knowing that the remainder of the night belonged to those with more energy and stamina. A late supper was offered to buffer the effects of the alcohol and a few people availed themselves of it, while the DJ blasted rock and roll into the grand ballroom.

Andrew was finally left on his own and he moved casually about the room to greet the few guests he hadn't already. Annie watched him surreptitiously, and realized that he was making his way toward her.

Her back was turned when he arrived at her table, quietly asking her, "Enjoying yourself?"

Although her anxiety had been mounting since her encounter with Lord Cowan, the sound of Andrew's voice washed it away. Goose pimples arose on her neck before she could turn around and respond, "It's been a lovely evening."

He watched her nipples harden under the soft jersey of her dress, something he'd come to recognize as a response to his near-ness. "You look more beautiful tonight than I've ever seen you," he whispered to her. "Will you dance with me?"

She almost said yes, but instead told him, "I don't think it's a good idea."

"Why?" he wondered, dropping his smile. "Haven't I danced with half the women in the room tonight?"

"I've not seen you with the same partner twice," she realized.

"Well, then," he smiled again, "it might be suspicious if I didn't have a turn with you."

She didn't want to do anything that might upset Janet, but she answered, "All right, we need to talk anyway."

"Let me just have a word with the disc jockey," he told her, "and I'll be back."

Her breath quickened as she watched him leave her.

The strumming guitar at the opening was unmistakable. The music deepened as he walked across the almost empty dance floor, and he reached her as the lyrics began. Annie had recognized it from the start and had not just seen, but had felt him coming to her. He smiled and offered his hand, and they embraced as they should not have in public. But they couldn't help themselves.

Robin was the first to take notice, the song being very familiar to him, too. It evoked memories of his visits to Andrew's sickbed, of

Andrew asking him to play it again and again, while he stared off into the distance and fought back the tears. So as the music began he was not at all surprised to see his friend moving toward Annie, and taking her to dance with him.

John and Lena had been near Annie when Andrew returned to her, and they felt the aura that surrounded the two as they came together to dance. Husband and wife looked at each other with knitted brows and just a touch of surprise, as Andrew lovingly took Annie into his arms.

Having suppressed her recollections of that time, Janet didn't know why the song bothered her, but she sought out her husband when she heard it begin. Her eyes found him just as he reached Annie. She'd been speaking with Diana on the far side of the room and they both took notice of Andrew. Diana instinctively understood that this was the woman he'd told her about, and deeply empathetic, she did her best to distract Janet in this embarrassing moment.

Lord Cowan had been engaged in quiet conversation with Nigel Bain. Both men recognized the intensity with which Andrew strode toward Annie, and both felt they now knew with certainty what was transpiring between them.

Andrew and Annie, however, were oblivious to the eyes that scrutinized them. They heard only the music, letting themselves drift backward in time, closing their eyes to the world outside of their memories. His hand gripped hers, his arm pulled her ever closer, their cheeks tenderly brushing. She forgot about her encounter with Cowan, about her promises to Janet, about her concerns for his children. She allowed herself be carried to another place by his embrace—to a May evening in St. Andrews when life was young and emotions more simple—and they went to that place together. The lyrics, "just like way back in the days of old," took on new meaning.

When the song concluded there was an eerie stillness to the place, as so many of the people in the room found themselves staring at the couple. After Van Morrison declared that it was, "too late to stop now," they awkwardly broke apart, even as the present forced itself upon them in the person of Alfred Cowan.

His smirk was downright wicked. "I say, old boy, shouldn't keep a splendid woman like this all to yourself and, anyway, I don't believe you've danced with Lady Kilmartin for quite some time, have you?"

Andrew seemed a little unsteady, though it wasn't drink that had made him so. "No, no, you're right," he responded, his voice strained and distant. "Thank you, Annie—it was most enjoyable."

It was not possible for her to answer him, as she could barely swallow her own saliva. For his part, he could do nothing more than walk away from her in a daze.

Eleven

As if it had been asked to wait, the rain held off until Sunday night, beginning after midnight and continuing through the morning. Its arrival added an air of melancholy to the close of the festivities, though, and everyone on Monday morning, including the staff at Crinan Castle, looked somewhat down in the mouth.

Janet and Annie had not spoken again since their brief encounter at the ball, and it was clearly the best way to handle things. But as Andrew was preparing to leave on Monday morning—with Annie and Marc—the two women found themselves unavoidably face to face.

Janet bristled at the sight of Annie standing next to her husband, ready to leave with him, and her instincts told her not to let it happen. But the knowledge that Andrew was determined to have his way in this forced reason to prevail and made her see that all she could do was issue a warning. So after embracing her husband and shaking young Marc's hand, she crudely grasped Annie's shoulders to kiss her cheeks.

"Don't forget our agreement," she said into one ear and then followed it with, "because I won't," in the other.

Annie nodded her concurrence, then stooped to say good-bye to little Malcolm before brushing something from her eye.

As the Range Rover took them off to the helicopter, Janet stood watching from a window in the morning room. *How very odd,* she thought, *for me to feel this way. In all these years I've never ached to see him leave, never worried that he might not return. Many was the time I watched him go, knowing that he would see that French woman, that he would be sleeping with her, and I hardly gave it a second thought. Why is this time so different?* The answer crept up on her, like the stealthy mists that rolled in from the loch: *It's not so much his going off with another woman, it's the importance of the journey he's embarking upon. He's going in search of his heart, and the path he's chosen to follow takes him away from me—it takes him to her. Will it ever lead him back?*

In another corner of the morning room, Lord Cowan was having coffee with Lady Mary, listening to her express vexation at her son's leaving with "that woman." Cowan sought to console her but he, too, was rankled by the way in which Andrew flaunted his departure with Annie. Seeing that Janet had remained immobile at the window for some time after they'd gone, he excused himself from Mary and made his way toward her. When she turned her face to greet him, he discerned a redness of complexion that came from fending off bitter tears.

He patted her shoulder as he said, "My dear, don't fret—boys will be boys."

She found his words unexpectedly reassuring. "It is like that, isn't it? When he's with her—it's as though he's still that young man." She dabbed at her nose with a tissue, then thought to tell him, "You know, I can't help but think that his father made a grave mistake in not allowing him his desire back then. It may have been the only way to get her out of his system."

As he considered that, Cowan pursed his lips, then rearranged them into a frown. "Who's to say? Perhaps Donald was wrong in keeping them apart, perhaps that wasn't the wisest thing the do. But we can't change what's done. The best we can do is play the cards we're dealt and I have to wonder, Janet dear, is it wise to let them be together now?"

With the barest shake of her head, she answered, "I don't know. I only know that if I try to stop them he'll hate me for it, and I'll lose him in that way." She was visited, suddenly, by a stark recollection. "I should have let him go then, followed my first instincts," she muttered to herself.

"When was that, my dear?"

She hadn't meant to say what she did aloud, but it was too late. She gestured with a tilt of her head for him to follow her to a more removed spot; although her mother-in-law was now occupied by another lingering guest, she worried that they might be overheard.

"After the car crash," she whispered, "when his mind finally cleared—he asked for me, he wanted to see me. But it was to tell me about her, to say how much he loved her, to explain that the accident had happened because he was desperate to get to her."

Cowan coaxed her into sitting on a nearby couch. He leaned close to offer, "That must have been difficult to learn."

The hurt that recollection carried with it darkened her eyes. "My first instinct was to release him, and I went away thinking that I would. But the next day, as I sat brooding over it, Donald came to see me." She began to fidget with the raised gold buttons on her cardigan. "He informed me that just after I saw him, Andrew had fallen ill with a fever. Donald said that he'd been up with him the entire night, hearing him call Annie's name, and it had broken his heart. He then told me about the lengths he'd gone to to keep them apart, and he was deeply remorseful; he had come to believe that the better course of action would be to stop interfering and bring her to him. But before he did that he asked for my permission, because it would, after all, affect me more than anyone; I would be the one to suffer the public humiliation."

Cowan was not surprised to hear this, but he gave no indication that he already knew these things.

"He left it up to me, he put it in my hands," she went on to say. "I had been feeling sorry for myself before then, but Donald's revelation and the power he was yielding, the chance to take my future into my own hands and be in control for a change, well, it was too heady a moment. And I wanted to punish Andrew, I think, I wanted to say to him—you can't walk away from me."

Janet smiled ironically now, as she recalled asking Annie if she loved Andrew enough to walk away, because in this moment she realized that she'd once been in that very position herself. Had she loved him sufficiently, unselfishly, she would have done just that, she would have set him free to be with Annie. Instead, she insisted Donald maintain his subterfuge, so she'd not have to suffer the disgrace of a broken engagement. But that hadn't been the only reason—there'd been the little matter of loving him, albeit in her own, reticent way, for as long as she could remember.

"So I told Donald to keep things as they were, and I could see that he was shocked, that he had expected another answer. But in my defense, I truly believed Andrew was in the grips of an infatuation, and that he would come to realize that in time." She looked into Cowan's eyes now, and her expression changed to one that conveyed pained befuddlement as she wondered aloud, "Isn't twenty years time enough?"

Cowan was unexpectedly moved by Janet's distressed state, and found himself overcome by a strong and unfamiliar protective instinct, something he imagined a father must feel toward his child. He softened his voice considerably to say to her, "My dear lady, there's no need for you to be the heavy in this; if someone need remind Andrew of his responsibilities, let it be me. You will recall that Donald was my closest friend, so as I see it, it's more my duty than yours. Mary has already called on me to do what I can, so if you find you need my help, you've only to ask."

Although she did appreciate it, his offer of service made Janet uncomfortable, but if she'd been asked, she would not have been able to say why. "Thank you, it's most kind of you, but there's no need, not at present anyway. I'm a bit overwrought just now, but I'll manage somehow." A thought suddenly occurred to her that filled her with worry, and in that instant, the button she was fingering came off in her hand. As though it was something precious that she didn't want to lose, she clutched it in her fist, asking, "Alfred — you won't share what I've told you with anyone, will you?"

He understood perfectly; now was not the time for Andrew to learn of Janet's role in his entrapment. "I'll carry Donald's secrets to my grave," he assured her, stroking the hand that held the button. He lingered in that action a moment, as his thoughts were drawn to one particular secret, the memory of which always left him wishing that life had taken a different turn. "Just remember, my dear," he added, as he let the memory fade, "that if it gets to be too much for you, I've no problem stepping into Donald's shoes. I know what he would do with her, and I'm prepared to do it." He punctuated that statement with a look of simmering pique.

She had closed her fist so tightly around the detached button, her palm began to smart. She unfolded her fingers now and stared at the thing, and had to ponder for a moment what on earth it was she was holding to.

Andrew flew with Annie and Marc as far as London and they spoke of little else but the Laird's Day celebration. Marc thoroughly enjoyed his visit and his time spent with Andrew's children, and neither he nor Annie could decide which part of the weekend they enjoyed more. They finally concluded that Sunday's events were the most fun, because it had been a rare treat to see so many people enjoying themselves to such an extent.

Before Andrew disembarked, he and Marc shared an embrace that was more like a father and son than anything else. Marc thanked him profusely and expressed the hope that they would meet again.

He was touched by the young man's sincerity and, for an instant, overcome with regret, wishing that this child of Annie's had been his. "Marc, you'll always be welcome in my home and any assistance or hospitality that I might offer will be yours but for the asking—no matter what."

"That's so cool!" he grinned. "Thanks a million, really, and tell your kids again what a great time I had."

"I'll do that, and you're very welcome." He gripped Annie's shoulders now and held her at arm's length. "And you, my dear friend, I'll see you soon."

"Yes," she answered, "soon."

In Barcelona, it was hard to say good-bye; Annie missed her son immediately and felt achingly alone on the return trip. But as they prepared to land at Le Bourget, her anxiety returned and it all but obliterated everything else as she realized that her moment of truth was near.

The staff at the Trianon Palace Hotel were skilled purveyors of discretion, and they ushered Annie to her elegant rooms without asking for the formalities. Once she was settled, a manager brought the necessary paperwork along with complimentary champagne and canapés, and after filling in a brief form and showing him her passport, she was left on her own to await her lover.

The clock annoyed her as it ticked on without a word from Andrew, and as her tension grew, she began to feel the need for air. The rooms had a view of the park grounds of Versailles—which the hotel bordered—and she thought to walk there. But the doorman informed her that it was not entirely safe, so she had to content herself with the hotel environs.

A bronze sculpture in the garden immediately drew her attention. From a distance she couldn't make out what it was meant to represent, but as she approached the piece it struck an old, familiar chord. She read the little plaque—Europa and the Bull—and it made her smile.

"Well hello, old friend," she said softly, "it's been a long time. But you've changed, haven't you?"

This was not the triumphant maiden she had known in the sculpture fountain at her old university: a strong and determined woman, ready to meet the challenge of whatever lay ahead. This rendering of Europa was entirely different: a yielding, vulnerable creature, who lay naked, stretched on her back over the bull's haunches, her pubic tuft rising with his withers, her flowing hair melding with his tail. And unlike the other bull whose massive bulk tensed as he readied to spirit the maiden away, the docile beast beneath this Europa bowed his head to the ground, like a dog craving acceptance, and stepped lightly, carefully with his burden.

Annie had lowered herself onto a nearby bench to sit in quiet contemplation when something occurred to her. "I got it wrong, didn't I? I thought it was about defiance, about swimming against the current, but that wasn't the message, was it?"

Night had fallen before she became aware of it, and in the darkness the vision was even more compelling. In the mutable electric light she watched the sculpture change, the bull's body transform to a sacrificial altar on which the compliant maiden lay offered. The evening deepened and the air turned somewhat chill, but Annie remained transfixed, as though awaiting an answer.

There was a message from Andrew that he would not arrive until two in the morning. She sat drinking in the Givenchy-designed bar for a time, watching the chic clientele come and go, the expensive scents they were wearing following them like vapor trails. When she returned to the suite, she discovered that flowers had been delivered in her absence, three dozen magnificent white roses, with crimson, curled edges that looked as though they'd been dipped in blood. The card read only—Soon!

The flowers were her companions as she picked at the dinner she ordered, washing it down with the champagne. She brought the flowers with her when she retired to the bedroom, and they were the last thing she saw as she fell into a deep, inebriated sleep, her nude body partially draped in the pale pink sheets.

She was walking—down a long road on a blustery day— housewives swept the sidewalks behind her. When she passed through the West Port she was flooded with a feeling of peace. South Street bustled as she walked among prams and bicycles and scarlet gowns, inhaling the aromas of meat pies and harvested flowers. She smiled and said "Fine day!" but no one returned her greeting. She saw her old friend Adam standing in front of Southgait Hall, but he didn't acknowledge her. She left him behind, and made her way toward the Whaum.

Andrew sat near the fire, a glass in one hand, a bottle in the other, his blue eyes glazed over. When she bent before him she realized that she was wearing an unusual gown, a sort of toga, which gathered over one shoulder and exposed one breast. She cupped the breast in both hands and offered the nipple for him to suckle, but he was unmoving, his eyes focused somewhere in the distance. No longer peaceful, she felt alone and bewildered, so she left him, and went to the cathedral.

Percy B. waited for her among the tombstones; the graveyard was abandoned and overrun by a jagged, sharp briar. A shadowy figure lurked behind the granite headstones and followed her, crouching among thickets of the dead. She quickened her pace and reached Percy finally, scratched and torn and bleeding. The furtive shadow grinned with gray, scum-covered teeth to see her wounded so.

Wild vines had entangled Percy and wound across his seat. She lifted her gown to straddle the motorcycle, exposing bare bottom as she sat, and the vine's thorns tore into her tender flesh. She cried out in pain and tried to remove them, but they only drove themselves deeper. The vines wound themselves around her body now, pulling her backward and pinning her to the seat, her legs entwined and spread apart.

The shadow crept nearer, and raised its hooded head to peer into her most private entrance. She felt the creature's rank, cold breath on her labia, its icy protuberance wriggling, stroking, then sucking at her wounds. She heard its lapping slurps, felt its slime trickling onto her flesh. Like a serpent slithering into a burrow, the prowler crawled inside; pulsing and dancing, it hunted down its prey, and her hips followed its rhythm.

Andrew's naked flesh felt warm and healing as he nestled next to her, lifting Annie from the depths of her nightmare.

He brushed aside her dampened hair and kissed the nape of her neck. Between kisses, he sighed, "God, how I missed you."

She opened her eyes, then closed them tightly again, trying to flush the dread and fear from her mind. "Andrew," she answered, "thank God it's you."

"You're perspiring, darling," he whispered. "Were you dreaming?"

The tender sound of his voice was like an antidote to the images poisoning her mind. "I was having a nightmare—an awful nightmare."

Stroking her arms now, he asked, "What was it about?"

She rubbed her eyes then turned to face him, saying, "I've had it before. There's something dark and evil—a man," she said at first, then decided, "no, not a man, some inhuman creature. It comes after me and I can't stop it—I don't stop it. It always leaves me with this horrible, sick feeling inside, as though I've been raped."

Her description made him recall what had happened to her before they met. "Is it the LSD thing, are you reliving that in your nightmare?"

"That's part of it, I think, but there's more to it." She didn't want to go any further, because the longer she kept it in her mind, the worse she felt. And, too, she wasn't ready to tell him that her first experience with the dream was after she'd left St. Andrews, as

she lay in a deep, druglike sleep on the floor of the Sherwood Forest. She and John had copulated like animals, and the dream had
been a vividly agonizing climax to their sexual frenzy.

He knew she wanted off the subject, so he told her, "Never
mind, my darling, it's over now. It was just a bad dream and I'm
here now." He lifted one hand to kiss the palm of it, then the wrist,
saying, "I'm sorry I'm so late, but it couldn't be helped."

She wanted to think of something pleasant, so she looked to
the flowers. "Thank you for the beautiful roses, they've a divine fragrance." Her vision was too blurry to read the clock, so she asked,
"What time is it?"

"Half past two," he answered, his voice silky and reassuring.

"What time is the appointment?"

"Eleven."

"That's good, we can sleep late." She pulled her arms into her
chest and burrowed into him as he enfolded her, working their bodies into the lush comfort of the mattress.

He rested his chin on the top of her head, and breathed deeply
of her warm scent, before softly questioning, "Are you frightened
of tomorrow?"

"No," she answered, "not anymore," her voice reverberating
through the muscles of his chest.

He seemed surprised, and wondered, "Why, what's happened?"

"You," she realized, "you've happened."

She lifted her face to him and they brought their mouths together in a delicate kiss, as their hands passionately grasped the
other's.

They ate breakfast in bed just before nine, and left the hotel
at half past ten. The clinic was only three blocks away so they
shunned the driver who awaited them, deciding to walk instead.
But before they left the hotel grounds, Annie led Andrew to the garden to show him the sculpture.

"What do you think?" she asked.

He took one turn around it before telling her, "Interesting—
beautiful—sad."

"Why sad?"

"I don't know, I can't put my finger on it, it just makes me feel somewhat sad."

She was looking again at the work, trying to see what is was he saw, when something occurred to her that hadn't the night before. "Do you think she's dead? Do you think the bull is carrying a dead Europa?"

"That could be it," he realized.

She shook her head adamantly as she decided against that possibility, for it was one she could not accept. "She's not dead — look at her right arm, it's flexed, it's not limp like the other. Dead limbs don't stay flexed like that. No, she's just totally relaxed, she's given in, she's stopped fighting her fate — that's what's going on."

He recognized that his suggestion had unsettled her, so he said, "Of course you're right, darling. That's it, of course." He glanced at his watch. "We'd better be getting on, or we'll be late."

It was a very well-appointed office, in a building fashioned of marble and granite, with long, echoing corridors that smelled of antiseptic and freshly applied wax. Annie had already been examined and her blood drawn, now she and Andrew sat side by side, hands clutched, waiting for Dr. Coupau to return to his office. Although they were eager to speak with him, when he came into the room they immediately tensed.

He greeted them cordially, before observing, "I take it you want to do this together," his accent heavy and charming.

"Yes," she responded, "although, as I told you, Andrew's not physically involved — he's not at risk."

"I understand," he answered, glancing only fleetingly at Andrew. "Well, I'll start by saying that in the examination I found no indication of AIDS; your immune system appears to be functioning well and normally. Let me ask you, Madame, did you have a viral illness before the blood donations in question were made?"

Annie looked at Andrew, then back to the doctor. "A virus? Like the flu, do you mean?"

"Or like Epstein-Barr, mononucleosis, that sort of thing."

She rubbed her forehead, and dropped her gaze to the floor. "Not that I know of, but let me think." Her heart had begun to race and flutter, and it was making her a little lightheaded. "That would have been last fall — I can't think — no, I don't think so. I think I was well all last fall."

"How about a vaccination against the flu?" he questioned.

Still grasping her hand, Andrew watched her anxiously.

"Yes," she almost shouted, as though she'd found something she'd long been searching for. "I did get a flu shot — I always do, ever since I started working in a hospital years ago. Is that important?" From the look on his face, she had already guessed that it was.

He responded calmly to her enthusiasm. "Well then, I think we may have found a reason for you to be a false positive."

"A false positive?" Andrew asked, his voice breaking slightly.

"There's been quite a bit in the scientific literature on it," he informed them. "Ever since the Red Cross began screening for HIV antibodies, they've been turning up a fair number of false positives, and some of the reasons for them have been discerned. Recent viral illness is one, and viral vaccination is another."

"But that's wonderful!" Andrew blurted.

Her mouth agape and frozen in disbelief, it was hard to get it moving again to ask, "Why didn't my doctor at home tell me this? Why didn't he ask me those questions?"

Dr. Coupau shrugged in an exaggerated way, typical of the French, then said, "Perhaps he didn't have the information at hand."

Andrew wanted the bottom line. "So you think she's all right, then?"

Smiling slightly, he told Annie, "We must wait for the laboratory results, of course, but when I look at the physical findings, together with your relating to me that neither of your partners have tested positive — it leads me to say that I find very little reason for concern."

Andrew had meant to stay in the background during this meeting, but he couldn't help himself. "Did I hear you correctly?"

"I find little reason for concern," he repeated, looking directly at Andrew now. "I think the probability is very high that she's well, but I want to hold off on my final pronouncement until we get the results of the blood work, because there's always the chance that a misdiagnosis was made with one of the male partners in question."

Although it was a struggle, she did her best to keep her excitement in check. "How long will that take?"

"Let me see, today is Tuesday—the earliest we could have it is by Friday. I tell you what, I'll personally see to it that we do have it by Friday."

Annie looked at Andrew as she said, "Friday—only three more days—"

Even if he'd wanted to, Andrew could not have stopped the smile that overtook him as he echoed, "Friday."

"I'll need a number where I can reach you," the doctor said, suddenly feeling as though he'd intruded upon a private moment.

Annie had begun to replay the doctor's words in her head, because she needed to be certain she hadn't misinterpreted them. As she verified that it was all real and true, she leaned into the back of her chair, and brought a hand to her mouth. "I'll be on location in Cauterets," she told him, a look of amazement filling her face. "I'll have to phone you when I get there."

"Cauterets?" he questioned. "That's a lovely spot, what are you doing there?"

"Shooting a commercial with The Band of Gypsies."

He seemed impressed. "Really? How fun—I do so enjoy their music. They're the most popular group in Europe, are they not?"

"Yes, they are," she answered, still feeling as though everything that was happening was perfectly astonishing, even miraculous. "We're very fortunate to have them."

Dr. Coupau recognized the look the couple gave one another now, one that said they were anxious to be alone. "Well, then," he told them, "let's part on a positive note. Here's my private number, you can leave a message if you can't reach me. May I suggest a restaurant for lunch? It's nearby and quite good—I think you'll enjoy it."

Annie beamed gratitude as she answered, "That would be lovely."

"Thank you so much, doctor, for everything," Andrew told him, as he enthusiastically shook his hand.

"Not at all, your lordship. It's been my pleasure to help."

As they left the clinic it was with such lightness of spirit, they nearly floated along the corridors.

The bistro was just the thing for them, small and bustling and very French, staffed with waiters of great aplomb and personality.

They were offered a table on the busy street, but chose instead the long banquette at the more quiet rear.

After hearing Annie converse with the waiter, Andrew grinned with delight, telling her, "I'd no idea you spoke such beautiful French."

They clinked their glasses of Pernod as she explained, "My grandparents taught us when we were young, and I've spent a fair amount of time with my cousins in Pau. I was at loose ends after my divorce and they were kind enough to invite us for a visit; Marc and I stayed with them for almost two months."

Because that seemed odd to him, he questioned, "Why'd you stay with them instead of your parents?"

After a small, barely audible sigh, she explained, "After Timmy died, what was left of the family fell apart. Even coming together for holidays seemed pointless and painful, because it always reminded us that he wasn't there. Eventually my parents moved back to New Orleans, and I just don't get there that much."

"But surely they need to know their grandson—they need to spend time with him."

"Marc visits them more than I do." Realizing she sounded selfish, she wanted him to understand: "My dad has taken to drinking too much, but my mother's company is the hardest to bear. She'll always use the occasion of being together to say things that hurt me—like when I graduated from college. That day was all about Timmy, all tears and musings over his lost life. And it's never stopped—when I told her about the award I won in advertising, instead of saying how happy she was for me, she said that Timmy was so bright and gifted, he would have been wonderful in that profession, or anything else he chose to do." Her suppressed anger was evident when she went on to say, "She always manages to make me feel guilty, like she wishes it had been me instead—she even said it once. She asked me, 'How can it be that you drove a motorcycle all over Europe without a scratch, and Timmy, who was so much better at it, was killed?'" She shook her head in despair. "I've got enough problems of my own with that—I don't need her adding to them."

He had wanted to understand why she seemed so disconnected from her parents, and now he did. But there was one more question he needed to ask. "And Carlos, what happened there?"

She looked away briefly, then back to Andrew. "He's not a bad guy, but he's very old world, a true Catalan, and he wanted me to be a good Catalan wife, you know, take care of home and hearth while he was out in the world doing what he pleased. And what pleased him was chasing after other women."

He frowned. "How did you meet?"

"He was finishing up his MBA at the Wharton School, where I was taking a couple of night courses. He was very intelligent and handsome, and there was a strong sexual attraction, which I mistook for love; we married because I was pregnant with Marc. It's ironic, but the personal attributes that attracted us to one another — for me, his southern European charm, for him, my feisty American independence — they were the very things that set us at one another." Her brow lifted and she pulled in her upper lip. "But don't get me wrong, it wasn't that simple. I have some very bad memories, to be sure, and there were some awful, awful moments, but Marc is worth everything I went through."

He took her hand in his and let his gaze settle there.

She forced a smile, asking, "Can we change the subject, please? This is such a good day, I don't want to waste any of it on painful memories."

He warmed her with a genuine smile when it dawned on him: "Do you realize where we are, after all these years? Do you realize that we're together in France, that I came to meet you in France?"

The happiness returned to her face. "Well, I'll be damned if you didn't! By God, that deserves a toast!"

"And I know the perfect one," he said. "Better late than never!"

"It certainly falls under that category," she chuckled.

As they were laughing and embracing, the waiter arrived with the first course. "Ah, l'amour," he said to them, "c'est la raison d'être!"

Annie raised her glass to the waiter, motioning her head toward Andrew. "Et il est le mien!"

The Frenchman bowed his head to her proclamation before wishing them, "Bon appétit!" then walked away with a knowing grin.

"And you are *my* reason for living, Annie d'Inard."

She could feel his heart in his words, and it set fire to her in-sides. "You know," she said tenderly, "while I was waiting for you last night, I was sitting near Europa, and I was thinking about love. That myth is all about love, isn't it? And I really like what this artist has done, because he's shown Europa giving herself over to it—even though it's come from such an unlikely mate. What I see in that sculpture is acknowledgment: the moment when Europa real-izes that love's power is greater than herself."

He had just lifted his fork and knife, but he laid them aside and touched her hand again.

She smiled slightly. "And there's no stronger, more important force on this earth, is there? Denying it must be the most arrogant and ungrateful act we mortals commit, and we do it all the time, in the name of logic or duty or whatever. I think we'd do better to accept the gifts the gods bestow—rather than reject them because we think we know better. Doing that is probably what ignites their wrath—it must infuriate the hell out of them to have their gifts rejected."

Andrew laughed at her.

She laughed with him before insisting, "I'm serious!"

"I know you are," he told her, reining in his smile, "and that's one of the things I love so much about you." He stroked her cheek to say, "I do wish I didn't have to leave you tonight."

"I do, too," she responded.

He wanted her to know, "My hands are rather full, just now, because Nigel's gone on holiday for a few weeks. It's bad timing re-ally, but it can't be helped." Although he intended to, he'd yet to tell her about what had transpired between the two men. "What I need to do is bring some key people up to speed, so they can pick up the slack and give me the freedom I need to be with you."

"Then that's what you should do," she assured him, adding with a grin, "and don't waste any time getting to it. I'll go on to Cauterets—we'll see each other as soon as you can get free."

They had hardly touched their food and the concerned waiter stopped by to ask if there were a problem; their smiles reassured him immediately. In French he offered, "Love—it fills the stomach as well as the heart!"

"I do so enjoy this country," Andrew said when he was gone. "For all its quirks and peculiarities and bloody strikes, they've the right attitude about love and life, about savoring life's pleasures and living in the moment. As far as I'm concerned, they've got their priorities straight."

She nodded her agreement, then wondered, "Have you spent much time here?"

He smiled at her again. "There was a time when I made every effort to come here, as often as I could. I told you about the woman I was seeing—I've had a relationship with her of one sort or another for the better part of seventeen years."

She was unsettled by his use of tense, but only questioned, "How'd you meet her?"

"At a diplomatic event." he easily recalled. "I was twenty-six and randy, always ready to have a go. She was thirty-three, amazingly beautiful and sophisticated, and married to a stodgy old Englishman, who reeked of cigars. She was very knowledgeable in the ways of love and a great teacher. Any skill I have as a lover I owe to Claudine." As he said her name, he was overcome by an unmistakable look—one that openly displayed his fondness for her.

Knowing that he had genuine affection for this woman brought her a sudden heartache. "You loved her," she had to say aloud, as though that might dispel the hurt. And as the jealously welled up, it made her ask, "Do you still see her?"

He read her as easily as she did him, and seeing her upset, he furrowed his brow. "I do, occasionally, but only as friends now. We've not slept together for quite some time—for several years, actually." He had wanted her to know this straight off, but he didn't hesitate to admit, "And, yes, I loved her; she was—is—a good and trusted friend." He stopped abruptly, then corrected himself. "No, it was more than that. We shared a passion, an insatiable, sexual appetite for the other. We loved making love, though there was never any deep, abiding love between us. Does that make sense?"

His response afforded her some consolation. "It does," she answered, "but what happened, why'd you stop?"

His eyes rested on the tiny vase of mauve flowers in front of him, just as one delicate petal drifted to the white tablecloth. "After my father's death," he said in a more serious tone, "after Malcolm was born, Janet and I became closer than we'd ever been. It was then that I made the decision to stop being with Claudine, so I might put more effort into my marriage."

That explanation made her increasingly anxious, for she realized that one day he could possibly—no, he would very likely have to make that decision about her. To distract herself from this disturbing idea, she motioned to the waiter for more mineral water. Once she'd moistened her dry mouth, she spoke again, trying her best to sound strong and unaffected. "Did it work, did you make things better?"

Looking at her now, he responded, "Yes, to some degree."

Her saliva evaporated again, and she had difficulty swallowing. "How's that?"

"It was better for Janet, but what I wanted to happen didn't," he said.

"What was it you wanted to happen?" she asked over her racing heart.

"I wanted to feel for her—with her—something of what I felt with Claudine. I wanted to find a passionate, sexual love between us, that was mutually satisfying."

Timidly, she questioned, "And you didn't?"

"No, I didn't," he told her. "Janet believes we did, though, and that's part of the problem now, because I let her go on believing it."

She looked into her lap and told herself to calm down, to stop this nonsense. He was, after all, married to Janet, and as for Claudine, what right had she to be jealous of her? And anyway, his situation was not so very different from her own—he had stayed with his wife because he loved her, and he had done what he felt he had to, in order to keep things going.

"So before we met again," she wanted to get straight, "you grew closer to Janet than you'd ever been, with her believing that everything between you was good and working."

It was with unmistakable regret that he answered, "That about sums it up."

"Great," she said plainly. "Then I came along and threw her whole world into disarray." The guilt made her feel heavy and cumbersome, and she sank into the banquette with the weight of it.

He had lifted his wine glass and was holding it near his lips when he corrected, "Not just her world, my world, too, because you've made it impossible for me to go on deceiving myself."

For the next few moments, they sat in silence, watching the bartender as he first dipped, then swirled, then rinsed, glass after glass, with assembly line precision. And as they observed him, the couple's thoughts were remarkably similar, both of them pondering the numbing dullness of routine, the detachment that so often comes from showing up every day, from repeatedly hauling yourself out of bed to do what is expected of you.

"I've got to stop worrying about Janet," she said after a time, her voice less than steady. "I can't be with you and be thinking about her feelings all the time."

"No you can't," he agreed. "Janet's my problem."

She sighed now, as she thought of her own problem, of the love she continued to feel for Mike. It didn't matter that he'd been with another woman, that he was probably still with her. And being with Andrew hadn't altered or lessened those feelings; in an odd way, they may have actually been reinforced by it.

"Why can't life be more simple?" she wondered.

Andrew took hold of one of her hands. "It's the price we pay for their gifts. That's why I laughed at you before, when you talked about the gods giving us gifts. They never give us anything—we always have to pay."

After lunch they strolled through the grounds of Versailles before returning to the hotel. Just before they checked out, Annie phoned the desk and asked that the young chambermaid who had turned down the bed last evening be given her roses.

"That was nice of you," he commented as she completed the call.

"She was very sweet, and I doubt very much that anyone has ever given her such beautiful flowers. Anyway, it's good karma to share my happiness."

He smiled at her, then moved nearer to kiss her forehead.

Andrew accompanied Annie on the flight to Pau, and because it was so difficult to say good-bye, he went in the car with her to the hotel. When they arrived, the driver stood outside while they shared a few more minutes, huddled together in the back seat.

"I'll come to Cauterets no later than Friday," he promised her, "but sooner, if I can."

She felt tears coming on as she told him, "I miss you already."

"What will you do tonight?" he wondered.

She shrugged. Since it was relatively early—just past nine— she decided: "Probably phone my cousin Jean-Marc, invite him for a drink. He's going to work with us on location as a translator—did I tell you that?"

He shook his head.

"I thought of him because he's already acquainted with one of the musicians, and he speaks Spanish and some Basque, as well as Béarnais, so he should be a considerable help. And he's got his own business," she went on to say, "so he's able to set aside the time. He's driving me to Cauterets in the morning."

"Don't forget to ring me on the private line and let me know how to reach you," he reminded her.

"I won't."

He embraced her now, whispering, "I'm praying for Friday," his lips touching hers.

His kiss made her body limp, and she cuddled into him saying, "Do you realize that we may make love for the first time on Friday, I mean, with you inside of me?"

"I've thought of little else," he admitted, breathlessly.

They looked into each other's eyes for one long moment, and then Annie left the car, without either of them saying another word. When she reached the top of the steps she didn't go into the lobby, but instead positioned herself with a long view of the boulevard, so that she might follow the Mercedes until it disappeared.

Twelve

The road to Cauterets goes nowhere else. It leads right into town and ends there; the only way out is to turn around and follow your own tracks. There are, however, several dirt roads that meander into the highest mountain areas, and it was one of these that Annie and her cousin received directions to follow.

After a brief stop at the hotel, they tackled the bumpy, rock-laden, wagon path, through stands of ancient beech and chestnut, up and up, along a wonderfully noisy stream, into crystal, mountain sky.

"I'm curious," Jean-Marc said, both hands gripping the convulsing steering wheel, "was it you who chose this location?"

She braced herself against the dashboard as she answered, "Guilty. The agent for the band told me they don't like to fly, so I needed a spot they could easily drive to—well, in distance anyway," she chuckled. "And we wanted breathtaking mountain scenery, so I thought of this place."

The car jostled them through a particularly rutty stretch, which gratefully smoothed out before too long. When it was easier to converse, her cousin asked, "And what's the advertisement for, cheese you said?"

"Sheep's milk cheese," she responded, "like your brébis. There are very good sheep's milk cheeses in Scotland, but they're virtually unknown outside of Britain. The earl wants to open up new markets by introducing them first to the Europeans, then to Canada and the United States. Most of the sheep farmers in Britain barely eke out a living now, and he sees this as a way to help."

Jean-Marc turned toward her with a skeptical frown. "Come on," he said, his voice jostling along with his body, "a rich aristocrat wanting to help little farmers? There must be something in it for him."

"There is," she answered confidently, as a sharp turn pressed her against the door. They could see the site ahead of them now, and she and her kidneys were most grateful. "When farms are about to go under," she explained, "the Highland Land Trust has been buying the land, then leasing it back to the farmers. They've also set up a co-operative network, through which farmers can sell their wool and lambs and cheeses, and make fair profits. Lord Kilmartin established the trust about five years ago," she went on to say, "in tribute to his dead father and grandfather. It's all meant to help independent farmers stay in business and keep their way of life from becoming extinct, a lifestyle tradition that is essential to the character of Scotland."

As Jean-Marc drew the overheating vehicle to a stop, he lifted his brow to say, "I get it. He's increasing his land holdings and at the same time, making himself the middleman, so he can get his percentage."

She was not offended by her cousin's cynicism; had she not known that the person in question was Andrew, she would have been skeptical, too. "Of course there's profit," she told him, "but it doesn't go to Lord Kilmartin, it goes back to the trust. And should a farmer become solvent again," she wanted him to know, "he or she can buy back the land at the selling price."

Still incredulous, he wanted to know, "If there's no personal gain, then why does he do it?"

Having just come from Kilmartin and seen it for herself, she was able to answer with certainty, "Oh, but there is personal gain. He does it because he loves his fellow Scots, and he believes very strongly that those who are in a position to help should."

Jean-Marc seemed to catch something in her expression, which led him to observe, "Sounds as though you're taken with this fellow."

She blushed, and glossed over his comment by responding, "I'm taken with the idea." Then, to steer their conversation in a different direction, she added, "And I'm excited to be on location, because this is the fun part of what I do—you'll see. The finished product will be funny and beautiful to watch, and it'll send people rushing to their cheese shops, asking for Scottish cheese."

"Even in France?" he scoffed.

With a self-satisfied grin, she asked him, "Why do you think we're using the hottest musical group in France?"

Jeremy Whitman was the man in charge and he had arrived Sunday night, commandeering an entire hotel for the week. Because the project was for Nether Largie, John Millar-Graham thought it best that he oversee the endeavor, so he arrived midafternoon on Tuesday. And although she'd advised the team that she couldn't be there until Wednesday, when Annie showed up, John was noticeably perturbed.

As she stepped from her cousin's Citroën, she had to pause a moment; the setting was exactly what she'd had in mind, and the beauty of it warranted a deep sigh. They were high atop the Hautes Pyrénées, on a deep green alpine meadow that was dotted with lupine in all shades of blue and purple. The sky above them sparkled brilliant sapphire, and the air was exquisitely fresh.

When John saw her, he scowled, "Nice of you to join us."

She ignored the rebuke, declaring, "You did a great job choosing—it's absolutely perfect. Where are our actors?"

He continued to frown as he informed her, "Jeremy had to make the decision on his own, and the gypsies arrive tomorrow."

Laughingly, she responded, "I meant our sheep."

"Over that rise, being tended to by three men who no one can communicate with," he complained.

She'd neglected to introduce her cousin, and told him now, "This is Jean-Marc d'Inard."

It was with some relief that he realized, "Ah, our translator. Pleased to meet you." Briefly, they shook hands. "Do you think you can speak with those men?" he asked, pointing to the three bemused shepherds. "I don't know if they're Basque or what, but whatever they are, we can't seem to connect."

"No problem," Jean-Marc answered, "and it's a pleasure to meet you."

Jeremy joined them now, and after briefing him on what was needed from the shepherds, he took Jean-Marc to meet them.

When they were alone, Annie told John, "I know you're pissed about it but I've a good reason for coming late."

"Well?" he demanded.

She lowered her voice considerably. "I went to see a doctor about some health problems I've been having."

"You mentioned that in our first meeting," he recalled, then questioned, "Serious, is it?"

"It has that potential," she told him, quickly adding, "but I'm hoping for the best. The doctor's going to call me here on Friday, to let me know the results of some tests."

Recognizing how in earnest she was, he softened somewhat. "Is there anything I can do?"

Smiling with gratitude, she replied, "Just continue to be my friend. Now, what can I do? I'm itching to get to work."

He motioned toward the production crew. "Since it's your vision we're trying to realize, I'd rather have you working with the director than Jeremy."

Touching her forehead in a playful salute, she answered, "I'm on it."

At the hotel in Cauterets, before going to the location site, Annie made four quick phone calls, leaving messages for her son, Andrew, and Dr. Coupau, about where she could be reached. The last call was to her home in the States, and her housekeeper had answered.

"Morning, Lucy—how's everything?"

"Annie! How you doin'? How's Marc?"

"He's great. I took him to Barcelona on Monday."

"Did you have a nice visit?"

"We had a wonderful visit," she told her, "but it was too short. Listen, sweetie, I can't stay on the phone, because I need to get to work. I'm on the road and I wanted to give you the number where I can be reached for the next few days—got a pencil?"

Annie could hear her rifling the kitchen junk drawer, just as she said, "One of these days I'm going to clean this damn thing out." Then, there was the zip of tearing paper, and "OK—go ahead."

Once Lucy had jotted it down, Annie asked her about Mike.

"He's out running now," Lucy informed her, "too bad you didn't call half an hour ago."

That seemed odd. "What's he doing home at this hour?"

"He's taken the day off," she explained. "The gardeners were coming to clean up your beds and he wanted to keep an eye on them, because he didn't want them ripping up your pretty blue flowers like they did last time."

"The delphinium."

"Yeah, those."

She wasn't sure she'd heard correctly. "Are we talking about my Mike, Lucy? He took a day off for that?"

"He sure did. And he took a few days off before Marc left, too, to spend time with him. Didn't you know?"

It was astonishing. "No, I didn't. What's wrong with him, is he sick?"

Lucy laughed, then told her, "Naw, just bothered I think."

"By what?"

"I think things at the office are buggin' him."

"What things?" she wanted to know.

More soberly now, she told her, "You know, Annie, he doesn't say much to me usually, just asks me about my grandkids and whatnot. But lately he talks to me more—I guess 'cause you're not here he needs somebody to talk to."

Since her fateful phone call to the Bellevue Hotel, she'd been imagining Mike in the company of another woman, not seeing him sitting alone in the house, needing someone to talk to. "What does he talk about?"

"He told me that he's getting sick of defending big companies and all the crap that goes along with that."

"I find that hard to believe," she protested. "He's had clients now and again that he's disliked, but he's always loved his work."

"Not to hear him tell it. He said he's loved the money and the success, but never what he had to do for it."

Annie was suddenly heartsick, and the sensation of it weakened her voice. "He never told me that, Lucy."

"Maybe he's just realizin' it," she offered. "Maybe with you gone he's been thinking more about things."

"Maybe—"

"Do you want me to have him call you when he gets in?" Lucy wondered.

Her mind was trying to capture the image of her husband that Lucy was painting, and it was not easily done. "I probably won't be back until late," she responded. "He can try me tonight, if he wants, but that's up to him."

Lucy always asked this, but that didn't stop her asking again. "When are you coming home, Annie?"

"I don't know," she sighed. "Things are still up in the air for me and until I have those things settled, I can't say what I'm going to do."

She thought to tell her now, "Mike mentioned to me that he might go over there, to see you."

That was another shock. "He did?"

"Yeah. He said that Scotch fella invited him."

"Andrew invited him?"

"Yeah, your friend Andrew. Mike really liked him, he said he seems to be one of the good guys."

"He is, Lucy," she agreed, just as she caught a glimpse of a clock. "Damn, look at the time! I've got to get going, my boss is going to shoot me if I show up much later."

"We can't have that, now," she chuckled. "You go on. It's been great talkin', Annie."

"I miss you, Lucy. Talk to you soon, OK?"

They put in a long, hard day. They argued about doing a filming run with just the sheep, and then decided that it was pointless, laughing at themselves for even thinking that it might be possible to rehearse sheep. At the end of the day the group of them occupied the hotel restaurant and enjoyed a traditional meal of mutton and white beans — the producer joking that this was the first time he'd ever eaten one of his actors — then they sat talking and drinking wine to await the arrival of the musicians. They were supposed to have been there for dinner, but the two tour buses finally arrived after nine, depositing the group of honest-to-God gypsies at the hotel.

There were ten actual band members, mostly guitarists, twelve members of their back-up orchestra, and an entourage of rough-looking young men and colorfully dressed women—about a dozen of these—whose purpose could only be guessed at. Jean-Marc was the first to greet them, and one of them knowing him put them all at ease. The hotel proprietors were thrilled to have as their guests the most popular band in western Europe and they fussed over them, whipping the kitchen into a frenzy to see to their wants. The drink flowed freely and there was some spontaneous guitar music, and it began to look as though they might stay up all night. It was only with considerable effort that Jean-Marc was able to persuade them to turn in before two.

It was almost noon before everyone was where they were supposed to be and ready to work. With each passing minute John grew more tense and upset, repeatedly admonishing that, "Time is money!" Annie did her best to calm him, explaining that there was nothing to be gained from fighting the gypsies and their ways, and that it would be better for everyone involved to just go with the flow. When the hotel brought lunch to the site at one o'clock and everything that had just barely gotten underway had to be halted for the next two hours, John almost threw a fit. After the meal, however, when the band was relaxed and well-fed, they cooperated with the utmost enthusiasm. John finally saw the wisdom in letting them be themselves, because it became evident—even to him—that it was their passion and natural vitality that would give the commercial its special appeal.

They'd finally gotten down to some serious work—some choreographed camera angles, some understanding on the parts of the players about what was wanted from them—when the windy rhythm of the mountaintop was broken by the sounds of an approaching helicopter. Annie watched from a distance as John and Jeremy rushed to welcome Andrew; she held back a few minutes, concluding her conversation with a cameraman before going to greet him herself.

John was still with him, explaining what they had thus far accomplished. "Ah, here's Annie," he said to Andrew as she approached.

His entire being seemed like one, enormous smile as he greeted her. "Hello—how are you?" he asked.

Her cheeks went hot and pink, and because looking at him made her long to embrace him, she averted her eyes before answering, "Very well, thanks. I'm so happy that you could get here in time for the shoot tomorrow. I think you'll enjoy seeing it."

"I'm certain I will," he replied. "Everything going all right with your gypsies?"

"My gypsies—I like that!" she laughed. "Fine, just fine. My cousin is sticking to them like glue, and everyone's getting along well."

"As a matter of fact, " John added, "I was somewhat skeptical at first, but now I'm quite excited about their participation."

"That's good to hear," Andrew told him. "What's on for the remainder of the day?"

"More camera work, more walk-throughs. It looks as though the weather will cooperate and we'll be able to do the actual shooting tomorrow, right on schedule," Annie answered him.

"So you should be finished by tomorrow evening?"

She nodded, saying, "Unless the weather changes."

"Wonderful," he commented, and grinned broadly.

He didn't know why, but watching the interaction between the two made John feel like an intruder. "Well now, shall we get back to work? We need to make the most of the light."

"Of course," Andrew replied. "Don't let my being here interfere in anyway."

John watched them smile at one another, and Annie blush and avert her eyes again, and it gave him an uncomfortable feeling.

Dinner was a wonderfully noisy and happy affair; the large serving dishes that were set upon the tables had to be refilled almost immediately, carafes of wine were emptied in the blink of an eye, bread disappeared with barely the trace of a crumb. To start, there were baby eels in garlic and peppers, caught in the nearby river, and steaming plates of fragrant wild mushrooms, gathered from the woods. For the main course they were served stewed capons flavored with Bayonne ham, accompanied by crisp green beans that had been sauteed with garlic and bread crumbs. There was a delicate salad of baby greens drizzled with walnut oil to follow, then several different cheeses, including the nutty ewe's milk brébis, served with a strong, local wine and more loaves of crusty bread. And when it seemed they could eat no more, there was the traditional Basque cake, followed by hand-rolled, bitter chocolates—both prepared that day by the wife of the owner—and thick, dark coffee.

Throughout it all, townspeople could be seen peering through the dining room window for a glimpse of the famous group. Much to their delight, various members of the band would look up from their plates long enough to wave and flash their teeth, which were, more often than not, colorfully decorated with bits of food.

To John's surprise, Andrew had elected to eat in the dining room with everyone else, sitting at a table with him and key members of the production crew, and Annie, of course. Despite the raucous atmosphere, Andrew appeared perfectly happy and at ease, though John strongly suspected that it was Annie's proximity that was bringing him the most pleasure.

After dinner there was more wine, ever increasing laughter, and the occasional squeal of a young woman whose breast or bottom had been pinched by an inebriated gypsy. Several young men left the room together and returned with guitar cases, placing them next to chairs that they arranged in a semicircle near the street windows. Without the slightest fuss and in a matter of a few minutes—as though it were the natural conclusion to the meal—the ten gypsies were seated in the circle, tuning up their guitars. And in another couple of minutes, the room was filled with the joyous strumming and singing that had made them famous.

With skirts lifted to the tops of their thighs, the young women began to dance; one had a table cleared for her, and she eagerly climbed on top. Hands clapping in double-time accompanied the musicians, the dancers stomped and made chirping noises, men shouted back at them in a mysterious language. The street audience at the window tripled in size and the hotel staff stopped what they were doing to watch with delight as the music intensified and the place seemed to transform into a gypsy camp.

It was positively thrilling to everyone who watched, even the staid British. But there were two people who found themselves especially enthralled; as the music grew more passionate, Annie felt a powerful need to be closer to Andrew and he sensed it.

He inched his chair nearer hers, then leaned in to ask, "Wonderful, isn't it?" his eyes on the dancers.

"It reminds me," she responded, "do you remember the letter I wrote you when I arrived in Saintes Maries? The town was filled with gypsies that weekend, I'd stayed up all night with my friends, listening to music like this, watching dancing like this, thinking of you all the time. I wrote you in the morning and told you to come to me, no matter what, I said you had to come — if only for the summer."

He took her hand under the table.

She'd had more than a little wine and though she tried to hold them back, her memories were bringing on the tears. "That's all I asked for, just the summer —"

He placed his other hand on hers and stroked it, just as the first two droplets trickled down her cheeks. "We have it now," he softly told her, "we have our summer."

She wiped her face with her free hand, and questioned, "Do we?"

He nodded, then bestowed her with a smile that was as satisfying as an embrace.

John could not hear their conversation but he could see the emotions they were experiencing. So could anyone else who may have been watching.

Soon after, a dark young man with penetrating eyes approached their table and, in broken French, asked Annie to dance. She declined at first but then she heard Andrew encouraging her, saying how much he'd like to see her dance.

Once among the other dancers, she protested that she was unaccustomed to dancing to this kind of music.

He laughed at her, then simply questioned, "You have a soul, don't you? Listen to it with your soul, and you will know what to do."

He began by whirling her around several times, then he pulled her tightly against his chest. The music had changed to something dramatic, like a tango, and he backed her around the floor in perfect step, his spine arched, his body tense. Occasionally he stopped abruptly and dipped her, burying his face in her neck and inhaling her perfume before bringing her upright again. He was such a compelling partner that Annie let go her self-consciousness. His friends offered their comments as the couple danced past, making those strange, suggestive sounds that she'd heard so often as a young woman, when she'd pass a group of young, southern European men.

John had had his share of wine, too, and was watching Andrew watch her. He felt he knew what was going on, but he was emboldened by the drink to seek confirmation. "Damned attractive woman," he said to Andrew, adding, "of course, she always was, wasn't she?"

He was so enthralled by Annie's foray into gypsy dancing, he didn't think before answering, "She's always had a rare and wonderful quality."

Encouraged by this admission, John continued to probe. "Yes—but just what is that, do you think? I know I was taken in by it before, but I've never been able to quite put my finger on it."

The familiarity implied in his remarks struck an old but easily irritated nerve, and Andrew's hands balled into fists. He brought one to his chest and pounded it over his heart twice, then he turned to face John full-on. "She lives from here, right from here," he said, his tone dramatically different.

The table had emptied and it was now just the two of them. John sat a few seats away but Andrew beckoned him to move closer. He waited patiently for him to rise and then reseat himself, and when they were side by side, he locked eyes with him.

Speaking in that low, commanding voice he'd learned from his father, he warned: "Don't fuck with me, John. I'm not the same fool you fucked over all those years ago."

John felt his chest tighten. His stomach jumped into his throat, his vocal cords failed to move, his head began to spin—for all he knew he might have been having a heart attack. But the only clear thought he had in this moment was that he'd just blown the firm's most important account.

In the same, steady tone, Andrew added, "I know you kissed her." His jaw tightened and John could see the muscles in it begin to twitch. "Don't be stupid," he hissed, "don't ever, ever do anything like that again."

John was unable to get words through his tightened throat, so he shook his head to say he wouldn't.

"I've never forgotten what you did," Andrew wanted him to know. "The only reason I've not moved my business is because I can use you, and I'm going to do just that, do you understand me?"

He nodded.

"Good," he said, his smile cruelly triumphant, "because Annie and I are together now, and we can use your help to cover our tracks. Am I making myself clear?"

"Perfectly," he told him, but it did not sound like John's voice.

"And just so there's no mistake about it, what I hate most about what you did before is that you used her—you didn't even love her." He paused to let his words sink in.

Dropping his head slightly, he mumbled, "My actions were reprehensible."

Andrew looked around first, then satisfied that no one could hear, he told John: "It's time for a little payback. You used Annie and now I'm going to use you. Tonight you're going to help me go to her room, and you'll make certain no one else sees."

Like an obedient servant, John responded, "I understand."

"There'll be more."

"I'll do whatever you ask," he wanted him to know.

It gave Andrew a rush of sadistic pleasure, watching John squirm like that. "Yes—you will," he added, smiling again.

When Annie returned to the table they both stood to greet her. Andrew was grinning like the cat with the canary, but John looked as though he'd developed a bad case of indigestion.

John swallowed a handful of antacids and sat quietly for the remainder of his time at the table. Annie left the dining room first and sometime later, on command, John took Andrew to her room after scouting the halls and discerning that the coast was clear.

After he left, Andrew explained John's presence by flatly stating, "I told him."

"Why?" she wondered.

"We need his cooperation," he replied. "Anyway, he pissed me off tonight so I finally said something I've wanted to say for a very long time."

Although she understood, she was still surprised. "When you included him in the invitation to Crinan Castle, I thought you'd put that behind you."

Obviously irritated, he explained, "You get on well with Lena, I did that for you."

She smiled. "That was very considerate, very thoughtful." When he didn't return her smile, she questioned, "Didn't getting that off your chest make you feel better?"

"You think that one little blow-off should do it?" He removed his jacket now, then hurled it at a chair. It missed its mark and landed in a heap on the floor, just as he folded his arms and glared at her. "I was there, you know, watching you leave that morning," he said, the anger seething through, "and I could tell that you'd slept with him. I should have pulled him off Percy and punched his lights out then and there, I should have pounded the shit out of him, but I didn't. Like a fool I let you leave with him. Then I went to The Scores pub and pummeled Patrick Ramsay instead."

As upset as he was, Annie knew it was wrong to laugh. But she couldn't help herself. "Did you really?" she blurted out. "God, I wish I'd seen that!"

Still enraged, he informed her, "The bloody bastard clobbered me with a chair!"

"Jesus — did you keep fighting?"

"Until both of us were so bloodied and bruised we couldn't see straight," he wanted her to know, adding, "and we were almost sent down because of it."

"God, that must have been something to see!" she exclaimed, some light, prolonged laughter following her remark.

Her reaction was perplexing, and he demanded of her, "What's so bloody funny?"

"This, us, everything," she giggled. "Knowing that you loved me so much you had to beat the shit out of Patrick Ramsay — being here with you now, in France with the gypsies, with John—you still wanting to tell him off after all this time—it's all so delicious!"

Part of him wanted to stay miffed, but another part had to admit that there was something deeply gratifying about it all. And seeing how the circumstance delighted her, he suddenly let go his anger and lifted his face to the ceiling as his own laughter escaped, although his was more release than amusement. Then he walked over to where she stood and took her in his arms.

They laughed again when they pulled back the coverlet to see human hairs in the bed sheets. But they casually brushed them away and cuddled their naked bodies together, then lay awake for a time, to go on talking about the past, until there was nothing more to say about it. In the wee hours, in that haphazardly decorated room, with its mismatched fabrics and tired furniture, frequently disturbed by the antics of gypsies who roamed the halls, they spooned against one another and drifted off with peaceful smiles, smiles that arose from having come together in this offbeat place, a place that made them feel like the young, renegade lovers they'd meant to be.

They awakened to insistent knocking and the call of "Breakfast!" Andrew swung his legs to the side of the bed and stretched before retrieving his shirt and boxers from the worn carpet.

As he opened the door, John offered a nervous, "Morning, mind if I come in?"

Andrew frowned at him, saying, "Annie's not dressed."

She had reached for her robe and was pulling it on, as she called out, "It's all right, I'm covered."

The anxiety John was experiencing made him speak with uncharacteristic abruptness. "I wanted to see you both first thing, because there's something I need to say." He stepped into the room with the tray he was carrying, and seeing no other place to put it, awkwardly set it on the bed below her feet.

As he returned to his place beside Annie, Andrew surveyed the tray, which was nothing more than a basket of croissants and jam, an earthenware jug of café au lait, and three cups and saucers, replete with nicks. In his haste to see the couple, John had forgotten the flatware.

"Join us, then," Andrew told him, though rather unconvincingly.

"Thank you," John answered. He settled himself into a chair and crossed his legs with exaggerated casualness, but he quickly uncrossed them again. He leaned forward now, and pressed his hands into his thighs. "You were right to treat me as you did last night, Andrew, I deserved every bit of it. All I can add this morning is that I'm truly sorry for what happened back then, although I know you feel any apology is a bit of the barn door."

Hearing nothing worthy of a response, Andrew chose not to. Instead, he nonchalantly poured Annie's coffee, then one for himself, deliberately leaving the third cup untouched.

John looked directly at Annie as he added, "I apologize to you both, because my actions hurt both of you."

Andrew found this admission somewhat more appeasing, and it led him to pour coffee for John, then hold it out to him.

Springing from his seat to reach for it, he once again uttered, "Thank you." After two obligatory sips of the now barely warm drink, he remained standing to continue: "I offer my apology along with any help or service I might render, in the hope that I might somehow make things up. But if you can't accept that, if there's still too much bitterness and resentment, then I think it's best for all of us if we part ways. I'll be wracked by the loss of your account, to be sure, but there's no good to be had from a business relationship where this kind of asperity exists." He paused to search their faces and seeing nothing there, he sighed, "All right then—I've said my bit, and I'll leave you to it." His cup rattled in the saucer as he set it on a nearby table. Then he made his way toward the door.

"John, come back," Annie called to him. "Sit down, will you?"

Andrew watched impassively as John sheepishly obeyed.

After a sideways glance at Andrew, which was an attempt at reading him, she told John, "About last night—I think you understand that Andrew needed to get that stuff off his chest."

"I understand perfectly," he responded. "It was a bloody awful thing I did to him. I can't imagine how I would have felt, had I been in his shoes."

With a lift of her brow, she nodded her agreement, then ventured, "And I believe, knowing him, that that's the end of it. Am I
wrong, Andrew?"

Andrew let the room fall silent while he slowly finished his coffee. When he was ready to answer, it was with a terse, "It could be."

John seized upon that. "Under what circumstances?"

A tad impatiently, he replied, "Under the ones I described last
evening, under the conditions that you'll be helpful to me and Annie."
Then he looked to Annie as he added the caveat, "But what we really
need is a friend. I'm not certain he can be that good of a friend."

His comment was unexpectedly hurtful, and John responded
meekly, "I think I can be."

With a defiant lift of her chin, Annie added her voice, "And I
think so, too."

Andrew exhaled first, then said, "All right. If Annie trusts
you, then so do I."

Buoyed by the realization that he would not lose Nether
Largie's account, John reacted with enthusiasm. "Tell me how I
can help and consider it done. And you needn't worry about any
rumors being brought back to Oxford—I'll extinguish any gossip
before it starts. After all, it's my business, isn't it, to tell people
what to think."

"Yes it is," Annie replied, smiling as she added, "and you're
good at it."

John was feeling considerable relief now, and it showed in his
face. "Right. Let me be off, we've a lot to accomplish today." He
made a hasty retreat, before anything more could be said.

When he was gone, Andrew questioned, "Why is it you
trust him?"

She considered that a moment, then shrugged as she answered, "He's no better or worse than the rest of us. He makes
dumb mistakes because he lets his libido override his judgment, but
at his core I believe he's caring and decent. To be fair, I don't think
he realized how much in love we were. Christ—we didn't even
know that! But he did feel bad when he saw it," she recalled, "and
in his own way he tried to make things up to me. Anyway, we were
all so young and stupid, don't we all deserve a second chance?"

Andrew smiled, telling her, "You know I believe that."

"And you have to admit," she added, "it did take balls for him to come see us this morning."

With a sardonic grin, he responded, "Balls, John was never short on."

His comment provoked such a belly laugh, Annie buried her face in a pillow to muffle it.

Thirteen

The Band of Gypsies were a somewhat listless group this morning, and Jean-Marc apologized profusely for failing to coerce them into a decent night's sleep. After about an hour of ineffectual direction, it seemed the only thing to be done was to have lunch, so have lunch they did. Happily, as had happened the day before, the gypsies were transformed by the wine and food and were ready, in a couple of hours, to tackle the job.

The plan was to have the gypsies and their orchestra playing music on the plateau, as the sheep wandered up the rise, ostensibly drawn to the sound. The milkers would then walk among them, and as the milking began the musicians would serenade them. Once edited, the commercial would end with a distinctly Scottish voice declaring: Nothing is too good for our sheep! A graphic would then credit the Scottish Cheese Producer's Association, in cooperation with the Highland Land Trust.

Having grown up around these animals, Andrew knew that getting sheep to follow direction would be exceedingly difficult, so he suggested leaving the flock in place and bringing the musicians to them. A single attempt to follow the original script proved him absolutely right; despite being controlled by their familiar shepherds and dogs, the sheep were not about to go anywhere near the noisy gypsies. So the decision was made to corral them on the plateau, and choreograph the action around them.

A living fence was formed around the jittery flock, pressing every available person into service, including Andrew. But the bolder sheep weren't deterred by their human guards and they continually attempted escape, inciting others to follow. There were times when a person in pursuit of a runaway would be doubled-back upon; the panicked animal would turn on its heels and become a hurdle to its pursuer, who would then find himself in an unavoidable collision. The second time this happened to Annie she fell so hard to the ground that Andrew came running to see if she was all right. He found her holding her abdomen and laughing hysterically, and when he reached his hand out to help her up, she pulled him down next to her. When they realized their section of the corral had sprung a major leak, they hurried to resume the chase, Annie scolding the sheep like mischievous children, Andrew shouting advice to her, warning her to watch out for the double-back.

When music was added to the equation, it became even more of a circus. But after about four takes the sheep seemed to have tired, and they were finally able to get them to behave as they wanted. There were several mishaps with fresh piles of dung, but it was mostly taken in stride and good spirits. Jeremy realized from the start that this would be a problem, and had enlisted five boys from the village to bring their shovels and buckets. Although theirs was the nastiest work, even they seemed to enjoy themselves.

Since they weren't using costumes, Annie had the idea to include the band's entourage in the shoot. The young women were asked to dance among the sheep, while the young men acted as milkers. Their inclusion added an air of gaiety and humor to the situation, and the camera worked splendidly with it all. There was so much spontaneity and fun that the actual filming went quickly, and the production crew were delighted with the outcome. In the end they had a solid hour and a half of good footage, which was just about right for editing down to three or four one-minute pieces.

The day flew by, and as the sun lowered on the horizon, the band members were the first to return to the hotel. The work had gone so well and they were in such good humor, they decided to gather on the stream-side terrace for drinks. The hotel owner was delighted to accommodate them and by the time the production crew returned from the mountaintop, the band had broken out their guitars and an outright party was underway.

In the excitement of the day's shooting, Annie and Andrew had forgotten that today was Friday, and that Dr. Coupau would be calling. When they returned to the hotel, the music and laughter beckoned them, and they joined their friends at the terrace bar.

As the crowd grew larger, they became separated, so Andrew had not witnessed a young woman from the hotel searching out Annie to deliver a note. He only became aware of it when he happened to look over and see her standing alone near the rushing water, the piece of paper in her hands.

Sensual, sambalike music was playing as Annie read the message: lively, sexy music with a compelling drumbeat. She read it through several times before feeling a hand on her arm; it was her dance partner from last evening asking for another dance. She tucked the paper into the back pocket of her jeans, then broke into a smile as he led her to the dance floor. As he grasped her hips, she tossed her head back and laughed, then positioned her hands on his shoulders. They dove into the rhythm, he backed her up, then she did the same to him. He grinned wickedly, saying things she didn't understand, while she continued to smile, moving her hips more seductively, tossing her silky hair from her face, then letting it fall across it again, obscuring it like a dark veil. The dance grew increasingly impassioned and by the time the music ended, the young man was driven to kiss her throat.

Throughout the dance, John and Jeremy had been talking to Andrew, but he hadn't heard a word they said. He'd kept his eyes on Annie, trying to read her, trying to know what it was she'd found in the note. He realized that there was a reason she kept this moment to herself, so he waited for a sign and followed her erotic dance with the young gypsy. Then, in a flash of insight, he understood.

When their dance ended, Annie approached Emmanuel, one of the older members of the band, to request a special song. She stood by as they took a moment to tune their guitars, then Emmanuel started it off as a solo, gazing into Annie's eyes with the ardent tenderness of a lover. "Un amor" was the song—a love lives on, the lyrics said, despite everything.

As the rest of the band joined in, Annie searched the terrace for Andrew. He was still watching her when she caught his eyes, and he understood that she was asking for a dance. They met in the middle of the dance floor and gingerly, tentatively, he took her into his arms. She melted into him, closing her eyes to his touch, breathing in the now familiar, sweet scent of his skin.

She reveled in his nearness for a moment, before she whispered, "We have it back, Andrew, we have our chance again. I'm perfectly well."

He stopped dancing to look into her eyes, then he embraced her so tightly it squeezed the air from her lungs. But her next breath was one of the happiest she'd ever taken.

Jeremy and John were watching the couple.

When they embraced, Jeremy expressed surprise. "You know, I'd got the clear impression at your dinner that the earl didn't care for Annie. But did you see them on the mountain today? And look at them now—whatever is going on, do you think?"

John feigned disinterest when he replied, "Nothing. They've just got over their past differences, that's all."

"But look at the way they're dancing!" Jeremy protested.

"So what? Didn't you see her dancing with that gypsy fellow?" he questioned, adding dismissively, "She's like that with everyone."

"I suppose," Jeremy responded, though he remained wholly unconvinced.

Annie and Andrew walked to a corner of the terrace and stood above the racing stream; a nearly full moon shimmered the water and set the buildings and mountain boulders aglow. From their location, they could see that a crowd had gathered in the street below, people of all ages who clapped and danced and sang along with the Band of Gypsies.

His racing heart made it difficult to speak. "Tonight I'll take you away," he told her. "We'll leave and be alone, and God, Annie— finally—we'll be lovers like we were meant to be."

Her heart had heard him and it wanted to run away, to run with his, to wherever it was he would take her. Breathlessly, she asked, "Do you want to go now?"

"Do you?" he asked, over the pounding in his ears.

Annie looked around them before realizing, "No, not just yet. This is all so perfect, isn't it? This night is ours, Andrew, it's like a fête in our honor—but we're the only ones who know what the celebration is about!"

"Yes," he agreed, "it is."

She motioned toward the crowd below them. "I wish we could invite them all to celebrate with us."

"That would be nice," he responded, "but I'm afraid there's not enough room." Then he had a crazy thought. "We might bring the party to them."

"Do you think?"

"I'll just go have a word with the manager—but come here first," he said, as he took her hand.

He led her down the narrow and slippery steps that brought them to the water's edge, to a landing that had been carved from the rock. When they reached the bottom they were hidden from view, and they stood looking into the other's eyes for a moment, listening to the sound the water made as it tore over boulders and broke upon itself, in its relentless rush toward oblivion.

He started to speak, but Annie put a finger to his lips. She ran the finger along them, slowly, tenderly, then she touched her lips to his. They tasted each other first, with softly probing tongues, then they wrapped arms tightly to quell their quivering bodies. Their mouths became their lifelines—the source of their beings and all their consciousness. For the next minute they drank the other's saliva to survive, breathed the other's exhaled air to live, every single cell within them deriving its energy from the connection.

It was only with great difficulty that they separated into two, distinct people again.

Andrew arranged for the townspeople to be included in the party by having the hotel set up two bars in the street for a period of two hours. Because it was France, there was nothing but cooperation from the local police, who enjoyed a party and appreciated the moment as much as anyone else. Andrew wrote the hotel owner a check for twenty thousand francs to cover the cost of the public bash. The man thanked him profusely, then went to find the nearest chair. Andrew then set about locating John, so that the two might coordinate his exit with Annie.

While he was busy, Annie went to shower and phone Dr. Coupau. The good man returned the call while she was still in the room.

"I take it you got my message," he said first.

"Yes." It had read simply: *You're healthy. Call me so I can elucidate.*

"I thought it best to say it outright," he explained, "so you wouldn't be worried a minute longer. You've been needlessly worried long enough."

"I appreciate that—and you can't know how much I thank you!"

"By the way," he said now, "with some difficulty an associate of mine was able to track down one of your Red Cross samples. It seems that it was barely reactive in the first place. It was a judgment call on the part of the technician who ran the test."

She couldn't think of anything to say, save to exclaim, "Jesus Christ!"

"My thoughts exactly," he chuckled. "Well, my old grandmother used to say that everything happens for a reason—perhaps there was a good reason for this to happen to you."

She was overcome by the irony: But for the judgment call of an anonymous technician, none of what was transpiring around her would likely have been. There would have been no rekindled relationship with Andrew, no commercial to film, no gypsies serenading them as they prepared to leave together. The thought of what she might so easily have missed brought on a shudder.

"Yes, I believe that," she realized, "I really do."

"Well, best wishes to you, Madame," he said. Then he added, "Make the most of this gift you've been given."

"Oh, Dr. Coupau, you're so right about that! It is such a gift!"

"That's the good thing about a brush with mortality," he mused. "It heightens the senses and makes us feel more alive."

"It does that!"

"Oh, I meant to ask: How'd it go with The Band of Gypsies?"

"It went very well," she told him. "Watch your television for the commercial; the first one should run in a couple of weeks."

"I will, and I'll think of you when I see it. Au revoir, Madame."

"Au revoir, Dr. Coupau, et merci mille fois!"

"Mon plaisir, Madame."

Andrew watched her descend the stairs. She was wearing a jade silk dress, a color that ignited the green fire in her eyes. He was standing in a corner, talking with the British crew, but his eyes followed her as she made her way to John.

"It's all set," John told her quietly. "Can you act a believable drunk?"

"I don't see why not. I've had a fair amount of practice over the years," she grinned.

"He'll be away by half-past ten, by eleven you'll be so drunk you'll need to be taken to your room. That's when I'll take you to him. In the morning I'll say you're sleeping in with your hangover and going back to Pau with your cousin."

"Sounds like a plan."

He thought to make her aware: "I told Andrew—Jeremy's suspicious. I'd recommend that you and Andrew keep some distance between you for the remainder of the evening."

She lost some of her smile. "All right, if we must. I'll just go find my cousin and tell him what we're up to."

They shared one more marvelous dance, but mostly for the next couple of hours, Annie and Andrew grinned at each other from across the room, in secret enjoyment of their fête.

They exited the hotel by a rear entrance and though they tried to do it quietly, Annie could not keep from giggling. Fortunately, the party was still in full force and no one heard or saw them leave.

"Are you really blotter?" John asked her, as they started away in the car.

She laughed again. "Yeah, but not on booze."

He remembered something now, and told her, "I take it you got good news on the medical front."

Grinning as though she'd won the lottery, she informed him, "The best! That problem I was worried about turns out to be nonexistent."

"I'm very happy to hear that, Annie." He turned his head to look at her, to say, "I want you to know that I appreciate you standing up for me this morning."

"Andrew wouldn't have stayed angry with you, John—that's not his style."

He pulled a face as he observed, "He seems to have stayed angry with you for quite a long while. But he's all over that now, isn't he?"

She understood the gibe and dropped her smile, saying, "You can be so sarcastic."

"That's one of my finer traits," he boasted. "Anyway, it was good of you." Now he took another tack. "Did he tell you that everyone's still talking about his address to the House of Lords on Monday?"

"No, he didn't even mention it."

It was his turn to grin, as he said glibly, "He's probably saving it for later."

He was obviously going somewhere with this, but wherever it was, she wasn't interested. "How far is it to the meeting place?" she asked, wanting to change the subject.

"Ten kilometers."

"I'm so happy I think I may burst!" she had to say.

John knew he should leave it alone, he knew it was none of his business. But he felt an obligation to Annie—an obligation that remained from all those years ago—that compelled him to be honest with her. Somberly now, he said, "That's what worries me."

His change in tone made her look to his face for explanation. "Why would that worry you?"

"Can I speak frankly?"

That obviously meant he had something unpleasant to say, so she grimaced as she asked, "Could I stop you?"

"Probably not." Unconsciously, he slowed the car. "Do you remember the morning we drove out of St. Andrews? I remember it well—how you cried and trembled so it almost made me lose control of Percy. It made me heartsick to see you that way. I was taking you away from him then—now I'm taking you to be with him, and to my surprise, I find that I'm feeling almost exactly the same way I did that day. Do you know why that is?"

She was obviously irritated when she responded, "That's very confusing, John. No, I don't know why that is."

"Because I'm worried about you, Annie."

He was bringing her down, and she resented that. "Because he's married? I accept that and I'm prepared to deal with it—so's he."

His response was swift. "If it were just his marriage, I'd say you could manage. But it's so much more than his marriage to the countess, Annie, it's like he's married to a whole country—to the whole of bloody Scotland. Are you prepared to deal with that? When we were at Crinan Castle, Lena told me something about his family I wasn't aware of; have you ever heard of the Stone of Scone?"

"Sure, the Destiny Stone," she answered confidently. "Andrew told me about it and how his ancestors were crowned on it."

"What else did he tell you?" he wondered.

"That the English stole it and that some people think the real Stone isn't in England at all, but hidden away in Scotland. He told me the whole story."

He raised an eyebrow as he inquired, "Did he also tell you that it's widely believed that the real Stone was secreted away by one of his ancestors, and that it's been kept hidden for hundreds of years by the Kilmartin earls, whom Scots believe to be the rightful heirs to the Scottish throne?"

She laughed abruptly. "No, but I guessed they had something to do with it. He had such a mischievous look in his eyes when he was telling me the story," she recalled.

"Well, it's not just an amusing story to the Scottish people—it's a crucial part of who they are and what they believe in," he informed her. "And if he is the guardian of the Stone, that puts him in an extremely portentous position. When Scots talk of regaining their independence—and there's more and more of that these days—they speak of revealing the Destiny Stone and restoring the rightful Scottish king."

"That's preposterous, John," she scoffed. "This is 1994 for Christ's sake, not 1694. Nobody restores monarchies. It's a miracle that yours continues to exist."

"That tells you something about the British people, then, doesn't it?" he rejoined. "And in the grand scheme of things, how significant is the time that's gone by since Bonnie Prince Charlie was exiled compared to the more than one thousand years of Scottish rule with Scottish kings?"

"I still think it's ludicrous," she insisted.

"Ask Andrew sometime how ludicrous he thinks it is," he proposed. "Lena told me their bloodline has been carefully controlled for hundreds of years, just for that purpose — just for the purpose of producing an heir apparent. Andrew's that heir apparent, you know."

Annie laughed at him again. "So what? Why should that affect me or us in any way? Kings have always had mistresses; in fact, it's made for some of the more interesting history."

As true as that used to be, John knew that modern Brits viewed these things differently. "Andrew's been held up as some sort of standard, you know, the Scots adore him. They see him as the supreme husband and father, the impeccable, irreproachable keeper of their sacred trust. Finding that he wasn't those things would be akin to Diana's fall from grace — no, scratch that — it'd be worse."

His words evoked a vivid recollection for Annie, of the woman's reaction in the grocery store that day, when Andrew's photo accompanied the tabloid headline: *Di steps out with Earl of Scotch!* The woman obviously revered him and was incensed by the sacrilege, the earl's honor being in her mind unquestionable.

"Times have changed, Annie," he told her, as he braked sharply to round a hairpin bend in the road. When they were out of it and on the straightaway again, he continued, "People like him used to be able to do as they pleased, but not anymore, thanks to our thriving tabloid industry, which exists to ruin people in high places. Absolutely nothing is private or off-limits for them, and the attitude of the public has changed, too. They demand to know everything and know it they will, and there are certain things they won't tolerate."

He was making her a little nervous, but she continued to dismiss his concerns. "We're going to be very careful, John."

"Oh? Like you've been thus far?" he wondered. "I didn't see it, but Jeremy told me there's already been something in the tabloids about you two."

He was now the second person to tell her that, the repugnant Lord Cowan having been the first. "That's why he's taking me someplace remote," she explained.

"And you think they'll leave you alone, you think they won't try to find you?"

He was really annoying her now, and she scoldingly remarked, "It's under his control, I'm not asking for anything or directing anything. He's making the decisions and I trust him to do what he thinks is best."

"I'm sure you do," he understood. "Look, I don't want to be the spoiler, I just want you to go into this with your eyes open. I don't want to see you hurt again."

With something like bravado, she protested, "It would be very difficult to hurt me, I've got very little to lose."

John didn't buy that and felt compelled to issue a warning: "Do you know what I think? I think you're the one who's likely to lose the most."

They had arrived at their rendezvous point, and Andrew and his driver could be seen standing beside their car.

John pulled his car in behind them, and when Annie's right hand went immediately to open the door, he grabbed hold of her arm. "One more thing—I want you to know that if you ever need us, Lena and I will be there for you." He released her now and with two fingers pointed to her heart, saying, "Take care of that."

Andrew's face beamed as he approached her, and upon seeing him, all the worrying thoughts that John had been provoking fled her mind. "Thanks, John," she hurriedly offered, then practically leapt from the car.

After they drove away John sat in his car a moment, pondering what he'd just witnessed. Annie and Andrew had gone off after embracing and kissing, in front of him and the driver, looking and acting for all the world like newlyweds plunging into their future,

with that kind of blissful ignorance that shielded them—however
briefly—from what was to come.

They huddled together in the back seat like teenagers. Feeling
completely safe and at peace, Annie drifted off in Andrew's arms.

He awakened her as the car drew slowly to a stop, asking,
"Feel up to walking a bit?"

"Walking?" she echoed, as she rubbed the sleep from her eyes.

"I thought to send the driver on the rest of the way with the
bags; it's only a short distance to the house."

"Sure—OK," she responded, although puzzled as to why he
would want to do that.

The stone drive crackled as the car continued on. Annie
breathed deeply of the damp air, then searched the moonlit landscape; it was markedly warmer here than it had been in the moun-
tains, and the late spring night teemed with life. There were no
houses in sight, no signs of civilization save the well-worn road,
which had just emerged from dense woods to wind alongside a
pond of considerable size. They stood now at the water's edge, listening as frogs called to one other, while a pungent scent wafted
past them that bespoke the life hidden beneath the surface. A cho-
rus of crickets accompanied the singing frogs, and the barest hint
of a breeze cooled their skin and tickled the leaves.

Andrew took her hand and began leading her along the road,
which rose now, upon a gentle hill.

At the crest of the hill she first saw it, its lights sparkling in the
distance: a magnificent gem of an old French château, elegantly
kept and tended to, not large, but splendid and welcoming. It stood
on its own, quietly commanding the deep night, like the sentinel of
the vineyards that surrounded it.

A little bewildered and sleepy, she sighed, "It's so beautiful! Is
this your place?"

He squeezed her hand and smiled as he replied, "Not exactly."

"A friend's, then?"

"Come along," he told her. "I'll show you whose place it is."

They had walked a couple hundred yards or so from where
they were left. They now paused to read a small, carved sign, which

appeared to have been placed there quite recently. The ground around it was freshly tilled, and there were delicate flowers planted in the newly formed bed.

Annie read aloud, "Château d'Audine — Audine — why, that's the name of my ancestor, the woman the baron loved — " then halted in midsentence.

As the meaning overcame her, she let go of Andrew's hand and sank to her knees. Burying her face in her hands, she began to cry.

Andrew knelt beside her and enfolded her sobbing body. "My Audine," he whispered, just before his own tears came.

Fourteen

The chauffeur had awakened the caretaker and housekeeper, Didier and Lisette, who came to the door in their robes and slippers. The bags were quickly taken upstairs and the driver, who had already been paid, exited the estate by the distillery road. Didier and Lisette stationed themselves outside the courtyard entrance to the house, grinning in anticipation as they watched the couple approach.

As Annie and Andrew drew nearer, Didier bowed, then exclaimed, "Madame la Comtesse, bienvenue au château! Bienvenue!" His wife Lisette curtsied.

Annie looked at Andrew, who was both saddened and embarrassed by the mistake. In his excellent French, he carefully corrected, "Didier, Madame is not the countess."

The poor man's face turned the color of a beet. Over and over again he apologized for his blunder. "I'm so terribly sorry, Monsieur le Comte, Madame!"

"It's not important," Andrew assured him. "Madame is the mistress of this house, so it's a natural mistake. Please don't worry yourself over it."

Annie overcame her awkwardness to say, "It's all right, really, it's not a problem." She offered her hand to Didier and he kissed it reverently.

The older man was not easily consoled, so Andrew added, "Any fault is mine, Didier, I should have explained to you beforehand."

"No, Monsieur le Comte," he protested, "it is not for you to explain yourself to me. I am at your service, sir, it is for me to know and understand, without being told."

Andrew's laugh was good-natured. "That's all well and good, but I don't believe you're skilled at reading minds, are you?"

Lisette chuckled at that, saying, "No—he's not, Monsieur le Comte, but he's very good at reading the heart." She made a point of greeting Annie now, with a warmly reassuring smile. "Welcome, Madame, a thousand times, welcome to the château. May you be very, very happy here."

Didier and Lisette remained a discreet distance behind them, as Andrew led Annie inside, through the spacious marbled foyer, to an adjacent drawing room. He grinned with pleasure as she looked around the beautifully designed room, her mouth slightly agape.

"This is so wonderful—so perfect!" she cooed. An enormous bouquet, set on a table at the room's center, overflowed a blue and white porcelain vase. Annie reached to touch a spray of magenta lupine, as she called out to the foyer, "Did you arrange these exquisite flowers, Lisette?"

"Yes, Madame," she answered. "The count specifically asked; he said that you're very fond of flowers."

The idea of that, of him planning ahead for her arrival, wanting to please her with the things she loved, filled her heart. "They're so fragrant," she sighed "I smelled them the moment I walked into the house."

Lisette explained, "They're from your garden, Madame."

"My garden?" she questioned, looking at Andrew.

In a tender voice, he affirmed, "Yes, your garden."

"Are you hungry?" Didier questioned. "Lisette has kept something nice in the kitchen for you."

"Want a bite of something?" Andrew asked her.

She was much too excited to eat. "No—thank you, but I could use some cold mineral water."

"How about some of your Armagnac?" Andrew wondered.

"My Armagnac?"

"Yes, from the château. Do you remember me telling you that I was buying an Armagnac château?"

"This is it? This is the château? Where are we?"

"About an hour north of Pau," he answered, "in Gascony, near Roquefort. Do you know it?"

Her eyes widened as she exclaimed, "Very well! I love it here! It's one of my most favorite places in all of France, Andrew. How did you know?"

Astounded by the coincidence, he shook his head to respond, "I didn't. This entire thing fell out of the blue, right into my lap. But as I stand here now, I realize that it was meant to be."

"So you only recently bought it?"

"I came here for the first time the very week I saw you on the flight to London, a few days after that." Still stricken with disbelief, he went on to say, "As I walked 'round the place, you kept popping into my mind: I'd see you stretched on a couch with a book, in the kitchen making breakfast, in the garden cutting flowers. I had been trying desperately to put you from my mind, so it was really very odd, sort of like what you experienced when you visited the Whaum."

"But you were still so angry with me," she recalled.

"I know—I can't explain it." His voice wavered with emotion. "When you told me you might be ill, that's when it started to make sense. I began to see it as a place where I could be with you and keep you safe, where I could care for you, if need be."

In this moment, as she realized that he would not have left her, that he would have stayed by her side—until the end—her heart wanted to burst. Swallowing hard and closing her eyes, "Oh, Andrew—" was all she could manage to say.

Balancing a tray with their water and Armagnac, Didier cleared his throat to announce himself. "This is sixty-three years old, Count Andrew, the château's very finest for you and Madame!"

Watching him set the tray on an antique side table, Andrew used the moment to recover his composure. "Won't you and Lisette join us in a toast?" he asked.

"Oh thank you, sir, that's very kind of you. But only a little one." He went quickly out of the room and was back in a flash with his wife and two more crystal snifters.

Andrew offered the sentiment. "To Madame d'Inard, the mistress of Château d'Audine: may she reign here in peace and happiness, and the very best of health!"

"Santé!" Didier and Lisette said in unison.

The very best of health—those words echoed joyously in her mind. "I'm overwhelmed," she replied, her voice soft and failing. "There's no earthly way to express how I feel."

In the way that they looked at one another now, Lisette understood that it was time to leave the lovers on their own. She tactfully inquired, "Would you like breakfast at a particular time, or shall we await your call?"

"We'll ring when we're up," Andrew answered her.

"The sweetest of dreams," she wished the couple, "on your first night here together."

As they started toward their apartment, Didier whispered to Lisette, "They're so in love, they remind me of us, when we were that age." He reached an arm around Lisette's waist and, grinning seductively, slid it down to rub her fleshy behind.

Now that they were alone, Andrew showed Annie around the downstairs, in and out of the various rooms. They were six in all on the ground floor, not including the kitchen and pantry, each one with a fireplace and high, molded plaster ceilings and cornices. The walls were either painted in the washed pastels of southern France or covered with old silk, and they were furnished with French antiques, of course, which looked as though they may have been in the house from its eighteenth-century beginnings. Although beautiful and adequately furnished, Annie sensed a bareness about the rooms, for some of the art and most of the collectibles that would ordinarily adorn such spaces were gone. But she was thrilled to see a baby grand piano in one of the rooms, and would soon press Andrew to play for her.

The tour revealed two airy drawing rooms, or salons, as the French prefer, and a walnut-paneled library with but a few, unimportant books. The library was situated at one corner of the château, boasting a second story with a spiral stairway to the balcony and upper shelving. When she saw it, she imagined it filled with books and the fire ablaze, thinking what a glorious retreat it would be on a rainy afternoon. An adjacent room, small and cozy and furnished with a day bed, appeared to have been the sewing

room, with its woven basket stand and petit point frame stationed
near the fireside chair and footrest.

A large, marble-floored dining room, with a long, wide table
that easily seated twelve, had its entrance from the foyer and access
at the opposite end to the butler's pantry, which provided transition
to the kitchen. The kitchen was another world altogether; lacking the
formality of the rest of the house, it had the character of an old farmhouse, with its primitive stone fireplace, copper pots suspended from
the ceiling, and chipped porcelain table, laden with fresh fruits and
vegetables. A large glass-doored cupboard commandeered an entire
wall to display colorfully painted, everyday dishes and sturdy blue
glassware. There were mixed aromas in the air, the unmistakable
pungency of garlic and olive oil that lingered from the afternoon
meal, and the more subtle scents of lavender and sage, which hung
from the wooden drying rack near the hearth, in neatly tied bundles.

Annie fell in love with it instantly, and couldn't help but be reminded of her own farmhouse kitchen. But she would not give into
the melancholy and guilt that always accompanied memories of her
home with Mike—not now, not tonight. She turned her thoughts
elsewhere and observed, "This room seems older than the others. I
wonder if it was part of the original structure?"

He nodded his agreement. "That would be my guess." Pointing to a door at the far end of the kitchen, he told her, "Didier and
Lisette's apartment is through there. It's an attached house with a
sizable sitting room and kitchen, two bedrooms and a bath. I'll take
you 'round in the daylight tomorrow to see it, along with everything else."

Lastly, he showed her a room in another corner of the château,
which, with its floral motif and comfy chintz chairs, looked as
though it belonged in an English country house. It appeared to
have been private space for the lady of the château and despite its
lack of personal items, it was intimate and warm, a feeling enhanced
by the glass doors that opened directly into the garden.

His hand gliding along the glossy surface of the lady's desk,
Andrew told her, "I thought of this as your study, if it suits you."

She giggled like a young girl. "If it suits me? It's so exquisite!
Are there lights for the garden?"

"I believe so." He located the switch behind the drapes and then opened the doors, saying, "That was the other thing about this place. When I saw this rose garden—well, I've no need to tell you what it reminded me of."

Once the subtle landscape lights were aglow, the space transformed magically, from one of shadows and promise, to an eighteenth-century vision of color, form, and texture. Stepping through the doorway to the terrace, she was so eager to discover what lay before her that she practically skipped along the gravel paths.

When she had traversed the length of it, she stopped abruptly and closed her eyes, breathing deeply of the fragrance-filled air. "It's like a dream," she called to him, "a beautiful, beautiful dream, the kind you never want to awaken from. No, it's better than that—it's my daydream, the one I used to have while I was working in the Whaum's garden—it's how I envisioned it!"

He plucked a rose, a deep red one with a heady scent, and brought it to her. Brushing the petals across her cheek, he asked, "May I take you upstairs now, take you to our bedroom?"

"Our bedroom—our bed—oh Andrew!" The galloping in her chest made her lightheaded.

He took hold of her hand, and slowly led her from the garden.

Their enormous bedroom was in a three-story corner tower that, Andrew explained, had been added to the château in 1777. Its many windows were long, virtually floor to ceiling, and there were two sets of French doors, both of which gave access to a large balcony; a scented breeze carried through the open doors and there were several vases set about the room, filled with peonies, roses, and cerulean hydrangea. The bed was massive, an old mahogany affair, with a deep feather mattress typical of the French, made up in linens the color of fresh cream. At one end of the room, there was a sitting area near the fireplace; Annie readily pictured the two of them cuddled there on cooler nights, glasses of Armagnac in hand.

"It's all so lovely, so very lovely," she sighed. "I don't know how it can be real."

"I'm wondering that myself," he replied, and although he knew it would make him seem eager, he could wait no longer.

"Annie my love, I'd like to undress you. I want to see your beautiful body, standing here by the bed, waiting for me to make love to you—it was the vision I had when I first saw this room."

She answered him by smiling tenderly, and moving to within his reach.

As they embraced he traced her neck with kisses, up and down, both sides. She was a mass of gooseflesh as he moved behind her and slowly unzipped her dress, using both hands to slip it off. It fell around her ankles and she stood quivering, her back to him, as he unhooked her bra and removed it. He pulled her panties down and she stepped away from her things.

She turned toward him. He took a step backward and let his eyes float along her contours, then he moved closer, so that he might explore her with his hands. He ran his fingers through her hair and caressed her face, then he worked downward to her chest, digits counting her ribs, palms massaging her abdomen, engaging her hips. When he reached her thighs she went to the floor, on her knees, and loosened his trousers. For a lingering moment she looked into his face, then she took his erection into her mouth.

The taste of him was intoxicating, and the knowledge that she could enjoy it fully, without fear of passing on that dreadful disease, almost brought her to tears. The sensual sounds coming from him drove her on; she massaged his scrotum and moaned over the shaft, until he could stand it no longer and nudged her away.

He pulled her up to him and took her mouth with his. They kissed as they had never before, as lovers preparing to give everything, to take everything, without boundaries. Their kiss went deeper and they moved to the bed.

But something distant grabbed Andrew as he lowered himself onto Annie. Whatever it was pulled him away from her, and she could only watch as the sorrow filled her lover's blue eyes.

He rolled onto his back and when he spoke, the anguish deepened his voice. "That pain, Annie—I'm full of it again—it's welling up inside of me. God, how I hate it."

She turned to her side, and reached a finger to trace the deep scar on his cheek. With tender certainty, she said to him, "Don't be afraid, Andrew, and don't turn away from me. You have to let me know all of you, even those miserably painful parts, that go back to your childhood, to that day at Eton."

He marveled at her intuition, for it was exactly that: memories of Philip that had struck him down and pulled him away. "I don't know that I can," he said, "I've never been able to be that open."

"You weren't able to because you weren't with me," she understood. "It needed to be me—it needed to be us."

She was so dead-on, it stunned him. His voice grew more strained as he struggled to explain, "Whenever a woman sucks me, I see him, I remember him, I have to go through it all again in my mind. I have to fight with myself to manage, and I feel sick inside."

"Did you feel sick just now, with me?"

"Yes," he admitted ruefully. "And there hasn't been a good time to tell you this, but something happened with Nigel that's brought it all back again, made it seem like it was yesterday." He avoided her eyes to say, "He revealed that he's a homosexual, and he made overtures to me. That's why he's away now—I sent him away because it sickened me—it reminded me of all the things I've tried so hard to forget." He closed his eyes and turned his face to the wall.

That was it—she realized—what she had picked up on at Crinan Castle: why they wouldn't look at one another, and the reason Andrew was so stern with him.

Although it broke her heart to know that he was still so deeply troubled, she told him firmly, "Andrew, look at me." She touched his arm and he turned back to her. "I understand what that sick feeling is—it happened to me for years, you know, after that godforsaken night with the LSD. It's not going to go away until you face it, because each time you run from it, it gets stronger, it has more power over you. You've got to bring it out in the light of day to dispel it, and you can do that with me, because I'll never judge you and will always forgive you—no matter what you've done."

He meant to say something to her now, but all that came out was a short burst of angst-ridden air.

"Tell me," she said, her voice tender with compassion. "Tell me what's so hard to say."

It took courage to meet her eyes, and to let her look deeply into his so that she might see his most secret, hidden self. "I enjoyed it, Annie, I liked it when he touched me, it made me excited when he sucked me, and God help me, had we not been caught, I think I would have let it go on. I came in his mouth that day—it was the first time I ever had an orgasm with anyone—and it happened with him, kneeling before me in that lavatory, with my trousers around my ankles. I know it was wrong, I know it's depraved, and I've never stopped hating myself for it, for being so sick, so weak." His eyes closed again and he winced with anguish, recalling as well, the impassioned eagerness with which Philip had swallowed him.

She realized now why this had come upon him: because she had taken him in the same position, kneeling before him with his pants dropped to his feet.

She let his confession settle out of the air, so that he'd know she'd heard it clearly and understood. Then she kissed his tightly closed eyelids, before whispering, "I knew that, Andrew, I've known that since the night you first told me. Had you not enjoyed it, it would never have affected you so. But you have to believe this—it only deepened my love for you. Because you trusted me enough to confide in me, I came away from that night feeling the deepest, truest love I have ever felt for another human being and nothing—not even all the years gone by, not even your hating me— nothing could ever change that."

Enormous tears of relief went chasing down his cheeks, splattering on the pillow slip. "Why?" he questioned. "Why would you love someone like that?"

With absolute certainty, she answered, "Because it's not someone—it's you. I love you because there's such depth to you, because you're filled with a rare and special sweetness that comes directly from your soul, from your generous and loving heart. It reaches out to mine and makes me feel more wonderful inside than I've ever felt with anyone else." She brushed the hair from his forehead, then combed her fingers through it as she realized, "And I would bet my life that it was those same qualities that appealed to Philip and made him love you."

He let her finish, then heaved a sigh. "I appreciate what you say, Annie, and God, I love you for it, but I don't know if you can truly understand, because it's never happened to you."

"No, not exactly like that," she agreed. "But don't you remember what I told you about Susannah? Had she taken the initiative, I doubt I'd have turned her away." She wanted to make him laugh, so she added now, "Christ, she taught me how to masturbate, you know. She dropped her pants one day to show me her clitoris, and then gave me instructions—can you imagine?"

For a fleeting moment, he felt like laughing, but all he managed was a brief smile.

Annie, however, had a good chuckle. "I can't tell you how many times I masturbated after that, thinking of her, imagining putting my fingers inside of her and playing with that little puffed-up protrusion she'd thrust in my face."

Her laughter infected him, and he wiped his cheeks and grinned widely, saying, "You're joking, aren't you? You're trying to make me feel better."

She put her hand to her heart and traced a cross over it. "I am not—I'm telling you the honest-to-God truth! And there were times you know, when I imagined myself with both of you, with you and Susannah—God was that a turn-on."

"But you're so completely feminine!" he protested.

"And you're so completely masculine!"

"Why is it, then, that you don't feel guilty about it?"

They had been facing one another, lying side by side, but now she flipped onto her back. "I think it's my perspective, my ability to see it for what it was," she recognized. "Susannah was always so kind and such a good friend, and coming on the heels of that rape, why should I chastise myself for responding to her affectionate tenderness, especially when it was something that I needed so much?"

"How I wish I could feel that way," he sighed.

She raised herself on one elbow so that she might face him again. "I can help you get there. I can help you see what happened to you for what it was, so you can accept it and move on, so you can stop hating yourself over it."

"How, Annie?"

"By loving you with all my heart and soul, in spite of everything, beyond everything."

He seemed very young and innocent now, as he searched her eyes and questioned, "Can love really do that?"

The warmth of her smile touched him, as she answered, "Look at me—I'm living proof of what love can do! Am I anything like the person I was that day you came to me on the cliffs, that day I almost tumbled over the edge?"

He tucked a lock of hair behind her ear. "No, thank God—you're my Annie again, my brave and marvelous girl again."

"Oh, Andrew, let me do that for you," she pleaded, "let me help you. Feel safe in my arms—I'll never betray you; I'll guard your secrets with my life."

He focused on the green in her eyes. "I want to, God, how I want to, but I've no idea how to go about it."

She reached and tenderly stroked him now, finding him soft, unaroused. "Let me do it again," she said, "and don't shut yourself away from me if the bad feelings return. Don't be afraid of them, just go through them and know that you're safe with me. It's the only way to lessen their power and free yourself."

He studied her eyes a moment, seeing there how very much she wanted to help him, and he suddenly realized that trusting her as he had never trusted anyone—enough to work his way through that very private hell—would only bring them closer, and be a gift to them both.

He took her hand in his and guided it to his penis; she lay her cheek against it at first, taking in the scent of him, then she lifted it to her mouth. His head pushed back into the pillow and he closed his eyes, as she massaged him with her lips.

When it grew stiff again, she paused for a moment and whispered to his ear, "You're safe, Andrew, there's nothing to fear or be ashamed of, and whatever you need, I want to give it to you." She went back to it, sighed over it, moaned onto it, swallowed the lubricating fluid as though she were dying of thirst for him.

As he relaxed, his thoughts drifted where they always seemed to go in this circumstance, and Annie became Philip. Her mouth was his, squeezing him with tightening lips, rough tongue dragging over the young boy's organ. He felt again what he had felt then, sinful, forbidden pleasure, the kind he'd never known before, the kind that incited feelings he could not understand. With each pass of her mouth he sank deeper into the memory, experiencing again the terror of being caught, the desire to have him go on, to do more—the pulsing in his rectum.

She looked to his face momentarily, observed the deepening pleasure, then slipped a moistened finger into him. His groan was a release of mammoth proportions.

He stayed with Philip and let himself be taken by him; he gave himself over completely, knowing this time he would not be seen. But even as his arousal grew, a warning sounded, and he understood why: the pleasure Philip brought was hollow, ephemeral, it passed quickly and left miserable shame in its wake. The sick feeling returned with a vengeance and Andrew wanted to push Annie away to end it, but he forced himself to stay with it. He let himself be consumed by the mental nausea and as he did, Philip began to fade from his thoughts.

Annie now took Philip's place in this muddled rapture; reaching into him, she chased away the sickness. Her presence cleared his mind of the guilt; it filled him, made him feel safe and steady again. He opened his eyes to see the woman he had always longed for, eagerly making love to him with her mouth, and the sight of it sent him flying. His penis throbbed with sweet pain, as he released what felt like gallons of himself into her throat, calling out her name as though he were dying.

She swallowed him, then brought her mouth to his, to give him back his life.

But the shame of it was still there, hovering over him like dark, gathering clouds, threatening to consume him with remorse and self-loathing—until her voice—as true and bracing as the garden breeze—chased it all away.

"I love you," she said simply, catching him, holding him, lifting him, clearing away the clouds of shame.

He passed into the kind of sleep that's like floating, like being swept away on a warm tide.

The birds awakened them, pouring their tiny hearts into each meaningful chirp and every soul-sustained warble, in a stupendous effort to chase the night. Andrew opened his eyes first and with awareness of the woman in his arms came the most contented feeling he'd ever known. He tasted the lips on which a salty trace of his juices still lingered.

She smiled with her eyes still closed, asking, "Is it morning yet?"

"Not yet, but soon. Hear the birds?"

She opened her eyes upon him. "It's glorious!"

He needed to apologize. "I hadn't meant for it to go that way."

She put a fingertip to his lips, saying, "Shhh, my love—it's all right."

"I want to be inside of you," he sighed.

She rose from the bed and stretched, then held out her hand. "First things first. Coming?" she asked, then led him to the bathroom.

When they returned, they stood at the side of their bed and held hands, looking into each other, saying nothing, saying everything.

Eventually, she whispered, "It's such a moment for us."

He lifted first one hand, then her other, to deliver them with gentle kisses. "When I kept myself from you all those years ago, it was because even then I knew that once we became lovers, it could never stop."

"I ached for you then, as I do now."

His penis was hard and getting harder, flexing up toward her, as though responding to her voice. He looked at it and smiled, as he said, "There's no hiding how I feel about you." He kissed her mouth, then nudged her into lying down. He moved down in the bed and began to explore her with his tongue, parting her folds with a delicate reverence, a tenderness beyond anything she'd ever experienced. The incredible intimacy of it brought her to tears.

When he looked at her again and saw the tears, he went to each one, to kiss them away. "Every woman I've ever made love to," he whispered, "you've been there—it's always been you who I've wanted."

She stroked his head and let her tears flow, as she told him, "It was the worst mistake of my life, leaving you."

Their words to each other were as soft as clouds. They were like billowy clouds, blowing into one another.

He lifted a breast and suckled it, quenching his thirst with her imaginary milk. When he kissed her mouth again, he told her, "Don't close your eyes, look into mine every moment. I don't want to miss a second of you—I want to see inside of you—I want you to look inside of me." He passed into her then, without the slightest effort.

She breathed him in. "Andrew—" Saying his name was like taking in oxygen.

He cradled her head, gently pumping her, as he said, "Look into me—what do you see?"

She didn't have to think or act, her body so naturally, so perfectly, responded to his. "Love—deep, deep, wondrous love."

"That's right, my darling, my dearest, my only love." He needed to thrust himself harder. "Do you feel me? Do you feel me inside of you?"

Her clitoris was hard and tingling. "I do—I feel you, oh God, Andrew, I feel you." She was coming to a small climax.

"I need to give it to you—I need to give myself to you!" His blue eyes mesmerized her. "Am I too rough? Am I hurting you?"

"No, no, never!" She held his hips to slow his movements. "But let me sit on you now, so I can come with you."

They rolled over without coming apart.

She rubbed her hands on his chest, still fixed in his eyes. "Be still a minute," she commanded, her voice deeply sensual. She raised herself, then moved up and down on his shaft, leaving her moisture glistening all over him.

He kept focused on her eyes and held himself back as long as he could, though it was pure, sweet torture. "I have to come in you—I have to give myself to you—"

She had been leaning forward, passionately, lovingly, rubbing herself on him. "I'm ready for you, Andrew—my love, my heart—"

There were cries and tears and sighs, but no human sound could possibly express the joy and relief that they felt all at once and together. There were breaths of untold depth, parts of their bodies that tingled and fluttered in ways they had never before, muscles and bones that seemed utterly depleted, completely undone. But most of all, overpowering all, there was something else, something alien and riveting, and absolutely extraordinary: powerful, exotic, spellbinding peace.

The solid peace within Andrew told him that he had finally gotten it right, that he was finally where he was meant to be. And Annie, whose life since the day they parted had been a futile search for someone to fill the emptiness, felt peace seep into her, much as his semen did now, bringing her a gift she had long ago given up hope of ever receiving: like a wanderer, exhausted from the journey, who has looked one last time to the horizon and seen—beyond reason—that she has come home, at last.

As they lay together, recapturing their breath, he continued to throb and move inside of Annie, her muscles rhythmically clamping and unclamping, helping him to deliver the very last drops of himself. Outside, first light was quieting the birds, satiating them with its arrival and promise. A waft of damp morning crept over them, and they could hear the crow of the château's rooster, proclaiming to all the world that he owned the day.

"It feels as though my whole life has been a quest for you," he murmured, pouring his sweet, warm smile, all over her. Then, in the tone of an apology, he said, "It's a little late, I know—I should have asked before—do we have to worry about you becoming pregnant?"

Her voice was as relaxed as her body. "I stopped taking the pill months ago, so I suppose we should, but right now, I can't."

"I don't want to be foolish or selfish, but God—I do want to be able to give myself to you, and to do it over and over again, without any kind of restraint."

"Then do that—I want that, too. It feels so good—so right."

They began to kiss. His fingers dove into her, making her even more acutely aware of his presence within her for the first time. Their kiss became visceral and then went beyond that, striking a need that Annie had long ago repressed. She imagined him making love to her in his bed at the Whaum—they were young and life awaited them—he had taken her to be his lover and he would never let her go.

She screamed into his mouth as it all released with a great shudder. Afterward, she moaned and pulled her knees to her chest.

He drew the bedclothes over her body and held her to him, asking, "Are you all right, my love?"

"F-fine," she stuttered out, then smiled up at him.

"What was that? I've never felt anything even close to that before!"

"That, my Andrew, was how I feel about you, about having you in me for the first time."

Physical exhaustion replaced the lovers' passion as they entwined their legs and nuzzled into one another. A lark serenaded them with his aria; just outside their balcony doors he sang of things mysterious, with wistfulness and longing. The vineyards were fully awake now, the dewy grape leaves glimmering in the early light, as Annie and Andrew cuddled under the covers, and let themselves be taken by blissful sleep.

Fifteen

It was after ten when Didier brought their breakfast up, and the couple were still in bed. The tray he carried was heaped with freshly baked croissants and slices of a thick, nutty bread, yogurt and perfectly ripened cantaloupe, homemade confitures and butter, and, of course, two pitchers, one of frothy hot milk, the other of rich, fragrant coffee.

"Slept well?" he asked them, as he ceremoniously laid the meal at their feet. "Lisette thought you'd be hungry this morning, Monsieur le Comte, Madame." He was a short, stocky man in his early sixties but he had a mischievous, little boy smile that was absolutely charming.

Grinning broadly, Andrew responded, "We're quite peckish, Didier, do tell her thank you. I hope we didn't keep you two up last night."

"No, Count Andrew—not at all, we didn't hear a thing." He smiled so pointedly at the lovers, it seemed as though he was offering congratulations.

Andrew laughed, "Good, that's good!" as he poured coffee for Annie.

"If you need more coffee or anything, I'll be in the kitchen with Lisette—just ring. Good morning to you!"

Annie giggled and choked on her coffee as Didier closed the door. "I think they heard us!"

He patted her back as she coughed. "Can't be helped," he said, laughing slightly, "anyway, how could they mind—they're French!" He broke off a piece of croissant, then painted it with raspberry jam as he informed her, "They've spent most of their lives here, you know, with the baron and baroness, and were kind enough to stay on for me. Lisette is purported to be a fabulous cook." He held out the slathered piece of croissant, which she ate from his fingers.

When she had swallowed, she asked, "This was a baron's château?"

"A financially embarrassed baron, I'm sorry to say. But I think I've helped his situation considerably."

"A baron like Audine's lover?"

He was nibbling at a piece of brown bread, so he merely smiled and nodded.

"I'm going to call you Baron from now on," she teased.

He reached to wipe a crumb from her lower lip, saying, "If you're to call me Baron, than I shall call you Audine."

"Let's," she grinned. "They'll be our secret names for one another."

"What would you like to do on your first day at your château, Audine?"

She took a long, satisfying drink of coffee, then responded excitedly, "Well Baron, I should like to see everything. I want to thoroughly explore the house, walk through the vineyards and sample the grapes, tour the cave, taste the Armagnac and Floc—we do make Floc here, don't we?"

Her enthusiasm delighted him. "We do indeed, Madame Audine—the very best you've ever tasted. And where would you like to have your midday meal, in the dining room, on a terrace—or perhaps Madame would prefer a picnic?"

"I should like to be in the dining room for our first meal," she answered, "and to start, I'd like an icy cocktail of champagne and Armagnac, with some fresh foie gras canapés. And if Lisette can manage, I'd adore a warm salad with goose gizzards and walnut oil, then, a bit of confit de canard would be nice, if she's put any up."

She had requested all the local specialties and Andrew was impressed. "My, you do know what part of the world you're in!"

With mock condescension she answered, "This is, after all, where my family has lived for hundreds of years, Baron—peasant though I am."

"So it is, so it is!" he chuckled, then more seriously added, "Peasant you may have been born, Audine, but you are my queen and the mistress of this château. Champagne and Armagnac it shall be, and I'll ring the kitchen straightaway, so Lisette can be prepared for Madame."

The adjoining bathroom was as wonderful as everything else, with antique black and white tiles, and an enormous old claw-foot tub. There was also a marble shower and a well-lit vanity with sink, both of which appeared to be relatively new additions to the large room. After their breakfast they went in to use it together, and Andrew began by shaving, as Annie drew the bath.

There were several canisters decorating a marble ledge near the tub, and Annie discovered they contained an assortment of bath salts. "Eventually, I'm going to have to do some shopping," she told him, as she added lavender salts to the hot water, "because I don't have the right clothes for this climate." As quickly as the salts dissolved, the room filled with fragrance.

He finished shaving the delicate area around his mouth, before responding offhandedly, "Haven't you?"

"All my summer things are still at home, in the States."

"Hmm." He rinsed his razor, then patted his face dry, as he moved toward the closets in the dressing area. "I wonder if there might be something—well, would you look at this!" he exclaimed, as he opened one.

The tub was full now, and Annie shut off the taps before joining him. He was standing in front of a closet filled with women's clothing—dresses and skirts and slacks, blouses and negligees, even shoes and handbags, all with the tags still attached.

"I wonder if any of this is your size?" he teased.

"Andrew," she nearly screamed, "how'd you do this?"

Grinning broadly, he answered, "A gentleman at St. Laurent was kind enough to oblige me—a friend of Claudine's, actually. I had a root through your things when you were at Crinan Castle to find your sizes, then I rang him and described you, told him you needed clothes for the summer in Gascony. I see he did a marvelous job of it."

She'd been pulling things out, one at a time, holding them up to herself before the mirror. "One's more beautiful than the next — I love them all!"

"I told him nothing too far out or extravagant, because that's not your style."

"They're so elegant and French! Which one should I wear today?"

"Let's see," he folded his arms and watched as she displayed several options, before deciding, "I rather fancy that blue one." He chose one that was reminiscent of clothing the gypsy women had worn in Cauterets, with its long full skirt, figure-hugging bodice, and neckline wide enough to expose her shoulders.

"Then the blue one it'll be." She threw open the lids of several shoe boxes. "Look at all this! You're too much, Baron, you know that? You're so good to me — so very generous — you're going to spoil me!"

"Oh, I do hope so," he admitted. "Spoiling you is just what I had in mind." He was standing with his arms folded in front of him, the towel he'd used for his face still in his grasp, when his gaze fell to the floor, and his expression turned thoughtful. Remembering the many gifts he'd given Janet over the years, realizing she'd never once shown this kind of excitement — always taking things in her emotionless stride — he was struck by the contrast in Annie.

Recognizing that his thoughts had gone elsewhere, she questioned, "Where'd you go, what are you thinking?"

His smile was restored by another memory. "I'm thinking of the first gift I ever gave you, remembering how you accepted that small token as graciously as you've done these."

She had located shoes to go with the dress, but now she set them down. "You surprised me with gardening gloves," she easily recalled. "You'd gone out and bought them for me because you'd seen the scratches I'd gotten from the roses. I don't think I'd ever received such a thoughtful gift."

As that dreamlike image from his youth faded, he was stricken by the pain of present-day reality, and it made him say, "All these years, it's you who should have been sharing my life, you, I should have been showering with gifts after the births of our children. That's the way it should have been, the way it was meant to be."

She stepped forward and grasped his hand, saying somberly, "No good can come of thinking that way; it'll make us crazy if we dwell on what we lost. Anyway, I'm so happy now none of what's gone before matters any longer." She brought his hand to her lips and after delivering it with a tender kiss, she rubbed it against her cheek, saying, "Come back to bed with me, let me make love to you again."

She asked him to lie on his back and pinned his arms to the bed as she took him into herself. In her most sensual voice, she told him, "I have you now, you're my lover, and that's all that matters."

He closed his eyes and moaned, then he opened them on her again.

She leaned forward, and whispered to his ear, "I'll never stop loving you, Andrew, I never can."

"God, how I need you, Annie."

The outside world seemed to fall away. Past and present, it ceased to exist beyond the vineyards, and the center of what remained, the source of all meaning and energy, was condensed into two warm bodies, bound by their love for one another, and an essential ache to become one.

In the revealing daylight, they explored the house more thoroughly, walked around the terraces and gardens, through the orchard, and over to the swimming pool, which was situated at a discreet distance from the château.

The pool was a large oval, decked with flat sandstones and decorated at various points with sculpture and enormous pots of cascading flowers. At the shallow end a chubby Eros spewed water from his mouth while at the other, a robust, vine crowned Dionysus poured from an urn; together, they generated the wonderfully soothing sounds of a sizable fountain. There was also a small, stuccoed pool house with all the amenities, which was tucked into the shade of a pine grove.

"What a beautiful pool!" she exclaimed. "I like how far away from the house it is—we won't need bathing suits."

Andrew raised a brow and grinned at her comment, saying, "I do like the way you think."

Opposite the pool house, in a clearing in the tall pines, there was another statue, a large rendering of Prometheus chained to the rock. The area around him was spread with tiny white pebbles, and he was flanked by two curved, stone benches.

As they approached the sculpture, Annie commented, "I understand the other two being here, but what's his connection?"

"Perhaps it's his association with fire," Andrew ventured. "They may have wanted to balance the water theme."

She shook her head. "They've not shown him with fire—no, this is about his perpetual torment."

He grimaced slightly. "Zeus chained him to a cliff face, and every morning sent an eagle to peck out his liver; then every night he restored it, so that the torture would be endless. I've forgotten why it was Zeus was so angry with him; do you remember?"

Greek mythology had long interested Annie, so she had the story readily available. "Prometheus knew something that Zeus didn't," she explained. "Fate had decreed that a son would one day be born to Zeus who would dethrone him and drive the gods from the heavens. Zeus knew this was to happen, but only Prometheus knew who the mother of this son would be, and he refused to name her."

"Did Zeus finally get it out of him?" he wondered.

"No, but he found out from someone else. By that time he'd tired of the game and decided to let Prometheus go."

"Bloody cruel, your gods," he observed.

"Damn right they are. You don't want to mess with them," she warned, only half-jokingly. She took his hand as they returned to the pool environs. "It's so lovely here, I don't think I've ever seen a prettier setting for a pool."

"If you'd seen it a few weeks ago you wouldn't have thought it nice; it hadn't been cared for in years. Nigel located a gentleman in Bordeaux who specializes in renovating them, and he commissioned the chap to get on it. The summers here are very hot and dry, as I'm sure you know, and I wanted you to be able to enjoy this."

What he said about Nigel surprised her. "Your secretary knows about me?"

"There's very little about the circumstances of my life that he doesn't know."

"Doesn't that worry you, I mean, in light of what just happened with him?"

He shrugged. "It might, if I let it, but I'm not going to. And while we're on the subject, I'm having some things delivered on Monday—a computer and fax—and they've already installed two additional phone lines. I hope you won't find it intrusive, but I've decided that it's the only way I'm going to get any time with you."

"I think that's a good thing," she responded, "and I don't mind at all. I bless anything that gives us more time together."

They ended their tour on the terrace outside her study, where they could take in the enticing aromas of Lisette's cooking. They sat in a pillowed settee and drank in the Gascony sunshine, while Didier served them champagne cocktails and canapés of foie gras.

"This is heaven," she declared, head tilted toward the sun, feet propped on an ottoman.

Andrew set his flute aside and reached for her hand. "I'm hoping you'll feel free to change whatever you like and add your own special touches, so it's that much more your own," he told her, then added, "and so you can do that, I've set up an account for you at Crédit Lyonnais—they've a branch at Barbotan. I've put two hundred thousand pounds in it to start."

Her eyes grew wide. "My God!"

"You need money to run the house," he continued, "and you shouldn't have to ask me for things. I want you to be able to go ahead and do whatever you will."

"But that's so much money!" she protested.

"It isn't really."

"Maybe not to you!"

He laughed at her. "I believe that's the point, isn't it?"

Lunch, rather dinner, as the French prefer, could only be described as divine. There was everything Annie had asked for and more, including savory slices of potato roasted in goose fat, that were crispy on the outside and satisfyingly gooey inside. Lisette was indeed a marvelous cook and the couple applauded her when the meal was over, raising their glasses to her talent. When she served her pièce de résistance—a sinful Tarte Tatin, hot from the oven—Andrew invited her and Didier to join them.

When the coffee was served, Andrew asked, "Might we take a few minutes to go over some things about the household?"

Lisette explained to Annie how things had been run thus far, how their neighbors supplied them with fresh milk, cheese, butter, and vegetables as needed, how the local boucherie always reserved their best meats for the château. There was a cellar full of excellent wines, and a kitchen garden for fresh herbs and summer vegetables, situated behind the château and near the hens.

"We keep a small number of hens for eggs at the house," Lisette told them, "but if chicken is required for cooking, one or another neighbor can be relied on to supply a fresh one."

"Geese, ducks, and rabbit are always plentiful," Didier added, "and Lisette is renowned for the different dishes she prepares around them." He'd said that with considerable pride.

The good woman blushed, then concluded by telling them how much money she spent for the kitchen, on average, on a monthly basis.

"That seems very little," Annie commented.

"In the past we've paid the neighbors for their food with bottles of Armagnac or Floc, Madame."

Annie considered this, then told her, "If they wish to be paid that way that's fine, Lisette, but there's no need for that any longer. You'll let them know they have a choice now, won't you? And that we'll pay them a fair market price."

As they continued their conversation, Annie and Andrew learned that the entire community was connected with the château in some way or other, over many generations. Didier informed them that when it was time for the harvest or if smudge pots needed to be put out to fend off frost, every able-bodied person within twenty miles would come to lend a hand. He also told them that several of the people who worked in the cave making the Armagnac and Floc also worked in the house as needed, doing the heavy cleaning, helping when there were guests and parties.

"Will this arrangement suit Madame, or do you think you'll require more household help?" Lisette asked.

"It should be fine as it is," Annie told her. "We've no intention of entertaining when we're here, in fact, the fewer people around the house, the better. What we seek in being here is time alone together."

"I quite understand, Madame. Didier and I appreciate that, and we'll do our utmost to respect your privacy."

Later, Didier accompanied them to the distillery to handle the introductions.

In the car Andrew explained to Annie that he had not changed the name of the château officially, that it and its products were still known to the public as Château de Lacon. "It's a very old and respected label, and it wouldn't make good business sense to change it."

"Of course not," she agreed. "Besides, Audine is our secret and I want to keep it that way."

Once inside the stone and wood structure, which was delightfully cool and as large as a warehouse, they were greeted by the pungency of fermenting alcohol. The employees were gathered and waiting for them and as the couple approached, a young man stepped forward to present Annie with an enormous bouquet of flowers.

"Welcome, Madame," he blushed, and Annie blushed, too, as she thanked him.

They were given a grand tour, shown the copper still, which was from the mid-eighteenth century and original to the château, the huge fermenting casks of Floc, the oak aging barrels, the bottling room and cellar. They were carefully told the details of production that had been followed, virtually unchanged, for 170 years. At the end of the tour everyone sat in the tasting room and sampled some of the château's finest accomplishments, glasses raised again and again to the good health and fortune of the new owner and his lady.

Didier drove the car back to the house, leaving Annie and Andrew to walk the road that left the distillery. It joined the driveway to the château just below the pond, and they kept along it for almost a mile before coming to the estate entrance. The boundary was marked by a set of tall iron gates, which opened to a quiet, rural road. In either direction, all that could be seen of their location were woods of knotty oak and beech.

"How far are we from a town?" she wondered.

"Lacquy is five minutes away and it's a wee place. Roquefort is the nearest town of any size—it's about twenty minutes from here. Then there's Barbotan-les-Thermes with its thermal baths, which is in the opposite direction, but if you head south, you'll be in lovely Aire-sur-l'Adour in about half an hour, more or less."

With delight she told him, "I know exactly where we are! I've driven through this area more than once, and I absolutely love it here!"

Once again, he was struck by the serendipity of it all. "You don't know how happy it makes me, to have pleased you so."

A vintage Renault delivery truck puttered by on the narrow road, and the old man behind the wheel removed his beret deferentially, realizing that they must be the Scottish count and countess he'd heard about.

Annie waved to him, calling, "Bonjour!" then she reached to touch the rusting iron gates. "These seem wonderfully old," she observed.

"I was thinking to have them automated," he responded. "It's a bit of a nuisance, getting in and out to open them."

"But I don't mind that," she said. "I bet they make a great clang when they're closed."

He seemed a tad concerned, when he next said, "I've been giving some thought to security for the estate, because I don't want any uninvited persons wandering in, especially when you're here alone."

That comment distressed her on two levels, although she only mentioned one. "It'd be a shame to lock this place up—it would change the atmosphere, I think." The other thing that bothered her was the thought of ever being without him.

"It would," he agreed, "but we needn't worry over that now. Want to go back to the house, or shall we do the vineyards?"

"Let's do the vineyards."

They headed along the drive for a while, before turning into the vineyard. As they walked the sandy ground in the late afternoon heat, they could smell the distinct perfume of young grapes, sharp and tangy in the dry air. In her excitement Annie went ahead of him, giving him pause to marvel at the picture of her among the vines.

The blow balls of dandelions were cast upon the breeze, and tiny white butterflies flittered around her, drawn to the brilliant blue of her gypsy dress. Her hair danced with the breezes, capturing and then releasing prismatic colors, and her cheeks glowed pink with warmth and joy. He delighted in seeing her this happy, in knowing that she was healthy and with him, his lover now, in every sense of the word, and he thanked the heavens for this day, for it and all the days to come. But he would not allow himself to think in terms longer than the next few, nor let his imagination carry him to the moment of their first, inevitable separation.

While he watched, she stopped to gather a cluster of new grapes in her hand, then plucked one to taste.

He smiled at her wry response, for they were far from being ready. Catching up with her now, he said, "I've a proposition for you, Audine."

Still beaming joy, she asked, "Yes, Baron?"

He reached to pluck a fluff of dandelion seed from her hair, then ran his fingers through. "How would you feel about getting involved in the running of Château de Lacon?"

"Doing what?"

"It's been losing money for years," he told her, "and it needs someone clever and creative to save it without destroying it. That's why the family approached me with the sale, they loathed the idea of commercializing it or selling it to the Japanese."

"I love a challenge," she smiled, "and it'll give me something to do with myself when you're away."

His heart sank suddenly, and he took her hand in his as they headed back to the house. He was quiet the rest of the way, obviously preoccupied. Filling his mind was the thought, the worry actually, of how impossible it was going to be to ever leave this place—to ever leave this woman.

They dined by candlelight under warm summer stars, drinking a fine, old Bordeaux, listening to the fervent chants of crickets.

Afterward, they cuddled on the settee and spoke very softly, though Didier and Lisette had long since retired and there was no one to hear.

"It scares me to be this happy," she whispered to him.

He pulled her closer. "Me, too."

"How long will it last?"

He sighed before answering, "I'm not sure I want to know."

"They can't just let us stay this way."

"You never know," he ventured, realizing that she was referring to her crazy gods. "Maybe like Zeus with Prometheus, they've tired of the game."

"I wish I could believe that."

A long call from the pines split the dark calm: a shrill, foreboding call, that startled them both.

She sat abruptly. "What was that?"

He stroked her arm. "Most likely an owl, I should imagine, swooping down on a mouse."

"Do you think?" Looking into his eyes now, she felt instantly calmer. "Well, that was damned decent, if you ask me. At least it called out a warning and gave the poor thing a fighting chance."

He pulled her back to him, and enfolded her with his arms.

Morning found them clinging to one another, like the lone survivors of a shipwreck, holding to the same bit of flotsam. He was stone hard again, and she reached for him before saying anything. He slid himself into her, into his own wet residue — it was then, that they spoke.

"God, how I love you," he sighed.

"How did we live, those twenty-two years, how did we ever survive?"

"We survived because this was waiting for us," he said, then connected himself to her mouth as they went running, falling — dying into one another.

They asked Didier to serve breakfast on the bedroom balcony, where they sat at a small table and looked into the garden, as the warming sun coaxed the flowers into releasing their fragrances.

Annie was wearing another of her gifts, a pale pink, diaphanous
gown that was reminiscent of something the ancient Greeks wore.
One or the other strap wanted to slide off her shoulder as she ate,
and Andrew smiled as he told her, "You look like a goddess in that
gown, and I love the way it keeps wanting to expose your beautiful breasts."

She smiled, too. "I could just as well sit here naked, if you like."

He laughed. "Later—we'll go for a swim before lunch."

"Have you ever made love in the water?" she wondered.

He searched his memory. "No, I don't believe I ever have."

"Then I'll be your first."

"Every time we make love, Annie, it's a first for me."

She reached for his hand and as she did a strap slipped to her
elbow, exposing a full, round breast to below the nipple.

As she moved to replace it, he softly commanded, "Leave it,"
then rose from his chair.

She lifted her face to him as he looked down upon her, thinking that what he wanted was to replace the strap himself. But that
wasn't it—he went to his knees and kissed the nipple, then suckled
her in the full morning light. She closed her eyes and cradled his
head like the tenderest of mothers, and felt him drawing from the
depths of her womb.

She answered what he asked of her, and her response came
from a secret, hidden place. "You can take my life from me, Andrew, if you need it."

He dropped the other strap and grasped the neglected breast.

Protected from the sun by his battered straw hat, Didier had
just come into the garden to do a bit of weeding. They hadn't noticed him, but he heard them on the balcony and glanced upward.
He should have looked away but the utter passion in what he witnessed struck him, and in a totally spontaneous gesture, he took his
hat off to the lovers, and held it over his heart.

Sixteen

There was a grouping of comfortable furniture set in the shade of a wisteria arbor, and the couple retired there after their midday meal, sinking into two large chaises. A rambling patch of white dianthus was set aglow by the afternoon sun, and its spicy aroma filled the garden. Didier and Lisette were routinely off on Sunday afternoons, and they had left the château to visit relatives in Mont-de-Marsan.

Andrew leaned into his chair and settled his eyes on Annie. "This is what I've always wanted," he told her.

"What's that, darling?"

"You—the simplicity of being with you."

She reached her hand for his, saying, "You have me." She rose from her chair and squeezed in next to him; she had sensed the deeper meaning behind his words and wanted to respond to it. "When you have to leave me and I know you will, you needn't worry if I'll be here when you get back."

Wrapping his arms around her, he questioned, "But will you be happy doing that, waiting for me?"

"I'll find things to do to make the time go faster, and yes, I'll be content, though being separated from you will never be easy," she admitted. "But I'll be content because I know you'll come back to me."

"And, Annie, I will; I promise you that. There's nothing that can keep me from you now."

How she wished that were true. "There'll be things, Andrew—like it or not, there'll be things. But you and I are different now, we understand the value of what we have and we'll treasure every precious moment."

"Yes, we will," he answered, from his heart. He kissed her forehead and rubbed her arms. "I should ring home, you know, I haven't done that since Friday morning. Malcolm was to have seen the doctor again yesterday; I want to see how things went."

"Of course you do."

"I haven't wanted it to intrude."

"It doesn't," she assured him. "And when you're finished, I'll phone Marc."

He needed to say this. "And your husband, you should let him know that you're well, that you got a clean bill of health."

She gasped slightly. "Lord, I'd almost forgotten that he's waiting to hear the news!"

"It'll bring him considerable relief," he ventured. "He carries a fair amount of guilt over the thing."

"He shouldn't."

Andrew almost laughed at that. "Since when do hearts behave as they should?"

"Never," she smiled.

His demeanor changed when he next told her, "He still loves you, you know. The two of you are going to have to deal with that some time or other." After a moment's hesitation, he added, "I invited him here — I invited him to come and see you."

Her expression indicated that she already knew. "My housekeeper said he's considering it."

He wasn't surprised by that, but he was momentarily distressed as he responded, "Well, there's no time like the present."

"There is no time *but* the present," she knew.

She waited on the terrace while he sat in the drawing room and spoke with his children, and then he waited for her while she talked with her son. She had misgivings about calling Mike and almost went back outside to be with Andrew, but she gathered her courage and dialed the number anyway.

She greeted him with, "Hi, Mike."

"Annie! I've been trying to reach you since Friday! Lucy gave me your message but by the time I called back, you'd already left

Cauterets. Then I tried your place in St. Andrews, your cousins in Pau, I even called the ad company in Oxford—where are you?" He seemed more upbeat than usual, and decidedly happy to hear from her.

"Sorry about that—I'm in France, north of Aire-sur-l'Adour. Andrew has a lovely château here."

Without wanting to, he instantly formed a mental picture of the two of them in that circumstance, and it disconcerted him. They had spent their honeymoon at a place not far from Aire, and the thought of her there now—without him—was more than upsetting. There was a long, still pause before he asked, "Is there any news, I mean, did you see that doctor?"

"Jesus—how could I forget? That's why I called! I'm well, Mike, I'm perfectly well." She gave it a moment to sink in. "The doctor said it was probably the flu shot I had last fall that made me a false positive. He said there's nothing for me to worry about and told me to have a nice life."

"Say that again," he quietly demanded, over the tears that were forming in his throat.

"I'm well." She paused for emphasis. "I don't have HIV, I'm not sick, I'm not going to die."

"You're really all right?"

"I'm really all right," she assured him. "The doctor Andrew took me to see, he's an expert on HIV. He wanted me to see the best, so there'd be no mistake."

There weren't just tears, there were words choking him, words that found their origins in his heart but weren't making the journey to his lips. "How can I ever thank him?" was all he could manage to communicate.

"Andrew? You don't have to thank him." It saw its opportunity now, and there was no stopping the truth. "He did it because he loves me," she said, then held her breath.

Mike hadn't wanted to hear it, but it was something he'd already begun to see. After their meeting in Philadelphia it had crept up on him, hounding his thoughts until it had finally captured them. "I know that," he told her.

"And I love him, Mike." That had to be said, too.

It seemed that several minutes passed, but it was less than one.

Somehow, he found the courage to break the silence. "A lot's happened."

Her tone softened and apologetic, she wanted him to know, "I haven't meant to deceive you. I asked Andrew not to say anything when you met, because I believed it would be better coming from me."

His response was somewhat terse. "He didn't have to say anything. I could tell how he felt about you."

She sighed before saying, "I wish things had gone differently. I tried time and again to speak with you and then, when I did reach you, well, I reacted badly. It's selfish and hypocritical I know, but it upset me to learn that you were with someone else, because in spite of my feelings for Andrew, I still harbored the hope that you and I might somehow find our way back together."

Her candid admission encouraged his own. "I didn't handle things well. I should have been forthcoming, let you know I was seeing someone."

"I hurt you horribly, Mike," she understood too well. "And as much as I would have appreciated being informed, you didn't owe me an explanation."

They were speaking with less constraint and more honesty than they had in a very long while, and it led Mike to observe, "We shouldn't be having this conversation with the Atlantic Ocean between us." Whatever would come of this frankness, it was wrong to let it happen over the telephone. They deserved better than that.

She had been thinking along the same lines. "Lucy said you were considering coming to see me, do you still want to?"

He fortified himself with a breath. "Yes—I do." He waited for a response, but not very long. "How do you feel about that?"

"I'd like to see you." Deafening silence followed.

"Will Andrew be there?"

"I don't know," she answered, because she didn't.

"If it's possible, I'd like to meet with him while I'm there," he told her, in an oddly affirmative way.

She responded meekly, "I'll tell him."

Through the wall of fear and hurt that encased Mike Rutledge's being, he managed to say, "Let him know I'm not angry, will you? He was obviously having difficulty with something when we met, and I understand now what that was about."

Still buoyed by boldness, she told him, "He didn't like keeping it from you, he did that for me. But it's important that I live my life straightforwardly now—no more sneaking and lying like I did with Glenn. That's one of the things I regret most, not only the lies, but the truth I withheld."

Something impelled him to put forth, "You know, very often I find that people who are lied to ask for it, in one way or another."

He had turned away from her, he had refused to let her inside of him, but if she was certain of anything, it was that he hadn't meant to. "You didn't ask for it."

"But I didn't make it easy for you, did I?"

She answered with her silence.

His next breath was a sigh. "I'll look into my schedule and see what works, then I'll call you."

"OK."

The silence returned, before Annie breached it with, "I'm deeply, deeply sorry for what I did, Mike, for all the pain I've caused you."

"It's time to end it," he said, then qualified, "the pain, I mean."

Her heart had skipped a few beats when she heard the words *end it,* but it regained its rhythm as she answered, "I'm looking forward to your visit."

"Good night, Annie," he said, and didn't wait for her response.

Andrew discerned something in her expression. He handed her a glass of mineral water that he had just poured, asking, "Everything all right with Marc?"

She had to push thoughts of her husband from her mind to recall the conversation with her son. "He's having a great time being the cool, American cousin. His aunt and uncle have invited him to stay for the coming school year—he wanted to know how I'd feel about that."

The ensuing smile filled his face. "Well now, that wouldn't be such a bad thing, would it? I mean, my jet can get you from Pau to Barcelona in under an hour."

She laughed at him. "No, it wouldn't be a bad thing, in fact, it could work out rather well. He's at such a great, receptive age," she recognized, "living in Europe would be a wonderful experience for him. And he wouldn't have to fly all the way back to the States for his holidays; he could spend them here with me, and we could invite our cousins up from Pau. But best of all," she added, holding back her delight, "I wouldn't be too far from him, I'd be at Château d'Audine, waiting for the Baron to come home." She set her glass down and questioned, "How are your children?"

He'd been smiling broadly as he listened to her work that out, but he turned more solemn when he answered, "Malcolm got the all-clear from his doctor, I'm happy to report. But the children miss me. I told them I might be home next Sunday—everyone will be there then, the older boys will be back from Eton."

"Why might?"

"I wanted to clear it first with you." They stared at one another, then he asked, "Did you reach Mike?"

"Yup," she nodded, "I did."

"And?"

"He does want to come for a visit," she informed him, "and he made a point of saying that he wants to meet with you."

He responded sincerely, "I want that, too. When we parted in Philadelphia, I'd said we needed to talk again." He was waiting for her to volunteer it, but since she hadn't, he asked, "Did you tell him about us?"

She nodded and appeared distracted. "He said to tell you he's not angry."

Anxiety made them both look away for a few moments, but then Annie said, "I know it's early but I'm ready for bed, Baron, how about you?" She was overcome by a sudden, powerful need to be held by him, to lie under the covers and feel safe in their bed.

"I was ready hours ago," he told her, then stood and reached out both his hands.

They lay naked alongside one another, looking, touching, lingering in their intimacy.

"I love this bed, this house, these vineyards," she whispered. "I never want to leave them."

"You never have to."

She traced one of the scars on his face. "I even love these scars."

"Why would you love them?" he wondered.

"Because they're part of you—part of us. They tell something of our story, don't they?"

"Yes," he sighed, "they unfortunately do." He lifted one of her hands to his lips to kiss the palm of it before resting his cheek there.

Seventeen

After luncheon on Monday they lay decadently naked in the sun, near the edge of the pool. Their lounge chairs were right up against one another and every so often they reached to clutch hands, as though they needed to reassure themselves that the other was really there, that they weren't dreaming. Occasionally, they rose from their reclined positions to rub lotion on pink skin or dip their overheated bodies in the cool water. Their conversation was sparse but terribly intimate because their bodies, not their minds, were in control. So it was a considerable shock to them both to hear the popping stones and see the car coming up the drive.

"Christ, I'd forgotten they were coming today," Andrew said.

"Who's coming?"

"The lads from London. Christ."

"What lads?"

"They work for me and they've driven here with the computer and things," he explained. "I've got to go and tell them where to set up. Sorry, darling."

"That's all right. You go ahead, I'll just stay here out of the way."

"Oh, and that's your car they're driving," he added, as he pulled his shorts on.

Annie sat up to see a pale yellow Jaguar sedan parked in front of the château.

"My car?"

"You need one, don't you? You can't stay trapped here when I'm away."

Shaking her head and grinning, she told him, "You're something else, Baron."

Quickly, he yanked his shirt over his head, then he kissed her. "I won't be long," he said.

It was an hour or more before he returned. She had had enough sun and gone into the pool house to browse through the left-behind collection of paperback novels, a fair number of which were in English.

She had located a yellow-paged copy of du Maurier's *Rebecca* — a perennial favorite of hers — and settled on the couch with it, when he walked in. Looking up from the pages, she asked, "Everything all set?"

"Almost," he told her. "Lisette's giving them something to eat, then Didier will drive them to the airport. I apologize for leaving you out here, I hate having to hide you." He went directly to the small refrigerator and pulled out a bottle of Badoit, a mineral water that Annie was fond of. He twisted off the cap, then held it out to her, asking, "Thirsty?"

"Thanks, but I just had some," she responded, as he poured the bubbly water into a glass. Watching his swift and almost jerky movements as he went about the room, she could tell that he was tense. "You seem upset about something," she cautiously observed.

He swallowed a few gulps, then joined her on the couch. Frowning now, he informed her, "They brought me a *Sunday Times*. There's an editorial, having to do with the speech I made to the House of Lords a week ago."

She recalled John mentioning something about that, but said only, "Oh?"

As though he were excessively thirsty, he finished what was in the glass before explaining, "Basically, I asked the rich and privileged of Britain to get off their duffs and do something, take some individual responsibility and quit asking and expecting the government to do everything. It was fairly well received, and now they want me to take the helm of a project I proposed in that speech, which involves setting up a nationwide system of job training with British corporations, to help get people off the dole."

She closed the book, then rose to return it to the shelf. "Will you do that?"

His frown deepened. "I'll have to see. Damn it all anyway."

"Why do you swear?" she asked, folding her arms and lean-ing into the book shelf.

"Because it spreads me even more thinly."

"Why'd you make that speech, then?"

He shook his head and affected a look of disgust. "Because so much of what I see going on makes me ill, and I take my responsi-bility as a peer very seriously. I can't keep quiet about things when I feel there's something I can do to make them better."

She looked at the floor and smiled softly, thinking that he was still very much the same young man she had fallen in love with so long ago, whose conscience and sense of duty guided him in all things. "Well then, you'll just have to find the time, won't you? And I might help you," it occurred to her, "from behind the scenes, of course. I'm very good at bullying corporate executives into doing the right thing."

His expression changed and became difficult to read. "Annie, sit down, will you?" he asked, patting the cushion next to him.

Something about his demeanor troubled her, and she began to worry that John's warning had come to fruition, that there'd been a story in the tabloids about them. Anxiously, she questioned, "What's wrong? You're scaring me."

"Nothing's wrong." He took hold of her hand, saying, "Don't be afraid. It's nothing bad. It's my damned time—my bloody time. There's never enough of it and I don't know how I'm going to find what I need to be with you. And first and foremost, I need to be with you." Gazing into her eyes, his expression warmed and softened. "I want to marry you," he whispered. "I want to ask Janet for a di-vorce and marry you." He smiled slightly. "Are you still scared?"

Twenty-two years ago those words would have been the an-swer to her prayers, but today, in this context, they only made her heart ache. "Your children, Andrew, your responsibilities—"

His response was adamant. "None of it means a damned thing if I can't be with you. How can I be a good father if I'm miserable because we're not together? And I will be, you know, when we're separated."

She understood his feelings too well, still, she felt compelled to respond, "But we haven't given it a chance, my love, we've only just started to work out being together. Why don't we wait and see how it goes before we plunge into something like that?"

Her response was unexpected, and it made him question, "Don't you want to be married to me?"

"God, Andrew," she answered, as a nervous laugh escaped, "that would be bliss, sheer bliss, if things were different. But they aren't—and those five, beautiful children of yours would suffer because of us, and because they were suffering, you would, too."

"But eventually they'll grow up and have lives of their own," he protested. "They'll understand eventually."

"Eventually could be twenty years," she sighed, struggling to stay focused and practical. "Janet wouldn't go easily, you know that. It'd be rancorous, horrible, and she'd make me the demon. Your children would hate me, they'd never accept me as their stepmother, and I couldn't stand that I took you away from them."

He left her eyes and looked at the floor.

She gripped his hand more tightly. "And there's something else. I've witnessed you with them, and I don't believe I've ever seen a more loving and natural father. And that's partly because you understand too well what damage a bad relationship with a parent can do to a child. You have a very strong need to be the best dad you can be to those children—you need to do that for yourself, as well as for them. Being their loving father has helped to heal some of the wounds you carry from your own father, I can see that."

He let go of her hand and ran his fingers through his hair, as the truth in what she'd said sank into him.

She went on to say, "I love you for wanting this, but it's not something we can have just now. What we can have we need to make the most of—like today. Let's take our clothes off again and get in the pool and forget about London and the House of Lords and all the rest of it. When we're here together we owe it to ourselves to revel in every precious moment, and not fret over the things we can't change."

He took up both of her hands and kissed them repeatedly. "Help me with that, will you?"

"I will." She tried to smile when she next told him, "You go ahead and make plans to be with your kids this weekend and let

yourself look forward to it. I'll be here when you get back, whenever that is. And every time we come together it's going to get better. You know that, don't you? Our love is only going to deepen."

When he'd left her to go to the house, she had donned only a
loose-fitting dress to cover her nakedness. He leaned into her lap
and kissed her thighs, then pushed the filmy gauze toward her hips.
The sight of her dark hair peeking from under the raised edges of
dress immediately aroused him, and too, there was the scent of her:
warm and earthy, and thoroughly intoxicating.

He stood and dropped his shorts to the floor; he didn't remove
his shirt, there wasn't time for that. In the next few seconds he had
pulled her from the couch and guided her to a built-in cabinet, then
lifted her to it: It was the right height to support her for what he
wanted, and what he wanted was to drive himself into her with impassioned force.

With strong and meaningful thrusts, he told her how very
much he needed to be with her, in her. He lifted her on his penis
and wrapped her legs around his hips, grunting with his powerful
exertions. With each successive lunge, books and various orna-
ments went flying, falling from the shelves around them, and something made of glass shattered. None of that affected him. The
intense frustration he felt over their circumstance had inflamed his
desire, made him go after her more aggressively, as though not
being able to possess her completely might somehow be undone by
force. She cried out a little from the pressure of him, so hard and
far inside, and bit down on his shoulder to release the pain, tugging
at his shirt with her teeth. But she understood what it was he
needed to give her and stayed tightly wrapped around him, clinging to his body as though she might save him from something.

His explosive ejaculation sent shock waves through both of
them, short-circuiting their muscles and collapsing them to the
floor amid the debris.

"I'm sorry if I hurt you," he whispered to her, still somewhat
breathless. "It was just—I couldn't get far enough inside of you—I
needed to be a part of you."

"You are part of me," she answered, stroking his face. "We're
not separate people, you and I, and we never have been."

They took their days one at a time, like careful, appreciative viewers walking through a gallery filled with priceless art—one-of-a-kind masterpieces that they would never see again. They talked about everything, laughed about nothing, and listened intently to one another, always eager to learn more, to understand more.

On Tuesday they explored the nearby village and despite her objections, went into the mayor's office to introduce themselves. Andrew presented her as his good friend and consultant, who would run the distillery in his absence and be in charge of marketing for the château. The excited mayor rang up several key townspeople and invited them to come raise a glass, and everyone shook Andrew's hand enthusiastically, thanking him for pledging to restore Château de Lacon to its former glory.

They went next into Barbotan-les-Thermes to meet with the bank manager at the Crédit Lyonnais, so he could obtain Annie's signature for the account Andrew had set up. Afterward they stopped in at the pharmacy, where they purchased an impressive supply of contraceptive sponges. In this town populated largely with retirees, they raised a few eyebrows among the shoppers, though the pharmacist looked upon Andrew with what appeared to be envy. Before they headed home, they sipped coffee in an outdoor cafe, idly watching the parade of those who'd come to take "the cure."

When Lisette announced that she was headed to the Thursday market in Eauze, they volunteered to do her shopping. Carrying her woven basket, they happily searched the tantalizing displays of fresh produce and all manner of local foods, which overflowed the colorful market stalls. They nibbled enough for a meal, but couldn't resist sandwiches of crusty baguette, Bayonne ham, and local cheese, which they enjoyed on a bench, shaded by ancient plane trees. Just before they left, they spotted a stall filled with old books. They both had the same thought and went home with a trunk load, then spent the remainder of the afternoon dusting and stacking them on the empty library shelves.

Andrew also arranged for some books to be sent to the house, so that Annie might learn about the business of growing grapes and making Armagnac. Each morning after breakfast, while he sorted through his e-mail and faxes and held conference calls, she would sit near him and read, occasionally asking questions and jotting down notes. She was keenly interested in all the varied aspects of the business, from the planting and grafting of vines to the laws governing exports, and he was delighted to see it.

They did more exploring of the estate, which was very large, four hundred hectares in all, and of that only twenty-five were planted with vines. Another fifteen were planted with a crop of sunflowers, typical of the area, which would be breathtakingly beautiful in late summer.

They located a second, more isolated pond on the property, that had a small wooden dock with a serviceable boat tied to it, suitable for rowing. The next day they returned with a picnic basket and spent the afternoon reclining by the water, after a languid bit of rowing. They made a bed under the tall pines for a nap, their blanket spread upon fragrant needles several inches thick, then made love twice, once before they fell asleep and again when they awoke.

Afterward, as he caressed her, he whispered, "I love making love to you in the open like this. It reminds me of that day, long ago, when we almost made love in the meadow. God, how I wish we had."

She said nothing to him, but ran a fingertip along the wide scar in his thigh, the place where his femur had broken through in the car crash.

On Friday night, Mike called to inform Annie of his plans; he would arrive a week from Wednesday and leave the following Sunday. Andrew decided that he would fly to Glasgow the morning of Mike's arrival, staying at Crinan Castle and doing business for a few days, then return on Saturday. Annie and he agreed that luncheon on Saturday would be the best way for the three of them to get together, as Mike wanted. But before all that, Andrew had to face the monumental task of leaving Annie for the first time, though only for the day on Sunday.

Along with the car and computer, the men who worked for Andrew had brought stereo components and a box of assorted CDs, everything from Bach to the Beatles. They set up the system so that they might listen when they dined on the terrace, and on the

Saturday evening before he was to leave, Andrew arranged with Didier and Lisette for a special meal under the stars.

He sent Annie up to their room to dress and asked her not to come downstairs for a half hour. When she did, she found him waiting at the landing dressed in his kilt; the rooms were lit only with candles and the terrace was ablaze with them as the first strains of music began to play. He led her to the terrace then took her in his arms as Bobby Short's soulful voice serenaded them with "The Nearness of You."

The summer night felt like velvet, rubbing against their skin; it was sweet and sensuous and they languished in it. They danced again and again and seldom spoke. They ate but little, drank not much, and took every occasion between courses to stand again in the candlelight and hold one another to music. When it was nearly midnight, they finally extinguished the flames and took themselves to bed.

Nuzzled into one another, she did her best to comfort him. "It's only the day that we'll be apart," she said.

"It's just so difficult."

She wanted to believe: "It'll get easier."

He left just after dawn and drove the car to the airport in Pau, where his jet and crew were standing by. As he had asked, she remained in their bed, listening as he pulled away from the house. When she could hear the crackling stones no more, she buried her face in his pillow and began to cry.

All five children were waiting by the helipad, even Donald, who was usually off with his friends when he was home from school. The girls ran to him first and fought with each other for his attention. Dumfrie wanted his attention, too, and he would not stop jumping on Andrew until he gave him his due. Andrew carried nothing with him, not even his attache, and Duncan recognized how unusual that was.

"Where've you been, Dad? Where are your things?"

"I have to go back tonight, so I didn't bother to pack."

"Go back where?"

"France."

"So soon? Why? Can't you stay longer?"

"Not this time, but I'll be home again soon, and I can stay longer then."

"What are you doing in France?" Donald wondered.

"I've a new business there and I'm catching up on some things, some important things." He understood the inappropriateness of telling them the truth, but nonetheless, he loathed the idea of an outright lie.

Maggie asked, "Will you watch me ride today, Daddy? I can take a three-foot fence now—bareback."

"Can you really? That's splendid! Your legs must be very strong."

"They are. I've a much better seat than Cat, you know."

"You do not!" Cathy protested. "She does not! It's just that I'm smaller than she is, but I ride just as well—our instructor even says so!"

"I'd like to see both of you ride today and I may even go out with you, if that's all right."

The girls squealed with delight at the prospect.

Malcolm had been very quiet.

"Aren't you feeling well?" his father asked him.

His little face was all pout. "You're not staying tonight." He had clearly been upset by that.

Andrew's heart was suddenly heavy, and he now felt selfish and regretful. And in the same moment, he realized how very right Annie had been, in the things she'd said about his children, about how much they needed him, and he them. "No, not tonight, but I'll return next Wednesday, and then I'll stay until Saturday."

"How many days is that?" Malcolm wanted to know.

"Four."

He took a moment to consider how long that was. "All right, then," he said, and managed a smile.

Neither Janet nor the dowager countess were anywhere to be seen. After a time Andrew asked a servant where his wife was.

"In her rooms I believe, your lordship."

"And my mother?"

"Gone visiting I'm told, your lordship. Is there anything I can get you, sir?"

"No, thank you."

He let himself into her study without knocking, and Janet looked up from her desk in irritation.

"Oh, it's you," she said, and went back to her correspondence.

"Hello to you, too."

She laid aside her pen with vehemence. "What do you expect? Hugs and kisses?"

"No, just civility."

"Then you expect too much," she informed him.

He winced slightly. "How are we going to manage dinner with the children if you're in this state?"

"I'll rally for them, I always do. It's just you I can't rally for."

He bit his lip, then lowered himself into an overstuffed chair.

"Well? What is it?" she demanded.

"I'm not going to stop seeing her," he stated boldly, "so I'm hoping you and I can achieve some kind of detente."

She fired back, "Do you now?"

"Why don't you tell me what it is you want," he decided to say, "what it is you'd like me to do."

She sucked in as much air as her lungs would hold. "What I'd like is to throttle you, but I don't fancy spending the rest of my life in prison so I suppose I'll have to think of something else. So what's left? Castration? Maiming of some sort or other? Or should I hire some thugs and have you beaten to a pulp?"

"How about hiring some solicitors and filing for a divorce?" he heard himself suggest, and it had just jumped out.

Janet's eyes went small and slit as a reptile's, as she hissed, "Not on your life."

Unperturbed by her fury, he told her, "We can't go on like this."

She sat fuming for one long moment, then thought to remind him, "Not so long ago you assured me you had no intention of divorcing me, so why have you changed? Is this what she wants?"

"No," he responded, "it's what I want. She, in fact, tried to talk me out of it."

Freshly infuriated by that, she railed, "You're both malicious liars!" Her voice climbed another octave as something occurred to her. "And what about her disease? What about that?"

"She's not ill," he responded. "I took her to see someone in France and he said that her tests were false positives."

Janet was still seated at her desk. She picked up her pen with both hands and tried to bend it, then through gritted teeth, seethed, "So I suppose you're having sex now, unprotected sex."

"There's no longer anything to worry about," he answered.

"Isn't there?" she threw back at him.

He saw where she was going with that, and closed his eyes in a sustained blink to express his disappointment. "She isn't deliberately going to get pregnant, if that's what you're thinking."

"We'll see," she scoffed.

He blinked slowly again, then exhaled as he focused on his wife. "You couldn't be more mistaken about her. Annie's conscience wouldn't allow her to do anything that would be destructive to my family."

"Think so, do you?" It was astonishing that anyone so intelligent and insightful could be taken in like that. "Well, we'll both see what she's made of, won't we? Because I'm not going to divorce you, no matter how much I hate you now I won't give you an easy out. I'll fight you tooth and nail if I have to, but I won't let you discard me — not after all I've been through with you, all I've lost because of you!"

Puzzled by that remark, he questioned, "What have you lost, Janet?"

She stood abruptly and the pen snapped in her hands, staining them with ink. "My dignity for one! From the first day of our marriage you've been stealing it from me. Just how humiliating was it, do you think, to wait alone for you in our marriage bed? How disgraceful was it, to face the whispers of servants, the looks from those who'd witnessed your debauchery that night? Do you think I was left with a shred of pride after that?"

Andrew's breathing became audible, and he hung his head in shame. They had never discussed this, in all their years together it had never been mentioned, but still, it had been there, festering, stinking, infecting their relationship. "I hate myself for that," he admitted to his wife. "I'd do anything to be able to go back and undo that. With all my heart I wish I could." But it wasn't just his wedding night spent with the girl from the caterer that he would undo, it was the entire day. He would never have entered that cathedral, never have stood at that altar.

Janet rubbed at her ink-stained palms like Lady Macbeth. "But you can't, can you? And now you've the chance to make it up to me—you could turn your back on her and give yourself over to me—but you won't. You're going after my dignity again, Andrew, but this time I won't stand by and let it happen. Not this time."

"We need to face reality, Janet," he found the courage to say. "We were wrong from the start—from the very start. We were only together because my father engineered it. Had I gotten her letters, everything would have been different."

Brushing aside the memory of her complicity in that, she railed, "But you married me! You stood in front of God and the world and pledged yourself to me! You impregnated me, you gave me your five children to carry!" Her fury generated an aura around her, like steam, rising from boiling water.

He hated what this was doing to her—what he was doing to her—and he was wracked with pain and guilt. Nevertheless, he needed to speak the truth. "God forgive me for saying this, but I did that out of duty."

Her face went pale when she heard that and she pounded the desk with her fist. "Damn you to hell, Andrew! And I gave birth to your children out of love!"

The remorse was burying him alive. "We should never have married. I was honest with you, I told you that I loved her, I asked you to release me then but you wouldn't. *You* made that choice, you went into this with your eyes open. You knew I could never give you the kind of love you wanted—you can't force yourself to love someone you don't."

"No, you can't," she agreed, "no more than you can stop yourself from loving someone, even if he hurts you, even if he's more cruel to you than any other person on this earth."

He folded one arm in front of him and rubbed his forehead with the hand of the other, murmuring, "Look, this isn't going anywhere." The strain made him sound hoarse. "I think it's better if I leave;

there's no use in going through the farce of a family dinner. I'll tell the children there's been some emergency, they'll understand."'

"That's just fine!" she screamed. "Turn your back on them, too, abandon them as you've done me!"

"I can't take this, Janet—I've got to get out of here." He stood, and as he did he scanned the room that was filled with Janet's personal things—the memorabilia of a mother: family photographs from past holidays, a finger painting that Duncan did for her when he was four, the ragged bunny toddler Cathy had always carried with her. These artifacts from their married life usually comforted him, reassured him that although it had not been his choice, he had done the right thing. But today they were nothing more than cruel reminders of what he had lost with Annie, what he could never have with the woman he loved.

"I feel like this place is my bloody tomb," he told his wife, "like it's a damned, bloody crypt. I've got to get out of here before I suffocate." He was through the door before she could respond.

Bounding down the corridor he almost collided with his eldest son.

"What's wrong, Dad?"

His breaths were coming rapidly and his face was flushed. "I'm sorry, Donald, I've got to leave. Where are your brothers and sisters? I need to say good-bye."

"What's happened?" From behind his father he could see his mother peering through her doorway. "Did you and Mum have a row?"

"Yes, we did," he admitted, "an awful one. Where is everyone else?"

"Cat and Maggie are at the stables waiting for you. I think Duncan and Malcolm must have gone there, too."

"I'm sorry to leave but I must," he told his son. "I'll try to come back soon, I promise."

Donald offered, "Let me walk with you to the stables."

As they headed for the staircase, they heard Janet's door slam.

Donald kept pace with his father, and waited until they were out of the castle and in the open to ask: "What's happening between you and Mum? She's been awfully on edge lately."

"I'm sorry, Donald, but I can't talk to you about this."

"Are you seeing another woman, Dad?"

The bluntness of that question caught him off guard, and he abruptly halted his brisk stride. "Why do you ask that?"

Donald was as tall as his father now, and when he looked into Andrew's eyes, it was with a penetrating directness. "I overheard Grand Mama and Lord Alfred speaking," he said. "They mentioned your American friend Annie and they weren't happy that you'd brought her here for Laird's Day. I couldn't imagine what could be wrong with that, until I gave it some thought."

Andrew not only saw the concern on his son's face, he heard it in his voice. He motioned toward a bench that was situated under an old copper beech. "Let's go over there a moment; you and I should have a word."

As they walked toward the tree, Andrew was struck with the realization that he was repeating history. As a young man he, too, had been aware of his father's indiscretions, although it had never been discussed, never dealt with openly.

After taking a seat, he tilted his head to gaze through the massive tree limbs. "I began climbing this tree when I was Malcolm's age," he told his son. "I fell out of it once, but that didn't stop me from getting right back into it, and going higher than before. I was forbidden to do it, of course, and Nanny used to run screaming after me, but I'd climb it anyway."

Chuckling, his son admitted, "I was forbidden but I climbed it, too."

Andrew smiled at him, to remark, "Then you know how extraordinary it is, to be up there on your own, how it makes you feel free as a bird sitting there on those great limbs. By God, I wish I had the wherewithal to climb up there now."

"Why would you want to do that?" Donald wondered.

He shrugged, then sighed, "It might make me feel young again, afford me a different perspective."

"A different perspective on what, Dad?"

Although he tried to steer the conversation away from his problems with Janet, Donald was not having it. And as Andrew weighed how to best handle the situation, he recognized how very much better it would have been for him as a young man had his own father allowed for some discussion, had there been some outlet for his concerns.

"On what your mother and I are going through," he decided to say. "I'm being selfish and I'm hurting her terribly, but in truth I can't help myself."

Donald had been putting two and two together already, so he came straight out with it. "You knew Annie before, when you were at university—does this go back to then?"

His son's perceptiveness astonished him. "It does," he answered him, adding, "I was just twenty-one and she was twenty." He meant to say something benign, something casual about their relationship, but he astonished himself by divulging: "We fell in love, Donald, deeply in love."

The young man seemed befuddled. "Then why didn't you marry her?"

The bluntness of the question shocked an already amazed Andrew. "I was unofficially engaged to your mother," he responded, "and her family and mine were strongly behind the match."

There was a certain incongruity to that answer, which led Donald to remark, "But you always tell me to make my own choices."

"I do."

"Why didn't you?"

"My father didn't trust me to do that," he explained. "He believed that someone of my age was not equipped to make such an important decision."

"So you let him decide for you? That doesn't sound like you," he insisted, with a dismissive shake of his head.

"I didn't exactly give in," he decided to tell him. "I determined to go against him. I was going to give up everything if need be—my title, my inheritance, any future I might have had in the family business—just to be with her."

That revelation astounded the young man. "You loved her that much? So what happened?"

"These scars happened."

"The car crash? The car crash had to do with Annie?"

He had gone this far and the world was not coming down around them, so he told his son, "I was to meet her in France and my father knew of my plans, so he locked my passport and birth certificate in the safe. There wasn't a chance in hell in those days of going over there without the proper documents, so I went crazy with fury. It all culminated in that horrible accident."

As Donald contemplated the tragedy in that, he exclaimed, "That's dreadful!" Then he sat quietly thoughtful for a few moments, before observing, "Then your marriage to Mum, it wasn't because you were in love—you married her out of duty."

Although he had long been aware of how sensitive his oldest son was, Andrew was admittedly bewildered by his reaction, because instead of the anger he was certainly entitled to, he was reacting with sympathy. "You don't seem shocked, why?"

He shrugged as he answered. "I'm surprised, but not shocked; how could I be? Look at Wills and Harry and what they've had to deal with. Compared to their parents, I'd say your situation is rather ordinary."

Andrew's smile for his son was sadly proud, the kind of expression that said he recognized Donald's maturity, but at the same time lamented the loss of his innocence. "Some of the things I've done with my life I'm not proud of," he wanted him to know, "but my relationship with Annie is not one of them. I loved her with all my heart and circumstances conspired most unfairly to take her from me." He would go no further with the story because he believed he'd said enough, and anyway, no good could come of Donald knowing about his grandfather's machinations—about the stolen letters.

The young man took a moment to digest what he had just learned. The faith and respect his father had shown by confiding these matters made him feel very much a man, and it encouraged him to respond, "I've never been in love like that, but I know what it's like to have strong feelings for someone. That girl I've been seeing, the one Mum doesn't approve of, I like her very much, Dad."

He had witnessed the telltale excitement his son displayed when going to see this girl, and had wondered, "Are you intimate with her?"

His response was preceded by a bright, red blush. "Well, yes," he said, looking at the ground, "I am."

Softly, he questioned, "Are you using condoms?"

Donald's blush deepened. "Of course!"

Andrew told him, "It makes me proud to know how responsible you are."

His father's approval chased his embarrassment, but he nervously cleared his throat before adding, "She's on the pill, Dad, and it wasn't her first time." He'd told him that because he didn't want Andrew thinking that he'd taken advantage of the girl.

Andrew understood, though it would never have crossed his mind that his son would behave selfishly. But he wondered now, "Was it yours?"

His son nodded, then looked away again.

With that admission Andrew couldn't help but think of himself as a young man in love with Annie, and grieve the loss of that once-in-a-lifetime experience, the experience of making love for the first time, to the girl who made your very heart beat. "I hope it's been good for you—for both of you. It's so very important for that to be right."

Despite his awkwardness, Donald grinned to say, "It has been." But as he thought of his mother now, his smile fled. "Mum would have a coronary if she knew—you're not going to say anything, are you?" In the next instant it occurred to him that his mother's objections to his girlfriend might stem from her feelings about Annie. He felt strong pangs of sympathy for his father, and at the same time, came to a deeper understanding of his mother.

"This conversation is between us," he assured him, "and I'm very honored that you've confided in me."

It felt so good, talking like this, man to man—he wanted more of it. Donald looked into his father's eyes again, to implore, "Don't leave, Dad. Everyone's so happy you're home, don't leave just yet. We all know something's up with Mum; it'll help everybody if you stay and spend time with us."

His heart heavy with guilt, he decided, "I won't go; I'll stay as I said, and I'll come back again soon." He put his arm around his son's shoulder. "Now that you know what's going on with your mother and me, can I ask you for your help?"

"Of course," he answered.

His heart ached anew, and his eyes began to burn as he said, "Reach out to your mother, be there for her. I think she must feel very alone just now."

Donald reflected on this a moment, and with much insight and wisdom, responded, "I'll do what I can for her, Dad, but I don't think I'm the one she needs."

Eighteen

It was late and Annie sat in the drawing room with a cup of tea; he had called just as they were landing so she knew he'd be arriving soon. She kept her eyes fixed on the drive and fancied she heard the clanging sound of the gates, though they were quite a distance from the house. When she finally saw it, the pale yellow Jaguar seemed gray in the moonlight.

He wrapped his arms around her as soon as he emerged from the car.

Through their embrace, she could feel his distress. "It didn't go well, did it?"

"No," he answered, then motioned toward the settee on the terrace. "Let's sit out here and talk awhile."

"Want a drink?"

"Yes, please, a large one."

She went into the house and returned with two snifters. They sat looking over the sleeping vineyards and went well into their drinks before either one spoke again.

"I can't live with her any longer," he sighed.

"What happened?" she murmured.

He sounded utterly drained when he next said, "I can't go on with her, but she won't give me a divorce. She's too angry to do that."

Annie gasped slightly. "You asked her for one?"

He took hold of her hand. "I know how you feel about it, but I can't see any other way. I can't go on pretending—the minute I leave those gates I feel as though I'm cut off from myself, Annie. I'm only half alive without you."

She squeezed the hand that held hers, saying, "I know, I feel the same way."

He emptied his glass. "I had a talk with Donald. He came right out and asked if I were seeing another woman."

Her eyes grew wide.

"He was so incredibly mature and reasonable, I can't get over it." Recalling their conversation, he shook his head in astonished disbelief. "It's good he knows," he decided. "He's been aware that something's troubling his mother, and now he understands."

"Does he know it's me?"

Nodding, he answered, "He'd guessed."

She worried now, "Did you tell him that you want to divorce his mother?"

"No. I didn't think it appropriate."

That was a relief, but she wondered, "What about the others? Do they know?"

"I don't think so. But according to Donald, they're all aware of Janet's distress."

Quickly and with certainty, she told him, "Then you need to spend more time with them."

He nodded his agreement, saying, "I've told them I'll be back at the weekend."

She looked into her lap, as she asked him, "Can you tell me what Janet said?"

"A load of ugly things," he sighed. "She's digging in for a fight to the finish."

She had been upset by his revelations, but her distress was now compounded by anxiety. "Does she know about this place? Does she know where we are?"

"She has the phone number, of course, in case of emergencies, but not the location. She's made it very clear to me that she doesn't want my honesty, so I didn't tell her about the château." He became aware of her increasing agitation, and questioned, "Why do you ask? Are you worried that she'll come here?"

She nodded slowly and deliberately.

He dismissed the idea. "I don't think she'll do that. I don't think she wants a confrontation with you."

"I hope you're right," she responded, though unconvincingly.

"You think she will—why?"

The anxiety was causing her breaths to come a little faster now. "Because I made a deal with her."

He recognized that her breathing pattern was changing, so he released her hand and began rubbing her back. "What sort of deal?"

His touch relaxed her, helped her regain some control. "I promised her that if it became too much for her, I'd give you up. It was the only way she was going to give us time, to let us be together. I had to agree that I'd end it when she said."

He frowned. "Why didn't you tell me this before?"

She inhaled deeply, to fortify herself with a good rush of oxygen. "Because she asked me not to."

He flashed back to that day in Crinan Castle and realized, "That's what you were talking about in her study."

Tears had been building with her anxiety, and they made their escape now. "I promised her, I gave her my word."

He reached to wipe her cheek, softly questioning, "And you think she's going to tell you time's up?"

"I'm sure of it," she sniveled.

"You felt that desperate to be with me?"

She nodded and dabbed at her nose, saying, "I can't go back on my word."

He reached his arms around her and pulled her to his chest, then began stroking her hair. "Janet held all the cards, my darling—all of them—you weren't even in the game. It wasn't a fair deal to make, so there's no shame in not holding up your end of it." He kissed the crown of her head. "The only promise you need keep is the one you made to me—to never leave me."

The caressing night belied their turmoil, embracing them with its warm stillness. Andrew released her so that he might cup her face in his hands and kiss the lips she'd been biting.

His kiss was passionate and understanding, it told her everything she needed to know—that he was not angry, that he realized what she had done and why. When they separated their mouths, she pleaded, "Let's go to bed—let's stop talking about this and go make love. I need to feel you inside of me."

They mounted the stairs in silence. He went into the bathroom and returned with a moistened washcloth. The cloth was cool and soothing and he wiped the tears from her face before undressing her, like an upset child he was putting to bed.

The bedroom doors and their shutters were open and when the lights were out and they lay together, the night came into the room and made them as still and quiet as it was. But despite their mutual need and for the first time since they'd come together, Andrew was unable to make love to her — Janet and the children were that much on his mind.

They wanted nothing more than to be alone, utterly alone, so in the afternoon they took a picnic to the distant pond again. Annie wore a sundress and sandals, and Andrew commented on how young she looked. "When I see you like this," he told her, "with your hair loose and no makeup, it brings me back. It makes me think that it's our summer, and we're together as we wanted to be."

"It's the magic of this place," she understood.

With certainty, he responded, "It was meant for us, it was waiting for us." Standing at the water's edge now, he picked up a stone and skipped it across the smooth surface. It jumped five times before finally plopping into the depth.

"That's pretty cool," she grinned. "I didn't know you could do that."

As he spread the coverlet in the shade of an oak, he said simply, "My father taught me."

That surprised her. "I never imagined him teaching you anything like that."

He smiled. "He taught me to fish and hunt as well. We'd go to the shooting lodge in Rannoch Moor and hunt grouse, or fish the loch for brown trout, the river for salmon. His favorite was deer hunting, though, and I disappointed him there. I could never bring myself to end the life of a creature with such soulful eyes."

As she pulled the plates from the basket, she questioned, "Do you miss him?"

"My father?" After a reflective moment, he answered wistfully, "I do. As difficult as things could get with him, I loved him, and that never changed."

Observing his melancholy, she offered, "It's too bad he died so young. You might have had some wonderful years with him, later on."

Andrew smiled at the thought. "What do you think he'd say about us being together now?"

She grimaced, then teased, "Oh, that's a tough one."

"I don't know, but I suspect he might have understood my need to be with you," he ventured. "Before he was killed, he told his valet Ambrose that he regretted taking you from me, that he was sorry for taking the passion from my life."

That was unexpected, and she questioned, "Did he use that word? Did he say passion?"

"Yes."

"That's interesting," she mused, as she unwrapped their food.

"Why?"

She poured their wine, then stopped her preparations to respond: "It tells me that he understood what we were about. Maybe it took getting on in life for him to realize just how important passion is."

"It's certainly taken that for me," he admitted.

She had been kneeling but now she sat on the spread and reached out her hands for him. "Are you hungry?"

"A little," he answered, as he settled beside her. Then he thought to say, "I want to apologize for last night, for not being able to make love to you."

She smiled tenderly. "Don't you think I understand?"

"No, I know you understand, you always do. It's so rare that I ever have to explain anything to you." He gazed off toward the pond. "If only I'd had that kind of relationship with Janet."

"I know you've tried," she told him.

"Probably not hard enough," he answered. "When I look back, I see things that I regret with all my heart."

Annie broke some pieces off a baguette and put them on plates with Lisette's olive and tomato salad, and a thick slice of her homemade paté. She handed one to Andrew, asking, "Like what?"

"Ta," he said, as he took the plate. "My wedding night may be my biggest regret."

As she recalled her conversation with Robin, she felt suddenly anxious.

Remembering that night robbed Andrew of his appetite, and he set the plate down. "I did something unforgivable that night," he told her, "and I shall probably burn in hell for it."

She had taken only a single bite, but as her stomach turned queasy, she also set aside her food.

He stared at the untouched meal, and in the monotone of confession told her: "It was an incredible production, our wedding, worthy of the royal family. There was so much done in advance — even before the official announcement — and so many important people invited, I know they did that to lock me in, to make it impossible for me to back out."

She lifted her wineglass and gulped nearly half of it. Then she reached for the bottle to refill it, all the while avoiding his eyes.

He avoided hers as well. "There was an initial reception after the ceremony, at a hotel in Glasgow," he continued, "as grand as all get out. There were so many people to greet and shake hands with, I don't think Janet and I said a word to each other. Then we moved on to Crinan Castle for more, but with a smaller crowd who were staying over. I was already blotter when we got there and one of the first people I encountered was a young woman working for the caterer. Her name was Jackie and she had dark hair that was straight and long, like yours, and eyes the color of emeralds." The vivid memory was like an accident scene he wanted to turn away from, but couldn't. In a voice devoid of emotion he told her, "As they were packing to leave, I accosted Jackie and asked if she'd meet me in the stables, in the tack room. She arrived half an hour later and stayed the remainder of the night with me."

Annie still could not meet his eyes as she said, "You made love to her."

"Repeatedly."

She lifted her gaze to the pond, saying, "You didn't go to Janet."

"No." The agonizing memory made him wince as he recalled, "I left her waiting alone, all night — our wedding night."

Something occurred to Annie that she just had to voice. "Did you want to punish her for marrying you?"

He took a moment to consider that. "I suppose," he responded. "But more than that, there was the problem of feeling nothing for her and knowing I wouldn't be able to get hard for her. Part of me wanted to save both of us the embarrassment."

"And the other part?"

He sighed as he answered, "The other part was dying. I'd killed it that day with those vows — mortally wounded it, anyway."

"And that was the part that went after Jackie," she understood.

His face had been turned away but now he looked into her eyes. "I called her Annie; I asked her to let me call her Annie and she did." He looked away again as the self-loathing filled his face. "In the morning I gave her a hundred pounds and went outside to vomit."

The image of that scorched her soul, and she felt suddenly hungry for cool air. She stood and walked away from him, over to the little boat dock. As though she'd had too much drink, she walked and sat awkwardly, then dangled her feet over the water, taking deep breaths with her eyes shut, trying to erase the image, trying to release it from her mind.

He was standing behind her when she heard him say, "I keep needing to say I'm sorry."

She opened her eyes and asked through her anguish, "Do you know what I'm wondering? I'm wondering where I was and what I was doing then, while this was happening to you. I'm wondering if I felt anything, anything at all of it. I should have felt something — I should have felt your agony all the way across the ocean." When she turned her face to him, it was etched with pain.

Although the anguish this revelation was causing both of them was almost impossible to endure, he had to do this; he needed to bare this dark corner of himself, and she was the one he needed to confess to.

"All the years that I fostered hatred for you, I told myself it was because you'd forsaken me. But that wasn't the real reason — I hated you because it was easier than hating myself. I despised myself for the things I'd done on account of you, for my wedding night and all the times afterward when I had sex with another woman and wanted her to be you. But most of all, it was because of that night in the stables, with a young woman I'd never seen before and haven't seen since. It was my first time, Annie—it was the very first time I had sex—and the pain of it, of me wanting it to be you when it wasn't, that was the real reason I began to hate you."

It had started burning and rumbling the night that Robin told her, but she'd been handling it. There was no denying it now, it was there and it wanted out. She tossed back her head and took several deep breaths, hoping that that would suppress it, but it had already gone beyond the point of control. It came out and echoed around the pond and sounded more awful than a woman in the throes of a cruel labor, and like the pains of birth, it kept coming until it had emptied out her insides. When the scream was finally delivered, she had to struggle for her breath.

He sat beside her on the dock and took her into his arms, burying his face in her shoulder, amid the strands of dark, flowing hair.

As though her misery was nothing more than a momentary disturbance—like the report of a shotgun or backfire from a passing car—the peace of their surroundings was instantly restored, and the afternoon carried on. Frogs splashed now and again, the birds performed their late day concert, and dragon flies kissed the surface of the water. A warm breeze had begun to blow and it carried with it the fragrance of impending summer: the green, bittersweetness of irrepressible life.

Nineteen

The week passed in a haze of contentment and there was no more mention of Andrew's wedding night, though truth be told, it was a difficult thought for Annie to keep from her mind. They went about their days as they had before, taking long walks around the estate, putting in some time at the distillery, and savoring the delights of Lisette's kitchen. Andrew spent Saturday with his children—a day he chose because Janet would be away at a riding competition in the Cotswolds—and he took them all sailing. He was back at the château in the wee hours on Sunday, and he and Annie spent the next few days in tender appreciation of one another. But Wednesday, the day that Mike was expected, seemed to arrive with undue haste.

As Tuesday drew to an end, Andrew sat propped in bed, holding Annie in his arms. Stroking her hair, he whispered, "I can't help but wonder what will happen with Mike. I feel in my heart that he's going to want you back."

Her response was disconcerting, though not wholly unexpected. "Would that be so bad?"

He tightened his grip on her, and sighed.

She nuzzled into him. "What I feel for Mike and what I feel for you—one doesn't take anything away from the other. If things weren't so rough with Janet right now, I imagine you might say the same of your feelings for us."

His churning insides kept him from responding.

She sat up now, and moved slightly away. "The joy you bring me has affected everything in my life," she told him, "even my feelings for Mike. It's allowed me to look beyond the hurt and rejection and remember why I love him. Does that sound totally nuts, or does it make a crazy kind of sense?"

"Go on," he murmured.

She was sitting cross-legged alongside of him, and she reached to stroke his thigh, saying, "My love for you, it didn't just begin the day we met and it doesn't just exist between us. It comes from all the time before and all the time that will be—it extends to all the other people I love, and all the people you love. It makes me whole and complete and endlessly capable of it; I even feel it for Janet," she realized. "She must surely be suffering and I've felt terrible anguish about that: There are times when I've wished I could put my arms around her and love her out of her misery."

He was listening intently as she gave voice to her heart, because in her words he recognized the yearnings of his own. "I have had similar feelings," he admitted. "There've been moments when I've wished I could carry some of what you give me back to Janet."

"And when you feel that way," she questioned, "don't you wish you could go on feeling that way? Isn't sharing your love what it's all about?"

He smiled slightly and nodded. It would be so liberating to do that, he realized, to love freely without being hobbled by jealousy or fear or possessiveness.

She rested her head in his lap again and in a soft voice, told him, "If Mike still loves me and asks me how I feel, what I want, I'll have to answer that I love both of you, and want to go on loving both of you; I don't want to be cut off from his love or yours, I just don't see the point in that. Look at all we've been through—you and me and Mike—the suffering and loss, the painful mistakes." Her thoughts were drawn now to Andrew's wedding night spent with Jackie, and she felt compelled to add, "And Janet, I shouldn't leave Janet out of this. Isn't it time for all of us to stop punishing ourselves, to stop denying what we know we need so desperately?"

Andrew sat quietly breathing, obviously deep in thought.

After a time, she said, "Tell me what you're thinking."

"What if you put it to him and he agrees? What then? How do we handle that, then?"

"I don't know exactly; we'll have to find a way."

He questioned, "Could you make love with him, Annie?" as the churning in his gut started up again.

She looked into his eyes, as she answered, "If everything else was right, I think so."

That response jolted his heart. "How? How could you do that?"

"What are our alternatives, my love? Divorce? Mine would be friendly and civilized so that's not the issue, but yours would be akin to world war. And what about the aftermath? How long would recovery take? Do you think it's possible that there'd be such widespread damage it might take forever?" She searched his eyes and let that sink in. "And if we're to stay married to them, why can't we have loving relationships with our spouses, too? Wouldn't that be preferable to the acrimonious relationship you have with the mother of your children now?"

His brow knitted, as he asked her, "How could you split yourself between the two of us? How could you go from my bed to his?"

"I don't imagine it'd be the simplest thing to handle emotionally," she conceded, "and I'm sure there'd be monumental problems. For one thing there'd have to be complete agreement, not to mention openness and honesty. And we'd have to adhere to behavior that would protect the four of us from diseases."

Andrew winced. "Christ, I hadn't even thought of that! With you living apart from Mike for a time, what would keep him from going out and being with someone else, as he has already?"

The simple answer was: "Nothing but his conscience. I don't know; it's an impossible idea and I can't see Mike agreeing, so let's not waste any energy fretting over it."

He shook his head, saying, "I have to tell you—I find the entire prospect unsettling, to say the least."

"I'll give you that," she frowned, then affected a look of disappointment. "It's just that I keep trying to find some way to work this, so that other people aren't hurt by us. Because besides my feelings for you, there's only one thing I'm certain of: We can never be happy if we make the people we love miserable. And you know that as well as I do."

Andrew slept fitfully. He alternately held Annie and released her, turning and rearranging himself in the bed. Annie was awakened several times by his restlessness, and it worried her to see him so. Just before dawn he began mumbling and moaning, violently grabbing at the sheets. He awoke with a start and sat bolt upright in the bed, perspiration dripping from his forehead.

"Christ," he said, as he opened his eyes.

Annie sat up too, and reached for his hand. "Are you all right?"

"Christ," he repeated.

She understood that it takes time to come out of those things, so she rubbed his back some moments before asking, "Can you tell me about it?"

He lifted the sheet to wipe some of the sweat from his brow. "It was all so strange. It started out fine enough, we were walking through the vineyards when I heard Janet call to me. I turned back and went to see what she wanted—but she didn't speak, she only grinned. When I looked for you again you'd gone, and the vineyards were gone, too. I started searching for you, calling your name—that's when it got really bizarre."

To chase the shadows from the room, she switched on the bedside lamp.

"Then I was someplace else," he continued, "it seemed to me the Nether Largie Cairns, but it was endlessly long, and there were carved-out shelves lining the walls, like in the catacombs. There were human remains everywhere, but there were also walking dead, people I knew to be dead but who acted the same as the living. Their speech was garbled and foreign, and I kept saying—I can't understand you—but they kept chattering away. I was terrified and wanted to get out of there, but I couldn't find a way out."

She grimaced at the image, and questioned, "Did you finally get out?"

He nodded, as he told her, "One of the dead took my hand and led me away. Then I heard your voice, calling me, asking me to help you. I followed the sound to the Temple Wood—but it was different, it was more like that Celtic site near St. Andrews, with the sacrificial bowl. When I looked into it, I saw that it was filled with blood. I knew it was your blood and I called to you, screamed for you, but you didn't answer."

"God—what an awful dream—"

"You were in trouble," he remembered. "You needed my help but I couldn't find you or figure out what was going on—it was the most helpless, horrible feeling."

She wrapped her arms around him and whispered, "I'm fine, it was just a nightmare—I'm here with you and nothing bad has happened."

He realized why the dream was so upsetting. "Even if it's a passing thought that lasts a fraction of a second, I can't bear the idea of losing you, Annie."

She understood, and told him, "Don't let what I said last night frighten you, my love. I didn't say it to take myself away from you— I said it because I'm trying to do everything in my power to keep us together."

"Stay with me, Annie," he pleaded, "you don't know how much I need you."

She answered him with her lips, her hands, and the warmth of her body. He dove into her depths and lost himself there, like a hunted man seeking refuge from his pursuers.

When they parted at the airport in the morning, they didn't use that other word, the one that they couldn't bring themselves to say.

"Soon," he whispered to her.

"Soon," she echoed, trying to smile.

As soon as his jet was off, Annie drove to see her cousins in Pau. She arrived in time for lunch and passed several pleasant hours talking with Jean-Marc's parents, Pierre and Jeannette. Jeanette was a dear, sweet woman, and Pierre had been first cousin to her beloved grandfather. They resembled one another strongly, Pierre and her grandfather, in appearance and personality, so it was always a bittersweet pleasure to spend time with him. They were excited to hear that Mike would be visiting—having met him on two previous occasions they'd become quite fond of her husband— and they invited her to bring him back for lunch tomorrow.

Before she left Pau she called Mike's hotel to see if he'd ar-rived, then went directly there as planned. He'd arranged to stay at

Eugénie-les-Bains, which was about halfway between Pau and Château d'Audine, and the hotel where they'd spent their honeymoon almost ten years earlier. The memories of that happy time flooded her as she drew closer to the village, and reawakened the tender feelings she'd long nurtured for her husband. And she had to wonder at his decision to stay here: Would he be affected in the same way? Was that what he wanted, she mused, to reawaken his feelings for her?

When she spied him seated at a patio table just outside the main entrance to Les Prés d'Eugénie, a quivering pulse shot through her. In his polo shirt and loose-fitting khakis, his relaxed appearance warmed and pleased her, for he spent so much of his time stiff and bound in his Brooks Brothers suits.

As for Mike, he'd been sitting outside for the last half hour, watching couples come and go, and it had been impossible not to remember. What he recalled most strongly, however, was that even then, on their honeymoon, he'd begun to be ambushed by the guilt. All too frequently, in their most tender, special moments together, it had already begun to rob him of his joy.

Mike stood to greet his wife and softly returned her smile. "Hello. You're looking well."

In the manner of French greetings, she kissed both of his cheeks several times, saying, "And so are you." It was in this moment that she realized how very much she'd missed him.

He helped her with her chair, asking, "What will you have?" A waiter had already appeared and was standing by.

"Is that Floc you're drinking?"

"It is. Want some?"

She smiled. "Chilled Floc is the perfect apéritif for a warm evening in Gascony."

He nodded his agreement.

"How was your flight?"

"Good," he answered. "Can't beat that Concorde for the time it saves."

"Did your connections go OK?"

"Fine. And the hotel car was waiting for me at the baggage claim." The garçon had arrived with her drink and Mike raised his

glass, saying, "To your health, your very good health," adding to
himself, *I thank God for it.* "You really are looking well," he said
again, then reflected on why that was.

In stark contrast to the pallor she wore the last time he saw her, her
skin was golden-brown, and the highlights in her hair had burst through,
as they always did in summer. A few freckles had emerged on her nose,
she'd lost some of the hollowness in her cheeks, and the dress she was
wearing—a silky, flowing thing—gave her a carefree, youthful air.

"Thanks, Mike," she answered, and had to catch herself, because she'd almost said: *Thanks, honey.* "I'm feeling great, as you can
imagine—very happy to be alive. It was like I was sitting on death
row and an angel came to deliver me with a full pardon."

Mike looked into his drink, as he said, "And it would be my
guess that you see Andrew as that angel."

She smiled briefly, then looked away.

"Well, no matter," he lifted his glass again. "To whatever or
whomever, I'm still grateful."

She thought it best to change the subject, steer it away from
Andrew. "How was Lucy when you left?"

"Good, but unhappy that I wasn't going to bring you home."

"I've not said very much to her about the situation."

"I know you haven't, but she's so damned smart, she doesn't
miss much."

She grinned. "And that's what we love about her, isn't it? She
keeps us honest."

The look he affected then was hard to read, as he considered
the irony of her statement. "She made cookies for you and Marc,
they're in my room. Remind me to give them to you."

The expression on his face distracted her, but she said, "She's
such a dear. She's all heart."

"Spoken to Marc lately?" he asked her.

She smiled. "Yesterday, as a matter of fact. He's having the
best summer, and he was absolutely thrilled that you were coming
to see me."

He seemed lighter now. "Do you think we might fly down to
Barcelona to see him? I was thinking maybe on Friday—if you've
no other plans, of course."

That suggestion delighted her. "I was hoping we could do that, and Friday's perfect!"

An awkward silence fell between them, almost as though they had run out of things to say.

Mike had been looking away from her when he asked, "How's about going to my suite before we go to dinner? I'd like some privacy for a few minutes, if you don't mind."

His desire for privacy told her that he meant to talk about the state of their marriage. She answered, "Sure," and as they made their way toward his rooms, she was overcome with dread.

He'd been given one of Eugénie's best suites, a lovely corner one on the second floor that, like the bedroom at the château, was wrapped around entirely by a balcony. When they walked in, it was clear that he'd intended to bring her here, for a bottle of champagne and a tray of canapés awaited them in the sitting room. Annie sat stiffly on the couch and after opening the wine and handing her a glass, Mike settled into a chair across from her.

He began by observing, "There've been a lot of changes since we were here." He kept his head down, looking into his champagne flute, because he wanted to avoid her eyes.

Besides worrying about what he would say, being alone with him was making her surprisingly nervous. "Yes," she agreed, "they've recently renovated the place."

There was disappointment in his tone when he told her, "I wasn't talking about the hotel." She was holding her glass with her left hand and he focused on it now, saying, "I see you still wear the rings I gave you."

"I haven't taken them off," she responded, then sipped at her champagne, trying to appear casual.

"How's Andrew?" he questioned.

The question restored her feeling of dread. "Fine. He's in London for the day, then Scotland tonight. He'll be back on Saturday."

Still avoiding her eyes, he told her, "I was reading about him on the flight over, in the *Financial Times*. He's stirred things up at the House of Lords."

"Really? What'd the article say?"

He tilted his head to one side, the way he often did when he explained something. "A lot of the Peers were put off by remarks he made about their lack of concern for the less fortunate—he told them to their faces that they're selfishly out of touch. But the Prime Minister and The Commons are solidly behind this proposal he's made, about requiring British corporations to train unskilled welfare recipients for decent jobs. The PM is now asking him to head a task force to see that it gets done."

She nodded as she informed him, "He did mention something about that."

He raised an eyebrow. "He's going to be a very busy boy if he says yes, what with all his other responsibilities." Noticing that her glass was almost empty, he asked, "Ready for more?"

While he poured, she said to him, "Speaking of busy boys, how have things been going for you?"

He waited until he was seated again to respond. "We just won an appeal for RJR, but it was hell to get there. I'm involved in something for one of the big pharmaceuticals now." He grimaced. "It looks like they're not going to be able to stay out of court, so they've called on the great litigator."

"Something you're not thrilled about, I take it."

He sighed. "I hate to say it, but these corporations are almost always in the wrong, and I'm getting pretty sick of defending the bad guy all the time. It makes for killer indigestion."

Although Lucy had mentioned his disillusionment in their last conversation, she was still surprised to hear him admit it. "But you always liked the challenge of finding them a way out, and the financial rewards haven't been hard to take, have they?"

He refilled his own glass now, still keeping away from her eyes. "If you want the truth," he said, "I'm finding it harder and harder to do the things I need to do to win."

A tad sarcastically, she said, "And of course, you have to keep winning."

Instead of returning to his chair, he walked toward the open balcony doors, then leaned against one and gazed out over the garden, musing, "You know, I wouldn't mind losing once in a while, if it was a fair fight."

Wryly, she observed, "And there's the problem. When your firm is stacked up against the little guy, it never is."

He recognized the veracity in that, and allowed their eyes to meet for the first time, though only for a few, fleeting seconds. "I've been thinking it'd be good to give myself some breathing room. Maybe I'll go stay at the beach house for a while, take some time to walk the beach and get in a little fishing. That always clears my head."

She opened her mouth as though she would comment, but nothing came out.

"What is it?" he wanted to know.

With an ironic smile, she recalled, "I was remembering the time we were at the beach and decided to change our lives. But once we got home and back into things—"

He didn't let her finish. "I wasn't ready then, I was still running from myself."

Her brow knitted, as she commented, "That's odd to hear you say."

"I guess it is." Now was the time, he realized, so he blurted out, "I've been in therapy, you know."

In the last few minutes he'd been revealing aspects of himself that she'd always longed to see, and it encouraged her to ask the question, "What were you running from?"

One of his hands balled into a fist, and he tapped the side of it against his mouth before answering. "My guilt, my loss, my fears—you name it."

She let that settle out of the air, like so much stirred up dust.

He mustered the courage to tell her now, "My coming here to see you—it was important for me to do that, because one of the things I need to change is that tendency I have, to run from anything emotional and difficult."

She'd been watching his face while he said this, but now she lowered her eyes. "I'm sure my involvement with Andrew hasn't made things easier for you."

"Easier, no," he admitted, "but it has made them clearer."

She held her breath, as she questioned, "How?"

Mike returned to his chair. He allowed their eyes to meet again, and they looked into one another through the ensuing moments of silence.

The intensity of his gaze was intimidating, and she nervously asked, "How has it made things clearer?"

He released her eyes, and looked away again. "In learning more about myself, I believe I've come to understand you better, and your relationship with him confirms much of that understanding."

She was almost afraid to ask, but did anyway. "How so?"

He propped an elbow on the chair arm, and put that hand to his face. His fingers rubbed the stubble of his beard, before he said, "Love is important to most people, but to you it's essential, and what you give, you need to get in return. When you don't get back as good as you get, it messes you up, makes you feel abandoned, unwanted, even desperate."

His assessment made her laugh in embarrassment.

He was glad she had laughed because it lightened the atmosphere a bit, but it also made him wonder, "You don't agree?"

"I do agree," she said. "It's just funny to hear you tell me about myself, that's all."

They allowed the quiet to return and their thoughts to take them where they would.

"Are you hungry?" he asked after a few moments. "How about some of these hors d'oeuvres?"

"Thanks," she said, and helped herself to one with a large dollop of caviar.

Now he laughed. "I knew you'd take that one."

She smiled back at him, and without thinking, said, "I've missed you, Mike."

He wanted to respond—*and I've missed you, and it took being with someone else for me to see that*—but he wasn't quite ready for that. First, he needed to know, "Where is this thing with Andrew going?"

Although she knew how important it was to answer honestly, she loathed the idea of hurting him. So it was with tremendous reticence that she responded, "He's, ah, he's asked his wife for a divorce, and she refuses to give him one. But I don't want him to do that," she quickly added, "I didn't ask for that. I prefer going on as we are, being together when we can. I think divorce would hurt everyone involved, most of all the children—and I include Marc in that."

The air he blew through his lips, made a slight whistling sound. "I hadn't realized it had gone that far," he said, as his eyes fell to the floor.

She responded defensively, "It's not like we just met, we've a long history—"

"So I'm beginning to understand."

The softened, vulnerable man she had been sitting with vanished suddenly, and she was once again faced with her husband's all-too-familiar protective veneer.

He shifted into flippancy as he questioned, "And where does that leave us?"

"I don't really know," she answered.

She was stung by his bitterness when he next asked, "Would you like me to free you, so at least that complication is removed?"

As difficult as the last half hour had been, it had felt very good talking like this, being open, being honest, and she didn't want to lose that. "Is that what you want? Is that why you've come?"

There was only one way he could say this: in anger. He answered, "No, it isn't. I'd actually had hopes in a very different direction, if you want to know. I'd thought that we might spend these few days together and see if there was anything worth salvaging." With that he folded his arms and glared at her.

She could see what was going on inside of him, that he was wounded and angry and feeling maddeningly foolish, as though he'd just made his debut before a packed audience and flubbed his lines. Fearing that she would say the wrong thing in this crucial moment, she was suddenly terrified to open her mouth. She set her glass down and rose from her seat, then walked onto the balcony. She put both hands on the railing and looked into the garden below, as she recalled the discussion she'd had with Andrew only last night, about wanting them both, wanting to love them both. *Is it mere selfishness,* she asked herself now, *or is it my cowardice, my fear of losing someone I love, having to once again say goodbye to someone I love?*

As she contemplated it, she was astonished by the irony of this situation. As though it were somehow meant to be, they were here again, in the place where they had spent their honeymoon, where she had begun to dream of their life together, of the beautiful children they would have, and the nurturing love that would grow with the years. Ten, barren years along the road, after all the endured loneliness, the unsatisfying affair, and that horrendous scare with HIV, incredible as it was, it occurred to Annie that fate could be offering them a second chance, the opportunity to start over and rediscover what they had lost. And most ironic of all, it was her second chance with Andrew that had delivered her to this place: It was Andrew who had brought both of them here.

Mike remained where he was in the sitting room, waging his own internal debate. He didn't have it in him to say good-bye just now, he knew that, but did he have it in him to fight, to compete with another man for her? He searched himself and couldn't find the answer, but something compelled him to follow her, and after a couple of minutes he was standing by her side.

The nearness of him, the scent of his cologne—a fragrance she had chosen—evoked vivid memories of how it felt to be taken into his strong and protective arms, feeling the suppressed power of his emotions, emotions that he would only reveal in their most intimate moments, in the night, in the dark, when he had lost himself in her.

She felt suddenly faint, and stepped back to sit on a balcony chair. She grasped the arms of the chair, then lifted her face to her husband, saying, "Let's do that, Mike. Let's spend these days as you said and see what comes of it—no pressure, no expectations, let's just see what happens."

Her words washed him with relief, but before he could respond he needed to know, "What about Andrew?"

It was important to make this clear from the start; it was the right and fair thing to do. She answered from the depths of her heart: "I love him, Mike, and no matter what happens, that's not going to change."

His brow furrowed and he felt the beginnings of a headache as he considered the risk to himself in what she was proposing. But even as he was ruling it out, dismissing it as utterly, ridiculously impossible, he realized that if he said no, she was going to walk out of his life, and it would likely be forever. He was not prepared for that, so he made an impulsive and admittedly frightening decision.

"All right, I'm game, after all, I'm here already, so why not?"
And then in the next breath, he asked her, "Ready to go to dinner?"

She was flabbergasted. "Just like that? No arguments? No
protestations about how selfish I'm being?"

"Nope. I'm hungry, let's go eat," was what he answered. But
in his thoughts he continued—something he was not prepared to
say aloud: *One of the things I've figured out these past months is that being
with you is worth it, Annie, at pretty much any price.*

She waited in the sitting room while he shaved and changed
his clothes for dinner, once again sipping at her champagne. When
he emerged from the bedroom he smiled softly, and it sent that familiar quivering pulse shooting through her body. When they
reached the lobby it had settled down, but the nervous queasiness
it left in its wake stayed with her stomach throughout the evening.

When she returned to the château and stopped the car to open
the gates, she was struck with an awareness of how completely
transformed her life was. And, too, there was the utter naturalness
of it, of living in a remote corner of southwest France, in a château
her lover had provided for her. It had all happened so quickly, with
such relative ease—how could that be? How had she gone from
wife and mother, living a fairly ordinary life in Bucks County,
Pennsylvania, to being the secret lover of one of the most important
men in Britain?

Once she'd driven through the entrance, she stopped again to
close the gates, and with their secure clang she recognized an essential truth: She was at peace here, and surprisingly happy living this
role, though it was certainly one she had neither envisioned nor
wished for. Here she was not the abandoned wife, waiting alone for
her husband to return, here she was the woman an important man
had chosen to be with, had risked his marriage and reputation to
share stolen moments with. Here she was the wife who had made
the choice to be with another, and was yet still so desired by her husband that he had swallowed his pride and come to her, seeking another chance. If there was anything she understood about herself,
it was that when it came to love, she had always needed more than

any one man had ever been able to give her. So was it really a surprise that she would find herself embracing this moment in her life?

Still, the rapidity with which these changes had transpired dizzied her. Anxiety suddenly flooded her thoughts, and as she continued up the drive to the house, she began wondering what unhinging, unpredictable events were in store for her in the days and weeks ahead.

Twenty

Didier left her a note, saying that the count had called, and she wasn't in bed long when the phone rang again.

"I really missed you today," he sighed.

"I missed you, too." She rubbed at the mattress, at the place where his body should be. "How'd everything go?"

"Pretty well, considering."

"Are you talking about work or home?"

"Both. Nothing was great but it's all relative. How'd it go with Mike?"

"My day was better than yours—I'd say it went well."

He was anxious to know, "How was it, seeing him again?"

"Good. It's nice to have most of the bad stuff behind us, it's very freeing."

"How'd you find him?"

"In a word, changed. I'd say he's going through some major changes."

"Want to elaborate?"

"Not now—later, when I see you." She paused for a moment. "We're going to have lunch with my cousins tomorrow," she said, "and then we're thinking of going to Barcelona on Friday, if we can arrange the flights."

He flashed on an idea. "Why don't you let me send my jet? That would make it worlds easier. You can set your own timetable that way, not waste any time."

"What would you do for transportation?" she wondered.

"I'd send my private jet and use the corporate one."

"I hadn't realized there were two."

"You all right with that, then? Shall I go ahead and make the arrangements for you?" That would make him feel better, he knew, make him feel somehow connected.

She understood why he was offering and answered, "That's awfully nice of you, Andrew. I think Mike will be OK with it, but I need to ask him. Will you call me tomorrow?"

"Of course. I love you so much, Annie," he told her, then with some trepidation added, "While you spend this time with Mike, please don't lose sight of that."

"I can't possibly, my love. I feel as though I carry you around inside of me."

"And that's where I am, inside of you—"

They both clung to the telephone receivers for a time, before feeling able to put them down.

Their arrival at Pierre and Jeanette's home was ceremonious. The d'Inards welcomed Mike with many kisses and many toasts to his health. Two more of Annie's cousins were in attendance, Jean-Marc's sisters Laurie and Valery, and they all sat down to a long and delicious family lunch. Special bottles of wine had been opened for the occasion and Jeanette, who was always a fabulous cook, outdid herself with a garlicky capon from a neighboring farm. They ate and talked and laughed until everyone was so full they could barely move. When they had been revived by coffee in the garden, Annie and Mike walked the village streets with the younger cousins before returning to the house to say their farewells. It was tearful but sweet, and Annie promised to return soon.

"It always upsets you to leave them," Mike observed, once they were on their way.

"That's because they remind me of my grandparents. And I always get this terrible feeling when I leave them, that it could be the last time I see them. They're getting old and Jeanette's health is plainly fading."

He'd been curious about this, because throughout the afternoon no mention had been made of it. "Do they know what's going on with us?"

She nodded. "I told Jean-Marc, but asked him to keep it to himself. He worked with us on location, you know, so we were able to have some good talks."

"Have you told them you're living just up the road?"

"They know I'm staying there for a time, with a friend, but no more than that."

"Why?" he wondered.

She shrugged. "Maybe because I keep hearing this nagging voice telling me that it's going to end, that it can't last."

"It doesn't surprise me that you're still having the same struggles," he commented, his head turned to regard the view.

It was oddly comforting to hear him make that observation. She sighed as she told him, "The people I love—I always seem to lose them, they get taken from me too soon."

"Not everyone," he responded, and left it there. "Want to stop in a cafe somewhere?"

"I couldn't possibly eat again."

"I couldn't either, but we could find a nice place to sit with a coffee or a glass of something."

"There's a pretty little place on the river bank in Aire," she remembered.

Noisy French rock and roll blared out of a nearby bistro, where young people had gathered to pass the evening. Annie and Mike went to the nearly empty cafe next to it and sat at a tiny table, very close to the river. They ordered mineral water and coffee, and sat quietly for a time, both of them looking over the water.

Mike had almost finished his coffee, when he asked, "Why don't you think your relationship with Andrew can last?"

She looked into the river as she collected her thoughts. "That voice I hear is my practical self, and it keeps reminding me of the facts. It's hard to ignore the facts."

"The facts about who he is?"

Nodding, she responded, "They're what kept us apart before, when I wasn't even aware of them."

"He's a very powerful and important man," he acknowledged, "and the more I learn about him, the more impressed I am. He's a man of conscience and responsibility."

Her memory flashed on the young man she knew in St. Andrews. "And he's always been that," she told him, smiling briefly.

"That's why I worry that our relationship will somehow bring him down."

"He appears willing to take the risk," he observed.

"He is," she said, "and that's what frightens me. He needs me so much . . ." She stopped herself. "I don't think I should be talking to you about this."

"No, you probably shouldn't," he agreed. "Want more coffee?"

"No thanks, this is plenty."

From the bistro they could hear the opening bars of a popular song by Sting. "If he loved you, like I love you," it began.

"How would you feel about a dance?" Mike asked her.

"Here? Now?" The request surprised her, because it was decidedly out of character. The Mike she knew would dance at a wedding or a ball amid the cover of a crowd, but alone, in the middle of a cafe?

"Why not?" He rose from his chair and reached a hand out. When she stood, he immediately took her in his arms. "It's been a long time since we've done this," he said, pulling her closer. Then, after a few moments, he questioned, "Can I ask you something?"

She was suddenly weak from the nearness of him, and she murmured, "Sure."

His voice was soft and deep and sensuous, as he said, "I need you to be very honest with me and I don't want you to worry about my feelings, all right?"

"OK," she responded, goose bumps rising on her neck.

"All things being equal, and all other things aside—Andrew's responsibilities, our marriage, Marc's needs—if you could have it anyway you wanted, how would that be?"

Here it comes, she realized, *my moment of truth*. They had stopped dancing but he still held to her, and she was relieved that she didn't have to see his face. "I'd have you both," she answered. "I'd stay married to and loving you, but I'd remain Andrew's lover."

He released her then, and met her eyes to say, "Thank you for your honesty." He was outwardly calm, though inside he felt like a man standing in the open hatch of a flying plane, wondering if he had the courage to jump. *I've come this far,* he told himself, *and in all likelihood I'll survive it, but do I want to take the risk? Will I look back on this and question my sanity for even coming here?*

"You're welcome," she answered him, laughing slightly, because he had surprised her again. "Is that all you're going to say about it?"

"For now." He allowed for some settling in, before adding, "I guess what I want is time to mull it over."

The song had ended and she searched his eyes, trying to read them. "Take all the time you need," she told him, meaning to smile but yawning instead. "I should probably bring you back to Eugénie now, we want to get an early start in the morning."

Mike pulled some francs from his pocket and left them on the table. "How far do you have to go after you drop me off?"

"It's a little over half an hour to the château," she answered, yawning again.

"If you're too tired to drive you can stay with me," he offered.

They had reached the car and as he opened the door for her, she turned to him. With a soft kiss to his cheek, she responded, "Let's the three of us talk about this on Saturday, Mike, before we go into anything like that."

"I'd take the couch," he told her, "if that's what you'd want."

Her expression was half-frown, half-grin, as she responded, "I don't know if I could let you do that."

"Oh," he answered, and smiled to himself.

On the drive back to the château Annie could think of nothing else but how different Mike's embrace felt as they danced. It was so completely different, is was almost like another man.

Mike readily agreed to Andrew's offer; he frequently flew on his firm's corporate jet as well as his clients', so he was keenly aware of the benefits of private aviation. The crew were by now familiar with Annie and greeted her with respect and cordiality, almost as though she was the one who paid their salaries.

"Welcome aboard, Ms. d'Inard."

"Thank you, Captain. This is my husband, Michael Rutledge."

"Welcome, sir," the captain said. "It's our pleasure to have you with us."

The steward added, "We're very pleased to be taking you to see your son. Have you had your breakfast?"

"No, actually, so some juice and coffee would be nice."

The young man smiled warmly as he responded, "I think we can do better than that," then took them to their seats.

Marc greeted his mother and stepfather at the door and although it had only been a couple of weeks, they embraced as though they hadn't seen each other for months. After about an hour of sherry and conversation with Carlos's brother and his family, the three left for lunch at a seaside restaurant recommended by Marc's uncle.

When they were seated in the bustling cafe, the first thing out of Marc's mouth was, "Does this mean that you two are over whatever it was?"

Mike looked to Annie before responding, "We're getting there."

Marc's face beamed delight.

Mike didn't want him to get too excited, so he added, "We've still some big hurdles to overcome and we need to take our time, but I want you to know that I'm terribly sorry for the hurt and worry this has caused you."

"You don't need to apologize to me," he told his stepfather. "I haven't suffered any. I've just been worried about the two of you, that's all." His curiosity got the better of him and it made him ask, "What were you fighting about, anyway?"

Annie started to speak, but Mike cut her off. "I've been very inconsiderate of your mother for a long time. I put too much time in at the office and too little at home, and you can't do that to a marriage. You need to nurture it and take care of it and put it first. I had this foolish idea that I could put it on autopilot and go away and everything would be all right when I came back, but it doesn't work that way."

He was doing it again, astounding Annie with the things he said.

"I've recognized this," he continued, "but now the problem is, can I change? That's why I say we're getting there, because I'm trying to change but I don't know yet if I can."

Marc grinned as he told them,"Well, I'm not going to worry about you two anymore, because I know you both well enough to realize that whatever you set your minds to, you can do."

It was time to change the subject, so Mike said now, "Your mom tells me you're thinking of staying for the school year."

"Yeah—what do you think?"

"I think you should go for it," he smiled. "It's a great opportunity and I know your dad's family will take good care of you."

"I just worry about Mom," Marc admitted, glancing sideways at Annie.

She responded quickly. "Well you shouldn't, because the ad firm I've been working for wants me to stay with them, so that means I'll be spending a considerable amount of time in Europe over the coming year."

"Really? You going to keep working for Andrew?"

She nodded.

"That's cool. I really like him. Have you ever met him, Mike?"

"Yes, I have. He was in Philadelphia recently and we met for dinner."

"What'd you think of him?"

"I share your opinion of him," Mike answered, after a brief glance in Annie's direction.

"It was so cool at his castle—man, you should see that place. I had a great time there."

Annie said to Marc, "Let's get back to you, honey. Would you want to come home first, maybe go to the beach house at the end of the summer?"

"The three of us, like always? Can we bring Lucy and Buddy?"

"Of course, honey. I know they both miss you terribly." She hadn't discussed this yet with Mike, and she worried suddenly that she had overstepped. But if he was perturbed, he gave no indication of it.

"Maybe I'll come home early, so I can see my friends and get all the stuff I'll need for school."

"Whatever you want," his mother said. "The more time we have with you, the better."

Annie and Mike looked at one another and smiled, and the sight of that warmed Marc's heart. "It's really great to see the two

of you together again—I missed having my parents together." He
blushed as he added to Mike, "I mean, you've always been more
like my dad than my stepfather."

Mike was deeply moved, and with downcast eyes he responded, "Since the day I married your mother, I've thought of you
as my son, and I don't imagine I'll ever stop thinking of you that
way, no matter what."

When it was time to say good-bye that evening, Marc lingered
in his hugs. "I'm looking forward to the beach," he said, "we're
going to have a great time together."

"I'm looking forward to it, too," Mike told him.

Annie kissed her son's forehead. "Take good care of yourself,
and be safe."

"You always say that, Mom," he chided, then kissed her
cheek, murmuring, "but I love you for it."

Because Annie was suddenly very tired, Mike drove to Eugénie from the airport in Pau. When they arrived they went into the
lobby and ordered some coffee.

"I worry about you driving back," he told her. "Why don't I
see if there's a room they could give you?"

She yawned, then said, "The coffee will rev me up, I'll be fine
after the coffee."

He continued to express concern. "You look very tired, Annie."

"I don't know what's wrong with me," she said. "I got plenty
of sleep last night, but this afternoon I kept wanting to lie down and
take a nap."

"The heat always does that to you," he remembered, "and it
was damned hot in Spain."

"That's probably it." She finished her coffee, then said, "I'd
better be on my way. I'll pick you up at one tomorrow, all right?"

"What time is Andrew getting in?" he wondered.

"Midday. A driver will be waiting for his flight so I can come
get you."

As he walked her to the car, he advised, "Play the radio and
keep the windows open."

She kissed him tenderly in response, and they lingered in an embrace when the kiss was over.

She rang down to the kitchen for breakfast because she'd slept later than she'd wanted to, and needed to get a move on. Didier came up the stairs with her tray, singing to himself.

"Slept well, Madame?"

"Too well. I should have been up an hour ago."

"The count returns today."

"Yes."

"You must be very happy."

"I am," she answered. As he was about to leave the bedroom, she called him back, because she decided to warn him, "Our guest for dinner today is my husband."

His brow raised slightly. "I see."

"The three of us need to discuss some important matters."

He got the point. "We'll serve the meal and keep well out of the way, Madame."

"It's not that, I know you'll do that. It's just that I don't want you put in an awkward position. I remember how embarrassing it was for you when I arrived and you thought I was Andrew's wife."

"Lisette and I don't mind about that," he told her, with a decidedly French facial shrug. "We know that love is a power unto itself, and not required to mind the boundaries of marriage. It happens when and where it wants, and we're mostly powerless to stop it."

She smiled at his remarks, telling him, "You're a philosopher, Didier."

He returned her smile and as he descended the stairs, Annie heard him resume his singing of an old Edith Piaf tune "La Vie en Rose."

Twenty-One

A ndrew arrived before they did and was sitting on the terrace with a glass of Pernod as they pulled up. His first instinct was to embrace Annie when she emerged from the car, but out of deference to Mike, he didn't.

He walked over to greet him. "I'm glad you could come," he said, as they shook hands.

Mike glanced at his wife, then focused on Andrew. "I think it's a good idea, getting together like this."

To Annie his response sounded less than sincere—as though he was trying to convince himself.

More nervously, Andrew said, "It's damned generous on your part."

They both looked to Annie now, waiting for her to take them to the next step. She realized this and blushed slightly. "Shall we go in?"

"This is a beautiful spot," Mike observed. "I see why Annie likes it so much. It suits her."

That comment heartened Andrew, and made him feel as though Mike was bestowing approval.

Didier was waiting inside to serve drinks to Mike and Annie; afterward, he made himself scarce. When he had joined his wife in the kitchen, Lisette told him, "I caught a glimpse of him when I was in the dining room. A fine looking man, her husband."

"Yes, and well off, from the looks of him."

"They don't seem estranged, do they?"

"No, they seem quite warm toward one another."

"The count is a little uncomfortable, though."

"I noticed that, too."

276

"I wonder what this is all about?"

"Who knows? Though it all appears very civilized."

"Yes, it does," Lisette agreed. "I hadn't realized Americans were so sophisticated about these things."

They made a brief tour of the house, then they went outside again; Mike particularly liked the pool. "What a great spot this is."

"We've been enjoying it," Andrew responded, then regretted saying that.

Looking now to the statue of the shackled Prometheus, Mike asked them, "What's he doing here? A bit off the hedonistic theme, isn't he?"

Annie smiled awkwardly. "We've decided that he's there to remind us that life isn't all love and wine."

Mike scoffed, "As if anyone over the age of twelve needs reminding of that."

Andrew nodded agreement, just as Annie suggested, "Why don't we finish our drinks here? There's a bar inside the pool house if we need anything."

Pulling a deck chair into the shade, Mike observed, "I can see that this would be a very hard place for you to leave."

"It's not so much the place," she responded, "but how I feel when I'm here."

With some hesitation, Andrew added, "It's afforded us the opportunity to recover some time together, in privacy." Every time he spoke to Mike he held his breath, as he waited to see how he would respond.

Mike emptied his glass and set it down, then folded his arms and fixed his eyes on Andrew. "Tell me something, Andrew, how does your wife feel about all this?"

His response came with swift certainty. "She's bitterly unhappy about it."

"Annie's told me that you asked her for a divorce."

"I did, but she won't hear of it."

"So what now?" Mike wondered.

"I don't know," he answered plainly.

Annie fidgeted while they spoke, then cautiously told her husband, "You know what I want in this—I don't want to lose either of you. But having made that clear, I'm willing to do whatever is best for you, Mike. You've a perfect right to free yourself of me and get on with your life, if that's what you want."

He looked off into the distance for several long moments, then back to his wife. "I don't know what I want just yet, but I do know that I'm not prepared to make any major decisions. I told you before, I came here hoping that we might find something to salvage in our marriage."

"And I think we have," she replied eagerly.

He didn't respond, and Andrew wondered if he should leave them alone. Then, just as he was about to offer to do that, Mike told him, "I'd like to know how you feel about all this."

His anxiety had already been rising, but Mike's question sent it soaring. "More than anything I want Annie to be happy, and I'm willing to do whatever I can toward that end. But in truth, what she's proposing troubles me, because it's replete with complications. After all, conventional, two-person relationships are challenge enough."

In her anxiousness to express her feelings, Annie blurted out, "I'm not naive, I know it'll be difficult, but it'll be worlds easier than walking away from one of you. And I know it's probably my cowardice that's driving me, but I can't help that. I love both of you, and both of you love me—at least, I think you still love me, Mike." She was putting him on the spot, she knew, but she needed to know how he felt.

The old, avoidance-driven Mike would have gotten up and walked away just now—hell, he would never have come in the first place. But the new, evolving Mike was determined to stay and see this out, so instead of leaving he merely lifted his shoulders and rearranged his position in the chair, saying, "I wouldn't be here if I didn't, Annie."

His response emboldened her. "Then let's at least give it a try. We might try and fail, but I think that's preferable to not trying at all, don't you?"

He kept his head lowered, but allowed his eyes to meet hers. "I can't answer you, not just yet," he told her.

She assured him, "All right, that's all right, there's no hurry. It's enough for you to even consider it."

He lifted his gaze, glanced at Andrew first, then looked directly at his wife. "The thing is—as much as I may want to, I don't know that I can give you what you need. A large part of what went on with us before was you needing more from me than I could give." An uncomfortable quiet settled on the trio.

Andrew shifted in his seat and avoided Mike's eyes, though he felt tremendous compassion for a man who could admit something like that, especially in front of another man.

"It wasn't all you, Mike," she told him, "there's what goes on inside of me—there's my fear, too."

He suddenly wanted to know this, and his eyes conveyed his vulnerability as he questioned, "Does *he* satisfy you, Annie? Does *he* give you everything you need?" He knew that he was taking some hazardous steps, but there was no going back now.

"Oh God," she whispered, as both men focused on her. She rose abruptly and turned away from them with a brisk stride toward the opposite end of the pool, then stood with her back to them, her arms wrapped around her middle.

Andrew and Mike found themselves unavoidably face to face, while the afternoon seemed bereft of sound, save the ever-present gurgling of pool water from Eros and Dionysus. They sat looking at one another—Mike's expression now sharply challenging, Andrew's softly penitent—waiting for her to return. When, after some long moments she didn't, it was Mike who went to her.

He laid a gentle hand on her shoulder to say, "Whatever it is, I can take it."

The stinging in her eyes made it difficult to meet his. "He brings me peace, Mike, and it's something I've been searching for all my life. I thought I'd found it with you, but it got away from me; you never let me in, and that's where I needed to go to find it."

Andrew remained seated where he was, but in the quiet of the afternoon, he could easily hear what they said to one another.

"I wanted to let you in, I couldn't," Mike sighed. "It was as though I was being disloyal to Michele — as if my being happy without her was wrong."

"I know, I understand, and I don't blame you; I never have."

He didn't want Andrew to hear this, so in a hushed voice he questioned, "What if I let you in now? How's that going to work with him in the picture?"

She closed her eyes and released the pent-up tears. "Don't ask me to give him up, Mike — don't make me choose. Please don't do that to me."

As though the words were stabbing him, he winced to tell her, "What you did with Glenn, it hurt so much —"

She could feel his pain as acutely as her own, and she put her hand to her heart, saying, "I hate what happened with him and I can never forgive myself for it, but he's not Glenn — he's Andrew. Andrew's been with me all along, he's always been a part of me. He's as much a part of me as Michele is of you."

"Michele is dead," he stated, and she could hear his ever-present anger.

"Andrew's not," she responded, almost apologetically, "and God help me, but I want to be with him while I can. What would you do if Michele came back into your life? What if she was the one sitting over there? That's how I feel about him, Mike, like a miracle has restored someone I'd given up for dead."

"How can it work?"

"I can make it work."

He shook his head in denial. "I think it's doomed."

"We're all doomed."

"Why do you want to keep on with me?" he asked, the suffering etching his face with lines. "Why don't you just end it and be with him?"

For the first time, there was true conviction in her voice. "It's there for us, Mike, I know it is. I know we can find what we need from one another if we put our hearts in it — if we're willing to open them up and try."

"I just don't see it, Annie, I only see it causing more hurt, more suffering."

"No, I don't believe that," she insisted. "My love for Andrew—it's opened my heart and let me know the wonderful things
again. I don't want to keep that to myself, Mike, I want to share
that with you."

He turned his face away so she wouldn't witness the pain he
felt over that. "I'm a man, Annie," he murmured, his eyes closed.
"These things are much harder for men."

Through her anguish, she found something to smile about.
"That's why men love women, Mike—we're the open gates."

He turned to look at Andrew then, who had been grasping the
arms of his chair; his face was solemn and compassionate, and Mike
could tell that he was feeling their anguish as well as his own. He stared
at the man who little more than a month ago was a complete stranger,
but who now was privy to one of the most awkward and painful moments of his life.

He pondered what he would say next, whether or not he
should take a stand and walk away, while he still had a modicum
of self-respect. In the next moment he decided to do that; he would
let them both know that his dignity forbade him to be party to this
insanity. But when his eyes found Annie again, standing so near
he could smell the sweetness of her sun-warmed skin, all his resolve faded.

Although it held potential for further heartache and humiliation, he whispered to her, "I do love you, Annie. I can't say more
than that. I love you."

After all that had happened between them and everything that
had been said today, those words were received as validation, as acceptance and absolution. She was almost too choked to respond.
"And I don't need more than that, because you've just given me
everything."

He had to make this clear. "I can't give my blessing to this, not
now, anyway."

"I understand."

"I'll go home tomorrow, I'll go home and give myself some
time and distance."

Her hand brushed aside the tears that had come chasing down
her cheeks. "Do whatever you need to, take as long as you need."

With a precipitous change of tone, he said now, "I don't think I can stay for lunch. Can someone take me back?"

The thought of him leaving so abruptly and in such an obviously distressed state, drove her to plead, "Please reconsider, Mike, please don't go like this. I'm going to miss you terribly when you're gone."

"But that's the problem, isn't it?" he realized. "How are we going to deal with the inevitable separations?"

That he was thinking through this, gave her hope, and she responded with alacrity. "You have your work, Andrew has his—I'm the one with all the time to fill."

"But when you're with him, I'll think of it. I'll think of him making love to you," he found the courage to admit. "How am I supposed to handle that?"

Andrew's empathy only grew when he heard him say this, for he had his own grave concerns regarding that very thing.

"I don't know," she answered, because she didn't. "That's going to be the hard part. That's the part where we're just going to have to wait and see if we can manage."

Mike was so drained, he couldn't muster a response.

"Please stay for lunch," she said again.

Andrew had come up behind him. "Please do. I don't want you to go away like this."

"Please, Mike—"

He brought one hand to his suddenly throbbing forehead. "All right," he muttered, "I guess I could use some food."

Annie rushed to say, "I'll get you some aspirin."

He eyed her suspiciously, asking, "How'd you know I need them?"

"I love you, Mike; I know when you hurt," she answered, then hurried along the path to the main house.

When they were alone, the awkwardness escalated as the two men were directly confronted with one another again, without the buffer of Annie. Andrew understood that this impossible moment had to be far worse for Mike, so he determined to reach out to him.

Mike was wincing with the pain in his head when Andrew offered, "The thing is, once you start loving her, it's impossible to stop. As hard as I tried, Mike, all those years, I never could."

He knew what Andrew was attempting to do and on some level he appreciated it, but a flame of masculine pride erupted suddenly. "And just how are you going to work this into your nice little life?"

"My nice little life is already turned on end," he responded readily. "And what will happen as time goes on, I can't say."

"But you can't face the alternative."

Standing within two feet of her husband, it took more than courage for him to admit: "No, I can't. I don't want to be without her."

Mike was revived by anger as he inquired facetiously, "And you're willing to share her with me, are you?"

Andrew was aware of the change in Mike, but he accepted his animosity because he was entitled to it. "It's what Annie wants," he answered.

Mike shook his head dismissively. "That's very easy for you to say, standing as you are: She's living here with you, tonight she climbs into bed with you. But I wonder how you'd feel if you were the one being left alone, sleeping alone, imagining her making love to me."

It was, admittedly, an unsettling thought, and he frowned as he responded, "If we do this, I'm going to be in that position sometime, aren't I?"

"But what if it were today? What if I took her back to the hotel and left you here, how would you feel about things then, I wonder?"

He allowed the picture to take shape in his mind, and as it did, he had to admit, "It would be impossible to bear."

"Precisely," Mike quipped.

They glared at one another, realizing that they had come to the same, disquieting place.

"Is that what you want to do," Andrew questioned, "take her with you tonight?"

Mike responded first with a grim smile, and then, as he was preparing to answer, Annie returned from the house.

She was carrying a bottle of aspirin and a glass of water. "Take these and then let's go eat," she told her husband. "Drinking on an empty stomach isn't good for anyone," she added, plagued as she was by her own nervous queasiness.

At the large dining room table Annie seated herself between the two men; dinner began quietly and tensions eased with the first glass of wine. Lisette prepared a tartar of salmon and oysters for the first course, and it was divinely inspired. Mike made Annie laugh to think of their Lucy ever preparing such a thing: Lucy, who felt compelled to cook everything to death. Their conversation about home and their housekeeper made Andrew feel left out, but he tried to smile and realized it was something he needed to deal with. By the main course, which consisted of veal panée, julienne vegetables, and gratinée potatoes, they were talking about the Armagnac and Andrew's desire to have Annie get involved in the business.

She was excited about it, and enthusiastically told her husband, "It's a fine, respected label and the production is very limited. Marketed properly, it could be one of the most expensive and sought-after Armagnacs in the world."

With a sardonic grin, he commented, "Just what Andrew needs, eh? More income."

Andrew was a little insulted by that remark. "Actually Mike, I'd like to deed everything over to Annie eventually, the house, the business, everything. I can't do it just yet because she couldn't afford to run it; it loses money, it hasn't made any for years. So I intend to get it up and running profitably first."

This was the first she'd heard of his intention and it left her dumbfounded. "You can't do that!" she exclaimed.

"Why not?" he wondered.

She would have preferred that they were alone just now, so that she might say this in private. "I couldn't accept it, Andrew. It's far too much and I don't need that from you."

His voice wavering with emotion, he told her, "This place can only be yours, Annie. I can't ever see it belonging to anyone else."

She understood why he wanted to do this; it was almost holy now, this protected, secret place that had witnessed their coming together. For as long as they continued to exist, this house, these vineyards, these groves and ponds would echo their memories. And too, she understood that he wanted to somehow make up for all the things he couldn't give her, for the public life they could never share, the children they could never have, the simple joy of being able to come home to each other at day's end, in front of the world.

For the poignancy of this gift she would have liked to express her gratitude and love, but she didn't, for she knew how hurtful a display of that nature would be to Mike.

Because Mike had done no less for her, at another time, in another place, giving her the home she'd always dreamed of, providing her and Marc a place of refuge they had long been in need of. But what made the gifts vastly different, she realized now, was that one came with a man's heart and soul, while the other—ironically the one from her husband—came instead of that.

Although she withheld the words, Mike read what was in her heart—he saw it through her eyes. "I guess that seals your relationship," he wryly commented, to cover the stinging he felt in his own heart.

"I've not done it for that reason," Andrew protested.

Mike was not going to let this go. "Still, it does obligate her to you."

"It's a gift," he stated emphatically. "I don't consider gifts to be contracts."

Tension was mounting rapidly in the room but Didier entered then, to serve the salad course. They thanked him, one by one, then sat in silent contemplation of their plates.

When they were alone again, Annie whispered a plea, "Please don't do this. You're not rivals, this isn't a competition."

Mike gripped the stem of his wine goblet and violently swirled the liquid in the bowl, splashing a bit of it onto the tablecloth. Andrew clenched his jaw as he struggled to rein in his anger.

When Annie looked to Mike, she could see that he was ready to erupt, so after a hard swallow, she asked him, "Is there something you want to say?"

He planted his glass on the table with the force of a hammer blow. It broke the delicate stem and spilled the remainder of the contents, but no one moved to handle it.

"This is a farce, isn't it?" he shouted. "I'm in some ridiculous situation comedy, aren't I? But where's the canned laughter? I don't hear the laughter!"

They glared at him in silence.

He had wanted it to be different, but the way it had gone—the pride he had had crammed down his throat—left him with no other choice. "Well maybe I can get a laugh with this," he decided to say. "I put something to Andrew earlier that I'm going to say to you. He's very calm about this whole, damned thing because he's in the cat-bird's seat. Here he sits, on his own turf, his servants scurrying about, dangling treasure in front of you. The way things stand it's his game, because tonight you'll go to his bed. I think he needs to change places with me and see things from my perspective before we decide on any arrangement. And you, with all your declarations of love," he said scornfully, "you and I haven't slept together for months, so this entire thing about you being able to love us both is mere theory. If this is for real we need to put the theory to the test, before we go any further with it, before we make any of these god-damned, fucking impossible decisions." Since his was now a stain on the table linen, Mike reached for Annie's wine. She had closed her eyes midway through his rant, so he demanded to know of her, "Are you listening?"

In a barely audible tone, she answered, "What do you want to do?"

He finished what was left in her glass, before telling her, "I want you to come back to the hotel with me. I want to see the proof of what you claim."

Andrew's fury was barely containable, but with classic British restraint, he said, "I must say, Mike, that's a damned ugly approach."

He responded mockingly. "Well, old man, sorry to offend you, but there are some things you just can't make pretty."

Annie's heart was fluttering and sinking. "When we sleep to-gether again, it should be out of love, Mike, not because we need to prove something."

He almost laughed. "That's a nice sentiment, isn't it? But I see a barrier here, one that needs breaking before we can even ap-proach that place. You slept with Glenn—you proved you could do the sex on the side thing—big, fucking deal," he scoffed. "But that's no proof of emotion, and it in no way proves that can you love two men as deeply as you claim to." He felt he had gotten his point across and he stared her down with it.

It was damned near impossible to swallow, let alone breathe, but she could still think and the logic in what he said was undeniable. Remembering her words to Andrew about protecting themselves from disease, she abruptly questioned, "That woman you were with, did you use protection?"

He responded smugly: "To the extreme."

"I don't ever want to be in the position of worrying about that again, Mike—not ever."

"I can assure you, I'm safe and healthy. I went through all that with you, remember?" His head snapped toward Andrew. "What about lover boy here? Surely he hasn't been celibate."

Andrew felt as though he were in a nightmare, one he couldn't rouse himself from—sitting at a luncheon table with Annie and her husband, negotiating how they would work out the sharing of her. It was inconceivable and insane, and yet he answered, "I've been tested recently—I'm in perfect health."

"Good," was all Mike could find to say in response.

Annie looked to Andrew now, whose complexion had blanched with distress. "If I go, will you be all right?"

He could only stare at her.

"There has to be a first time," she whispered, as though Mike might not hear. "Surely the first time is the worst."

"This is not what I want," he said, his eyes unable to leave hers.

She looked to Mike again, and a thought hardened her expression. "Are you doing this to hurt him?"

"No," he told her. "I can honestly answer that as no. In fact, right now, I feel rather sorry for him." And as incredible as it seemed, he did.

"Then what the hell is going on with you?" she railed at him. "Was the reason you came here to get back at me?"

Mike pounded the table with a fist, rattling the dishes and startling Annie. "Let's get at least one fucking thing straight today, shall we? Do you think for one, fucking second, that I'd be sitting here, putting myself through the humiliation of having lunch with you and your lover if I hadn't realized that I love and need you, and want you back in my life?" His body flushed with intense heat: the fever of vehemence.

Andrew already knew this, so he was not surprised to hear it said. Still, the emotional power behind Mike's declaration affected him like a punch in the gut. He had to respond to it somehow and when he did, his voice was the calmest of the three, though his insides may well have been undergoing the most upheaval. "Annie, you don't have to do this—there has to be another way."

Her husband's impassioned words left her in a tailspin. "Give me some time alone with Andrew," she demanded of him. "Go for a walk or something, go see the distillery; Didier can run you over there, if you like. When you come back, I'll go with you to the hotel."

Mike glanced at Andrew, and his wretched expression struck at his heart; in that instant, he decided he could no longer be party to his torment. "All right. I'll see you later." His chair scraped across the marble floor as he wiped his mouth, then flung his napkin at the table. Without looking back, he left the dining room.

She rose from her seat and walked to Andrew; her legs felt leaden and her heart even heavier. Reaching out her hand to him, she pleaded, "Please, come upstairs with me."

Andrew stood near the open balcony doors, watching as Didier and Mike left for the distillery. When they were out of sight, he turned his attention to Annie, who sat on the edge of their bed, staring at the floor.

He sat next to her, saying, "This is impossible, Annie. What you want, it can never work."

She brought his hand to her heart and closed her eyes tightly. "God, but it feels awful in here."

"Don't do this to yourself, don't do this to us."

As she lay back upon the bed, tears dropped straight to the pillow from the corners of her eyes. "I have to try," she told him, "I can't do anything but try. You heard what he said—he's never declared his love for me like that before. I might have agreed with you, had he not said those things, but they're the words I've always wanted to hear. I can't, I won't turn away from him now."

Andrew nestled next to her, and took her in his arms. He understood—God knows he would rather have not—but he did. Her betrayed husband had swallowed more pride than any man should ever have to do, and come to see her—living now with another man — because he wanted to tell her how much he loved and needed her. It would be beyond cruel to reject him now, it would be savagely sadistic, and Annie would have to be utterly soulless.

He wiped her damp cheeks with his hand, and as he did, realized how very much he wanted to be inside of her. Covering her face and throat with the tenderest of kisses, he slowly began to undress her, while her tears continued unabated.

Andrew stayed in the bed while she packed a small overnight bag. He studied the curves of her body as she bent and twisted and moved about the room, trying to commit them to memory, though they were already etched there.

When she was ready, she asked, "Will you come downstairs with me?"

He answered simply, "No."

"I'll see you in the morning, then," she told him.

He turned his face away when she walked toward the door, and because he could not hold her, he clutched at the sheets, nearly ripping them through.

Mike had come back some time ago and settled himself in the salon. When he saw his wife standing in the foyer, he knew immediately that they had made love. The realization tore at him, but he managed to ask, "Ready?"

She nodded slightly.

"Andrew not coming down? I wanted to say good-bye."

"It's too hard for him," she knew.

His empathy welled up again as he recalled Andrew's admission the night they had dinner in Philadelphia. He quietly observed, "It must feel something like the time you went off and slept with that John fellow."

"How'd you know about that?"

"He told me the night we met."

"Oh God—" she responded, repeating it in her head. She was holding to her overnight bag and it dropped to the floor, as her body began to move in the direction of the stairs. Everything within her said to go back to him, not to leave him like this, and just as she was about to mutter —*I can't go with you, Mike*—she saw her husband's face, and realized how very deeply that would hurt him. In these critical moments, the torrents of emotion flowing through her were so powerful and contradictory, her physical self seemed to shut down, and she felt suddenly paralyzed.

Mike recognized how torn she was, and he was not without sympathy. But dammit all, he needed her, too, so he strode toward her, bent to lift her bag, then gently took hold of her arm, saying as he led her away, "He's a big boy, he'll be all right."

When they exited the house, Annie looked toward their bedroom balcony. It was lifeless and silent, but just beyond it, from inside the room, she could feel the approaching storm.

Twenty-Two

In Mike's suite there were flowers that had not been there before. There was also a room service cart with a cold supper and wine.

He smiled self-consciously, as he admitted, "I called ahead."

"You didn't need to do this," she told him, attempting her own smile.

He affected perplexity. "Is Andrew the only one allowed to seduce you?" Standing opposite her, reading her face as she stared blankly at the dinner cart, he said, "You know, you put me in mind of a condemned woman just now—looking at her last meal."

"I'm sorry—it's just so hard—I knew it would be—but—"

He smiled again. "You're making my point, aren't you?" He seated himself on the couch, then patted it to beckon her to sit.

When she did, she looked through his eyes. Their soft brown seemed deeper than usual, and she imagined she saw something dark behind them.

He allowed her the probing look, before questioning, "What is it you see?"

"I see what you're doing—I see you trying to teach me a lesson."

"Oh? Is that it?"

He leaned in closer and as he did, she could smell the distinct aroma of his flesh. It had been warm today, and with all the stress he'd undergone, his scent put her in mind of summer days at their home, when he'd just come in from his run. It reminded her of the early days of their marriage—of the times when she would join him in the shower, making love to him with her mouth, under the steam and running water.

He sensed that she was remembering something about their time together; he leaned in and kissed her neck in a way he knew she liked, then waited for her reaction.

When it came, it was not what he expected. "OK," she said flatly, "Andrew's not here, so no more posturing. Let's do this straight, with as much honesty as we can bear. We owe that to one another, don't you think?"

He moved slightly away, saying, "All right," then settled himself into the corner of the couch.

She seized him with her eyes. "You challenged me because you doubt me, but that should cease as of this moment, because what I've risked by coming here—the hurt I've caused Andrew— that should put all doubts to rest."

His eyes lowered as he considered this, then he told her, "There's no more doubt."

"Good. And there should be no more hiding behind anger or fear or whatever, because that's all total bullshit—it's a fucking waste of our time."

He sat up a little straighter and went back to her eyes.

"Because you and I both know what it is to have someone you love with your heart and soul taken from you. So you should understand why you're not going to persuade me to change my mind about this— I won't choose to suffer through another loss, I just plain won't do it."

He allowed her words to resonate in him, before he asked, "Not even if I told you that I love you more than I've ever loved anyone, even Michele?"

That was completely unexpected, and it shocked her. "Do you really believe that?"

The open, vulnerable man she had caught glimpses of in the past few days made a sudden reappearance, as even his physical self seemed to soften in this moment. "With all the garbage I've had to wade through in that psychiatrist's office, it's one of the most important things I've discovered."

She closed her eyes, but the echo of those words stayed with her. There were so many thoughts just now, it was hard to sort anything out. But before she would respond, she had to get this absolutely straight, in case he had any idea that what he said would change things. In a hushed voice, she told him, "I can't leave him, Mike, not yet." When she looked at him again, she could plainly see his pain and bewilderment, so she explained, "He needs me, he really needs me. You've never needed me like he does."

You're wrong about that — he said to himself — *very wrong.*

"And I need him," she continued, "because he gives me something I've been desperate for."

It was forced sarcasm she heard, when he flippantly inquired, "And what's that?"

She hated doing this to him, but it needed to be said. "He lays his insides bare, he shares himself with me, the good and the bad, he lets me know him."

"And I don't?"

"You only go as far as absolutely necessary, then the walls go up, every time. Like right now, I know you want to be close but you still can't let yourself go that distance."

He seemed intensely frustrated, when he told her, "Christ, at least give me credit for trying." Then something occurred to him that he wanted her to know, that would show her he was changing. "That woman I was with, she was beautiful and smart and made all the right moves, and I gave in because I wanted to see what there was for me after you. But when she came to spend the night with me, I couldn't do it, I couldn't get hard, and all that happened — well, she gave me a blow job. But there was nothing afterward — nothing but emptiness and remorse." He lowered his voice to add, "I found myself longing for you, for that connection we always had."

She started to say something, but stopped herself because she knew she'd been hurtful enough.

Her reluctance was not lost on him. "Go on, say it; we're to be honest, aren't we?"

OK — she decided — *he's right, and better to get this out now.* "Not in the beginning, but as time went on, as you withdrew from me, that emptiness you described — I'd feel that after being with you."

Her words plunged into him; they were a jagged sword, twisting in his gut. "It was how I survived," came out of his pain.

"I came to understand that, Mike, and that's why I let it go," she told him. "That's why I gave up trying to make it different."

He had never said this to anyone, and in recent years he hadn't even let it into his consciousness, but it was a bitter, buried truth, something he now realized that she should understand about him. "I had some very bleak days after Michele's murder, Annie, very bleak months. I would have put a gun to my head, had I not cut myself off from my feelings. The fact that I didn't own a gun saved my life."

In all their years together, he had never even hinted that things had been that bad. His revelation was jolting, and it cast her back in time, made her see him—not as he was now—but as he was when they first met: living alone with Michele's possessions, her clothing-filled closet still carrying faint traces of her perfume, the hairbrush she had used on that last morning still near her sink, tenaciously holding what remained of her blonde locks. And there were the crib and changing table that gathered dust in the silent, dark nursery, the pastel animals of the layette peeking from behind the cellophane windows of their boxes, still waiting for the baby who would never come.

Annie had carried these memories and images throughout their life together: They were the excuse, the wedge, the barrier to their intimacy. But she had never imagined that the bereaved husband and father who stared out the window of his den, watching her and her small son in the park, was contemplating how he would kill himself.

"You never told me this," she murmured, over the aching in her heart.

He was recalling that time more vividly than he wanted to, so he bolstered his courage and tried to force it from his mind. "When I shut down the feelings, I put those memories away, too," he told her. "Anyway, you didn't need my garbage. You had enough struggles of your own."

There it was in a nutshell—the root of all their problems. "Oh God, Mike, you're so wrong about that. People in love don't see their partner's problems and needs as garbage. It's a gift when someone trusts you enough to share those things with you, a downright gift!"

He shook his head. "I saw it as weakness. I wanted to be strong for you and Marc."

"Sharing those things about yourself would have made you stronger," she knew with certainty. "It would have made us all stronger."

"I hated what I was inside," he remembered. "I was weak and broken and guilty. That's why I went after winning my cases with such vigor, so no one would see what was inside. And the last person I ever wanted to see there was you. I thought that if you knew the real me, you'd leave."

She asked herself — *How could he have felt that way? Did I send him the wrong message because I depended so much on his strength?*

"No, honey, no," she insisted. "I would have loved you more, and deeper. And that guilt Mike, I could have helped you with it, if only you'd have let me."

What he said next was what had hit him the hardest in therapy, when, after weeks of struggle, he'd looked inside and realized: "All those years we might have been moving in a very different direction, we might have grown closer and more in love, but we didn't, because I lacked the courage to act beyond my fears."

"We both lacked that courage," she said. "I should have fought harder for you, tried harder to find you."

Even if it sounded whining and childish, he knew he had to tell her this: "But you're turning away from me now. I've come to you to bare my soul and you're shunning me in favor of him." His eyes were beginning to sting, and he rubbed at them.

Watching him fend off tears, brought on her own. *Dear God,* she lamented, *to see him this way, to know that he was protecting me — that he didn't want me to think less of him — God — how could we have grown so far apart, when all we ever really wanted was the other's love?*

"I don't mean to do that," she whispered.

His eyes and throat burning intolerably, he pleaded with her, "Then let me in, Annie, let me be with you again, it's my only hope."

The man sitting next to her — he was her husband — but he wasn't. He was more like the man she thought she'd married, the one who seemed to be an illusion after a time: She had always longed to see that man again.

She may have been deluding herself, but the longer she looked into his tormented eyes, the more she inhaled the scent of him, the more she believed. Slowly, she reached her arms around him, and put her mouth to his.

At first he didn't move his lips, but when he kissed her back, it was with painfully raw sentiment. That experience was compelling, it was both liberating and terrifying, and he wanted to know more of it. He reached deeper within himself, and when he connected with his feelings for her, it was as though he'd tapped into a geyser. For there was more to them now, more than just the love and need; there was the anguish he still felt over her betrayal, and the fear that she would only continue to hurt him. And it was still there—the big one, the intimacy killer—the ever-present terror of losing someone he needed so very much. As their kiss deepened, his emotions grew more powerful, even more dangerous, seeming to overflow and spill into her.

Annie responded to the rare sensation of it, to the acuteness and urgency of her husband's emotions, and with her heart aching and racing, she invited him to take them deeper. She leaned backward and pulled him with her, then reached to unzip his trousers. When she held him in her hand, he groaned and closed his eyes.

But he raised himself and pulled away, asking, "Are you sure this is what you want?"

She nodded and rose from the couch, took his hand in hers, and led him to the bedroom. When she began to undress in front of him, he did the same. They climbed into bed and in their awkwardness pulled the covers over themselves. They lay at first without touching, and it might have been any night in their struggling marriage, but it wasn't, because Andrew was there now, very much between them. But after a few silent moments, Mike banished him from his thoughts and reached out for his wife.

It was still there in his kiss, that raw urgency, and it made Annie brush aside her own thoughts of Andrew and pull her husband in. He buried his face between her neck and shoulder, shuddering when he entered her, grasping her upper arms to steady himself. She wrapped herself securely around him, so that she might shelter him, body and soul.

But then, as he began to move inside of her, he became aware of the presence of an unusual amount of moisture. In a moment of shock he realized that it was what Andrew had given her: He hesitated, lifting himself slightly away so that their eyes could meet. Over the pounding in his chest and the emotions that were cascading out of him, he was driven to say, "It doesn't matter—" and then, to plunge himself deeper.

She understood what he was telling her, and for only the second time in her life—since knowing this depth of intimacy with Andrew—she felt the wholeness of her being, and the completeness of love.

It was late morning when Annie returned to Château d'Audine, and the iron gates at the entrance made a reassuringly solid clang as she closed them behind her car. She drove rather quickly up the drive and leapt up the stairs to the house. The rooms were silent and Andrew was nowhere to be seen. She discerned familiar aromas that told her Lisette was preparing lunch, so she went into the kitchen. Didier was peeling potatoes for Lisette and they were uncharacteristically cool toward their mistress.

"Bonjour," she said.

"Bonjour, Madame," they returned.

"Where's Andrew?"

They looked at each other before Didier answered, "We haven't seen him, Madame, since you left yesterday."

Her heart seized when she heard that, but she managed to leave the kitchen.

The bed was made but that meant nothing; Lisette did that first thing every day. She looked for his suitcase—it was still there—then fearing he may have left without it, she searched the room for a note. When she found nothing, she went out onto the balcony and scanned the grounds. The pool suddenly beckoned her, and she went there next.

She found him sitting inside the cottage, his back to her, a book opened in his lap. He was not reading it, he was staring out the window, and although it was a sunny day, all the lamps had been left on.

"Andrew—"

He couldn't answer her, his heart was too full from the sound of her voice. He had survived the night and she had returned to him, and this time there had been no storm, no destructive rampage of wind, only the incessant chants of crickets calling through the night, as though to lead him to the day.

When he did not turn to face her, she walked around to the front of his chair, and in one seemingly continuous movement, sat at his feet and rested her head in his lap. Absentmindedly, as though she had been there with him all along, he began to stroke her hair; the night had been interminable, and her presence had brought it to an end.

And when he spoke to her, it was as though there had only been a brief interruption in their conversation. "I almost left after you did. I called the crew and told them to be ready, but then I changed my mind."

"Thank you my love, thank you for staying."

He kissed her hair and with the kiss, detected an unfamiliar fragrance. "I thought about before, in St. Andrews, when I kept away from you. I didn't want to do that again."

"Thank you for not leaving me." The enormous relief she felt made her cry.

She could hear the exhaustion in his voice, when he told her, "We're in a hell of a predicament, the three of us."

She meant to sound certain, but her voice faltered as she responded, "We're in a much better place today than we were yesterday, my love."

"Are we?"

"I believe so," she said, wiping away the tears.

He continued to stroke her head. "What time is it?"

"Just past noon."

Throughout the night, he'd been riding out an emotional tempest, and had struggled to maintain some sense of reality. "I've been out here all night," he said, "I should have a shower."

"Stay a minute, please." She looked to his face; there were dark circles under the somber blue. "It's going to be all right, Andrew, I know it is."

"How do you know that?" he wondered.

"We're moving in the right direction," she thought to say now, "not the easy one, but the right one."

"I hope so. It's an awful price to pay, if it's not." He spread the fingers of his hand so that he might gather up strands of her hair. "Such a beautiful color. I've always been fascinated by the way it catches the light."

Annie smiled through her anguish. "I have to work at keeping it that way."

"Do you? I couldn't tell."

"The grays are setting in." She tried to elicit a smile from him, but it was impossible, and what she discerned in his face made her ask, "What's been going through your mind?"

He sighed. "I've been thinking about how things change. No matter how hard we try to keep certain, precious things, it's inevitable that we lose them."

Her arms resting on his knees, she looked far into his eyes to tell him, "You haven't lost me, Andrew. What I did last night I had to do, for myself, for Mike, but maybe most of all, I had to do that for you."

The pain in his eyes kept them unfocused. "I want things to be more simple," he told her.

She shook her head in dismay. "They always had other things in mind for us. From the start, they never gave us anything simple."

"Your gods." He took several deliberate breaths before he asked her, "How'd you leave it with Mike?"

I must do this carefully—she warned herself—*he seems so very fragile right now.* "We left it with love and tenderness, that we both needed to feel from one another. But about the last thing he said to me, before we parted, was that he understood about us, and that he'd do nothing to interfere with that."

Andrew's next breath was easier. "When will you see him again?"

"He wants to make it soon, but he can't say. We're planning for me to take Marc home in August, and we'll all go to our beach house for a couple of weeks."

"That'll be nice for Marc," he said, as though it didn't hurt.

"He loves Mike very much."

"And you—you love Mike very much."

"I do love him," she admitted, "but I struggle with that love. It wasn't easy being with him last night, but it was worthwhile and honest."

Throughout the night he'd been imagining it, seeing them naked together, their bodies moving in the familiar rhythm of husband and wife, but he had told himself he would not pry. But seeing her now, observing the glow in her cheeks, inhaling the different scent she carried, he could not help himself asking, "How many times did you make love?"

"Oh, Andrew—please," she pleaded, "don't torture yourself with this."

"I want to know, Annie," he insisted, connecting to her eyes again.

Looking into his, she whispered, "Three."

He suddenly let go of her hair and brought both of his hands to cover his face. In the next instant she stood and put her arms around his torso, then pulled him up from the chair. She held onto him like he had held her at the pond while she screamed. His scream, however, was inaudible.

"Trust me to do the right thing for us," she begged him. "I can't bear the thought of us being separated any more than you can."

He let his hands fall away as he said, "I thought I would die last night, for want of you."

She kissed his forehead, his temples, his nose and cheeks, and finally his lips, saying, "What we have can't be touched by anyone else. It can't be altered or taken away, and we have to trust in that." She kissed him again and probed his mouth with her tongue. Then, because her words did not seem to comfort him, she backed away and removed her clothing.

He ran his hands along her shoulders and arms, saying, "Such strong shoulders. I need your strength, Annie, I always have."

She helped him undress, and with delicate urgency, pulled him to the floor. She lay back on the carpet and as she reached for him, he told her, "There's a different scent to you."

Sitting up now, she said, "I've had a shower, but I'll go have another."

He gripped her arm as she was about to stand, "No, don't. It's not unpleasant, it's just different." Lying her back again, he tenderly separated her labia, then inserted his fingers. The sensation it carried to Annie was that of an examination.

In the next seconds, he underwent the same shock Mike had, as he realized what it was he was feeling. It might have been repulsive, it could well have been upsetting — but surprisingly, it was neither of these things. And what it was, was incredibly intimate, on a level deeper than anything he had ever experienced. Annie had been with her husband because she loved him, and now she was back with him, to say again how much she loved *him*, to make certain that he knew it.

He withdrew his fingers and in a wildly erotic impulse, painted her mouth with them. She parted her lips and made a little gasping sound, as she recognized the taste of her husband. Her response made him repeat the action, this time giving her his fingers to suck.

Like a becalmed schooner that is suddenly captured by a gale, the powerful sensuality in what they were doing grabbed hold of them. In the next moments he hardened and throbbed unbearably, and as he entered her, he put his mouth to hers. With the sharing of that kiss, they went plunging over the edge.

He lifted his mouth away and hovered over her, sighing, "God, how I love you."

"Oh, Andrew," she sighed, "I've never felt this whole, this loved." Mike and Andrew had given themselves completely to her — they had let themselves be vulnerable and trusted her to take them where there were no rules, no boundaries. It had to be the most liberating moment of her life; she had never felt more desired, never been more free.

A fantasy began to form in her mind; she imagined Mike was there with them. He had just made love to her — in front of Andrew — and now he was giving her to him, watching as Andrew entered her, then leaning in to kiss her mouth.

From the depths of her belly, she moaned and sighed, swept away by the fantasy. She had left the constraints and conventions of the pedestrian world behind: She was Europa, giving herself to the bull, embracing the dangerous and taboo.

"I know what you're feeling," Andrew whispered to her, his heart pounding with fierce strength. "I feel it, too."

They clung to one another, in a frenzied, yet synchronous dance, until they reached what they sought. Their coming together now was like an imploding star, far off in the heavens, that drew everything else into it, into the fathomless gravity of its newly formed reality. It transcended the physical and left them in a place they had never before been, in a forbidden, secret corner of the universe. Annie had led them there, she had taken Mike and Andrew and led them where they would not have gone but for her, where it was darkly compelling, and disturbingly beautiful.

As they lay in the aftermath of their passion, Mike was boarding his flight in Pau. Having just used it for their trip to Barcelona, he recognized Andrew's jet as it sat on the tarmac: it meant that he was with her, that he hadn't left the château as he'd imagined he might. He couldn't help but picture them together now, Annie's naked body sunken into the sheets, Andrew's hands exploring the very places Mike had just been. That image might well have unsettled and angered him, but as the plane lifted off and left behind the beautiful city of Pau, he discovered to his surprise, that he was not only comfortable with it, he was aroused by it.

Twenty-Three

He was supposed to go to London on Tuesday to confer with the Prime Minister, but he postponed it. Nigel was back from his holiday and they were supposed to meet on Wednesday, but he canceled that. There were numerous other things that needed his attention that week but they were all put off, because Andrew could no more leave Annie than he could swim the ocean.

What they had begun with Mike's visit they continued, seeking refuge from the world in their lovemaking, and uncovering more of the mysteries of their secret universe. They denied themselves nothing, letting their bodies take charge and bring them wherever they would, into things they had never before done, into carnal pleasures so deep they might have drowned in them.

On one warm, lazy afternoon, as they lay napping after lunch, Mike phoned. His tone was relaxed and seductive, sounding very much as he used to in the beginning, when he first began to love her. "Annie," he simply said, then breathed in as he waited for her response.

She had merely turned in the bed to answer the phone, and with her back to Andrew, she sighed into the receiver, "Mike," her body tingling in response.

In the days before Mike's visit, Andrew would ordinarily have removed himself to give them privacy. But that no longer seemed necessary, and indeed, a rather empty gesture, so he nestled in and enfolded her with his arms.

Mike said to her, "I'm not interrupting anything, am I?"

She yawned, then answered, "We were just having a nap." Reaching her free hand to rub Andrew's thigh, she questioned, "How was your return flight?"

"Fine," he told her. "There were ten whole passengers on the flight."

"Everything all right at home?"

"Yeah—Lucy says hi, and Buddy ran around for an hour to show me how much he missed me."

"What a good dog," she said, laughing slightly. "And the office? How's it going there?"

"I've started making some changes," he told her, "that's what I called about actually. I met with the other partners and told them that I want to back away from the litigations, get more into the boardroom stuff, the mergers and acquisitions."

She wondered, "How'd they take it?"

"Fairly well, but I think they've decided that I'm in a midlife crisis that'll pass."

"They could be right."

"We'll see." Assuming that Andrew was beside her he almost didn't say this, but then he decided—*what the hell*—*I'm in this deep, I might as well go deeper.* "It's been hard for me to think of anything else since we were together—our lovemaking—it struck me very differently." He didn't wait for a response, and was a little tentative when he next said, "There's the possibility that I'll be in London in a week or so, do you think we might get together if I am?"

"Of course," she answered, "just let me know."

He sounded relieved. "Good, because there's much more we need to say," he told her, then added impulsively, "I take it you two weathered my visit well enough. I meant what I said about keeping clear of that. I'm not going to ask you to give him up."

"You and I have a better chance if you don't."

"For me it's pretty much come down to one thing," he said, "can I live with it?"

"We need more time together for you to know that."

"That's why I'm hoping to see you in London."

"I'll make every effort to be there," she assured him, then added, "I love you, Mike, and I thank you for being who you are."

He concluded their conversation with, "And you know how I feel about you."

She sighed as she moved to replace the receiver, then rested her head on the pillow again. Andrew lifted her hair and kissed her warm, slightly damp skin, just at the hairline; the scent of her was at once aphrodisiac and tonic, and as he filled his lungs with her, he hardened against the flesh of her buttocks.

Mike sat with his hand on the telephone, lingering there as though it still connected him to Annie. He let himself miss her, and with the ache that came of his longing, he experienced an intense desire to rekindle their intimacy, to feel again her baby-soft skin, to suckle her full breasts and taste her mouth, to lose himself in the warm moistness of her depths. He closed his eyes and conjured up the memory of their night together in France, of passionately making love to her as he hadn't done in years, but when he opened them again he was forced to remember where she was in this moment: in bed with Andrew, the two of them most certainly naked in the afternoon heat. In his mind's eye he now pictured Andrew nuzzling against her back, and what he next envisioned—and what was in reality happening an ocean away—made him want her all the more.

When they were up and about, Andrew told her, "I've an idea for us today. Let's get in the car and head off somewhere, find a secluded spot for dinner in the countryside. What do you say?"

She loved the idea. "Let's do that, and let's throw our toothbrushes and a change of clothes in a bag, in case we want to stay overnight."

"You're on."

They headed northeast; it was a sultry summer afternoon and the driving couldn't have been nicer. With no particular destination in mind, they merely followed the road, but Annie soon thought of a place she'd like to go.

"We're headed toward Pech Merle," she realized, "have you ever been there?"

"No. I was in Perigord once, years ago, with Claudine, but we didn't get down there."

"I was there on Percy," she informed him. "The Lot River Valley is amazingly beautiful—I must have written you from there."

"You did," he just recalled. "You sent me a postcard with the spotted horses on it. It was one of the ones Ambrose had."

The memory was bittersweet. "I wanted you with me so badly. Everywhere I went, every time I saw something beautiful, I'd think — 'God, how I wish I could share this with Andrew.'"

He smiled tenderly, saying, "Then let's go there. We'll go there and you can share it with me now."

Annie took the map from the glove box. "According to this, we're halfway there." She thought back to what he'd said about Claudine. "You traveled with Claudine?"

"No, not really," he responded. "Sometimes we'd stay at friends' places, friends of hers. There's a countess in Sarlat with whom she's very close. It was less risky, staying at private houses."

"When you were with her, how long would you stay?"

"Most often it was just overnight, but every so often I'd manage a couple of days. At the countess's château in Sarlat," he remembered, "Claudine stayed there for three weeks once, and I must have visited her four or five times. Why do you ask?"

"I don't know," she answered at first, then admitted, "I guess I'm jealous."

He laughed to hear her say that. "Why?"

"Well, let's see," she teased, raising her fingers to count on them. "She had you for so many years, she had you when you were younger, she spent countless hours making love with you . . ."

"Well, I'm envious of Glenn," he informed her, "and Mike. I would have liked to have been both of them."

Now she laughed. "If you'd been Mike, there wouldn't have been any need for Glenn."

The thought that followed upon her declaration, sobered him. "I'm not so certain of that," he said. "Your husband was painfully honest when he questioned if he could ever be enough for you, and I have to confess, I've had moments when I've wondered that about myself."

Looking away and out the window, she sighed. "It's true I need a lot — more than most women, I think."

Still driving, he reached for her hand and brought it to his lips. After he kissed it, he told her, "And I thank God that you're not most women."

They passed the prehistoric site of the Grotte du Pech Merle —
which was closed for the day — and followed a narrow road that led
into a shadowy woods. They'd seen a sign advertising an inn some
miles back and decided to pursue it, and when they reached the place
Annie squealed with delight. It was completely isolated in a deep
woods, near a wonderfully noisy tributary of the Lot river, with an expansive lawn that was naturalized like a meadow. The late afternoon
sun cut through the tall trees and split across the lawn, casting shadows that were like dancing silhouettes on the green. As they emerged
from the car, the distinct call of a cuckoo greeted them.

"God it's perfect," she declared, "it's absolutely perfect! I'll die
if they don't have a vacancy!"

Seeing her reaction, he was only half-joking when he responded, "Not to worry, I'll buy the place if they don't."

When they were in their quaint, old room, Annie threw herself backward on the bed, which was a tall, canopied affair, with
brocade curtains all around. The walls of the room were exposed
fieldstone and the furnishings all old and heavy and rustic. There
was a slightly musty odor to the air, but it was in keeping with the
antiquity of the place.

"God, I love it!"

"I love you," he answered.

"Come here." She held out her arms and he dropped into
them. "This is what I dreamed of, you know. I could never afford
to stay in places like this when I was on Percy, but I saw enough of
them. I'd try to imagine what they were like inside, and then I'd
think of being there with you. And now here we are, finally! It's too
delicious!"

"You're delicious." He planted kisses all over her throat.

"What a great idea you had, Baron, taking us for an outing.
After we see the grotto tomorrow, we should drive on and find another place. I like being a nomad with you and where no one can
find us."

He rolled away from her. "Tomorrow's Friday, isn't it?"

"I think so, I lose track of time when we're together."

It wasn't that he'd forgotten to tell her this, it was because he
hadn't wanted to think of leaving her. "Maggie's pony club is having

their gymkhana on Saturday, and she's very keen on having her dad there. I told her I'd come."

Smiling and smoothing back his hair, she answered, "No matter. That's more important, we can go off again anytime."

In a quiet voice, he said, "Thank you for being so understanding about my children."

She lost a bit of her smile, when she responded, "It gets taken from you so quickly—childhood, I mean. It should be nurtured and protected, while there's still time."

He reached for the hand that stroked his head and kissed the palm of it, then the wrist and along the forearm. "We've a couple of hours before dinner, what shall we do with our time?"

"My dear Baron, do you really have to ask?"

They shared a pleasant meal in the hotel restaurant, having ordered from the regional specialties: trout from the Lot, wild boar and mushrooms from the forest, and a sinful gateau, drenched in a walnut liqueur from a local distiller. There were four other couples in the dining room and no rush on anyone's part; courses arrived slowly and lingered, wine flowed freely, candles burned down and were replaced. The conversations were hushed and the night was full of woodland music that drifted in through the windows and lulled its listeners into a trance. When at last they left the dining room, they strolled out to the meadow to be closer to the orchestra. As the night deepened, so did the melodies—the delicate rustle of leaves, the rolling trill of frogs, the serenade of a nightingale—all lending to the harmony of a perfect night.

They stood listening for some time, before Annie whispered to her lover, "This kind of happiness—it's worth everything."

Both his arms were around her waist, and she held onto his forearms. "It's worth all we've paid—and then some," he told her.

"This night, this place, they're a part of us now."

"Like Château d'Audine, and all our days there."

"Thank you for all of it, Andrew—thank you for giving this to me."

The way she said that—it almost seemed as though she was saying good-bye. He felt his throat closing with that idea and it made it damned difficult to tell her, "Annie, all the thanks — I owe you so much —" but was unable to continue.

"Listen," she said, holding tighter to his arms. "They're singing to us, they're singing us a lullaby."

She heard the rattle of the breakfast tray and opened her eyes to see Andrew, already showered and dressed, coming through the door with it.

He greeted her with, "Well, sleeping beauty, it's about time. It's going on half past nine."

Annie yawned and stretched, as she responded, "It's all this contentment, it makes one rather somnolent."

"Hungry, my love?" he asked, as he waited for her to arrange herself.

"I think so — ready for coffee anyway. What's the weather like?"

"Splendid — as splendid as the sight of you, naked in this bed." He handed her a large café au lait.

As she brought the cup to her mouth, the aroma turned her stomach; it smelled as though they'd used some chemical to clean the pot and hadn't rinsed it well. "This doesn't smell very good," she said.

He took it from her for a whiff. "Smells fine to me."

She tried again but had to put it down. "I think I'll just do the juice this morning."

"As you wish, but we'd better get a move on, the grotto closes for lunch."

They thoroughly enjoyed their tour of the prehistoric cave, where they saw drawings believed to be from about 15,000 B.C. It was an incredible experience, visiting this place where man saw his civilized beginnings, where he transitioned from nomadic forager to nurturing community member. And it was enlightening to envision the life that would have been, here in the womb-like caverns, through the long, cold winters. Privacy would have been nonexistent, human functions handled in full view, nudity certainly prevalent, and sex performed at will, very likely in front of whomever, with whomever. Annie smiled to herself as she contemplated this hedonistic utopia, and wondered how long it had been before shame and modesty arrived, and the idea of monogamy took hold.

When they were in the car and heading home, Andrew questioned her about other things she'd done while traveling on Percy.

"Most of what I saw of France was around here," she told him. "I visited Cordes and Albi and Carcassonne — oh yeah, and St. Cirq-Lapopie. Have you been to any of them?"

"Carcassonne, once."

She frowned. "Let me guess, with Claudine?"

"That's a lovely shade of green you turn," he teased, "whenever she comes up. It goes nicely with your eyes. And no, I was on holiday with Janet and the children."

She winced at her blunder, saying, "Sorry."

"Were you traveling alone when you were here?" he wondered.

"My girlfriend Issie was with me," she informed him, "and we stayed overnight in most of those places, in the cheapest hotels we could find. But one night near Cordes, we decided to save money by sleeping outdoors." She giggled as she recalled, "We drove a few miles out of town to this isolated spot and laid our sleeping bags out, just before it got dark. We had no light save Percy's headlight, no flashlight or anything. When it got dark it got really dark, pitch-black. There were no houses or lights of any kind, not even a moon. We were right next to each other, Issie and I, and we couldn't see one another. We zipped up the bags and lay there with wide open eyes, getting more scared by the minute. Then we started to hear noises — rustling — like someone walking in the woods. It came closer and closer, then we saw these eerie red eyes; it scared the crap out of us. We both screamed and I jumped up and turned on the headlight; it ran off, whatever it was. We rolled up those sleeping bags faster than you'd ever think possible and headed for town, then got a room. When we told the people at the hotel what had happened, they said it was a good thing we got out of there, because there were wild boar in those woods."

He laughed heartily, before commenting, "That's quite a story."

"One of many," she chuckled.

When she said that, it made him recall, "You said you'd tell me sometime how you came to lose the knife I gave you. Will you tell me now?"

Annie had been smiling as she told the story of the night in the woods, but with this recollection her mood changed dramatically. "Only if you promise not to be upset," she told him.

He was instantly worried, and turned to see her face. "All right, I promise."

She had to give some thought as to how she would tell this. "Right after I wrote you that first letter, Issie and I left Saintes-Maries and went to Paris," she remembered. "We stayed a week — we found a very cheap room that turned out to be in the red light district."

He grinned. "That must have been interesting."

She nodded emphatically, saying, "It was. I'd get up at night to go to the communal toilet and run into the ladies and their customers. It was an education, seeing the kinds of men who came to do business: not the seedy types you'd expect, but respectable looking people. I even witnessed a well-dressed couple — man and woman — going into a room with a hooker. I was so intrigued by that one, I debated going to peep through the keyhole."

He laughed.

"When we left Paris we stopped briefly in Brussels," she continued, "then we went to Amsterdam. We weren't there long when we ran into some students from one of the universities."

"And?"

She glanced at him briefly, then looked away again. "We had intended to stay in a hostel, but they offered to let us stay in one of their dorm rooms — one of the guys said we could have his and he'd bunk with his buddy. We jumped at the chance of a free room, because obviously, the less we spent, the longer we could travel."

"They were guys?" he questioned.

"A whole group of Indonesian guys," she easily recalled, "who'd come to the university together. There was one in particular, Jeffrey, who was their leader. The guy whose room we stayed in told us that Jeffrey was the son of some very important person on Bali, and that Jeffrey's dad had paid for all of them to go to the university, so that his son would have friends from home." She frowned as she continued, "Jeffrey had all the money and he was generous with it. He'd treat us to meals and take us out to the discos, and showed us a good time, generally."

Recognizing that a frown should not have accompanied what she'd said, he asked, "But what happened? I know something happened."

"Jeffrey was interested in me, but I wasn't at all in him. I played along with it, though; after all, he was my benefactor." She grimaced, recalling her naive stupidity. "When Issie and I decided to leave, he tried to talk us into staying longer, but we'd been there a week and were ready to move on. Besides, I was anxious to get back to Saintes-Maries because I expected to hear from you," she said. "I even fancied that you might be there already, waiting for me."

He was growing more upset, and when he spotted a roadside picnic area ahead, he pulled the car into it. So that he might listen more intently he turned the engine off, then asked her, "What did he do to you?"

She couldn't look at him, so she stared at her knees. "On our last night they said they wanted to do something special, they wanted to make an Indonesian dinner for us, at Jeffrey's. Issie and I went over to meet them and they were all there."

There was something in his throat when he asked, "How many of them?"

"Six."

"You're scaring me, Annie—"

She still couldn't look at him. "They managed to take Issie off on the pretext of needing something from the store—the guy who was cooking insisted on taking her with him to get it. I got a really bad feeling and I tried to go, too, but they whisked Issie out of there faster than I could do or say anything. Jeffrey held my arm and said he wanted to talk, privately, in his bedroom. I tried not to go but the rest of them were standing there, glaring at me, and it scared the hell out of me. Jeffrey pulled me into the bedroom and they closed the door behind us. I could hear them on the other side, speaking in their language and chuckling."

Andrew had taken her hand when he'd stopped the car. He held it very tightly as he asked, "What happened?"

She closed her eyes to say, "He forced himself on me," then she opened them again. "At first I resisted, but inside of a minute, I knew what I had to do. What I kept thinking was, there's four other guys outside that door, four guys who are devoted to this creep, who'd do anything for him. They're not going to like it if they hear me fighting him. I knew I could end up in a much worse situation if I resisted."

His heart pounded out the growing anger he felt. "Didn't your friend come back?"

"They planned it well. She told me later that they'd gone to several different markets, supposedly in search of this one ingredient. It took a long time."

"What did he do to you?" he had to know.

"Nothing horrible, just had sex with me. I rattled on and on while he did it, I was so scared, I guess I needed to hear my own voice. When he decided he'd had enough he got up and unlocked the door—I was so grateful I think I even said thank you. When Issie came back I immediately pulled her out of there, because I was afraid for her, too. We raced to get our things from the other place and then tore the hell out of there on Percy. It wasn't until the next day that I realized I'd left your knife behind. That made everything worse. I hadn't cried before then but I broke down at that moment and just sobbed."

His rage and frustration building, he seethed, "I'd have killed him."

"He wasn't worth it," she said, in no uncertain terms. "And anyway, I considered myself damned lucky to get out of there as easily as I did. I could have been gang raped—or worse. The way that whole thing was orchestrated, there's no telling what might have happened." In a pointless attempt at lessening the awfulness of it, she suggested, "I'll never know, of course, but I think my nervous ramblings turned him off, maybe even made him a little sorry for me."

He shook his head and stared at the steering wheel, roiled with anger, thinking that he would like to locate this man and pound him senseless.

She could easily see what was going on inside of him, and reminded him, "You promised."

Despairingly now, he said to her, "I should have been with you, I should have been there to protect you. But I had to have been in hospital then, thinking of you every waking minute, praying for you to find out somehow and come to me."

"It's funny, isn't it, how things worked out."

"It's bloody tragic," he knew, absolutely. "My heart breaks for you."

"I know—I can feel it." But she had to tell him, "I learned an invaluable lesson, though, and I was much more cautious after that."

"That's a lesson no woman should have to learn. And God, to suffer through that twice!" he exclaimed, thinking of how she'd been raped at college.

She still cringed with the memory. "That was much worse. At least in Amsterdam I got out of there with my sanity."

They sat in silent contemplation for a time, holding hands while they gathered themselves. Then she asked, "When are you leaving for Scotland?"

He exhaled heavily. "I'd intended to go tonight, but now I think I'll leave at dawn. That'll get me there in time for breakfast."

"It's OK if you want to go tonight," she told him. "You don't have to stay with me. I'll be all right."

"But I won't." He reached to tuck a lock of hair behind her ear.

Didier and Lisette welcomed them as though they'd been gone for weeks. They had supper on the terrace under flickering stars, and went to bed about eleven. When four o'clock arrived, Andrew had to drag himself from her.

"It's always so difficult to leave you."

She took up both his hands and kissed them. "When can I expect you back?"

"Tomorrow night," he responded. "I want to have Sunday dinner with everyone—do you mind?"

"Not at all," she said. "Enjoy your children."

"I will."

They walked downstairs together and lingered in an embrace.

When she yawned, he told her, "You should go back up and get more sleep."

"You can count on that," she smiled.

"Soon, my love—"

"Soon—"

Annie was sleeping very soundly when she felt a hand touch her arm. Lisette was whispering, "Madame, forgive me, but something important—"

She was instantly gripped by terror and sat up, tugging the sheet to cover her nakedness. "Is Andrew all right? Please God, tell me nothing's happened to Andrew!" Her first thought was that his plane had crashed.

Recognizing how frightened she was, Lisette patted her arm. "No, Madame, it's not the count," she consoled, then hesitated before revealing, "it's the countess, she's downstairs and insisting on seeing you."

"The countess?"

They heard Didier's voice then, insistently calling after someone. Lisette opened the door to see what the ruckus was about and found Janet just outside it. Didier, red-faced beside her, was trying to persuade her to go back downstairs.

"Madame la Comtesse," Lisette scolded, "please!"

When Annie realized what was happening, she called to them, "It's all right, let her come in if that's what she wants."

Janet, attired in her usual masculine garb, pushed past the guards and into the bedroom where her husband had spent much of the last several weeks.

"It's all right," Annie said again to the couple. "The countess and I are acquainted with one another."

They clearly heard her, but remained standing in the doorway.

"Have you had your breakfast, Janet?" she asked, trying to diffuse the tension.

"I'd like some coffee," she answered, flatly.

"Could you bring us some, Didier?"

He nodded and turned away with his wife.

"Please close the door," she called to them, then reached to the floor to retrieve her gown, the pale pink one that Andrew loved her in. "Mind turning your back a moment?" she asked her visitor.

Janet obliged and looked toward the balcony doors. "I think my husband's whore is falsely modest," she scowled.

"I don't want to embarrass you, Janet." When she had donned the gown she rose from the bed, then walked toward the bathroom saying, "Make yourself at home—I'll just be a minute."

When she was alone, Janet surveyed the room, and in doing so, noticed some of her husband's clothing which had been left on a chair. She picked up the shirt and inhaled its scent, but when Annie returned she dropped it as though it were a filthy rag. Janet resumed her glaring stare at Annie, who now stood rather regally in the middle of the room, the silhouette of her body showing through the diaphanous gown.

She had considered getting dressed while she was in the bathroom, but then, defiantly, stayed in her night dress, telling herself: *She's barged into our bedroom and awakened me from a sound sleep, I'll be damned if I'm going to hustle around to accommodate her.*

Janet had remained standing, so Annie motioned her toward the sitting area, asking politely, "Won't you sit down?"

Janet occupied the chair as though she were angry with it. She began with, "This is all very cozy, isn't it? I imagine you're quite pleased with yourself and what you've got from my husband."

Lisette had to have made coffee in record time, for Didier was already knocking at the door. He set the tray on the table between them, then turned to his mistress, pointedly asking, "Do you require anything else, Madame?"

Annie deferred to her uninvited guest. "Janet?"

"Nothing," she uttered impatiently, then as an afterthought added a brusque, "thank you."

Didier left the room, but not before gesturing with his eyebrows, to let Annie know he'd be nearby.

Janet didn't wait to be served, so Annie seated herself on the love seat and tucked her legs beneath her. Once Janet had taken what she wanted, Annie leaned toward the table to stir milk and sugar into her cup. But when she brought it to her lips—for the second morning in a row—the aroma put her off. She had a moment's flood of worry, and frowning, set it back on the tray. As she settled into the cushions, one of her gown straps slipped off a shoulder, and with her thoughts gone elsewhere, she reached in slow motion to pull it up.

Janet observed her rather dramatic rejection of the coffee and decided she was putting on airs, seeking to show Andrew's wife how discriminating she was. But her apparent composure was infuriating, and the fact that she hadn't lost her cool over the unexpected visit further inflamed an already fuming Janet. It led her to remark, "You feel very secure, don't you, sitting here in your boudoir, with my husband's things about."

There was no response.

Janet looked toward the bed, as she questioned, "What time did he leave?"

"Half past four this morning," she answered.

Then, in an effort to demean them as much as possible, Janet observed, "I suppose he had you before he left."

She debated saying this, but then couldn't help herself. "He's never *had me,* Janet. We make love together."

"Yes, I'm sure he's getting his money's worth," she acridly commented, hoping that it would hurt.

"You're wasting your time, trying to get a rise out of me by calling me a whore," Annie wanted her to know. "I'd be his whore, I'd be his slave, I'd lick his boots if he wanted it."

She was getting to her now, she knew, and it made Janet smile wickedly. "That's what makes a great whore—and I can see you are one."

Why is it—Annie wondered—*that asexual women want to see women who enjoy sex as whores—to make themselves feel less deficient?* She wanted to say this to Janet, to throw it in her face, but she wasn't going to give in to that impulse and escalate the situation.

"Thank you," she said instead. "I appreciate the compliment. Now, tell me, is that why you came, to call me names?"

That blithe response rankled Janet to such a degree, the cup and saucer she held in her hands began to rattle. *I despise you—you vile creature,* was what she wanted to say to her, but instead she set her coffee down and seethed, "You and I made a bargain, and I'm here to tell you that time's up. You've had your little fling, you've had your time, it's over now and when Andrew returns I want you to end it."

OK—Annie told herself—*I knew this was coming; I'm prepared for it.* She looked her square in the eyes to respond, "I'm not going to do that. I told him about our arrangement, I told him everything we said, and I'm not going to do that."

She had been holding back as best she could, but the moxie with which Annie communicated that tidbit had the effect of flipping a switch in Janet. "Why in bloody hell did you do that?"

"Because I can't keep anything from him—because we share everything."

Her glare was piercing. "You gave me your word!"

"I know, and I accept full responsibility."

"What bloody good does that do?"

"None," she answered flippantly.

Janet stood abruptly, shouting, "Damn you! Damn both of you!"

It was becoming increasingly difficult for Annie to maintain her composure. "I know he's asked you for a divorce," she informed her, "but you should know that I'm against it. I'm trying to persuade him to keep on with you, for your children's sake as well as your own."

Her words only deepened Janet's outrage. "Just who the bloody hell do you think you are, even having an opinion about me and my family? You're nothing and no one—a bloody tramp who my husband uses for sex—that's all you are! How dare you even speak of my children?"

She was doing the best she could, but her restraint was slipping, even as her gown straps did, when she stood in front of Janet. But she lowered her voice to inform her, "I'm an important part of your husband's life who's not going to go away—that's who I am—and you know it. That's why you're so enraged and terrified, that's why you're so threatened."

Janet scorched Annie with her eyes. "I'm not afraid of you. I could crush and ruin you if I chose to."

She responded with absolute certainty: "If you even tried, you'd only drive Andrew further away and you know it. What you'd ruin is any chance you had of keeping him."

The confidence Annie applied to everything she said wasn't just adding kindling, it was throwing petrol on Janet's flames. "Don't presume to know anything about my relationship with my husband—you know nothing of it, absolutely nothing!" she railed at her.

"I know that you love him—I know that you don't want to lose him."

It was absolutely maddening that she could argue so calmly and with so many truths. "I'd sooner see him in hell than give him over to you!"

"You can send him to hell," she responded swiftly, "you can ruin me, ruin him, but it'll only make him hate you, and it won't make you feel better. You'll end up more miserable than you are now."

For the first time in her life, the usually placid and proper aristocrat wanted to spit, she wanted to spit in this woman's face and pummel her with her fists. And her desire to do these things was so strong and compelling, Janet felt dizzy from having to hold back.

Annie blinked slowly and shook her head at Janet. "You're fighting a losing battle," she told her, "and you know it. The sooner you accept that Andrew and I are part of one another, the better off you'll be."

"You listen to me, you piece of filth—" Without thinking, she moved in, her fists balled at her side, stopping just inches short of Annie. But as she drew closer, she was suddenly aware of a familiar scent, and when she recognized what it was, it deepened her discomposure. "You smell of him!" she exclaimed. She hadn't meant to say that, it had just bolted out.

Annie moved closer, too, so that their bodies were almost touching. The strap of her gown slipped again, but she let it stay where it had fallen, and as it slid even farther, it exposed the top of one breast. With eerie self-possession, she responded, "That's because we made love this morning and I haven't bathed yet. What do you do, Janet, jump up and wash him out of you as soon as it's over?"

Janet had tolerated as much as any human being could be expected to, so no one was going to fault her for this—for the slap she delivered to Annie's cheek. And in the aftermath, feeling the smart in her hand and watching the red shadows of her fingers visualize on Annie's skin, she experienced an exhilarating surge of power that felt damned good. It felt so bloody good, it prompted her to do more. With the gown Annie was wearing now slid completely off of one breast, Janet reached with that same hand, then squeezed and twisted. "You filthy whore," she hissed through clenched teeth, squeezing and twisting a few seconds more, before releasing the breast.

In her horror and outrage Annie might have struck back at her, but she didn't, because as angry as she was with the woman, she was also very sorry for her, for the depths that she had been lowered to through fear of losing her husband. And she knew damned well that she had provoked her, that she had said what she never should have, things that had to have been brutally painful to hear.

She was instantly flooded with pain and shock, and it was through wincing tears that she next told Janet, "There's a part of Andrew you can never have—that's what makes you so crazy. All these years you've tried, but you could never have it because it's mine." The pain in her breast intensified suddenly as the blood rushed into it, and she rubbed at it with both hands.

Janet backed off now, slowly realizing what she'd done. She saw in Annie's face and on the appendage itself how much she'd hurt her, and for a few seconds she wanted to apologize. But something else was happening inside of her, something disturbing and distracting. She felt herself being aroused by the sight and nearness of Annie—watching as she massaged her breast—and confused by the familiar aroma her skin gave off. Her imagination began running into places it had never gone before, as she recalled the full, sensual feeling of her breast, so unlike her own, and she had to struggle to bring it under control.

Beads of perspiration were forming on Janet's chest, under her necklace, and on her forehead. A large droplet slid down her belly. "You're wrong," she whimpered. There was a lump in her throat and they both heard it.

The pain was worsening and Annie told her, "I need to sit down," in an urgent but weakened voice. She covered herself again and continued to rub at the ache.

Regret and sympathy were mixing in to further muddle Janet's emotions, and she asked, "Are you all right? Can I get you something?"

Annie shook her head.

She needed to act, to undo this if she possibly could. "How about a warm compress?"

"All right," she answered, and moaned slightly.

With an unsteady gait, Janet made her way to the lavatory, then reemerged with two moistened cloths. "Here, put these on it."

So that she might apply the compresses, Annie dropped her strap again, and Janet felt her heart break into a gallop. It was unclear whether it was seeing the extent of injury that caused her heart to race, or just the sight again of the breast itself. At any rate, Janet turned pale and needed to take a seat.

She hid her face with her hands and asked through her fingers, "What's happening to me? Why are you doing this to me? What did I ever do to you?"

"Nothing," Annie answered, her voice faltering.

"You're punishing me for loving my own husband."

It was hard to speak over the pain. "I'm not—I'm trying to get you to see the truth of things, that's all." Annie bit her lip and looked at the ceiling, thinking how very much she needed Andrew now. "Because we need more time together," she muttered, almost to herself. "He's just beginning to heal, don't take him away before he's healed."

Her plea implied that it was in Janet's power to do that, to take him from her, so she asked abruptly, "How do you mean?"

It was hard to think, just now, but Annie realized that Janet wouldn't understand his need for healing, because Andrew had never shared his secrets with her. "Just be patient and don't make him hate you," she decided to say. "He wants to go on loving you, so don't do something stupid and make him hate you." She continued to hold the compresses to herself, and her eyes closed frequently with the agonizing waves of pain.

"He's going to hate me for this," Janet knew with certainty, though there was very little else she could be sure of.

She was right, he would. "I'll do what I can," Annie told her. "I'll tell him that I provoked you, which I did. I should never had said the things I did."

That almost sounded like an apology, and it led Janet to mumble, "I should never have come here." She was imagining her husband's reaction: He'd be enraged and unforgiving, and more determined than ever to divorce her. *What was I thinking*—she asked herself—*what on God's earth possessed me? And what I did—dear God—I can't believe what I did! I need to get hold of my anger—I need to stop before I destroy everything.*

She was frantically trying to decide how to handle the inevitable aftermath when Annie spoke to her again, and what she said gave her chills, because it was almost as though she could read her thoughts.

Her voice raspy and wavering, she told Janet, "It's your hostility and anger that are pushing him to divorce. If you could get control of them, he'd calm down and back off, I know he would. He doesn't want to walk away from you, any more than he wants to walk away from the children."

There she was again, adding to her confusion; if the woman were trying to steal her husband, it wouldn't make sense for her to offer such advice. So for a moment, Janet almost believed Annie, but then she remembered how she'd already been betrayed by her.

She hissed, "I'd have to be a perfect fool to believe anything you say."

Annie had reclined with her head on the arm of the love seat; her color had not returned and her breast was shot through with stabbing, unrelenting pain. The distress it caused was plainly evident and it made Janet question, "What can I do?" as she watched her face contort.

Her complexion ashen, she moaned, "I'm going to be sick—"

Horrified by the way she looked, Janet stood abruptly to help Annie to the bathroom. They arrived just in time, as a trembling Annie knelt in front of the toilet and began to heave. Janet stood back and watched, and as she did, she experienced a flash of comprehension, which was followed instantly upon by an adrenaline rush of fear: fear for her own survival.

Watching her now as she vomited, Janet recalled Annie's refusal of the coffee, and the full, heavy feeling to her breast. As the realization settled in, it felt like small lightning bolts charging through her core; it moved her into high gear, sent her mind racing to form a battle plan. In the few brief moments it took to filter into her consciousness that Annie was pregnant, any possibility of appeasement between the two women was lost, flushed down the toilet with her sick.

"I'll go and fetch your housekeeper," Janet offered, her voice decidedly stressed.

Annie nodded agreement and remained with head hung, pathetically, over the bowl.

Lisette was appalled by what she found and insisted upon calling the local doctor. Once she had settled into bed, Annie asked her about Janet.

"The countess left, Madame, right after she came to get me."

"Did she say she'd return?"

"No, she just said good-bye, that's all."

Annie lay back as Lisette mopped her face with a cool cloth. The sweet woman mumbled something in a dialect she wasn't familiar with. "What did you say?"

Lisette fumed, "I just said—good riddance. I'd prefer not to see the likes of her around here again."

"That makes two of us."

Janet returned her hired car to the airport in Bordeaux, where she had more than two hours to wait for the next available flight to London. During that time she made several phone calls, but mostly she sat thinking, contemplating her next move.

A car met her at Gatwick. The Rolls brought her first to the home of Lady Evelyn, from where she telephoned Crinan Castle. She informed her butler that she would be unavoidably detained until Sunday afternoon, and asked him to let the family know that she was staying with her longtime friend. She chatted briefly with Lady Evelyn over sherry, then took a hot, soaking bath.

The driver of the Rolls waited patiently while she did these things. When she emerged from Lady Evelyn's house he transported the refreshed and energized Lady Kilmartin to the opulent Mayfair town home of Lord Alfred Cowan, who enthusiastically awaited her arrival.

Twenty-Four

The butler brought Janet to Alfred Cowan in his upstairs sitting room.

He kissed her hand as he told her, "How lovely you look, my dear."

"It was good of you to accommodate me, Alfred, at such short notice. I was sitting there in that airport, trying to decide what I should do next, and all I could think of was coming to see you."

"I'm so very glad you did. Won't you sit down? I was just enjoying a glass of our very fine Scotch—won't you join me?" His possessive reference stemmed from the fact that he was a major shareholder in Nether Largie, Inc.

"Yes, thank you. I feel quite the need for drink these days."

"I'm sure you do, my dear," he consoled.

When they had toasted one another's health, Janet settled into a chair. "You must know why I've come," she began.

He frowned sympathetically. "I assume it's the situation with the American woman."

"Precisely."

He seated himself very near her, so that they might speak softly. "Become a bit much for you, has it?"

"Something's got to be done, Alfred, before it's too late."

Cowan chuckled as he recalled, "I heard those exact words from Donald, many years ago, concerning that very thing."

"Have you any idea how far it's gone?"

He shook his head.

She sighed with exasperation. "He's bought her a château in France and he spends most of his time with her. He's canceling important meetings; he even postponed one with the PM. He's neglecting his duties as earl, his children, everything—because all he cares about is being with her. He's letting the businesses go to hell and Nigel told me that rumors are beginning to circulate in the offices."

"My," he exhaled, "I hadn't realized."

"And that's not the worst of it." She hesitated briefly, because she loathed the idea of revealing this to anyone. "He's asked me for a divorce."

"Gracious! What did you say, how did you respond?"

"I said I'd rather see him in hell."

"Gracious," he repeated, shaking his head.

"I need your help, Alfred."

"I can see that."

"I don't know what to do."

"No, I'm sure you don't." He set his drink down. "My word, this has come to a head, hasn't it?"

Janet emptied her glass. "It may even have gone beyond that, I'm afraid."

"How so?"

"I went there this morning—to France—to see her, and I'm afraid I've made a bad situation worse." She inhaled deeply, feeling the whisky loosen her knots. "I knew that Andrew would be with the children," she explained, "Maggie's gymkhana was today and he promised her he'd be there. So I went to Nigel and coaxed him into giving me the information about where they've been living."

"Go on."

"She was still asleep when I got there, it was going on ten. I didn't wait for her to come down, I barged into her bedroom."

"What happened?"

"I confronted her," she said plainly. "When she was at Crinan Castle, she made me a promise; she gave me her word that she would give him up if it became too much for me. I let her know that it was time to do that and the bloody tramp refused. Her word meant nothing to her, and she refused me outright."

"Excuse me for saying this, my dear, but I can't believe you put any store in that to begin with."

"I was a perfect fool," she admitted, looking into her empty glass.

Alfred rose and went to the drinks table, to pour Janet another, more generous Scotch. "What did you do then, did you leave?"

"I wish I had," she answered, taking the refilled glass from him.

He remained standing in front of her, as he questioned, "Why do you say that?"

"We exchanged angry words and then she provoked me into doing something I now regret."

"And what was that?"

She shifted uncomfortably in her seat, before telling him, "She was wearing almost nothing and smelling of sex. She flaunted herself in front of me in this gown you could see right through, one strap kept slipping off her shoulder and exposing her—well, her bosom."

Alfred sat down quickly, because he felt the beginnings of an erection and he wanted to hide it. "If you want me to help you I need to know everything," he encouraged, as he began forming the mental picture of their encounter.

"This can go no further than this room," she insisted, "and I must have your word on that."

"That's understood," he assured her.

She could not look at him, as she recounted, "She moved right up against me and boasted about how they'd made love this morning. She said this to me, standing within inches of me, with one breast uncovered. It was as though she were asking for it."

"Asking for what?"

"I slapped her face. And then I grabbed her."

"Where?"

"The breast, the exposed breast," she blushed to say.

As his penis stiffened to the point of discomfort, Alfred swallowed hard and pulled a pillow to his lap.

"I grabbed it and twisted it and hurt her so badly she cried." She stopped short of saying: *And then I held onto it and kept squeezing it—though God only knows why.*

Dearest lord—Cowan bemoaned—*I'd have given anything to have been there—anything.* "What then?" he sighed.

"We said more things and she was sick."

"Sick?"

"She vomited."

"From the pain?" he wondered.

"I hope so, but I don't think that was it."

He understood what she was getting at. "My word, you don't think she's pregnant, do you?"

"I do," she answered, nodding several times for emphasis. "Her servant brought us coffee and she'd started to drink it, but she turned up her nose and put it down. Coffee always sickened me early on—and then there were her breasts."

"What about them?"

"They were very full. I could see that, and when I touched her I felt it, too."

Alfred mused—*oh, this is too delicious!* "They felt like pregnant breasts?" he asked, hoping she would describe them in more detail.

Unfortunately for Cowan, Janet merely nodded again. "When she was sick, that's when I put it all together. I was watching her vomit and it hit me like a bolt of lightning that she was pregnant."

The image of Annie bent in agony over a toilet, her ass showing through a flimsy nightgown, was as exciting to Cowan as the picture of Janet hurting her. "Did you ask her?"

"Absolutely not. I left and got the bloody hell out of there."

"Good. That's very good you did that," he realized.

"Why?"

"Because if she is, you don't want Andrew to know that you know," he told her, already forming a plan of action. "Is there anything else, anything else at all, that I should be told about? Because if I'm to help you, I need to know everything." *Oh please*—he said to himself—*let there be more!*

She looked at the floor as she answered, "No, that's it."

He brushed aside his disappointment. "Does Andrew know yet that you went there?"

"I doubt it; he should still be busy with the children."

"Good, because you need to be the one to tell him."

Her eyes widened. "Oh, no, Alfred, I can't do that! He's going to be furious with me!"

In a calm, paternalistic tone, he told her, "You've no other choice, my dear. You have to tell him and apologize profusely when you do, because that's your only hope out of this. Not doing so will only compound your problems, you have to see that."

"It'll be bloody awful," she knew, and shivered with anticipation.

"When is he going back to France, do you know?"

"After dinner tomorrow."

Cowan's crafty mind was in overdrive. "You should take him aside and tell him just before he goes. That'll lessen the time he has to rant at you, because he'll want to get on his way to her, to see if she's all right. And you must be very contrite and even cry if you can manage it. He's got to believe that the incident hurt you as much as it hurt her, and that you did it because you were pushed to your breaking point. Do you see what I'm getting at?"

She did, and it was making perfect sense. "I want him to feel as sorry for me as he does for her."

"Exactly."

"But what if she gets to him before I do?"

He put one hand to his chin and stroked it. "That's a chance you'll have to take, but I'd be willing to bet she won't ring him with news like that. She's a clever woman, she'll most likely wait until she sees him."

"But then what? He's going to go to her and stay with her, that seems certain. Am I supposed to just let him do that, after all this?"

He grinned sadistically. "That's precisely what you'll do, and not only will you do that, but you'll change your attitude toward her. You'll be understanding and let him go to her and stay out of it, because I'm going to handle it from here on."

He seemed so in command just now, it brought her tremendous relief to think of giving this over to him. Still, she needed to know, "What are you going to do?"

At this juncture he wasn't certain how he'd bring about their separation, only that he would. "I've some ideas I'm kicking around, but it's better if you don't know any of the details. When he returns to you — and he will — he should believe you completely innocent of any part in what occurred, so that it's easy for him to come home."

She saw the wisdom in that. "But if she is carrying his child, what can you do about it?" she worried. "That seems to me the one thing that neither of us can do anything about."

His mouth twisted with malevolence, as he responded, "With what I have in mind, her pregnancy won't matter."

The assistance he was offering had eased her disquietude, but the malice she discerned in his voice brought it on again. "Don't do anything to hurt her, Alfred," she warned him. "If she is pregnant, Andrew will be fiercely protective of her. He always was with me and I imagine that he'll be tenfold more so with her." And as she realized the truth in that, her heart began to ache.

"You have to trust me," he beseeched. "You've come to me for my help because you've nowhere else to go, and now you must give this over to me and trust that I will do the right thing by you and your family. I promise you, I'll act with the good of the family in mind." Remembering that he was dealing with a relatively devout Church of Scotland woman, he added, "And you're not to suffer any pangs of conscience, either, over doing whatever must be done to bring your husband back into the fold. Remember that your right to keep your family intact supersedes everything."

She liked the way in which he'd put that, and it reassured her once again. She smiled gratefully as she said, "Thank you."

"Now you should be on your way, we don't want to run the risk of Andrew finding out we had this meeting. He'll know my role in what happens soon enough, that can't be helped, but he doesn't have to know yours. If you need to contact me, be very careful and discreet about it, all right?"

"I will." She smiled again.

He had her write the address of the château out for him, then left her with an admonishment. "Remember what I said about how you tell him what you did. Don't let yourself be pushed into anger."

"I'll do my best."

Janet stood and Lord Alfred did not. "You'll forgive me, my dear, if I don't get up. My gout seems to be acting up and it's quite uncomfortable for me to stand just now." With the excitement of his plans for retaliation further arousing him, his erection was still in force.

After Janet was gone, Cowan went directly to his bedroom. He was still so turned on by the images she had evoked that he locked his door and removed one of his favorite magazines from

hiding place. He had a collection of these things, of contraband pe-
riodicals that featured real—not staged—photos of sadomasochis-
tic sex. He opened it to a particularly brutal layout of a woman in
wrist and ankle shackles, who was undergoing sexual torture from
two hooded men. He exchanged Annie's face for the hapless
woman's and in no time at all, he was squirting himself onto the
dog-eared pages.

When Lisette saw Annie's injury, she had insisted upon calling the doctor. He arrived quickly and left her with some potent
pain medication, and the promise to return tomorrow.

She had drifted off to sleep from the narcotic, so Lisette answered the phone. The two women had already discussed this, so
she knew what to tell him. "She's been ill today, Count Andrew, and
she's just gone off to sleep."

"Ill? How?"

"Her stomach has been upset, and she's been unable to keep
anything down."

"Oh dear—should I change my plans and come home tonight?"

"That's up to you, of course, but I don't think it's necessary.
you to come back tomorrow afternoon?"

Yes. I'd planned to arrive early evening."

I believe that'll be soon enough. She is somewhat better than
earlier in the day, but what she really needs just now is sleep."

answered reluctantly, "All right. But I want you to ring
gets worse or she decides she wants me sooner; promise
that?"

course."

her I'll ring again in the morning, Lisette."

er not too early," she advised. Her mistress had been
lot and very late these days, and Lisette believed she

I'll just come home without phoning. If she's still un-
n't want the phone to disturb her."

she's awake, I'll let her know what you've said."

you. And, Lisette, do give her my love."

It was a very touching request and in light of what had happened today, it brought a tear to the woman's eye. "I will, Count Andrew." She hung up the receiver, feeling relieved and pleased with herself for handling that just as Annie had asked.

Janet arrived at Crinan Castle in time for the Sunday family meal; the children were delighted to see their parents together for once and even Andrew expressed his appreciation for her earlier-than-expected arrival. Everyone gathered in the family dining room, everyone except Nigel, and dinner went on in its usual, noisy fashion. Even Lady Mary, who was usually perturbed by the casualness of the affair, seemed in good spirits.

Andrew spent an hour on the lawn with the children afterward, kicking around the football. As he was preparing to leave, a servant came to say that his wife was requesting he stop in her study; he braced himself for another confrontation.

She was standing at a window, watching the children on the lawn below, when she whirled around and told him, "Please sit down."

He did not oblige, and questioned impatiently, "What is it, Janet?"

She'd been rehearsing the performance since her talk with Cowan, and like an anxious actor new to the stage, she plunged headlong into her lines. "There's no easy way to do this, so I'll just come out with it. I went to France yesterday and did something I regret with all my heart. It's unpardonable, I know, but I'm asking for your forgiveness anyway."

His heart slowed to a deadly pace. "What did you do?"

"I confronted her. We had a nasty argument and I assaulted her."

He couldn't believe his ears. "You what?"

"I assaulted her," she repeated, though with less enthusiasm.

"How, in God's name?"

"I lost control of myself," she said plainly. "I was so filled with anger and frustration that I took leave of my senses for a few minutes. I slapped her, then I grabbed one of her breasts—I twisted it until she cried." With her best effort at looking remorseful, she added, "I'm afraid I caused her rather a lot of pain."

"Jesus Christ! Why? Why would you do something like that?"

She affected a penitent posture, rounding her shoulders and lowering her gaze, to respond, "I reached my breaking point, Andrew, that's all I can say. I'm mortally ashamed of what I did and I can never apologize enough, but I wasn't in control of myself at the time. I don't know, nothing like this has ever happened to me before," she sniveled, shaking her head in apparent disgust at her own actions. "But I thought yesterday—this is how people do it, this is how they get to the point of murdering someone; they get pushed so far they just completely lose control." She was only able to squeeze out a few tears, but she mopped at her cheeks with a tissue as though there were a torrent of them.

"My God, Janet!" He remembered his conversation with Lisette and realized, "That's why she wouldn't speak to me last night."

"You rang her?"

"Yes, to say good night. The housekeeper told me she'd been ill and needed to sleep." He looked off into the distance as it settled further in.

"So you haven't spoken to her?"

His eyes were filled with concern for Annie, but when he glared at his wife, there was no mistaking how furious he was with her. "I need to leave. I need to go to her, but I'll deal with you later," he said. "We'll finish this after I know she's all right, do you understand?"

"Yes, you do that, go to her," she readily agreed. "And please tell her how dreadfully sorry I am. I'd do anything if I could take it back." She was trying valiantly to bring on more tears, but they weren't cooperating.

He gave his wife one more menacing look, then exited the room with heavy steps and haste. When the door slammed she heaved a sigh of relief and grinned, as she congratulated herself on a job well done. But even as she did that, she became unaccountably anxious, and began to worry about what it was that Cowan meant to do.

The doctor called in again on Sunday, because he was concerned about the extent of Annie's injury. He had also taken a urine sample with him the day before, and wanted to speak to her about the results.

After examining her, he said, "I was a little worried that it might be worse today. I'm pleased to see it's not. How are you feeling?"

"Groggy—from the pain pills."

"That's to be expected, Madame. But you may want to limit how many of those you take. I ran the urine sample and you are pregnant."

Her eyes welled up before she closed them.

The young man touched her hand. "Unhappy news?"

"Not the best," she answered. "My husband is not the father, you see, and the father is married to someone else."

"Oh," he responded, as he settled into a chair at her bedside.

"And then there's my age." Over the last week, as the idea that she might be pregnant began to take hold, she'd been overtaken by an avalanche of concerns.

"There are tests, you know, to make certain the fetus is all right."

"I know. But my main fear—I don't want to make things more difficult for Andrew—for the father—or for my husband, for that matter. And then, I'm not certain I want this, at this time in my life. My son is almost fifteen—I'm not sure I want to start over again with a baby just now."

"It would be a big adjustment," he recognized.

"An enormous one. But on the other hand, it's something I've always wanted, since I first fell in love with Andrew. Of course, it can never be like that, like what I dreamed of as a young woman." Several more tears chased after the others.

He handed her a tissue from the box at her bedside. "You've time to decide. It's very early yet."

"I know," she said again.

He thought to make her aware of this: "Lisette said that it was his wife who attacked you, so I've some appreciation for how tangled things are. And you should know, too, that Lisette's guessed at your condition." He waited for Annie to respond, and when she didn't, he questioned, "Will you tell the count about the pregnancy?"

"I may wait a bit, while I think it over. It's bound to complicate things to such a degree, I need to be sure of myself before I make any moves."

"Well, you should take care in the meantime, act as though you intend to carry it through—no caffeine, no alcohol—and take vitamins. Shall I prescribe some for you?"

"Sure," she answered, her eyes focused somewhere in the distance.

"The pain pills are safe but use them sparingly," he told her, scribbling out a prescription form. "Keep up with the medication I gave you for the bruising, and keep applying the heat. Make certain to get plenty of rest over the next few days, and no lifting of any kind or doing anything strenuous," he advised.

"OK," she answered, although she wasn't fully listening.

"Call me if the pain in the breast worsens; have Lisette get in touch with me right away if that happens, all right?"

"Yes, thank you, doctor, you've been very kind."

"It's been my pleasure, Madame. I'll stop in again on Wednesday, after office hours."

When he left the room, Annie walked onto the balcony. As she gazed into the garden, she envisioned a child playing there: a pretty little girl, about three, with long, dark hair, which lifted with the breeze as she chased tiny white butterflies through indigo spikes of salvia. Just before the vision faded, the apparition turned to look toward the house, smiling a bright, warm smile, which shone in her cobalt blue eyes, and struck at Annie's heart.

Lisette answered the call that came from Andrew's jet.

"I'm so sorry, Count Andrew, but she's asleep again."

"I know what happened," he was loathe to admit. "My wife told me what she did. Is she really asleep?"

"Yes, Monsieur, she really is. The doctor gave her something for the pain and she's been sleeping like a baby." *Oops,* she said to herself, *not the best choice of words.*

"I'll be there in two and a half hours, will you let her know when she wakes up?"

"I will."

"And please tell her that I know, so she doesn't fret over how to tell me."

It was just past seven when she heard the car on the drive; she had wanted to get up to greet him but couldn't, because with the slightest movement, the combination of narcotics and pregnancy made her want to vomit.

Andrew took the steps two at a time to get to her. He reached for her as she sat up, but she held her hands out to fend him off.

"Sorry," he whispered, realizing why she'd protected herself.

"I can't be hugged, not just yet. I can be kissed, though."

He touched her arms very gingerly, and put his mouth to hers. Then he unbuttoned her night dress to examine the injury. His face contorted when he saw that part of her which he had always treated so reverently, black and blue and swollen. "How could she have done this!" he exclaimed.

She lowered her gaze, as she answered, "I provoked her."

"What?"

"She barged into our room while I was still sleeping and called me ugly names—she kept calling me your whore. I tried not to let it get to me but it did, and I fought back with my own nasty digs."

"Dear lord." He was imagining the scene, and with his intimate knowledge of Janet's acerbity and vindictiveness, the picture he formed wasn't pretty.

"She wanted me to end it with you and I told her I wouldn't. Then we got right in each other's faces and said more hurtful things, and she finally snapped. I was still in my nightgown and the strap had slipped and that poor breast was just staring her in the face." She looked down at it.

He winced, as he contemplated the moment. "Dear God, it looks so bloody painful." Then, glancing at the prescription bottles on the bedside table, he questioned, "Who was this doctor? Is he good enough, do you think? Shall I take you to Pau for a second opinion?"

"No, that's not necessary. He seems very competent and he's been most attentive."

"I can't believe Janet would do something like this! I've never known her to be violent; to my knowledge she's never even spanked the children!"

"I told you, I taunted her. It wasn't all her fault."

"You were worried she'd come here," he remembered. "You were right to worry. What a mess, what a bloody, awful mess." He looked now to the bedside table. "What are all these?" he questioned, picking up one of the pill bottles.

"One's to dissolve the clots, one's for pain, and the other's vitamins."

"Why vitamins?"

"To help with the healing." She had just lied.

"Can I get you anything? Have you eaten?"

"Not yet, I was waiting for you. Lisette's going to bring dinner up here."

As they talked, he was struck by her composure. "You seem extraordinarily calm about all this."

"It helps being drugged," she answered, trying to smile. "But really, the truth is, I just want to put it behind me, and I hope you will, too."

"Put it behind me? Not bloody likely," he responded. "Janet and I need to have this out."

"Please reconsider doing that."

"Why? I know you claim equal responsibility, but the fact is she was the one who came down here and started the whole damned thing, and no matter what her excuse, she had no right to hurt you, no right at all."

Annie had watched his eyes darken with anger, and it disturbed her. "If you confront her it's only going to make everything worse. I think we'd all do well to settle down and see how we feel about it a week from now. Would you do that for me, give it a week?"

In truth, he didn't relish the idea of rehashing things with Janet just now, mostly because it would mean leaving Annie again. And he did see the wisdom in giving everyone time to cool down, so he reluctantly agreed. "If that's what you want."

"It is. Now let's talk about something else, shall we? How are your children? How was the horse show?"

He exhaled first. "They're all well. Maggie took third place in her class for the cross country, and fourth for the stadium jumping. She's become quite the horsewoman. She performed brilliantly, actually; I was awfully proud of her."

"I'm glad you went."

"I'm not," he sadly realized. "If I'd been here this wouldn't have happened."

"Janet would have come some other time," she knew. Still wanting off this subject she asked, "How's my little Malcolm?"

It made him smile to hear her call his son that. "Very well. He played football with us today; he's growing amazingly these days."

Imagining Malcolm playing soccer with his daddy led her to reflect on the child she was carrying. If it were born, it would probably be in early March, she realized. She wondered if it would resemble its father as much as Malcolm did.

"When's his birthday? When will he be five?"

"In August, just before our twentieth." He closed his eyes and sighed, as he contemplated the tragedy of twenty years married to the wrong woman.

That saddened her, too, as she thought of it, but her stomach was engaging in that weird waltz of pregnancy, vacillating between nausea and hunger, and it made her say, "I'm getting hungry, are you?"

"I'll ring the kitchen." He turned away from her and picked up the house phone.

She was overcome with anxiety suddenly and touched his arm, saying, "Andrew—"

"Yes, my love?"

"It scares me how much I love you."

Something in her face troubled him. "This thing's upset you much more than you want to let on, hasn't it?"

She nodded and then looked away, out through the open doorway, toward her garden. She listened as he spoke his beautiful French to Lisette, and allowed the melody of his voice—such a cherished and reassuring sound—to lull her into peace. But even as she relaxed, a thought settled into her head that plunged her into despair: *I know someday I must—but how can I ever give him up, how will I ever live without him?*

After dinner, they talked for a while in soft, bedroom tones, and as they fell asleep—her back to him—he rested his hands on her lower abdomen, so as not to disturb the tender breast. His hands felt strong and protective, and she was grateful to have them guarding her tiny, vulnerable child.

As expectant mothers often do, she spoke to her child in her thoughts: *Poor little thing, you were conceived here in this beautiful, magical place, after twenty-two years of waiting and wondering and giving up hope—you've come to us out of love, out of the purest expression of our love—but how can I know if giving you to your father is the right thing? How can I know if your precious new life will bring him joy or misery?*

Swallowing her tears she laid her hands on top of his, and although she did not really believe in God, Annie began to pray.

Twenty-Five

It took all the powers of persuasion the three of them had, Annie, Lisette, and Didier, to convince Andrew to go to London and meet with the Prime Minister as planned.

"We'll take good care of her, as we always do, Count Andrew."

"I know you will. I just don't feel right about leaving. The last time I left it was a disaster."

"Andrew, please," Annie pleaded, "it worries me to see you neglecting your responsibilities."

"I'm going to have Nigel look into getting this place secured," he insisted. "I don't want people wandering in here anymore."

"All right, do that," she agreed, for she knew it would make him feel better, make it easier to leave her.

After much effort, he finally succumbed to their reassurances and encouragement and left for London on Wednesday morning.

As he said he would, the doctor returned that afternoon to see Annie. His name was Bernard Huron and he was a very appealing man, in his early thirties she guessed, with a competent air and sweet way about him. Annie greeted him at the entrance to the château.

"Bonjour, Madame. It's good to see you up and about. You're looking much better."

"Thank you, doctor, I'm feeling much better, except for the constant queasiness, which can't be helped."

"Were you sick all the time with your other pregnancy?"

"Only the first eight months," she laughingly answered, as she led him up the stairs to her bedroom. Once inside, she sat on the bed and unbuttoned her blouse, so that he might examine the breast.

"I'm pleased with the way it's healing," he told her. "How's the pain?"

"I haven't needed a pill since Monday night."

"That's quite good. Any other problems?"

She did up her blouse again. "No, just the question about what I'm going to do."

They moved to the sitting area in the corner of the room, as Dr. Huron asked her, "Can I help?"

"How long do I have to wait until I can know if the baby's all right?"

"We can do the tests at the end of your first trimester."

That worried her, because she remembered, "You become very attached during that time. Soon after that, you start to feel movement."

He nodded understanding. "Have you told the count?"

"No. I decided against it, for now. He has so much on his plate, I hate to add to his burden."

"Does he have other children?"

"Yes, five. Why do you ask?"

He raised a single brow. "In that case, I shouldn't think you'll be able to keep this from him much longer," he ventured. "He's bound to notice the changes in your body."

"You're right," she realized.

"He can help you make your decision."

She smiled at the young doctor. "I think I already know what he'll say. He'll tell me to follow my heart, and he'll support me in whatever it is I choose to do." Her smile lessened somewhat when she added, "And then there's my husband, who will be hurt by this turn of events, but still, I believe he'll say virtually the same thing."

"That doesn't sound bad," he said.

"They're both wonderful men, good men," she told him, "and they both love me. I feel very blessed in that."

"But? I sense a 'but' somewhere," he grinned.

"I like you, doctor," she laughed, and made him blush. "But bringing a baby into these confused circumstances — I'm not sure it's fair — to anyone, most of all the child itself."

In a very sweet fashion, he retorted, "It's been done before, I think."

"Yes, it has," she laughed again, and thought to tell him something. "My ancestor was one of the Barons d'Inard, from Béarn, you know."

"I know your family name, there are d'Inards in and around Pau."

"My cousins."

"It's a very old family, I believe."

"There's an interesting story attached to us, would you like to hear it?"

"Of course," he answered, still smiling.

"About mid-sixteenth century, one of the barons fell in love with a woman of low birth, a woman he could never marry. Her name was Audine Laborde-Hourcade."

"Did you name the château after her?" he wondered.

"Andrew named it that. You see, the baron impregnated Audine, then gave the child his name. And so they might live in comfort, he also made a gift to her of some land and a small château. The child was named Arnaud and he was quite prolific—the d'Inards alive today are all his descendants, all descendants of their love-child."

He was curious to know, "Is there still a Baron d'Inard?"

"The aristocratic line died out a couple of hundred years ago. We survive only through Audine's son."

He made one of those sounds with his mouth that the French do so well, to show when they're powerfully affected by something. "That's quite ironic, isn't it?"

"If Audine had terminated that pregnancy somehow—I guess there were ways women could, even then—none of us would be on the earth." She rested her hands on her belly. "Since you told me I'm pregnant, I keep thinking about Audine. I keep thinking how brave and strong she must have been, and how very glad I am that she had her child."

He smiled more broadly, as he said to her, "I can see how you would."

Annie's eyes lost their focus for a moment, as her thoughts returned to her ancestral grandmother, and the choices she made.

The doctor sat quietly with her, until she looked at him again. "I'd like you to come into the office when you feel up to it. I'll want to do a pelvic examination and determine your general health."

"Of course."

"Will you phone the office for an appointment?"

"I'll do that," she answered. They made their way out of the bedroom, headed for the front door. "By the way, I really appreciate the house calls—they're obsolete in the States, you know."

"It's customary, Madame, for the doctor to call in at the château," he informed her, then added, "I'd like to meet the count sometime, if I may."

"He'd be delighted to meet you, I'm sure. Thank you so much, doctor, and not just for your care," she thought to say, "thank you for listening."

They descended the steps from the terrace and he opened the door to his Citroën, but hesitated a moment before getting in. "I know life is difficult," he said to her, "under the best of circumstances it's a challenge. But don't you think it's worth the struggle?"

His question made her think of Tom Keegan's deathbed letter to her, regarding his regret over having cut himself off from pain, and in effect, having disengaged himself from life. She thought also of the precious gift she'd just received, when she'd been reprieved from death by the blessing of good health. She'd made a promise to herself then, to relish every moment of life—good and bad—from here on in.

A smile arose from deep within, as she answered, "Every bit of it."

Dr. Huron grinned. "Remember that, remember what you just said." He started the engine, then waved good-bye from his car, bidding her, "Au revoir, Madame."

Lord Alfred Cowan was a man of means. He'd inherited a fortune and made it again, several times over. He'd been married and divorced three times, with no issue from any of them, so his wealth was his to do with as he pleased. At age sixty-six he enjoyed excellent health and patrician good looks, and when asked, always declared that this was the best time of his life. He associated with the most influential people in Britain, including and especially royalty, entertained lavishly, and had his finger on the governmental pulse. He had other fingers in the most lucrative business pies in the United Kingdom, sitting on the boards of many of them, wielding power and influence as freely and as often as he swung a nine iron. Lord Mortimer Cowan, his father, had formed a partnership with Andrew's grandfather after World War II, pooling their resources to help bring Scotland's economy out of the ashes. Together they revitalized the British textile industry and saw to it that Scottish plaids were worn all over the world.

Lord Alfred became fast friends with Donald, Andrew's father, when they were young men. Their fathers were business partners and their hereditary seats within fifteen miles of one another, so they knew each other as children, although they attended different schools. They both served in the last days of the war and when it was won, took to celebrating their survival extensively. Donald's father, the twenty-second earl, disdained the relationship and tried to convince his son to find other company. At an early age he saw something in Alfred that troubled him, and he recognized that when his son spent time with him, his behavior seemed to change for the worse. But the venerable man was unsuccessful in turning Donald away from Alfred, and eventually he just gave the matter up.

Cowan sat with the widowed countess at the twenty-third earl's funeral, and eulogized his longtime friend. In the years following Donald's death, he took it upon himself to call in frequently at Crinan Castle and make himself available to the family, for whatever they might need of him. Everyone but Andrew seemed to like Cowan, and treated him as they would a member of the family. Andrew didn't know it, of course, but he experienced the same kind of apprehensive intuition about Alfred's character that his grandfather had, and it made him wary of the man.

Andrew's instincts regarding Alfred were reinforced by a conversation he had with his father, about four years before his death. Andrew was working closely with Donald at the time, learning all he could about the businesses. Cowan had come to the offices in

Glasgow for a meeting and argued with Donald about his decision to lower their wool prices. When he left, Donald closed the door to his office and spoke privately to his son.

"Don't turn your back on that man, Andrew, always be on your guard with him."

"I am already," he informed him. "I've never trusted him, though exactly why I can't say."

"Good."

He was curious to know, "Why don't you? I thought you were close friends."

"We used to be," Donald answered, "when we were younger, but I would no longer bestow that honor. If only I had it to do over."

His father's change in demeanor was troubling; his bowed head and remorseful expression were decidedly uncharacteristic. "Had what to do over?"

Donald's brow furrowed before he answered. For some time now, he had wanted to reveal this to his son, to save him from the fate that so many had fallen prey to, but embarrassment kept him from saying anything. On this day, however, freshly affected by an encounter with the odious man, he located the courage. "You know how he gives those elaborate weekend parties at Lunga House?"

Cowan owned the small island of Lunga off the west coast of Scotland, and his household staff and groundskeepers were its sole inhabitants. The only access was by sea, and there were intriguing rumors about mysterious goings-on at the thirteenth-century castle.

"Yes, I've heard," Andrew responded.

Donald's reluctance was overcome by his anger. "Cowan's like a spider with those parties, drawing victims into his web. He makes himself out to be Britain's answer to Hugh Hefner, encouraging his guests to indulge in whatever they will, all at his expense. He'll coax them into revealing their secret desires and then take it upon himself to fulfill them. He procures partners for them, of either sex, provides illegal drugs if that's what they enjoy, he's even orchestrated orgies that would put Caligula to shame, all the while portraying himself as the kind of person who can be trusted with that sort of thing. Then he files away the information in that diabolical brain of his and adds it to his arsenal. Should one of those unsuspecting friends ever cross him — well, I think you can guess the rest. I know all this because in the days when we were closer he boasted of it to me." He shook his head as he recalled, "Your grandfather made every attempt to get me away from him. Dammit all, how I wish I'd listened to him."

Andrew was not shocked to hear this, the rumors he'd heard having been along those lines, but he was instantly struck with concern for his father. He looked him straight in the eyes to question, "Has he done that with you, has he something to use against you?"

Donald sighed heavily. "He thinks he has," was the answer.

Father and son stared at each other a moment, but Donald would go no further than that simple response. He picked up the telephone to take a business call then, and that quickly, the matter was dropped, never to be discussed again.

Janet made certain she would not be disturbed when she rang London from her study.

With saccharine articulation, Cowan answered, "Hello, my dear. How did it go?"

"Just as you predicted," she answered excitedly. "He was so anxious to get to her, he didn't take the time to give me what for."

"Excellent, excellent. And you, did you manage to evoke some sympathy?"

"I think so. I said nothing but how sorry I was."

"Wonderful, there's a good lass. Now you must keep this up. You mustn't let your anger get the better of you, it's wholly counterproductive. In fact, a call to your husband asking after her health would be a strategic next move."

"Yes, I'll do that." Janet paused as she remembered something. "She told me much the same thing, you know."

"Annie?"

"She said it's my anger that's pushing him away."

"When did she say that?"

"That day, in France."

"That's curious," he responded.

She wanted to know, "What are we going to do next?"

"If you're up to it, I'd like you to have a private word with
Nigel on my behalf."

She was anxious to help, and happy to do anything at this
point. "What do you want me to say?"

"Tell him I've come to you—not the other way 'round, mind
you—because I'm very concerned about the circumstance with
your husband. Tell him that I feel it's my role as his late father's closest friend to step in and see if I might prevent disaster befalling him.
In that light, tell Nigel I'd like to speak with him, to see if I might
discern a way in which to help Andrew see the error of his ways.
Think you can do that?"

"That shouldn't be a problem. He's here a good bit of the time,
anyway, waiting for Andrew to deign to leave her."

"Good lass. Have him ring me here, and that should be the end
of your involvement. Just be certain you tell Nigel that I approached you, all right?"

"I understand. Thank you so very much, Alfred, for everything."

"It's my pleasure, my dear, really it is." And in truth it was, for
the hatching of this plan was more fun than he'd had in quite some
time.

In his conversation with Nigel, Cowan learned that he would
be joining Andrew in London in the morning, so he invited him to
come down that very evening to have dinner. Nigel had been rather
bored of late and was delighted to have something to do, so he happily accepted the invitation.

Twenty-Six

D idier had driven Andrew to Pau when he left on Wednesday morning, but it was Annie who waited on the runway Friday evening. She leaned against her car and watched the Gulf Stream jet roll in after a flawless landing, thanking the powers–that–be for returning him to her once again.

He had called her three times a day while he was away, to see how she was getting on, but he was still enormously relieved to see with his own eyes that she was looking much better.

"God, how I love coming home to you," he sighed as they embraced, and then with surprise added, "You cut your hair!"

Fluffing it with her hands, she asked, "Do you like it?"

"It's very chic, but what possessed you?"

She almost said something about the pregnancy, about how women often act on odd impulses when they're pregnant. "I just wanted a change," she shrugged, "I get that way sometimes. I went to the salon at Eugénie for a facial and then decided to have them do my hair. I was thinking about the heat and getting it off my shoulders." They had given her a more sporty cut, which was youthful and trendy.

"Well, you look lovely," he told her, "though you were perfectly lovely before."

"And you're perfectly sweet."

They embraced again once they were inside the car.

He was anxious to know, "Did you see that doctor again?"

"This morning, I stopped in his office before I went to Eugénie."

"What did he say?"

"He thinks the injury has healed beautifully, and he's very pleased."

Annie was driving now and he lifted her right hand to kiss it. "I'm so happy to hear that, my darling. Did he say anything else?"

"Not really," she answered. But in truth, Bernard Huron had determined that her cervix was already closed, indicating that the pregnancy was secure. He'd also deemed her to be in excellent health for carrying the child. "Do you know what I was thinking today? It's almost Bastille Day—do you recall how we wanted to spend Bastille Day in France together, all those years ago. Do you remember that?"

"I do," he answered, with a hint of melancholy.

"We should make a big fuss over it, I think. We should plan something wonderful for ourselves, a celebration of being together after all this time, of beating the odds and defying the will of the gods. What do you think?"

He smiled broadly as he told her, "I think we should storm the Bastille and free all the prisoners, and set off fireworks that'll rival Paris, that's what I think."

"In or out of the bedroom?"

"Both."

They laughed at each other.

The summer had deepened around them. The days dawdled with the heat, and the parched earth held to it, even through the night. The grapes were a substantial size now, though they still wore the soft green of new life, and the garden beds overflowed with lavender, roses, and poppies, a veritable feast of color and fragrance.

They dined on the terrace the night he returned, amid dancing moths attracted by the candlelight. When a Band of Gypsies CD that Annie had queued up began to play, Andrew told her, "A secretary in the London office was playing a radio at her desk the other day, and when I walked past I heard this song. She saw me smile and asked if I liked them."

"What'd you tell her?"

He laughed as he recalled the surprised look on the young woman's face. "That they're my favorite group."

That reminded her of something. "John called the other day. They've started running the first ad and it's getting rave reviews."

"Yes, he rang me, too, and he sent a tape over. I've brought it with me, I thought we'd see it together."

"What a wonderful souvenir!" she realized. "Every time we see that we'll remember being there and finding out that I wasn't sick, then coming here for the first time."

"And making love for the first time," he added, "like it was the first time ever."

And creating a child, she almost said, but didn't.

When they rose from the table, he noticed, "You've barely touched your wine, don't you care for it?"

"Didn't I tell you? I'm still on that medication for the bruising, and Dr. Huron said not to take alcohol with it—the two don't mix." She wanted a little more time to know her mind in this, and maybe, hopefully, to know his.

"How much longer need you take it?"

"A few more days." That was all she thought she could manage, anyway. Her breasts were growing more full and tender and with the bruises all but dissipated, he'd have to notice. Besides that, he was bound to realize sooner or later that she hadn't menstruated.

He took hold of one of her hands, to ask, "Are you well enough to make love tonight, if we're careful?"

"Make love to me as you always have," she told him. "Nothing you do ever hurts me."

He held her carefully, kissing her mouth as he sent himself into her. He didn't remove himself afterward, and he softened very little.

He spoke to her ear in the tenderest of tones. "I think I can stay here a moment, then go again."

"What are you, twenty-one again?" she teased, as she nibbled at his ear.

"How I wish!"

"You're better than that—we're better than that," she knew.

"Yes, we are."

He began to dance inside her again. As he did, she released an explosion of joy, and arched her back to meet his body. They both lay quivering at the end.

She brought one of his hands to her chest. "Touch them, you haven't touched them."

"I'm so afraid of hurting you."

"You won't. I need you to touch them."

He massaged the uninjured one, then cautiously touched the other, saying, "They seem very full."

She answered anxiously, "They are." She put her hands on his and moved them to her belly now—it was time to tell him.

He gently rubbed at her abdomen, then suddenly turned on his back and stared at the ceiling. Touching that breast for the first time since Janet had, he couldn't help but think of her assault on Annie. And with those thoughts came the unavoidable guilt, the understanding that it had been his selfishness, his need to love and be with Annie, that had driven Janet to such baseness.

"What is it?" she questioned. "Where'd you go?"

He flipped to his side and propped his head with his arm. Looking into her eyes, he told her, "I think I'm finally coming to terms with the nature of our relationship."

"How so?" she wondered.

"How it's going to have to stay this way," he explained, "at least for the near future. It's taken time, but I understand now what you've been trying to tell me, I know what I've got to do. I've got to find a way back to Janet and keep on with her as best I can." He began to caress Annie's abdomen again.

She felt suddenly, deeply anxious.

"It's no good thinking I can have it any other way," he went on to say. "It's selfish of me to seek my personal happiness, when there are so many other people affected by what I do. You were absolutely right when you said that we needed to stay married to our spouses, that it was our only recourse."

She didn't respond.

"It was unbearably painful that day with Mike, but I'm grateful for it now," he continued. "I know why you did it—it was to show me the way."

She pressed his hand into her flesh and held it there.

"I know you'll continue to help me, to guide me to do the right thing," he told her. "Without your help and support, I don't know that I can."

It was a loud sigh and the anxiety that prompted it showed right through.

"What's wrong?" he asked.

She was unable to speak.

"Talk to me, tell me—"

She shook her head, then mustered, "I can't say—"

That was so unlike her. "Why?"

"I'm just worried, that's all."

"About what?"

"About having to live without you."

"But you won't have to do that." He smiled softly. "We'll be together whenever and as much as we can."

She doubted that now, very much. "Will we?"

"Being with you is still the most important thing in my life, that hasn't changed. I can't see that changing."

It was more than doubt that prompted her to reply, "If you find your way back together, Janet may agree to accept it at first, but then she'll do everything in her power to keep you from me. She made it very clear that she won't have me as any part of your life."

"She's going to have to learn to compromise," he responded. "Just as you've done with Mike, I'll let her know that I'm not giving you up."

Shaking her head again, she told him, "I can't see that working with her. She's not like Mike—or any of us for that matter—she hasn't experienced the things in life we have, the things that would allow her to be more generous."

He was bewildered by her reaction. "But this is what you've been trying to convince me to do."

"That was before."

"Before what?"

"Before she came here, before I knew certain things."

"What things?"

He needs to know this about her, she decided, *he should know what Janet said.* "She'd rather destroy you than share you with me; she said that, in exactly those words."

As his confusion deepened, he sat up and folded his arms. "I didn't get that impression when we talked yesterday," he told her.

"She rang me at the office and we had rather a good chat, considering. She called to see how you were doing, if you were all right. And the way in which she did it — she was so timid about contacting me — I realized it was sincere." He paused a moment as he reflected on this. "And it also left me feeling horribly guilty for what I've done to her."

She sat up now, and evidenced irritation as she frowned at him. "She's becoming more clever, Andrew, dangerously clever."

"You don't believe her?"

"Not for a second."

He exhaled slowly. "But her approaching me could mean she's truly sorry for what she did. The experience may have changed her."

"Is that what she said? Did she say it changed her?"

"Yes, she did, actually. She's realized how destructive her anger is, she understands now that she's got to let go of it and get on with her life."

Annie's intuition sparked and it made her warn: "Don't let yourself be fooled. You didn't hear all the things she said, or feel the ardor with which she said them. She didn't change that quickly, she's up to something, I know it."

His brow knitted, but he said nothing in response.

Seeing his disbelief, she became intensely frustrated, and also utterly conflicted. She rose from the bed and wrapped a silk robe around her body, then walked out onto the balcony, asking herself — *What am I going to do? I understand why he believes her — it's because he wants to — he needs to — this is the mother of his children, for Christ's sake, his wife of twenty years! No, I can't tell him about this pregnancy now, not now that he's decided to make things better with her — how unfair would that be? But what am I going to do? What I need is more time to think this through — I've got to have more time.*

Shortly after, Andrew was standing beside her, wrapping an arm around her waist and asking, "Why has what I've said distressed you so? Something's troubling you and I've a feeling it's more than just my conversation with Janet."

She gripped the railing as though she were on the deck of a pitching ship. "We've gotten so close, you and I. We don't take a breath without thinking of each other, without feeling each other."

Her voice trailed off as she added, "If I lost you, I don't think I could go on living."

"But you're not going to lose me. We're going to go through some adjustments, that's inevitable, but we're going to come out of it all right. I know that now, don't you know that, too?"

"Sometimes I do," she answered, "other times I get so frightened. It's very scary, loving someone this much. It's like being up on the high wire without a net, without even a frigging umbrella."

He laughed slightly and wrapped his other arm around her, resting his chin on her head. "You needn't fear your love for me, my darling. Don't you know that my life begins and ends inside of you?"

Yes — your life, inside of me — she heard it differently than he meant it. "Dear God," she prayed aloud, "give me the strength."

"To do what, my love?"

"The right thing."

"Give us both the strength for that," he said.

In the distance, a thunderstorm lit the night. They remained on the balcony watching its approach, until it was so near they were forced inside for cover. When the rain arrived it came in torrents, washing through the garden paths and down along the hillside vineyards. It pounded the tile roofs and overflowed the planters, breaking tender shoots and flowers. After the initial flurry it went on rumbling and flashing, lightly showering for most of the night.

Just before dawn Andrew began mumbling and turning fitfully. Annie was awakened by his movements and watched him for a minute, before he sat upright with a start and a muffled scream.

She embraced him. "Another bad dream?"

He didn't answer at first.

She reached for the water glass at the bedside. "Here, sweetheart, have a sip of this."

After he drank, he shook his head. "It was that nightmare. It started out differently this time but it ended the same."

"The one with all the blood?"

"Yes, that one — but this time it was worse. I heard you screaming, like you were being tortured — God, it was horrible." He wiped the perspiration from his forehead.

She pulled him into her body and stroked his hair, saying, "It's all right, it was just a bad dream. Try to think of something nice, something happy."

"I have such an awful feeling—such foreboding."

"It'll pass, give it a minute, it'll pass."

He relaxed in the comfort she offered him, and after several minutes, they drifted off again.

The morning was spent attending to some business with the distillery. They dined just after one and then retired to the pool on this perfect gem of a day that saw everything sparkling in the brilliant summer sun.

They were nude sunbathing and Andrew was reading, while Annie passed in and out of sleep: The voice that awakened her was as disturbing and frightening as any nightmare she'd ever had.

"Ah, the happy couple, contentedly naked and satiated. How perfect, how Edenic!"

In the pit of his stomach Andrew reacted to the voice. He reached for a towel to cover Annie first, then pulled his shorts on, then reeled around to face the voice.

"What are you doing here, Cowan?"

Annie sat up. Andrew was standing next to her and she reached for his hand. She could tell by the way in which he grasped hers that he was as worried as she.

"I've come to have a chat. My, it is warm here, might you offer me something cool?" He leered at Annie who held the towel against her torso with one hand.

"In the cottage; help yourself," Andrew told him, wanting him to go inside so that Annie could dress.

Cowan disappeared into the cool darkness of the pool house.

As she pulled the loose-fitting gauze over her head, her heart was racing and her face was pale.

"I'll get him out of here," Andrew said to her. "Damn it anyway, but I wish I'd locked this place up."

He was back again, tinkling gin and tonic in hand. "What a lovely spot this is. Perfect little hideaway for illicit lovers."

Andrew scowled indignation. "You've no business here, Cowan. This is my property and you're trespassing."

"Going to call on the local gendarmes, are you? That should be fun!"

"No, I'm going to throw you out of here personally, on your bloody ear if I have to."

"Not very hospitable of you, I'd say. Not at all like the young earl I know."

"You're not welcome here," he persisted. "If there's something you want with me we can meet in London, or any bloody place you like, but not here. Now I want you to go."

Cowan sat defiantly on a chaise, crossing his legs and leaning back. Andrew walked toward him and stood menacingly over the smirking creature, saying to Annie, "Please go into the house."

She moved to stand behind him, and grasped his upper arms. "That's not going to work. Look at him, he wants to get a rise out of you."

"Very astute of you, my dear. Won't you sit down, both of you? It's too bloody hot to do this standing up."

"To do what?"

"To have this chat we need to have," he answered, adding disdainfully, "Oh do sit down, Andrew, and try to get hold of yourself."

Annie coaxed Andrew into a chair, then sat next to him.

"That's better now, much better." He grinned at Annie over his drink. "I say, I did prefer the first outfit you were wearing."

She cringed to know that he'd seen her naked.

Andrew's voice vibrated with rage. "Did Janet send you?"

"Janet? Oh heavens no," he lied. "Janet knows nothing of my visit here, in fact, I hope she never learns of it. What I have to say would upset her just as much as it will you—well, maybe not quite as much." He drank his glass down to the ice cubes, then looked at Annie. "Would you be a dear and get me another? I'm just so bloody comfortable now I don't want to move."

With quick sarcasm, she questioned, "Aren't you afraid I'll poison it?"

"Hadn't thought of that. Keep arsenic behind the bar, do you?"

"I wish," she said, as she sprang to her feet.

Cowan watched her every move, saying to Andrew, "She is such a tasty morsel, I do understand you old boy, always did. I remember that day I met her in St. Andrews. I told your father she was going to be trouble, knew it then, I did. But who could have foreseen just how much?"

She was back, handing him a fresh glass.

"Thank you, my dear."

When he looked at her, it made her skin crawl.

Andrew had been struggling to bring himself under control. "Do you want to get on with whatever you've come here about, Cowan? I find your company tedious and the sooner you say your piece, the better."

"Of course, quite right." He put both feet back on the ground. "Something rather upsetting has come to my attention, something ugly that is about to be committed to print." He affected a more serious look. "Ugly as it is, I'm terribly grateful it has come my way, while I might do something about it, while there's still time to act."

Andrew glared at him.

"One of those muckraking reporters," he continued, "the one who obtained the recording of that obscene phone conversation between Camilla and Charles, he came to me with his rough copy for verification of the facts, that's how I came to know of this. And so far, I've been successful in keeping it out of the papers, but I don't know how much longer I can manage, without your help. I mean, if the royals can't keep things like this down . . ." He shook his head for emphasis.

Andrew fumed in silence, while Annie began to feel beads of perspiration dripping from her underarms.

"At first I thought it just a little tidbit about you and Annie," he went on to say, "but when I read it, I found myself wishing that it had been about the two of you. That would have been so much easier to deal with."

Andrew folded his arms and tilted his head. "What did you read, Cowan?"

"It's a sordid allegation about the ongoing affair between you and your personal secretary, the homosexual Nigel, and how you've just spent three weeks hidden away in the Greek islands with him." He couldn't help chuckling and congratulated himself on his brilliance, when he realized, "You've even matching suntans, haven't you, to add veracity to that."

Andrew laughed but Annie knew from the sound of it that it wasn't real. "That's utterly preposterous, complete crap," he said. "Anyone who printed those lies would be destroyed by a libel suit, and they know it. Someone's playing games here, and I'm inclined to think it's you."

Lord Alfred calmly reached into the pocket of his blazer, which he had draped across the chair. He retrieved some folded papers and held them out to Andrew. "I thought you might doubt me."

Andrew refused to take them from him. "You're capable of creating that yourself, Cowan."

"All right then, don't believe me. I'll just be on my way, and don't ring me Monday morning and say you need my help. It'll be too late by then."

Annie was staring at Cowan, because she was afraid to look at Andrew.

"If it is real, let them go ahead and print it," Andrew decided. "Within hours I'll have a retraction and them on their knees. They'll be out of business faster than the time it takes to set a match to one of those rags."

Alfred shook his head again. "I was afraid you'd say that. Very well, if that's the way you want it, if you want to open the flood gates, that's up to you, I can't stop you. You can probably destroy one paper but you won't get them all."

"I won't have to."

Cowan feigned sympathy. "I know you weren't with Nigel, I know you've been right here with her, and unfortunately that's going to have to come out for you to prove your innocence. You're going to have to expose her to save yourself, you know."

Annie blurted, "I don't give a rat's ass if he does!"

He laughed at her choice of words. "No, of course not. You'd willingly sacrifice yourself to help him and that's very noble, but I'm afraid that won't be enough."

"Why not?" she asked, with increasing rancor.

He affected his wise, understanding face. "These people are students of human nature, they know that where there's smoke there's fire. You shoot them down on the one story but you'll have to give them another to do it, and then they'll have their taste of blood. They'll know he's not the model figure he's been made out to be and they'll go looking, delving into dark corners, leaving no stone unturned. Who knows what they'll come up with then?"

Annie turned to Andrew, in time to watch the flush wash from his cheeks.

Cowan spoke directly to Andrew now. "Most easily, when they're flashing their reward money around, they'll likely discover the young woman your father sent to that private clinic in the Netherlands, some three months after your marriage. The records from the abortion are probably still hanging around somewhere." He couldn't help smiling.

The shock that delivered to Andrew, slowed his breathing dramatically.

"Donald never told you?" he innocently inquired. "He'd said he probably wouldn't, that he didn't see the point in your knowing. It was the young woman from the caterer, you know, the one you spent your wedding night with. She came to your father asking for money and help."

Andrew dropped his jaw.

Cowan struggled to conceal his delight over Andrew's reaction. "When the debasing details come out, the depths of humiliation they'll plunge Janet to, I can't begin to fathom. Imagine the whole world knowing that her husband preferred sleeping with a stranger on their wedding night." He waited for the impact. "And then there's the accident. Donald did do a splendid job of keeping the fact that alcohol was involved out of the official records, but there were witnesses. Quite a few of them, too, as I recall. Not so bad in itself, the drink, but a man was killed, his children orphaned, the public won't take kindly to that. They'll likely say that you got away with murder."

Andrew was weakened and equivocal, but still he told him, "I'll own up to it all if I have to. I'm sick to death of carrying it around all these years anyway."

"A virtuous man such as yourself," he mocked, "I'm sure it's been terribly difficult for you. Yes, it may be a relief once it's all over, but you'll be awhile getting there, I'm afraid. They'll keep digging into your past, going on and on, back and back, all the way back to your days at school." He sipped his drink, then cocked his head to one side and raised his brows, savoring the moment. This was going to give him the most pleasure, this was going to be his coup: "I hope there's nothing that happened at Eton that you wouldn't want the world to know about."

In a flash, Andrew had him by the shirt. "Get out of here right now you vile, despicable creature, before I kill you!"

Annie jumped in and tried to pry him away. "Andrew, Andrew—don't, please!"

He tightened his grip on the man's collar and twisted it, as Cowan started to choke.

"Andrew, please, let him go, listen to me and let him go!"

Reluctantly, he let up and Annie backed him away from the wretched man.

"Please, sit down, Andrew, let me talk to him. He came here saying he could prevent this, let me talk to him and see how he proposes to do that, please!" It took a great deal of coaxing but when she had him settled, she turned her attention to Alfred. "Are you all right, can I get you anything?"

Cowan coughed and rubbed at his neck. "No, I'm fine, just a bit shaken." The sun shown behind Annie and he could see her body through the thin, cotton dress she was wearing. That perked him up considerably.

Andrew was stricken; his complexion was alabaster and his breathing was awkward. She was terribly worried for him and to keep him connected she took up one of his hands, saying, "What do you want, Alfred? What's the bottom line to all this?"

He cleared his throat. "Well, I've managed thus far, as I said, to fend them off. I could do better if I had his cooperation."

"In what way?"

"First off, he's got to go home and give up this self-indulgence. None of this would have happened if he'd been doing what he's supposed to. Credence was given to that rumor about Nigel because of his mysterious disappearance."

She was so furious, she wanted to scream. But she remained outwardly cool as she said, "All right. Then what?"

"Then I'm going to put myself on the line and pull out all the stops to keep this from going public. I'm going to call in favors on Fleet Street and use whatever means I have to, but I'll get the story extinguished if it's the last thing I do."

Andrew emerged from his stupor to question, "Why would you do that?"

"I'd do it in memory of your dear father, and in exchange for a promise from you."

He loathed having to ask, "What sort of promise?"

Here it comes — Cowan gloated — *my crowning touch.* "For your promise that you'll walk away from her and stay away, forever."

Both their hearts felt as though they'd been shot through; they could do nothing more in this moment than glare at Cowan, through eyes clouded by pain.

In an effort to stay credible, he pretended to be sympathetic. "I know it's hard, but think of the alternative. Things could come out about Andrew that would not only disgrace and ruin him, but all of his family. Centuries of nobility could be destroyed in one fell swoop, his precious children, humiliated beyond repair, their futures forever altered by his shame. All the good he's done, all the charities that benefit from his patronage, the businesses themselves, all affected and possibly damaged by his ignominy, all for what? For a few nights of torrid pleasure?"

They could not look at one another, so they kept their eyes fixed on Cowan.

Turning it on even more now, he beseeched, "And all that aside, your sons, Andrew, think of your sons. What will it do to them to have the father they adore and model themselves after accused as a homosexual, a bisexual, at least? How will it affect them and how they see themselves? Donald's just going off to university, he'll likely be treated as an outcast. Duncan's still at Eton, good lord, what he'll have to endure I can't imagine. And poor little Malcolm, he'll grow up with it, this is how he'll come to know you. How confused will he be about his own sexuality, I wonder? It'll be dreadful, just dreadful. And of course there are the girls. "

Andrew put one hand to his forehead and grabbed at his hair. He stayed that way a few seconds before looking again to Cowan. "This is extortion, pure and simple," he managed to say. "I don't believe there's any story in the press. What I do believe is that my father made the grave error of confiding things in you he never should have, and now you're using them against me, for what true purpose I don't understand."

He affected a look of disappointment. "Think that, if you like, it doesn't matter what you think of me. I know my motivation. I'm acting on behalf of your father, out of respect for your father. I know he would have wanted me to do this."

Andrew was coming out of the haze, coming back to himself as he retorted, "You know nothing about what my father would have wanted. He wasn't your friend, he didn't even like you. He knew what kind of manipulative creature you are and he warned me against you."

"Donald respected me," Cowan insisted.

"Donald distrusted you," he knew.

"You don't know what you're talking about."

Annie broke in now. "What kind of assurance could we get from you, Alfred?"

"Regarding what?"

"If he did as you ask, what kind of assurance would we have that you'd act to protect him, and to keep him protected?"

He answered simply, "My word."

Andrew laughed sharply, abruptly.

Annie deliberately kept her voice soft, as she questioned, "Only your word?"

Leeringly, he responded, "What else could I give you?" then answered himself: *I know what I'd like to give you — I know the kind of treatment women like you deserve, and it would be delicious, oh so delicious, to see you get what you deserve.*

She sensed something obscene in his response and in her revulsion looked away from him as she muttered, "Nothing, I suppose."

Andrew told him, "I don't believe anything about this, not this fabricated crap about Nigel, not what you said about the press being on my heels, and if any of it were true I wouldn't trust for one minute that you'd do anything in anyone's best interest but your own."

Cowan seemed almost hurt. "Since you were very small I've looked upon you with affection, Andrew, and since you've become a man that affection has grown and been joined by respect. It pains me now to see you destroying yourself and your family over this woman." He glanced briefly at Annie. "I'd do anything I could to stop it, but I would not concoct a situation such as this. I understand how horribly painful all of this is for you, and I would not bring these matters up unless I absolutely had to."

Andrew scoffed. "I'd like to believe you capable of acting out of something other than complete selfishness, but I don't."

"I act out of duty. You seem to have forgotten yours," Cowan rejoined.

"I haven't forgotten," he insisted.

"You put it from your mind all too often."

"Lord Alfred," Annie interjected, "you don't understand about us. We're not going to let our relationship go any further. I'm going to stay married to my husband and Andrew will keep on with Janet. All we want is to be able to spend some time together, now and then." She ended on a pleading note.

"Don't beg him, Annie," Andrew said. "Don't lower yourself."

Cowan's eyes were drawn to her chest; her nipples had hardened and he could discern their dark color through the thin fabric. "I'd like to believe you, my dear, really I would, but I've known our Andrew since he was born and I've never known anything or anyone to affect him the way you do." His smile turned rancid as he added, "As I see it you're like a cancer to him, the only treatment for which is removal."

Hearing that, Annie dropped her head and wanted to sob.

Andrew was suddenly standing again. "Leave this minute, Cowan, this very minute or I swear, I'll kill you."

Neither Annie nor Cowan had ever seen Andrew so angry. Annie stood, too, and Alfred rose slowly from his seat, grinning all the while. "All right," he said, and nothing else.

As he was leaving he deliberately brushed against Annie's chest; his touch sparked a memory, a sick and powerful memory that she could not quite bring to conscious thought.

His parting words were like the delivery of a verdict. "I'll expect to hear that you're safely ensconced at Crinan Castle tomorrow and when I do, I'll begin my efforts on your behalf."

Andrew held blanched fists at his side as he watched Cowan make the walk back to his car. It was only Annie's presence beside him that kept him from acting at this moment, from going after him and pounding him into the dirt. When the car had disappeared from sight he turned to Annie; their embrace was unlike any they had ever shared.

Her voice quavered. "What are we going to do?" She waited for his response, then understood why it wasn't coming: He simply could not bring himself to say the words. She led him into the pool house and guided him into sitting down, then poured a large glass of Scotch. She offered it to him, but he shook his head in refusal.

She sat next to him, still holding to the glass, and questioned, "Do we have any choice?"

His silence answered her.

"But you don't believe him."

"No, I don't, but I know what he's capable of, and I fear him."

"Why?"

"Because he's diabolic."

"Is there no way to go against him?"

"I can't think just now." He closed his eyes and inhaled deeply.

"No—don't even try." She set aside the drink and began to rub his neck and shoulders, saying, "I'll think of something."

He looked at her now, and there was something akin to fear in his expression. "I don't want you near him, not anywhere near him. He's the devil incarnate, Annie."

"But there must be something we can do," she persisted.

He seemed resolute, when he answered, "If he's telling the truth, we have to do as he wants, and I'll have to defile myself by asking for his help. If he's not, we still have to do what he asks, because he's the kind of man who would plant a story like that, just to teach me a lesson about going against him. Jesus Christ," he suddenly called out, "Jesus Christ!"

"It's going to be all right," she told him. "We'll find a way to deal with this. We've been through worse, my love, we'll get through this."

"Have we been through worse?" he wondered. "I don't think so. This involves my children, Annie. By far, the most horrible thing he said was how this would affect my children. I can't take a risk like that."

His children: It was like a punch to her gut. Over the last half hour she'd forgotten about his child inside of her.

"I don't give a damn if the whole bloody world knows, but I can't face having my children dragged through this muck. There's no way on God's earth I could knowingly do that to them."

"No, of course you couldn't." She felt a strong urge to touch her abdomen, to comfort the little thing inside, but she resisted.

"What he said about that girl, Jackie, about her having been pregnant. It was a complete shock. Why didn't she come to me, why didn't she tell me she was pregnant?"

When Annie swallowed, it was with some difficulty. "I'm sure she thought she was doing the right thing, keeping you out of it."

"But it was my child, too! To have an abortion without even discussing it with me —"

"You had no relationship," she anxiously defended. "And you were married to Janet, what else could she do?"

"I would have helped her. I would have done everything I could have for her."

"Yes, you would have, because that's the kind of man you are." And that realization made everything worse, because for her and her child, she knew absolutely that he would go to the ends of the earth.

"That was my responsibility, not my father's. I did that to her and I should have been the one to help her out of it. God, all of this, it's so overwhelming! That excrement about Nigel —"

"Have you and he had the talk you were supposed to?"

"No, we haven't. He's just gone right back into his role and we haven't even mentioned the incident again."

Something occurred to her. "Do you think he has any complicity in this?"

"For his sake, I hope not." His anger had cooled a bit but it flared again at the thought. "But Cowan's cleverness, it reeks of evil. That bloody bastard is so cunning, he may have gotten something out of Nigel without his even knowing it. My father told me once how he lures people into things, into doing things in his presence that compromise them, sexual things mostly, then he holds that over them. I think he did that to my father, that's why Donald stopped trusting him, but he went on pretending to like Cowan because he feared what he might do. My father was a much tougher man than I—if he was afraid of Cowan . . ."

A cold shiver emanated in Annie's spine and spread to her limbs.

"How do you go up against the devil, Annie? How do you counter an implacable enemy like Satan?"

"There must be a way out from under this, there must be," she needed to believe.

Andrew lowered his head into his hands. As Annie massaged his neck again she felt him begin to shake. It was barely noticeable at first, but then it grew more intense, as his strength waned and the power of it increased. His sobs went first into his hands, then, as she pulled him to her, onto her shoulder. He gave himself over to them, because there was nothing else he could do. He had not cried that way for many, many years, not since that night on the West Sands, when Annie drove away and out of his life.

Today was in many ways worse than that night, for today he knew with certainty what it was he was losing: their newborn happiness, which had just been mercilessly strangled in front of them — without the slightest warning on this exquisite summer day—both of them forced to watch as the life drained from it, as the promise and beauty within it seeped away. Their love affair lay like a corpse now, as they sat powerless and stricken, enclosed by a wall of grief that severed them from the joys of the world.

But beyond those walls life continued unabated. Birds called to one another, butterflies visited the garden, the fountains of Eros and Dionysus bubbled and soothed. Heated by the late afternoon sun, the large clumps of lavender planted near the pool imparted their fragrance to the summer air, and literally hummed with bees. Everything seemed fluid, metamorphic, everything, that is, but the statue of Prometheus, which, as she held to her sobbing lover, took dead center in Annie's line of vision: His intractable suffering seemed directed at her, hurled at her, like a fiery meteor, propelled from the slingshot of Zeus himself. In one compelling moment, her mind took a flight of fancy and ran her out of the little pool house, to Prometheus—ax in hand. She wielded the heavy thing and swung away, shattering the rock to which he was chained, freeing him from his shackles.

Twenty-Seven

It took a long while, but Andrew finally composed himself enough to speak to Annie again. Still in the pool house, they were sitting on the floor, leaning against the couch, because it was where they had collapsed when their strength left them.

He forced himself to say it. "I'll have to leave tomorrow."

She already knew it, but that didn't lessen the anguish hearing those words caused. "I understand."

"There's nothing else I can do."

"No, there isn't," she agreed.

His eyes were glazed over, and he trembled now and again. "Never in my life have I felt this way—not even before, back then, did I feel this horrible, this hopeless. He might as well have killed me, Annie."

"Please, Andrew, don't say that," she pleaded. "It sounds as though you've given up."

"It's not just about you and me, he's made it about them, too. I have to act to protect them, all of them. I can't sacrifice them for—" he stopped abruptly.

"For me."

"That's not what I was going to say. I can't put my needs ahead of theirs—that's what I meant to say."

"No, you have to go now," she agreed, "that's clear, but we don't have to accept what he dictates to us. He has no right to tell us that we can't see each other."

"All of this, it's all because of me," he told her, "because of the things I've done, the mistakes I've made. I'm the most miserable

I've ever been in my life, and I've no one to blame but myself." That realization breathed new life into his suffering.

"You're not the only one who's made mistakes."

"But most people could have their sins made public and no one would give a damn. With people like me, it's entirely different."

"There has to be a way around this," she said. "I refuse to accept defeat, I absolutely refuse."

"I don't have the courage to go against him, I wish I did, but I don't."

"You don't have to—I'll do it," she decided.

His forlorn expression turned to one of deep concern. "Annie, listen to me. He's an evil, corrupt man, who's capable of anything. You have to promise me that you'll stay away from him; with everything else I can't be worried about you coming into the hands of that reprobate."

She only looked at him.

His voice had regained its strength, when he demanded of her, "Promise me."

She'd already started lying to him about the pregnancy, what harm would a few more lies do? "I promise."

"It's not just Janet and the children I need to protect, I need to keep you safe as well."

As crazy as it was to even think of now, she longed to tell him about the baby. "Do what you have to do for them," she said instead, "but don't give up on us. Will you promise me that you won't give up on us?"

He knew this absolutely: "If that day ever came, I think my heart would stop."

"And mine, too." She laid her head in his lap now and he stroked her. "That's why I can't let you talk this way, I can't even hear it without wanting to stop breathing."

His eyes burned intolerably, as he said, "My Annie, my dearest, dearest love."

"Tell me we'll make it through this, say we'll be together again—say that to me, Andrew, please."

He obeyed, but his voice lacked conviction. "We'll make it through, somehow we'll be with each other again."

"Keep saying that to yourself," she insisted. "Say it and believe it, and never stop believing it."

"I won't."

In the ensuing silence, they were both flooded with crushing doubt that neither would admit to the other.

"There are some things I need to tell you," he finally said. "I've had some papers drawn up, and executed a codicil to my will."

She shook her head, as she told him, "Please don't talk about this."

"I must—in case anything happens to me, you need to be protected."

She pleaded, "Please, Andrew, I can't hear this now."

He knew this would upset her, it was why he hadn't brought it up before, but with everything that had transpired today, he no longer had a choice. "I can't just hand the château over to you as I'd like, because you need money to run it. Besides, Janet could easily contest that. So I'm going to put you under contract as my on-site manger of the Armagnac distillery. Every month there'll be five thousand pounds deposited in your account as compensation for that, and living in the château will be part of your contract. Mike and I discussed this," he informed her, "and he feels it's the best way to protect you, to allow you to stay on, should you want that. I or my estate will go on paying everyone's wages, of course, Didier's and Lisette's as well as everyone else's. All that remains is for you to add your signature, after Mike looks everything over."

She sniveled and reached for a box of tissues. "You discussed this with Mike? Why?"

"He was the only one I could trust to protect you," he answered. "The contract was his idea, because it would be very difficult for Janet to break."

After blowing her nose, she looked up to say, "I can't believe it—when did you do this?"

"A few days after he left here. I called him because I wanted to get some things off my chest."

"Like what?"

"I wanted him to know how very much I love you, and how grateful I am to have you in my life again. And I needed to say how sorry I am for hurting him, because I know how much he loves you, too."

"God, Andrew." She remembered now, how Mike phoned her, reiterating that he wouldn't interfere with their relationship. That comment had to have been spurred by his conversation with Andrew, and neither man had said a word to her about it.

"And I'm going to transfer more money to your account straightaway, to make it an even half-million pounds. The codicil is about that, about leaving that money to you, should I die."

"I don't need that," she protested. "It's so very generous of you, but I don't need it."

"I know you don't. I know that you can take care of yourself, and that Mike will always look out for you, whether you two find your way back together or not. But I need to do this for you, don't you understand why?"

The things he was saying, the way in which he said them—there was such finality to it.

"And there's something else I need to say," he continued. "I need to thank you for what you've done for me, for giving me back my spirit and opening up my heart again."

"Please, Andrew, I can't bear this!"

He reached and embraced her, saying, "When we met in St. Andrews, I was so locked up inside, I didn't trust myself to feel anything after that experience with Philip. You brought me such a gift—you loved me and reached inside of me and made me feel love for you—no one has ever done anything more wonderful for me." He kissed her tear-streaked cheeks several times before he continued. "After all the time and everything that went between, you came to me and freed me once again, you gave me that gift all over again. No matter what happens now, nothing can change what I feel for you, not time, not distance, not anyone or anything. You've given me what every human being strives for, Annie: absolute acceptance and forgiveness and love, love that is stronger than life."

She crumpled into his lap again and sobbed to break his heart.

"There's no possible way I can thank you for that. Out of all the good things that have happened to me, not one of them, not even the births of my children, can begin to compare with you."

She could barely get out, "But I've brought you so much hurt, too."

"I love even the hurt you've caused me," he knew with certainty. "I'd rather be hurt by you, than loved by anyone else, Annie."

"Andrew, don't leave me," she begged him. "Stay with me, we'll find a way to deal with this."

"What I feel, it frightens me," he admitted, shivering with the stark, brutal realization. "I could kill Cowan with my bare hands for what he's done to us. But I have to keep my mind focused on the children," he knew. "I have to think first of them."

She opened her mouth to tell him, to say: *Yes, and there's another child you need to consider*; but she closed it again because she understood, without a doubt, that the knowledge of that would do anything but help him.

"Someday, somehow, there might be a way to tell them everything, to defuse the situation. Cowan might even die—God, that he would! But until then, I've no other recourse. I know you understand, I know you'll help me to do what I must."

"I'll help you," she managed to respond.

He pulled her to his chest and inhaled deeply. "I love the scent of you, recognizing it always makes me feel so safe, so happy. I'm going to miss that terribly."

She choked on the tears those words elicited.

His voice quavered as he said, "We have to stop this now, we shouldn't say any more. We have tonight and we should enjoy it as much as humanly possible, we can't do that if we keep talking like this."

Annie grabbed his shirt with both hands as she thought of it, and her pleading face and eyes tore at his heart. "You won't take your things, will you? Please don't take your things away! I want to go on seeing your clothes in the closet, your razor on the sink— I want to go on thinking you'll be home soon—" She was choking and beginning to struggle for air.

In an effort to calm her, he stroked her head almost frantically. "I'll leave everything, Annie, even my heart."

Those words brought her beyond anything she could bear. "God! God! Why?" she sobbed. "Help me! Help me to understand why this is happening! I don't understand any of it, not any of it!"

Andrew no longer had words to give. He rose from where they sat and bent to lift Annie, who was by now prostrate with grief. In his arms, he carried her to the house.

In their bedroom, he pulled her dress off over her head, then settled her into the pillows.

"Tonight, we'll make love as we always have, we'll make love until we have no more strength. In the morning I'll go off, as though for a long business trip, and we'll say what we have to say in that light." He kissed her forehead. "All right, my darling?"

She understood that he needed her help to make it somehow bearable. She suppressed her sobs and nodded, then pulled his body into hers.

Didier and Lisette had been napping in their apartment when he arrived, so they had not seen anything of Lord Cowan. They were surprised and disturbed by the demeanor of the couple as they served them their supper, when they had seemed so happy and at peace at luncheon. After a time, Annie realized that she must say something.

"Andrew's just learned that he must leave tomorrow, and he can't say when he'll be back."

Their faces conveyed sympathy and understanding, Lisette's especially, who sought to console her. "But surely it won't be too long, Madame."

"He doesn't know, just now, how long it will be."

Didier couldn't think what to say, so he questioned, "Is there anything we can do, Count Andrew, anything at all?"

"Take good care of Annie for me, will you both?"

Lisette answered, "The very best care, as though she were our own daughter."

Their thoughtfulness brought on the tears again, and Annie had to leave the table. She walked into her moonlit garden and stopped in front of a newly opened rose. It was white with curled, crimson edges—like the ones Andrew had sent to her in Versailles—with a fragrance that seemed to intensify in the night air. Standing alone before the flower, she reveled in the sound of his footsteps as he traversed the pebbled path behind her. The realization that after tomorrow there'd be no more sound of him bore mercilessly into her soul.

He wrapped his arms around her and snuggled against her back. "That's new, isn't it?"

She laid her hands over his. "Yes, just opened."

"It's lovely."

"Didier told me it's always a late bloomer. The bush is filled with buds; in a few days, it'll be the highlight of the garden."

Such a simple thought, such an insignificant thing really, but it made Andrew want to die when he realized that he would not see it in its glory. "I'll think of you here while I'm away, I'll think of you here and by the pool and in the vineyard, and I know it'll comfort me."

All evening her stomach had been churning, threatening—now it felt as though the acid was eating her from the inside out. "I can't finish my dinner, Andrew, do you think we might go in now?"

"Let's do that. I said my good-byes to Didier and Lisette and they've retired for the night, so we can be alone."

They held hands as they made their way—very slowly—to the house.

Their lovemaking was quiet, delicate.

"The feel of you, still wet with me inside, I can't describe how it affects me," he whispered to her. "It's always so right and perfect; even sharing you with Mike, even that was all right, somehow. It was an intimacy I never expected to enjoy."

They lingered in an impassioned kiss.

Annie's voice had changed into that sexy, throaty one that he loved. "I've never felt so much love as I did that day, never in my whole life. When you took me back, when you loved me enough to wait for me, to accept that I'd needed to be with my husband—I've never felt closer to anyone in my life than I did to you in that moment."

He smiled softly. "I'd have to say that it was a crucial moment for me as well."

"We can do it, you know—if we can get out from under Cowan's threat, we can go on, we can be together."

He put a gentle finger to her lips. "I don't want to hear his name—I don't want even to think of it."

"No, nor do I."

He was still inside of her and had not moved as they spoke. He slowly began to thrust himself again, kissing her throat and face. When he climaxed he was overcome with tears.

When they separated their bodies, she whispered to him, "I won't believe that this is the end."

Lying alongside her, Andrew took up both of her hands. "I want to tell you something, something very secret and important, something that I'm sworn to tell no one except the mother of my children, and when he's old enough, my heir. I want to tell you because you're closer to me than the mother of my children, closer to me than anyone in the world. I want to tell you to show you how much I love and trust you."

She looked far into his eyes, eyes that always made her think of the skies over St. Andrews.

"The Stone of Destiny—I'm entrusted with it. It's my duty to keep it safe and hidden until Scotland is free again. My ancestors took it more than six hundred years ago; all the Kilmartin earls since have guarded it and kept it out of English hands, sometimes at the cost of their lives. It's been our most sacred and important obligation, it's what we're born to do and what we pledge to pass on to our sons. It's the most crucial reason I could never marry you, why I had to marry Janet. Tradition dictates that our wives be chosen from certain bloodlines, to keep the succession intact. I had very few choices; Janet was the best of them."

In understanding the gravity of what he had just confided to her, Annie was plunged backward in time and overcome with sympathy for a young man to whom honor and duty were everything, but whose heart sought to tear him away from those things. A series of memories flashed through her mind—the torment in his eyes that night at the Kate Kennedy Ball when he told her about his engagement, the battle that always seemed to be waging inside him when they'd come close to making love, the ways in which he fought to keep his distance—all the things he'd done that had left her confused and hurt, they all came back to her now and made perfect, sad sense.

"I wanted with all my heart to be able to change that," he continued, "but it wasn't up to me. I was compelled to uphold what was passed on to me — I could never have lived with myself if I hadn't. Everything I do, everything I am, none of it is confined to me. My actions reflect on the family, on my country. That's why I must do everything in my power to defend them, even at the very great cost of losing the most wonderful thing in my life, the only real love I've ever known."

"I understand," she whispered, staying in his eyes. Her memory flashed to that day in the market when she'd laughed at the tabloid photo of him, dancing with the Princess of Wales. The woman beside her was a stranger, an ordinary resident of St. Andrews whom he'd never met, but who defended him with obvious and deeply held pride. And on the heels of that recollection she realized now what it was that John had tried to tell her, that night he drove her to meet him; he warned her about the importance of his heritage, and predicted that in the end his responsibilities would win out.

"Trusting me with your secret," she said, "it shows such faith in me. Thank you for that, my love."

They lay in silence for a time, before Andrew spoke again; something Sir Walter Scott once wrote, had come into his mind. "What Scott said, it's so very true: 'One crowded hour of glorious life is worth an age without a name.' We've had that, Annie, we've lived these weeks together gloriously and intensely, and we'll never have to look back and wonder what being together might have been like. We'll have these memories with us always."

He pulled her to him again and pressed his heart to hers; they could feel them beating against one another, even as they felt the night close in around them.

The morning was cruelly beautiful. The sunlight gave an acute, intense quality to everything, to the polished wooden floor, to the folds of drapes flanking the French doors, the flower-filled vases set about the room. It should have been one of those gentle, lingering mornings, when they enjoyed their breakfast at the little table on their balcony, gazing into the garden, then bathed together, loving hands soaping, caressing one another. They should have welcomed the light that brought them another day—but they could not—for it was a pitiless, ruthless morning that broke upon them, a morning that had come racing out of the night and overtaken the world, with fierce rapidity.

As she awakened she listened first to his breathing, then opened her eyes to see him already alert and looking upon her. They didn't speak. Their hands connected with each other first, and the rest of their flesh followed. The sexual act that blossomed from their touching was the most intense physical sensation either of them had ever experienced. It was more primal and essential than the throes of birth, more poignant and affecting than the struggle against death.

When it concluded, Andrew spoke to her. "We should leave it like this."

She closed her eyes and nodded.

As he rose from the bed, she turned her face to the wall.

When he was dressed, he sat next to her. Both her hands were resting on her abdomen; he lifted one and kissed it. "I'm telling myself that it's a long business trip. It won't be soon, but I will be home someday." He kissed the hand again.

Annie could not open her eyes, she could not speak, she could barely breathe. She felt the mattress lift as he stood again. She heard him walk across the room and turned to see him one last time. He was standing frozen at the door, his hand upon the handle, his back to her. Her circulation seemed to be slowing, her blood thickening.

"I don't think I'll be able to phone," he told her. "The sound of your voice—I don't think I could bear it." He moved the handle and held it a few seconds, then he opened the door and went out.

She heard him descend the stairs, the front door close. The car started up, perfectly, indifferently. She listened to the crackling stones as the tires rolled across them. She wanted to run after him—to call him back and forbid him to leave—but her voice failed her, and all that came of her effort was a mournful expulsion of air. She tried to rise now but her body had become a baleful mass, that took herculean effort to move. Mustering the effort, she dragged herself to the edge. She lowered deadened feet onto the floor and stood, but her legs gave way and she slumped, naked, to the carpet. She kept moving, though, and managed to raise herself to crawl. Every inch she gained was torture. She kept her eyes on the goal, on the glistening brass door handle that a shaft of sunlight had illuminated. She kept after it, on hands and knees until she reached it, then she pulled herself up, grasping it as though it were something tender and alive. It was the last thing she had seen him touch, and she brought her lips to kiss it. Her mouth tried to bring it alive with him, with anything of him, but it gave up nothing of Andrew.

He stopped at the gates. He got out of the car to open them and turned to look behind. Nothing could be seen of the house, nothing. It was lost to him; all that remained was a pebbled road that he could not turn back on. He moved the car through and got out again. He held onto the gates with both hands as they clanked shut, as they transformed in one split second from opening to barrier. A moan originated in his gut—a response to the finality of that sound. Churning and rumbling, it grew louder and louder, until it reverberated in his throat, then expelled itself. It was the primal report of pure misery, and Andrew had to hold to the iron bars as it took everything from him.

Annie released the brass handle and sat, her nude body leaned against the door. Like the scavenging opportunist it is, Death began whispering to her. It offered to end the despair, it promised to bring her peace. Not so very far from where she sat, a nearly full bottle of potent narcotic called to her; all she need do was get it, sit quietly with the pills and swallow, one after the other, until they were gone. It would be so easy, all her pain would pass away and she would forget. She would tell herself that she was going to sleep and in the morning Andrew would be there, lying by her side; she would drift off like that, never to awaken and feel this pain again.

She listened to what Death had to say, listened quite intently, until she heard another voice come from behind it. The second voice was not nearly as trenchant, nor was it as seductive: It was

tremulous and weak and pathetically unsure of itself. But its quavering cries were so overwhelmed by the other, it evoked her sympathy. While the ensuing voice lacked the distinction and emphasis
of Death's, it gradually grew louder, calling to Annie, asking for
something, compelling her to hear it out.

Death's bid was refused, as the timorous voice of Andrew's
unborn child asked Annie to protect it, and give it life. She pulled
her legs into her chest and instinctively began to rock, saying
aloud, "Hush now, it's all right, everything will be all right. I'm not
going to let anything bad happen to you, my little one, my precious,
little one."

The rocking went on, for how long, it was impossible to say.

Twenty-Eight

Janet received an early morning call from Lord Alfred. "He should be home today — and home to stay."

"What happened? What did you do?" She could barely contain her excitement.

"It's best that you know nothing of that. Be completely surprised to see him, welcome him with open arms, and be endlessly sympathetic — all right, my dear?"

"Of course!"

"I expect he'll accuse you of taking part in this. Steadfastly deny it and be crushed that he'd even imagine you capable of such a thing."

With his warning Janet's excitement shifted into unease. "I'll do my best," she answered.

"If you want him to be your husband again, you need to do better than your best. I can get him home to you, but I can't make him return to your bed," he said frankly. "That part is up to you."

"I understand."

"Good luck with everything. Let me know how it works out, will you?"

"I will," she answered.

Andrew focused on the clouds and sky, trying his damnedest not to think. He waited until they were preparing to land in Glasgow before ringing Crinan Castle. The head butler answered.

"I'll be there in half an hour; is Lady Kilmartin at home?"

"She is, your lordship. Shall I get her?"

379

"No," he said curtly. "Tell her I'm arriving and that I want to meet with her in my study as soon as I'm in."

"Yes, right away, your lordship. Is there anything else, sir?"

"Is Nigel Bain about?"

"I believe so, sir."

"Get a message to him, too. I want to see him when I'm through with my wife. And, William, I don't want to see anyone but my wife when I arrive, do you understand?"

He hung up without waiting for a reply and the poor butler, who knew the earl as the kindest and most polite of men, wondered what it was he'd done to offend him.

Janet had received Andrew's message but she thought it better not to wait in his study. She was concerned about Cowan's warning that he would blame her for whatever happened, so she decided to meet him first where there were people around, and drove the Range Rover to the helipad.

When he disembarked and caught sight of her, he glared with such vehemence she wanted to cower. He didn't speak, not even to say hello. She was standing by the driver's side of the vehicle but Andrew brushed past her and got behind the wheel. He waited for her to walk around and get in, then drove the car quickly away and toward the wood. He followed an old trail up to a spot that overlooked the loch and braked to an jarring halt. He slammed the door and walked to the edge of the promontory, then stood rigid, forcing the cool air into his lungs.

Though her knees felt weak, Janet bravely followed him. Her heart was beating wildly, as she said to his back, "I can't know what you're so upset about until you tell me."

He turned suddenly, violently. "What have you done, Janet?"

What she saw in his face terrified her. "What have I done? I don't understand—is Annie worse?"

His glare burned through to her core. "You think you've helped yourself by bringing that animal into our personal business—"

"What animal? Whom are you talking about?"

"You know damned well."

"I wish I did," she answered.

"This is no game, Janet, no bloody, fucking game."

Her insides were a quivering, short-circuiting jumble of nerves, but she managed to say, "Please tell me what you're on about."

He sat on a boulder and tried to breathe more slowly. For the first time in his life he wanted to strike a woman and the sensation of it was adding to his distress. "Bloody, fucking Cowan, Janet. Bloody, fucking Cowan."

She remained standing and at a safe distance. Still feigning ignorance she questioned, "What about him?"

With quiet, deadly rage, he informed her now, "He came to see us yesterday. He made threats, threats that should they be followed upon, will destroy all of us, and I do mean all of us—you and the children as well."

She didn't have to pretend when she asked, "What kind of threats?"

He exhaled, then fumed, "Cleverly disguised ones that he purports exist in their potential to be discovered, but that are really his threats. He knows things, things he shouldn't, and if I don't do as he dictates, he's prepared to use them against me. He's effectively made all of us his hostages—you, me, Annie, the children—we're all hostage to one of the most cruel and frightening people I've ever known, and you've done this, you've brought this on us."

Janet felt her thin veneer of composure melting away. "What sort of things? What does he know that he shouldn't?"

"Things that you don't even know, that only my father and I knew." Andrew had a sudden thought: Were these the things that Cowan tried to use against his father?

"Please, tell me what he knows!" she demanded now.

His face flushed and his voice grew weaker, as he answered, "He knows about incidents from my past, episodes that I'm ashamed of. If the press got wind of these things, they'd have a field day. We'd all be right there on the covers of those tabloids every day, right alongside Diana and Charles and Camilla. Our personal lives would be splattered all over the media and none of us would ever be the same again." He raised his voice to reiterate, "None of us!"

Fear was overwhelming her. "Can you tell me what these things are?"

He scrutinized her: Either she didn't know what Cowan had done or she was a damned good actress. "For one, there's our wedding night. If Cowan follows through with his threat the whole world will know that I slept with a girl I'd never seen before that night, and made her pregnant."

The implications hit Janet very hard, and she gasped.

"I didn't even know about the pregnancy until yesterday. Donald confided in that jackass that the girl had come to him for help and money. My father sent her to Holland for an abortion and never even mentioned it to me."

"My God, my dear God," she began to pray.

"Think of that, Janet, think of the world knowing that. You'll never be able to hold your head up in public again."

"My God," she repeated.

He lifted a stone from the ground, squeezed it in his fist, then hurled it at the loch. "And there's more—there's the accident. I'd gone to the pub before it happened and put away a few, but my father pulled his laird's strings and kept that from the official records. As Cowan himself said, it wouldn't have been so bad, if a man hadn't been killed."

Janet closed her eyes.

He watched her face contort with anxiety. "Are you thinking of how this will affect your children? Are you thinking about how learning these things about their father will affect your children?"

"Yes," she admitted, for in fact, she was.

His smile was cruel. "Good, because it doesn't end there. There's yet another thing he knows, the worst thing of all for me, personally. It's something I only ever had the courage to tell one person in my life, the only person I felt I could trust with such a thing—I only told Annie."

Her legs suddenly wanted to buckle beneath her and she looked around for a place to sit. Andrew watched her every move, her every blink, as she perched herself on an old tree stump.

"You only told Annie?" she asked, once she had braced herself.

"That's right—the only person I could trust with that information." He knew those words stabbed his wife, but he didn't care, because what he was reading in her, in her slouched posture and timid responses, was telling him that he was right, that she was the one who had brought Cowan upon them.

"How does Alfred know this?" she wanted to understand.

"My father knew," he spat at her. "He was so ashamed of it he never even told Mother, but he told that snake. I can only imagine it was done in a moment of drunken weakness."

She swallowed hard before asking, "Will you tell me, will you tell me now?"

"No," he answered curtly, emphatically. "It's bad enough that monster knowing, I'm not going to give you that kind of power, too."

To realize that he saw confiding in her as a risk, that he trusted Annie with something he would not trust her with—dear God—of all the things he'd said in recent weeks that had hurt her, this was by far the worst. Stunned and bewildered, she questioned, "You told your mistress but you won't tell your wife?"

He answered quickly, "I told her long before we were even lovers, I told her twenty-two years ago."

She hadn't thought she could feel any more miserable, but it was growing worse with each passing second. "You told her back then?"

He responded with searing bitterness, "I knew then that she was the only person I could trust. I'm even more certain of that now."

His words kept finding spot after spot of previously untapped pain in Janet, and although it wanted to grind to an agonizing halt, her heart kept beating so that she might ask, in a pathetic whisper, "So what are we to do now?"

"Be good little hostages," he quipped.

"What do you mean?"

"He told me to go home and stay there, to stop seeing Annie, and if I did that he'd help me through my upcoming troubles." Then, almost as an afterthought, he added, "He fed me some rubbish about there being a scandal ready to break in the papers, a story about my ongoing love affair with my homosexual secretary." He glared at his wife again, to make certain she understood. "It's my belief that he's fabricated that filth himself and is poised to use it, just to show me that he means business."

In the next moment, the realization of what she'd brought upon her family by going to Cowan settled into her gut. Sudden, violent pains overcame her. She stood abruptly as her head began to throb, her stomach to sting and spasm; folding her arms around her middle, she gagged and coughed as though she meant to vomit.

Andrew waited while she brought herself under control, then, with chilling detachment, said to her, "My sentiments exactly."

He turned away from her and strode toward the car. Following like a whipped dog, Janet took her seat quickly and kept her face to the window. *God help us* — she prayed, as she watched the trees whip past them.

Annie had not wanted breakfast, then she refused lunch. She did not move from her room, though the day was very warm and it was uncomfortably hot upstairs. And she'd made herself less tolerant to the heat by donning a long-sleeved shirt of Andrew's, the only one she could find that hadn't been washed.

It was Sunday and their afternoon off, but seeing her distressed state Didier and Lisette canceled their plans to go visiting. When it was time for supper, Lisette took it upon herself to visit her mistress, though she'd called through the door that she didn't want to eat or see anyone. But Lisette entered the room anyway, and what she saw made her realize that she was right to be concerned.

Annie was still abed, her eyes mere slits, her face a pale, swollen mass of flesh. "What is it?" she asked, slightly confused by the good woman's presence.

"Didier and I are worried about you, Madame."

"I'm perfectly all right," she answered, "I just need to be alone."

Moving to open a window, she told her, "It's not good for you to stay here this way, you'll dehydrate in this heat if you don't at least drink something."

"I'm not thirsty."

Approaching the bed now, she offered, "I can make you a nice infusion, something that will calm your nerves."

"I don't have any nerves left," Annie informed her, then turned her face away.

"I can see how unhappy you are — let me help you, Madame. I promised the count that I'd take care of you."

When Annie heard her say *the count*, the tears started again; this time they went directly into sobs and curled her into fetal position. Lisette stood helplessly by, offering unheard words of consolation. Annie attempted to stop the sobs by getting up from the bed and going to the bathroom, but as she stood her unreliable legs gave way, and she crumpled to the floor.

Dr. Huron's face was close to hers, listening to her heart through his stethoscope.

"There shouldn't be anything to hear," she told him, "because it's been killed."

He was stern and somewhat scolding when he said, "I hear a rapid heartbeat and I see a woman who needs very badly to take fluids—and not just for herself." Lisette was behind him and he nodded in her direction. "And you should thank Lisette for calling me, you might have done yourself some real harm."

Lisette lowered her eyes and smiled before saying, "I'm going to make you something to eat, something easy to digest. And Dr. Huron will stay here until you eat it," she added, then left the room.

Bernard Huron pulled a chair close to the bed, then lifted a glass of orange juice from the nightstand. "Now, you can drink this or not, it's up to you," he told her. "You may not want it, but that poor baby needs it."

Reluctantly, Annie took the juice.

Once she was drinking, he demanded to know, "What's happened to put you in this state?"

"The world has ended."

"Nonsense," he told her, then smiled as though what she'd said amused him.

She was not amused, and would not return his smile. "Andrew's had to leave, and he doesn't think he'll be able to come back."

"Why?"

The pallor she'd worn all afternoon was replaced by a bright crimson flush of anger. "He's got to stop seeing me because some pathetic excuse for a human being is blackmailing him. He's made horrible threats that can't be ignored."

"I see," Bernard responded. "And what about the baby? Have you told him about the pregnancy yet?"

"No."

"Why? Did you decide not to keep it?"

"I decided just the opposite."

"So why didn't you tell him?"

The man was positively infuriating in his persistence. "How could I, under the circumstances? He had no choice but to go. It was hard enough for him, for both of us, without bringing that into it."

"Then what are you going to do?"

She was becoming increasingly resentful of his intrusive questioning. "I don't know—I can't think past today." She knocked back the remainder of the juice, then slammed the glass to the table.

Aware of her growing irritation, he softened a little. "Can you stay on here?"

"He's arranged that," she informed him.

"Well, that's good, that's one thing, then. Do you have money?"

"Much more than I need," she answered coldly.

"Well then," he decided, "all that remains is for you to get over your grieving and get on with things, get on with taking care of yourself and your baby."

The look she gave him was one of total bewilderment, as she wondered, *How can anyone be so insensitive?* "That's so unbelievably callous," she hissed. "Obviously you have no idea how much I love this man!"

"It is a bit cold," he granted, "but it's what you must do. It's not at all good for the child to have its mother so emotionally distraught, it's not good at all."

She screeched, "Then why are you grilling me like this? Why don't you go away and leave me alone?"

He was unperturbed. "I know it's hard, life is terribly hard at times, but those are the times that test our character. So the only question is, will you buck up and do your best with the circumstances, or will you give yourself over to despair?"

Lisette knocked on the door then. Didier was behind her, holding a tray.

"Ah, supper, just what the doctor ordered," Bernard grinned.

Didier set the tray over Annie's lap and removed the covers from the dishes. Lisette had prepared an herb omelet with dry toast, a bowl of peeled and diced fruit—the sort of thing you would do for a small child—and a cup of chamomile tea. "Bon appétit, Madame," he said, as he backed away from the bed.

"She needs a glass of milk, too, Lisette," the doctor said, "pasteurized milk. Have you any?"

"We have only the raw milk from the neighbor, doctor."

"Well, boil some up and put a bit of vanilla and sugar in it. That'll be good for her, it'll help her sleep."

"Of course, doctor, right away."

Annie stared at the omelet and wondered at the audacity of this man to decide things for her as he did.

"It doesn't do your baby any good just looking at it," he scolded. "He, or she, is depending on you."

"All right!" she exclaimed, as she picked up her fork and began to eat.

He watched her attempt a few, tiny bites before informing her, "Didier tells me there's a day bed in one of the cooler, downstairs rooms. I think you should move down there for the time being; it's altogether too hot upstairs for a pregnant woman."

She glared at him and swallowed with difficulty.

"And I want you to get into the habit of resting after lunch, when the day is its warmest," he continued. "You're healthy but you are older, and we do consider women of your age to be high-risk pregnancies."

She was doing the best she could with the meal but Annie suddenly had to give up the effort, and motioned for him to take the tray away. Dr. Huron telling her the things he just had forced her to see into the future, a place she hadn't wanted to look, to see herself as she was, as she would be—alone—going through what would surely be her last pregnancy—quite alone.

He seemed annoyed with her when he questioned, "What is it?"

"My stomach."

"Drink your tea, it'll calm you."

"I can't."

"Why?"

She was so aggravated now she screamed. "Because my insides are all tied up in knots, that's why, and if I put anything else down there I'll throw it up!"

He removed the tray then returned to his seat, making sure to capture her eyes. "How long do you intend on being like this?" he demanded to know.

"I don't intend anything," she fumed. "If you knew me you'd understand that I'm a neurotic mess who's dealt badly with the series of trials my life has been—one after the other—and I don't think I have it in me to take any more."

"What kind of trials?"

"What kind?" She opened her eyes as wide as they would go in their swollen state. "The kind that make me believe that happiness is just a colossal joke perpetrated on us by a gang of cruel and criminally deranged gods!"

"Could you be more specific?" he asked, a little arrogantly.

She was indignant. "You want specifics? I'll give you specifics: I lost my little brother in a motorcycle accident, doctor, when he was just eighteen years old. He was the person I loved most on this earth and he died clutching my hand, asking me to help him. Before that I'd lost Andrew, despite loving him with everything that was in me. He was the man I should have married and spent my life with; instead I married an abusive control freak, who left me depressed and addicted to sleeping pills, then took my son from me because of that. I got through it all, married a wonderful man whom I loved but who couldn't bring himself to love me, found Andrew again, discovered I'm pregnant with his child—and then couldn't even tell him about it, let alone share this time with him. Is that enough for you, or should I go on?"

"That's enough," he decided.

"Really? I was just getting started."

"You're very angry."

"You're damned right I'm angry! Some asshole walks in here yesterday and threatens Andrew with ruin and takes my life away, just like that, and there's not a fucking thing I can do but sit here and be sick and sorry for myself—not one fucking thing!"

Lisette knocked timidly at the open door, carrying the cup of hot milk. She spied the uneaten omelet and glanced disapprovingly at Annie.

"Please, don't look at me like that," Annie implored. "I just can't do it."

Bernard smiled and took the milk from her, saying, "It'll be all right, Lisette." As she headed back downstairs, he closed the bedroom door. "Let's get back to what you were saying. Why isn't there anything you can do?"

She said impatiently, "Because the creature who came here is horrid and capable of anything, and Andrew's afraid of him."

"Why does he fear him?"

"Because he's made a career out of this sort of thing," she snapped. "He learns things about people, tricks them into showing him their weak underbellies, then uses what he knows against them."

"I assume you're talking about sexual weaknesses."

Nodding, she responded, "Apparently he's skilled at seducing people, at getting them to do things in front of him that they don't want others to know about."

Bernard seemed increasingly thoughtful, as he quieted for once, and looked away from her.

Although she was happy for the respite, she needed to know, "What are you thinking?"

He pursed his lips, then lifted one brow, saying, "A man like that, he can't be at all virtuous himself, can he?"

"What are you getting at?"

"A mind such as his," he realized, "one that works in such a way, it has to be a very sick mind."

"You have a gift for understatement, doctor," she scoffed.

He disregarded the sarcasm. "I wonder if anyone's ever tried to give him a dose of his own medicine? I mean, a person like that, I doubt extortion is his sole form of entertainment. I'd be willing to bet his sexual proclivities fall along the lines of those whom he blackmails, and then some. How else would his mind come up with such things?"

Annie flashed on the times she's seen Lord Cowan. She remembered his lascivious stares at her body, the drooling way in which he spoke to her when they were dancing at Crinan Castle, the painful pinch on her hip. "I'd bet you're right," she said. "He's so repulsive, every time I've seen him he's impressed me as being one of the most lewd creatures I've ever run up against—and that's in public. God only knows what he's like behind closed doors." The idea gave her a shiver.

"You knew him before?" He seemed surprised.

She was less agitated now and answered, "Slightly. I met him years ago and I've seen him again very recently. He made a pass at me, he tried to tempt me away from Andrew." She laughed at the absurdity of it.

Bernard folded his arms and looked directly at Annie. "That's very interesting."

Her brow furrowed, as she wondered, "What are you thinking now?"

"His attraction for you—it might work to your advantage." He paused and looked away again, out one of the windows.

"Where are you going with this?" she asked, although she believed she already knew.

"Your reference to weak underbellies, it's made me wonder if there might be a way for you to see his."

Annie stared at him, realizing, "That could be dangerous."

He saw where she was taking the idea and was quick to tell her, "I wasn't thinking of you going on an undercover mission. I was thinking more along the lines of hiring a detective agency to look into his activities, starting with that, at least. With what you learned, well, you could go from there."

It was the first glint of hope she'd seen and she considered the idea carefully. She was thinking out loud, when she said, "A good agency would cost money, and I've plenty of that."

"And a good agency would see to it that you're not discovered. The last thing you'd want is for this man to find out you're going after him."

"Christ no—I wouldn't want that," she agreed.

They stared at each other for a moment.

"Now you tell me what you're thinking," he said to her.

"Do you know what's got me the most upset right now? It's being unable to help Andrew," she recognized. "Years ago, something

awful happened to him and he really needed me. I couldn't help him
then, I was powerless to do anything because I didn't know what was
going on. In spite of that, I still feel perfectly horrible about not being
there for him. Can you imagine how it feels now? I know what's going
on, I know he needs help, but I'm every bit as powerless."

In a quiet voice, he responded, "Then for both your sakes, I
should think you need to do something to change that, unless you
like being a victim."

"No, I don't," she insisted, "I fucking hate it!" It was now clear
why Dr. Huron had provoked her: he'd been trying to rattle her out
of despair. "At the very least, I need to try," she said, evidencing the
beginnings of a smile. "I'll phone someone tomorrow, someone I
know in England. John promised to be our friend and help us in
any way he could—he can help me find the right kind of investigators for the job." She looked off into the distance as she began for-
mulating her plan.

There was an immediate and profound change in her attitude
and Dr. Huron approved. He held out the cup of now tepid milk,
saying, "If you're going to get out of this bed and do something,
you're going to have to fuel up first."

Annie dutifully consumed the milk, then motioned toward the
supper tray. "Would you mind bringing that back?" she grinned.

He readily obliged, and stayed with her until she had finished.

At Crinan Castle, Janet had gone to her bed feeling ill.

Nigel felt ill, too. The summons was worrying enough, but
when he walked into Andrew's private study he was gripped with
a sudden terror as he looked at his employer and read what was
in his face.

"Sit down, Nigel." It sounded like the voice of doom.

Nigel perched precariously near the edge of the leather couch.
"Has something happened, your lordship?"

Andrew was ensconced behind his desk, grasping his pen like
a dagger. "When was the last time you saw Alfred Cowan?"

It felt suddenly as though a small boulder had become lodged
in his throat. "He invited me to dinner in London, and I stayed over.
It was about a week ago."

"You stayed over?'

"At his house; he insisted. I'd had quite a lot to drink, I'm afraid." He was doing his level best to keep from trembling.

"Was it just the two of you at dinner?"

"Yes, it was."

Andrew lowered his eyes briefly, opening and closing his hand on the fountain pen. "What did you talk about?"

"My holiday mostly," he explained, "he asked about my holiday on Mykonos."

That slimy, fucking bastard—Andrew said to himself—*I knew it.* "What else?"

"We talked about you, a little," he reluctantly admitted. "He asked what I knew about your relationship with the American woman."

"And?"

"I told him that I did not discuss your personal affairs—with anyone."

"Is that all?"

"No, he pressed me," he decided it safe to add. "He said he was very concerned about the matter. He said he was afraid of what it would do to your marriage and reputation, if you kept on with it."

"So?"

"So I told him again that I wouldn't discuss it with him. Then he asked me about myself—" he hesitated.

"What about yourself?"

"About—he, ah—" He glanced fleetingly at Andrew, and what he saw in his expression compelled him to continue. "He said he knew one of my friends quite well. He said he knew that I preferred the company of men."

With his eyes, Andrew pressed down on Nigel, forcing him to go on.

"He was very kind and sympathetic," he added, "he wasn't rude or judgmental."

"How so?"

"He suggested that it must be very difficult for me, working around someone like you, someone who—" He wished he hadn't said that.

"Go ahead," he insisted.

"Someone as attractive as you." Nigel looked to see if he might stop, if what he had said embarrassed Andrew enough to make him stop questioning him, but that wasn't the case. "He asked me if I had feelings for you."

His jaw tightened, as Andrew questioned, "And you told him?"

"I told him I didn't, but I don't think he believed me."

"Why not?"

"Because he kept on with it, he kept driving the issue, giving me more and more to drink. When I decided to get up and leave, I wobbled a bit, and it was then he insisted upon my staying."

"So you slept there?"

"Yes. A butler saw me to a guest room."

"Then what? Did you talk again in the morning?"

"No, I slept rather late, so the butler brought breakfast to my room, and then I hustled off to the office to meet you. That was Wednesday, you came into the London office on Wednesday last, if you recall." For emphasis he nodded, but it was a little overdone.

Andrew thought back to that day, and when he did, he recalled that Nigel had seemed a bit under the weather. "So nothing else was said between you?"

"No, nothing," he told him, avoiding his eyes.

"And you haven't seen or spoken with him since?"

"No." That was true.

Andrew softened a bit to ask, "Have you told me everything, Nigel? Has there been any other occasion when the two of you have spoken privately?"

"No, your lordship," he answered honestly.

"And that's the extent of it—what you've told me—are you certain that's all that was said between you?"

"Yes, I'm certain," he said, in a diminished voice.

Andrew stared his secretary down for a moment, allowing oppressive silence to fill the space between them. Finally, he declared, "All right, you can go now. I'll talk to you later." Throughout the discourse, he had maintained his death grip on the pen.

Although it took superhuman effort to keep from shaking in front of Andrew, Nigel managed, and made his way to the door. Once through, he closed it softly, then released a sigh, hoping it hadn't been heard. The walk back to his apartment seemed like miles, and once inside he turned the lock with a trembling hand. He made his way to his bed, then sat upon it for a long while, unable to move, thinking of what had happened that night with Alfred Cowan, which he now regretted with all his heart.

It was fuzzy, his memory, but clear enough in certain aspects. Lord Alfred had hounded him to the point of tears over his feelings for Andrew, and Nigel had overdone it with drink in an effort to keep himself calm. When he tried to leave, Cowan turned conciliatory and offered him a bed. He had not been in the room long when Cowan came to him, clad only in pajama bottoms and dressing gown, a glass of something in his hand.

"This is my special remedy for distress," he offered. "It'll also help fend off the hangover I fear you're due."

"What is it?" Nigel wondered.

"A family secret, I'm afraid, but quite harmless, I assure you." Nigel took the drink and Cowan made himself comfortable in a chair, saying, "I'll just stay a few, until you get sleepy."

"It was a lovely dinner, thank you for the invitation," Nigel thought to say, though in truth, he wished he hadn't accepted.

"I care very deeply for our Andrew, you know," he grinningly informed him. "Never had any children of my own."

"No—"

"Not for lack of trying, though. Tried it with three different women."

"Yes, you've been married three times," he recalled hearing. He yawned and set his empty glass down.

"Couldn't quite seem to keep the marriage thing together—it's not as easy as it looks." He laughed slightly, as he watched Nigel yawn again. "Ready to turn in now?"

"I believe so, thank you." Nigel stood and held to the back of the chair for balance, then swaggered as he headed for the bed.

Alfred followed and put an arm around him. "Here, let me help you."

"P-retty p-owerful stuff, your secret drink," he slurred.

"You'll sleep like a baby, and you'll thank me in the morning."
He guided him into lying down. "Comfortable?"

"Yes, quite." Although Alfred was still beside him, Nigel
couldn't help but close his eyes.

The next thing he remembered was the sensation of someone
fondling his penis, then being rolled onto his stomach. He roused
out of his overly sleepy state enough to realize that he was naked
and had not gone to bed that way. He felt his ass being touched,
the cheeks spread, and then the cold, familiar sensation of lubricating jelly being squeezed over his anus. His arms were under his
belly and felt bound at the wrists, and he was unable to move to
free himself.

"Just relax and enjoy it, darling," the husky voice said. "I'm
the man you love, I'm Andrew. Open that sweet little bum to me,
the one I watch you wiggle in front of me every day, the one that
drives me crazy with desire for you."

Nigel felt himself being penetrated.

"Yes, that's right, that's good, relax to me, relax to your Andrew."

The voice was so irresistible and his libido so heightened by
whatever it was he had drunk, Nigel was powerless to do anything
but what it said. He called out to his seducer, "Take me, Andrew,
take me—I love you so much, I've loved you so long—take me, do
whatever you will to me."

Nigel moaned as Cowan thrust himself deeper, saying,
"There's a good lad. Tell me all the things you've wanted to say to
me, tell me all those things now, darling, while I'm enjoying you,
while I'm in your sweet, little bum."

Twenty-Nine

Janet lay, eyes fixed on the brocade canopy cover over her head, going over and over what her husband had said. After about an hour of paralyzing worry and although she was in terror of being found out, she decided she had to place a call to Cowan.

"Where are you ringing from?" he demanded to know.

"Home."

"Is he there?"

"Yes."

"Then you should ring off immediately," he warned. "There are far too many extensions."

She made no attempt at hiding her outrage when she told him, "I'm not bloody ringing off. I need to know what you're going to do next. I had no earthly idea you'd handle things in this way and I'm absolutely infuriated. How could you? If I'd had any inkling of what you would do I would never have even discussed it with you: Never!"

He shifted now, to his seductive voice. "My dear countess, calm yourself. I'm not going to do anything next, not to your husband at least."

She was so distraught, she missed that qualifier. "You're threatening my family, Alfred, my children!"

There was not the slightest hint of remorse in his tone, if anything, there was the ring of triumph when he responded, "I grant you, it's unfortunate things needed to be handled in that way, but matters were such with that woman as to require extreme measures. And anyway, it's the very severity of the consequences that will keep Andrew in line. As long as your husband does as he's told—and I've no reason to believe that he'll do anything but—you and your family have nothing to fear. Nothing at all."

What she had missed in his earlier response hovered over her, and it now came to roost. "What do you mean, not to my husband at least?"

"There's one other matter that needs to be tended to directly, and that's Ms. d'Inard."

Janet had heard the rumors about how Lord Cowan enjoyed the unconventional. Now, as she listened to him speak of tending to Annie, the dismissed whispers intruded upon her thoughts. "Alfred, I'm warning you, don't harm her in anyway. Andrew will do whatever he has to to protect her, especially if she's pregnant." Janet's distress over that possibility was undeniable, and in spite of herself, it compelled her to set aside her anger with Cowan and ask, "Have you discovered whether she is or not?"

"No, not yet," he was sorry to report. "And that's exactly why I must pursue this. If she is it can't be ignored and allowed to progress, that just won't do at all."

Janet agreed, but was loathe to say so.

He needed to know, "Now, you haven't admitted to anything, have you?"

"No."

"I assume he did accuse you."

"He did."

"Well, that's all right, that was to be expected." He sounded now like the kindest, most concerned of friends when he next said, "I don't want you to lose any sleep over this, my dear. You've trusted me thus far and you must continue that trust while I tie up loose ends. Now we should ring off before someone picks up an extension and discovers us."

In her most earnest and insistent manner, Janet repeated, "Don't hurt her, Alfred, all bets are off if you hurt her. Andrew will forget about the danger to himself—and all of us—and do what he has to, to help her."

He smiled to himself, as he responded, "I'm aware of that, my dear, and I know what to do. Try to stay calm. We'll speak again some other time when he's not around, all right?"

"All right," she answered, albeit reluctantly.

"There's a good lass." Grinning widely, he replaced the receiver.

For reassurance, Janet moved to her study window so that she might view the estate grounds. But while this simple act usually anchored her, reminding her of her place in the world as the Countess of Kilmartin, today it did nothing of the sort. Gazing over the magnificent gardens of Crinan Castle, she found herself falling into panicky despair, as she realized that her neatly ordered life was drifting out of her control. As her gaze lifted to the loch, her anxiety intensified and brought on an out-of-body experience: She felt cast upon the waning tide in a boat she could neither steer nor navigate, watching helplessly as the shoreline faded into the distance, the castle battlements and turrets sinking into the misty curvature of the horizon. Her soul began to ache with longing, for from this imagined distance her life with Andrew seemed more beautiful than it had ever been, and a thousand times more precious.

Annie rose at half past seven and prepared breakfast for herself. Lisette and Didier watched in amazement as she put away two eggs, fruit and yogurt, bread and jam, then washed it down with a large glass of milk. Shortly thereafter, before the day turned hot, she went for a walk through the vineyard. She was back by nine-thirty and settled at her desk to place the telephone call.

"Good morning, Lena, how are you? It's Annie."

"What a lovely surprise! Where are you?"

"I'm in France."

Lena hesitated, then boldly questioned, "With Andrew?"

"John told you," she realized.

"Yes, I hope you don't mind."

"I don't mind at all. I trust both of you with that information."

She knew that Annie appreciated forthrightness, so she went ahead and told her, "John expressed concern about the relationship but I for one think it's marvelous, you know, absolutely marvelous. If ever two people deserved to be together, it's you."

"Thank you for saying that, and I wish I could report to you how blissfully happy we are, but John was right to be concerned. He warned me, in fact, and he was right. Something's happened, something awful, and that's why I'm calling."

"Hold on a moment, let me close the sitting room door." Lena was back quickly. "Go on," she told her, anxious to hear what this was about.

"This is all in the strictest of confidence —"

"That goes without saying."

"Thank you." She took another fortifying breath. "I'm going to get right to the point: Someone is blackmailing Andrew, someone with power and influence, that Andrew is unwilling to go up against. He knows things about Andrew, things from his past that if they were to be made public would destroy him and his family. This person pretends the threat is coming from elsewhere, but Andrew doesn't buy that. And what he's demanding of us — he wants us to stay away from each other and for good. If we don't comply, Andrew believes he will go to the press with at least some of this information."

As that all settled in, Lena exclaimed, "Annie! How perfectly awful for you — for both of you!"

Tears were threatening, and she had to fight to keep her composure. "I love him so much, Lena," she admitted freely, "and to have someone come along and do that to him — to us — it makes me homicidal to think of Andrew being controlled by a person like . . ." She hesitated, because she wasn't sure if she should name him.

Lena told her, "You don't have to say who he is."

"But I do," she realized, "because I'm going to ask for your help, yours and John's. But before I tell you who he is, let me tell you what it is I'm planning, to see if you're willing."

She was decidedly intrigued and said, "I'm listening," with some excitement.

Sounding more in control, Annie continued, "From the little I know and the few times we've met, I get the very strong feeling that this man is a depraved individual, with probably more than a few skeletons in his own closet. I'm thinking of having him investigated to see what I can come up with, to see if there's any way I might turn the tables on him and get him to back off of Andrew."

Lena's response was, "How can I help?"

"Whatever I do," she was certain, "Andrew can't be connected to it in any way. If he were to think that Andrew was going after him, it would surely make matters worse. And it's probably dangerous — what

I'm thinking—I'd say it's at least potentially dangerous, so you're going to want to consider that before you agree to anything."

"Why is it dangerous?"

"His depravity aside," she responded, "he's as wealthy and powerful as they come, and Andrew says that people are afraid of him. Andrew's father was his friend at one time, and even he feared him."

Lena remembered well, the impressive persona of Andrew's father, the handsome and charismatic twenty-third earl of Kilmartin, highly visible in the upper echelons of society. She responded with widened eyes, "Bloody hell," because in her admiring eyes, he'd always seemed the sort who could slay dragons.

"Shall I stop now? Have I succeeded in frightening you off?"

She scoffed, "Not bloody likely."

"Maybe you'll want to discuss this with John before I go any further."

"John's in Hong Kong," she informed her.

"When's he due back?"

"Thursday."

Disheartened, Annie told her, "Oh, well, I guess I'll have to wait until then."

"Why?"

"So you two can talk."

Sounding slightly vexed, Lena responded, "Since when do I need his permission for anything, let alone to help a friend?"

"Think about this first, will you?"

"All right," she paused a moment, "there, I thought. Now what do you want me to do?"

Annie's heart felt suddenly lighter. "I need a really good detective agency, the best money can buy."

Lena's grin filled her face. "That's easy. I know the exact one and I know the director personally. In fact, I used to call him uncle when I was growing up."

"Really? Who's this? What agency?"

She answered proudly, "He's Daddy's oldest friend, Sir David Whetfield. He was a commander of British Naval Intelligence at the end of World War II and during the cold war, a true hero, knighted for service to queen and country and a member of the Royal Order of the Garter. When he retired from the navy he started a private intelligence-gathering service. It's very hush-hush, they don't even have an official name or headquarters, it's that discreet. I only know about it because of Daddy's connection to him. Their clients are VIPs—royalty, heads of state, and the like. People of Andrew's sort."

"Would they do something like that, investigate a private individual for someone like me?"

With some cockiness, she responded, "If I asked personally, they would."

"Will you, then? Money's no object, Lena, I'll pay whatever it costs."

"Who's the bloke?" She was trying to sound cool and savvy, like someone on that television show she enjoyed: "Inspector Morse".

"Lord Alfred Cowan."

She laughed as she pictured him. "The one who escorted the Princess of Wales at Crinan Castle?"

"The same."

"He's not so frightening," she said.

Annie knew better. "What's under that surface, Lena, makes my skin crawl."

"Why would he do such a thing?" she wondered. "Do you think someone put him up to it?"

"Andrew suspects his wife," she informed her, "and I feel certain Janet's got a hand in this somehow. She paid me a visit recently, she came here when she knew Andrew would be away and showed me, with perfect clarity, what she's capable of."

She recalled the cold hostility with which Janet had treated Annie at Crinan Castle, and said sarcastically, "*That* must have been delightful. Do you want me to ring up Sir David today?"

"The sooner the better."

"What shall I tell him?"

She had already given this some thought. "To be certain there's no possible connection to Andrew, I think we should lie, if you can do that."

Lena laughed again.

Encouraged by her friend's amused response, she told her, "Let's say I'm a wealthy divorcee, who's being courted by Cowan, and I want him investigated before I take the relationship any further. I want to protect my vast assets, you see, and I've heard things about him, rumors. I don't want to involve myself with anyone whose morals would compromise my own."

"Do you have a name?"

"Anne Rutledge, that's my alias."

Lena's sharp mind searched for loopholes. "How do I know you?"

Annie hesitated briefly, before deciding, "We're old friends who met years ago when we were students, and I was on a tour of Europe."

"Where can I reach you?"

Annie gave her the number at the château, before saying, "You're a good friend, Lena. I've grown very fond of you, you know. I truly admire the woman you are, and the strength and grace with which you handle everything, including and especially, me."

Lena responded warmly. "It's mutual, darling. The truth be told, once I got to know you, I couldn't blame poor old John for falling for you. He's only made of flesh and blood, after all."

They both laughed, then blew kisses to one another over the phone.

Annie had been up from her prescribed afternoon nap little more than a half hour and was composing a letter to her son when the phone rang.

Lena's tone was that of suppressed excitement when she greeted her with, "Hello there!"

"That was fast."

"I'll say. I just rang off with Sir David and I thought you'd want to know straightaway."

"Know what?"

Lena was thoroughly absorbed by the mystery. "His first response was to go all quiet, then he asked if my friend was a nice person. When I said that you are, he answered that his best advice to you would be to forget that you ever met Cowan and pack your bags and go back to America. That's from a man who's seen it all and isn't easily impressed by others."

Annie's only response was, "Jesus."

"Bloody hell is what I said. And when I realized that our story wasn't going to get us anywhere, I took the liberty of changing it."

"What'd you say?"

She'd had to think on her feet, and hoped that Annie would approve. "I said I hadn't told him the truth—the truth was that Cowan was blackmailing you, over something he learned about your past, something personal that would ruin you if it were known. I said you're not the kind of woman to take this lying down and you want to see if there's some way you might turn things around, so you don't have to go on being harassed by the likes of him."

"Well done!" she congratulated her friend. "What'd he say to that?"

"He answered that there are many people who would like to do that very thing, but that it wasn't advisable."

Annie exhaled her frustration. "Jesus! Why not? Did he say why not?"

This had been deliciously intriguing, and Lena couldn't wait to pass it along. "He said that for many years he's heard tales of Cowan's exploits, seen the response people have to him, and heard more than one person say that they're afraid of him—important people, powerful people. For you to get mixed up in a game of espionage and blackmail with him—he said it would be suicide. Sir David's exact words were: 'Cowan's no match for an amateur.'"

"Dammit!" she despaired. "So did he refuse to help? Did he refuse to investigate him?"

She was pleased to report, "Not exactly. I pleaded with him to at least try to find out something, anything. I told him that you were positively distraught and wouldn't go to the police, but you'd not give up without a fight. I said I feared that you would do something rather clumsy on your own."

"That was clever," she realized.

"I think it worked," she said. "He's going to see if he can put someone on it tomorrow, but he wants you to know he's not promising anything."

Because she didn't want to waste a minute, Annie anxiously questioned, "Does he need a retainer to get started? I can wire the money."

"Not yet," she responded. "He'll charge appropriately when and if he finds something."

She felt enormously relieved. "This is great! For a minute there, I thought it wasn't going to work."

With a measure of self-satisfaction, Lena replied, "I used all my powers of persuasion on Uncle David."

"God bless you, Lena! Thank you so much!"

"Don't thank me yet," she answered, more sedately.

Sunday had been an intolerably slow day. After the family meal, Andrew was relieved to find that the children weren't underfoot, so that he didn't have to uphold the pretense of normalcy. On Monday morning he was dressed and at the helicopter by six, packed and prepared to stay at a hotel in Glasgow. Janet watched him leave from her bedroom window, her heart in her mouth, having made no effort to speak with him again, save a total of about a dozen words at Sunday dinner.

Andrew could think of no better way of dealing with his torment than by burying himself in work, so bury himself he did. By midweek, however, he found that he was feeling a little less burdened, though not with regards to his separation from Annie. While he had not believed Cowan's threat regarding the tabloid story, he had nonetheless worried, and the fact that nothing had come of it by now was somewhat reassuring.

Late on Wednesday, while he sat through yet another meeting, one of his office assistants interrupted him with a note: Ambrose's wife Sarah was on the private line, asking to speak with him.

Knowing that it must be important, he did not hesitate to take the call. "How are you, Sarah? Is Ambrose all right?"

Her voice betrayed her fatigue when she responded, "He's just home from hospital, your lordship, and doing remarkably well, considering. We didn't think we'd take him home this time, truth be told, and we're ever so grateful."

He was genuinely concerned. "I didn't know, Sarah, and I apologize. I haven't been around much these past few weeks," he thought to explain. "Is there anything I can do?"

"No need to apologize, your lordship, we managed very well," she told him, adding, "and I've engaged a young woman to help me with him, so that's working out. But I've rung because Ambrose has asked especially to see you; he was wondering if you might find the time for another visit."

He responded readily, "When would he like me to come?"

"At your convenience, sir."

"Would tomorrow be all right?"

"That would be fine. Will you come for tea?"

"Yes, thank you," he answered, knowing that would please her. "I'll plan to arrive around half past three, if that suits you."

"I'll look forward to it, your lordship, and I know Ambrose will be most happy to see you."

It was a blue-white summer's day on the green Isle of Arran, with very little wind, and the wild foxglove that were at the height of their bloom made a showy display. The traffic on the narrow coastline road was heavy with holiday makers, and as the earl's helicopter landed in an unplanted field near Ambrose and Sarah's cottage, several curious motorists pulled to the shoulder to watch.

He found Ambrose on the lawn, tucked into a lounge chair, basking in the sunshine. Sarah and a nurse's aide were by his side and he greeted Andrew warmly, saying, "I'm so happy you could come."

Remembering that Ambrose was fond of baked goods and fragrant flowers, he'd brought him a basket of treats from the finest bake shop in Glasgow and three dozen stargazer lilies. "I apologize for not coming to see you sooner," he said softly, "but no one told me you were ill."

Sarah had informed Andrew's mother, Ambrose knew, and it was odd that the dowager countess had made no effort to come see him; she hadn't even telephoned. He didn't see the point in mentioning that, but he had wondered if her aloofness was directly related to the letters he'd saved for her son.

"Thank you for your gifts, your lordship, these flowers are splendid, their fragrance will fill the cottage," he said, drinking them in before giving them over to Sarah. "And it's just as well you didn't come to hospital, for I wouldn't have enjoyed your visit near as much."

Sarah smiled her gratitude and after peering into the basket of goodies, asked, "Can I offer you some refreshment, your lordship?"

He returned her smile. "Tea would be lovely, Sarah, thank you."

The young nurse's aide had been standing by silently, in awe of the man she had only seen on television or in photographs. Sarah introduced her to Andrew and when he smiled at her, saying that he was glad she was here to help, she nearly swooned.

Ambrose was noticeably weaker than the last time they'd met as he offered, "Have a seat, your honour," then coughed and closed his eyes for a moment.

Before Andrew arrived, Ambrose had informed Sarah that he wanted time alone with him. She tactfully said now, "We'll leave you, then, so you can have your chat in peace. Fiona and I will make the tea."

Andrew settled into a wicker chair next to him as Ambrose questioned, "Is all well at Crinan Castle?"

"Yes, all's well." His response lacked conviction and that was not lost on the man who'd known Andrew all his life.

"Really, sir?"

Andrew sensed his concern, and it led him to wonder, "Why do you ask?"

He smiled fleetingly. "You may think I've gone 'round the bend as I tell you this, but while I was in hospital, I had the very strong impression that I'd been visited by your father. That's why I've rung you and asked you to come."

Andrew settled deeper into Sarah's embroidered cushions and bestowed the old man with a patronizing smile.

Ambrose had expected him to be skeptical. "I'll understand if you think me daft, but I'll appreciate it very much if you will hear me out."

Andrew smiled to reassure him. "I don't think you daft. I know that when one is very ill, a great many strange sensations may be experienced."

Ambrose recognized that as dismissal, but did not let it stop him. "I lost about three days this time; that is, I don't remember where I was those three days. They tell me I was very close to death, and I believe that. I believe it because I saw and spoke with your father, and he was as real to me as you are now."

Andrew's patronizing look gave way to a more serious expression, and it encouraged Ambrose.

Shaking his head, he went on to say, "He was not at peace, the earl, not at all. He seemed quite distressed, in fact. He said something that odd to me, at least it was at first. He said, 'Warn him, Ambrose,' and he waited for me to understand. I finally did."

Andrew's tone was softly hesitant when he questioned, "What was it you came to understand?"

As though it were the only way to say this, he blurted out, "He wanted me to warn you about Lord Alfred Cowan."

Andrew felt the sudden chill of foreboding, and searching the old man's face, the sincerity he read there filled him with dread. "What about him?"

He prefaced what he was about to reveal by assuring Donald's son, "You must understand, I know these things only because your father trusted me enough to confide in me. I've never told another soul and I never will again, but I'm that certain it was your father who came to me and asked me to tell you. He's deeply concerned about you, young master."

His unease growing by the second, Andrew looked toward the cottage. Sarah and the young woman were still inside, so there was no one to overhear, still, he dropped his voice to a whisper. "Then by all means, Ambrose, tell me what you think he wants me to know."

Ambrose carefully lifted the glass of water next to him, and took a sip before continuing. "They used to be good friends, you know, though, I must say, neither your grandfather nor I ever liked him. Your grandfather did his best to discourage the relationship but Lord Alfred gave your father something he needed, I think, in that he provided an outlet, if you'll permit my saying so, for his unsatisfied desires. Your father wasn't in love with your mother when they married, you see." The old man waited to see what effect this information would have on Donald's son.

"That's never been a secret," he let him know.

"No, I suppose not," he realized. "But while your father wanted to do things, to have affairs I mean, he wanted to be discreet—for obvious reasons. Lord Alfred helped him with that, as he did many other important men, in similar circumstances."

"I'm not surprised to hear this," he thought to inform him. "Father told me something about Cowan once, about how he enjoyed facilitating sexual activities for people."

Emboldened by that, Ambrose felt his face flush with heat when he said, "Your father went quite frequently to Lunga House. That was where Cowan held his wildest parties, orgies, I'm told." He shook his head slightly when he added, "I never liked seeing him go. He'd be hungover and remorseful when he returned."

Andrew exhaled and closed his eyes, trying his damnedest not to form that mental image.

"The last time he went," Ambrose continued, "and I recall very clearly that it was the last time, the earl seemed quite overwrought when he came home, so much so that he took to his bed for better than a day. I was very concerned about him, and asked if there were anything I could do. He sat me down and told me what had happened, it was that distressing to him, you see, and he needed to tell someone."

Although he knew he should hear him out, Andrew dreaded learning more.

Ambrose read his face, and asked now, "Shall I go on, sir? I know this must be terribly upsetting to you."

"It is, Ambrose," he sighed, "but I suppose it's something I need to know."

"Truly, I believe it is," he responded quickly, then nervously cleared his throat. "There was a young woman, a very pretty young woman who was a special favorite of your father's—Cowan always had her there for him. But on that particular weekend . . ." his eyes went briefly to the cottage door to assure himself that Sarah was not yet returning, "your father could only recall that he'd fallen very soundly asleep on the bed afterwards, with her beside him. When he awakened in the morning she was still there, but unconscious. She had been severely beaten and there was blood coming from her, ah, her private parts, if you'll forgive the expression—both, ah—both orifices."

Ambrose paused to conquer his embarrassment and Andrew looked away to help him do that, while he swallowed back his nausea.

Ambrose mustered what little strength he had to convey these things to Andrew, but with the telling, the recollections became clearer, and the outrage he still felt over what had been done to his beloved employer brought him unexpected energy. "The earl called for help, and Cowan came immediately. Cowan stopped him calling others; he said he'd take care of it. Your father protested that he hadn't hurt her, but Cowan insisted that he'd heard him beating her during the night. He hadn't interfered because he trusted him—Cowan said—and decided to leave the earl to his own vices. Then he persuaded your father to let him handle it. The young woman in question was brought to hospital and treated, and from what the earl learned she recovered completely. Cowan even handled the matter of paying for her silence. Your father never saw or spoke to her again, as Cowan recommended he not."

"Jesus Christ," Andrew hissed, his own outrage building.

"That's exactly what your father said," he recalled, "over and over. His instincts told him that Cowan had set him up, but while the earl never accepted that he had been the one who harmed that young woman, he had no way of proving it." Blushing again, he explained, "There'd been blood on his hands and genitals, you see, when he awakened, though he knew Cowan to be quite capable of smearing it there himself."

Andrew spat his disgust, saying, "Quite," vividly recalling his father's anger with Cowan that day in his office, and the stern warning he'd issued his son. He questioned, "When was this—do you recall the year?" wanting to know if it had already happened by then.

"Not exactly," Ambrose answered, "but it was before your grandfather died, to be sure, for we were still at Crofthill."

So that was what Donald meant, he realized; when Andrew had asked if Cowan had anything on him, it was why he'd answered: *He thinks he has.*

"Your father even wondered if Lord Alfred hadn't slipped something to him," Ambrose remembered now, "some drug that might have made him sleep as soundly as he did, and left him unable to remember. Lord Alfred always had drugs around, you see, cocaine and the like."

His insides churning with fury, Andrew said, "I wouldn't put anything past that man."

Ambrose raised a single brow to observe, "You don't seemed surprised by any of this, your lordship."

"I'm not," he seethed. "I've learned more than I care to know about Alfred Cowan in recent days, and I believe him capable of anything."

"Your father was quite changed after that," the old man continued. "He kept as far away from Lord Alfred as he could, though he never severed the relationship completely. He told me that he feared making him angry, feared that if Cowan became angry with him he might tell someone what had happened. And, sadly, the more time that went by, the more that fear grew."

Andrew softened a bit to acknowledge, "I know this was exceedingly difficult for you to tell me about, but I'm most appreciative, for the more I know about Cowan, the better equipped I am to handle him."

Sarah appeared in the doorway and Ambrose waved her off, saying, "That brings me to your father's warning, sir. Has something happened between Cowan and yourself? I ask because that's the very strong impression I was left with, after his visit. I wondered if Cowan had perhaps come to you and told you of that horrible incident, blamed your father for it."

Quietly fuming, he answered, "He came to see me, but not to blame my father for anything. You know the young woman whose letters you kept for me?"

"Yes, the one you've seen again," he recalled.

"We've been together these past weeks, Ambrose, and in many ways it's been the most wonderful time of my life, being with her again."

"I want to say I'm happy for you, sir, but I know it isn't all happiness you feel."

"No, there's been terrible guilt, too," he admitted, "over what this is doing to Janet, and the potential harm to the children."

"I can see that," he nodded, noting that Andrew wore uncharacteristic circles under his eyes, and seemed depleted of his usual vitality, almost defeated.

"We were managing, though," he added, "trying to work our way through things, when Cowan showed up on our doorstep and threatened me."

Ambrose seemed increasingly anxious when he questioned, "How'd he do that, your lordship, with your father's disgrace?"

"With my own," he answered bluntly. "Donald had to have told him things about me, very personal things, and now Cowan's using them to keep me away from Annie."

"Oh dear," he muttered. "The car crash, sir?"

It was Ambrose who'd witnessed his hysterical rage as he'd tried in vain to recover his passport, Ambrose who'd smelled the alcohol on his breath and tried to stop him going off, Ambrose who'd rung up Donald with the brutal news that his son was near death.

Remembering how intimately involved he'd been in those events, Andrew answered, "That's one thing," realizing that this kindly old servant likely knew as much about him as anyone.

"Oh my—he knows more?"

Andrew nodded.

"Dear me," he whispered, as his distress grew.

Andrew tilted his head to one side, to question, "You know the things I'm talking about?"

Ambrose looked away from Andrew, before he responded, "I believe so, your lordship."

"Then I'll say no more."

"No sir, no need to say more."

Andrew sighed his frustration. "If my father wanted you to warn me, it's too late I'm afraid. The damage has already been done."

Still feeling the potent courage of his outrage, Ambrose looked first into his lap, then directly at Andrew. His eyes were filled with concern and his voice ominously heavy when he spoke the words, "Perhaps not all the damage," then told him of his gruesome vision.

On the return flight to Glasgow, Andrew was so affected by Ambrose's vision—that was eerily, chillingly similar to his own nightmare—he knew that he must take whatever means necessary to protect Annie.

Thirty

Before Ambrose and Andrew met on Thursday, Annie received another call from Lena.

"Can you come to Oxford? Sir David has some information for you and he'll bring it by here tomorrow afternoon, if you can make it."

Annie thought quickly of Mike, who she was due to meet in London on Monday evening, and realized that she had plenty of time to spare. "No problem. I'll come tonight, if I can get a flight."

"Oh do try, we can spend the evening together, maybe go out for a meal."

"Isn't John due home today?"

"Not until late," she answered, "then he'll head for bed and sleep most of the day tomorrow."

Annie felt hope swelling inside of her as she told her friend, "This is the best news I've had in a while. I can't wait to give this bastard what he deserves. I hate what he's doing to Andrew, I absolutely hate and despise him for it."

"I wouldn't get too excited," Lena advised. "You've no idea if Sir David's come up with anything you can use."

Annie had to rush to catch the next available flight. As she was going out the door, she decided to tell Didier and Lisette that she was headed to Barcelona, for a visit with her son, because the more people who knew what she was up to, the better chance there was of Cowan finding out.

She wasn't gone an hour when the phone rang at Château d'Audine.

Lisette answered, "Count Andrew, how good to hear from you!"

412

"How is she, Lisette, is she well?"

"She's doing much better, I think, though it's plain that she's pushing herself and trying to keep busy."

"May I speak with her?"

"I'm afraid you've missed her. She ran out of here about an hour ago to catch a flight."

"A flight? To where?" For a moment he feared hearing that Annie had returned to the States.

"Barcelona. She's gone to visit her son for a few days."

He exhaled relief. "Oh, that's good, she should be safe there. Did she say exactly when she'd return?"

"No, she didn't." Her curiosity sparked, she questioned, "What do you mean, safe?"

Didier and Lisette had to be informed, so he didn't hesitate to tell her: "I'm concerned that someone may try to harm her, and because of that I'm sending two bodyguards to the château to watch over her. They'll also oversee the installation of a security system. I'm going to have the immediate area around the house locked up so people can't wander in."

"Mon Dieu! Is it that serious, do you think?"

He answered honestly, "I don't know, Lisette, it's more a hunch than anything. But I'm quite certain it's better to be safe than sorry."

Lisette was thinking of her pregnancy, when she responded, "Yes, of course, especially now."

He thought he understood. "Right, since I can't be there with her. The bodyguards will arrive tomorrow, they'll show you identification and they're to contact me as soon as they get there. We'll need to put them in two of the guest rooms."

"That won't be a problem," she assured him. "Didier and I will make them comfortable."

"Thank you," he told her. "Will you ring me when you hear from her? And be sure to get a telephone number in Spain. I imagine she's staying at a hotel."

"Of course."

"And let's not tell her about this just yet," he decided. "I'll explain everything when she's back at the château. I don't want to ruin her visit with Marc and frighten her unnecessarily."

"No, that wouldn't be good," she answered, thinking again of her condition.

It occurred to him now, "And Lisette, if you see any suspicious people around the estate, I want you to ring the police immediately, do you understand?"

She responded anxiously, "Yes, of course!"

"And ask Didier to speak with the employees in the distillery, tell them the same thing. Any suspicious persons seen on or around the estate should be reported to the police immediately."

"You're very worried, aren't you?" she realized.

There was no point in pretending otherwise. "Yes," was the answer, "I am."

Sir David arrived at Fargate just after noon on Friday, and was shown into the sitting room where Annie and Lena awaited him. Annie was immediately appeased by the sight of him, for with his military officer's carriage, his small, gray mustache—neatly trimmed, of course—and the worn but quietly proud face that said he'd survived the worst and was wiser for it, he looked exactly as he should, like the decorated and knighted war hero he was.

After embracing him, Lena nervously used her friend's alias, Anne Rutledge, to introduce her.

Sir David was about the same age as Alfred Cowan, and his surprisingly cynical smile reminded her of him now, as he shook her hand and said, "How do you do, Ms. d'Inard?"

Annie turned to Lena for an explanation, but she was as baffled as her friend.

He hadn't liked that he'd been lied to, and was pleased with himself for shocking them. "What kind of investigator would I be," he questioned, "if I weren't capable of discovering a client's true identity?"

The women stared with their mouths agape.

No longer smiling, he went on to say, "Now, what I need to know is, why did you think your little deception necessary?"

Annie recovered herself enough to answer. "Because I'm trying to protect someone very close to me, someone whose life I value more than my own."

He inquired bluntly, "Your husband, Michael Rutledge?"

Realizing she had no recourse save frankness, she answered swiftly, "No, not my husband, my lover."

He seemed satisfied with that response, and questioned, "And who would that be, Ms. d'Inard?"

She almost named him, for in spite of his inquiry, something told her that he already knew. Still, she would only answer, "Must I tell you? It's so very important that he be protected."

He respected that, and decided, "No, you needn't, not now."

The initial tension eased, Lena invited them to have a seat. They made themselves comfortable at a small round table, which was already set for tea.

As Lena poured and prepared his — remembering exactly how he liked it — he brought his attaché to his lap, and popped open the locks. He reached for the folder before saying, "Let's discuss what I've come up with, shall we, and then we'll see if I need to be told more." After a sip of his tea, he opened the file on the table top, telling the women, "What I have here are condensed financial records and the flight history of Lord Cowan's personal jet, covering the last two years. I've also collected personal data regarding his ex-wives and estate holdings, his various addresses and private phone numbers, and other general information, of the sort that is easily obtained by any competent investigator."

Annie's nausea had been in force all morning, so she didn't take any tea. She asked, "Is any of it meaningful?"

He responded coolly, "It could be. For instance, two of his three ex-wives have moved away from Britain, after no-contest divorces. It seems they also walked away from the enormous settlements they were entitled to. I find that very interesting, myself."

Lena suggested, "They wanted out very badly, wanted to sever their connections."

He concurred. "That would be my guess."

Annie wondered, "Do you think you might contact them, see if they'd talk about him?"

"I can try," he said, "though I think it unlikely that they would speak with an investigator about any personal matters. There's also the possibility that they might alert him to the fact that someone's asking questions about him."

She was disappointed by his response, but curious to know, "What about the third one, the one who didn't leave?"

"She lives a very reclusive life on the Isle of Wight," he informed her, "which doesn't bode well for her being of any help, either."

While she had been full of hope in anticipation of his arrival, she was beginning to feel it slip away. "What else is there?"

He finished what was in his cup, but refused Lena's offer of a refill. Still holding to the handle, he rubbed his thumb on the smooth surface, as he continued, "The flight record of his private jet is rather curious. It seems he makes frequent trips to the Netherlands, but while one would expect to see business interests or property there to explain that, we came up with nothing of the sort."

She saw possibility there. "That's intriguing."

With consistent aloofness, he suggested, "It could be easily explained by the sexually permissive nature of the country. Perhaps he goes there to visit prostitutes; he wouldn't be the first."

That would make sense, she realized, if what he's into is so kinky and disgusting he has to pay women to participate.

"And it may simply be a desire for privacy," he theorized, adding, "I actually have some information about that, albeit hearsay."

Lena and Annie simultaneously leaned forward in their seats.

He observed their eagerness, and deliberately settled into his chair before telling them, "I had an off-the-record discussion with someone who's had connections with him over the years, and he had quite a lot to say. It seems Cowan was much more open about his sexual exploits when he was younger, but as he's gotten on he's became more discreet—secretive, actually. He still gives lavish parties but they're not the orgies he was once famous for, and for his part, he's seen occasionally with various respectable women at the theater or the opera. As a result, he no longer carries the nefarious reputation he once did."

Annie questioned, "Are you telling me that he's reformed? Because I know he isn't! I've been the recipient of his unwanted attention and I can say with certainty, Sir David, this is no honorable man."

"I didn't say he was," he responded. "I said he's keeping a lower profile. My contact suggested that he may have become more secretive for the very purpose of protecting himself from exactly what it is you're trying to do to him." His brow furrowed as he added, "He's done it himself, often enough, to enough important people, he may have developed a healthy paranoia about having the tables turned on him."

Lena had a thought. "So if that's the case, his trips to the Netherlands, they could well be what Annie's looking for."

Sir David nodded agreement.

Trying to regain some objectivity, Annie questioned, "Do you know where he goes when he's there? Do you have an address or phone number, anything?"

The answer was simply, "No."

Increasingly frustrated, she asked, "Can you find out?"

He pulled in his chin and cocked his head to one side. "We can try, although it would mean having him followed, and that carries risk as well as considerable expense."

She informed him, "The expense isn't a problem. What's the risk?"

He removed his hand from the porcelain teacup, and brought it to his mustache. "The risk lies in being found out," he told her, stroking the gray hairs with the same absentmindedness as he had the cup. "Following someone isn't as easy as it looks in the cinema."

Annie responded soberly. "No, I'm sure it isn't."

He went on to say, "And even if we come up with what we think is something, say we follow him to Holland and discover where he's been going, it could well turn out to be nothing more clandestine than visits to a married woman."

Annie wasn't buying that and declared adamantly, "No, he's into something evil, something really foul, I can feel it." And in the next moment, she vividly recalled her first encounter with Cowan, how twenty-two years ago in St. Andrews, just by looking at her, he'd made her feel sick inside, as though she'd been raped.

Sir David knew enough about Alfred Cowan to concede, "You may be right, but proving that may be next to impossible."

Annie stood abruptly and walked to a window at the far end of the room, cursing, "Dammit!"

Seemingly unaffected by her agitation, he asked in a calm voice, "Do you want me to keep on with it?"

She whirled around to face him, saying, "Of course I do! What other choice do I have? I can't just sit back and let Cowan continue his threats! I can't let him do that to . . ." She halted precipitously.

He heard the desperation in her voice, saw it in her eyes, and determined it was a good time to ask, "Do you want to tell me now who it is you're protecting?"

Deeply sympathetic to Annie's plight, Lena tried to help. Sounding somewhat childlike, she implored, "Uncle David, couldn't you just let that go for now? Protecting this man is more important to Annie than anything."

His stern demeanor dissolved suddenly, and he bestowed Annie with a look that may have been mistaken for a smile. For from his sleuthing, he had already surmised that it was the Earl of Kilmartin she was protecting, and that was why he was willing to get involved. But his respect for Lord Kilmartin and his gentleman's discretion dictated that he wait for Annie to reveal it, so he decided to say to the women, "I suppose I don't, not just yet," but he would not let it go for long, for that was not how he conducted business. He always demanded complete honesty and frank discussion from his clients.

Handing the dossier to Annie, he told her, "This is your copy. Look it over, perhaps you can come up with some ideas on your own. Just heed my advice and don't try to do anything on your own, all right?"

Lena touched his arm in gratitude, asking sweetly, "Won't you stay for lunch? I've asked Cook to make one of your favorites, cheese and leek pie."

He seemed softer and more approachable, like a kindly older relative, when he responded, "I'd like to, Lena dear, thank you, but some other time." He turned to Annie to say, "I've no one I can assign to follow him just now, and it could be a few weeks before I do. But I'll be in touch."

The prospect of weeks was so disheartening she wanted to cry. But she bit her lip instead and told him, "I'm grateful for your help. I've a retainer for you, if that's all right."

He merely nodded.

Annie moved to retrieve her handbag, then pulled out a bank envelope. "It's a cashier's check for ten thousand pounds, is that enough?"

"It's more than adequate, thank you." He tucked the envelope into his jacket, saying, "It was a pleasure meeting you, Ms. d'Inard."

"The pleasure was mine," Annie answered, though pleasure seemed to be the last thing she was feeling.

When he'd gone, Lena excused herself to awaken the jet-lagged John for lunch. Annie remained in the sitting room with the dossier and read it through three times. She found nothing there to grab hold of, and that, combined with the discouraging things Sir David said and the wait that she seemed doomed to, brought her to the boiling point. It was intolerable, knowing that Andrew was being dictated to by such a person, that they were being kept from each other by such circumstances. It was unendurably frustrating, maddeningly infuriating, and not to be borne.

A refrain began to play in Annie's mind. Like a song whose lyrics were at first poorly understood, it became clearer with each replay that the key to finding what she was after lay in Holland, and if Sir David's men could not yet follow him there, then she would. But while actually following him seemed out of the question, getting him to invite her there was not.

She reread the opening paragraph of the dossier's brief summary, which said that at the time the information was compiled, the subject was at his London town home. The address and phone number were on the next page.

He was not in, so Annie left her name and Lena's number, then went to join her hosts for luncheon, though her stomach was still in a state of turmoil. Lena had been filling John in on the situation with Alfred Cowan and as he listened to his wife, he gave Annie one of those looks, one that said: I told you so.

Although it was totally unnecessary, he reminded her, "I tried to tell you, I did do my best to warn you."

That irritated her and she snapped, "It was already too late and anyway, it wasn't up to you, was it?"

"This sounds a terribly sticky business," he was compelled to add. "Lord Cowan's no minor player."

Their housemaid interrupted them to announce that Annie had a phone call. John and Lena both regarded her with suspicion as she left to take it in another room.

His voice was like warm syrup, as he inquired of her, "You rang me earlier?"

"Yes, Lord Alfred, I'd like to talk."

"How'd you come by this number?"

"It took a great deal of time and effort."

"I see." There was a long and ominous silence. "What is it you wish to discuss?"

"I asked you before about assurance, assurance that Andrew would be protected."

"And I gave you my word," he recalled, "provided he complies."

She was making this up as she went along. "I'd like more than that. I'd like to not have to worry about it at all."

His curiosity roused, he asked, "What do you propose?"

"A truce," she answered, "and as an overture to that, I'd like to show you that I'm not the insidious influence you think me." She swallowed back her worsening nausea.

There was the taint of sarcasm, when he responded, "Oh? And how will you do that?"

"By keeping my promise to Janet." She'd said that as a test.

He wondered, "Will you return to the States, then?"

"Eventually, not just yet." The fact that he hadn't asked, *What promise to Janet?* said that he already knew about it, and he could only have known if Janet herself told him.

"Why delay?" he questioned.

"There are some things I'd like to pursue first, some possibilities that may exist for me in Europe." She braced herself and cringed to say, "And you, Lord Cowan, are one of them."

He was obviously amused. "Am I now?"

Trying to sound coy, she asked, "Do you recall the offer you made me at Crinan Castle?"

If she could have seen the lascivious grin that filled his face when he responded, "I do," she would have vomited then and there.

Her heart began to race in fear as she suggested, "Then why don't we get together for dinner or something, see if we might put this mess with Andrew behind us."

He sounded almost human when he told her, "You're very transparent, my dear, sweet, but transparent."

She waited, catching her breath, pondering what she would next say.

The smooth, saccharin voice returned, "It's not assurance you're asking for, it's insurance you're hoping to buy for your Andrew, isn't it?"

She feigned exasperation over having been caught so easily. "I guess I'm not very good at this."

"No, you're not. But still, I am tantalized."

Despite her best efforts, her voice quavered when she continued, "Why don't we, then, what harm would it do at this point? I'm not going to be able to see Andrew anymore, that's pretty clear, so what harm would it do? And my hope—if I'm to be honest—would be that if you and I got to know one another better, I might persuade you to ease up on him, so he could go about his life without your threats hanging over him."

"Is that all you want?"

"That's all." She was so filled with disgust over her own words, it was hard to go on. Still, Cowan seemed not yet persuaded, so she thought to convince him by adding, "It would be my parting gift to Andrew, a way of making up for the grief I've caused him."

He taunted her with, "How very noble of you, my dear, to offer yourself up to the likes of me, in exchange for freedom for a man you'll likely never see again."

That miserable prospect strengthened her resolve. "It's not that noble," she protested. "And if I'm to continue being honest . . ." She paused for dramatic effect.

Mockingly, he encouraged, "Oh, do!"

The toxic taste this outrageous lie and come-on left in her mouth, made her grimace as she said, "You do fascinate me, Lord Alfred, and in spite of everything, I find myself attracted to you.

And I'm not the sort of woman who can be without the company of a man for long."

He was eerily silent for several, long moments, and Annie imagined she could hear the whir and hum of his diabolical brain.

His tone smooth and confident, he said now, "I was just preparing to leave for the weekend on the continent. Perhaps you'd like to join me."

She felt a rush of adrenaline and the fight or flight terror that accompanied it, when it occurred to Annie that he was inviting her to the Netherlands. "The weekend sounds good."

"The number where I've reached you, it's an Oxford exchange, isn't it?"

She answered quickly, "I'm here to do some work at the ad agency."

"Ah yes, the one Andrew employs," he realized. "Hasn't he had you sacked yet?"

Suppressing her indignation over that remark, she responded, "There's no need for that, I'm finishing up here."

"Good, because we don't want him running into you, do we?" She could hear the moisture in his mouth, as though he were salivating over a delectable meal, when he said, "You're not far from the airport, can you be there in two hours, meet me at my jet?"

She was running low on courage and responded quietly, "Sure."

"You needn't pack but a few things," he advised, "because we'll return Sunday night." Then, in a cool and businesslike manner, he gave her the instructions.

When Annie hung up the receiver, she turned to see Lena standing near.

Having heard most of Annie's side of the conversation, she had gleaned her intentions, and her voice raised in shock and disbelief: "'I find myself attracted to you? The weekend sounds good?' What in God's name do you think you're doing?"

Still standing alongside the telephone, Annie was overcome with a sudden weakness that sank her onto the couch. "I'm going away with him, Lena. I can't believe I agreed to it, but at the moment it felt like the right thing to do."

"Where are you going? Tell me you're not going to the Netherlands!"

She avoided Lena's eyes when she responded, "I don't know, he didn't say."

Lena declared, "This is insanity! If he is what you suspect he is — Annie think! You could be putting yourself in terrible danger!"

She sounded completely drained when she admitted, "But I've got to do something. The only thing that's keeping me going right now is the possibility of putting an end to this. You can't know how terrible it is being kept from Andrew again. It makes me feel so desperate."

Once again overcome with sympathy, Lena sat next to her and took up her hand. "But you haven't even given Uncle David a chance. Give it time, let him see what he can do."

Annie's other hand went to her abdomen as she told her, "I don't have a lot of time."

"You managed for twenty-two years being apart," she reminded her, "what difference will a few more weeks or months make?"

"A world of difference," Annie knew, thinking of the tiny life inside of her. "Lena, please understand, Andrew needs me to do this for him. I'm the only one who knows what's going on, who understands what it's doing to him, and that makes me the only one who can help him. So I've got to do something; at the very least I need to try."

"Dear Lord," Lena sighed, realizing there was no dissuading her. "I pray to God you are able to help, and I hope and pray that you don't do more damage in the bargain."

Annie recognized that as a very real possibility but with so much at stake, she had to take the chance.

Her voice heavy with resignation, Lena asked, "Will you phone me when you get wherever you're going? Someone needs to know where you are."

Making a feeble attempt at a smile, Annie nodded. It occurred to her now that she'd better say for the record, "Andrew can't know. If for whatever reason you or John speak with him, he can't know about this."

Lena understood perfectly. "He'd stop you."

She nodded again, though more somberly. "So promise me you won't tell him."

Lena responded with, "Damn you for asking."

Annie squeezed her hand, then gave her the dossier. "I'm going to leave this with you. I can't risk Cowan finding it on me."

Shaking her head in disapproval, she told her friend, "I wish that were the only risk you're taking."

They returned to the dining room to finish their lunch. Annie didn't want John to know what she was up to, so she announced that she was leaving for Spain tonight, to visit her son for the weekend. Lena had to look away while she listened to the lie.

The Millar-Grahams offered Annie their car and driver and as she waved good-bye from the back seat, she began to worry about how she would protect herself. She came up with an idea and reached into a zippered compartment of her small carry-on bag, the only one she'd brought with her. She was relieved to find what she was looking for, what she had left there after her trip to see Dr. Coupau; it was the letter from the Red Cross, warning her about her positive antibody tests. She tapped the driver on the shoulder and asked him to stop at a chemist's before the airport, where she purchased a box of condoms. Her plan was to play Cowan as far as she could to find out as much as possible, but if things got out of hand, she'd show him the letter, tell him that she was probably infected. And if that didn't scare him off, she'd insist he use the condoms. His repugnant narcissism was suddenly cause for optimism; it made her believe that he'd find protecting himself more important than screwing her.

As she contemplated the idea of having sex with that vile man, she wanted to be sick, but she reminded herself that she'd been through things just as awful before — maybe even worse. She'd survived them well enough, and if enduring one more abhorrent sex act was what it would cost to free Andrew, it would be well worth the price.

Thirty-One

Janet hadn't wanted to go, but she was persuaded by Lady Evelyn to come to her house in the Cotswolds for a riding party. She left Crinan Castle on Friday morning and didn't bother to tell Andrew, who wasn't taking her calls anyway.

On Friday evening, still at his office, Andrew spoke to Château d'Audine for the third time that day. The bodyguards had arrived earlier and phoned him from the house, but he was anxious over the fact that no one had heard from Annie yet.

"Lisette, still no word?"

"None, sir."

He sighed. "I can't believe that I don't have the number there, perhaps it's time for you to have a look 'round her desk, see if there's an address book, a letter from her son, anything."

"How about her husband," she suggested, "do you have his telephone number? Surely he knows how to get in touch with their son."

"That's an excellent idea, Lisette," he told her, berating himself for not thinking of that. "I'll ring him straightaway; meanwhile, see what you can come up with, in case he's not available."

"I'll do that."

Vicky, Mike's secretary, handled Andrew's call personally.

"I'm afraid you've just missed him, your lordship. He was only in for a few hours this morning; his flight left this afternoon."

"When will he be back?"

"He's scheduled to return a week from Sunday."

He cursed under his breath. "Will he phone you, check in with you?"

"Yes, but it's the weekend, that won't be until Monday."

He couldn't help himself and in frustration, exclaimed, "Dammit!"

Vicky gleaned the urgency, so she suggested, "I'm not at liberty to give out this information, you understand, but I can phone his hotel and have a message waiting for him at the desk, if you like."

His distress was momentarily alleviated. "Would you? I'd be ever so grateful. It's terribly important that I speak with him."

Annie stepped from the Millar-Graham's car and onto the tarmac, her heartbeat more pronounced with each step toward Cowan's jet. She was escorted inside and ushered to him with only the barest civility; he had his back to her and was reading the newspaper.

He whirled around in the swivel chair, saying, "Ah, you've arrived. Let's get on our way, then, shall we?" Gesturing toward the steward, he asked her, "Glass of something?"

Her mouth was filled with invisible cotton puffs and she answered with difficulty. "Just some water, please."

He affected disappointment with an obnoxious pout. "That's not very festive. How about some champagne or a lovely mixed drink?"

"I'm not drinking these days."

"Oh? And why's that?"

"I'm trying to lose a few pounds," she thought to say.

His passed his eyes over her body and everywhere they rested—her hips, her waist, her breasts—she felt as though bugs were crawling there.

"You have gotten more plump," he observed, "but it's not unattractive."

Taking her seat and snapping her belt in place, she responded curtly, "Thank you. But mineral water's all I want."

Once the steward had served her, he lifted the phone and said, "Let's go," then returned his attention to the newspaper.

With great effort, she smiled and questioned, "Where are we going?"

From behind the pages of his financial paper, he responded only, "You'll see soon enough."

Cowan spent most of the short flight reading, saying next to nothing, and she kept her head turned toward the window. Just before they landed, she finally saw him put the paper down.

Distance was not what she wanted, after all, she was trying to seduce him into revealing himself, so she said, "You seem angry with me," as though her feelings were hurt.

"Do I? I'm not, you know, just distracted," he grinned. "Once we reach our destination, I'll be in better spirits."

It seemed a good time to ask again, "What is our destination?"

Still grinning, he answered, "The far east of Holland, almost on the German border."

She made a little gasping sound that was born of anticipation, which she tried to cover with a cough. "What's the name of the town?"

"You ask a lot of questions, my dear."

"It's one of my little quirks," she quipped. "I like to know where I am."

He smiled with evil patience. "You will, soon enough."

As they made their approach, Annie turned her eyes again to the window, to watch the dusky landscape come into focus.

A black Mercedes, its windows so dark they were almost indistinguishable from the body, waited for them on the deserted landing strip. When the steward opened the cabin door, there was a rush of fresh, cool air, and in her sleeveless dress, she felt chilled.

As they descended the steps of the small Lear jet, Cowan offered his arm in a gentlemanly gesture. She was growing more nervous by the minute and slid awkwardly into the back seat of the limousine, then to keep herself from shivering, folded her arms across her chest. The chauffeur seemed sullen and the look he gave her cruel, as he closed the door behind her. She now noticed a second man in the front seat, who kept his eyes elsewhere. Once the car started up and drove away from the private airfield, this man turned around to look at her.

Cowan was seated to her left and as the man in front glowered at her, Cowan grabbed her left arm and held it painfully extended. Before she could protest that he was hurting her, the other man leaned over the seat and yanked the arm, pulling her entire body

with it. With one large hand squeezing her upper arm like a tourni-
quet, he jabbed the needle he held in his other hand, directly into
her bulging vein. Everything changed to slow motion after that, the
stinging burn did not last long, and she was guided to rest in Alfred
Cowan's lap.

Andrew didn't sleep that night, staring at the clock, at the telephone, wondering, worrying, trying to come up with a plausible explanation why no one had heard from Annie. His elegant hotel suite
in Glasgow seemed more like a rank prison than a posh accommodation, a prison in which he lay chained to interminable time.

He went to the office in the morning, though there was no one
there but Nigel, who had come in to take calls and help with any
work. When Nigel told him that Mike Rutledge was on the private
line, he took the first easy breath he'd taken in more than twenty-
four hours.

He could not hide his anxiety when he told Mike, "Thank you
so much for getting back to me."

As he'd checked into the Claridge, the desk clerk had handed
Mike the note. "My secretary said it was urgent. Is Annie all right?"

"I don't mean to alarm you, but the truth is I don't know."

Mike immediately demanded, "Explain yourself."

He did not want to worry Mike unnecessarily, but there was
no getting around how concerned he was. "I've reason to believe
that because of her connection with me, someone may try to harm
her. As soon as this came to light, I sent bodyguards to the château,
but the problem is she'd already left for a visit with Marc. She's
been gone since Thursday and hasn't phoned—she's probably perfectly all right," he wanted to believe, "but I'll feel much better
when I know that for certain. I rang you to see if you might give me
Marc's number."

When Andrew said "I sent bodyguards to protect her" Mike
instantly conjured an image of kidnapping and ransom; Annie
would be an easy target, he recognized, a rich man's mistress, living
on an unsecured estate in the remote French countryside. Because
Andrew did not strike him as someone who worried needlessly,

Mike did not question the situation and responded quickly, "I'll do better than that, I'll call him myself. Will you be at this number?"

"All day. And do you have my mobile number?"

"Yes. I'll get right back to you."

In less than ten minutes Mike and Andrew were on the phone again.

His voice now betraying his own concern, Mike told him, "Marc hasn't seen her, and he got a letter from her only yesterday that said nothing about a visit. Are you certain she said she was going there?"

"Dear God." Andrew's voice almost failed him.

Increasingly insistent, Mike questioned, "When was the last time anyone saw her?"

"The housekeepers saw her leave in her car for the airport on Thursday, she was hurrying to catch a flight. She said she was going to visit her son for a couple of days. That was the last time."

Mike's mind downshifted, as he ran the possibilities through. "Have you sent your bodyguards to the airport to look for her car?"

"No, I kept hoping that someone would hear from her."

"Then you should do that, and if they find it, tell them to look for credit card or ticket receipts. And you should probably get the police involved at this point, have them check the hospitals, accident reports, that sort of thing." As he considered the awkwardness of Andrew's situation, Mike momentarily hesitated, then offered, "Do you want me to handle this? I'm in London, you know."

"London—I'd forgotten you were coming." He seemed dazed as he muttered, "She could be anywhere, Mike, anything might have happened."

He was thinking more clearly and with less emotion than Andrew, and wondered now, "How about her cousins in Pau, have you tried them?"

"I don't have their number, either." He cursed himself for not thinking of these things, but knew it was his distress and fatigue that had kept him from it.

"I do," Mike said, "I'll call. How about the ad agency? Have you checked with them?"

Mike's levelheadedness made Andrew infinitely grateful that he was now involved. "Not yet," he told him, "but I'll do that next."

"Why don't you let me?" Mike decided, recognizing that it might be better if Andrew stepped back a bit. "You handle things in France, phone the château and have the bodyguards check on the car and file a missing person's report with the local police. By the way, who is it you're afraid may hurt her?"

As he spoke the words, Andrew was filled anew with foreboding. "Lord Alfred Cowan. Regrettably, an old family friend, and a most sinister human being, Mike, whom I fear is capable of anything."

That did not fit with Mike's theory of what may have happened to Annie and because it was so out of sync with what he'd been thinking, it worried him even more.

He tried Jeanette and Pierre first, and they hadn't heard from Annie since Mike's visit. Then, because it was Saturday, Mike called John at home.

"Is this John Millar-Graham?"

"Speaking."

"This is Mike Rutledge, Annie d'Inard's husband."

"Yes, how are you? What can I do for you?"

"I'm trying to locate Annie and I was wondering if you'd seen her recently?"

"Why yes," he readily responded, "she was here yesterday, at the house."

Mike's relief was audible. "What was she doing there, John? Was she working?"

Although Annie hadn't wanted him to know what she was up to, Lena had filled John in anyway, for it was too worrying a secret to keep. He took a moment now to consider if telling Mike was the same as telling Andrew, then answered plainly, "She was visiting my wife."

Aware that his hesitation meant something, Mike evidenced disbelief when he responded, "Now that's odd, because the problem is, she said she was going to visit her son in Spain, and when she didn't show up there, people started getting worried."

John realized that he was caught in a quagmire, so he extricated himself by saying, "You should speak with Lena, my wife.

She'll know more than I do. I'll just get her for you." Before Mike could say anything else, he'd set the receiver down.

Instead of her delightful, cordial self, Lena was awkward and reticent. "This is Lena Millar-Graham."

He was somewhat brusque in his response. "Mike Rutledge, Annie's husband. I don't mean to be rude, but I'm worried about my wife. Can you tell me where she went when she left there yesterday?"

She cringed as she told this lie: "Why, yes, to Spain, to see your son."

"And she was going yesterday?"

She responded meekly, "Yes, why?"

"Because she's not there." His reproachful tone told her that he knew she was lying. "Now, Lena, I realize that she may have asked you to say what you just did, but you should know that Andrew is very worried that someone may try to harm her, and it's extremely important that we find her and prevent that."

"Oh my. Andrew rang you looking for her?"

"That's right."

She had never imagined any connection between the two men, and that caught her off-guard enough to ask, "So you know about her relationship with him?"

"I do," he answered, "but that's beside the point now. We need to find her and make certain she's safe."

Lena had been standing but she suddenly felt the need to sit. Grasping the receiver with two hands, she questioned, "How much do you know, do you know everything?"

"Why?"

"Because I don't want to say more than I should."

In no uncertain terms, he told her, "Annie may be in danger, Lena, and we need to find her, so this is not the time to worry about broken promises or hurt feelings."

"Who's Andrew worried about," she wondered, hoping against hope that it wasn't him, "is it Lord Cowan?"

Mike's heart slowed with apprehension. "How do you know that name?"

She was happy for the opportunity to come clean and quickly recounted what she knew, from Annie's first phone call telling her about the blackmail, to the meeting with Sir David. "He had some information," she explained, "but it wasn't much to go on, so she decided to try to find out what she could on her own."

The dread enveloped him, as he murmured, "Oh, no."

She reported anxiously, "She phoned him and suggested they get together. That's when he invited her to go off with him for the weekend, on his private jet."

Incredulous, he questioned, "And you let her go?"

She was decidedly apologetic as she answered, "I did my best to stop her, I really tried, but you know how she is."

"Do you know where they went?"

"No, she didn't even know where he was taking her."

It was so maddeningly like her, so impulsive and emotional and reckless: Annie in desperation mode. "Christ!" he exclaimed. "How could she? What was she thinking?"

"You don't think he might . . ."

With each passing second, his feeling of dread grew. "I don't know what to think—only, my God—Andrew's beside himself with worry. He was so worried about what this guy might do, he sent bodyguards to France to protect her."

"Dear Lord," she said, then thought to make him aware: "She didn't want Andrew to find out, that's why she's lied about where she is."

"But the truth is we don't know where she is," he realized, "do we?"

"She may be in Holland."

"Why Holland?"

"Sir David showed us his flight records; he often goes there."

Mike had to act quickly, he knew, and run down every possibility until she was found. "I want you to phone Sir David," he instructed Lena, "and tell him what's happened, tell him she may be in danger and we have to find her, see if he can help us. I've just arrived in London, I'm at the Claridge. I was supposed to meet Annie, you know, we were supposed to get together. I rearranged things and arrived early so we could have more time."

"No, I didn't know that," she mumbled, "she didn't say."

"It must have slipped her mind." There was sarcasm there, but it was overshadowed by his concern. "I'm going to call Andrew back and tell him what's going on. I'll get back to you in a few minutes."

Nigel answered the call.

Mike didn't have time for niceties, and demanded, "Who's this?"

"Nigel Bain, the earl's private secretary. Is this Mr. Rutledge?"

"Yeah—I need to speak with him."

"His lordship asked me to await your call," he explained. "He's had to leave because of a family emergency."

Mike exhaled, "Christ. What's happened?"

"One of his children is being flown to hospital this very minute. She was trampled by a horse at the estate and appears to have sustained a skull fracture, I'm afraid."

Mike couldn't believe what he was hearing. "Will she survive?"

"We don't know, and as her mother is away, his lordship is rushing to be with the child."

Andrew was already so distraught, and now this, a critically injured child who needed him—how could he possibly tell him where Annie was? It had to be decided quickly. "All right, Nigel, let's not bother him with this. Just, when you can, give him this message: tell him Annie was in Oxford yesterday with the Millar-Grahams and he's not to worry because I'm in the process of tracking her down. Tell him the situation is under control, so he can give his full attention to his child. He can call me tomorrow or whenever, and I'll fill him in on the rest. And tell him I hope his daughter recovers quickly, tell him I'm praying for that."

"I'm leaving for the hospital straightaway," Nigel responded, "and I'll give him the message as soon as practicable."

Andrew only caught a glimpse of his unconscious daughter as they were wheeling her into the operating theater. While they prepared little Cathy by shaving her head, dropping her wavy blonde locks into a plastic bag, the neurosurgeon took a moment to speak with him.

They walked to a corner of the family waiting area as the doctor explained, "It's going to be tricky. First off, she's eaten very recently and that makes anesthesia more difficult. Second, it appears
that a shard of bone is embedded in her brain and the prognosis for
that kind of injury isn't good."

Andrew was standing, but he could not feel the floor beneath
him.

Although he said nothing, the doctor read the suffering in Andrew's eyes and touched his arm to add, "What we can hang our
hopes on, is the fact that at nine years old the brain is capable of recovery after such injuries. If she were an adult, the outlook would
be considerably more grim." A nurse interrupted them, with a gesture of readiness for the doctor. "I need to go in now, your lordship."

"Yes, of course." He couldn't know, but Andrew stood in the
very same spot his father had, twenty-two years earlier, watching
as the surgeon walked away from him and back to his mangled son.
As the automated doors of the operating suite parted for the doctor with a great swish of air, then closed in near silence behind him,
he remained unmoving and alone—just has his father had—with
nothing but his regrets, and the picture of that precious blonde
head, that he had so often stroked and kissed good night, crushed
and bloodied.

Lena had arranged for Sir David and Mike to meet at her
home, and Mike arrived first.

As she greeted him, she took one of Mike's hands in both of
hers. "It's so very nice to meet you, though I do wish the circumstances were different."

His dour response was the best he could do at the moment. "I
would have preferred a night on the town, myself."

John came into the entrance hall, saying, "Mike, it's a pleasure."

Mike merely nodded recognition, and couldn't help thinking
that this was the man Annie had slept with twenty-two years ago,
another impulsive act, and one that had broken Andrew's heart.

"Let's go into the morning room, shall we?" Lena suggested.
"We've some coffee in there waiting for us."

When they were seated, John asked whether Andrew would be joining them.

Mike shook his head. "I didn't have time to explain over the phone, but in the midst of all this, Andrew's had an emergency with one of his children. His daughter suffered a skull fracture when she was trampled by a horse."

Lena was immediately and genuinely distressed. "Oh no! Which one?"

"I don't know."

"Poor child—the poor child! Will she be all right?"

"I don't know that, either."

"Andrew must be beside himself," she realized. "He adores his children."

"I gathered that," Mike said, "so I told his secretary that everything's under control with Annie, so he wouldn't have that preying on his mind, too."

John was somewhat surprised. "That was very considerate of you, Mike."

Mike frowned at him, as he questioned, "Would you have me kick him when he's down?"

John blushed and fumbled out, "No, I just meant, under the circumstances—"

"I like the man, very much," he wanted it understood, and left it there.

Sir David now entered the room. Once the introductions were complete, he wasted no time in telling them, "Cowan landed at a private airfield near Eindhoven just after eight last evening, and his jet remains there. I've got two operatives in Holland who I pulled from another assignment, and they're trying to track her down as we speak, starting with the flight crew and anyone who might have seen them leave the airfield. If we can't come up with something in that way—well—I hate to be pessimistic, but with all the time that's gone by, she could be anywhere."

Mike looked at his watch, then to Sir David. "Should I go there? Maybe I can help your investigators."

"Do you speak Dutch or German?"

"Neither."

"Then best stay here and wait."

"She was supposed to try and ring me," Lena just remembered. "I told her I'd be worried and she said she'd let me know where she was."

Sir David wondered, "Is the line free?"

She nodded, "It should be, none of the children are home."

"Instruct everyone in the household to keep it that way," he advised.

Lena excused herself and went to find the maid.

"Can you put a tracer on the line?" Mike asked him.

Because it wasn't legal, he responded, "I'll see what I can do. What I could use is a photograph, have you anyway?"

Mike reached for his wallet, then pulled from behind the cloudy plastic a photograph he'd taken of her on the beach, as she sat daydreaming over the Atlantic. It was only three summers ago, he realized, but it now seemed a decade.

Lena returned to the morning room, announcing with bravado, "Won't it be wonderful when the phone rings and we hear her say she's just fine?"

Mike nodded slightly as he tucked his wallet away, then checked his watch again.

Annie's throbbing head awakened her. She had to put some effort into opening her eyes, because the lids were altogether too heavy. Her struggling consciousness began to tell her that she'd had too much to drink, but then it realized its mistake. Her left arm hurt, at the wrist and near the shoulder, and she moved to rub the wrist pain. The cold metal of the handcuff was startling.

When her eyes opened, reality came at her like a speeding freight train. She lay in a darkened room, her left arm handcuffed to a bedpost, and she knew nothing of where she was or how she'd arrived. She quickly became cognizant of the fact that she was without underpants, though her dress was still on her body. As her eyes accommodated to the darkness she began to discern things, unusual metal objects, heavy old furniture, black velvet drapes suspended from the ceiling. There was an oddly familiar scent to the air, a pungent, human scent. She made some feeble efforts at freeing herself from the metal cuff, but to no avail. Her bladder was uncomfortably full and the need to urinate quickly overrode all else, as she strained to sit up.

She began to call out, "Please, someone," repeating it several times.

After several miserable minutes her captor arrived in his rolled up shirt sleeves, smiling, tinkling drink in hand. He flicked on a light and it pained her eyes.

"You look a mess," he declared.

Averting her eyes from the light, she implored, "Please unlock this, I need to go to the bathroom."

He set his drink down and she heaved a sigh of relief. He moved nearer, then shook his head, telling her, "No, I don't think I will."

She wanted to spit on him, but realizing that bondage and begging must be part of his game, she kept it up. "Please, Alfred, please release me."

Bending now, he lifted something from the floor and held it out to her. "Use this."

She was overcome with disgust, but pleaded, "Won't you let me use the toilet?"

He was obviously enjoying this and grinned as he told her, "Either use this or wet the bed, but if you wet the bed, you'll have to lie in it."

The pain in her bladder gave her no other choice, and she reached for the chamber pot with her free hand. He stood about two feet in front of her and did not move, as she asked, "Can't you at least turn your back?"

"Actually, no."

"Fuck you, then," she hissed at him. He only laughed.

When she stood at the bedside, her legs felt heavy and cumbersome, like they were someone else's. Hiking her dress up around her hips, she awkwardly used her free hand to position the pot between her thighs. Then she closed her eyes and chased the idea of him away, so that she might relax enough to void.

He became aroused as he watched, and when she finished and opened her eyes again, he was rubbing himself. "Very nice," he commented, as she squeezed out the last drops. Then he took the pot from her and left the room.

With the immediate stress of an urgent bladder behind her, she sat down on the bed and started to cry, as with each passing second, her terror grew. The quiet loneliness of the room made everything worse, and she was almost glad to see Lord Cowan return.

Still smiling, he motioned toward the cuff. "I suppose you'd like out of that." Remembering what she'd come for, she told him, "Please, if you would. Really, there's no need for this — I'll cooperate." She was thinking now that what he'd wanted was to watch her urinate; with that behind her, maybe he'd let her go.

He removed a tiny key from his shirt pocket, then unlocked the handcuff in tormentingly slow motion.

Rubbing her wrist, she said in a faltering voice, "Thank you, thank you so much. But I'd have done that for you without the cuffs, you only needed to ask."

"Would you now? Are you that adventurous of a woman?"

She swallowed back her revulsion to respond, "With the right partner."

"Do you consider me that?"

She tried, but couldn't meet his eyes. "I told you that you intrigue me. There's no need to drug me and force me into things."

He responded with joyful malevolence, "Ah, but that's half the fun, you see, the applied force."

She had experienced a momentary gain in courage, but his last remark wiped that out. She rethought her position and decided it best to leave; with what he'd already done to her, she had enough ammunition, anyway, enough to threaten him with the police and pressed charges.

The corners of her mouth trembled as she tried to form a smile, saying, "Well, maybe some other time, Alfred, but whatever you gave me in the car has made me quite unwell and I need to ask for a rain check. Do you think I could get a cab to the airport from here, wherever here is?" She stood and walked a few tentative steps toward the door.

He watched her awkward retreat with amusement. "There are no taxis, my dear. You're quite at my mercy."

"Well, would you be so kind, would you ask your driver to take me?" Until now she'd been valiantly keeping it together, but those words, *at my mercy*, made her chest begin to heave.

Lord Alfred observed her mounting anxiety and affected a kind, almost fatherly expression, as he approached her. Something in his eyes made her think that he pitied her now, that he felt some sympathy as he watched her struggle for air. He stopped when he was right up against her, close enough for her to smell the alcohol on his breath, and for a second she thought that he would say "All right, you can go," so she tried to smile again, as she awaited liberation.

But it was not liberation that Cowan had in mind. He took his right hand out of his pocket and she flashed on something metal in his fist, just before his arm coiled back and hurled at her abdomen, with enough force to fold her in two and send her to the floor. In a few seconds he had pulled her to her feet and the fist, wrapped in brass knuckles, found its mark again—this time she spat blood as she hit the tile floor. She coughed and moaned and pulled her knees in, wrapping her arms around them as she struggled to breathe.

He stood over her, languishing in this moment of dissolute pleasure and arousal, to say with menacing delight, "I ran one of those little tests you get at the chemist's, you see, on your water. It came up distinctly positive, I'm afraid, and we can't have that, now, can we?" He circumnavigated her huddled body, looking for an opening, a vulnerable spot where he might deliver his foot.

Her eyes closed tightly in anticipation of more pain, she heard a door creak open and shut, then a voice in a thick Germanic accent say, "Alfred, you greedy bastard, you've begun without me."

Cowan's laugh was at once sinister and gleeful. "You've not missed anything," he said, "I'm just getting started. Hold her for me, will you?"

"Where's the blindfold?" the other demanded. "You know I like the blindfold."

He responded impatiently, "On the bureau."

As she lay trembling, in mortal terror of what the next moment would bring, two strong and gentle hands lifted her head and wrapped a silk kerchief around her eyes. Then those same tender hands pulled Annie to her feet and slid through her damp underarms. Standing behind her, he leaned his body into hers, so that he might act as a support and provide the resistance to Alfred Cowan's blows.

Thirty-Two

The hospital in Glasgow offered an empty office to the earl, so that he might await the outcome of his daughter's surgery away from the public eye. Nigel remained with him, keeping guard and fielding calls from three different cell phones. The Countess of Kilmartin was being flown in from Lady Evelyn's and had been granted special permission to land at the hospital heliport. Knowing that Janet would soon be there—and while the phones were momentarily quiet—Nigel decided that it was a good time to deliver Mike's message.

"He asked me to tell you that Ms. d'Inard was in Oxford yesterday, visiting the Millar-Grahams."

His careworn face lit with relief. "Was she all right?"

"Mr. Rutledge's words were that everything was under control, that he was in the process of tracking her down today, and you were not to worry over the situation, he would take care of it. He said you should give your attention to your daughter and you can phone him in a day or two."

Andrew almost smiled. "I thank God for that at least. What good fortune it was that he happened to be in England."

"He added that he hopes for the best with young Lady Catherine."

Nigel answered an urgent knock and opened the door to find Janet, flanked by security guards. He stepped out of the office as she rushed to greet her husband with an emotional embrace.

When the door was closed again and they were alone, Andrew allowed his pent-up tears escape. In this moment, Janet was no longer the cold and distant women he had never shared much intimacy with: She was the mother of his children, the only other

440

person on the face of the earth who could truly understand and share his grief.

"I'm so frightened," he told her.

"This is my fault, all my fault." She began to sob.

He held her at arm's length. "How is this your fault? You weren't even there."

There was a wildness about her eyes, a destabilizing fear. "I spoke with one of the grooms—it was Rage, Andrew, that bloody, hateful animal. If I'd put him down, if I'd listened to you, this never would have happened."

The rise of his ire was like a great wave swelling within him. "How could this happen? I thought you kept him apart—you promised me you would."

She suppressed her tears enough to explain. "He *was* safely stabled and the children all had strict orders not to go near him. But Maggie got it into her head to ride him, to prove to herself that she could handle him. Cathy came running after her, raising her voice, telling her to leave off—that's when it happened. He doesn't react well to that sort of thing, he gets excited by noise." She reached for the box of coarse hospital tissues that she spied on the empty desk, and paused long enough to dab at her nose. "Maggie had him by a rope lead and he reared up, then he came down on Cathy. Maggie couldn't control him, he knocked her down and then went after Cat again, he kept after my poor baby daughter." She buried her face in her hands and sank onto a couch, as the sobs overpowered her again.

Part of him wanted to vent his outrage; after all, he had warned her often enough, even predicted something like this would happen. But the other part understood firsthand what guilt and regret felt like, how it scorched your soul and made you feel less than human, less than alive. For their daughter's sake he decided to let the anger go, and say instead, "You mustn't do this to yourself. You need to be strong for Cat, for all of us. We all need you to be strong for us." He approached her now, putting one hand on her shoulder, with the other, he tentatively stroked her head.

His touch felt like heaven, like a bit of heaven brought down to Janet in her living hell. "But it's my fault," she cried, "it's through my stubbornness that he still breathes. He should have been destroyed long ago."

He stroked her more compassionately, saying, "We mustn't dwell on what's done, what we can't change. We have to deal with what we have and do our best with that."

She reached around Andrew's hips and buried her face just below his ribs. Her sobs had changed to silent, endlessly running tears, and when she lifted her eyes to him, questioning, "Where are our other children? Are they safe?" the desperation he saw there touched him.

"They're safe," he assured her. "I thought it best to leave them home for now; Mother and Nanny are with them. If after the surgery, things don't look good," he swallowed the tears that prospect gave rise to, "well — we'll bring them here to see Cathy then."

She tilted her head toward the ceiling, crying out, "Dear God, please forgive me for what I've done, please don't punish me, please don't take my little girl from me! My children are my life — don't you know that?"

He'd never, in all their years together, seen Janet express this much emotion. He sat next to her now, saying, "Shhh, don't go on so. We have to pray for her and believe that she'll be well. We mustn't let despair take us."

"Hold me, Andrew, hold me."

He drew her body into his chest, then wrapped his arms tightly around.

When night had fallen without a word, neither from the detectives nor Annie, Mike grew increasingly restless. He was up and down, browsing through John's books, choosing one that he would scan distractedly, before replacing it and choosing another. John and he had remained in the study, while Lena came in and out. At one point in the evening, John turned on the BBC news only to hear that Andrew's daughter was in extremely critical condition. That report was ironically followed by Annie's commercial with the Band of Gypsies, which Mike had never seen.

For a few precious moments, watching the ad, he felt the presence of the woman he'd fallen in love with, recognizing her unmistakable touch as the piece unfolded. It was charmingly off-beat, earthy and sensual: Annie as she was when she was happy, when she felt grounded, when she was loved. As he listened to the gypsy music and followed the sweeping camera over the high Pyrénées, he lamented the loss of that woman, even as he recognized that she had returned, and that it had been Andrew who had brought her back.

"How about a drink?" John offered, when he'd turned off the news. "It might help."

Still struck by what he'd seen and felt, Mike mumbled, "No, thank you."

"Why don't we step outside then, have a walk 'round the grounds? The fresh air will do us good."

"I should call France again," he decided, "and Marc, too."

"They all know to reach you here," John reminded him. "They'll ring straightaway if they hear from her. Anyway, you don't want to alarm your son, do you?"

He didn't need this man to second-guess him and said in anger, "I have to do something, anything. Sitting here is driving me insane."

Lena had been trying all day to get Mike to take some nourishment and came now to the study, asking, "How about something to eat?"

He had to admit, the burning in his stomach wasn't helping, so he finally relented, saying, "All right, a sandwich and a glass of milk, that's all I need."

But just as she was headed toward the kitchen, the phone rang; Lena answered and Mike picked up the extension.

They could hear his fatigue when Sir David informed them, "We've discovered only that a black Mercedes sedan met the jet and that a woman fitting Annie's description was with Cowan. The witness said that he believes it's the same car that always calls for Cowan, but he doesn't recall the license number, and he doesn't know where it comes from or where it goes."

"Goddammit!" Mike shouted.

Sir David continued calmly, "They're combing the countryside in a fifty-mile radius, circulating her photograph and looking for that car, and they've been joined by four others I sent in from Belgium. The good news is, at least now we have something to look for."

"Yes, that's something," Lena said, hoping it was.

He concluded with, "If you don't hear anything further from me tonight, I'll ring first thing in the morning."

"Yes, thank you, Uncle David."

When Mike said nothing, Sir David added, "Don't give up. We may yet find her tonight."

"No, we won't give up," Lena answered, then looked across the room to Mike, who stood with telephone in hand and a blank, emotionless stare that only heightened her concern.

As night fell, Janet was overcome with fatigue, so she went to the hospital office to curl up for a few hours. But Andrew stayed at his daughter's bedside, holding her hand, talking softly to her, telling her that she would be all right. She was not expected to awaken for at least twenty-four hours, but he fervently prayed for it to happen sooner. Just before dawn, he fell asleep for a time, his head resting on the mattress next to Cathy's little hand.

The nightmare began again and as before, he saw the pool of blood, but this time he also saw his father. Donald was at Kilmartin's Temple Wood, gazing downward at the circle of stones, where the remains of a sacrificed woman and child had been unearthed. His face seemed tired and etched with regret as he said: *You'll do the right thing, Andrew. Trust yourself to do what must be done.* The father who had always seemed so aloof and unforgiving was now reassuringly warm and understanding, and Andrew was comforted by his presence. He wanted more of it, and when he awoke from the dream he was stricken with a sense of loss, for that brief intimacy had been nourishing, and something he'd always longed for.

When he looked again to his comatose daughter, he wondered at the meaning of his father's message, for like Ambrose, he was quite certain that it had been that. It seemed to him that it had to do with Annie, perhaps with his decision to abandon her in the wake of Cowan's threat.

Lena and John invited Mike to stay the night with them, and since Annie would likely phone Lena if she phoned anyone, he accepted their offer. They sent for his luggage and Lena made up a room for him, but he could not bring himself to call it a day. He remained dressed and upright on the bed, fighting sleep, until jet lag and emotional exhaustion took its toll, and his eyes closed against his will.

It was still evening when Annie awoke to the warm, oozing sensation. Every fiber of her being ached and throbbed and everything she experienced she did so first through pain, as she opened her swollen eyes and tried to focus. The room was deadly quiet again but she was now grateful to be alone. She moved her arms slowly to see if they were still bound and almost cried out in gratitude to find they were not. Someone had taken the trouble to put her torn dress back on her body, and a towel between her legs. That strangely familiar odor that she'd noticed earlier was everywhere now, and she realized that it was the scent of blood. She slid herself cautiously toward the edge of the bed and pulled herself up, grasping the headboard. As she moved across the sheets the towel slipped away and the oozing changed to a steady flow. When she stood it trickled down her legs, and after a few steps it gushed forth and stopped her dead in her tracks, flowing away in clotted torrents.

She began to have a conversation with herself at that moment, one that said she had to get out, that she could not die in this place. She kept repeating that mantra with each step, edging closer and closer toward the door, congratulating herself when she finally reached it. The stairs were a different matter but the mantra continued to work, and when she reached the lower landing and heard the sounds of another human being, she seized up in fear, clinging to the railing.

The front door opened and a man stepped into the house—an older man, with a kind face. He saw her and immediately turned his head away, shaking it in disgust. It took all her strength and courage to speak to him.

"Please," her voice was barely audible, "can you help me? Can you take me to a hospital?"

He looked at Annie again, then at the blood running down her legs. He walked away and into another room, while she waited, trembling, still clinging to the stair rail. He was back before long with several towels, which he had tucked under an arm, and her hand and carry-on bags. He moved slowly closer, his free hand extended with the palm opened toward her, as though he were approaching a cornered, wounded animal.

It was almost midday on Sunday when the call came from Sir David. As before, Lena answered and Mike picked up the extension.

Grimly, he informed them, "We've located her. She's in a hospital at Eindhoven."

Mike tried to swallow, but couldn't. "Please tell me —"

"She's in guarded condition," he answered quickly, "though she needed emergency surgery last night, and a transfusion. I've taken the liberty of stationing two men outside her room and there are police there, too. They're waiting for her to be alert enough to answer questions. If you'd like, I can fly you there; I'd like to question her myself when she's up to it."

"Yes, please, I need to go to her." Mike's voice dropped very low, to ask, "What happened, do you know?"

"Hospitals are hard to get anything out of, but a nurse told my man that she'd been beaten and raped to the point of serious injury. I'm sorry to have to tell you that, but there it is."

Lena put the phone down and walked toward John. She threw her arms around her husband and told him what had happened.

Mike kept himself together. "When will you leave?"

"As soon as you get to the airport."

When they ended the conversation, Mike meant to go immediately out of the room, but he sat suddenly and involuntarily. He stared at the floor as he was overcome with memories, memories he'd worked very hard over the years to keep down. Against his will they came rising up, taking forefront in his thoughts, attaching themselves to what was happening now, making it seem as though they weren't part of the past at all. Michele's face came to mind, then it was Annie's, then it was Michele's again. He struggled to remind himself that Annie wasn't dead and that he would be with her soon, but the memories kept wanting to put her where Michele was, gone far beyond his help.

Though she knew nothing of his previous loss, Lena was struck by the paralyzing depth of his anguish. She went to him and knelt in front of his chair, to say, "We're going with you, Mike. You shouldn't be alone."

They recognized Annie's room from far down the corridor, for the police and detectives standing in front of it. As they neared it a doctor came forward and asked if he might have a word before they went in. Sir David left them to speak with his operatives.

Mike introduced himself as Annie's husband and the doctor ushered them to a small waiting room. The middle-aged man spoke English very well and was proud to tell them that he'd done a fellowship at a London hospital.

"I'm so terribly sorry for what's happened," he offered.

Mike responded simply, "Thank you. How is she?"

Trying to sound optimistic, he answered, "Getting better by the minute. The blood we gave her helped enormously."

"What kind of surgery did you perform?"

The doctor looked at Lena and John, then back to Mike. "Would you prefer speaking about this alone?"

Lena and John started out of the room, but without thinking, Mike asked them to stay.

"All right—here goes," the doctor said. "There were some tears in the vagina, but most of the blood was lost from her rectum, I'm afraid. There were lacerations to the anal mucosa that we needed to suture, there was also some damage to the musculature—the anal sphincter— which we carefully repaired. We did a colonoscopy after we put her to sleep to see the extent of the damage, to look for perforations and the like. Most fortunately, we saw only two tiny areas of perforation, which were easily closed. There was also some bleeding from her cervix but that appears to have been caused by trauma to the cervix itself—we don't believe it's coming from her uterus. So the good news is that at this point, her pregnancy is intact. She suffered repeated blows to the abdomen so I can't guarantee that it'll stay that way, but for now, at least, she doesn't seem in any imminent danger of losing the child."

Mike looked behind him for a chair. He sat down and clasped his hands together, then began twisting them. "How pregnant is she?"

The doctor realized that Mike hadn't known, and he blushed with embarrassment. "Forgive me, I assumed you knew."

"How far along?"

"Four weeks, I estimate."

Lena moved nearer to John and as she began to tremble, he took hold of her. They said nothing aloud, but Andrew's name bounced between them.

"Could the baby have been harmed?" Mike asked.

"By the assault, do you mean?"

He nodded, as the word *assault* brought images to mind again: of Michele after her assault, attached to a ventilator, robbed of her child's life, robbed of her own.

The doctor answered, "At this stage, if it has been, we'll expect to see her abort spontaneously. The obstetrician we've brought in says the earliness of the pregnancy is actually in her favor, because if the fetus were larger, it would have been more susceptible to damage."

Mike said, "I see," but what he really saw in his mind's eye was another specter from the past. It was what he'd always imagined his baby had looked like when they removed it from Michele's bullet-torn uterus: a limp, blue, handful of promise, the umbilical cord still attached, then callously severed.

The doctor continued, "I'm not ruling out damage, you understand, it's just not of very great concern at the moment. But there is something else; she's worried about a drug they gave her. Apparently her assailants drugged her with a syringe. We're running toxicology studies on her blood to see if we can identify it. If we can, we'll be able to answer her questions about potential harm there."

"Assailants?" That word brought him out of the past and back to the moment. "There was more than one?"

"At least two."

"My God—"

"I'm awfully sorry to have to tell you that."

He inhaled deeply, before asking, "Can I see her now?"

Somewhat more timidly, he explained, "She looks dreadful, be prepared for that. She's suffered some contusions to the kidneys and ribs, her face is swollen and bruised, and there are marks around her wrists and ankles were she was bound, and some on her neck, where one of them tried to strangle her."

It had suddenly become too much for Mike, and he covered his face with his hands. Lena went to him immediately.

"Please accept my condolences," the doctor offered. "I do hate to deliver this kind of news, but it's better to prepare you than to have you go in there unaware. Can I get you something? Do you need anything?"

"Just a little time, " Lena answered for him.

When the doctor left them, Lena embraced Mike and let herself cry with him. John stood apart from them, too stunned and sickened to move.

Thirty-Three

She was lying on her side, her face turned toward the wall, when she heard one of the dearest sounds that had ever reached her ears—the tender sweetness of her husband's voice.

"Annie—"

It was too good to be true, so she didn't believe it at first.

"Annie, honey—"

His hand touched her arm and she turned her face to him. He flinched when he saw her, and that reaction was a mirror, it was as though she'd looked into a mirror and seen for herself.

Still disbelieving, she grasped his hand. "How'd you find me? Did the hospital call you?"

He had not expected her to be so lucid and found solace in that. "Andrew called me," he said softly, as he pulled the bedside chair closer. He bowed his head to kiss the palm of her hand, then the bruises he saw at her wrist.

Her voice was raspy and weak, as she questioned, "Why?"

"You said you were going to visit Marc," he reminded her. "When you didn't show up there, he worried that you'd fallen into that creature's hands."

"So you know who did this?"

He nodded, then briefly explained how he'd found her.

She seemed anxious, when she asked, "Is Andrew here, too?"

"No, he doesn't know yet what's happened to you. The last time we spoke, we were still looking for you."

She was visibly relieved and gripped his hand more tightly, as she said, "Then you mustn't tell him, promise me you won't tell him."

The conversation was immensely taxing, he could see that, so he said to her, "Let's not get into this now, you need to rest."

"You have to promise that you won't tell Andrew what happened," she insisted.

"Why?"

She answered plainly, "Because he'll want to kill him. It was my fault, Mike, I should never have gone, but that won't matter to Andrew, he'll kill him anyway."

He couldn't imagine Andrew killing anyone, no matter how angry he was, but to calm her, he responded, "All right, you have my promise."

Satisfied with that, she closed her eyes. After a few moments of silence, she whispered to her husband, "I thought of you, Mike, I thought of you and I stayed alive for you. I knew you'd never get through losing another wife."

"No, I never would have," he realized, choking back a tear. He looked to the marks on her throat, and the blue fingerprint bruises on her upper arms. The rest of her body was covered by blankets, but he focused on her abdomen, imagining the trauma there. He lowered his gaze to say, "The doctor told me you're pregnant."

A tear came welling up and ran down one, swollen and purple cheek.

Mike's face turned hopeful and questioning, like a little boy's, as he looked into her eyes and asked, "Is there any chance it's mine?"

She released his hand to touch the childlike sweetness of his face. "When we made love, I was already feeling like I might be. I was so tired then, tired all the time, just like I was with Marc."

As he remembered that, he averted his eyes so she wouldn't see his disappointment. "Does he know?"

"No."

"Why haven't you told him?" he wondered.

Her speech was slow and pained. "It's all so complicated, isn't it? I worried that it would be terribly wrong, terribly selfish."

Quietly, he asked, "So you were thinking of an abortion?"

After a small sigh, she answered, "At first, but then I realized I couldn't. But now—God—now I feel as though I have no other choice." She looked away from him as her tears stepped up with burning intensity. "I can't believe I have to go through this again."

"Go through what again, honey?"

"Worrying about being infected with HIV."

It hadn't occurred to him until she said it, and when the concept settled in, it made him want to scream. But he would not compound her suffering with his own, so he kissed her hand over and over, because there was nothing he could possibly say that would make it any better.

It hurt awfully to cry, and when she moved to readjust her position, she winced from the myriad pains that caused.

"Are you all right, sweetheart?"

"I guess it's time for more Demerol. They say it won't hurt the baby."

"Let me call the nurse, then."

When she'd delivered the medication, the nurse suggested that it was time for Mike to leave.

"Oh no," Annie said. "Please don't leave me. I don't want to be alone."

He returned to the bedside chair and took up her hand again to assure her, "I won't. I'll stay right here."

She'd been reading his face since they'd been together, and what she saw there made her say, "I'm sorry to have to put you through this, I know it must bring back terrible memories." She closed her eyes again as the narcotic flushed through her body, with a wave of nausea and a rush of heat. "But I'm so glad you're here. I feel safe now," she murmured.

"You are safe," he told her. "Let yourself sleep sweetheart, I'm not going to leave you."

When Catherine Stuart-Gordon opened her eyes on Sunday evening, the first thing she saw was the weary, tear-ravaged face of her father. She had been extubated and taken off the ventilator that morning, so she was able to speak to him.

"Daddy, what's wrong?"

Like Annie, who had found it hard to believe that it was Mike's voice she'd heard, Andrew thought he was imagining hers.

"What's wrong, Daddy? Are you crying?"

Brushing at his cheeks, he answered, "I was, my wee one, but not anymore!"

"Why?"

He reached to stroke her forehead, the small patch of skin that was not covered by bandages. "Because you've been hurt and I've been worried, my angel."

"I was hurt?"

Janet had been out of the room for just a short time, to telephone Crinan Castle. When she returned and found her daughter speaking to Andrew, she called out in delight, "Cathy! Cathy, my darling girl!"

"Mummy—Daddy's been crying," she said with concern.

Janet and Andrew looked at one another and began to laugh, in that slightly hysterical way that relief of that magnitude can precipitate.

The Dutch police officers who'd been waiting to speak with Annie confronted Mike when he emerged from her room.

"We need to speak with her, Mr. Rutledge. We need information about her assailants."

"Have you seen her, have you seen the shape she's in? Can't that wait until tomorrow?"

"The sooner we swear out warrants, the better."

Sir David had been standing by and he put a hand on Mike. "Might we have a private word?"

"Excuse us a moment," Mike said, as they walked out of earshot.

"I'd like very much to speak with her first, Mr. Rutledge."

It seemed important, so he responded, "All right. When she wakes up, I'll take you in."

Within a half hour of her waking, Cathy had been examined by the neurosurgeons, who were beside themselves with excitement. When they came out of her intensive care room to speak with her parents, they were grinning like schoolboys.

"She's moving all her extremities, your lordship, your ladyship. Her reflexes are slow but all present, and the only residual problem seems to be the loss of her short-term memory, which is nothing, really, nothing at all, considering."

Andrew drew Janet to his side with one arm, sighing, "Thank God!"

"We've still a long road ahead of us, recovery from these types of injuries needs to be slow and careful, but her prognosis at this point is excellent, unbelievable as that is. We had hoped for this, of course, but we really didn't expect it."

Andrew squeezed Janet's waist, as he felt her tremble and begin to cry again. "I thank you so much," he said to the doctors, "I thank all of you, so very much."

Later, when things had settled down a bit, Andrew met with Nigel in the hospital office they'd been occupying.

"With everything that's happened, I've forgotten to ask if you've heard again from Mike Rutledge."

"I've tried to reach him, your lordship, but he checked out of his hotel yesterday," he informed him. "He left the Millar-Graham home telephone for forwarding, but the maid tells me they've gone somewhere, the three of them. They left around midday and she doesn't know where they've got to."

Furrowing his brow, Andrew said, "That's odd."

"Perhaps they've gone to meet Ms. d'Inard," Nigel ventured, "or perhaps they're simply off touring and having a meal."

"How about the château? Have you tried the château?"

"Yes, nothing new there."

He was troubled by this report, but with the circumstances as they were, he needed to trust that Mike was with her. Still, he told Nigel, "Keep on it, will you? I want to hear with my own ears that Annie's safe."

"I will, your lordship."

Even though it hurt, Annie smiled to see Mike next to her. Their earlier visit was like a dream, and in this moment of awakening, when things were just coming into focus, she feared that it had been.

He touched her arm with his fingertips, and brushed it tenderly. "How are you feeling, honey? Do you need anything?"

"A little water would be nice."

He held the cup and carefully guided the straw through her lips, which were covered with dried blood. "There are a couple of things we need to discuss," he told her, "do you mind? Are you up to it?" She nodded, as he set the water down. "I phoned Marc; he knew we were looking for you so I didn't want him to be worried."

"What'd you tell him?"

"That you'd been in an automobile accident and had gotten banged up," he answered, "and that you'd be fine in a week or so."

She responded with a small, but grateful smile. "Was Marc OK with what you said?"

"He seemed fine, worried but fine. He wants to come to see you as soon as you get back to the château, and I told him I'd keep him informed."

"I'll call him myself, as soon as I'm feeling a little better."

"And without going into too many details, I've told the partners at the firm more or less the truth, so they'll understand the importance of my staying with you. George is flying to London tomorrow to take over the merger negotiations for me." He watched her face more carefully as he said, "And I really should phone Andrew and let him know that I've found you. What do you want me to say to him?"

Andrew — dear God, she thought — *what do I do about Andrew?* She closed her eyes to think, and it was not an easy thing to do in her present state.

Mike had yet to tell her about his daughter's accident, because she didn't need that on top of everything else. And he didn't see the point in compounding Andrew's troubles by telling him about Annie. "I've got an idea," he offered. "What if I tell him that you were with one of your French cousins, that instead of going to see Marc you went to Paris with Laurie to do some shopping or something?"

That was plausible, and she was infinitely grateful. "That's good, that's very good, Mike. But what if he wants to speak with me, phone me?"

He answered, "I'm sure he will."

"I can't do that," she knew, "because I'll break down if I hear his voice." She ran some possibilities through her fuzzy mind. "All right, I've got it. You can say that speaking to him right now would not be good for me, because I'm trying to come to terms with our separation. I'm having a terrible time of it and I know talking with him will make it all worse. He'll believe that. The last thing he said to me was that he wouldn't phone, that hearing my voice would be more than he could bear."

He responded placidly, "I'll tell him," though he was roiled by jealous twinges. "And the next thing is Sir David, he wants to speak with you before the police do."

She was instantly alarmed. "The police? I don't want to speak to the police!"

"Why not?"

"I can't speak to the police, Mike."

"Why?"

"Will you ask Sir David to come in? I'll tell you why; I'll tell you both."

With all the terrible things he'd seen in his military career, Sir David still was taken aback by the sight of Annie's battered face and body. He felt some unavoidable guilt, too, and he wanted to get that out of the way. "I should have realized you'd do something on your own, I should have anticipated that."

"There's only one person to blame for this," she told him.

"He didn't act alone, though, did he?"

She didn't respond directly, saying instead, "I'm going to tell you now who it is I'm protecting."

As he took a seat, Mike walked to the window to gaze distractedly into the street below.

With difficulty, she brought herself perfectly upright in the bed, and chased, as best she could, the narcotic induced cobwebs. "Cowan said that if I press charges, his first act will be to release to the press all the information he has about the man I'm protecting. Everything I tried to do, everything I went through, it'll all be in vain, and my actions will have been the direct cause of this man's ruination."

Sir David pursed his lips and frowned before asking, "I do beg your pardon, Mr. Rutledge, would you prefer not to be present while we discuss this?"

His back still to them, he responded, "I know about her love affair. We've been very open about it."

He relaxed his frown. "I see. Well then?"

With downcast eyes, she answered, "He's the Earl of Kil-martin."

"Thank you," he told her, smiling ever so slightly. "And for your information, I knew that already, but I've too much respect for the man to have named him on my own."

"So you understand the importance of this?"

"I believe so."

"Then you'll help me protect him? It'll mean lying to the police."

Sir David sighed and settled his back against the chair.

"Cowan is sicker than you can possibly imagine," she continued, "and what he did to me . . ." She closed her eyes in a sustained blink. "But we can't use the police to get him. We need to find another way to keep him from doing any more damage—not just to Andrew—but to anyone."

That worried Mike, and he whirled around to ask, "Are you certain you want to lie to the police? They could prosecute you if they find out."

"I have no other choice," she knew, "it's what I have to do for Andrew." She settled her eyes on Sir David again. "Can you help me? Will you help me?"

He thought of all the times over the years that he'd seen the ingratiating Lord Cowan at royal events and charitable fund-raisers; the man had never failed to rub him the wrong way, and he'd always been unsettled by the things that were said about him. But to see with his own eyes those whispers and innuendo substantiated in the person of this battered, violated woman, it made his blood run cold, and it turned his aversion to outrage. His hand went to his mustache and he stroked it twice before nodding and saying to Annie, "I'll help you. God knows, you're going to need it."

The hardest thing was convincing them that she'd taken a train ride up from France, to do a bit of touring and sightseeing for a couple of days; Eindhoven, they knew, was not a tourist destination.

They were very obviously incredulous, but recognizing how determined she was to keep the facts from them, they gave up after about forty-five minutes of difficult questioning. Before they left, however, the chief inspector summed up her statements, and left everyone in the room with the certain understanding that he in no way believed her.

He read from his own notes, with his pen held like a band leader's baton, marking time to a monotonous refrain. "So, you took a train up from Bordeaux, you don't remember the exact one, got off at Eindhoven, you don't remember the exact time, walked to get a taxi, you don't remember where, and got into a car with a strange man instead. You don't recall the kind of automobile it was or even what color it might have been, you only recall that the driver was English and you thought him very kind to offer you a lift to a hotel. After that there's almost nothing you remember, because you were drugged and taken somewhere, where you were repeatedly assaulted by two men whose faces you never saw. Oh, and the man who brought you to the hospital, you don't recall his face or anything about the automobile because you kept passing out on the ride here. Is that it? Have I got it all?"

That last bit was the only completely truthful thing she'd said. "That's it."

He clicked his pen, slid it into his breast pocket, then slapped his notebook together with disingenuous satisfaction. "Very good. That should do it, then, that should really help us find and punish these men. Thank you ever so much, you've been more than kind to speak with us."

Mike could think of nothing else but to plead for his wife's need for rest and usher them from her room. When they were alone again, he sat close and quietly asked, "How are you holding up, sweetheart?"

"That wasn't fun."

"No, I guess not. So where do we go from here?" he wondered.

She'd been agonizing over this, and had decided that it would be intolerably selfish of her—not to mention wrong—to involve her husband any further. "You don't have to go anywhere with this, Mike. You can leave now and wash your hands of the whole thing."

He frowned disbelief. "How could I possibly do that?"

She watched his facial muscles tense, his eyes grow dark. "It's got to be fucking humiliating for you," she said, "hearing me talk about Andrew, about how I need to protect Andrew. It's got to be hard as hell."

He exhaled so forcefully, it stopped her from saying more. "You're right, it's hard, it's beyond hard. But I'm not walking away from this—from you—not this time. Besides, if you're not going to let the courts wield justice on those criminals, the least you can do is let me have a piece of them," he said, his face burning with rage. "They beat and raped you, they sodomized you, left you bleeding to death—there's no way in hell I'm going to put my personal discomfort ahead of that. I am still your husband," he added with indignation, "no matter what, and I won't rest until I see them punished for what they did."

Reason told her that she should try to dissuade him, but the police interview had taken everything out of her, and her body was pulling her into sleep again. She reached for his hand, saying, "I don't have it in me to argue with you. I just don't want to see you hurt any more, because I love you, Mike, I love you."

Still a tad resentful, he responded, "And I love you, don't you know that?" He glared at her a moment, because he wanted to add: *every bit as much as Andrew, probably more,* but he didn't. "The hospital says I can stay with you," he said instead, now noticeably calmer. "They're bringing a cot in for me. John and Lena have gotten a hotel room, but I'm not leaving you alone tonight." He lowered his face to hers, then touched his lips to her forehead.

Late on Sunday evening, after Catherine had gone to sleep, Andrew and Janet decided to take the helicopter to Crinan Castle, so they might give some attention to their other children. When they arrived Malcolm was fast asleep, but the others had waited up for news of their sister. The dowager countess and Nanny were there, too, and after hearing the good news they retired, so that the family might have some privacy.

Maggie was understandably the most upset, and the most happy to see her parents. "Promise me she'll be all right, Daddy."

Andrew pulled her close and stroked her hair. "My sweet lass, we've every reason to believe your sister will be completely well in time."

"Promise that, Daddy."

He kissed the top of her head. "I promise."

She added timidly, "It's all my fault, you know, and Cat will never forgive me."

"She will forgive you, and you must stop blaming yourself, my darling girl."

Janet sat quietly while her husband comforted the children, saying almost nothing and staring off into space. Andrew glanced several times in her direction, and felt a growing unease about her demeanor. After a time she stood and kissed the children, then said she was off for a hot bath. Her husband watched her leave the room, looking somewhat stiff in posture, and obviously following a distracted mind.

The telephone rang about an hour after they'd arrived at Kilmartin. It was Nigel, who'd remained at the hospital with Cathy.

"Lady Catherine has been sleeping very peacefully since you left, your lordship, and all's well."

"I'm so happy to hear that, but you'll ring straightaway if she needs us?"

"Of course. There is one other matter, sir, if you've a moment. Michael Rutledge just rang and he had some news."

Andrew became instantly anxious. "Yes?"

"He's located Ms. d'Inard, sir, and he's with her now."

"Thank God! Is she all right, then? Where on earth was she?"

"Apparently she'd changed her mind about going to see her son, and after a brief stop in Oxford she went on to Paris, to meet a cousin and do some shopping."

"Christ, is that where she was, shopping?"

"Apparently."

He chuckled in gratitude. "Well, I'm glad I was worried over nothing, far better that than what I'd imagined."

"If I may be so bold, sir, what was it you were concerned about?"

"Some other time, Nigel. Did he say anything else? Did he leave a number?"

"No, he didn't, but he said he'll try to ring again tomorrow, so that he might speak with you personally."

"Good. Be certain to put him through to me immediately, will you?"

"Of course, sir. I offered to let him speak with you tonight, but with the lateness of the hour he declined. He sent his heartfelt wishes for your daughter's continued recovery, sir. He was genuinely pleased that she is better."

"Thank you, Nigel. I don't mean to rush you, but if there's nothing else, Maggie's waiting for me."

"No, there's nothing else. Get a good night's rest, sir. You and the countess need that very much."

Andrew stood by the telephone for a minute, picturing Annie walking the Champs-Elysées, loaded down with shopping bags. He smiled at that image, and thanked the gods that she was safe.

Thirty-Four

Andrew took Maggie to her room and, at her request, stayed to read a bedtime story. Her response to her sister's accident was troubling, because she was acting less like the twelve-year-old she was and more like her baby brother. When she was finally fast asleep, he kissed her furrowed brow and went to his rooms, worrying over how she would deal with things as time progressed.

His first inclination was to get into the shower and stay there an hour, but before doing that he decided to check on Janet. She failed to answer his knock so he went in and searched for her. Finding her bathroom untouched he went next to her study and saw no evidence that she'd been there. He rang the servant's hall and asked if anyone knew her whereabouts.

"I was locking up," a footman told him, "and I saw her ladyship some minutes ago, sir, in the downstairs gallery."

"Where was she headed?"

"She was going into the armory."

Andrew replaced the receiver precipitously, then sprinted in that direction.

The door to the armory was slightly ajar and Andrew was sorely disappointed to not see his wife there. He knew that she'd been there, though, for his father's engraved Korth revolver had been taken from its locked case. He stood frozen for one awful moment, and when he realized what she must be up to, he bolted from the room.

It was past midnight and the stables were deserted and peaceful, save an occasional snort and the rustle of hooves on straw. Andrew crept along the dimly lit corridor, so that he might listen as he walked. When he reached Rage's stall and found it empty, he exhaled frustration. He was ready to call out Janet's name when he had another thought about where she might be.

The breeding stalls were separate and removed, to keep the potent scent of mares in heat away from the stallions. They were large, roomy spaces, more modern than the others, some designed for foaling, others equipped with hobbles—leather devices that fastened around the neck and restrained the hind legs, to prevent a mare kicking at her mate. Andrew entered this building with the same quiet caution, and it was thus that he heard the sound of Janet's voice, tenderly reprimanding Rage.

With great difficulty, she had hobbled him; now she stood near his head, watching as he struggled against his restraints. "You don't like that, do you? This is how it feels to be a mare, you know. At least you don't have some brute mounting your bum, biting at your neck, ramming two feet of organ into you." She stroked his nose for a time, scratching him between the eyes, then suddenly plopped down on the straw beside him, saying, "You and I, we've had some fine times together, haven't we? As difficult a beast as you are, you're always a tremendous thrill to ride. The others are so easily managed, but you, old thing, you're a challenge. Some days I hate you for your obstinacy, other days I understand it perfectly. But I never dreamed it would come to this, I never imagined you'd hurt one of my babies." She began to weep softly.

Andrew had halted while he listened, now he stepped forward and made himself known. When he peered into the stall Janet was sitting on the floor, her back against the wall, bits of straw in her hair and on her clothing. Her knees were drawn up and the revolver lay on top of them, grasped by her right hand. She was startled when she looked up and saw her husband.

"Janet," he said quietly, "you needn't do this yourself. Let the vet take care of him." He moved inside cautiously, his hand outstretched, saying, "Give me that, will you?"

She seemed oddly different, and her face was at once twisted in befuddlement and set with annoyance. As her husband drew nearer, she lifted the gun and pointed it at him, saying, "Go away, Andrew."

It was his turn to be startled. "What on earth? Put that damned thing down!"

Her eyes were cold and unnatural, and she kept them trained on him, along with the gun. "Not until you leave us. I don't want you here, I want to be alone with him."

"Why are you pointing that at me? You're not thinking clearly!"

"I'm thinking very clearly," she said, her quavering voice belying that. "In fact, I clearly see the truth of things, and maybe for the first time."

All evening he'd been sensing this change in her, this emotional overload, but he wasn't certain what he should do, except to keep her talking. "What truth?"

She answered with conviction, "About you, about myself, about this bloody charade of a marriage we've carried on for twenty years. That truth."

He exhaled in a short burst. "Janet, listen to me; you're overwrought. So much has happened these past days, let's just put the bloody gun down and go inside and talk this out."

Her response was, "No." It was punctuated by a more pronounced aiming of the revolver, this time at her husband's heart.

Although he couldn't imagine her capable of pulling the trigger, there was something about her manner that made him fear her. He implored, "Please think what you're doing! Your children are finally asleep. They've all been through hell the past two days and they're resting peacefully now, even sweet Cathy. You don't want to do anything that will disturb that, do you?"

"No. But you need to go away. Go away, Andrew." Her left hand lifted to release the safety.

"Jesus bloody Christ! Put that down now!"

She went to her feet, still aiming the gun at her husband, then she turned to Rage and put the barrel to his head.

"No, Janet! Don't!"

Her hand began to tremble and she closed her eyes for a moment; it was then that Andrew lunged forward and pried the gun from her grip. When it was out of her hands, she fell back in the straw and sobbed. Andrew kept one eye on her as he replaced the revolver's safety and removed the bullets, slipping them into his jacket pocket. Then he laid it outside the stall, on a shelf with grooming supplies, before returning to his baleful wife.

"You can't do this, darling," he told her. "The sight of it—it would be more horrible than you could possibly imagine. You can't do this to a horse you love, you'd never get over it."

She glanced up at him and forced her puffy lids open. "You haven't called me that in so long."

"Called you what?"

"Darling."

He hadn't even realized he'd done it. She bent her head to her knees and he sat next to her, asking, "What made you think to do this alone? Why didn't you talk to me about it first?"

When she looked at him again, he was relieved to see that the coldness had left her eyes. "It should be done by someone who loves him, and I love him more than anyone."

"And that's the very reason you shouldn't, Janet. Honestly—I'm very worried about you. What's going on with you? Why did you point that thing at me?"

She seemed surprised at the question. "Because I love you more than anyone, don't you know that?"

"So you pointed a gun at me?"

It had seemed perfectly logical, and recognizing that now, gave her a shiver. "I thought, for a moment, to put you out of your misery."

His eyes widened and he pulled away slightly. "So you really thought of doing it, you really thought to shoot me?"

She shivered again. "I thought it better than watching you suffer, and better than leaving you to hurt my children, to hurt me."

As it sank in, he muttered, "My God." Then he removed his jacket and draped it around her trembling shoulders.

Although her forlorn expression still conveyed heartbreak, she was enormously comforted by his gesture. "You'll never be happy without her, will you? And you'll go on hurting all of us so long as you love her. When I looked up and saw you standing there, I suddenly realized that. I understood that it won't end until you do, until you die."

"Dear God," he said, looking off into a nonexistent distance. "My poor Janet, what have I brought you to?"

As though he understood the gravity of the situation, Rage had been relatively still over the last minute, but he started up again and tried to wrest himself from his bonds, pounding the floor with an impatient hoof.

Janet looked to the horse, saying, "People say he's evil, but look at him, Andrew, he's not evil, he only does as his nature dictates. He's not like us, he can't plot or seek revenge, or do things that are deliberately hurtful. He can only follow his nature." She briefly tilted her head to one side, to rub her cheek against her husband's jacket and inhale its scent.

"But his nature is violent," he protested.

She wondered: "Why do people expect him to act like a kitten when he's a seventeen-hand stallion, full of muscle and sex drive?" She was more like herself now, and yet, she remained burdened, weighted with melancholy. "Keeping him away from everyone else, I thought that would keep him safe. Trouble seems to come looking for him, though."

It was clear that his wife's distress was about more than Cathy's accident, so he said, "Tell me what's going on inside you. I want to know what's brought you to this."

It seemed ages since they'd been like this, this close, this connected, and it encouraged her to open her heart. "I wanted to keep you safe, too," she told him. "I wanted to protect you and keep you here with me, but you went looking for trouble. You had to find her again."

He couldn't think how to respond.

"I didn't understand it at first," she added, "that's why I was so angry with you. But I do now."

"What is it that you understand?" he questioned.

"The feelings, the need." Her head had been bowed and she had looked mostly at the stall floor, but she lifted it to search her husband's eyes. "I was at Caroline Evelyn's you know, when Cathy's accident happened."

"What's that got to do with anything?" he wondered.

She grasped the jacket's lapels and pulled it tight around her. "On Friday night," she began, "I couldn't sleep, it was the middle of the night and I couldn't sleep, so I dressed and walked out to her stables. That's what I do here, you know, when my mind is so full I can't rest; I come out here to see my horses. They calm me, they make me feel more peaceful."

"I wasn't aware of that," he admitted, the guilt creeping in. "Does that happen often?"

In a more subdued tone, she responded, "Far too often, lately."

He touched her hand and whispered, "I'm sorry."

His sincerity moved her, and she smiled fleetingly. "Friday night, what kept me from sleeping was thinking how miserable you were, because you had to be away from her and back with me. This past week, with you so estranged from me, I don't think I've ever felt more lonely." She released the lapels and plucked bits of straw from her trousers, to distract herself from her own, disquieting feelings.

Andrew reached for one busy hand, and took tight hold of it.

That simple connection, brought her much needed strength. "When I went to Caroline's stables," she continued, "I heard something and realized that it was the sound of two people making love. I should have left, I know, but I was curious to see who it was. I thought to find one of the grooms with someone, you see."

"And did you?"

She shook her head. "No. It wasn't a groom, it was two people I know, two riding friends of mine."

Andrew raised a brow. "Illicit lovers, I assume, in the middle of the night, in the stables."

"Yes, quite illicit," she agreed. "It was two, respectable, married women, making passionate love with each other, lovemaking of the sort I'd never imagined."

Andrew exhaled surprise.

"They were in an empty stall," she said, "one was against the wall, her blouse was open and her breeches were around her ankles, the other woman was sucking at her breasts and going at her bottom with her hand, the way a man does. They kissed too, and the one against the wall was moaning and sighing and wriggling. The other one took something from her pocket and pushed it up into her. I think she must have climaxed on it, judging by her screams."

"Good lord, that must have been quite a scene," he realized. "Did they see you? Did you leave?"

"They were too carried away to see me, and no, I didn't leave. I was so intrigued; I've never seen anyone else make love, you know."

He commented, "No, I suppose you haven't."

She tilted her head to one side and looked wistfully at her husband, to say, "I didn't know lovemaking could be like that, Andrew. And as I stood there watching, I realized that you and Annie must be like that, that she must make love to you with the same abandon. Does she?"

His face filled with heat, and he said only, "Janet—"

"It's all right," she assured him, "you can tell me. Knowing will help me understand why you left me, why you went to her."

He could see that she meant to have an answer, so he reluctantly admitted, "Yes, our lovemaking is passionate."

"Not like ours."

He was ashamed to say it. "It's very different."

Amazingly, she didn't seem upset by that. "I thought so," she said calmly. "I watched them and I thought, that's how they do it. That's why he longs to be with her, that's why he risks everything to be with her. That's why those women risked what they did to be together, because it felt so good they couldn't deny themselves the pleasure. I knew it already actually, but I hadn't allowed myself to see it. I knew it from that day I went to see Annie in France. I was standing very close to her and I felt it."

"Felt what?"

"The sex, the attraction, it rolls off her like a scent. It pulls you in, it intoxicates you."

He didn't respond, but he studied his wife's face, wondering what was going on inside of her, what she would say next.

She looked now to Rage, who continued to fight his restraints. "I felt it," she repeated, "that's why I got so angry with her, that's why I hurt her. I didn't want to feel it, you see, it made me angry that she did that to me." She took her hand away from his, and wrapped her arms around her knees, saying, "When I grabbed her the feelings got stronger—holding her breast in my hand only made the feelings stronger. That's why I twisted it and didn't let it go. I wanted to hurt her, I wanted to make her stop doing that to me."

As his confusion grew, he muttered, "I don't understand."

In a tone that conveyed some impatience, she explained, "She made me want her. She exposed her breast to me and smelled of you and it made me want her—I wanted to touch her and lie with her and know what it is that you know. For one awful moment I wanted to put my fingers in her. I had this terrible urge to push her down on the bed and rape her with my hand."

He was stricken and at a loss for words, so he searched her eyes again.

"I realize now that it was a need to be closer to you," she explained. "I thought that if I could go through her, maybe I could find you again."

His bewilderment gave way to some limited understanding, but the gravity of her confession made him bow his head.

"When I watched those women, that's what I thought of again, I imagined myself doing that to Annie. That's when I realized that I'd hurt her because I was fighting those feelings, those powerful, frightening feelings. I've never experienced anything like them before." She paused, trying to read her husband's reaction. "I know I've gone and shocked you," she said, "I'm sure you must think me quite perverted for what I've just told you. I know that I'm terribly ashamed of myself, mortally ashamed."

"I am somewhat shocked," he admitted, "but I'm more surprised than anything."

She was suddenly anxious. "You mustn't tell her any of this. She'll think me a sexual deviant."

He might have laughed at that comment, had everything not been so intense, so deadly serious. "You needn't worry about that," he told her, remembering how Annie had admitted being attracted to Susannah. "If anyone would understand your feelings, she would."

Janet's voice changed, becoming more tentative and childlike, when she questioned, "Do you think I'm sick, Andrew, do you think something's wrong with me? That's what I've been thinking, you know. When I heard about Cathy's accident I thought—God's punishing me for my impure thoughts."

He shook his head and frowned, for he did so dislike this puritanical tendency of hers. "No, I don't think you're sick, I don't think that at all. I think you're very human, and I don't believe that God means to punish us for being human."

She smiled, though barely. "You're so wise, so strong and wise. It's always made me feel safe being with you, being around you."

"I've done anything but make you feel safe these past months," he said, his voice soft and apologetic. "I've put you through hell."

"You couldn't help it."

"No, I couldn't," he readily responded. "I needed Annie's love, I needed to feel it again. It was the only way to heal that wound."

She could suddenly hear Annie's words to her, that day she'd hurt her. She was nearly collapsing from the pain, but she'd pleaded for him: *He's just beginning to heal, don't take him away before he's healed.*

"I understand that now," she said to her husband. "I only wish that you could feel that kind of need for me. If only once, I'd like to know how it feels to be loved and needed like that." The regret and heartbreak that filled her made her close her heavy lids.

Janet stood abruptly, tossing Andrew's jacket back to him. She released Rage from the hobble and when he was free, Andrew jumped out of his way and pulled the half-door, just as Rage made for it. When he realized that he was thwarted, he delivered it with a good kick.

"Look at him," Janet said. "He's just a big baby, isn't he? He wants to go back to his own stall."

"Then let's take him back," Andrew said to her. He retrieved the revolver from the shelf and they both stared at it incredulously before he concealed it under his jacket.

Janet took up the rope lead and they returned him to his stall together, walking in silence along the wide corridors, only encountering two stealthy barn cats who were stalking a mouse. Once inside his home, Rage put his head over the door as he always did, asking Janet for a treat. She reached into her pocket and pulled out an apple, then she rubbed his nose where he liked it, reassuring him in a tender voice that Andrew had only heard her use with the children.

He suddenly felt strong pangs of sympathy, not only for his wife, but also for the horse. Watching Rage crunch the apple, he seemed no more threatening than one of the family dogs, and when he finished and nudged Janet's pocket in search of more, Andrew made a decision.

"I don't see why we have to put him down," he told her. "I think we should be able to manage him. I don't believe anyone will go around him again, least of all the children."

She removed Rage's halter and flashed astonishment at her husband, asking, "Do you really mean that?"

Nodding slightly, he answered, "I do."

Her relief and gratitude brought the pink back to her cheeks. "Thank you, Andrew, thank you so much." They started away and when they reached the tack room, she said of the halter and lead she was carrying, "I won't be a minute, hanging these up."

They both went in and Andrew closed the door behind them. He walked to a table and switched on a lamp, then extinguished the overhead light.

Looking surprised again, she questioned, "Don't you want to go in?"

He responded, "Not yet," then had to steady himself and chase the memory that being in this room always evoked, the memory of their wedding night. He never regretted that night more than he did in this moment.

That regret sent him to her now. He walked to where she stood and took hold of her upper arms, then kissed her gently on the mouth.

"That was very nice," she said afterward. "We've not kissed like that in a long while." She wanted to smile, but was afraid to, for the expression she read on her husband's face was not a happy one.

"No, we haven't." Studying her face, he added, "We've been through a lot these past weeks, you and I."

"Yes, we have," she said, then waited expectantly.

He stroked her cheek. "It's remarkable, really, the way you hang in there with me."

"It's not remarkable at all," she answered. "I love you, Andrew, I always have."

Something stirred inside him, something he had not felt for her in a long while. He leaned in and kissed his wife again, this time more ardently; she was kissing him back with an adamant passion, as though determined to awaken dormant feelings. Their kiss was that, but it was something more: It was the singular connection of two people who have just survived a near tragedy, who have felt things together, as parents desperate to hold onto the life of their child, that no other person on the face of the earth could share.

As their kiss evolved, Andrew unbuttoned her blouse. He massaged her breasts, kneading them with gentle hands, and as he pressed himself against her, she could feel his erection grow.

Janet's heart was pounding, when she whispered to his ear, "Make love to me the way you do to her. You can pretend I'm her, if you like."

That brought a stark reminder, once again, of the night he'd spent in this very place with Jackie from the caterer: when he had pretended that she was Annie.

"No," he answered, "I want to make love to you, to the mother of my children." Slowly, he undressed her, then surveyed her nakedness, saying, "You're very lovely. I'd forgotten how lovely."

"Am I? I'm such a rail, and I've such small breasts. They're not like hers."

He led her over to the couch, and she kept her eyes on him as he undressed. Janet suddenly reached for his penis and began to suck it, something she'd rarely done over the years. The sick feeling threatened him when she did, the one that only Annie had managed to remove, and he had no other recourse but to think of her now, to chase it from his heart.

Still holding him in her hand, she looked up to say, "I meant what I said. I want you to make love to me the way you do to her. Do that for me, Andrew, please."

He coaxed her into lying back on the couch, then put his hands on her flexed knees. Spreading her legs, he went to her labia to kiss them; she gasped and moaned and became instantly wet. Fearing the loss of his erection, he quickly slid himself into her.

She cried out, "I love you, I love you so much!" and bit into his shoulder. She let herself move and do things in ways she hadn't before, imagining that she was responding like Annie. He kept a rhythmic pace, then lifted her to sit on him. Taking hold of her waist, he moved her small body up and down on his shaft. She threw her head back and called out again, saying this time, "Oh God, oh God!"

He withdrew himself and positioned her with her ass to him, then entered her again. He was trying to find a way to bring her to climax, and this seemed to be what she needed, for she called out his name as he drove into her, saying over and over again how good it felt. Then he felt her vagina clamp down as she shuddered, and the rush of hot fluid that accompanied it. He stilled and held her belly while she quivered and moaned, kissing the nape of her neck.

She had never experienced an orgasm like that before, and gasped, "God! God! I never knew!"

When she had relaxed, he started up again. He went slowly at first, gradually increasing the intensity until he had returned her to that unbearable point, and this time he went with her. There were tears in her eyes when he rolled her over and took her in his arms, and she kissed every bit of him within her reach.

"My husband," she said, as though those words had new meaning. "Thank you, my husband, thank you so very much."

He tucked her head down onto his chest, so that she would not see what he was feeling.

They slept that night in Janet's bed, holding to one another at first, but then moving apart. When his back was turned Andrew brushed aside more than a few tears, as he thought of Annie and how much he missed her. His mind kept seeing her in the most simple and poignant of moments, like when she strolled through the garden at the château, stopping now and again to inhale a fragrance or touch a delicate petal. He saw her dip her tanned body into the cooling waters of the pool, watched her eyes close when the water reached her lips, heard her raspy morning voice as she sat across the table from him at breakfast, her hair still mussed from sleep. An ache settled into him that deepened with each recalled detail, an ache he was powerless to ease. It was all he had of her just now so he gave into it and let it bring what comfort it could, let it capture him and numb him into sleep.

Janet lay beside him, thinking also of Annie. In an uncharacteristic move she'd gone to bed without bathing and most of her husband's semen was still within her. It brought her a smug satisfaction, knowing that it belonged to her now, that she had deprived Annie of it. But as she was drifting off to sleep, a wildly erotic vision captured her thoughts: She imagined Annie sleeping next door in her husband's room, as she had only recently. In her imagination, Janet rose from her bed and went to her, then slid beneath the sheets next to her nude, voluptuous body. She took Annie's hand and brought it to her bottom, forcing her to acknowledge the warm, wet prize. Annie pushed her fingers inside and sucked at her tiny breasts, with ardor and abandon. Then she brought her mouth to Janet's bottom and hungrily, passionately, drank what remained of Andrew. The fantasy aroused Janet so much she clamped her legs together and fingered her clitoris, then burst into climax once again, while her husband made the soft, snoring sounds of sleep.

In the middle of the night at Eindhoven Hospital, Annie began to call out. She'd been heavily sedated and her mind was caught in a netherworld that she could not shake herself out of. Cowan was coming after her again, with fists and unbridled sexual anger; she was bound and defenseless, her insides already screaming with pain. He told her how much he hated her, that he hated all women, and that he meant to kill her bastard. She begged him through exhausted, dry tears for the life of her unborn child—he only laughed—his cruelest, most chilling laugh. She struggled against the pain and tried with all her might to free herself from the bonds, but her suffering only incited him further, aroused him the more. He used his penis as an instrument of torture and when it tired and could work that way no longer, he used other things, more brutal things.

She wrested herself free of the two IV lines that were in her arms and knocked over the pole. Mike jumped to his feet and found her soaked with perspiration, pitifully confused, and struggling to awaken.

His voice was tender and soothing. "Annie, honey, it's just a bad dream, you're having a nightmare. Wake up and see me, your Mike is here, you're safe now."

Her face was contorted and she was in agony. "Help me, Mike, help me—"

"I will, I'm here, I'll help you. It's all over now, they can't hurt you anymore, honey."

She focused her bewildered eyes. "They can't?"

"No, they can't."

"You've caught them?"

He realized that she was still not out of it. "Not yet, but I will." There was a great deal of blood running from the open IV sites; Mike lifted the buzzer that called the nurse, then put pressure on one, the worst one. "Relax, honey, take some deep breaths and relax, sweetheart."

"I can't, it hurts too much."

Mike bowed his head and tried not to cry as two nurses entered the room.

When they'd replaced her lines they sponged her down, then gingerly rolled Annie to her side to change the damp sheets. Mike saw for the first time the raw lashes across her back and buttocks, the marks left by the application of a whip, and the bruises at her kidneys the size of a boot. She cried when they moved her and though she at first refused, the nurses administered more pain medication before they left. Her husband stood aside while they tended to her, and kept himself in check by contemplating his revenge on Cowan and company.

With the nurses gone and the lights turned off, Mike sat next to Annie's bed, holding a glass of cool water while she sipped it. "Do you think you can sleep now?"

Her eyes had glazed over again. "I don't like this stuff. Starting tomorrow I'm not taking any more."

"But I'm sure you'll still have pain, honey."

"I can handle pain," she told him. "I can't handle having more worries about this baby."

"No, I understand, but let's talk to the doctor first." He saw tears begin their run down her cheeks. "What is it? Can I do anything?"

"I was just remembering—that's another reason why I don't want to take this crap anymore. It takes my mind away and I can't control what I think."

"Why don't I tell you about your garden, about how beautiful your garden was this spring?" For her sake, he forced himself to smile. "The delphinium were spectacular, absolutely splendid. And the foxglove, they were everywhere, in all shades of purple, and there were columbine and pink poppies—"

Her swollen face scrunched up and contorted again.

"Have I said something?" he worried.

"They tied me into this thing, this leather thing, they called it the toy."

"Annie—try not to think—"

"My arms and legs were spread apart, I was standing, spread open, and there was a collar around my neck like a dog. I couldn't move."

Mike held tightly to Annie's hand.

"Then they came at me, one in front, one behind. They forced their way in, trying to touch each other from the inside. Cowan said it was their favorite game, both of them inside one woman, a game to see how much she could take. I felt something pop, something rupture, and the blood gushed out. They finally stopped, only Cowan didn't want to stop, the other one made him. He said it was no good leaving my dead body there. It would never do, he said."

"My dear God," he whispered.

"While it was happening I felt my mind slipping away, slipping out of reality, but I reached and pulled it back. I didn't want to go crazy, Mike, I know what going crazy is and I didn't want to go there again."

"The bad trip—the LSD that guy gave you," he easily recalled.

She nodded and blinked. "So I thought of you and Andrew, I thought how horrible it would be for both of you, if I died or went crazy. I couldn't hold too tightly to what was real, it was too scary to do that, so I played a game, too, with myself. I imagined that they were you, that they were the two of you. That's how I managed. I told myself you'd gotten a little overzealous but that it was love that was driving you. I stopped fighting them and accepted what they did to me, because they were you. That relaxed me inside, it kept them from hurting me so much." She closed her eyes. "It saved me, that thought. You and Andrew saved me." Her breathing slowed and her face relaxed, as she was carried off by the morphia.

As she told him, he prayed that there would be some way to free her of these memories, that they might somehow, find something to take this away. But the only comfort he could offer just now was what he'd already done so many times during that day, he lowered his head to her hand to kiss it. He kept tight hold of that hand so she would know that she was not alone, and didn't allow himself to cry again, until she had gone deeply, mercifully into sleep.

Thirty-Five

A ndrew's helicopter landed at the hospital before Janet was even up. He left a note for her at the bedside, suggesting that she get as much rest as possible before joining him. But there was a more important reason for leaving early: He wanted time alone, time to think.

The night had been so bizarre, so irreconcilable: the chilling look in her eyes, the terror he'd felt when she pointed the gun at him, and then the powerfully sympathetic response he'd had that had led him to make love to her. And now, in the remorseful light of day, he was nothing if not burdened with guilt, miserably conflicted about what it all meant, and deeply worried about how she would perceive it.

Once at the hospital, he went straightaway to see his daughter. He found her awake and having breakfast, and delighted to see her daddy.

"Where's Mummy?"

He kissed her bandaged forehead several times. "On her way, sweetness. I wanted her to sleep in this morning. How was your night?"

"Fine, Nigel was here. He said you and Mummy were very tired and needed to sleep, so I understood why you weren't here."

He was amazed at how coherent and alert she was. "So Nigel kept you company, did he?"

"I woke up and I was scared, so he read me a story."

"That was very nice. Was it a good one?"

"It was a funny one, it made me laugh."

Her little girl's grin lit the darkness in her father's weary soul.

When the surgeons stopped in to see Cathy, Andrew went to speak with Nigel, who was waiting outside.

His gentle smile expressed his gratitude as he suggested to his secretary, "Why don't you go on to the hotel and have a good breakfast, then get some sleep? You've put in a very full couple of days, and you could use a day off."

"I may do that, sir, if you don't mind. I am a bit ragged at this point."

As awkward as their relationship had become in recent weeks, Andrew needed to say this to Nigel, to make certain he knew how appreciated he was. "I'm very grateful, Nigel, for everything. You've been splendid through all this, just splendid, and it's times like these when you really prove your worth."

Nigel felt a blush coming on, but he managed to keep it down. "It's I who should thank you, my lord, for allowing me to be of service to you."

Andrew furrowed his brow, then said what had yet to be discussed. "I'm very glad we didn't part company after that unfortunate incident."

"I'll be forever in your debt, my lord, for that."

He briefly laid a hand on Nigel's shoulder, and his touch lingered there like a salve. "You go on, now, and get some good rest. Don't come back until you feel fully up to it, all right?"

"Thank you, sir. Oh, before I go, let me give you the mobile, the one Mr. Rutledge will ring on."

"Yes, thank you. I'd almost forgotten." He'd almost forgotten the phone, but he hadn't forgotten about Annie. She was as much on his mind as ever, maybe even more so.

John remained outside Annie's room, while Lena went in to see her. She was carrying a floral arrangement, and the flowers poked their heads through the partially open door before she did. "Good morning! Up to some company?"

Mike answered her. "Of course, we've been waiting for you."

When she looked at Annie, her cheerful smile disappeared. "My poor darling, how are you?"

Annie reached for her friend's hand, saying, "Much better today. Oh, look at what you've brought me!" They were a colorful mix of stock and snapdragons and Gerber daisies, tucked amid sprays of feathery fern.

Lena wanted to kiss her cheeks, but the bruises she saw dissuaded her. "I should have bolted the doors and not let you go off with that monster," she told her.

"Like that would have stopped me," she scoffed.

Mike offered Lena his chair, then said what he'd been holding back until now. "Really, Annie, it boggles my mind, trying to understand why you took such a risk."

She responded meekly, "I know it was an absurd risk, but the things Cowan threatened to disclose about Andrew would have been so damaging, I felt it was worth it."

That explanation did not satisfy Mike, and he rebuked, "So you were willing to sacrifice yourself because he might suffer some personal embarrassment?"

His disapproval was upsetting, because she wanted— needed—him to understand. "It was more than that, Mike. The things Cowan knew about," she explained, "were three very painful incidents from his past. If they were made public, it would not only destroy his reputation and his family, it would destroy Andrew at his essence, at his core. But there's even more to it than that. Two of those things would never have happened but for me, for what I did to him."

Mike remained skeptical. "How do you figure that?"

"It was because of what I did with John, the hurt that caused him, that those things were set in motion."

Lena was noticeably upset, and muttered, "My bloody husband, the bloody stupid man."

"Bloody stupid both of us," Annie corrected her. "We did that together."

Lena frowned and shook her head.

Still doubtful, Mike wanted to know, "And the third?"

"The third was something that happened to him when he was very young that's haunted him ever since, that no one can ever make up to him. But the other things—I thought if I could somehow get control of the situation and stop Cowan threatening him, I might make up to Andrew for the pain I caused him."

Mike looked into her eyes now. "What'd he do, Annie?"

"I can't tell you that."

He seemed increasingly annoyed. "If I'm to help you, I need to know these things."

She shook her head. "I'm sorry, Mike, but I just can't. Telling you, telling anyone, it'd be just another betrayal, wouldn't it?"

John knocked at the door, asking, "Is it all right? Sir David's got some news."

"Yes, come in, both of you," Annie answered, relieved to have the diversion.

Mike nodded at him, but Lena frowned at John, who got the odd sense that he was being talked about. When he got a good look at Annie, he declared, "Good heavens! I'm so terribly sorry."

She attempted a smile. "Good morning, Sir David."

"Did you pass the night well enough, Ms. d'Inard?"

"Having Mike with me made all the difference," she answered, glancing at her husband, "and I wish you'd call me Annie. What's the news?"

"One of the emergency room orderlies recognized the man who brought you here, and my operatives have located him. He's going to take us to the house where your assault occurred."

That surprise brought Mike abruptly to his feet, to demand, "When are you going?"

"Now."

"I'm going with you."

Annie leaned forward and tried to grab his arm, but he was already moving away. "Mike, I don't think that's a good idea."

Sir David agreed. "It may not be, Mr. Rutledge."

"To hell with that," he declared. "I'm going and that's the end of it."

"Mike, please!"

He was resolved, and said sternly, "This is something I need to do." He turned away from her and left the room with Sir David.

Annie recognized the fever in his eyes: it was the same burning darkness that always came of remembering Michele's fate, like when he picked up a newspaper and read of something similar, or when the anniversary of that terrible day came around. The patient, eloquent lawyer was being pushed aside by the outraged husband and father, the man who'd never overcome his loss, and never forgiven himself for not being where he was most needed.

When he'd left her room and closed the door behind him, she said to John, "I want you to go, too, because I want you to stay with him and keep him from doing anything foolish. Will you do that for me, John?"

He and Lena were both puzzled as to why she would ask that. To their eyes, Mike was the steadiest of persons: angry, naturally, but steady.

Annie lowered her voice to explain. "You couldn't know this, but Mike's first wife was murdered, shot during a robbery when she was five months pregnant. He's never gotten over it, and now this. I can see what's happening to him, he's getting angry, very angry, and I'm worried. That's why I need you to stay close to him. Don't let him do something that he might regret."

Lena looked somber, and went a little pale.

John nodded, saying simply, "I understand."

"See if you can get Sir David aside," she added, "and tell him that, too, so he understands why I want you along, so he can help you."

Lena told John, "I'll distract Mike so you can do that."

"And John," she said more soberly, "whatever you do, when you go to that house, don't let Mike go upstairs. I don't want him to see that room."

One of the private detectives remained at Annie's door, but at the hospital entrance, two cars waited for everyone else. The Dutchman who'd transported Annie to the hospital was in the lead car, accompanied by two of Sir David's men. Mike, John, Sir David, and another of his men were to ride in the other. When Mike spied the Dutchman sitting in the back seat, he stormed in that direction, but was forcibly pulled away from the car by a burly detective.

Sir David said to Mike, "Let's have a little chat, shall we?" and opened the car door for him.

Once they were underway, Sir David told him, "I think it far better that our informant not know you're Annie's husband, so let's not give that away, all right? He doesn't speak English but he may well understand more than he lets on, so let's be very cautious about what we say. At any rate, you need to let me and my men do the talking and questioning. Are we clear on that?"

Mike didn't respond.

"Believe me, I do understand your need to be here," he went on to say, "but let's not jeopardize the investigation by going off half-cocked. Now, he seems prepared to tell us what we want to know, but he's already alluded to the fact that he's paid well to keep his mouth shut. If we want him to open it, we're going to have to pay better than well. Is that going to be a problem?"

"No," Mike fumed. "Give the bastard whatever he wants."

"Fine. The more we offer, the more we're likely to get, and we want to get as much as possible from this man. Handled properly, he may turn out to be a gold mine."

The rest of the drive was mostly silent. John glanced repeatedly at Mike whose expression seemed to grow darker and more obscure each time he looked at him.

They went far into the countryside, through deep, thick woods, following a narrow road. A half hour after they'd left the hospital, they arrived at the entrance to a locked estate. The Dutchman stepped out of the car and unlocked the gate with a key he carried. When they passed through they closed the gates but did not lock them again, in the event a hasty retreat was called for.

The man's name was Steiner and before unlocking the front door to the house, he made a statement. One of the operatives was Dutch and he translated for the others.

"He says there shouldn't be anyone here, because he was supposed to come today and clean."

"He cleans the place?" Mike wanted to know.

The operative translated again. "He says he does the special cleaning, the cleaning after one of their episodes."

They entered the house and stood in the dark foyer. Steiner switched on the lights.

"What does he mean, one of their episodes?" Sir David asked.

Steiner went into a long explanation.

"He transports prostitutes to the house, most often after picking them up at the local train station. Sometimes it's just one, sometimes it's two or three. They're mostly women, but there are men, too, young male prostitutes sometimes. He also brings them back to the train, and he sees how they look afterward."

"And how's that?"

"Very often they've been beaten, but not beaten as badly as the woman he brought to the hospital. He says that was the worst he's seen."

Mike squinted and seethed, and John kept his eyes on him.

"What are his other duties?" There was a hint of sarcasm in Sir David's usually unaffected tone.

"He's the one to clean up afterward. Sometimes there's blood, sometimes there's human waste. He says he thinks they scare their victims so much they soil themselves."

Mike began to feel sick. "What else can he tell us?"

"Nothing, until we make a deal with him."

Through a painfully tensed jaw, Mike demanded, "How much does he want?"

"He says he wants enough to retire on. He'd like never to have to see this place again, or drive another battered woman to the station again."

"How much is enough?"

"He asks for two hundred thousand American dollars."

Mike's face relaxed slightly. "He'll have it tomorrow. I'll have my firm wire it tomorrow, tell him that."

Steiner seemed to understand, because he smiled. He continued speaking in a very measured fashion, as though he were negotiating a deal to sell his business.

"He has a Swiss account where he's been stashing the other money," the interpreter explained. "He wants it wired directly there. Once the bank's confirmed the deposit, he'll talk to us again."

"What can he give us? Can he give us names and dates?" Sir David wondered.

"He's been keeping a sort of journal, as an insurance policy," the operative informed them. "He says we'll be quite pleased with its contents."

Mike exclaimed, "For that amount of money, we need something more than just his scribbles in a journal!"

Steiner smiled like the cat with the canary, and the operative translated. "His bringing us here is his demonstration of good faith. He won't reveal anything more until the money is safe in his account."

Sir David seemed exasperated. "Let's get the sampling equipment, then, and the cameras, and comb the house. Maybe we'll find what we need in there."

Mike was working so hard at keeping his anger under control that he only partially heard what Sir David said. "Sampling equipment?"

"We have the ability to do DNA tests and we're going to collect evidence and take photos, just as the police would, only we'll do a better job of it. With any luck we should have some very damming evidence for you when all is said and done, should you decide to use it."

"It may be damming, but it's illegally obtained," Mike knew.

He responded, "If you are not going to press charges and all you mean to do is threaten the man, it should have considerable effect." Sir David excused himself and went outside to give instructions to his detectives, who were gearing up.

John was fascinated by the sudden flurry of activity and failed to pay much attention to Mike at that moment, who stood in the foyer, taking in everything he saw around him.

Mike spied several reddish-brown spots on the otherwise clean floor and followed them with his eyes as they led to the staircase. He quietly moved in that direction and halted at the foot of the stairs, noticing a rather large, flaking spot on the last step, near the railing. It was preceded by many more spots, on almost every step, some larger than others, going all the way up. He mounted the stairs, careful not to step on the spots, and made it to the second

floor unnoticed. The stains led to a set of double doors: heavy, or-
nate doors that were slightly ajar. He had the presence of mind not
to touch the handles, and he pushed one of them open with a foot.

He was greeted by an odor, a somewhat rank scent. It took a
few seconds for his eyes to accommodate, for despite the bright
daylight outside, there were black velvet drapes overhanging the
windows. Using a corner of his shirt he turned the wall switch he
found, wholly unprepared for what the dim lights revealed.

John had realized too late that Mike had gone upstairs, and
he leapt after him and into the room with the open door. He gasped
and halted behind him, as Mike stood frozen, stricken.

The bedclothes were covered in dried blood, the sheets disheveled and torn. There were four sets of handcuffs, one attached
to each of the bed posters, and ropes wound around the posts as
well. A noose hung from the ceiling directly over the bed and there
were more ropes suspended from metal loops. There was a riding
crop on the floor near the bed and a set of brass knuckles, both
seemingly tossed aside, and a rack on one of the walls, hung with
various leather articles and phalluses. A steel and wood apparatus
dominated one corner of the room, complete with chains and
leather cuffs, that resembled something from a medieval dungeon.
On the floor, underneath this device, was the largest bit of blood
yet, larger than the pool that lay at the site where Michele had
been shot. Very near the dried puddle, on the floor and covered in
blood, was a steel dildo that was more than a foot long. Mike spied
that at the last, just as he felt the contents of his stomach rising into
his throat.

John saw him begin to retch and put his hands on his shoulders. He guided him toward the bathroom, which he had noticed
off to their right. Mike positioned himself over the toilet, while he
willed himself under control.

Once recovered, he looked around the bathroom. He noticed
the chamber pot near the sink, still with urine in it, and the pregnancy test alongside, indicating a strong positive. John saw that,
too, seemingly at the same moment, and they looked to each other
in shocked astonishment.

John couldn't believe the conclusion he was coming to. "They
did this to her, knowing she was pregnant?"

Mike was incensed by the prospect. "Maybe that's exactly why."

"No—no!" John protested. "That's too horrible!"

Sir David came into the lavatory then, scolding them like schoolboys. "You shouldn't have come up here, you've corrupted the crime scene! Besides, it's no good for you to see this, no good at all."

Mike pointed to the urine and pregnancy test, saying only, "Look."

It took a moment to register.

"It's almost as though this were the point of the thing," Mike said soberly, "to find out and then to do something about it. Why else would he have taken the trouble?"

Looking as though he might comment, Sir David stared at Mike a moment but then he turned suddenly and went back into the room. One of his detectives had come in and was now absorbing the lurid details of the scene, clicking his tongue in disgust.

"After you've taken all your photos, we'll dust for prints," Sir David instructed him. "Start with the shackles and the handcuffs. They'll have fastened them on her so any prints there should be theirs. And, ah," he cleared his throat and pointed at the dildo, "the base of that thing, too."

Mike looked again at what he'd already seen, and the impact of it was still too great to bear. He quickly left the room, making his way out of the house and into the fresh air. John, fully cognizant of the fact that he'd not done as Annie had asked, followed him now like his shadow.

The nurses helped Annie out of bed and into a chair for her lunch, which was nothing more than clear liquids. Sitting on a hard surface for the first time was not the most pleasant experience, and she needed several pillows underneath to manage.

Lena removed the covers from the various dishes, then declared in disappointment, "You'd think they could give you something more than that to eat, what with the baby and all." She'd said this deliberately, wanting to get the fact that she knew out of the way.

"They don't want anything tearing through there, just now," Annie explained, then motioned her toward a chair. When she was seated, she questioned, "Were you there when they told Mike?"

Lena nodded, and avoided her gaze.

She didn't need to ask anything more, because Lena's reticence told her that it had been perfectly awful for Mike.

 The women sat in awkward silence for some moments, before Lena sprang to her feet again, to retrieve the shopping bags she'd brought with her. The bed had been made, so she sorted her purchases out there, casually announcing, "Mike asked me to do some shopping for you. I hope you approve of my choices, I wasn't certain if we have the same taste."

After chasing the floating clouds of grease away from her spoon, Annie tasted the broth, then pushed it aside to smile and respond, "I think you have impeccable taste."

Lena returned her smile and lifted a bottle of shampoo, saying, "I decided on these aromatherapy products, because they're supposed to have calming properties—and this knit, which I thought very comfortable." She held the simple beige dress against herself, pinning the turtleneck under her chin and stretching the sleeves over her arms. She wouldn't say, but she'd had a devil of a time finding the appropriate thing, something soft and sedate, that would cover Annie's bruises and not pinch or bind her in any way. "I thought I'd help you fix yourself up," she said now. "I know how I am when I've been unwell for a few days. There's nothing that makes me feel better than getting myself back in order again."

Back in order—how she wished she could get back in order. Order was such a rare commodity in Annie's life, and it seemed such a staple in Lena's. Thinking of that made her say suddenly, "I envy you."

Lena had been rooting through the shopping bags, her blonde curls falling about her face. She finally located the hairbrush she was searching for and turned to Annie with a doubtful look, questioning, "Me, darling? What on earth for?"

Annie had had enough of her miserable lunch, so she pushed the tray table away. "For everything," she answered wistfully. "Your stable marriage, your well brought-up children, the unflappable way you always handle yourself. But I guess it's your love for John that I envy most, for the self-confidence it affords you, because you know he's in it for the long haul."

Lena turned pensive as she approached Annie, hairbrush in hand. In the next moment she began the difficult task of untangling her hair, and she kept at it for fully a minute before responding. "My love for John, it's like those lens filters they use in films, you know, for the older movie stars, the ones that blur the lines and make it difficult to see their flaws."

Annie was puzzled by her comment, but ventured, "Maybe that's what makes for good marriages, that filtering."

"Perhaps." The brush caught on a knot, and Annie's head jerked back with her downward stroke. "Sorry, darling," Lena said, rubbing at her shoulder, "didn't mean to do that." She set the brush aside and began using her fingers instead. After some moments, she blurted, "Truth be told, I envy you."

"You envy me?"

She'd gotten the worst knots out, so she went back to brushing. In a quiet voice, she said, "I've never told anyone this, but I had an affair once. It lasted twenty months and ended eight years ago. It'll be eight years next month."

Annie refrained from comment, for the way in which she'd put that, as though she'd been counting the days, told her a lot.

Satisfied with her work on Annie's hair, Lena opened the face cream and a box of tissues, then placed them in front of her. Annie dipped her fingers in the jar, then gingerly applied the jasmine-scented cream to her tender skin. For one precious moment, the scent carried her back to summer afternoons in New Orleans, biking along the buckled sidewalks of her neighborhood with Timmy, through the wafts of jasmine that seemed to drift from every garden.

As she screwed the lid back on the jar, Lena reported matter-of-factly, "He was younger than I was, with no attachments, and he wanted me to leave John and marry him."

With the tissues, Annie carefully removed the cream from her skin. "Why didn't you?"

"John begged me to stay," she answered, without emotion. "He broke down and sobbed, and begged me think of our children."

Annie sighed, then wadded the tissues in her hand.

"But while it lasted," Lena said, her face warming and light-ing with the memory, "it was the most wonderful—no, that's too tame of an adjective—the most thrilling, exhilarating time of my life; I never felt more alive. There's no describing the joy I'd feel, at simply hearing his voice on the telephone. And those afternoons together in hotels, those stolen moments when John was away, nothing else mattered then, our bed would become the center of the universe." Her eyes filled with pain, when she added, "God, I'd give anything if I could go back and feel that again."

Annie wondered, "If you could, would you decide differently?"

Lena shrugged, and dropped the corners of her mouth. "It's not been a bad life," she answered, "and the children are secure and happy; you can't underestimate the importance of that."

"No," Annie agreed, "you can't."

"And yet," she mused, "there's never again been anything like it. I've never felt so full, so loved, as I did then. But you never know, do you, if that sort of thing can last, if it can hold up in the long run." As her thoughts took her away, her eyes lost their focus.

"Did you never see him again?" Annie questioned.

"Once," she answered, her face looking suddenly older, more weary. "I rang him about three months later, asked him to meet me for lunch. We chatted about this and that, then I told him that I was dying inside, that living without him was killing me. He said nothing, and signaled for the waiter. I lit with anticipation, thinking that we would leave together, go to a hotel. But after he settled the bill, he looked me straight in the eyes and said: 'I can't do this anymore.' Then he rose from his chair and started away, but he turned back, just to say: 'I'd have given my life for you, you know.' That was the last thing I heard him say, the last time I saw him." Her eyes closed in this moment of intensely private pain. When she opened them again, she said, "I suppose that's why I didn't try that hard to dissuade you, when you went off with that horrid man. I understood what it was you were trying to hold to, what it was you were desperate to not lose."

Annie reached to take hold of her hand, and the women sat together in heart-wrenching silence. After a time, Lena buoyed herself enough to ask, "When they discharge you, will you and Mike come stay with us, let me look after you? You mustn't recuperate in a hotel, and what with Andrew's daughter as ill as she is, I don't imagine he'll be able to look after you."

Annie's face grew pale with concern. "What do you mean, ill? What's happened?"

"Oh dear," she said, "my big mouth. I'm so sorry, I'd thought Mike told you."

Sir David and John had taken rooms at the same hotel and when they were finished with Steiner, Mike went there with them; after what he'd seen today, he'd never felt more in need of a shower. John offered Mike the use of his room and left to have a drink in the lobby. When Mike had finished his shower and shave, he dressed in the change of clothes he'd brought, then sat at the small desk to make some phone calls.

First he called Marc to let him know that his mother was improving, then he phoned one of his law partners and arranged for the money to be wired to Steiner's account. It was an awkward request, but the man was more than partner, he was a trusted friend who would not ask for an explanation; he replied that he would see to it without delay. Those tasks completed, Mike helped himself to John's bedside bottle of single malt whisky. Then he placed the call to Scotland.

When the mobile in his pocket began to ring, Andrew walked out of his daughter's room and into the corridor to answer. "Yes?"

"I'm trying to reach Andrew Stuart-Gordon."

"You have. Is this Mike?"

"Andrew—sorry. I didn't expect you to answer."

"My secretary's off for the day," he explained.

"How's your daughter?"

"Greatly improved, miraculously well, Mike, thank you. We may even be taking her home by the end of next week."

"That's wonderful news."

Andrew wondered, "Where are you, Paris?"

He fortified himself with a breath, before responding, "Yes, we're in Paris."

Andrew heard the weariness in Mike's voice, and told him, "You don't sound well, is anything wrong?"

He answered quickly, "Just the usual jet lag and lack of sleep."

"How's Annie? Is she there with you?"

"Yes—well, no—she's gone out with her cousin."

There was disappointment in his tone. "I was hoping to speak with her."

The lies had gone well thus far, but now came the hard part. "She wanted me to call after she went out, because she doesn't want to speak to you just now."

His words pierced Andrew's heart. "Why?"

"It's all so difficult for her, she's not handling it very well. That's why she had to leave the château, there were too many reminders."

"I see."

"She knows that if she hears your voice . . ." He halted.

He answered despairingly, "I understand."

"But she wanted me to tell you how very concerned she's been over your daughter, and that you've never been out of her thoughts."

"Tell her I've felt that," he said, his voice slightly tremulous.

"I will." Even over the telephone, Andrew's suffering and his need for Annie were so strong as to be tangible, so Mike added, "You shouldn't think her frivolous, but she's been trying to keep herself busy, trying to keep from thinking about things too much. You know how she is; it's the only way she can manage right now."

"I don't believe her capable of being frivolous," he said, with barely contained emotion.

"No, she isn't, is she?"

Andrew took several breaths before saying this, before asking her husband to say these things for him: "Would you tell her that I miss her from the depths of my soul? Will you do that for me? In the depths of my heart I miss her, and I don't want her thinking that it's any other way for me."

Mike hesitated, before responding, "I think she knows. I believe she knows how much you love her, but I will tell her for you."

"Thank you," he responded. "I'm so very glad she knows that. It gives me some comfort."

Mike found himself wanting to console him. "Somehow, you'll both get through this and to a better place. I know it doesn't seem so now, but you will."

Michael Rutledge never ceased to amaze Andrew. He was continually surprised by the ways in which he would set aside his ego and do what he felt was right, regardless of the personal cost.

He wanted to tell him this, to let him know how much he appreciated his generosity, so he said, "You are, Mike, without a doubt, the most noble of gentlemen. I apologize profusely for the problems I've brought you, but I thank you from the bottom of my heart for the very fine way in which you've handled everything. I could never imagine that a man in your situation would be as understanding and forgiving as you've been, and as truly honorable. I admire you greatly for the kind of man you are, I sincerely do."

There was silence, then a meek, "Thank you," as Mike lowered his head in shame for the lies he'd just told this man, and the truths that he'd been forced to withhold.

Thirty-Six

The doctor came late in the day to see Annie. "You're looking much better," he told her. "The swelling in your face is all but gone."

"Have you got anything on that drug yet, the one they gave me?"

"Oh, yes, we have. It appears there were two: something called propofol, which is what knocked you out, and fentanyl, which is what kept you asleep for a while." He gave her a quizzical look, when he added, "Whoever arranged that knew what he was doing because anything more than the proper dose would have killed you."

Her heart was racing. "Could they have harmed the baby?"

He patted her hand. "The studies on both those drugs seem to indicate that they're safe."

She pursed her lips and exhaled, with a slight whistling sound. "Thank God for that. At least that's one less thing to worry over."

He was less reassuring when he said, "But the matter of the HIV—you wanted to know how long it would be before we could detect it, if they've infected you."

She nodded tentatively.

"Ten days to two weeks," he said. "But even if you are negative initially, your CDC recommends continued testing over six months, to be absolutely certain."

She knew this from before, but she'd been discounting it, trying to tell herself that in this circumstance it would be different—it had to be. "Six months? The baby will be fully viable by then," she worried. "I won't be able to do anything about it then, it'll be too late."

"That's right," he responded. "But the chances are good that the first test will be accurate. I should think that you can make your decision then, with reasonable certainty."

The door had been left half-open and Mike came in as they were speaking. He went directly to his wife and leaned to kiss her.

She could see the beginnings of tears, welling up in his eyes, and it made her question, "What is it?"

"Nothing," he lied. "I've just missed you."

Holding to his hand, she told him, "I've been begging the doctor to release me tomorrow, and he's considering it."

Mike brushed at his cheek before turning to ask, "Really?"

He nodded, saying, "I'll see how she is in the morning, and then decide."

"Are you sure she's ready?"

"Not to get up and back to things," he answered, "but to go somewhere else to continue her recuperation."

"Lena and John have offered to take us in," she told her husband.

"Yes," he responded, a tad absentmindedly, "they told me."

"Is that all right with you?"

"That's fine, I can't think of anything better."

Something was off, she knew, and it made her ask, "Are you sure you're OK, honey?"

"Yeah, I'm fine," he answered, unconvincingly.

When the doctor was gone, Mike walked over to the window and looked down into the busy street. It was that time of day when people scurried about, hurrying to the shops before they closed, thinking about what they would have for dinner, and how they would pass the evening. He found himself longing for that normalcy, for simple problems like deciding whether they would eat in or out, whether they would accept an invitation or beg off.

Now that they were alone, she asked him, "Did you find the house?"

He didn't answer, and kept his back to her.

"Mike?"

"I called Andrew," he said, his voice constrained by tension. "I told him the lies we'd agreed upon."

"Please don't say it like that. It's not like I wanted to lie."

Still gazing out the window, he responded, "I know that, but I can't help thinking how I'd feel in his shoes, how it would be if that were my child in you, when you'd been beaten and raped to within an inch of your life, and everyone conspiring to keep it from me. It makes me want to explode just thinking about it."

She lowered her voice to a whisper. "You know what it is I'm afraid of."

That reminder set him off, and he turned on his heels to demand, "Does it never cross your mind that I might want to commit murder myself, that I might want to grab that dildo and ram it up the asses then down the throats of both of those animals, just for the pleasure of watching them choke on their own shit?"

She couldn't meet his eyes, and spoke to the bedclothes. "You went into that room."

In this moment, he was so incensed he found it impossible to answer.

"I told John to keep you out of there," she muttered. "I didn't want you to see that."

He railed: "Not fucking John, not fucking Sir David, no fucking one could have kept me from doing what I needed to do!"

She was consumed by burning tears. "It has crossed my mind, more than once. I can see how horrible this is for you, how it reminds you. Right now I'm more worried about you than I am about anything else, and that's saying a lot, Mike, a fucking lot."

They stared at one another a moment, before he turned toward the window again, and pounded the sill with his fist. "God, how I hate what those animals did to you!"

Annie slid herself to the bed's edge and stood, using the IV pole for support, then walked to her husband and reached him just as his tears began. She wrapped her arms around him and held on as tightly as she could. He met her hands with his and supported her weakened frame against his back.

He recovered himself quickly, to say to her, "I wish that child were mine. Why couldn't you have let it be mine?"

She rested her cheek against him. "Because it's not the truth, and you deserve the truth."

"What do you care about truth?" he chided. "How much has truth meant to you?"

That stung her, but she answered bravely, "Just because I haven't had the courage to speak it, that doesn't mean I don't revere it."

He bemoaned his remarks and faced her now with an apologetic sigh. He helped her to the pillowed chair, and sat on the stool at her feet. Looking up and into her eyes, he was compelled to say what was in his heart. "If you don't want to involve him, then why not let it be mine?"

"Is that what you really want?" she questioned, brushing at her cheeks. "You know how much I wanted that, but you refused me, again and again."

He didn't allow her to finish. "I was a fool, a coward and a fool. But that was then, and the idea of being this child's father is what's getting me through, because this tiny life is the one good thing that could come out of this."

She flinched as though she'd been struck with a sharp pain. "It's wrong to do that to you, to let you take on that responsibility."

He didn't see it that way. "How can you be so certain it isn't mine? We made love, Annie, not three weeks ago, which is just about right. And they could be wrong about the dates, they often are."

As it began to throb with tension, she put a hand to her forehead. "I don't know, Mike, I just don't know."

His eyes pleaded with her. "I'll take you home. We'll go home and be a family again, you and me and Marc, and we'll raise this baby together. I'll proclaim to all the world that I'm its father; we'll give it more love than any child ever had."

His eyes were so hungry, she had to look away. "You're forgetting something," she said, "what if I have that disease? Both those men, they're so sick, so depraved, the things they do . . ." She couldn't finish.

"We can't think that way, honey."

She shook her head. "I can't think any other way, and I can't imagine willingly bringing a child into the world with a fatal illness. I could never do that. I'd much rather end it now, put an end to it now."

"What do you mean?"

She lifted her shoulders and took a deep breath, bracing herself to say it aloud. "In two weeks time I should know if I'm infected or not, and if I am, I'm going to have an abortion. I've decided that."

He reached to touch her face. "Listen to me, honey. When I thought that you may have been ill before, I read everything I could about HIV. I know that they treat pregnant women with this drug AZT, and that they have very good results with it. Some of the reports say that the baby has as much as an 80 percent chance of being healthy, even though the mother's infected."

Although he meant to appease, he riled her. "Do you think I could do that, make that choice, and leave my child motherless at who knows what tender age?"

"Yes, that's exactly what I'm saying," he responded, "because even if they have infected you, you could live for ten years or more without developing AIDS, and you could have many wonderful years with this child."

"But that's not a given," she argued, "that's only an outside chance, and why should I take all these risks? Why should I give birth to a child whose father can never marry me, whose life will be difficult and complicated from the start, and burden a wonderful man who's not its father with the responsibility of having to raise that baby on his own, without me? How could I do that to you?"

Mike stood now, then bowed his head and said nothing for a time, seemingly defeated. When he spoke again his voice had changed, and she could feel the regret and grief behind his words. "I've been through this before," he somberly told her. "I've been called to the hospital before, to sit at my wife's bedside and hold her hand, feeling the helplessness, the burning regret, the wishing—if only. But in the before I had to let them go, I had to sit by and let them both go, there was nothing else I could do. There wasn't even one more day, not one more word, no more chances to say how much I loved them, how much I would miss them, how my life would never be the same without them. And every day since, I've suffered for what could have been."

Annie reached for his hand.

He squeezed down on hers. "Fate decided to bring me here again, for whatever reason it's brought me to the same kind of place again, but this time it's given me a choice. I don't have to let you go, either of you, not this time, and I've no intention of doing that. It's not time to give up, it's time to fight, and that's what I'm going to do. And I fully understand that we may be in for a hell of a blow, two weeks from now we may be delivered an awful blow, but that only makes me want to fight harder."

She closed her eyes to say, "I'm so scared, Mike. I was frightened before, but that was nothing compared to now." One of her hands went to her abdomen. "Because it's not just me this time. I can hear this little thing, I can feel her voice inside of me."

He sat again on the stool, then put his hands on her thighs, asking, "Her voice?"

"I know it's a girl; I feel it so strongly. And you, just now, asking to be her daddy, it made her voice stronger."

He knelt and leaned in toward Annie's belly. She moved her hand away and he carefully rested an ear there, as though he might hear her, too. Then he said tenderly, "I'm here for you, little one, I'm here to protect you."

Stroking his hair, she began to cry. "Oh, Mike, what am I going to do?"

He lifted his head to look directly into her eyes and answer, "You're going to fight, that's what you're going to do, for me, for Marc, for her."

"But what if she can't escape? Have you thought of how that will be, when your life revolves around her, when you live just to see her little smile, just to hear her call you daddy? How will it be watching her die?" The very idea threatened to suck the life from her.

Although that image wrenched his heart, Mike remained strong and determined. "I'll treasure every moment I have with her, every single moment, just as I'll treasure each day I'm given with you."

Annie was suddenly overcome with weariness, and with the throbbing in her head growing worse, she said, "I haven't wanted to take anything, but I need an aspirin or something. My head hurts so much."

Mike called the nurse, then helped her return to bed.

Once she was tucked in and medicated, she told her husband, "I want you to have a say in this and I will hear you out, but in the end it has to be my choice."

"I know that," he said softly, "and I'll respect your decision. But you need to know that I'll be beside you, wherever that decision takes us, because I'm not going anywhere."

His assurances were as comforting as a favorite cuddly toy, brought to the sickbed of a frightened child. She clung to that comfort as tightly as the child would, and it afforded her the first restful night she'd had in days.

With Cathy improving in leaps and bounds, Janet and Andrew decided to alternate staying with her. In the early evening, the helicopter flew Janet to the hospital to relieve Andrew, who'd been there all day. He flew back to Crinan Castle just before nine to find the silver Bentley belonging to Lord Alfred Cowan parked in the drive.

He was beyond tired and Cowan's gall provoked him. He brushed past the butler who'd come to greet him with, "Where's Cowan?"

William read his face and responded without hesitation, "In the small drawing room, with the dowager countess, my lord."

He didn't wait for him to take his attaché, but dropped it to the floor instead. With heavy strides he made swift work of the long gallery, and his unannounced entrance had the abrupt thunder of a one-man police raid.

Cowan was sitting on a sofa next to his mother, holding one of her hands and patting it. When she looked up and saw her son, her face crinkled with concern. "Andrew! What's wrong? Has Catherine worsened?"

"Cathy's fine," he said, with rancor. "What the bloody hell are you doing in my house, Cowan?"

She pulled her hand away from Alfred and in flustered bewilderment, smacked it against her chest. "Andrew! That's no way to speak to Lord Alfred! He's come here to express his sympathy over Catherine's accident, as the old and dear friend he is."

"Dear friend my bloody ass."

"I won't have you speaking that way!" she scolded. "What on earth has gotten into you? There's no excuse for such rudeness, none whatsoever."

Ignoring her rebukes, he persisted, "You're not welcome here Cowan, and I want you to go."

From the moment of Andrew's entrance, Alfred had affected an arrogant smirk. But he grinned now to say, "I'm going to forgive you, my boy, because I know you've been through an ordeal these few days, but I do wish you'd stop upsetting your dear mother this way."

He sharpened his insistence. "Get away from my mother, you snake, and leave my home now, before I throw you out."

Alfred stood with calculated ease and still grinning, told him, "You are your father's son after all, aren't you? You do have Donald's fire and hubris."

"And I share his hatred for you," he seethed.

He had the audacity to laugh. "What on earth are you talking about? Your father and I were the best of friends."

He would respond to that, but not in front of his mother. "Leave us, Mother," he commanded.

"I won't," she insisted, "not until you stop this attack on Alfred."

"Leave us now, Mother, and I do mean now, goddammit."

She bristled, "With God as my witness, I swear —"

"Go!"

She'd never seen her son this irate and in her frightened confusion, she obeyed, warily pulling the doors behind her.

Cowan blithely observed, "You do like to push it as far as you can, don't you, old boy? Aren't you the least bit concerned that you'll anger me to the point of acting?"

He responded sharply, "Pushing it to the limit is your game, not mine," then glowered at the man. "I know what you did to my father, Cowan, I know all about the young woman you beat and raped, and how you tried to convince Donald that he'd done it."

"I don't know where you got your information," he responded, "and I'm sorry to be the one to tell you, but Donald did do it. He was just too bloody far gone to remember."

"You lie with as much facility as you commit crimes."

That seemed to have struck a nerve, for Cowan lost his disingenuous grin. "Now you listen to me, you get a check on that temper of yours, within this next minute, or you'll regret it for the rest of your life, do you understand me?"

Andrew set his jaw, then seethed, "You understand me. I want you to leave Crinan Castle and never show your face here again. I don't want you within a mile of my family, not my children, not my mother, not my wife."

The smirk was back and it was more obnoxious than before. "And what about that nice little bit of American ass? How close can I get to it?"

He had never in his life felt this intensely angry, as though he could pummel another human being senseless. "You filth," he hissed, "if you so much as touch a hair on her head, I'll castrate you with my bare hands."

Alfred threw his head back and laughed. It was the same laugh Annie had heard when she pleaded for her child's life: a cold, mean cackle that although disguised as a laugh, was really an expression of the pleasure he derived from hurting others.

Alfred began walking slowly away. When he reached the doors he turned to glance at Andrew, who stood tall and menacing, with fists balled and muscles taught, outrage coloring his face. Cowan felt a nostalgic twinge of longing for the man he had loved above all others, for in this moment, Andrew never looked more like his father: just as his father had that day in Cowan's secret room.

He dismissed that sentiment to tell Donald's son, "We'll see about that, my boy, we'll see." Traversing the gallery with studied nonchalance, he left the castle without haste.

When Cowan was in the gallery, Andrew shut the doors behind him with such vehemence, he nearly pulled them from their hinges. His concerns for Annie's safety were now instantly renewed, and he cursed himself for not thinking to send the bodyguards to Paris. But more than that, he rued his insufferably impotent position, his inability to personally protect her. The possibilities sickened him and fueled his rage, and in fury-driven frustration, he lifted the thing nearest him—a valuable Chinese porcelain—and flung it at the marble hearth.

Thirty-Seven

Before he did anything that morning, Andrew put in a call to Nigel, who was still asleep at his hotel in Glasgow.

He began with, "I'm sorry to awaken you."

"That's quite all right, my lord. Is the Lady Catherine not well?"

He assured him, "She's still improving and her mother's with her. But I'm ringing for another reason; I spoke with Mike Rutledge yesterday, he rang on the mobile and I neglected to get a number where I could reach him. It didn't show on the screen so I've tried the call-back option, but all I get is a mobile company recording, saying it's out of the service area. Is there another way to trace that number?"

"I could ring the mobile company," he suggested. "I don't see why they wouldn't give it to me." He suppressed a yawn, then questioned, "Is there anything else I can help you with?"

Although hesitant at first, he needed to ask, "Have you told me everything about Alfred Cowan and that visit you had with him?"

Nigel swallowed the lump in his throat. "Why do you ask, your lordship?"

"Cowan's an evil man," he answered, "a horrid cancer of a man, and I've reason to believe he may try to hurt Annie."

"Has he threatened her?"

"Not exactly, not outright, but I have a dreadful feeling about it and I won't rest until I'm assured of her safety. Those two bodyguards I hired are sitting in France guarding nothing and I want to send them to her, but I have to find out where she is first. All I know is that they're in Paris."

"I'll get on it right away, sir."

"Nigel," he said, pausing deliberately, "you didn't answer my question about Cowan."

He could feel the heat rush to his cheeks. "Sorry, my lord. I don't believe I've anything else to tell you about the matter, I believe I said all I could about it when we first spoke."

Andrew wanted to trust him — needed to trust him — so he determined that he would. "All right, then. Shall I see you later?"

"Of course, sir. I should be there within the hour."

Annie was set to be discharged on Wednesday afternoon and Sir David was to drive them to the airport and his waiting company jet. As she was getting ready, a nurse brought Mike her carry-on and handbag, and a plastic sack, which contained her torn and bloody dress. He recognized it as one he'd seen her in many times before: a tight-fitting, black shift that she'd looked wonderful in.

While Lena was helping her dress, he opened her clutch bag; it still contained the box of condoms and the letter from the Red Cross. He was at first puzzled as to why they were there, but then he reasoned her intent. It tore at his already aching heart to picture her when she went off with that monster: as lovely as she was desperate, as hopeful as she was terrified, stoically putting aside her fear to help Andrew. Inside of a moment he wanted to shake her for her stupidity, then embrace her for the love that drove her to it.

When Sir David came in, he asked Annie, "Mind if we have a chat before we get on our way?"

"We'll be in the waiting area," John said, as he and Lena made their way out.

Mike stayed where he was.

Sir David was somewhat less formal today, and his manner was gentle, almost fatherly. "I've waited to do this until you were feeling better," he told her. "But I need to ask you some questions, and I want you to tell me everything you remember." He turned to Mike to say, "It might be better if you waited outside."

Annie touched his arm. "Why don't you do that, honey?"

He responded sternly, "I've been to that house, I've seen that room. What I've imagined happened to you can't possibly be worse than the truth. It's better for me to hear the truth now than to go on wondering."

She was adamant. "No," she said, "I can't go through this in front of you. Please understand."

Sir David was setting up a tape recorder and when she saw that, she thought to say to her husband, "You can listen to the tape afterward, if you must, but you can't be here now. Please, Mike, help me with this, don't make it harder for me."

"All right," he sighed, "I'll be outside."

The interview was exhausting, and Sir David felt sorry that she had to relive it as such, for as difficult as it had been for him to listen to, it had to have been hell for her talk about.

In order to tell her story, she'd found it necessary to affect detachment, so much so, it had often seemed as though it had happened to someone else. "At the end, when I was bleeding so badly," she remembered, "the other man, Hans, he finally convinced Cowan to leave. But before he did, he warned me that if I made any attempt at all to connect him with what had happened, the very first thing he'd do would be to give everything he knows about Andrew to the press. Then he'd come for me and he'd finish what he'd started, and he said it wouldn't be nearly as enjoyable as what I'd just experienced. He got right up in my face and said these things while he squeezed my breasts, and when he was through, he punched me one last time. Then he went away laughing." He'd said something else to her at the last, but she withheld that.

"Did Hans say anything to you?"

She nodded slightly. "Yes. He said I'd be wise to heed Cowan's warning because he doesn't make idle threats."

Sir David sighed and looked troubled.

"When they were gone, they left me hanging in that thing for a while," she recalled, "everything was getting very fuzzy and confused by then, like I was passing from one dream to another. Then I was freed and laid on the bed; I think it was Hans who did that, but he didn't say anything. I went in and out of sleep, hearing voices, thinking I was somewhere else. Then I awakened more lucidly and realized I was dressed, and there was a towel between my legs. I managed to get downstairs and I saw that man Steiner come in. The rest you know."

"So you never saw his face, this Hans?"

She bit her lip before answering, "They kept me blindfolded."

"I assume you can recall his voice."

"Very well," she told him, "and his cologne, he wore an expensive cologne."

"Anything else?"

"No, nothing else," she responded, and averted her eyes.

There was something amiss about her response; Sir David began to feel that she was holding back, because throughout the interview, whenever she mentioned Hans, she seemed reticent. "If we can go back to the pregnancy test on your urine, was there any conversation beforehand about your pregnancy?"

"None whatsoever."

"Did Cowan ask you about it?"

"No. The only thing was, in the plane, he offered me a drink and I refused. I told him I was on a diet and not drinking alcohol. He looked me over and said I'd gotten more plump, then he dropped it. That was the only thing even remotely related to my pregnancy."

"Do you have any idea why he thought you were, any guesses?"

She shook her head. "The only people who knew were my housekeeper and the doctor in France."

"Could either of them have told anyone?"

She answered with conviction, "That's very unlikely. But Cowan was at the château, he sneaked up on us when we were at the pool. He may have been snooping around the house before that, but what would he have seen? There wasn't anything for him to have seen unless he saw me throw up, which he didn't." She ended by making a gasping sound.

"What is it? Have you thought of something?"

Cowan's words came back to her now, the ones she'd withheld a few moments earlier, the last thing he said as he twisted her breasts: *And that's for Janet.* "Oh no, not her."

"Who?"

"Andrew's wife came to see me about a week before Cowan showed up. We had an ugly scene in my bedroom and I got ill in front of her. She left then, without another word. My housekeeper suspected after witnessing that; I have to wonder if Janet did, too."

"Would she have gone to Cowan with her suspicions?"

"Andrew thinks the very reason he got involved was because Janet asked him to." She looked at the floor now, thinking, *Christ — his own wife — how the hell will he deal with that?*

Sir David turned off the recorder. "Well then, that's all for now. My men have had Steiner under surveillance and we're to meet with him at four. The money was wired through this morning, so he's ready to talk."

"What money?"

"Steiner wanted money before he'd give us detailed information," he explained, "and your husband took care of it."

When Mike was back with her, she thanked, then scolded him. "But it's not right, you shouldn't be paying for that."

He responded, "Without the police involved, what else were we to do?"

An attendant arrived with a wheelchair just then, asking, "Ready to go?"

"More than ready," she told him. She hadn't been this anxious to leave a place since the last time she was in this country, twenty-two years earlier.

It was later in the day when Nigel heard back from the wireless phone company. Andrew was still at the hospital and Nigel approached him with such a quizzical look, it alarmed him. "What is it?"

"It's odd, my lord. I mean, the call did not come from Paris."

"Where then?"

"Eindhoven, in the Netherlands."

"What?"

"It was a hotel, the Hotel Europa in Eindhoven."

"Are you certain?"

"Quite certain. The only other calls were from me."

He'd been standing in the center of the hallway, but now he moved nearer the wall to lean against it. He stared at the floor a moment, trying to reason why Mike would have lied to him. Then he wondered, "Have you rung the hotel?"

"I did," Nigel answered readily. "There's no Michael Rutledge registered, and there hasn't been over the last week."

He folded one arm across his chest and raised the fist of the other, tapping it against his mouth. "How about Annie? Did you check under her name?"

Nigel had anticipated him. "Yes, I did. No Annie d'Inard, either."

His puzzlement gave way to disquietude. "This isn't right," he knew, "something's not right here. Why would he tell me he's in Paris when he's not?"

"I take it you didn't speak with Annie herself."

"No," he said. "Mike told me she'd gone out."

Nigel questioned, "Why would he lie?"

Andrew knew that it was not in Mike's character. "He wouldn't, not to me, anyway. He and I—we've had an awkward relationship—but it's been an honest one."

"Yet he must have," Nigel reminded him. "The phone companies just don't make mistakes on these things."

"No, I suppose not," he acknowledged. "Then there must have been good reason."

Recognizing how worried he was becoming, Nigel asked now, "Shall I contact his law offices, speak with his secretary?"

Andrew rubbed his forehead before deciding, "Call the château first, see if they've shown up there. And if they haven't, call John Millar-Graham, see if he knows anything. She was there before, maybe John and Lena know something."

It didn't take long, and once again, Nigel walked with him into the busy hospital corridor. "They're not at the château," he told Andrew as a stretcher was pushed past them. "And no one there has heard from them. As for the Millar-Grahams, the maid said they've been away since Sunday and are due back tonight."

"Where've they been, did she say?"

"Holland."

"Holland?" he repeated, then raised his voice to question, "What the bloody hell is going on?"

There were two urgent messages awaiting John and Lena when they returned. One was from Sir David, who'd called only minutes before, asking Mike to ring him straightaway, the other was from the Earl of Kilmartin's personal secretary. After Annie was settled in her room, John showed them to Mike.

Mike sighed heavily. "Christ—Andrew. What the hell am I going to tell him? I despise having to lie to him about this. I don't agree with Annie, I think he has the right to know what's happened to her."

John ventured, "Then maybe it's time to tell him the truth."

"Maybe," he agreed, "but let's hold off on that. Let me see what Sir David wants first."

Sir David and his men were at Eindhoven airport, waiting for the jet to return for them. Mike called Sir David's cell phone from the privacy of John's study and being the cautious detective he was, Sir David returned the call on a conventional line.

"Sorry about that, just a precaution, you know. We're at the airport and will momentarily be on our way back to England."

"So soon?"

"We struck gold," he informed him. "Steiner was poised for this opportunity and he sang like the proverbial canary. He'd already done most of our work for us, and his journal reads like a pornographic novel complete with photographs—it seems our man is also into photography. Cowan is a very sick fellow, Mr. Rutledge. Very sick indeed."

"We already know that. Give me the gist of it."

"He doesn't just enjoy torturing prostitutes, he's fond of children, too."

"My God." That settled in the pit of his stomach, and made him want to vomit. "Steiner has proof?"

"He has names and dates. He's also offered to testify and believes he can convince others to do so as well."

"What's in the photographs?"

"The ones Steiner has are discards, the Polaroids which didn't develop well, but they're good enough. There are photos of men having sex with girls who look to be no more than ten years old, and men sodomizing and performing oral sex on young boys."

"Jesus Christ, I'm going to be sick."

He'd already had his own bout of nausea, and his, like Mike's, was followed upon by a burning need to see Cowan get what was coming to him. "There's enough there to send him to prison for the rest of his life, if he'd survive it; prison inmates don't take kindly to pedophiles. But I think we're looking at just the tip of the iceberg."

"Why?"

"I think he's part of something very large, something that extends over the continent that has to do with pedophiliac pornography. And I've been giving this some thought; this information might be best turned over to Interpol. We might act behind the scenes and bring him down with it in a big way."

Mike liked that idea, but decided, "We can do that afterward, but first I want the personal satisfaction of facing him with what we know, because I need to bring that monster to his knees." His fury welled up, and he took a few seconds to bring it under control. "What about the other one? What have you got on him?"

"Nothing at the moment, not even his real name. Steiner says he uses a different one each time he visits. He's apparently covered his tracks better than Cowan, and Steiner can't even give us a good description of him."

That troubled Mike, but first things first. "Well, the important thing at the moment is to neutralize Cowan."

Sir David answered emphatically, "I agree. Annie told me he threatened to finish her off, and I don't like that, I don't like that at all."

"Finish her off?"

Sir David explained, while Mike listened, gap-mouthed. When he concluded, Mike was more determined than ever to do what he'd been planning.

"I'll be there first thing in the morning," Sir David said, adding, "I should tell John to make certain everything's locked up tonight and I wouldn't let any strangers into the house: no deliverymen, the like. You never know, but Cowan may have gotten wind of our investigation somehow."

"Where's Cowan now? Do you know?"

"Of course," he answered, smiling to himself. "Since he returned to Britain, he hasn't been out of our sight. He's at Arduaine, his hereditary seat. It's just up the road from Crinan Castle."

"Andrew's estate?"

"That's right." He waited to see if Mike was going to say anything else. "I'll be by at half-past seven tomorrow, if that suits you."

"It suits me fine. See you then."

John had been standing nearby while they spoke. "Cowan threatened to finish Annie off?"

"Make sure the house is well locked up, John, and don't let any strangers in. I'm going to sleep in Annie's room tonight."

"Right. What about Andrew?"

Mike expelled all the air from his lungs. "Sir David's coming here in the morning. He's going to give me all the information he has on Cowan and then I'm going to see that animal in person. He'll rue the day he was born when I'm through with him. After that I'll go to Andrew and tell him everything, but tonight we'll have to stick with the lies. It's not fair telling him something like this over the telephone."

As they'd done the day before, Andrew spent the day with Cathy, then Janet came to be with her for the evening. Andrew arrived at Crinan Castle around eight, and Nigel accompanied him. Inside the great house his children had waited to greet him, and he sat upstairs with the four of them for the better part of an hour, telling them how their sister was getting on.

When the younger ones had gone off to bed, Donald accompanied his father to his study, observing, "You look awfully tired, Dad."

"It's the stress of everything," he explained.

With some awkwardness, Donald broached the subject, the reason he wanted time alone with him. "I was coming downstairs last evening and I saw several of the servants fussing in the small drawing room. They said you'd quarreled with Lord Alfred and afterward had smashed something in the room. Is that true?"

Reluctantly, he admitted, "It unfortunately is."

"Why?"

"I can't tell you that, Donald."

"Does it have to do with the American woman?" he wondered.

"Why do you ask that?"

"Because so much lately seems to have to do with her."

He considered his response carefully. "It has to do with Lord Alfred and the terrible person he is."

"What's he done?"

Andrew softened his expression. "Donald, I love and trust you and appreciate your concern, but I really can't get into this with you. Someday soon I'll tell you what my father said about him and the dealings he had with him, and then you'll understand. I'll tell you that for your own good and safety, but I'm just not up to it tonight. I'm too bloody drained just now."

"All right," he answered, "I understand." Struck with a sudden urge, he walked over to his father and embraced him.

Andrew returned the embrace with warmth and gratitude. "My father and I never hugged like this, never," he said to his son, quietly, wistfully. "How I wish I could go back."

"What would you do differently?" he questioned.

"Many things, son. A great many things."

As Donald was preparing to leave, Nigel knocked at the door, saying, "Sorry to disturb, your lordship, but John Millar-Graham is on the line."

"Put him through, Nigel." He turned to his son to say, "Sorry, but I need to take this in private."

"I'll see you at breakfast?"

"You will. I'll stay late and have breakfast with everyone."

When Donald smiled at Andrew, it was like seeing his own father as a young man, as he had never known him. He watched him walk away as he waited for the line to ring through.

"John, thanks for getting back to me."

"What can I do for you?"

"Do you know where Annie is?"

"I believe she's with her husband, though I'm not sure where."

"Are you certain of that? Are you certain she's with Mike?"

"They had planned to spend some time together, the last I heard."

It was all too evasive, and he frowned to himself before questioning, "What were you doing in Holland, John?"

He wasn't prepared for that. "Ah, I was, ah, there on business. Why do you ask?"

Andrew heard the reticence, the spinning wheels of fiction. He observed with sarcasm, "Now that's odd, because Mike called me the other day, he was also in the Netherlands, but he said he was calling from Paris. You wouldn't know anything about that, would you?"

Anxiously, he responded, "Me? Why would I know about that?"

He stated calmly, "I'm asking you."

"No, I don't know anything about that."

Andrew waited, and as he did, he fancied he could see John perspiring.

"I'm sorry I can't help you, Andrew," he said now, hoping to end this ordeal.

"I'm sorry, too," he scowled. "Just do me one favor, will you? Should you hear from Mike or Annie, will you get a number where they can be reached and get in touch with me immediately?"

He answered, "Of course," then added for effect, "is there some problem?"

"You know there is, John. You know damned well there is." He hung up the receiver without saying good-bye.

Mike had been standing near and John looked to him with widened eyes. "He knows something's amiss."

"And why wouldn't he?" Mike responded. "He's too close to Annie not to sense that."

With the extra pillow and quilt Lena had given him, Mike crept into the bedroom where Annie slept. It was the same suite of rooms where Andrew had stayed when he visited just two months earlier, where he had stood looking out the window and seen Annie walking across the lawn. Mike removed his trousers and shoes and settled himself on the small couch, positioning his head so that he might keep watch over his wife.

She appeared to be sleeping soundly at first, but it wasn't long before she began to stir and moan and claw at the sheets, and then to cry out, "Please—please don't—please stop—"

It was a pathetic plea and it tore through him. He went to her and touched her arm. "Honey, it's OK, I'm here, Mike is here."

As she opened her eyes, perspiration dripped from her forehead. "Mike."

He lifted a corner of the sheet and tenderly mopped her brow, saying, "Yes, baby, I'm here. You're safe, you're at Lena's house."

She reached her arms for him, saying, "Lie down with me, hold me."

He lay beside her and carefully took her in his arms, asking, "Is this all right? Am I hurting you?"

"No, it feels good."

"Do you want to talk?"

"No. I want to sleep in your arms."

"Then sleep. I'll watch over you."

As she listened to the quiet of the room, it made her remember. "I thought of this, you know, I thought of your arms around me. When they left me bleeding on the bed that last time, I imagined you on one side of me and Andrew on the other. It made me feel safe, being between you. I knew nothing bad could happen to me with both of you watching over me. That thought kept me together, it kept me from giving up."

He kissed the nape of her neck; it was damp with perspiration and smelled strongly of her. He thought to tell her this now, and hoped that it would bring her some comfort. "When I spoke with Andrew, he asked me to tell you something. He said that he misses you from the depths of his soul."

Her face twisted up and her throat tightened. "Did he say it that way?"

"Yes."

She swallowed hard, before she could ask, "Does it hurt you, Mike, to know that?"

"Sometimes," he admitted. "There are times when it feels like burning coals in my gut."

"Please forgive me," she begged, just at the onset of the tears.

"For loving him? There's nothing in that to forgive," he realized now. "I can accept your feelings for him because I understand why you love him. My only problem is what it takes away from us."

"But it's funny, Mike," she said, gulping her tears, "I don't think it takes anything away. I feel closer to you and more love for you than I ever have." She moved one of his strong hands and rested it on her belly. "What you said about wanting to be her father, do you still feel that way?"

Ever so gently, he rubbed her abdomen before responding, "I dreamed about her last night. She was about three and she was playing near the pond behind the house; you and I were sitting on the porch watching her chase butterflies. She had long, dark hair like yours, and it was shimmering in the sunlight, the way yours does. When she caught a butterfly in her hands, she came running to show us. Her sweet face was all smile, and when I looked into her eyes I saw that they were the blue of her father's. It broke my heart to see that, but then she called me daddy and climbed into my lap. The hurt dissolved with that word; that one word healed everything."

She was astounded by the image of the child that Mike's dream had brought him: It sounded identical to the vision she'd experienced when she first learned she was pregnant. And then, as she contemplated this, she was overcome with the strong understanding that it was meant to be this way, that Mike was the one meant to raise her. That realization brought her some solace, but it was not a joyous moment, and resignation imparted a heaviness to Annie's voice when she said, "We'll have to tell him. We can't live under the weight of a lie like that."

"I know," he said, "and I agree, but I believe we can convince him that it's for the best. He'll want her to be happy and secure and loved; he'll understand that I can give her those things in ways he can't."

Annie closed her eyes. The deep ache in her chest was so draining, she could no longer think. All she could do was give into it and feel it and let it take her where it would, and pray that wherever that was, it would be the right place.

Thirty-Eight

Lena had breakfast ready for Sir David's arrival. After they were seated in the dining room, he handed Mike a copy of the file he had created on Alfred Cowan, along with a copy of the tape he'd made when he questioned Annie. A stack of photographs filled a second envelope, most of which were taken by Sir David's men at the house, focusing on the room where Annie had been imprisoned. There were also copies of the photos that had been taken of Annie in the emergency room, just after her admittance. These showed her lying on a stretcher in her torn dress, her face swollen almost beyond recognition, caked blood under her nose and at the corners of her mouth, and bright red blood soaking the sheets beneath her.

Mike had taken a sip of coffee before looking at them, and it congealed and sat like a clump of mud in his throat. "How'd you come by these?"

Sir David informed him, "In suspected rape and assault cases, the emergency department admission clerk is authorized to take pictures."

His voice was slightly tremulous. "She looks dead."

Sir David gave him a moment, before questioning, "Where do you want to go from here?"

"Is he still in Scotland?"

He nodded.

Mike inhaled deeply, then closed the folder before him. "I want to confront him today, this morning. I don't want to wait."

Sir David told him, "All right, but I'd like to accompany you and add my voice, because I think it'll help seal things. He knows me and the weight I carry in Britain."

"Fine," Mike responded, adding, "I appreciate that."

"There's an airstrip at Oban," Sir David went on to say, "that will accommodate a small jet like mine. And I've a good friend who runs the Isle of Eriska Hotel, which is quite near the airstrip. I'll ring him, ask him to have a car there to meet us. It's a bit of a drive down to Cowan's estate."

Annie walked into the dining room then, looking gaunt and frail in a nightgown and robe that were too large for her. "You're going to see him?"

Mike jumped up and helped her into a chair, tenderly scolding, "You shouldn't be out of bed, honey."

"I'm feeling much better, Mike, really I am. You didn't answer my question."

"I am," he said now, "and Sir David is coming with me."

She knew better than to protest. "OK," she sighed, "but take John with you, too."

"Why?"

"Because I'll feel better if there's two of them to pull you off him."

"I won't let it get to that," he assured her.

She was not comforted. "You don't know what will happen. You can't know how it'll make you feel to see him in the flesh."

"All right," he responded, realizing that she had a point.

"And I want you to call me afterward," she added. "I want to know that you're OK." Looking to John and Sir David now, she asked of them, "Promise me, both of you, that you won't let my husband kill him."

That was the main reason Sir David wanted to accompany Mike in the first place, so he answered without hesitation, "You have my word on that."

Annie refused to go back upstairs and she waited quietly, semi-reclined on a couch, while the men made ready to leave. Just before they left the house, she said to her husband, "I haven't tried to stop you because I understand why you need to do this, but I want you to remember this: When you see Cowan, you're seeing the devil. The devil wanted to kill that little girl chasing butterflies, failing that, he'll be happy to see her fatherless."

He leaned and kissed her forehead, saying, "Go back to bed, honey, and rest peacefully. Nothing bad will happen."

She tried to smile. "The little girl and I, we need you with us, not in prison. Remember that, and don't let your anger get the better of you."

Annie and Lena stood watching from the open front door as they drove away, with their arms wrapped around one another, holding tight, looking for all the world like wives who had just sent their husbands off to war.

Sir David placed a call from his jet to Arduaine House. He waited while a butler brought the telephone to Lord Cowan.

It was a warm and sunny day, and Alfred was seated on a terrace overlooking Loch Melfort, reading the morning papers that the stiff breeze kept wanting to blow away. He answered cheerfully, "Yes, David, how are you? I've not seen you in quite a while, not since the Queen Mum's birthday last year, I believe."

Sir David responded brusquely, "This isn't a social call, Alfred. I've come across something rather disturbing, something I've discovered in the course of my investigative business. I'd like to have a sit-down with you to discuss it."

There was silence, then, "This disturbing something has to do with me, I take it."

"I'm afraid so."

He kept his cool, and inquired casually, "When would you like to have this chat?"

"I can be there within the hour."

"It must be important," he realized.

"It is."

The silence punctuated things before Cowan responded, "I'll tell them at the gate to expect you, then."

"Cheerio, Alfred." Sir David grinned at Mike and John as he disconnected, saying, "I'd say I've got his attention."

Mike held out his hand. "Can I use that phone?"

Andrew was enjoying a leisurely brunch with his family. His mother and Nanny had relieved Janet this morning, so he and his wife were together for once, talking with the children about Cathy's anticipated homecoming the following week. When William whispered to him that there was a call from a Mike Rutledge, he excused himself abruptly, leaving Janet to wonder what could be so urgent.

A smoking room that hadn't been used as such for years adjoined the family dining area, and this was where he took the call. "Hello, Mike? Where are you? You sound as though you're flying."

"I am," he answered solemnly. "I'm flying into Oban."

That instantly worried him. "Oban? Why?"

"I've got some business there. Listen, Andrew, you and I need to talk. Where will you be, midafternoon?"

Andrew swallowed his anxiety to respond, "I can be anywhere. Where do you want to meet?"

"I'll come there, if that's all right."

"What time?"

"My business shouldn't take long. Before one, I should think."

"I'll be waiting. Do you know the way?"

"John's with me, he knows."

"John? Why is he with you?"

"If you can just hold off, I'll explain everything when I see you."

His heart had begun to do sprints with each exchange, and he had to say now, "You've got me very worried, Mike."

"I know I have," he recognized, "and I apologize for all the intrigue, but it can't be helped."

"Just tell me Annie's all right, please tell me that."

"She's safe, Andrew. She's at John's house with Lena, and she's safe."

He was finally able to exhale. "Thank God."

"I'll see you soon."

"Yes, soon." With the wild pounding in his chest, Andrew suddenly needed to take a seat.

At the Scots baronial estate of Arduaine House, the butler Danvers showed the three visitors to an impressive library, with floor to ceiling mahogany shelving that was neatly packed with fine, old books. At the room's center, there were several locked glass cases that displayed the more rare editions of Cowan's collection. John was intrigued and immediately drawn to examine them, finding two leather bound, hand-illuminated manuscripts that looked like Lindisfarne gospels.

"My God," he exclaimed, "these must be worth a fortune!"

Sir David was unimpressed and settled into a club chair, while Mike positioned himself near a window, his back toward the doors. He began to have an internal conversation at this point, coaching himself as he would before a tough case, and in the midst of that, he heard a door close behind him.

Cowan used his slick, business voice to offer, "Good morning, David. I didn't know that you were bringing friends."

"I believe you know John Millar-Graham, Alfred."

"Do I?"

"You met at Crinan Castle, at Laird's Day."

He indicated some recognition. "Oh, yes. How do you do?"

John nodded in reply. Mike had not as yet turned around, for he was still working on his self-control.

Cowan inquired, "And who's this gentleman?"

When Mike looked at the man, the first thing he saw was the smirk. Then he took in the refinement, the graying country squire who looked every inch the picture of civility, the product of polite society that he was. It brought his simmer to a boil when he contemplated the deliberateness of that public persona, a performance that had carried him through all these years, concealing and deceiving, luring who knows how many victims into his web.

"This is Michael Rutledge," Sir David said. "Mr. Rutledge is a highly regarded barrister from Philadelphia."

Cowan offered his hand, but Mike merely looked at it. "Judging by your demeanor," he observed, "I gather you've some unpleasant business with me."

Mike wanted to respond, but his churning fury kept him from it.

Sir David suggested, "Why don't we all sit down?"

Cowan moved away from the men to station himself behind his desk, where he chose a pipe from the rack, packed it, then, rather defiantly, set it ablaze.

Sir David cleared his throat and began with, "We've just returned from Eindhoven, Alfred, the three of us. We went there to retrieve Mr. Rutledge's wife from hospital; we went there to get Annie d'Inard."

Cowan said nothing, but worked at the pipe until puffs of smoke billowed out like small, gray parachutes, obscuring the space around him. He was buying time and scrambling to come up with a strategy when he asked, "Tell me, David, how did you come to be involved?" He glanced briefly at Mike, and there was no mistaking what he saw in his face.

He answered frankly, "Ms. d'Inard engaged me to investigate you."

Blithely, Cowan inquired, "Oh? And why did she do that?"

Beneath the collected exterior, Mike saw Cowan begin to squirm, and that recognition brought him what he needed. "You threatened her lover," he answered him, "and she wanted to bring you down."

Alfred assumed the benevolent grin. "As her husband, I should think you'd want to thank me for that."

Mike moved now, to the front of Cowan's desk. "What I want," he paused for effect, "is to kill you."

His companions simultaneously slid to the edge of their seats, readying themselves to act.

"But I'm going to do better than that," he seethed. "I'm going to see to it that from this day forward you live in such fear, you won't want to set foot out of this house."

Having decided on his tactics, Alfred laid his pipe aside. He arched his brow to affect concern as he questioned, "And how is the poor woman, recovering, I hope?"

Mike was too galled to respond.

Cowan now contrived a look of disgust. "I was the one to have her taken to hospital, you know. I warned her about Hans but she wouldn't listen. He tends to lose control sometimes, I'm afraid, but he really doesn't mean to. I blame myself, though, I should never have left them alone. That's what they wanted, of course, but I shouldn't have allowed myself to be persuaded."

Mike got hold of Cowan's eyes. "What you should never have been was born. Your mother should have impaled you on the end of a coat hanger and flushed you down the toilet with all the rest of her shit."

Cowan stood and puffed out his chest to rail indignation. "Now you see here, you rude man, I'll not tolerate your American vulgarities and if you don't desist . . ."

Mike rested his hands on his desk, and leaning forward, said, "Go ahead, threaten me, you bastard, you breathing glob of scum."

"Threaten you? I don't need to do that," he realized, as his composure returned. "All necessary warnings have already been delivered."

Mike straightened himself again and slapped a palm against his forehead, saying, "That's right! Silly me, how could I forget! Your fucking lordship has already delivered his threats to a bound and nearly comatose woman, hasn't he? To a pregnant woman he'd beaten to a pulp and raped to the point of exsanguination: What a formidable man you are, what a terrifying and awesome man! We all quake in recognition of your power and might, your supreme authority over women." Mike was suddenly aware of his companions' presence on either side of him.

Cowan had unwittingly allowed himself to be taken off the strategic track, so he attempted now to get back on it. "Mr. Rutledge, I'll have you know that your wife gave her full consent to accompanying me to Holland. I introduced her to Hans at that time and as I've told you, I did try to warn her about his dark proclivities. It was her choice to be with him and I am not responsible for what occurred after that. I can't help that she's an out-of-control little whore, with a voracious appetite for sex. I'm sure you've witnessed her seamy side; did she happen to mention that she wanted me to watch while she urinated?"

The self-possessed way in which he told that lie angered Mike more than the lie itself. "You lying pile of filth, how dare you think that I'd believe you, how dare you think that I could possibly take your word over hers? I could kill you right now for your audacity, if for nothing else."

Cowan's tactics were failing, he knew, so he said, "I want the lot of you out of my house, this instant, or I'll ring the constable and have you arrested for trespassing and slander."

"So soon?" Sir David asked, with uncharacteristic sarcasm. "We haven't even come to the point of our little visit."

The anger seethed through Cowan's deportment as he asked, "And what might that be?"

Sir David lifted his attaché, then laid it open on Alfred's desk. He removed a single sheet of paper: the typed summary of his investigation. Sliding it toward Cowan, he tapped it once with his index finger, saying, "This. This is the point. One word from me and this goes to Scotland Yard."

Cowan snatched the paper and scanned it. In about thirty seconds all the color had washed from his face.

Now Mike smirked at him. "The details of this and more have gone for safe keeping to a friend of Sir David's at Whitehall. It's also gone to my law offices. There are names and dates and photographs, too, just to make it more interesting reading. Any further threats against Annie or Andrew—or anyone of us for that matter—will be dealt with immediately. And make no mistake, Cowan, nothing you say or do from now on will go unnoticed. We'll watch you like an eagle watches its prey. Every time you fire up that jet of yours we'll know. Every place you go we'll be watching. We'll know what you've had for dinner and if you've bothered to change your underwear. If you so much as make a move to repeat any of the disgusting actions that have been elucidated here," Mike leaned forward and poked his finger at the paper in his hands, "we'll pounce on you so fast it'll make your sick head spin. Your life as you know it will be over and your buddy the queen will be so appalled to see what you've been up to, she'll ask Parliament to bring back beheading."

Cowan sat back down. He carefully laid the paper in front of him, then looked at his pipe. He picked it up as though he meant to smoke it, but then he halted. His face remained the color of his white shirt.

"Any questions, Lord Alfred, my man? Any fucking questions?" Mike demanded.

Cowan looked past him, toward the glass cases. He took several slow, pompous breaths before asking, "Is it money you want?"

Mike let go of his remaining restraint and walked quickly around the desk to grab Cowan by his lapels and pull him to his feet. "You sodomizer, you filthy fucker of innocent children, you steaming heap of shit. I'd make a bonfire with your fucking money and put you on top of it, but not before I sliced off your balls and threw them in it, just so you could hear them sizzle." He felt hands on his shoulders and he heard the echo of Annie's voice, telling him to keep control: He shoved Cowan back into his chair.

When Mike backed away, Sir David spoke, and he sounded as though he were summing up a board meeting. "All right then, Alfred, are we clear on everything?"

"I'll be ringing my solicitors, " Cowan answered.

That excited Mike. "Oh you do that, you go on and do that! There's nothing I'd like better. I'm only holding back because of Annie. She's asked us not to turn this over to the law but that's not the way we want to handle it. Sir David here wants Interpol on this yesterday, and I want to wipe my ass with you, so you just go ahead and push me, you push me with your little, aristocratic pinky, Lord Asshole. Go on, I'll make you my fucking legal career." He came close to laughing at the man.

Cowan tried to face down their glares, but he didn't have what it took. He stood and reached for the servant's buzzer. In a few seconds the butler was in the room. "Show these gentlemen out, would you?"

Mike tightened his fists and stepped closer to Cowan, but Sir David and John both put their hands on him and turned him around, then ushered him away.

"You've accomplished what you set out to," Sir David said to him as they left the library, "and a hell of a job you've done of it, too."

Mike's breaths were coming rapidly now, like when he finished his morning run. "I haven't accomplished everything," he told them, "I need to see Andrew."

"We're going there now, old man," John answered, patting him on the back.

Lord Alfred Cowan sat at his desk for a long while, staring at Sir David's investigative summary. Sometime later he left the library and went into the adjacent secret study, which was entered only through deftly hidden, hinged shelving. This room, known only to his head butler and himself, had been built in the early eighteenth century as a hiding place for firearms meant to be used against the English. The head butler had been informed so that he might personally see to the cleaning, but none of Alfred's three wives even knew of the secret chamber's existence.

There had been one other person, though—the only person Alfred had ever trusted enough to reveal it to—and he was now dead. Alfred had considered him his best friend, his only true friend, and he had experienced feelings for this man that went far beyond friendship. He often thought of that night, that one drunken, intimate evening when they were alone, when he'd taken this man into his confidence as he would no other and disclosed his secrets. Standing inside, hidden from all the world, Alfred had put an arm around his friend's shoulder and followed his heart's desire. He pulled him close, saying, "I've loved you, you know, for so very long," intending to kiss his mouth. Revulsed, Donald Stuart-Gordon had pushed away with a blistering slap to Cowan's dejected, wounded face.

The secret room housed the tools of his extortive trade, the neatly organized files that were indexed under the names of each important person they pertained to. There were handwritten accounts of weekends of debauchery attested to by explicit photographs, names of the accomplices and victims, even some follow-up data regarding their dispositions. In the file on the twenty-third earl of Kilmartin, for instance, there were hand-written notes pertaining to the pictures of the battered young woman, sprawled unconscious on the bed next to a soundly sleeping Donald. There were also color close-ups of her swollen and bruised genitalia, as well as her bloodied anus, with cheeks spread apart by someone other than the photographer, and recently updated notes regarding her whereabouts.

Once inside the room, Cowan poured himself a large glass of the limited production single malt that was Nether Largie's most expensive whisky. Then he placed a phone call to Geneva, Switzerland. When the call was completed, he unlocked a drawer that held the 455 Webley revolver he'd had since the war. He removed it from its velvet-lined resting place and stroked it tenderly, lasciviously; aside from his own cunning, it was his most cherished weapon.

Thirty-Nine

Driving through the wide open gates of Crinan Castle's main entrance, Mike said aloud, "Damn!" As are most people who first see it, he was immediately struck by its beauty and grandeur, but beyond that he was impressed by its welcoming facade. And the contrast to the place they had just visited, Arduaine House, was dramatic. Cowan's baronial manor, while grand and imposing, had nothing of the character of this estate, and the message it conveyed as one approached was clearly: Keep out. Crinan Castle oozed gracious hospitality and seemed to invite the passing traveler in.

Andrew had intended to go to the Glasgow office this afternoon, but the phone call from Mike had forced a change in plans. He sent Nigel in his stead and as he anxiously awaited Mike's arrival, attempted to occupy himself with his children. As they sat in the sunshine on the south lawn, Andrew's eyes constantly sought the entrance drive for sight of an automobile. When it finally arrived, he jumped up and went straight to it, without so much as a word to anyone.

Offering his hand to Mike, he said simply, "Hello."

Mike was noticeably subdued in his response. "Hi. I believe you know Sir David Whetfield."

He was confused by the man's presence, but he greeted him with appropriate politeness. "Yes, I do. It's very nice to see you again, Sir David."

"The pleasure is mine, Lord Kilmartin," he told him.

Andrew quickly acknowledged John before asking, "Shall we go in?"

Janet had noticed their car and her curiosity brought her downstairs, just as they were making their way through the gallery.

Andrew introduced her to Mike after she'd greeted the others, and she plainly understood that she was meeting Annie's husband. "How do you do, Mr. Rutledge?"

"I've been better." It was not exactly a cordial response, but he changed the tone of it by asking, "How's your daughter today?"

"Steadily improving, I'm happy to report. We expect to bring her home next week."

"That's wonderful news," he said, "I'm happy for all of you. I apologize for intruding on you like this, but what we have to discuss is best done where we can be assured of privacy."

She glanced sideways at her husband before responding, "I see."

Andrew avoided her gaze. "Let's go into my study, shall we?"

They were still in the gallery, so Mike pulled Andrew aside and lowered his voice to tell him, "I'm sure you realize that I'm here about Annie, and I'll leave it up to you whether or not you want your wife in on our discussion, but in my opinion she might just as well be. This is far too serious a matter to be kept from her."

The content of that statement was worrying enough, but Andrew didn't at all like the manner in which it was delivered. Still, he kept his cool and turned to Janet. "We need to discuss Annie; do you want to sit with us?"

The mortally serious expressions her visitors wore were not lost on the woman. "Yes, I do." Once they were inside and the door closed, they sat in a relative circle and made feeble attempts at being comfortable.

"We've just come from Arduaine House," Mike began, "the three of us. We've had a discussion with Alfred Cowan regarding his behavior and his future, and I have to be honest and say that it was all I could do to keep from killing the man."

Andrew had been stoically keeping it together, but his face went pale as he questioned, "Why, Mike?"

He sighed, then answered, "Annie hired Sir David to investigate him; she wasn't going to stand for his threats and would not have you controlled by him. She had a strong feeling about Cowan, that he was hiding things about himself, but Sir David only discovered that he made frequent mysterious trips to Holland.

Annie then took it upon herself to accompany him there, in the hope that she'd uncover something to use against him, to stop him blackmailing you."

Anxiety brought Andrew to his feet. "She went off with him?"

For Andrew's sake, Mike answered calmly. "Last Friday evening. That's why we couldn't find her. Sir David's men didn't locate her until Sunday; they found her in a hospital in Eindhoven."

"Dear God, dear God." His knees gave out and he needed to sit again. "What happened? Tell me what happened!"

Janet was sitting on the couch next to her husband, and she nervously straightened the creases of her trousers, then yanked at her shirt cuffs.

Mike met Andrew's eyes to tell him, "He beat and raped her, he and another man. They drugged and bound her, then tortured her with their sick sexual games until she almost bled to death. I saw the room where it happened; her blood was everywhere."

Andrew closed his eyes as the nightmare began to replay, seeing the pool of blood, hearing Annie's screams, feeling the helplessness, the insufferable helplessness. From deep in his gut he moaned, "No, this can't be, tell me this isn't so, please tell me this isn't so . . ."

He would not equivocate, for he understood that Andrew felt the pain of it as deeply as he did. "She needed three pints of blood and emergency surgery."

"Emergency surgery?"

"They sodomized her, they tore her rectum. It had to be repaired to stop the bleeding."

Tears broke through his shock, and Andrew's eyes now filled and overflowed.

"When I saw her she could barely open her eyes, she could hardly move for the bruises, the excruciating pain she was in. He almost killed her, he wanted to kill her, but the other man stopped him."

Andrew's hand clutched at his chest, at his heart that was so inexorably bound to hers. "You should have told me, I should have gone to her immediately."

"No," Mike said. "You needed to be with your daughter."

Janet meant it as consolation, but it didn't come out that way. "That's right," she told her husband, "you were where you should have been, where you were needed most."

Andrew snapped his head to the side to glare at her and she reeled back as though he'd struck her in the face.

She felt a sudden desperation, and said to Mike, "But there must be some mistake about this. Lord Alfred's an old family friend, we've known him all our lives. He wouldn't do something like this."

"There's no mistake, Lady Kilmartin," Sir David said. "I, too, have known Cowan a great many years. I've heard the whispers about his misdeeds and I've generally discounted them as rumors — until now. He's a very disturbed and dangerous individual, my lady. We've solid evidence of that."

Janet continued to protest, though silently, with a look of disbelief.

Mike had seen her upper lip quiver as she spoke, and he said to her, "Deny it all you want, Countess, I understand why you would. But Cowan should be in prison for what he's done to my wife, there's no getting around that."

Mike Rutledge's words and the images they created had ignited a fire of grief in Andrew that quietly consumed him and showed in his face, in his positively wretched looking face, as he said now, "I need to know everything."

"Annie's intuition about Cowan was right on," Mike explained, "and because of what happened to her, we've uncovered his heinous secrets. We went to Arduaine to confront him with the vile truth of it, and we made it very clear that he's never to threaten Annie or you again. When we left him it was just beginning to sink into his sordid little mind that he's finished, because with one word from us, he'll spend the rest of his worthless life behind bars."

Andrew's head had been bowed, but he lifted it to meet Mike's eyes. "What else has he done?"

"Besides his execrable hobby of rape and torture, he's into pedophilia."

Janet's first thought was of how often he'd been around her children. "My dear lord, this is unbelievable, totally unbelievable! I refuse to believe this!"

"We've photographs, my lady," Sir David told her.

Mike watched as a twitch developed under one of Andrew's eyes and his limbs became infused with nervous energy, his hands rubbing his thighs, his right leg bouncing then stilled, then bouncing again. "Tell me how Annie is now, where she is," he demanded of Mike.

"She's at John's; Lena's taking care of her. Physically, she's recovering quickly, she's getting out of bed and eating and looking much better. I don't know how long that will last, though."

"Why?"

"Because she's so much more to deal with, and I've no idea how she'll handle all of it. She's on the edge, I can see that, and she's just barely keeping it together."

His eyes now shot through with red, Andrew questioned, "How do you mean?"

Mike looked at Janet, then back to Andrew. "It's time for you and me to have a few words alone, can we do that?"

Janet stood mechanically and attempted a gracious smile. She felt happy for the chance to return to some semblance of normalcy, to put what they'd just said about Annie and Cowan out of her mind. "Have you gentlemen eaten?" she asked John and Sir David, as they obligingly followed her from the study.

The two men sat in silence for a few moments, warily regarding the other, before Andrew asked, "What is it? What haven't you told me?"

"There's no easy way to say this to you, so here it is: Annie's pregnant." He inhaled deeply after he got it out.

Andrew thought he'd felt the worst of it. He thought the pain that already consumed him was the worst thing he'd ever experienced, but he quickly discovered that that was not so. He looked to Mike with sadly questioning eyes. "My child?"

"She feels certain of that."

For one, precious second Andrew felt a burst of joy, of absolute joy. But the nightmare returned with the sound of Mike's voice.

"For whatever reason, Cowan suspected that she was; he tested her urine with one of those home kits and when it came up positive, he went after her. He repeatedly punched her in the abdomen with brass knuckles. He told her that he meant to kill her child, then he set about keeping to his word."

Andrew was in such deep shock, it was hard to take everything in. "He punched her in the abdomen? He punched a pregnant woman?"

"He did that and more, much more."

The enmity and rage that welled up in Andrew were too much for one human being to bear; it put him into overload and then swept him into a state of confusion. He looked at Mike, then searched the room, rubbed at his hairline and swept his fingers through, then asked, "How did he know she was pregnant? Why would he suspect that?"

It pained Mike to see him this way, a man of such strength, such character, looking so lost, so utterly defeated. "This is tough for me to say," he wanted him to know, "and God knows I wish there were some other plausible explanation, but we think it was your wife who told him. When she was at the château, Annie got sick in front of her."

The confused look vanished as the antipathy Andrew felt toward his wife burgeoned to new levels. "It was Janet who asked Cowan to get involved, I've no doubt of that," he informed Mike. "She must have gone straight to him when she left France; everything happened too quickly for it to have been otherwise."

Mike refrained from comment.

"Has the baby been harmed?"

"They don't think so, not by the beatings anyway. But there are other things—"

"What other things?"

"Her big concern right now—and mine—is HIV. She's back where she started—no—she's in a much worse place than before. In my mind it seems very likely this time that she has been infected."

"God, no. God, dear God, say that isn't so—"

"Cowan's bisexual," he answered solemnly. "Our informant said he regularly brought male prostitutes to the house where he held Annie. And the other man, he may also be, but we don't even know who he is. Sir David hasn't found that out yet."

"No, no, I won't believe this! This can't be happening to her, Mike, it can't be! Annie's already been through hell with this; life can't be so cruel as to put her there again, it can't be!" If there had been some way to shut himself off at that moment, even if it meant never seeing Annie again, Andrew would have done it. He would have done it because the pain he felt was so intense, so inhuman and unrelenting, it made him dread and despise every contraction of his heart muscle, every breath that came against his will, every swallow and blink he was forced to participate in.

"If they've infected her they've infected your child and she knows it. She's talking about an abortion, she wants to have an abortion." Now that he'd revealed most of what he'd set out to, he was overcome with a sudden exhaustion.

The despondency that arose from Andrew's infernal, burning insides, insides that seemed to burn hotter and hotter with each second, was impossible to fight as his mind went from Annie to his child, and back to Annie again. He had wild thoughts, crazy ideas that cropped up as possible answers. One of those thoughts was about aborting the baby; for an instant he wondered if that might help Annie, if it might help to make her well. He determined that he would make that sacrifice, but then logic prevailed, leaving despair to take a firmer hold.

He heard the strain in Mike's voice when he spoke again. "I don't want her to do that, I've asked her not to abort that child, Andrew."

Nothing was making much sense to him, and he questioned, "Why?"

"Because even if she is sick, I know that she can be treated with this antiviral drug called AZT to give that baby a fighting chance. It's very possible she could be born healthy with treatment." Mike called upon his waning courage to say to Andrew, "I've told Annie that I want to raise her child as my own. I want to be her father."

Andrew's expression was pure confusion again. "Her father? It's a girl?"

"She feels that. She says she can hear her little voice."

Andrew covered his face with his hands.

"I love that child already," Mike wanted Andrew to know, "as though she were my own, and I want her to live. I'm terrified of losing Annie, absolutely terrified, and I think she's got an outside chance at best. That thought is killing me. The only thing that's keeping me going right now is the idea of that baby, that she might be healthy and live on and be a part of Annie that I wouldn't lose. Do you understand that, Andrew, can you understand what I'm feeling?"

As he imagined that, imagined losing Annie, it was all he could do to keep his heart beating. "Yes," he muttered.

"Then help me with that, help me convince Annie that she needs to give that child life, and let me be her father. I can give her the kind of life you can't. I swear to you, she'll never want for anything, least of all, love."

When Andrew uncovered his face, Mike read his bewilderment. "You want me to give you my child?"

Mike was stung with sympathy, but he answered, "Yes, that's what I'm asking. You can't be a father to her without upending the lives of your other children—possibly shattering those lives—and when you've had time to think about it, I believe you'll see the truth in that."

"And what if," he almost couldn't say it, "what if she's sick, what then? What if the baby is sick?"

"Then I'll devote myself to her and love her even more," he knew with certainty. "She'll have the very best medical care there is, and the very best possible life."

There was silence now as the two men sat apart and without looking at one another. From a corner of the study a tall clock began to chime; its gentle reverberations brought a certain calmness and order to the room, a feeling that the universe had not succumbed to chaos, that it still marched ahead with a certain rhythm.

As he tended to do when it chimed, Andrew mechanically noted the hour, then broke the ensuing silence. "I need to see Annie, I need to go to her."

Mike dreaded having to tell him this. "She doesn't want that, she doesn't want you to see her the way she is now."

"I don't care about that."

"She does. She's adamant about it, in fact, she didn't want you to know anything about this."

"I need to be with her, Mike."

"Call her then, talk to her," he decided. "I'll leave you so you can speak in private."

Mike stood and when he did, he realized how weak his knees had become. He left Andrew sitting in his chair, looking confused and frightened and so very alone: the portrait of a man faced with the most difficult moment of his life.

When the maid said who was on the telephone, Lena was not surprised.

It was a woeful and broken voice that asked, "How is she, Lena?"

"She's getting better, she's much stronger today."

"I need to speak with her."

"I take it you've already spoken with Mike." John had rung to let her know that they were finished with Cowan, and to tell her they were on their way to Crinan Castle.

"They're here now, the three of them," he said. "They've just come from seeing Cowan and Mike's told me everything."

"I'm so very sorry about all this, I truly am, Andrew."

"Thank you, Lena," he managed to say, "but there's nothing for you to be sorry about."

"I should have stopped her, I should have stopped her going off with him."

"You mustn't blame yourself. In all of this, there's only me to blame. Please, let me speak with her, I need to hear her voice."

"She's in her room. I'll just be a minute."

Lena had thought Annie asleep, so she hadn't told her about John's call. But she found her awake and sitting by the window, looking down into the garden.

"You've a phone call, darling; Andrew's ringing."

She was instantly worried. "Oh no!"

"Mike and John are with him now," Lena explained. "They've told him."

"Why'd they do that? I asked Mike not to do that!" If she'd had the strength, she might have been more angry, but her vexation was quickly overridden by her concern for Andrew. "I can't speak with him, Lena, I'm not ready for that!"

Lena walked to her friend and took up her hand. "His heart is breaking, my darling, I can hear that. You can't be so cruel as to not let him hear that you're all right, not let him tell you how much he loves you."

Annie rubbed her forehead and rested it a moment in one hand. Then she rose from her seat and made her way to the telephone, lifting it with two, trembling hands, and saying, "Andrew."

When he heard the sound of her voice, he began to cry.

"Andrew, please, I'm all right, please my love, I'm OK." She heard the door latch as Lena left the room.

"Annie — God, Annie — why? Why did you do it? I need to understand why you did it."

"Because I couldn't help you the last time. When you needed me I wasn't there. This time was different; at the very least, I had to try."

"My darling, my beautiful, wonderful darling, what he's done to you . . ."

"Please, Andrew, I can't talk about it, not to you, not now."

"I'm coming to you, as soon as we ring off I'm coming there to be with you."

"No, you can't, I don't want that."

"Annie, don't keep me from you. I can't exist without you; there's nothing else that matters, only my love for you."

"Time, Andrew, I need time. Trust me, it's going to be better if we give it a little time." She had to face the HIV test alone, she knew, for if she decided on abortion, she could never do it with him by her side.

"My darling, I hear what you say but I can't do as you want. I have to be with you."

Her breathing had become difficult. "No, Andrew. Please go and talk to Mike, he'll make you understand. In a week or so we'll meet, I promise you, as soon as I'm ready I'll let you know." She began to gasp for air. "I have to hang up now — I have to stop talking — I can't stand all this right now — I'm sorry — I'm so sorry —" She replaced the receiver and collapsed onto the bed into physically painful sobs, punctuated by deep, noisy aspirations.

Lena had remained outside the room. She heard the gut-wrenching sound of Annie's tears and struggle for air and went to her, carefully stroking her back as she lay across the mattress, before Annie sat up and hugged her. The phone rang again and in a short time a maid was at the door, saying that the earl was ringing.

Lena pulled herself together to answer. "No, Andrew, she can't," she insisted, "she's not up to it. You have to respect that and do as she wishes."

"There's nothing more important to me than Annie."

"Then let her get her strength back before she sees you."

He could hear Annie in the background, sobbing and gasping. "Was she horribly battered? Tell me the truth, Lena."

"Yes."

Every cell in his being was stricken by the imagining of it. "God, how I hate that monster! He has no right to live, none at all!"

"Let me go to her now, she's very upset and she's having trouble breathing."

"Tell her how much I love her, please tell her that for me," he pleaded. "No matter what happens, she must always know that. Tell her that I value her life more than my own."

Lena's heart broke for him, and she answered tenderly, "I will. I'm hanging up now, all right?"

"Tell her, Lena."

"I will, Andrew, straightaway."

The dial tone that returned to the line had a powerfully hypnotic effect on Andrew; its humming sound sent him into a strangely detached state, one where he felt disconnected from everything and everyone who had ever mattered to him. The private study that had been his sanctuary, a place where he'd spent countless hours, both as a child with his grandfather and now as a man, had become alien, inhospitable. The portraits of his children, his family, his life as it was and never would be again, now seemed wholly unfamiliar, like a random window display, touting a sale on frames. Everything about him, even the clothes on his back and the watch on his wrist, the very veins that overlaid the bones of his left hand—it all seemed wrong somehow, and as though it needed to be put to right.

Although he could not feel it beneath him, he remained unmoving in his desk chair, still holding the receiver to his ear as though listening to a voice message. But the message he was hearing was not from any living person, it was from the grave: his father's voice repeating what he'd said in a dream, only a few nights before: *You'll do the right thing, Andrew. Trust yourself to do what must be done.*

Since the staff was cleaning the formal dining area, Janet had the visitors seated in the more intimate family dining room, where she served them lunch, though none of them, least of all Mike, had any hunger. She refused to acknowledge the purpose and seriousness of their visit and fussed about them in a hostess charade, making silly, small talk as they picked at their food. It was such a ludicrous performance, they found themselves regarding her warily, like spectators under a tightrope, watching a performer make all the wrong moves.

Janet's chatter grew less rational as time passed and her husband did not join them. She excused herself to search him out, saying how rude it was of him to keep himself from his guests.

John raised his eyebrows and made a whistling sound as she left them, wryly commenting, "That nut's about to crack."

Sir David and Mike nodded their agreement.

At first she walked quickly, but her pace slowed before she reached her husband's study. She knocked tentatively, then more authoritatively. When there was still no answer she opened the door and called to him; she found the study deserted. The formal dining room was her first thought, maybe he'd gone there, or perhaps he'd stopped in at the lavatory. She started back when something gripped her, like an icy hand on her shoulder; having just passed the armory she'd noticed the door ajar.

She took four backward steps and peered in. It was very dark—there were no windows in this room—and she switched on a light. Her eyes found the case where the Korth revolver was kept, the gun she had removed only recently when she meant to kill her horse. Andrew had personally replaced it, locking it up and keeping the key himself. It was gone now, the case left open, and so was her husband. From deep inside, from Janet's deepest, darkest fears, she heard a terrifying rumble. It sent her out into the corridors, running, seeking Andrew in every possible location.

Donald was descending the staircase and witnessed his mother's frantic search. He stopped on the last landing and watched, through confusion and concern, as she called to Andrew, sprinting from room to room. At last she went to the main entrance doors and opened them. It was then that she caught a glimpse of the Aston Martin as it tore up the driveway, leaving a cloud of dust in its wake. She stepped onto the terrace and called his name with such desperation and foreboding, it stopped everyone who heard dead in their tracks.

Mike, John, and Sir David came running from the dining room. Servants rushed, too, and everyone found Donald embracing his hysterical mother outside the entrance. When she saw Mike she broke free of her son's hold and ran at him, grabbing and nearly tearing his shirt. Donald made a gesture that sent all the servants scurrying away.

Clutching at Mike, Janet looked and sounded like a madwoman. "Stop him, please stop him!"

"I don't understand."

"He's gone to kill him—he's taken a gun—you have to stop him—you can't let him do this—please help me!"

Mike looked quickly to his companions and in seconds the three were running for their automobile. Donald took hold of his utterly distraught mother and stroked her head, as she continued her pleas, calling after the men.

"Don't let him do it! Please—don't let him do it!"

John got behind the wheel and Mike turned from his seat to look behind. As they sped away from the great house, he saw its mistress falling to her knees in a wretched fit of sobbing.

Forty

Danvers, the head butler at Arduaine House, heard the raised voices in the foyer and came to see what the fuss was about. He was surprised to see the young earl in such a state and so that he might handle him personally, he tactfully dismissed the other servants.

"Your lordship," he said, "won't you have a seat in the drawing room? I'll bring you a nice glass of something."

"I don't want any bloody seat, Danvers, I want Cowan. Where the bloody hell is he?"

"I'm not certain, your lordship," he answered, with perfect composure. "I've not seen him this last hour."

"Did he leave?"

"No, I don't believe he's left the estate."

Andrew pushed past him and headed down the hallway.

"Your lordship," Danvers called after him, "why not allow me to locate him for you?"

"Stay out of my way, Danvers," he warned.

Andrew began throwing doors open, crashing them against walls with the force of his wrath. When he reached the library he scanned the room, just in time to witness the closing of the hidden door as it was pulled shut from the inside. Danvers came into the room just after that, unaware of what Andrew had seen.

He turned to the butler to demand, "Get me in there."

"In where, your lordship?"

He pointed to the shelving. "There, I know he's in there." Danvers' face told him everything he needed to know. "Do it now!"

The butler did not move, so Andrew went to the shelves to search out the opening himself.

"Please, your lordship," he implored, "if you'll be so good as to wait in the drawing room, I'm certain I can locate him for you."

He pulled priceless books from their protected resting places and broke bindings as he sent them to the floor. After emptying nearly all the shelves in that area, he finally located the lever and turned it. The heavy door swung open to reveal Cowan standing behind it, looking more smug and evil than Andrew had ever seen him. As every muscle in his body tensed, Andrew snorted fury.

Danvers was standing behind him, and he apologized to Cowan. "I'm terribly sorry, your lordship."

"Never mind," Cowan told him, "it's good he's here. We've much to discuss, he and I." He looked to the heap of first editions, scattered about the floor. "Tidy up this mess, will you?"

Andrew stepped toward Cowan and he closed the door behind them. He turned his back on him and casually returned to his desk to take a seat. Picking up his glass he sipped at it, while Andrew glared his hatred. Outside the secret room, Danvers replaced the fallen books.

Cowan set his glass down again to ridicule Andrew. "My, my, you are in a state. The three musketeers must have paid you a visit, too. Only you seem to have taken them more seriously than I."

Andrew moved to the desk and was now within three feet of the man. "I came here to kill you, Cowan, but not before I tell you what you are."

"Did you now?" He laughed again. "You'd kill me for the likes of that little whore, who loved every minute of what we did to her, who begged us not to stop?"

"You lying piece of shit."

"Sorry if the truth hurts, old boy, but she is a wanton bit of ass, and as I told her husband, in possession of a voracious appetite. No wonder she needs the two of you to keep her satisfied."

Andrew had taken tenuous control of his fury. "You horrible filth, you're not even human, no human being could do what you've done and then sit there and lie so calmly about it. Your death will be a blessing to everyone."

"You know, my boy, you're sounding more and more like your father every day. I'm happy to see that, I did so love your father." He affected a curious, wistful expression.

Andrew was incensed by Cowan's effrontery. "You didn't love my father!"

"Oh, but I did, and I told him so, in this very room. He was the only person I ever brought here, you know, the only person I ever trusted enough to reveal my secrets to. He feigned shock when I showed him my files and told him how I used them, but he had to do that, I understood that."

"Your amoral pastime repulsed my father," he knew absolutely. "He told me all about you, about what you did. He feared and despised you, he only pretended to be your friend because of the blackmail, because of your fabricated evidence on him."

Cowan grew defensive. "I would never have done that to your father, had he returned my affections."

"You vile, disgusting creature, my father would never have . . ." It was so repugnant a thought, he had to chase it from his mind.

A corner of Cowan's mouth lifted to a half-smile. "He might have, had he not been so self-righteous. We enjoyed sharing women, you know, before everything, in the old days. I liked him to go first. It was one of my great pleasures, dipping into a woman he'd just come in."

Andrew's face contorted with his disgust.

Cowan laughed. "Don't be so quick to judge me, my boy. I dare say that's a pleasure you'll know one day with your Annie, if you don't already." He smiled a maliciously knowing smile. "But Donald had such an unpleasant tendency toward moral indignation. Take your situation, for instance; he was so appalled by what you did at school he couldn't see past it. I took your part, you know. I tried to help him see that it wasn't such a bad thing, that loving another man is nothing to be ashamed of. It can be infinitely more rewarding than relationships with women." His upper lip twitched when he added, "They're such bloody bitches."

"I'm very glad what I did appalled him," he responded. "He saved me from that depravity."

Cowan was beginning to lose patience. "You stupid, little hypocrite; you loved that boy and he loved you," he told him, as though it were an irrefutable fact. "He loved you so much he went home and killed himself over the loss of you."

"That's not true," Andrew protested. "He killed himself because of the expulsion."

Cowan's mean cackle chilled him to the bone. "Your father told me about the note he left, did he never tell you?"

In the next instant, Andrew lost some of his color. "What note? He didn't leave a note."

"He most certainly did." He was definitely enjoying this; it was making up for some of the unpleasantness he'd had to endure this morning. "He wrote that he loved you and was not ashamed of what he'd done. He said that if he'd had it to do over again, he would not change what happened. He closed it by saying that he knew he would never be allowed to see you again, and that he could not live without you. You bloody, stupid twit," he sneered, "you ranting hypocrite, how could he have loved you so much if he hadn't been encouraged, if it hadn't been returned? It's the same bloody thing with your Nigel, with your lovesick secretary. Why do you keep him around if you don't feel something for him?"

Andrew's feet felt suddenly leaden as much of the blood emptied from his head and pooled in his legs.

Cowan could see the effect he was having. "Struck home, have I? Struck a nerve, Andy, my boy?"

"I was very young," he responded. "I had no experience, I couldn't tell the difference between sexual arousal and true feelings."

Cowan smiled knowingly again, even sympathetically. "I know that's what you've told yourself all these years and more's the pity, for they're lies that only you have believed. As much as he didn't want to, even your father saw your potential as a homosexual."

"No."

"No what?" he scoffed.

"That's not true, not any of it."

Cowan laughed again. "The proof's in the pudding, isn't it? You know how Nigel feels about you, yet you keep him close, you keep torturing him with your constant presence when you know that he would die for you, that he would lay down his life for you."

"I've made things very clear to him."

"Right," he mocked. "So why haven't you sent him packing?"

"Because his sexual preference is none of my business; he's a damned good assistant and I trust him."

This was almost too easy. "You trust him, do you? Did he tell you about our night together, about how easily I slipped into his little bum, because I passed myself off as you? Did he tell you how he demonstrated his love for you, how he sucked me off, calling your name, saying how much he loved you, how he swallowed every drop of my come like it was the life force itself, because he fancied it was yours?"

Andrew could not believe his ears. He wanted to shut them off, wished they would fall off so he wouldn't have to hear through them, so he wouldn't be forced to listen to the filth that spilled from Cowan's rank mouth. But it was impossible not to hear, and Cowan's words brought him freshly to the memory of Philip, to that day in the lavatory when he'd given in, when he'd allowed himself to be seduced.

Cowan would not let up. More than beating a defenseless woman, more than raping a hapless victim, it pleasured him to torture another human being with the exposure of his own weaknesses. "You stupid, stupid man," he continued, shaking his head. "You've preferred the company of that adulterous slut to Nigel's, and you've been doubly stupid, because you've refused to see how much I've loved you. I've seen Donald in you since you were very young, you know. All the things I've done, all my efforts at keeping you out of trouble with that little whore, they've been motivated by my love for you. You've just been too bloody stupid to see it." He picked up his glass and emptied it. When he set it down he opened the drawer where he kept the Webley and removed it. Then he pointed it at the shocked and stricken man in front of him. "But that's over," he calmly stated. "I'm out of patience with you, my boy, I've been very patient for very many years but I've run clean out of it now."

Having taken a shortcut through back roads and driven very fast, Andrew had arrived nearly fifteen minutes before them. When they pulled in front of Cowan's house, they found his car with the driver side door still open. Sir David pounded the enormous knocker, and the door was cautiously opened by a young and nervous footman, saying, "Good day, sirs."

They barged past him.

"I beg your pardon, sirs."

"Where's Lord Alfred? " Sir David demanded.

"I'm afraid I don't know, sir."

"Has he gone out?"

"No, sir."

"Then he's in the house?"

"I believe so."

"Is Lord Kilmartin here?"

"I believe he arrived earlier."

Mike touched John's arm and looked at Sir David. "We'll have to spread out. John, you look around the grounds. Sir David, you go upstairs. I'll search the first floor and downstairs."

They quickly dispersed, leaving the footman gap-mouthed.

Andrew smiled as Cowan aimed the revolver at him. In an oddly liberating way, this immediate threat to his life invigorated him. "All your efforts, all because you loved me?" he mocked. "You beat and raped Annie because you loved me? You punched her abdomen, you attacked my unborn child, because you loved me? You loved my father, too, and that's why you beat and raped a young woman he cared for? You sick, twisted man, you pathetic excuse for a human being, you know nothing of love, absolutely nothing of it, and you hate me because I do. And you resented my father because he did," he now understood. "I suspect Donald actually loved that woman, and that's why you attacked her, because you were so jealous of that you couldn't see straight."

Cowan seemed amused and grinned at him.

It was Andrew's turn now, and despite the unalterable fact that he was looking down the barrel of Cowan's pistol, he was almost enjoying it. "You try to paint me as sick as you are, you distort the facts of everything to bring me into your putrid, profligate world, so you won't feel so alone, so you'll feel better about the dissolute life you've led, about your paltry, loveless existence. What's it like, living on the outside, watching others give and receive love, when you're totally without and totally incapable of even the slightest twinges of it? It makes you angry, doesn't it? It makes you want to kill, doesn't it?"

Cowan relaxed his aim slightly. "You're not helping yourself, my young earl, not in the least."

"I don't give a damn," Andrew told him, and meant it. "I won't beg the likes of you for my life. But I will go on about how much contempt I have for you, for everything you are, and most of all for what you did to Annie. Never would I have believed that I could feel so much hatred for someone as I do you."

Having seen no sign of either of them, Mike returned to the library for the second time and stood at its center, scanning the large room. There was something about it that bothered him, something out of place, and when Danvers came in behind him, he questioned, "What's different about this room?"

"I beg your pardon, sir?"

"Something's different in here, what is it?"

Danvers' eyes darted and went several times to the location of the secret door, concerned that he'd left it visible. "I'm afraid I don't know what you're referring to."

Mike caught the nervous movements of his eyes and followed them. He walked to that section of shelving, demanding, "What's here? Something's here."

"Books, sir, rare books."

He bristled impatience as he fumed, "You listen to me: This is no time for games. Cowan and Lord Kilmartin are around here somewhere and something terrible may happen if you don't tell me where they are. Do you understand what I'm saying?"

When Danvers didn't answer, Mike grabbed his lapels. "I'll beat it out of you if I have to, you little twerp."

He could see that Mike meant what he said, and Danvers was suddenly concerned for his lordship's safety. Although reluctant to divulge what he was sworn not to, he once again looked to the bookcases. Mike seemed to understand and released Danvers to do as Andrew had done, indiscriminately throwing books to the floor.

The butler cringed to see the priceless collection treated that way again, and he stopped Mike by putting a hand on his back. Then he reached and pulled the lever himself, walking quickly from the library afterward and closing the door behind him.

It startled them both when the door opened and Mike stepped into the chamber. Cowan stood immediately and moved to the side of the desk, to alter his aim and point the pistol at Mike. Mike stopped a few feet behind Andrew and slightly to his right, uttering, "Fuck," when he realized what he'd walked into.

In his most mocking, cynical tone, Cowan declared, "Ah, enter the husband, the noble defender of dubious virtue. You know, Andrew my boy, for all your intelligence and intuition, I should have thought that you would have surrounded yourself with more of these, the truly selfless and loyal, instead of the traitorous. That plotting wife of yours," his brow knitted into grimace, "what a mistake. But then, what would you expect from a Campbell?"

Andrew's expression nearly mirrored Cowan's as he questioned, "What in bloody hell are you talking about?"

Cowan looked suddenly thoughtful when he next said, "But then again, you've always sensed her treachery, haven't you? That's why your marriage has been marred by your own perfidy."

Excessively irritated now, Andrew demanded of him, "Why don't you just say what it is you mean to say, and quit playing games?"

"And there's another of your mistakes, blaming your dear father for a decision that was ultimately not his." At the mere mention of the man, his face was infused with dreaminess.

"What are you hinting at?"

"The snare, old boy, the noose. Donald meant to free you from it, did you never know?"

In this moment of bewildered shock, guessing at his meaning, Andrew might have set aside his anger and sat down with the monster, his curiosity having been that sparked by his allusions. But this was not to be; Cowan tensed his jaw and refocused his aim directly at Mike's head, saying, "I'm bloody weary of this; it's time to get on with it."

Andrew was overcome with a new terror, and pleaded, "Let Mike go, let him walk out of here right now. This is between us, isn't it?" He meant to sound sincere, and indeed, he was. "And besides, we need to talk, just the two of us, in private. This moment is long overdue."

"And why should I let him go?" Cowan questioned. "Before you interrupted me I was contemplating going off to the after world on my own, but now that I've company, I've a mind to bring your two sanctimonious souls with me. Who knows, but it might win me favor with Satan; he might see his way clear to better accommodations for me, when he knows that I've gone to the trouble of wiping the smugness from your pious faces."

Andrew's tone turned even more conciliatory as he realized he must do whatever he could to save Mike's life. "Please, Cowan, I'm begging you now. You've taken enough from Annie; don't take her husband, too."

His plea made Cowan look off into the distance for a moment, though he still held the gun aimed at Mike's head. "It will be dreadful, won't it, when she's faced with the loss of both of you at once, as if the woman hasn't been through it already." He grinned his odious grin to add, "It was rather pathetic really, the way she pleaded with me, the way she begged me to stop hurting her, to let her little bastard live."

The image of Annie painted by those words affected Andrew dramatically and unfolded before him with the intensified horror of his nightmare. Until that moment he'd been a man horribly impotent, utterly powerless to help the woman he loved—but no more. He lunged at Cowan and grasped the hand that held the gun with both of his, putting himself in Cowan's line of fire. In a few seconds of incredible strength, Andrew forced Alfred's arm backward and around, bringing the gun to Cowan's face. With his free hand Alfred struggled to regain control, but just as the barrel touched his jaw, he grinned at Andrew, because he saw his face lose the set of its rage and his will weaken. And in that instant, recognizing that Andrew would not kill him, he also understood that he had no future, that walking away from this alive meant being locked up for the rest of his life. Just as Andrew's grip was relaxing, Cowan's wicked grin deepened, and he said to him, "I've got a better idea," then squeezed the trigger himself.

His smirk was frozen as the bullet tore through his jaw and out the back of his head, spraying blood, bone fragments, and brain everywhere, especially onto Andrew's face. As Cowan's dead weight dropped to the carpet in a heap, the floor beneath Andrew seemed to undulate, and his body began to sway. He looked down upon the corpse, its hand still clutching the gun, and he had to blink several times to bring it into focus.

Mike had been behind Andrew, riveted by terror, but within seconds of the shot, he sprang into action. Touching his shoulder, he asked Andrew, "Is that your gun?"

He recovered himself enough to shake his head.

Mike exhaled forcefully. "Good. But you have to come with me."

Andrew didn't respond.

"Come with me now," he insisted. "We've got to wash your hands."

Andrew's face contorted with horror and disbelief as he looked into Mike's eyes.

Mike was overcome with sympathy, but there wasn't time for that. "There'll be gunpowder residue on your hands," he whispered. "We've got to wash your hands now; do you understand me? Are you listening to me, Andrew?"

He nodded slightly.

Something else occurred to Mike, another danger that was equally as pressing. "And we need to get this shit off your face, too," he told him. "We need to hurry, Andrew, everyone will have heard the shot."

As they left the library, they encountered Sir David and John in the hallway.

"What in bloody hell happened?" John asked, while Sir David only stared.

Mike abruptly demanded, "Where's the nearest bathroom, do you know?"

"I saw one just down the hall," Sir David answered, "under the stairs."

"Take us there now," he insisted, "we need to wash the blood from his face. If Cowan has HIV—it's possible to get it through the eyes, from blood splattering in the eyes."

They hustled him into the lavatory and John turned on the tap to fill the basin. Andrew remained zombielike, so Mike pushed his head over the sink and splashed him with water. It seemed to revive him, and he began doing it himself.

Mike emptied the basin and filled it again, encouraging, "You've got to keep doing that, keep flushing your eyes with clean water, it's the only way."

Sir David was outside the bathroom door when Danvers ran to him, bellowing, "Lord Cowan's been shot, my lord's been shot!"

Mike stepped away from Andrew, to proclaim with authority, "He shot his own fucking self, no one shot him. He blew his brains out right in front of us, right in front of Andrew. That's why he's covered with blood. Go and call the police, we need the police here. And don't touch a goddamned thing!"

As Danvers went running off, they could hear his suppressed sobs.

Sir David decided then, "I'd best keep guard at the library," and hurried away.

After repeated rinsings, Mike handed Andrew a bar of soap. "Use this now, soap kills most of the virus." He encouraged him to lather his hands and then to scrub his face. When he'd done that three times, Mike breathed a little easier. "That's better, we don't need you getting sick from this bastard, too." He handed him a towel, then patted Andrew's back as he said, "Let's go have a seat somewhere, while we wait for the police, OK?"

They located a nearby sitting room. Before they went in, Mike asked John to go back and rinse the wash basin carefully, then dry it with the hand towel Andrew had used. Although he didn't see the necessity, he said he would, then agreed to bring the towel to Mike before the police arrived.

Inside the room, Mike spied a decanter of cognac and poured a glass. He handed it to Andrew, then sat next to him, saying, "I know you're in shock but you've got to pay attention to everything I say." He looked into his eyes for some acknowledgment, and when he saw that Andrew was listening, he lowered his voice to a near whisper. "You left your house with a gun, didn't you?"

Andrew nodded, though just barely.

"And when you did," he told him, "your wife went screaming all over the place that you were going to kill him, that you meant to kill Cowan."

"I did," he answered, in a voice that didn't at all sound like his.

Christ—he said to himself—*Jesus Christ; he's in a hell of a fix, a fucking hell of a fix, and I put him there.* He was thinking out loud when he next said, "I don't trust the legal system to help you in this, I wish to hell I did but I know too damned much about it to trust it'll find for the truth."

Andrew sat staring at the floor, holding to the glass without drinking.

Mike was working this out even as he was communicating it to Andrew. "You're too high profile, too much of a target," he recognized. "Some ambitious little prick of a prosecutor will try to make himself famous on you. They'll find ample motive in what happened to Annie and charge you with murder, and that'll just be the beginning. The tabloids will have a field day; they'll publicize every sordid detail of it. Annie's just barely holding it together now, she'll never make it through that. And Jesus Christ—the baby— the poor baby," he suddenly realized. "There'll be no escaping her past. Her conception and what happened to her before she was born will be public record, and she'll carry that stigma for the rest of her life."

Andrew looked into Mike's eyes now. "God," he whispered, as he contemplated that.

"What worries me as a lawyer are the facts leading up to his death, they'll all point to your intent to kill him. I can't imagine a jury believing you intended anything but murder."

"I did mean to kill him," he said again, sounding slightly more like himself.

"I know," he said despairingly, "and so does everyone else. Look, this is an impossible decision to make and it's not up to me, it's up to you. We can walk out there and tell them the absolute truth, if that's the way you want it. Either way, I'm with you one hundred percent."

Andrew took a sip of his drink before telling him, "But the truth is, Cowan pulled that trigger himself, Mike, at the last. I lost my nerve, and he did it for me." It came to him now, what Cowan's final words meant. "He did that so he'd be certain to ruin me, to ruin everything. He wanted me charged with his murder. That's why he said: 'I've got a better idea.'" That realization made him tremble, and as he tried to set his glass down, it spilled over the rim as though he were on a rocking ship.

Mike had heard Cowan's words, too, but hadn't made sense of them—until now. "My God," he hissed, "I've never doubted that evil exists, but that creature, what he is is impossible to contemplate."

Andrew muttered, "Was, what he was," as the image of Cowan's shattered skull flashed through his mind. "What am I to do, what will I tell the police? Will they believe the truth?" It was settling in now, why Mike was worried about gunpowder residue, why he'd told Danvers that Cowan had shot himself when he actually believed that Andrew had pulled the trigger.

Mike's thoughts were a cacophony of concerns as he tried to work out how best to help Andrew: *God, the cruelty, the irony, the terrible injustice that could come of this. That monster nearly kills Annie and her baby—may yet have killed them with HIV—but he wasn't content to have ruined only her life, he may have also ruined Andrew's.*

He had to think fast. Andrew was in no state to decide rationally and he needed to think for him, for all of them, Annie and her baby included. "If we tell them exactly what happened, there'll be an inquiry to decide if you're telling the truth. And as I said, what worries me most is the fact that you came here with a gun, intent on killing him; if they find that out, they'll have to charge you and bring you to trial. But if we tell them that Cowan did it entirely on his own, with you standing just next to him, it's more likely to go away with just the coroner's inquest. Cowan's own gun is in his hand, and the gunpowder residue they'll look for will be there."

Andrew took several deep breaths as he thought of Annie, of what she'd already endured, and of how a trial would likely perpetuate her torment. And—God forbid—if she were sick, if she had

HIV: he'd be little help to her if he were embroiled in a long trial, or worse, locked away in prison. He thought also of his five children, how a trial would devastate their young lives. "But if they find out, if somehow they find out that I've not told the whole truth, what then?"

"Then we're both in for it," he knew, "and I'll be disbarred."

Andrew was struck with another idea. "What if I admit struggling with him, but say that it was to stop him killing himself?"

"That does make sense, if what you wanted was to see him brought to trial and imprisoned for the rest of his life." Mike's eyes darted from one end of the room to the other as he worked through this possibility. "But admitting that might compel them to do the gunpowder test on you and look for bruises on him, for signs of a fight. With my testimony, it might fly, even if they find traces on you, but the down side is I think it's likely to put you right smack in the center of their inquiry. That'll raise new questions and may generate some doubt—precisely what I'm hoping to avoid."

Andrew nodded, though barely. "All right," he said, and his voice quavered. "We'll tell them he killed himself, and say nothing about my struggle with him over the gun."

Although he'd hoped for it, Andrew's agreement twisted Mike's stomach into knots. Going ahead with this meant putting himself on the line as well, for if his complicity were ever to be discovered, besides being disbarred, he'd also be prosecuted. He said a quick prayer, and made a fervent plea to God.

"Listen well," he told him, "we can't have any discrepancies. We'll keep to the truth as much as possible: The three of us confronted Cowan first, then went to tell you. You were so upset that you left your place immediately and without us knowing. When we realized that, we went after you, because we knew the agitated state Cowan was in and feared for your safety. We couldn't find you when we arrived, so we grew more concerned by the second. Danvers and Cowan's other servants will attest to those facts, so we can't deviate from them."

Mike paused to see if he were listening. When he stopped talking, Andrew turned his head toward him, in anticipation.

"Then I found you," he continued. "You told Cowan that we were going straight to the police when we left, that's when he pulled out the gun. He threatened us, he held the gun on you and then me, threatening to kill us both, saying that he was going to take us to hell with him. We told him that it was too late, that the information was already on its way to Scotland Yard. His facial expression changed and he must have had a change of heart, because that's when he turned the gun on himself."

Andrew nodded understanding.

"It's important to add that bit, about telling him the information was already on its way to Scotland Yard; they'll want an insti- gating factor for the suicide and that'll give them one. I think—and I pray I'm right—that this is the simplest, most plausible of stories, the explanation that is most likely to get them to wrap this up quickly. Are you still with me?"

"Yes."

"Good, good man. You've got to do this for yourself, and for Annie. Annie could never stand your going to prison, it would put an end to her. She needs you, Andrew," he said, "she and the baby. You have to do this for them."

Andrew picked up the cognac again but set it down, then looked off into the distance. "The sight of his head, Mike . . ."

"You've got to put that from your mind and focus on what I said happened. We're in this together; I'm an accomplice after the fact and I can't have you fucking us both up."

"No," Andrew realized.

"If this thing does end up in a trial, they'll discredit me as a witness and charge me as an accessory to murder."

Andrew sighed deeply.

"If we're lucky they'll question us together but if they're smart, they'll separate us as soon as they arrive." Mike had a sud- den, terrifying thought. "Where's the gun you took from your house? Is it on you?"

That seemed ages ago. "I left it in the car, it's under the seat in the Aston Martin. I'd decided to kill him with my bare hands."

He exhaled relief. "Good. Don't volunteer anything about that, but if they ask you or search your car, then you can tell them that you feared the worst from him and brought it along for protec- tion; after what he'd done to Annie, you knew he was insane and capable of anything. But when you arrived, you were so incensed and beside yourself with anger and worry over Annie, that you forgot and left it in the car. They may find that hard to believe, but you'll have to stick to that explanation, and hope that the other facts will be compelling enough to dismiss any doubts."

"Right."

Mike was glad to see him perking up, because it meant he'd be better able to handle the questioning. "Don't doubt for an instant that you did the right thing; your actions saved both of us. If you hadn't grabbed that gun we'd both be dead right now, we'd be dead and Annie wouldn't be far behind. Concentrate on that thought and you'll be all right."

"All right," he repeated, and his eyes seemed focused somewhere far away. "I don't know that I'll ever be all right, Mike."

There was the ominous sound of the door knocker, echoing through the hall. It was instantly followed by John's rap on their door, and his urgent voice saying, "They're here!"

Mike looked into Andrew's eyes then, and when he did, the impact of what he had done hit him hard. In his need to come clean about everything, he had gone against Annie's wishes and told Andrew the things that had sent him here, that had brought him to the point of killing Cowan. Annie had warned him, she had known how angry Andrew would be, how he would not be able to let Cowan get away with this. Dammit all, why didn't he listen to her? And why did he leave Andrew alone after he told him? He should never have left him alone with his raging grief; he should have known better, he should have remembered how he felt after Michele, how he had wanted to hunt the animal down and plug him full of holes.

And beyond that, Andrew had acted to save him, he had pleaded for Mike's life then put himself between him and the gun. The responsibility Mike now felt for Andrew's predicament was suffocating, overwhelming, and he knew that regardless of the risk to himself, he must help him in every way possible.

The depth of suffering he discerned as he looked into his tormented blue eyes—eyes that he now associated with the image of Annie's little girl—sent his heart into a sinkhole, and made him repeat his prayer to God, adding to it a plea for mercy—for all of them—that they may somehow be delivered from this hell.

Arduaine House was only a couple of miles from the village and the constable arrived in no time. And as luck would have it, the chief inspector from Oban had been conducting in-service education at the village station when the call came in; when he heard that there had been a shooting at the estate, he was eager to go to the scene, for if it were murder, it would end up in his lap anyway.

John, who was holding the damp hand towel, stepped into the sitting room when Mike opened the door; he handed the towel to Mike, who slipped it into his jacket's inside pocket.

They traversed the hallway and met the police at the library door. The constable recognized the earl immediately and greeted him respectfully, though they were all obviously disturbed by the blood on his shirt and neck, and scattered about his hair. When the chief inspector asked if there'd been any witnesses, it was Sir David who answered him.

"Excuse me, Inspector, if I may introduce myself, I'm Sir David Whetfield."

The young policeman was impressed to be face to face with this legend of British Intelligence. "A pleasure to meet you, sir. Your reputation precedes you."

"Thank you. I'm somewhat involved in this matter and I was wondering if we might go through the questioning in a less public way." He glanced at the hoards of servants and others who had gathered in the corridor outside the library.

"All right, let's go in here, shall we?" They went into the library and closed the door.

In all there were six policeman, a photographer, and someone from the coroner's office, who were mostly in the secret chamber snapping photographs and gaping at the body.

Sir David began by saying, "We came here this morning, Mr. Rutledge, Mr. Millar-Graham, and I, to speak with Lord Cowan on a delicate matter. We returned a second time to continue that discussion."

"And what matter was that, sir?"

Mike answered brusquely, "The matter of the brutal rape and torture of my wife—my pregnant wife."

"Your wife?" the young man gulped.

"That's right. And tell your coroner in there that I want his rotting carcass tested for HIV."

"Sir?"

"You heard me, he may have infected my wife and we've a right to know."

The inspector blushed and cleared his throat. "Very well, it's not the usual thing but I'll have a word with the doctor." He shook his head to dispel the shock. "So you came to see Lord Cowan to accuse him of a crime? Why didn't you go to the police?"

"Because I wanted the personal satisfaction of telling him what I thought of him, that's why. We came back the second time with the earl," Mike thought to say now. "He's a close friend of my wife and he was every bit as angry about what had happened. He wanted the same thing, he wanted to let the bastard know what he thought of him."

"And did you do that?"

The inspector looked at Andrew but it was Mike who answered. "We did. And we also informed him of what we'd learned about him. It seems he's made of habit of beating women and sexually abusing children."

He blushed again. "Lord Alfred Cowan, sir?"

Andrew added his voice. "That's right, Inspector. Sir David has proof of what Cowan's done."

The young police officer was trying to remain aloof and professional, but he said, "Sorry, your lordship, it does seem rather difficult to believe."

Mike drew the officer's attention again. "When he realized we had him nailed and that we meant to go to the police, he pulled out his gun and threatened us. Then Andrew told him that killing us would do no good, because the information was already on its way to Scotland Yard. That's when he turned the gun on himself. The earl wasn't two feet away from him, that's why he's so bloody."

"And where were you?" he wondered now.

"Behind Andrew."

"What did you see?"

"Everything."

"Your view wasn't obstructed?"

"Not at all."

The inspector glanced at Andrew, who appeared somewhat dazed. "Do you have anything to add, your lordship?"

"No, it happened just as Mike said," he answered, mechanically.

"You seem quite upset," he observed.

"I've never seen a man's skull blown up before, Inspector," he found the courage to say, "and certainly not at close range."

"No, I suppose not," he realized.

"Was it just the two of you with him?"

"Just the two of us."

"Did anyone else hear or see anything? Did you, Sir David?"

"No, John and I were waiting outside."

Incredibly, in this moment of crisis, John had begun thinking like the advertising and image executive he was, and it gave him the audacity to break into the conversation. "Listen, Inspector, Lord Kilmartin's had quite a shock, as you can see. Do you think we might take him back to Crinan Castle so he can do a better job of getting the blood off?"

"A better job?"

"We had him wash the blood off his face right afterward," he informed him. "It splashed in his eyes and Mike was worried that if Cowan had HIV, the earl would be at risk. They say you can contract the virus that way."

"I'm aware of that," the inspector answered, a tad flippantly. "Where'd he wash off?"

That question made Mike nervous, because if they were clever enough they could test the sink and drain for gunpowder residue.

"The lavatory under the main stairs, just down the hall," John answered.

The young man looked directly at Mike as he observed, "You seem much calmer about this whole thing, sir, if I may say so."

"I wasn't right next to him as Andrew was. I didn't get hit by fragments from his shattering skull the way he did," he explained.

"No, I can see that."

"How about it, Inspector? " John asked again. "This is the Earl of Kilmartin we're talking about; surely you can grant him the favor of a wash before you question him."

He exhaled slowly and ran his eyes over the quartet. If ever he was confronted with a situation like this involving high-powered, influential people, he couldn't think when. "I've a passel of questions for the lot of you, not the least of which is what this information is that you have about Lord Cowan." He took a deep breath. "But I suppose it'll be just as well to let you go on to the castle, seeing as how it is the earl. I expect it'll be a couple of hours before I finish up here."

"We'll all be there, Inspector, and we'll answer any and all questions," Sir David responded. "We're most grateful to you for this."

As they walked out to the cars, Sir David whispered to Mike. "I don't want to know what went on in there, because I trust you to do what's right."

Mike nodded slightly.

"Where's his gun, does he have it on him?"

"He left it in the car, under the seat."

"Good," he sighed, obviously relieved. "If there's opportunity, it should be returned to its case."

"I was planning on that."

"I'm going to have a chat with the countess as soon as we arrive. I think it unwise for her to mention anything about his going off with it."

"I agree."

"You should drive his car, he's in no shape for it. John and I will take the hired car and follow you."

On the drive back Andrew looked straight ahead and said nothing. When they had gone a few miles he asked Mike to pull over. Sir David and John stayed in their car as Andrew walked into the wood. Mike followed after a minute and found him vomiting.

When the retching stopped, Andrew wiped his mouth and leaned against a tree. "What he said, Mike, about how she begged him to stop hurting her and the baby — I could see her, I saw her bleed and heard her cries for help. I wanted to kill him, but when the moment came I couldn't pull that trigger. I lost my courage, because I just couldn't take a life, not even his."

"That's because you're a human being," Mike told him, "a sensitive, compassionate human being, who respects life. What died back there was inhuman, a demon. You need to keep that in mind every time you remember it, in everything that lies ahead. And be glad that he did it himself, so you can go about your life with a clear conscience."

A clear conscience: Would he ever again have such a thing? "I'm not certain that I'm doing the right thing, Mike, keeping details from the police."

Mike frowned and sighed, then said to him, "As for courage, Andrew, I've never witnessed anything more courageous. You thought not of yourself, but of Annie, of me, of your unborn child, and were ready to sacrifice your life. That kind of bravery . . ." his voice cracked before he could add, "I'll be forever in your debt."

A misting rain had begun to fall, that smelled strongly of the sea; Andrew lifted his face to it, and the cleansing sensation it imparted fortified and revived him. It made him think of his yawl, *The Cloud*, and how it feels to be at her helm and sailing free. He pictured himself there now, somewhere west of Mull, with Annie next to him — and no one else in the world. That momentary flight of fancy brought him a much needed change of focus: the ability to look ahead to better times.

They slowly began the walk back to the car. When they were almost there, Mike, who had been troubled by the doubt Andrew expressed, told him, "After you've had a shower, I want you to sit down and listen to something. I'm going to play the tape Sir David made, when Annie told him what Cowan did to her. I want you to hear that before you talk to the police. Once you've heard her voice telling that story, there will be no question in your mind about what you should do, about protecting yourself so you can be certain to be there for her. You'll trust yourself to do the right thing."

Mike laid a supportive hand on Andrew's shoulder, and that somewhat tentative display of affection put him in mind of his father. Thinking of Donald, his words from the dream came back to him; with Mike nearly echoing them, Andrew now believed he understood their meaning.

Forty-One

Sir David had rung Crinan Castle from his mobile to inform Janet that they were on their way back. He told her that everything was all right, so she was relatively calm when they pulled up to the entrance. Donald had stayed with his mother to offer comfort, but after she received the call she sent him upstairs to see to his brothers and sister. The Aston Martin arrived first and when it drew to a halt and the men got out, Janet gasped at the bloodied and disheveled sight of her husband, his hair dampened and darkened by the drizzling rain.

She exclaimed, "God! What happened?" and sprinted for him, but Mike intercepted her and gently led her away. They had not discussed it, but Mike was keenly aware of the things Cowan had said about her in his final moments, and he wanted to save Andrew from an ugly confrontation—the last thing he needed—before he saw the police.

"Cowan blew his brains out in front of us," Mike explained. "Andrew was standing next to him when he did it."

"No!" She broke free of Mike's hold and attempted to embrace him, but her husband recoiled from her touch.

Sir David and John were beside them now, and Sir David, while he could not have known what Cowan had said about Janet, had grave misgivings about her presence and influence. "Why don't you come with me, Lady Kilmartin? John and Mike will see to your husband. Where are the children, are they about?"

"Yes, why?" She could not take her eyes off Andrew.

"Might someone take them off somewhere?"

"Why?"

"Because their father's in a very bad state and the police will be here soon to question him. It would be better for them if they didn't witness all of this just now, don't you agree?"

Janet's heart began to pound. "But you said Alfred committed suicide —"

"That's right, he did."

Andrew glared at his wife as he and Mike moved inside and away from them.

"Why does he look that way, why is he looking at me that way?"

"Let's go inside, shall we? It's no good talking out here in front of everyone." Sir David grasped her arm firmly. "Let him be for now, my lady," he said as they made their way in. "Where can we have a private chat, just the two of us?"

"The music room, there should be no one there this time of day."

Andrew and Mike had halted near the armory doors and watched in silence as Sir David led her away and up the marble stairs. Janet stopped at the first floor to look back anxiously, and what she saw in their faces made her quicken her pace down the long gallery.

Once the music room door was closed, Sir David coaxed her into a chair, saying, "Your husband's suffered an awful shock, my lady, he needs time to recover."

Her eyes lifted to his, like a small child, asking for reassurance. "He looks so very odd."

"Seeing someone die in front of you, in that way especially, it affects you deeply."

"I suppose, I can't imagine," she muttered.

He pulled a chair near her and when he was seated, removed his eyeglasses to massage the bridge of his nose. He exhaled one short burst, then replaced the glasses, to say solemnly, "Let me get straight to the point. The police may have questions for you. The important thing is not to volunteer anything. You can answer their questions, of course, but don't be too eager and don't volunteer information."

That unmistakable sensation of coming unhinged — the rise of panic — brought Janet to her feet. "Why are you telling me this? Why would they question me?"

"Because your husband went out of here very upset and with a gun," he said plainly. "If they should stumble on that bit of information, it's sure to make them ask more questions about Cowan's death than are necessary."

"But if he killed himself—"

"What we all want just now is to be able to put this mess behind us," he decided to say. "Your husband needs to do that, especially."

She nodded thoughtfully, said, "Yes, of course," and sank into her seat, though she couldn't feel it beneath her.

"Then let's do our best to see to that, shall we? An evil, twisted man is dead, by his own hand, and it's for the best. It thankfully means he'll never hurt anyone again, so we've nothing to be sorry about. But the sooner the police can close up their investigation, the better it'll be for your husband, for all of you. I hope you can see that."

"I can," she said, because she wanted this behind them more than anyone.

"That's good, that's very good. And while we're at it, I don't think it wise for them to know anything about his relationship with Annie either, or about her baby."

She looked stunned. "Her baby?"

"Oh, I do beg your pardon. I assumed you knew." One eyebrow raised slightly.

"Well, I suspected, but I didn't know for certain," she explained, her eyes unable to meet his. Then she thought to ask, "After everything that's happened to her, does she still carry the child?"

He answered, "Yes, she does," and observed her response carefully.

"My God," she exhaled, and looked away. Although she had not wanted to believe it at the time, she recalled what had been said earlier and it drove her to ask, "Did Lord Alfred really do all those horrible things to her?"

"Yes, I'm afraid so, and much more than we said. He discovered her pregnancy, you see, and set out to injure her so badly she'd abort the child."

Janet's distress was genuine as she lamented, "The poor woman, the poor, poor woman. Is she recovering, will she be well after all of it?"

"I do believe the physical injuries she's suffered will heal, but the psychological damage, that will likely last forever," he ventured.

"Oh, I can't imagine, I simply can't imagine." She twisted the rings on her fingers, then tugged at the digits. She stood abruptly again, then paced the length of the room before saying, "Sir David . . ."

"Yes?"

"I feel terribly upset by this."

"I can see that."

Her upper lip quivered and she pulled it in and bit at it to make it stop. "In some way, though it wasn't deliberate, you understand, but in some way, I feel partially responsible."

"Why's that?" he asked.

She scrambled to find a way of putting this that would vindicate her, make her less culpable at least. "Before all this happened I went to see her to ask that she give up my husband, which I had a perfect right to do." She waited for his agreement but it was not forthcoming. "When she refused, I asked Lord Alfred for his help. I was desperate to not lose Andrew, you understand, desperate, for my children's sake as well as my own."

Sir David looked directly into her eyes.

"I can't recall exactly," she lied, "but I believe I may have mentioned to Alfred that I suspected her to be with child."

"You believe you did?"

Janet lowered her gaze, because in his eyes she could clearly see the doubt. "I know I did," she was compelled to admit before looking up again. "But you must believe me when I say, I had not the faintest idea that he'd do anything like this to her, not the faintest!"

His expression turned skeptical. "Despite the rumors you'd heard about him, my lady?"

"It may have been naive on my part, but I could never imagine that people did such things."

"No," he realized, "I'm sure it was beyond you."

She wasn't certain if she'd just been insulted, but she dismissed it because there were far more important things to be handled. "Sir David, if my husband were to find this out . . ."

"Your husband already knows, my lady."

She held her breath as she asked, "How?"

"When they spoke privately," he said, "Mike told him that he suspected the information came from you. He informed me of this as we drove to follow your husband."

Andrew's apparent anger and the way he had responded to her when they returned now made perfect sense. "I see," she mumbled, feeling her dignity slip away. "I don't suppose he'll ever find it in his heart to forgive me."

"I should think that's up to you," he ventured.

She caught a glimpse of hope in that statement. "How so?"

"I think his forgiveness may come in time, depending on how you handle matters from now on. I know that he prizes honesty and forthrightness, so that should be a start."

She looked away and said nothing, but she very clearly understood his meaning: *Tell your husband the truth, and tell him everything.*

"Well, then, I've said enough," he decided. "Will you see to the children as I suggested, get them out of the house? I should think it far better that they don't see their father in this state and being questioned by the police."

"No, indeed not," she agreed. "I'll have them taken to their grandmother's, to Nethergate Lodge. They'll be safely looked after there."

His lordship's valet was quite put out by John and Mike, who would not allow him to attend the earl. The two waited in his bedroom while Andrew stood motionless under the hot water, reliving that horrendous moment again and again. But he didn't just dwell on that, his thoughts went everywhere, recalling the things Cowan had said to him about Philip, about his father, about Nigel: Nigel! How could Nigel have betrayed him so? Andrew thanked God that he was in Glasgow today, because he hadn't the fortitude for dealing with him just now.

But beyond all that, there was what Cowan had revealed about Janet the plotter, and his words: *blaming your dear father for a decision that was ultimately not his.* He could only have meant one thing, and confirmation of that would end twenty-two years of painful charade and bring about a sea change: the dissolution of a marriage based on deception.

As they waited for Andrew, John asked Mike, "What can I do to help?"

He answered carefully. "We none of us need mention anything about his taking a gun to Cowan's, because we don't want to open that can of worms. And in that same light, the police shouldn't be told about his relationship with my wife. That's why we've gone to the trouble of replacing his gun, to keep the questions to a minimum, because the more there are, the more will come out." While Sir David was speaking with Janet, the three had stopped in the armory and replaced the revolver.

John had gleaned the importance of that already, if for no other reason, to protect Andrew's image. He answered, "I agree, and you needn't worry about me holding up my end of things." But something was bothering him that he just had to know, and he seized this moment to question, "Tell me Mike, I didn't see the body, was he still holding the gun?"

He knew what John was asking. "He shot himself, John, he really did. And yes, the gun was still in his hand."

When Andrew finally emerged from the shower, he mechanically went to the sink and began to shave. When he was finished, he stood staring at himself in the mirror, seemingly unable to recognize the man he saw there.

Back in his bedroom, the perturbed valet had brought a tray of tea and sandwiches and a portable radio that played cassettes, as Mike had asked. John had gone to the hired car to fetch the report on Cowan, the packet that contained photographs of the house outside Eindhoven and Annie, and the audiotape.

John sat next to Andrew at the tea table and poured him a cup with two sugars and plenty of milk. "Put something in your stomach, old boy, will you? You need to get your strength back."

Mike queued up the tape, then sat with them. "Come on, Andrew, eat something," he coaxed.

Andrew obliged them and choked back two small sandwiches. Then he drank his tea. When John saw that Mike was ready to play the tape, he left them alone and went in search of Sir David.

Mike prefaced it by saying, "This isn't going to be easy to listen to, but you need to hear it before you talk to the police."

The first voice was Sir David's. When he heard Annie's, still weak and tremulous, tears began to roll. They continued, unabated, until the end, until the part when she gasped and thought of Janet as possibly having told Cowan about her pregnancy. At that point, Andrew's careworn expression turned bitter. When the tape ended, Andrew could only stare at Mike. Mike reached into the packet and removed the photographs then, handing them to Andrew one at a time.

Mike sat quietly with him and waited for him to speak.

When he did, his voice was impossibly strained. "How will she ever manage, Mike, how will she overcome this? She'll be so sick inside."

"The nightmares have already begun," he told him, "and I'm very worried about what she's in for in the weeks ahead."

Andrew looked into his lap and sighed again and again. "God, how I hate him, with every fiber of my being I despise him and what he did to her," he knew absolutely. "What about the other one? What about this Hans?"

"Sir David will keep after that. That fucker isn't getting off the hook, believe me."

"I want to help with that, I need to be a part of that," he told him.

"We'll do it together." Mike glanced at his wristwatch. "Are you ready to face that inspector now? He should be here soon, he'll have spoken with Cowan's staff and he'll have doubts," he ventured. "When that twit Danvers wouldn't tell me where you were, I stupidly said that something terrible might happen if I didn't find you. Shit! Why the hell did I have to say that?"

"Don't worry about that," Andrew assured him, "that's easily handled. The inspector won't be a problem; Janet's the one I don't want to face. I'm so angry with her, I don't know how I'll manage."

"Then maybe it's better if you don't talk to her just yet," he suggested. "Maybe you'd do better to let it settle a bit before you talk."

"No. I need to understand why she did this and how much of it she knew, if she knew what Cowan was going to do to Annie."

"I have to admit, I'd like to know that, too."

A footman knocked and informed them that the police were waiting in a drawing room.

Mike wondered, "Have you a safe in this room?"

"Why yes," he answered, nodding toward the bed, "behind that painting."

Mike reached inside his jacket and removed the still damp towel, saying, "Let's put this in there."

Andrew held out his hand to take it from him, but Mike told him, "No, don't touch it. Just open it for me, and I'll put it in."

He quickly obliged, and Mike decided to put the audiotape there as well, saying, "They don't need to hear that and find out about the two of you."

Andrew nodded agreement, and when the safe was secured, the two men looked deeply into the other; what passed between them was a silent, solemn pledge that would bind them inexorably.

The young inspector decided to speak with Janet first.

"I'm James McEwan, Lady Kilmartin, Chief Inspector of Police at Oban. I do apologize for this intrusion."

"That's quite all right, Mr. McEwan. I understand the circumstances."

Janet motioned for him to take a seat. He settled himself into a straight back chair and crossed his legs, then quickly uncrossed them. He'd never been in the presence of a countess before, and wondered if crossed legs might be considered rude.

"I don't wish to take up too much of your time, I've only a few questions for you. The servants at Arduaine House say the earl arrived there in a most agitated state. Were you here when he left to see Lord Cowan?"

"I was."

He waited, but Janet offered nothing further. "Can you describe his state of mind for me?"

"His state of mind, Inspector? Do you imagine I've supernatural ability?" She smiled slightly.

"No," he said, returning her smile, "let me rephrase that. Would you say he was upset when he left?"

"I would."

"Can you elucidate?"

"Certainly. Annie d'Inard is an old and dear friend of my husband's. When Mr. Rutledge told us what Lord Alfred had done to her, my husband became quite upset."

"According to the servants at Arduaine, he was considerably more than upset."

"They're correct in that. He was distraught, and I believe that was because he felt responsible."

"How so?"

"He introduced them, Inspector," she was cagey enough to say.

"I see. And when was that, do you know?"

"Why yes, it was here, at the Laird's Day celebration."

He seemed increasingly thoughtful when he inquired, "Is that the extent of it, do you think?"

"How do you mean?"

"Your husband's distress, was it simply because he felt responsible?"

"Not simply. I've said already that they're old and dear friends, Inspector. Andrew's quite fond of her, but he's also a man of honor. It's been my experience that honorable men are incensed by such nefarious conduct, is it not yours?" she asked, with a trace of flippancy.

He acknowledged her putdown with a slight grin, cleared his throat, then made an awkward face. "It's very difficult to ask this sort of question, and I apologize for it beforehand." He waited to see if she understood.

"What is it you're after, Inspector? I've already told you, I'm no mind reader."

"I hadn't wanted to suggest—it's only that—it's occurred to me that there might be more, more of a relationship."

Janet dismissed it all with a lighthearted laugh. "She's the old flame, Mr. McEwan. She and my husband kept company while he was at university. She was his first love, that's why they've retained such fondness for one another. Surely you remember what impact first love has on a young man; you can't be far removed from that experience yourself, now can you?" In an effort to embarrass him, she looked him square in the eyes.

Jamie blushed and looked away. "Do forgive me for prying."

Janet smiled benevolently. "Nothing to it. Is there anything else?"

"No, thank you ever so much, Lady Kilmartin. I won't trouble you any further." He shuffled next to his seat for a few seconds, wondering about the proper way to leave the presence of a countess, then simply exited the room.

Jamie McEwan's interrogation of John was brief, as it was with Sir David. Both men were straightforward and unflinching in their statements, but in spite of this, the young police officer still experienced a certain skepticism. When he tried to analyze it he recognized that what bothered him most was not what Danvers had said about Andrew's agitated state, what troubled him most was the proximity of the earl to Lord Cowan at the time the gun fired. He couldn't imagine why someone would kill himself with another standing that closely by, and indeed, why he hadn't waited until he was alone to do it. It also seemed to Jamie, that as near to Cowan as he was, the earl should have made some attempt to stop the man from doing himself in.

He separated Mike and Andrew and asked the same questions of them, cleverly changing the wording. First he interrogated Andrew, then Mike, then Andrew again, but as hard as he tried he could not uncover discrepancies.

His most pointed question to Mike, began: "Mr. Danvers told me that you were quite agitated yourself, and I wonder why it was you told him that something terrible was going to happen?"

Mike was instantly annoyed. "Danvers misquoted me. I said that I feared something terrible *might* happen if I didn't find them, because Cowan was so angered by our earlier visit, and I already knew him to be insane. My fear was for Andrew's safety, and who knew there was a secret room, for Christ's sake? When I couldn't find them, I grew more worried by the second; I pictured him lying wounded or worse, somewhere in that house."

The second time he questioned Andrew, Jamie McEwan asked, "Why didn't you make any attempt to stop Lord Cowan shooting himself?"

"First off, Inspector, he held the gun on me, then Mike. When he turned it on himself, I have to admit, I felt enormous relief."

"I can see how you would, but his lordship was a man you'd known all your life. I should think a normal reaction would have been to make some effort at stopping him."

"My honest reaction was: Good, this will be better," he told the inspector, "because the disgrace that awaited him—and everyone connected with him—would be somewhat averted."

"That's a hard line for you to take, your lordship," the young man observed.

"You've not had time to read Sir David's report yet, have you?"

"No, I haven't."

Frowning now, Andrew told him, "Read it first, then see if you still feel that way."

Jamie made some brief notes on his writing pad, then looked again to Andrew. "One more thing," he said casually. "Which lavatory was it you used to wash? I ask because the one you indicated, the wash basin was clean and nearly dry, and there were no damp towels to be found." He kept his eyes trained on Andrew's, as he awaited a response.

"I used the one in the hall, nearest the library, as I said. And there's no mystery about the dry basin; it's an old habit of mine, learned at boarding school, to wipe the basin dry so that it's clean for the next fellow." He was thinking on his feet, and scrambled for this one: "And the reason the towel wasn't there was because I took it with me."

Jamie pulled a face. "Why would you do that?"

"I was feeling quite unwell, Inspector, as though I would be sick at any moment. And indeed I was, on the drive back here."

"Where is it now, your lordship, the towel?"

He hoped this would do it: "In the wood, a few miles out from Arduaine, covered in sick. If you need me to, I'll take you there and you can retrieve it."

Jamie shook his head and grimaced. "Never mind," he said. "I'll take your word for it."

Key members of Crinan Castle's household staff had been questioned, too. They all attested to the same thing, that the earl was indeed upset when he left the house, but no one gave the police reason to believe that there was anything beyond that. In the end the inspector allowed the esteem in which he held Lord Kilmartin to sway him, to persuade him that he was being told the truth. He left the estate fully three hours after he'd arrived, not completely satisfied, but adequately. When he returned to the station he read through the summary Sir David had supplied him. During the course of it he pulled out his Scotch bottle and knocked back a stiff one, to quell the taste of disgust. Before he left the station that night, he filed the report as probable suicide, pending the coroner's findings.

Janet had remained at some distance from Andrew while the police were about. When they were finally gone she approached him in his study, where he had settled with Mike, John, and Sir David. Everyone but Andrew looked at the floor when she came in.

"Andrew, might I have a few minutes of your time?" she asked timidly.

The men had risen when she entered and they moved toward the door now.

"Mike, I'd like you to stay," Andrew told him. He didn't trust himself just now to be alone with her.

Janet lowered her head like a scolded child. "All right," she decided, "it does concern him as well."

Mike waited for Janet to sit, but she remained standing. He then sat across from her and folded his arms.

Andrew had been at his desk, standing behind it; he remained there, looking at the desktop, not at his wife. When he spoke, his slowly simmering fury surrounded him like an aura. "I've suspected all along that it was you who brought Cowan upon us, Janet. Now I've learned that it was also you who told him about Annie's pregnancy."

His words were like a blow and Janet flinched as she received them. "I was terrified of losing you, Andrew, so yes, I asked him for his help; I didn't know what else to do. But you have to believe me when I say that I never dreamed he would act as he did."

Every muscle in his body tensed, and he aimed his eyes as though they were a weapon. "He nearly killed her, he nearly killed the child. It's only by the grace of God that they still live."

Janet's voice grew more plaintive. "You have to believe me when I tell you that I only asked him for his help; I never wanted her hurt. I was more frightened than I've ever been in my life, can't you understand that? You'd already asked me for a divorce, and when it occurred to me that she was pregnant, I panicked. Her pregnancy threatened me more than anything ever has in my life."

His voice tremulous as he described it, he told her, "Another man held her while Cowan punched her. He beat her until she lost consciousness, but that wasn't enough. He impaled her on a dildo; she bled so much she nearly died. He meant to murder my child, Janet, and he nearly killed Annie in the bargain."

She had been standing defensively, defiantly straight in the middle of the room, but her shoulders drooped now as she exhaled despair.

"Would you have been happy then? Would you have felt less threatened then?"

From her aching heart she answered, "I'm glad he didn't do that, I'm very glad she'll be all right."

"All right?" he railed. "You think she'll be all right? She's been raped by two deranged, sexual criminals, she's undergone horrors you couldn't possibly imagine, and on top of it all it's anybody's guess as to whether or not they've infected her with HIV: How is it you imagine she'll be all right?"

She was quietly sobbing now. "Please, Andrew. I only meant that she and the baby are still alive."

"She wants to have an abortion, Janet," he seethed, "because she can't face what they may have done to my child."

She clasped her hands together as in prayer, saying, "I'm so sorry, Andrew, you have to know how sorry I am. I'd give anything for it not to have happened."

He turned away from her and ran one hand through his hair, trying to regain some composure. When he turned back to her, there seemed something dangerously amiss in his eyes. "Cowan called you my plotting wife, he said you were treacherous. And he said that my father meant to free me—what did he mean, Janet, what in bloody hell was he talking about?"

In this moment, hearing from her husband what she had always lived in mortal fear of—his finding out what she had done—she willed herself to die, to simply die on the spot. But as earnestly as she wanted that, her heart went on beating, throbbing out the unmerciful pain that came of knowing that she had lost him, that she would never again feel his love. She moved slowly toward the leather couch that put her directly across from Mike and carefully lowered herself onto it. She stared at the Oriental carpet and waited for the pulsing in her ears to quell, hearing along with that pulse Sir David's advice about telling the truth.

Andrew remained unmoving, eyes intent on her, waiting for—but dreading—what she would say.

At first she wanted to ask Mike to leave, but couldn't muster the courage. And then, in some odd way, she was grateful for his presence, glad that there would be a witness, however unobjective, to what she was about to reveal, because in the far reaches of her imagination, she fancied that she might someday make him an ally.

After several long moments, Andrew intensified his glare, asking, "Well?"

"Donald came to see me," she began, "just after they brought you home from hospital; he had sat up all night with you, while you were delirious with fever. He told me that you had called Annie's name throughout the night, and that it had broken his heart. Then he told me what he had done, how he had intercepted her letters and not told you about them. He explained his reasons, but said he wanted to stop interfering, he wanted to find her and bring her to you. But before he did that, he needed my permission, because he knew that it directly affected me, that it would mean a broken engagement and public humiliation."

She had kept her eyes on the carpet until now, but she lifted them to Andrew to say, "I refused to give it to him. I told him to keep on with that deception, because I loved and wanted you, and knew that I could make you happy. He was shocked by my response and tried to dissuade me, but I was firm in what I wanted, and insisted he respect my wishes. I also reminded him that he had entered into

an agreement with my grandfather and that it would be dishonor-
able of him to renege. He left there that day, vexed and with an admonition, and he used my family motto to make his point."

She looked away momentarily and expelled a barely audible,
seemingly regret-filled sound. "I recall his exact words," she told
her husband. "Donald said: 'I do *not* respect your wishes, and I
think you're making a grave mistake, but I will abide by my agreement with the duke. *Ne obliviscaris* — do not forget — that from this
day forward, your life together will be a lie.'" She paused to rally
what little courage she had left, but the growing indignation and
fury she saw in Andrew's eyes nearly took it from her. "Then Donald added: 'Trust me when I say this, for I know it too well — he will
always be hungry, Janet, never satisfied, because only the truth can
satisfy.' He walked away from me then, and went home to you."

Mike sighed deeply and covered his eyes with one hand as he
contemplated the tragedy in this — for all of them — but most of all
he lamented what Annie had been denied: a husband who would
have loved her completely, unconditionally, who would have given
her the children she always yearned for, provided the stability she
always needed. He thought of how she would have blossomed as
wife and mother in those circumstances, and likely become someone great, someone to be admired in this position as countess. Instead, she had lived a life haunted by poor choices and their
consequences, forever trapped in a cycle of self-doubt and self-
destruction. He felt sick inside thinking of this, and knew he had to
leave the presence of the woman who had stolen these things from
her before he lashed out.

He lifted himself from his seat and made his way to the door,
then opened it slowly, laboriously, turning to say to Andrew, "I'll be
waiting for you." There was no question in Mike's mind that when
Andrew was finished here, he would take him to Annie.

As the heavy door latched shut, Andrew's gaze fell to his desk,
to a picture of himself with his father, fly fishing on their Rannoch
estate. He was little more than eleven, he recalled, and yet to go to
Eton. He remembered that day well, how proud his father had been
of him, how he'd brought in three enormous salmon to his father's
one. It had been a sparkling day, a triumphant day, and he had

Barbara Bérot

never felt closer to his father, nor more loved by him. He lifted the glass framed photo and brought it into clearer focus: the smile Donald wore, the joy in his eyes as he regarded his son's largest catch: and young, beaming Andrew, growing rapidly then, standing straight and pleased with himself.

In little more than a year all that would change; his father would never again see him in so benevolent a light. He would be regarded with suspicion, with anxiety and mistrust, even disgust. His misgivings about his son would give way to life-altering decisions, to interventions that would nearly destroy the young man. And for all that, Andrew would never stop loving and trusting his father, never stop craving the affection that he had been denied.

To know now that his father had loved him enough to want to right his wrong and restore Annie to him tore at what was left of his heart. And to understand that it had been Janet who had prevented him from doing what his heart bid him do made him despise her in ways he'd never thought possible.

Still, there was Donald, smiling before him, reminding him of what was forever lost, and at the same time, this precious moment from his past was an altogether different message from his father, one that said with perfect clarity: *Seize the day, son; the moment is really all we have.*

He had been standing all the while Janet spoke, too tensed to take a seat, but he collapsed into his desk chair now as the enormous weight he'd been struggling beneath for so many years, was precipitously—improbably—taken from him. With a surprisingly steady hand, he returned the photo to its place on his desk, then looked to his wife as she sat with downcast eyes, trembling in anticipation. The rain had begun to tap at the windows and save that, the room was unearthly quiet.

With cold indifference, he questioned, "Is there anything else you have to tell me, any more plots or deceptions to reveal?"

She shook her head despairingly, and did not look up. "No," she whispered, "there's nothing more."

"Then leave my sight," he told her. "I don't want to see anything of you before I leave this house."

She stood and walked the short distance to his desk, then asked meekly, "Are you leaving me?"

"Yes," he answered, almost without emotion. "I'm going to do today what I meant to do twenty-two years ago."

She choked on her pent-up tears. "And the children, Andrew, what shall I tell our children? What about our darling Cat, who lies waiting for her parents to take her home from hospital? What shall I tell her?"

"You're not going to say anything to them," he told her, un-equivocally. "When Cathy is fully recovered and completely out of the woods, we'll deal with it then. When the time comes we will tell them together, and what I will say to them is this: I am not leaving them, I'll never leave them. But I am leaving you, Janet; I'm putting that lie behind me."

Forty-Two

From the sound of Lena's voice, Mike could tell straight off that something was wrong. "What's the matter?"

"Annie's gone," she said. "She left after she spoke with Andrew; she was afraid he'd come here and she didn't want him to see the way she looks. She was afraid of what he'd do."

"Where'd she go?"

"She was going to leave on her own, Mike, and I couldn't have that, not in the state she's in."

"Where'd she go, Lena?"

"I gave her my car and driver, where he took her I can't say."

"Can't you phone him?"

"I've tried, actually, for the last few hours. She must have had him turn the thing off."

"How long has she been gone?"

"It's hours—since early this afternoon."

"Hours? Jesus Christ! Cowan's dead, Lena, did you know?"

"I heard it on the news. They said he committed suicide."

"Annie shouldn't hear that on her own, we should be there to reassure her. Did she give any hints, any clues at all as to where she might be headed?"

"No, I'm so awfully sorry. She wouldn't say, because she knew I'd tell. But she said she'd ring here tonight to speak with you, to let you know where she is."

"Dammit. Goddammit! She shouldn't have gone off on her own!"

Andrew was standing next to him and had gleaned much of the conversation. A certain serenity overcame him as he listened, and it showed in his eyes. Touching his arm, he told Mike, "It's all right, I know where she is, I know where she's gone."

"How?"

The answer was simple. "I can feel it."

Sir David and John waited inside while Mike went with Andrew to the helipad. The rain had stopped but the wind had risen with the evening sky, and even before the massive blades disturbed the air, they found themselves having to brace against it.

"I'll ring you from the mobile, as soon as I've seen her."

Mike nodded.

"Thank you for letting me have this time alone with her," Andrew said. "I appreciate your generosity more than I can say."

He offered his hand and when he took it, Mike told him, "She needs both of us now, and every bit as much love as we have to give. I would never deny her what she needs so very much."

Andrew smiled—a sad, weak smile—before responding, "This has undoubtedly been the worst day of my life. But I shudder to think what it might have been like, were it not for you, Mike Rutledge."

Annie's cottage, closed up for so long now, was musty and stale smelling. The Aston Martin was gone and it worried her at first, but then she recalled Andrew saying he'd send someone for it. She stood looking around the parlor for a minute, remembering sitting by the fire with him, the meals the hotel sent over, the roses, the picnic. She closed her eyes and felt him undress her, caress her with his strong, gentle hands. "If only," she sighed, "if only we could go back."

She hadn't the strength to battle with the old, uncooperative windows, so she left the front and back doors flung wide, and went out onto the lawn. She still ached terribly and the long drive had made her stiff, so walking was slow and painful, but somehow she managed the steep downward slope.

The tide was out and standing in front of the pile of rubble, she cursed herself for not having brought a shovel. She began with the smallest rocks, the ones she could manage most easily. After moving only a few, she spied a corner of the stack, sticking up most decidedly through the decayed remains of flowers: the wet and ruined letters called her name, despite their blurred and unrecognizable writing.

As she pulled them to her heart, the weight drove Annie to her knees. If she could, she would have burrowed into the sand then, like a tiny, panicked crab, clutching its hard gained nourishment. She bowed her head and her tears fell directly onto the beach.

The approaching helicopter sounded at first, as though the sea had turned angry. She lifted her head to look and caught the sight of it. As it neared her she knew, and her heart began to race in anticipation. She held the letters to her chest and would neither rise nor turn around as it landed in the meadow beyond her cottage and returned the quiet it had stolen. His footsteps were inaudible but she could feel him coming. She kept her head bowed and her back to him, and waited for the sound of his voice.

"Annie."

She wanted to sob.

"Annie, my love, I've come to take you home."

"Please go away, Andrew, please."

He moved closer and whispered to her, "I'd sooner die than leave you again."

She shook her head. "He'll never let us be, we can never be together again."

"He can't hurt us anymore."

"Please, Andrew, you have to go. Go be with your daughter — your family needs you."

"Cathy's fine, my darling, she doesn't need me just now. She's doing just fine and she'll be home soon."

She felt him moving closer. "No — don't come around. I don't want you to see me."

Despite her wishes, he circumnavigated the pile of rubble she sat amidst; although he'd seen the photographs only hours before, the sight of her battered face and body stunned him and sent him to the sand with her.

The manner in which she held her arms across her chest revealed the rope burns and numerous bruises, some now turning a sickly shade of yellow. The light, summer dress she wore, which would ordinarily give her a carefree air, prominently displayed the blue imprints that Cowan's fingers had left on her throat.

Wretched, burning tears boiled inside him and wanted escape, but Andrew kept them in check through sheer will; instead, he put his lips to each mark and bruise he saw, every one he could reach. Then he recognized what is was she was clinging to; her desperate clutching of his letters struck him with even more tragic poignancy.

All the while he regarded her, she avoided his eyes. "Mike should never have told you," she said.

"Mike did the right thing."

She looked to him now, and he could see that the green in her eyes had gone dark with fear and grief. "But if Cowan finds out you've come . . ."

"He can't hurt us anymore," he whispered to her. "He's dead, Annie. He shot himself."

She didn't believe him. "No—he wouldn't do that. He loves himself too much."

"Mike and I told him that we were going to the police with what we knew," he explained. "He shot himself before we could."

"No," she insisted, "Mike wasn't going to do that—I asked him not to do that."

"He changed his mind, Annie. He couldn't let Cowan get away with everything he'd done. Neither could I."

"No," she said again, "he promised me."

"It was no use keeping that promise. Cowan had to be dealt with." For a few, horrendous seconds, the scene of Cowan's death replayed in his mind.

"He's dead?" she questioned timidly. "He's really dead?"

He nodded and kissed her arms again, forcing the ugliness from his thoughts. Then he bent himself to caress and kiss her abdomen. "Why didn't you tell me, my love? I would never have left you."

With his acknowledgment of her pregnancy, tears of relief began pouring down Annie's cheeks. "It would have made things impossible for you, it would have kept you from doing what you had to."

His hands remained over her belly, and he went deep into her eyes to tell her, "I'd do anything for you, anything to be with you, anything to protect you. I should have been with you, none of this would have happened had I been where I belonged. You needed me to protect you, and she needed her father to keep her safe."

She turned her head away. "Please don't do that, don't call yourself that. It'll only make it harder for me if I have to end it."

Andrew unfolded her arms and took away the soggy letters, laying them on the sand. Then he kissed her hands. "Whatever happens with her, we'll go through it together."

"But we can't be together," she said, shaking her head and still not looking at him. "And there's Mike; he wants me to go home with him, he wants to be her father."

"I know, we talked."

"I think that's what I should do, I think that's the right thing to do—for everybody." She looked to him now and let her tears flow. "He loves her, Andrew, he'd be a wonderful father to her."

"I've no doubt of that," he said tenderly. "But he no longer feels that way."

"I don't understand—"

"He's coming to the château tomorrow," he told her. "The three of us, we'll take our time and decide what to do together. He loves you very deeply and he realizes that whatever lies ahead, we need to face it together."

They were quiet for a moment, as Annie looked away and over the water, easily imagining Mike as he said those things to Andrew. He could and would be that generous, she knew, but there was another member of this improbable foursome who would not. "What about Janet? What about her?"

He exhaled in a short burst. "I've left her, Annie; our marriage is over. She admitted her responsibility in what happened to you—and other things. It's made it impossible for me to be with her any longer."

She stared at him in disbelief, as a gust of wind swirled around them, carrying the pugent scent of seaweed. It blew Annie's hair across her face and scattered the sand, as Andrew removed his jacket and draped it over her shoulders, gently turning her back to the wind.

"You shouldn't be out here in the damp," he said.

"I came for the letters," she explained. "I wanted to take them home with me. They never made it to America; I was going to take them with me this time."

Andrew stared at the remains of his letters. "My heart was in those. I poured it out to you until there wasn't anything left, until I was so empty inside I thought that my love for you had died—but it never died."

"I should have come back to you. I should have known."

"It was I who should have known; I should have recognized who had really betrayed me."

She didn't understand, but didn't ask him to explain. Fatigue was tightening its grip on her and with each passing minute it was growing more difficult to talk, to even think.

They sat in silence together, before he said, "Let me take you home to Château d'Audine. Mike will be there tomorrow; come home to be with both of us."

Fear compelled Annie to ask again, "Is Cowan really dead? Did he really kill himself?"

"Yes, Annie. He shot himself in the head. Mike and I witnessed it."

With melancholic yearning, she told him, "I want to go home with you, Andrew, God how I want to. I want to go back to France with you and start over as if nothing happened."

"Then come with me," he implored, "and let me—let us—take care of you. With love and time, I know you can heal and put this behind you."

Though they were dry now, her eyes were glazed over with misery. "I'm so scared," she said. "There's so much to face, so many horrible possibilities looming ahead; I don't have the strength for it. With each passing hour I feel that much weaker. I keep hearing her tiny voice, and it's zapping my strength."

Instantly, his eyes filled with water. When he blinked, huge, hot tears ran away from them. "What does she say?"

She closed her eyes. "I'm trying not to listen; I need to keep my distance. It seems so unlikely that she'll be all right, I need to prepare myself to say good-bye."

"How can you even think that?" he questioned, his eyes pleading and soulful. "She's us, Annie, you and me come together at last, how can you even consider ending her life?"

"I can't watch her suffer," she knew.

Andrew bowed his head; he'd promised himself that he would not break down in front of her, that he would not add his suffering to hers, so he reined in his emotions and batted at the uncooperative tears. "Mike said we'll know in a week or so."

"Maybe, maybe we'll know. But if it's negative they told me to keep getting tested—for six months—just like before. Six months, Andrew, six agonizing months. I can't go through that again. She'll be seven months grown then, old enough to live on her own."

He grasped both her hands. "We don't have to decide anything now, Annie, and we don't need to think that far ahead. All we need do is get through this day, that's all." *This day*—he said to himself—*this cruel, cruel day—let it be over, let it be taken into the past.*

"And I'm too old," she said now. "We'll have to do tests—there could be something wrong with her because of my age."

"We'll get through that, too."

She shivered suddenly, overcome with an eerie chill, an inexplicable foreboding that the superstitious say happens when someone is walking on your grave. With solemn conviction, she said to him, "Tom Keegan told me something once. We were talking about choices, about how in the end we find ourselves hemmed in by the consequences of our choices. My choices—they feel like they're the nails in my coffin."

He shook his head in adamant denial. "I won't let that be. I'll rip the nails out with my bare hands, with my teeth if I have to. I'll never give up on you, Annie, never. Giving up on you would mean the end of everything for me."

She muttered in response, "I feel so weak, Andrew. It took all my strength to survive, I don't have any left to fight with. Sometimes when I close my eyes to sleep, I think I won't have the energy to wake up again."

"You don't need to be strong," he told her. "You'll take your strength from Mike and me." He stood and reached out a hand for her. "Come home with me; let me bring you home and take care of you."

Annie looked up at him, then turned her face away, with a slight twist of her neck. She was so forlorn, she seemed to have gone beyond hope. "I think it's gone again."

"What's that, my darling?"

"My spirit. I had it back for a while, but I'm afraid it's gone again."

That had troubled Andrew, too; her eyes were so dark—the vacant eyes of someone who has given up, who will soon surrender to death. He had to find a way to bring her back.

"Do you know what today is?" he asked. "Today is Bastille Day, Annie, the day we were to spend together in France, so many years ago. We talked about how we would celebrate it this year, do you remember that?"

Her head moved in the barest of nods, as she responded, "We were going to free the prisoners today." She looked in the direction of the path, then up at him, still with his hand held out for her, and said, "I don't think I can make it, Andrew."

"With my help, you can." He took her hands and gently pulled her to her feet. Bending to lift her, he cradled her in his arms, and she winced from the pain it caused.

As he began walking away, she stretched an arm toward the letters, saying, "Wait—I need those."

He stopped walking and looked to the ruined bundle. "No," he told her. "They belong to the past; the past is our prison, Annie."

She sighed heavily, then said in response, "We'll never be free. They'll keep playing with us and taking from us and driving us insane with their cruelty."

"Let the bloody gods do their worst," he said defiantly. "Whatever comes, we'll survive it."

"Will we?" She shook her head again. "They're so cruel, Andrew, crueler than I ever imagined. Beyond all hope they brought you back to me, and just to make it more complicated, they let Mike really love me for the first time. Then they brought me the rarest, most beautiful gift, the one thing I was sure I'd never have—your child. It's their cruelest trick of all, can't you see that? They've given me everything I wanted, then made it impossible for me to enjoy any of it."

Andrew touched his cheek to Annie's. There was nothing he could say to counter her foreboding, no placations, no clichéd offers of hope. He understood as well as she that they were in the

hands of Fate, and that Fate would have its way with them, no matter their efforts. Slowly, he began to ascend the cliff path.

Annie kept watch on the letters as they left them behind.
Halfway up the path her face relaxed a little, and she looked into
Andrew's eyes, asking, "Am I heavy?"

"As light as thistle, lassie."

His playfully exaggerated accent brought her an elusive
smile. "That's a perfect symbol for me, the thistle."

"It's Scotland's most beloved one."

Her mood had changed suddenly, and she had gone soft, almost limp in his arms. "What you said about the past—before you
came here I was thinking about it. I was thinking that you and I are
doomed to repeat it, that we're destined to be separated again. I've
had this song stuck in my head because of that, all day. I keep hearing the same few lyrics, over and over."

"Which song is that?"

"An old Bob Dylan one: 'Memphis Blues.' Do you remember it?"

"No, I don't think I do. How does it go?"

Unconsciously, she mocked the singer's distinct intonations:
"And here I sit so patiently—waiting to find out what price—you
have to pay to get out of—going through all these things twice."

A powerful smile arose from inside Andrew, as he caught the
flash of her green sparkles and saw again—for one fleeting moment—the young Annie he had fallen in love with so many years
ago. That burst of green fire told him that she was not lost, that she
was still there, and that she could be recovered. In that instant hope
reinstated itself, helping Andrew to understand that in Annie's de-
liverance, he would find his own.

They were almost to the clifftop when she sighed again.
"Nothing is ever easy for us, is it?"

"No, it never is."

"I'm sure there must be plenty of times when you've wished
you'd never met me."

With palpable tenderness, he told her, "My life began the day
I met you, Annie, and it'll end the day I lose you."

She wrapped her arms around his neck and buried her face
there, while Andrew mounted the last few feet of steep path. The

pilots rushed to help him when they saw that he carried her, but he would not give up his burden.

The helicopter skirted the cathedral ruins of St. Andrews like a mighty, bellowing bird. Inside its belly, Andrew held Annie in his arms and stroked her head, their eyes fixed upon the majestic, invincible remains. Their thoughts were caught in the same, distant place, and as they passed away into the sky over the pier, the couple witnessed a strange and mystical sight.

There is a fog called the haar that sometimes overtakes St. Andrews, that is born in the warmth and stillness of a summer day, as it languishes over the cold waters of the North Sea. Stealthily, it grows, into a massive, opaque entity that rolls in like a tidal wave, chasing the St. Andreans along the streets, and chilling everyone to the bone. From the helicopter Annie and Andrew witnessed this phenomenon as it began its assault on the old gray town.

Although it was July and there were very few students about, two scarlet-clad young people walked hand in hand along the ancient wall of stones that is the pier of the town harbor. His sand-colored hair caught the rays of the late setting, summer sun, poised to vanish beyond the West Sands; she brushed aside the long, dark locks that blew, ever so softly, across her face. They stopped at the jetty's edge and looked toward the east, out over the North Sea, and seemed oblivious to the helicopter's presence.

Instead of running from the enveloping fog as the townspeople now did, the couple seated themselves at the pier's end and remained there as the wall of sea cloud closed in on them. Holding tightly to one another, they were absorbed into it, and seemed to welcome it as a hiding place, as an obscuring place of refuge.

Personal Journal, Château d'Audine, 16 July 1994

I have not written here since Andrew and I came together again, because I have not needed the release it offers. But I find need for it now, for there are things I cannot say to anyone, not even to them.

I spoke with Marc yesterday. He wanted to see me but Mike convinced him to wait until I was better. He asked about the car accident I was supposedly in; I said I didn't remember much. I miss him terribly—every time I think of the baby, I think of him.

Dr. Huron came by yesterday; Andrew phoned and asked him to. I let them tell what had happened, because I don't want to be forced to remember. I listened though, and it seemed to me that it had happened to someone else.

I like Bernard Huron more each time I see him. He handled being introduced to my husband and lover with perfect grace, and when he examined me it was with such tender consideration, it brought tears to my eyes. He calls her the tenacious little thing, and says her survival is a miracle. I asked him to be the one, the one who will tell me. I imagine it will make it easier somehow.

In the afternoon I heard them whispering; they thought me napping but I was unable to rest. Sir David had phoned for Mike; he spoke quietly with Andrew afterward. I understood that it was about Cowan's funeral. Andrew didn't want to go; Mike told him he must. Their voices became softer, but I made out that there had been a fire that destroyed the house at Eindhoven. They also spoke of Hans. I heard them say that they want to hunt him down and make him pay. I don't want them to do that, and why that is, is one of the things I cannot tell them.

In the night I fell into a deep and mortal terror; I was trying to protect her from them, but could not. Andrew lay next to me, and I thought him at first to be someone else. He brought Mike to the room and together they tried to comfort me—it seemed a long while before I knew who they were. I finally returned to a relatively tranquil sleep, with Mike to my right and Andrew to my left. The man whose eyes she would have held my hand and kissed it, the man who would be her father caressed my abdomen and guarded my back. They spoke to me, each of them in their turn, and told me that in time everything will be all right. I listened and pretended to find sol-

ace in their words, but I did not, because time is a vise, and I feel its pressure.

I awakened again to the clocks chiming three all about the house. Lisette had filled the bedroom with flowers for my homecoming; their mingled fragrances came alive in the predawn damp and crept over us. I listened to Andrew's deep breathing, his hand still clinging to mine, and felt Mike's gentle snoring into my neck. They are two latched gates and I am safe between them. I heard a breeze stir the garden, as though spirits moved among the roses, and I knew a moment's peace.